ACCLAIM FOR MOSES ISEGAWA'S

ABYSSINIAN CHRONICLES

"Epic, sprawling, brimming with life—and death, Moses Isegawa's *Abyssinian Chronicles* blasts open the tidy borders of the conventional first novel and redraws the literary map to reveal a whole new world. . . . Eloquent, harrowing, and compulsively readable."
—Francine Prose, *Elle*

"The first richly imaginative treatment of contemporary Uganda in fiction. . . . It is in parts haunting, and grippingly good." —*The Hartford Courant*

"There are few first novelists who write with the assurance and authority of Isegawa. This is a young writer who will command attention from the literary world for many years to come." —*Rocky Mountain News*

"As Salman Rushdie's *Midnight's Children* was for modern India, *Abyssinian Chronicles* will likely prove to be a breakthrough book for Uganda." —*Time Out New York*

"Isegawa's style is an intriguing and at times baffling mixture of exuberance on the one hand, and, on the other, a hard, journalistic realism, which dramatises its scornful insights in language rarely less than elegant." —*The Independent* (London)

MOSES ISEGAWA

ABYSSINIAN CHRONICLES

Moses Isegawa was born in Kampala, Uganda. In 1990, he left Uganda for the Netherlands and is now a Dutch citizen. This is his first novel.

INTERNATIONAL

ABYSSINIAN CHRONICLES

ABYSSINIAN CHRONICLES

MOSES ISEGAWA

VINTAGE INTERNATIONAL

Vintage Books

A Division of Random House, Inc.

New York

FIRST VINTAGE INTERNATIONAL EDITION, NOVEMBER 2001

Copyright © 2000 by Moses Isegawa

All rights reserved under International and Pan-American Copyright Conventions.
Published in the United States by Vintage Books, a division of Random House, Inc.,
New York, and simultaneously in Canada by Random House of Canada Limited,
Toronto. Originally published in the Netherlands as *Abessijnse kronieken* by
Uitgeverij De Bezige Bij, Amsterdam, in 1998. Copyright © 1998 by Moses Isegawa.
Copyright Nederlandse Vertaling © 1998 by Ria Loohuizen. This English language
edition first published in hardcover in the United States by Alfred A. Knopf,
a division of Random House, Inc., New York, in 2000.

Vintage is a registered trademark and Vintage International and colophon
are trademarks of Random House, Inc.

The Library of Congress has cataloged the Knopf edition as follows:
Isegawa, Moses, [date]
[*Abessijnse kronieken*. English]
Abyssinian chronicles / by Moses Isegawa.—1st ed.
p. cm.
ISBN 0-375-40613-1 (alk. paper)
1. Uganda—Fiction. I. Title.
PT5881.19.S24 A2413 2000
839.3'1364—dc21
99-089888

Vintage ISBN: 0-375-70577-5

Author photo © Jerry Bauer
Book design by Susan Carroll

www.vintagebooks.com

Printed in the United States of America
10 9 8 7 6 5 4 3 2 1

CONTENTS

List of Main Characters   vii

List of African Words   ix

Book One
   . . . 1971: VILLAGE DAYS   3

Book Two
   THE CITY   83

Book Three
   AMIN, THE GODFATHER   113

Book Four
   SEMINARY YEARS   185

Book Five
   NINETEEN SEVENTY-NINE   265

Book Six
   TRIANGULAR REVELATIONS   341

Book Seven
   GHETTOBLASTER   417

Acknowledgments   465

MAIN CHARACTERS

Mugeẓi: narrator and principal character
Serenity: Mugezi's father
    (also called Sere or Mpanama)
Padlock: Mugezi's mother
    (real name Nakkaẓi, also called Virgin or Sr. Peter)
Grandpa: Serenity's father
Grandma: Grandpa's sister, Serenity's aunt
Tiida: Serenity's eldest sister
    (also called Miss Sunlight Soap)
Dr. Saif Ssali: Tiida's husband
Nakatu: Serenity's other sister
Hajj Ali: Nakatu's second husband
Kawayida: Serenity's half-brother
Lwandeka: Padlock's youngest sister
Kasawo: Padlock's other sister
Mbale: Padlock's eldest brother
Kasiko: Serenity's concubine
Nakibuka: Padlock's aunt, Serenity's mistress
Hajj Gimbi: Serenity and Padlock's neighbor in Kampala
Lusanani: Hajj Gimbi's youngest wife, Mugezi's lover in Kampala
Loverboy: client of Padlock's (real name Mbaziira)
Cane: Mugezi's friend in primary school
Lwendo: Mugezi's friend at the seminary
Fr. Kaanders: librarian at the seminary
Fr. Mindi: treasurer at the seminary
Fr. Lageau: Fr. Mindi's successor
Jo Nakabiri: Mugezi's lover in Kampala
Eva and Magdelein: Mugezi's lovers in Holland

AFRICAN WORDS

boubou: a kind of wide garment for a man (West Africa)

busuti: a kind of woman's garment (central Uganda)

kandooya: torture method whereby one's elbows are tied together behind one's back

Katonda wange!: My God!

kibanda: black market

Kibanda Boys: Kampala mafia

mamba: poisonous snake

matooke: plantain

mpanama: hydrocele

mtuba: an African tree

muko: brother-in-law

muteego: AIDS

nagana: a tropical cattle disease

panga: large cleaver

posho: corn bread

shamba: plantation

ABYSSINIAN CHRONICLES

BOOK ONE

THREE FINAL IMAGES flashed across Serenity's mind as he disappeared into the jaws of the colossal crocodile: a rotting buffalo with rivers of maggots and armies of flies emanating from its cavities; the aunt of his missing wife, who was also his longtime lover; and the mysterious woman who had cured his childhood obsession with tall women. The few survivors of my father's childhood years remembered that up until the age of seven, he would run up to every tall woman he saw passing by and, in a gentle voice trembling with unspeakable expectation, say, "Welcome home, Ma. You were gone so long I was afraid you would never return." Taken by surprise, the woman would smile, pat him on the head, and watch him wring his hands before letting him know that he had once again made a mistake. The women in his father's homestead, assisted by some of the villagers, tried to frighten him into quitting by saying that one day he would run into a ghost disguised as a tall woman, which would take him away and hide him in a very deep hole in the ground. They could have tried milking water from a stone with better results. Serenity, a wooden expression on his face, just carried on running up to tall women and getting disappointed by them.

Until one hot afternoon in 1940 when he ran up to a woman who neither smiled nor patted him on the head; without even looking at him, she took him by the shoulders and pushed him away. This mysterious curer of his obsession won herself an eternal place in his heart. He never ran up to tall women again, and he would not talk about it, not even when Grandma, his only paternal aunt, promised to buy him sweets. He coiled into his inner cocoon, from whose depths he rejected all efforts at consolation. A smooth, self-contained indifference descended on his face so totally that he won himself the name Serenity, shortened to "Sere."

Serenity's mother, the woman who in his mind had metamorphosed into all those strange tall women, had abandoned him when he was three, ostensibly to go to the distant shops beyond Mpande Hill where big purchases were made. She never returned. She also left behind two girls, both older than Serenity, who adjusted to her absence with great equanimity and could not bear his obsession with tall women.

In an ideal situation, Serenity should have come first—everyone wanted a son for the up-and-coming subcounty chief Grandpa was at the time—but girls kept arriving, two dying soon after birth in circumstances reeking of maternal desperation. By the time Serenity was born, his mother had decided to leave. Everyone expected her to have another son as a backup, for an only son was a candle in a storm. The pressure reached a new peak when it became known that she was pregnant again. Speculation was rife: Would it be a boy or a girl, would it live or die, was it Grandpa's or did it belong to the man she was deeply in love with? Before anybody could find out the truth, she left. But her luck did not hold—three months into her new life, her uterus burst, and she bled to death on the way to the hospital, her life emptying into the backseat of a rotten Morris Minor.

As time passed, Serenity crawled deeper into his cocoon, avoiding his aunts, his cousins, and his mother's replacements, who he felt hated him for being the heir apparent to his father's estate and the miles of fertile clan land it included. The birth of Uncle Kawayida, his half-brother by a Muslim woman his father was seeing on the side, did not lessen Serenity's estrangement. Kawayida, due to the circumstances of his birth, posed little threat to Serenity's position, and thus attitudes remained unchanged. To escape the phantoms which galloped in his head and the contaminated air in his father's compound, Serenity roamed the surrounding villages. He spent a lot of time at the home of the Fiddler, a man with large feet, a large laugh and sharp onion breath who serenaded Grandpa on the weekends when he was home.

Serenity could not get over the way the Fiddler walked with legs wide apart. It would have been very impolite to ask the man why he walked that way, and Serenity feared that if he asked his children, they would tell their father, who in turn would report him to his father for punishment. Consequently, he turned to his aunt with the question "Why does the Fiddler have breasts between his legs?"

"Who said the Fiddler had breasts between his legs?"

"Have you never noticed the way he walks?"

"How does he walk?"

"With legs spread wide apart as if he were carrying two jackfruits under his tunic." He then gave a demonstration, very exaggerated, of the way the man walked.

"It is very funny, but I have never noticed it," Grandma said, humoring him the way adults did to get out of a sticky situation.

"How could you not have noticed? He has large breasts between his legs."

"The Fiddler has no breasts between his legs. He is ill. He has got *mpanama*."

Serenity's sisters somehow got wind of the duckwalk and could not resist telling their village peers and schoolmates about the Fiddler, his breasts, and the little clown who portrayed him in silly mimicries. As a result, Serenity got the nickname Mpanama, a ghastly sounding word used out of adult hearing that dropped from gleeful lips with the wet slap of dung hitting hard ground from the rear of a half-constipated cow. Once again he was cured of an obsession, though he continued with his visits to the poor man's home, faintly hoping to catch him pissing or, better still, squatting on the latrine, for he really wanted to see if the Fiddler's breasts were as large and smooth as those of the women in his father's homestead.

Apart from his secret fantasy, Serenity also wanted to learn how to play the fiddle. He could not get over the one-stringed moans, groans, sighs, screams, grunts and other peculiar sounds the Fiddler conjured, squeezed and rubbed out of the little instrument. The Fiddler's visits formed the high point of his week, and the music was the only thing he listened to with pleasure uncoerced or influenced by adults or peers. He wanted to learn how to hold the instrument proudly against his shoulder and tune the string with a knot of wax. His aim was to charm strange women into his magic circle and keep them rooted there for as long as he wanted. In school he was known for his beautiful pencil drawings of fiddles. His wish never came true.

Grandpa, a Catholic, was unseated and replaced by a Protestant rival in a contest marred by religious sectarianism. As the fifties ended, his power gone and the heart taken out of his life, Grandpa's homestead shrivelled as relatives, friends and hangers-on left one by one or in little groups. The women dropped out of his life, and the Fiddler took his talent elsewhere. By the time I was the age Serenity was when he ran up to strange tall women, Grandpa was living alone, sharing his house with the occasional visitor, relative or woman, a few rats, spiders and the odd snake that sloughed behind his heaps of coffee sacks.

Grandma, his only surviving sister, was also living alone, three football fields away. Serenity's bachelor house, a trim little thing standing on land donated by both Grandpa and Grandma, separated the two homesteads. It was a sleepy little house, now and then kicked from the slumber of disintegration, swept and cleaned to accommodate a visitor, or just to limit the damage wreaked by termites and other destroyers. It only came alive when Serenity's sisters or Uncle Kawayida visited and hurricane lamps washed it with golden beams. The voices and laughter made the rafters quiver, and the smoke from the open fire wound long spectacular threads round the roof and touched off distant memories.

The exodus of wives, relatives, friends and hangers-on had left a big howling lacuna which wrapped the homestead in webs of glorious nostalgia. The fifties and sixties were spanned by that nostalgia and provided us with stories pickled, polished and garnished by memory. Every migrant soul was now a compact little ghost captured in words, invoked from the lacuna by the oracle of Grandpa and Grandma and made to inject doses of old life into our present truncated existence.

The hegemony of lacuna'd ghosts in their stories was broken only when the characters, like resurrected souls, braved the dangerous slopes of Mpande Hill and the treacherous papyrus swamps to come and state their case in person. The Fiddler never returned, but was most prevalent because he was immortalized by the poor rendition of his songs Grandpa showered on his homestead as he shaved, as he toured his coffee plantation—the *shamba*—to supervise work, as he reminisced in the shade and as he wondered how to get a young girl with an old soul to see him through his last days.

Late in the sixties, no one's visit was awaited more eagerly than Uncle Kawayida's: the man was a wizard, a gold mine full of fascinating and sometimes horrifying tales, a fantastic storyteller endowed with a rare patience who answered my often tedious questions with a cheerful, reassuring face. When he stayed away too long, I became restless and worked out the days and months he was most likely to come. On such days I would climb into the branches of my favorite tree, the tallest jackfruit in the three homesteads, and fix my eyes on the distant Mpande ("Manhood") Hill. If I was lucky, I would see his motorbike, a blue-bellied eagle encased in silver flashes, glide down the notoriously steep slope and disappear into the umbrella-shaped greenery of the papyrus swamp below. With "Uncle Kawayida, Uncle Kawayida!" on my tongue, I would speed down the tree—dry, sharp sticks pricking my skin, the sweet hypnotic smell of jackfruit in my nose—and rush into Grandma's courtyard to break the good news.

Uncle Kawayida was a meter reader for the Ugandan National Energy Board. His job was to visit people's homes and take readings used to calculate the monthly energy bills customers had to pay. Courtesy of his travels and, I believe, of his large imagination, he told stories of women who used sugared promises to try to bribe him into under-reading their meters, and of men who tried to impede his work by accusing him of flirting with their wives. He amazed us with stories of people living in congested urban squalor, ten to a little house, with parents fucking in the vicinity of children who cleverly feigned sleep. He spoke of women who committed garage abortions by slipping stiff leaf stalks or bike spokes up the condemned birth canals of unfaithful wives or sneaky daughters, an occasional fatal or near-fatal hemorrhage the price for puncturing the wrong things. He told tales of men who beat their wives with electric cables, sticks, boots or fists and afterward ordered them to serve their dinner or to fuck them, and of women who drank and fought like men, cracked open men's heads with beer bottles and subsequently emptied their pockets. In those places were wild children who did not go to school and got into a life of crime: stealing, robbing, mugging, sometimes even killing people. In the same places lived rich people's children who went to school in big cars, laughed at teachers and wrote love letters in class. There were also people who could hardly make ends meet, who ate one meager meal a day after doing backbreaking work. In that world roamed fantastic football hooligans who fought their rivals in epic battles in which rocks, piss bottles, shit parcels, clubs and even bullets were exchanged to the point where police had to intervene with tear gas or bullets. There were men and women, devout churchgoing Catholics and Protestants, who worshipped the Devil and offered blood sacrifices during nocturnal orgies; and people of different religious denominations who deposited featherless, headless hens, dead lizards, frog entrails and other ritual garbage in other people's yards, outside shopfronts or at road junctions. He once told us of a skinless lamb left to roam the streets encumbered with unknown curses and armies of greedy flies. I remembered the story of a man who kept three sisters: he started with the one he had married, progressed to her next younger sister and ended up with their youngest sister, who needed accommodation near a reputable school. As with all his stories, the last one was open-ended, game to all kinds of endings and interpretations.

When Uncle Kawayida came, I made myself indispensable around the house, making sure that I was not sent away on long errands. When I suspected that he had some particularly juicy information about a relative or someone we knew and that Grandpa was going to send me away, I would voluntarily go off to play, double back, hide behind the kitchen and listen. Many times, however, Grandpa and Grandma were so enthralled that they forgot all about me, or just ignored my existence and intelligence, and I would listen to the story as if the future of the entire village depended on it.

Uncle Kawayida pricked my imagination so much that I wanted to verify some of his stories by visiting the places and the characters he talked about. For example, what sort of parents did whatever they did in bed with children snoring, falsely, on the floor? Were they

Catholics? If not, did Protestantism, Islam or traditional religion allow such behavior? Were such people educated and well-bred? Unable to tame my raging curiosities and doubts, I begged Uncle Kawayida to take me with him, at least just once, but each time he refused, bolstered by Grandma and Grandpa. Most annoying were their weak excuses. Later I found out the real reason why: Kawayida's wife, a woman from a very large, polygamous household, was not on good terms with my mother, who came from a very Catholic family, and none of the trio was ready to risk Padlock's anger by sending her son to the house of a person she disliked and disapproved of so much.

The tension between their wives had driven the brothers apart. My mother despised Kawayida's wife's background because she believed there was no morality and no salvation in a household with thirty girls and ten boys born of so many "whore" mothers in a climate of perpetual sin. Kawayida's wife despised Padlock for the poverty of her parental home, and for her guava-switch-wielding propensities. A cousin called her disciplinary activities "beating children like drums." She also accused Padlock of standing in the way of Kawayida's progress by stopping Serenity from helping his brother to get loans from the bank and able individuals. Kawayida's ambition was to own a business and make and spend his own money, but he lacked capital and needed his brother's recommendation. The truth was that Serenity, who had helped Kawayida get his current job, did not believe in retail business, hated it for personal reasons, and would not help anyone get into it. Because he had remained very laconic about his stand, Serenity's position got interpreted ad libitum by each of the warring parties.

Nowadays, the brothers met at weddings, funerals and when Muhammad Ali fights took place. Uncle Kawayida conveyed to us the details, wreathed in the sheen of his saliva, redolent with tricks of his imagination, on the wings of the blue-bellied eagle. Grandma listened to the endless accounts with the same vague irony that had entertained Serenity's revelations about the Fiddler's burden, and the same sparing laugh that had rewarded the famous duckwalk. Kawayida took us through Ali's flashy arsenal of jabs, hooks and wiggles with the same appetite that animated his usual stories. Behind his back Grandma called him "Ali," a name which never stuck because, apart from us, only one family, the Stefanos, knew of Muhammad Ali's exploits, and they could not see the appeal of this lanky substitute.

Aunt Tiida, Serenity's eldest sister, was the most unpopular, albeit imposing, visitor we received all year round. Her visits put everyone on edge, especially when she first arrived. In order to blunt the arrogance of his eldest child, Grandpa would greet her with generous, half-mocking cheer. Grandma, a great believer in countering vanity with candor, would receive her with an indifference which diminished only in direct proportion to Tiida's arrogance. Both strategies had their limitations, for as soon as Tiida opened her bags, she made sure that things were done her own way. I always had the impression that we were being visited by a government health inspector in mufti.

Tiida was like a member of an endangered species threatened with extinction, her life made more precarious by this inevitable contact with our backward village environment. She never came unannounced. Days before her arrival, Serenity's house had to be aired all day, swept, and the bed doused in insecticide. I had to combat the prolific spiders, dismantling their nets, puncturing their webs, destroying their eggs. I broke the veins the termites built on doors and windows. I scraped bat shit from the floor and windowsills with a knife. It was my duty to smoke the latrine with heaps of dry banana leaves, a duty I detested most of all because it reminded me of my first proper thrashing at the hands of Padlock.

During these visits, Aunt Tiida bathed four times a day, and I had to make sure that there was enough water for all her ablutions. This was a record performance in a place where one bath a day was enough, and where some went through the seven days of the week with only foot, armpit and groin washes. Little wonder that the villagers called her Miss Sunlight Soap or Miss Etiquette. Tiida was not happy with the first name because of its insinuation of odor, and also because the only other fanatic bather from the village, an air hostess, was only called Miss Aeroplane.

Unlike Miss Aeroplane, Tiida was very elegant, very attractive and very articulate, and despite her fussiness, I felt proud when I was with her. If the Virgin Mary had been black, it would not have been hard for Tiida to claim that they were sisters. At night I saw her wrapped in frothy muslin clouds, her white nightie blowing softly in the breeze, her long slim fingers intertwined below the belly, her regal grooved neck bent in the direction where dreams merged with reality. But my awe did not last long: it became dented courtesy of Grandma and Grandpa's after-lunch conversations. Tiida had not been a virgin when she married. She had lost her virginity to a married village friend. This man's daughter was famous for sitting with her legs open and letting passersby see her exposed genitalia. Grandpa was angry with the man for jeopardizing his daughter's marriage chances. I remember that Aunt Tiida once asked me whether this man was still married to the same ugly wife. I said yes and she laughed victoriously. I wanted to tell her that I knew her secret, but those were adult matters—I could not insinuate with impunity. As I boiled her bathwater, the smoke getting into my eyes, I would try to imagine what she had looked like at the time when men had rejected her. How did she fight back? I could see her telling a man that he'd refused her because he was impotent and not because he preferred virgins.

It was logical that Tiida got married to a doctor who, we found out years later, was only a medical assistant. Grandma had her on the run on a number of occasions. "He is not a real doctor, is he?" she would prod for the umpteenth time. "He could not prescribe a cure for my sugar."

"You and your sugar," Tiida, chafed, would fire back. "It is as if everyone was going to put it in tea and drink it."

"Don't get angry, Tiida. You are the one who started it. Why did you lie to us that he was a doctor?"

"A medical assistant with his experience is as good as any doctor. My man can do everything a doctor does. He also wears an immaculate white gown. Who can tell the difference?"

"You mean *you* cannot tell the difference!"

"My man is progressive, admit it. He is always looking for chances to improve his lot. That is more than you can say for many men who married into this family."

"I know, but still we would have accepted him as he was. He did not have to pull that snobbish stuff on us."

"He is always looking for the edge."

"Let him not try too hard." Grandma relented and then laughed. "Poor devil, how can you be married to Miss Sunlight Soap and not look for edges?"

"Don't start, Aunt," Tiida said uneasily.

The strange thing about Tiida's visits was that by the time they ended and she departed in a cloud of bottled perfume, I got the feeling that we had lost something.

This time a year passed without hearing any news from Tiida. Grandpa missed her, not least because she resembled her mother very much. She was the only daughter who, in his mind, reflected the nebulous shades of a love that had ended with so many unanswered questions. He talked about her almost every day. It was Uncle Kawayida who solved the riddle of the missing Tiida. Dr. Ssali, Tiida's husband, had converted from Protestantism to Islam! In the sixties, this was considered downward mobility, because in the political scheme of things, the Christians were on top, with the Protestants having the lion's share of the cake, the Catholics the hyena's, and the Muslims the vulture's scrawny pickings. With the phantoms of his defeat at the hands of a Protestant rival reawakened by this bizarre conversion, Grandpa fumed, "Impossible. How could he do that?" He got the feeling that his daughter was going to tumble down into the abyss. After all, the doctor now had license to marry four wives, and Tiida was most likely going to have to contend with younger co-wives, jealousy and witchcraft. If it had been in his power, Grandpa would have precipitated her divorce. Tiida did not seem the type of woman to share a husband. The whole conversion nonsense did not seem the kind of phenomenon that would occur in her world. Loyalty was not a quality I associated with her, and I still expected to see her gliding down Mpande Hill in a car loaded with her rich leather bags. We were all wrong: Tiida remained at her husband's side.

If the convert had any plans of taking on three more wives, in the near future or thereafter, it was the least of his worries. His biggest concern was the ulcerated circumcision wound which made his penis very painful and very hard to handle. Banal functions like urination had become a living hell, an ordeal to psych himself up for. Long and pendulous, the penis rubbed against the cloth of his skirt or sometimes of his wrapper; thread bit into the wound, and hairs somehow got embedded in the crust. Consequently, sitting, sleeping and standing became endless torture sessions. Sometimes a scab formed round the edges of the ulcer, covering the terrible pink and angry red, giving him surges of hope, and then, devil of devils, he would get a nocturnal erection and the scab would burst. Painful urination would begin all over again, thread would bite into the wound and caustic medicine would bring tears to his eyes. He shaved every other day, and the itching of incipient pubic hair added to the ulcer made his hours trickle with murderous sloth. He had himself tested for blood poisoning and various blood cancers, but the doctors returned negative results each time. He was as healthy as a bull. The doctors ascribed his ulcer to age, although he was only in his forties.

On top of all that came the flies. Tiida went out one morning and let out the scream of her life. The two avocado trees behind the house were full of flies, large green things the size of coffee beans. She dropped the basinful of soaked clothes in her hands on the ground. Ssali came to the door and his skin crawled as if it were being peeled off. It was as if a goat or a pig were rotting at the foot of the trees. The connotation of putrescence made Tiida vomit onto the clothes. Ssali, who had been about to make her go find out what was happening, decided to do it himself. With legs spread wide apart, he hobbled to the foot of the trees. There he found a large heap of chicken entrails.

Normally, the flies would have clustered on the entrails, and maybe on the lower reaches of the trees, but now they were high up in the leaves. With a sick feeling in his stomach, Ssali returned to his bedroom and sent for a laborer. The man dug a pit and buried the entrails. The flies lingered on for a day and disappeared with the dusk.

Four days later Tiida saw the flies again. This time a heap of dog entrails was buried, and the flies went away. A week later another heap of dog entrails was buried. This was very worrying to Ssali: somebody was sacrificing dogs to bring disaster on his house at such a difficult moment in his life. Goat and sheep were understandable sacrifices, but dogs! With blood-caked dog heads left on the heap of entrails to make sure that he knew which animals were being killed! This was a warning, a naked act of terrorism. And it could only be coming from one person: the mother of the man who had sold him the land on which he had built his house.

He had bought the land five years before with the intention of raising cattle. At the time he did not know of the disputes inside the land-seller's family. The purchase had been aboveboard, with no bribery or any form of corruption involved. It was only after the purchase had been ratified that the troubles surfaced. The mother of the seller appeared, with claims that her son had stolen the title deed and changed his father's will to suit his greedy ends. The claims did not stand in court, and the woman had threatened to fight to her death to regain the land. That she had chosen this particular moment to strike back irked the convalescent very much. Did she think that he was too enervated to fight back? That he would just surrender or lie down and die? He sent her a delegation asking for peace, but she dismissed it out of hand, offended that he could even think her capable of sacrificing dogs to the gods of terrorism.

Ssali employed a guard to look out for whoever brought the heads and the entrails, but in vain. The terrorist struck with impunity. Some said it was a curse, a punishment meted out by a dead relative to avenge Ssali's defection to Allah. The convert was at his wits' end. He tried running away for weeks. But the heads kept coming, and the ulcer kept crusting and bursting. The mere presence of flies and their insinuation of filth made his medical mind sick. Putrescence! When he had devoted his entire life to its eradication!

As if that was not enough, some tongues put religious significance on the curse of the dog heads and the flies. They said that the heads and the entrails and the flies had started coming seven, others said six, days after his rebirth as Saif Amir Ssali. Seven was a cursed number among many peoples. Three sixes was the number of the Antichrist. Now he had become something between a walking curse and a demon, and he deserved the terrorism! As a former Christian he could not entirely scoff at these nebulae, but to make sure he was safe, he invited some sheikhs and two famous imams to offer prayers and sacrifice. Two days afterward, a new head and a heap of entrails appeared. This was a concerted effort to drive him out of his house and off the land.

At the same time a new fear struck him: the possibility of Tiida's leaving him. He agonized about asking her what she thought about the situation. He could, however, not broach the subject directly for fear of annoying her by appearing to doubt her. What if it was all in his mind and she had never contemplated quitting? How long would she put up with this? A woman who bathed four times a day staying in a house besieged by entrails and dogs' heads? It seemed unthinkable.

It was well known that older converts were more susceptible to penile cancer, everyone told him, as if it helped. He wondered how long would this go on. His children were now being severely teased by schoolmates using words like "fly-man," "sick penis" and "skirt-daddy."

I was impressed by the siege of flies. It must have made Ssali feel like he had shit on him all day. What a turnaround! He had visited us twice looking like a real doctor. On both occasions he consented to take tea, but I had to wash the cups three times in very warm water and a mountain of soap suds which climbed up to my elbows. He sat there watching me and Grandma, saying nothing, bored by everything and everyone. He was wearing gray trousers, a white shirt, a blue tie and very black, very shiny shoes. He had a gold watch which cut the air like a yellow blade when he raised his hand to feel his neatly parted hair. Tiida was beside herself with pride. She was all over the place directing things, looking at him now and then as if seeking tacit approval or covert gratitude. I must have dried the tray six times, the spoons four times. There was always a little speck or a minute drop of wet left. In a bid to mend fences, she said, "Dr. Ssali has got such a delicate stomach!" I figured she was now saying, "He has got such a delicate penis! It should never have got cut in the first place."

Fourteen months after his circumcision, the skies cleared and the ulcer healed. But that was not the end of his troubles. The prize he had been anxiously awaiting, and indeed one of the things which had kept his sanity intact, was denied him. The representative of the Conversion Committee informed him that he was no longer eligible for a brand-new Peugeot because he had not fulfilled all the stipulations of the contract. His fellow converts, he was told, had spent the past year campaigning all over the country, addressing people in mosques and schools, at public grounds and community centers, fighting for the spread of Islam. He, on the other hand, had missed all that, spending his time in hospital wards getting treatment. The Committee was going to pay his medical bills and offer him a consolation prize: a 125cc scooter.

"You gave your word, sheikh," he pleaded.

"Look at this mountain of bills! You broke your word too, and never participated in the jihad."

"It wasn't my fault."

"It wasn't ours either. Do you want to go on a solo tour now?"

"I have to go back to work."

"Don't forget your skullcap, you have to wear it everywhere you go. Be proud of your new religion, Saif."

The story ended with Ssali collecting his prize: an overtly feminine Italian-made Vespa scooter. I awaited more twists to the tale, but Uncle Kawayida never mentioned it again. I tried to tempt Grandpa into telling me more about it, but he just sent me off to play. When Tiida came to visit, she created a wall around herself and would not divulge any more details. I gave up.

I was high up in the tree hoping to catch sight of the blue-bellied eagle when I saw a car headed for Grandma's compound. My heart sank. Visitors who came in cars tended to overstay their welcome, crowding us, knocking us out of our rhythm, filling me with impatience. Visitors with children were the worst: they expected you to babysit for them, as if you had nothing better to do, while they went visiting or having a good time. The children shat, wet themselves, crawled all over the place, and you were supposed to be responsible for their safety. And when departing, these parents would not even thank you or throw you a coin for pocket money.

As I slowly kneed my way down the tree, I wondered how many children this visitor had brought with her. Oh, the thought of those dreadful nappies soaking in the basin or flying in the sun!

By the time I arrived at Grandma's the car had left. In the courtyard were two large suitcases and things in cardboard boxes. My heart sank deeper. This woman had indeed come to stay, to disorganize our program, to boss us. Again! It was Aunt Nakatu, Serenity's second sister. She was a short, dark woman with deep curves on a compact body which bespoke great energy. She had a soft, melodious voice more suited for singing than giving orders, which was possibly the reason why she had to repeat things twice or more before her orders were obeyed. She was the only daughter of the house who had married in church. She looked more impressive in the wedding picture, the masses of bridal tulle and the three-meter bridal train giving her the air of compressed royalty. Her husband was a very tall man, whom I imagined bending over to tell her something if he was not to shout. As I stood in front of this short, fattish person, mouthing the obligatory words of welcome, I tried to work out how things were going to be for the duration of her stay. Joy of joys, she had not brought any children with her for me to mind and to keep from eating caterpillars, millipedes and earthworms.

Grandpa was away on a visit. The news he got on his return made him sad: Nakatu had run away and had no intention of returning to her husband's house. He was fond of Nakatu's husband, a bond of loyalty linked to the new Raleigh bicycle this son-in-law had given him before wedding his daughter. It was the same bicycle Grandpa rode around on now. The news made Grandpa look away in the trees, as if worried that his son-in-law was going to appear and demand the bicycle back.

Grandpa sent me away, but I doubled back as usual. Nakatu had left her husband after almost ten years of marriage. Grandpa was annoyed by her refusal to go back. As a compromise, he offered to invite the man over in order to hear both sides of the story, but Nakatu replied that even if he were to invite the pope, she would not change her mind. She insisted that her husband's concubine had tried to kill her. "It began with nightmares. As soon as I closed my eyes, I would dream of lions closing in on me and tearing me apart. I started sleeping with the light on because then the nightmares relented a bit. I consulted a seer, and I was told that it was a concubine who wanted to drive me out of the house. When she realized that I was not leaving, she got someone to try to run me over."

"There are too many drunks and freaks with cars."

"I got stomach infections and migraines which disappeared as soon as I left the house and slept elsewhere but returned as soon as I was back. The woman wants me out of the house, and now she can have it."

"Does she have a child with him?" Grandpa asked.

"Not that I know of, but I guess he would not bring children home with all those illnesses plaguing me."

This vague answer did not sit too well with Grandpa. In his experience, it was usually concubines with children who mounted campaigns of terror in order to get recognition for their children and equal treatment for themselves. Kawayida's mother had tried the same tricks. Her plan had been to become the official wife after the death of Serenity's mother. Grandpa had never had any intention of installing her as such, but her son was recognized and welcomed into the family. My guess was that, despite having a son with her, Grandpa was ashamed of her two buckteeth.

"Isn't it strange that a childless woman is driving you out of your house and your marriage?"

"Such behavior is not exclusive to women with children. Maybe she wants to have the children when she enters the house," Grandma said. Saddled with amenorrhea and barrenness, Grandma's marriage had been wrecked by a young girl who took over and produced six children with her husband. It was this piece of real-life experience that shut Grandpa up. He grumbled unintelligibly and later said, "All my daughters are marital failures."

It was another way of saying that Padlock had been right. It was she who had said that Serenity's family was full of marital failures. Normally, Grandpa would not have cared a hoot about such an observation, but his daughter-in-law was not a woman to be ignored. He had tried to block her entry into his son's house and failed. Her observation hurt now because she was still his son's wife and she showed no signs of leaving. Grandpa did not like her much: she was too strong-willed. What he admired about her, on the other hand, was her sense of commitment, a quality he felt Nakatu could do with.

Grandpa's worries were far from over. Nakatu left only two days after her arrival. She went off to visit her sister, Tiida. I was ecstatic. Grandma and Grandpa were mystified.

A month later, she was back, a brand-new marriage proposal in her bag. She had met and fallen in love with Hajj Ali, a former schoolmate ten years older than she. It was unclear whether she had always had him on her mind or whether he was a new phenomenon, but seeing her glowing face left no doubt that Nakatu wanted to marry this former football player who had transferred his competitive skills to the field of trade. Grandpa had so far sent two letters to Nakatu's husband without getting any reply. He was worried that there might be a clash between the two men in his house, which would do nothing to enhance his reputation. He wanted to avoid any unfairness. But then why was Nakatu's husband not coming to state his case? Grandpa did not dwell too much on that. He had a more pressing problem: he felt that he had to quell the fires of the latest Muslim invasion.

"This has gone too far. It has got to stop," he bellowed. "Look what happened to Tiida's husband: the ulcers and those filthy things left in his garden! Why do you women never learn? You looked around and thought your sister was getting something special, and so you decided to get a share too?"

"Sir, it was you who began the invasion, if I may use the word. Kawayida's mother is our mother too, and she is a Muslim. I can assure you that Tiida and her husband are happy. Shared suffering has brought them closer to each other. The madwoman who deposited dog heads in their garden confessed and withdrew claims to their land. Ssali is a better human being now. He is not the arrogant imp he was before."

"Was that why you decided to try the wonders of Islam by finding a Muslim man for yourself? Think about it: you left your husband allegedly because of the sinister activities of his concubine, and now you are entering a relationship in which four wives are legal. Why are you doing this?"

"Hajj Ali is not going to marry any other wives. I am enough for him."

"Foolish woman talk. I believe that Ssali won't marry again because he is highly educated. But what will stop Hajj Ali from doing what he wants? Are you a virgin, or do you still think you are?"

"If he was after virgins, sir, he would not have come knocking on my door. He has had enough of virgins who have to be taught everything. And save your worries for your other children, I know what I am getting into."

"So it is a question of a Muslim man getting tired of Muslim women and trying Christian stock for a change!"

"Sir, I am in love. I am old enough to know that. I also know that something special is going to happen. I can feel it."

Something special eventually did happen: she became pregnant after a drought of about eight years. Grandpa sanctioned the marriage, but without the knowledge that Nakatu was going to convert. By the time he got that particular detail, he had given up.

"They are not going to circumcise you, are they?" he asked in an attempt at humor.

"Whoever heard of women getting circumcised?" Nakatu, victorious, asked.

"Right. You can do what you want. If your husband wanted you, he would have been here already."

That was how Aunt Rose Mary Nakatu became Aunt Hadija Hamza Nakatu. The wedding took place six months after her departure from her husband's house, but most relatives boycotted it. For the first time in many years, Serenity, who had ignored all the dramas in the family, appeared.

This was vintage Serenity, "Cocoon Serenity," as Nakatu called him now and then. Withdrawal was his best form of attack, and after all the storms which had preceded his marriage to Sister Peter "Padlock" Nakaza Nakaze Nakazi Nakazo Nakazu, he had decided to lie low. He had visited Tiida once, when the ulcer and dog-head upheavals were about to end. He was a hands-off type of brother-in-law who never intervened in marital dramas except when especially requested by both parties. He was the first person in the family to address his sister Nakatu as "Hadija Hamza."

Serenity had had his share of a bachelor's troubles, like getting rid of Kasiko, the woman he had cohabited with at the end of the fifties, fathered a daughter with and then decided to send away in order to marry somebody else. Kasiko, a real peasant girl despite her long limbs and good looks, was the husband-has-said kind of woman, ever waiting for commands and ready-made directives to follow, all out to please and to obey. This, for a man who had spent his life maneuvering and outwitting the treacherous rapids and precarious depths of his father's female entourage and his army of female relatives, was frightening. He found himself being studied, analyzed, manipulated and negotiated like a river choked with papyrus reeds, or a steep hill with a soft crumbly surface. It made him nervous and angry. He wanted to be the one doing all the negotiating. Worse still, he could not care less for domestic affairs. Those were matters beneath him, but Kasiko wouldn't learn that. Instead of seeking advice elsewhere, she just kept on dragging him into it, asking whether to buy this or that thing, and cook this or that dish on this or that day. Worst of all, she tried to find out what he thought and what he liked or disliked, things he would rather have kept to himself.

Kasiko was nice, kind, shallow, limited in her ideas—very good in bed, very good in the kitchen and wonderful in the garden—the type of woman many men would have kept as a second wife or a concubine. But polygamy was not on Serenity's mind, at least not at the time. He was looking for a total package: a self-motivated, self-contained, self-regulating woman, good in bed, good in the kitchen, good around the house. A woman who would give him time to prepare his lessons and plan for the future without being distracted by things he considered beneath his dignity.

When Serenity finally informed Grandpa that the time had come for him to part company with Kasiko, he got the green light, with the tacit knowledge that Grandpa would help him find a suitable girl. Arranged marriages were slowly dying out but were not ended yet. To Grandpa, this was an opportunity to show paternal concern for his son. It was time to bring him closer to his heart, and give him a few useful tips on how to be a man and a husband. This was the time to fill a hole or two left gaping, because back when he was chief, he did not have much time to talk to Serenity. So, by suggesting that his son marry the daughter of one of his former colleagues, Grandpa was offering Serenity a hand in friendship and male comradeship. The time had come to introduce him to the clan as a potential clan leader, or at least as one of the leaders. Nowadays clans needed educated leaders. Serenity, with his schoolmaster background, stood a good chance against the traders and the like who often headed clans. If the elders and prominent members of the clan liked him, Serenity might gradually assume the administration of clan land; it would give Grandpa great satisfaction if that privilege remained in his family.

"It is a fine idea that you have finally made up your mind to wed officially. It is a sign of maturity and commitment. A former colleague of mine has a very well-bred, educated, attractive, nubile daughter who is very well suited to your temperament. I know that she will cost us heaven and hell in bride-price, but we are in this together, son. I will give whatever is demanded. What do you say?"

"Ah . . ."

"You see, son, some people put great emphasis on religious denomination, but we are not like that, are we? Not after what has happened in this family. The girl has a Protestant background, but her mother was formerly a Catholic. Maybe she can convert, though

Protestants do not often cross over to Catholicism, but that's beside the point. One needs to marry from a good house, and she comes from a fantastic family. We can always work out the differences."

Overcome by his father's avalanche of saliva and words, Serenity could hardly feel his feet. He seemed to be sinking in mud. His father's green-roofed brick house seemed to be moving, disintegrating, turning to liquid mud, sweeping forward to swallow them.

Serenity wanted the house to disintegrate; he had never liked it. It had given shelter to too many people he had not liked or understood, people who had neither liked nor understood him. It echoed with the shouts, the sighs, the screams, the whispers of all those women, some with children, some without, who swarmed the compound when favor and money were still plentiful. He had seen them do a lot of peculiar things. He had seen mysterious dusts sprinkled in cooking pans, dry leaves set on live coals and sprinkled with magic incantations; he had also heard plots and counterplots whispered in the dark. The walls of that house crawled with the schemes and counterschemes, the struggles and counterstruggles, between male and female relatives and strangers. Those walls reverberated with the fights, some ugly, some comical, between hangers-on and friends, greedy relatives and competitive in-laws. The green roof was laden with the curses of strangers who never got justice or got it too late because the big county chief had people round his house who, intentionally or unintentionally, stopped some people from gaining audience with him.

At the time of Grandpa's fall, when the spirit of the fifties was surging to its climax, the place was no better than a temple inhabited by thieves, each trading, each competing, each scheming for this or that gain. At the time of his fall, the place had gone mad, careening out of control and disorienting everyone in it, despite the fact that some people believed they were in charge. At the time of his fall, Grandpa was just like any other lodger, fighting for his sleeping place, antagonizing as few fellow lodgers as possible, working out shaky alliances in the hope that things would improve in the end.

At the time of the fall, Serenity had stopped eating meals there, and by so doing avoided the intrigue, the jealousies, the diaphanous festivity and the brittle joy that hung in the air like the smell of cow dung. All he was searching for at the Fiddler's house, with its chipped plates, its mutilated mugs, its naked children, was freedom of spirit. At the Fiddler's, surrounded by runny-nosed and runny-assed children, he felt at ease, accepted, not looked at as if he had stolen or was about to steal something.

In the beginning, Serenity had missed his mother terribly, believing that she was about to return. After the blessing from that mysterious woman, after that push into serene hemispheres, he stopped thinking about her, and filled the gap with indifference and dreams of education and music. At the onset of adolescence, he had waited for somebody to say something about his mother, or things a mother said to a son at that juncture. When no one said a thing, not even his aunts, who were the traditional sex educators, he put the ghost to rest. He luxuriated in detachment. His parents became mere shadows, ghosts, and he felt them floating away to the dark confines of a sealed abyss. At that time a close friend lost both parents in a spectacular bus accident which left all on board dead or injured, except for the driver, who escaped without a scratch. At that time he felt that his parents had done him a favor by saving him such pain. He was like that driver, surrounded by wreckage and carnage, but unscathed; surrounded by screams and lamentation, yet unaffected.

He stood looking at the orange tree, lean, gray-green, its thin branches loaded with blighted leaves, short thorns and small green balls. It was said to be his late mother's favorite tree. How little it evoked in him! It left him emotionally untouched, like a desecrated temple or a looted grotto. He had swept its leaves, together with the leaves of the acacia, the jackfruit and the mango trees, thousands of times without feeling anything special.

A storm was blowing in the thick forest of coffee trees around the house. He saw them being uprooted, overturned, broken like straw, swept over the village and ultimately dumped in the papyrus swamp at the foot of Mpande Hill. How many sacks of coffee had he picked in his life? How many wasps had bitten him in the process? How many liters of tears and sweat had seeped into the soil of this coffee shamba? Uncountable. Money from coffee sales had seen him through school up to Teacher Training College, but it had also seen useless people, like his father's women, through many superfluous storms. Many had come, many had gorged and all had moved on to worship at trees sturdier than his father's. Many had come under the clan's umbrella to partake of the proceeds from clan land, and had stayed till his father lost power. Serenity now wanted the storm to rake up all clan land, grind it up and sweep the dust in one mighty, furious river of erosion into the swamps. He wanted the storm to leave behind mean, uninhabitable craters and hostile, snarling gorges into which men would fall and break their necks. He wanted the remains to be so barren that no one would have anything to do with the place. He wanted another family to take over all clan land and all clan land troubles.

Religion? It seemed like poetic justice that his father had lost his power because of a religion he never practiced. At the same time he would not mind if the storm stretched its cadaverous hand to Ndere Hill and flattened the mighty church of his youth, sprinkling the bits in the surrounding forest. The aluminum church tower reminded him of all the fruitless Sunday masses, all the squandered prayers for the return of his mother and all the energy expended on church affairs. It also brought to mind the Virgin Mary: he had begged her to visit him, to turn into his mother. She refused. She would not wipe his tears, the few bitter ones he had ever shed. Now he wanted the tower and the church razed.

In the new life he dreamed of, there was no place for the county chief's daughter flaunting her laudable background, her looks or her suitabilities. This person, whom he had never met and would not care to meet, however qualified she might be, did not figure in his dream. There was already somebody waiting. She was the new star, the new wine, the new Virgin, his ticket to freedom, success and happiness. With her at his side, he would be free of obligation to his father and to his other relatives. She would be the buffer against all the things he hated on his side of the family.

"Sir," he stammered, "I already have somebody."

"Do I know this person?" Grandpa, staggered, hoped it was not a village wench, the type he had spent his life dreading as a potential daughter-in-law. Had Serenity failed to get his priorities right? He closed his eyes for a moment.

"No, sir. She is new. She lives in another county."

"Have you already proposed to her?"

"Not yet, sir."

"I don't like the sound of this, son. How can you build a house on sand? Do you know this person well? Her family background? Her education? Her temperament? How do you know if she is not epileptic or possessed by evil spirits?"

In Serenity's ideal world people never promised things; they just did them. He could not bear to be promised anything. He distrusted all promises and the people who made them. The hunch on his Virgin was good. He was confident that there was nothing to worry about. If she had promised to marry him, he would not have trusted her.

"Do not worry about that, sir."

Grandpa gave vent to his anger. "What sort of seed are you bringing into the family, son?"

Serenity knew what Grandpa meant. He wanted his women tall and elegant, wasp-waisted but firm-butted, and without the kind of boobs "which fell in the food while it was being served." Without buckteeth, too. All Grandpa's women looked alike. He admired consistency of choice—it demonstrated character. He believed that a man fell in love with one woman who appeared in different guises.

Serenity felt uneasy. His Virgin, his new star, was built differently: she was petite, the kind of woman who dried up with age instead of bulging all over and widening like a door. In a way she looked like Grandma, his aunt, though a touch more intense, more ambitious, more hard-willed, more self-contained.

"Some things one leaves to chance or to God," Serenity said, instead of simply asking his father to trust him.

"I am trying to be understanding, son, but all these gray areas and don't-knows do not sound convincing to my experienced ears. I would strongly urge you to consider my proposal. I will arrange for you to meet the girl; maybe that will help to make you realize what I am talking about."

"That won't be necessary, sir."

This was a shrill trumpet blast announcing his first major victory over his father. The risk involved, the total investment in his hunch about his Virgin, made the victory even sweeter. He was beaming. Now it was just him and the Virgin. He had gone for broke; he had put all his eggs in one basket. It made him feel both giddy and good.

"Have you thought about clan land and establishing yourself in clan circles?"

Another triumphant trumpet blast: "Sir, I would like to concentrate on the wedding first."

"It is all up to you, son," Grandpa said heavily, realizing that Serenity was determined to go his own way, and that there was no stopping him. He capitulated. He had done his best. A man was judged by the way he provided for his offspring, by the education he gave them. Serenity could not blame him for anything. Perhaps he should say a few words about the boy's late mother.

"Remember this, son: your mother was the love of my life, but things turned out badly. She must have done what she believed was right. It was just a shame that she could not take anyone into her confidence. If she had let me know about what she felt, I would surely have done something to alleviate the pressure. She hid her feelings from everyone, with catastrophic repercussions. I had planned to grow old with her. I think about her every day. You have a better chance to make things work for you and your family. Grab it."

Serenity had won his freedom. The storm in the coffee shamba ceased. He heard birds chirping, twittering. He saw black migratory birds crossing over from the Northern Hemisphere. He had watched them all his life, waiting for them at the change of season. They were his mascots. One day he would follow them and fly the same route. Right now, there was one person from the village who could follow them: that Stefano girl, Miss Aeroplane, the air hostess. His dream now was to become the second person from the village to fly.

Unlike most prospective grooms, Serenity was not worried about how big a success or how crushing a failure his wedding was going to be. The prospect of marriage had a more insidious effect: it ate away at his crust of indifference and corroded the bulk of his serenity, exposing the deep-seated hate, contempt and fear he reserved for shopkeepers and shops in general. Whatever happened now, he would not be able to escape the claws of those phantoms.

He had to buy new clothes and new shoes, new household goods and countless other things. He was going to spend hours shopping, carrying the ghosts of his fear from shop to shop. Those shopkeepers would touch him, feel him, measure him, dizzy him with their curried, garlicked or scalding breaths, pocket his money and smile their corny smiles. But he would see through them all. In the same mad vein, others were going to enter so many shops, come out with so much stuff and bring it all to him redolent with congratulations. Those goods would be his launchpad into the turbulent waters of married life, parenthood and adult responsibility. He wished there were a better way of expressing the same sentiments and intentions. Shops and shopkeepers had collaborated with a few other elements to make his life a cold, dark-chambered hell. How many times had he been beaten for refusing to go to the shops, or for going there too late and arriving when they were closed? How many times had he been punished for sending others in his stead who, now and then, stole all the money or all the goods or delivered half measures? His biggest problem had been that he could not explain to anybody the reason that he feared or hated shopping. He had been ashamed of his own terror.

One thing was clear: he did not belong in the shops. He did not trust shopkeepers, and he had never entertained the feeling that they trusted him. He always saw those Indians and those few Africans who owned shops, and the faceless financiers and manufacturers, as a species of silver-tongued man-eaters ready to tear people to bits. He saw them as well-dressed robbers with hidden knives, which they used to slice up people for the little they had and the much they hadn't. He saw them as two-faced devils, forever preying on people's peace of mind, sanity and confidence.

Who would believe that sacks of sugar, salt and beans, packets of sweets, matches and exercise books, released the worst fears in him? The fact was that the sight of all those things opened wells of insecurity, canyons of instability and craters of panic in him. Those objects exuded an indifference far bigger, far deeper and far meaner than his; they made him shrivel with insignificance. They exuded an air of preciousness, desirability and indispensability so profound that he could not bear to look at the way they were cared for and secured.

It was the diabolical lure of those very same things that had taken his mother away from him. If they hadn't been so desirable, and if the shopkeepers hadn't polished them so much, he reasoned, his mother would still be with him. Alive. Those precious things, and the shopkeepers, and the man in question had all conspired to take his mother away from him, with her tacit cooperation. The man who took his mother away met her at the shops, bought her things, promised her more and sealed her fate with the phony blessing of a shopkeeper's crocodile smile. How, then, could he control himself, feign or demonstrate indifference, when he was in the snarling jaws of this ring of conspirators? How, then, could he put it all behind him when he could not pinpoint a single conspirator, dead or alive, who had facilitated the dismemberment of his life? Ergo, whenever he was near them, the locusts in his stomach worsened, his tongue disobeyed him, he trembled and failed to express himself. Occasionally, he forgot the items he had traveled kilometers to fetch. Sometimes he bought the wrong brand. All of this had got him in trouble at home. How come, the people queried, it was him alone, and not the girls, who messed up things all the time? Had he shit his brains down the toilet? Or was he just doing it to spite them?

Born in 1933, the year the locust plague laid waste to large areas of the country, Serenity often dreamed of evicting all shopkeepers, exiling and marooning them on a barren island in the Indian Ocean, and of demolishing all shop premises and washing all the rubble into the waters of Lake Victoria. As a victory celebration, he would plant mango and jackfruit trees on all the sites.

Over time, and with a lot of hard work, his confidence had grown. Nowadays he managed his nerves better, and in case of emergency, he could grip the counter, or thrust one arm in a pocket, or present a neat shopping list and elicit a bad-toothed smile from the man behind the counter.

Grandpa's reference to evil spirits might well have been a hunch, a telepathic intimation or even a whiff from the nostrils of the hydra which brandished its three nefarious heads in Virgin's family.

The first head breathed the harsh poison of ultraconservative Catholicism: the type which stifled personal enterprise, glorified poverty and hard labor, extolled stoicism, execrated politics and focussed on heaven. The second head spewed dictatorship: the all-authority-is-from-God type and obedience without question. The third head was responsible for violent temper, Virgin being a second-generation sufferer, and the defense of indefensible contradictory positions, like the Church's stand on abortion, contraception and celibacy.

Grandpa should not have worried: Serenity was ready to deal with anything short of rock-throwing, shit-eating madness. With a touch of idealization kicked up by the Virgin's independence and self-control, he believed there was no female problem he could not handle, and no family conflagration he could not extinguish. A woman or two had made him tremble, a girl or two had started a fire in his balls and released a warm balmy oil in his thorax, but the intensity and the depth of those feelings had not come anywhere near what the Virgin ignited in him. This double-barrelled magmatic flow was his definition of love, and he felt that there was enough of it this time to go where he had not dared to go with Kasiko.

The groom's party made two big visits to the bride's home, or so Serenity remembered. As the two hired oily-white Peugeots packed with men in white tunics, black coats and black shoes went up hills and down valleys, Serenity had locusts on his mind. He could see them swarming in the air, flying, alighting, eating, shitting, shitting and eating. As the locusts on the ground ate and shat, those in the air advanced to virgin territory to eat and shit and shit and eat.

Virgin's village was crammed under a chain of hills that evoked images of a wolf's swollen teats, or the back of a monstrous crocodile. The village and the hills were flanked by a thick forest, stripped bare in 1933, divided in two by a laterite road with red dust that turned to red mud in the rains. The seasonal road into the village was lined with elephant grass and homesteads which stood hundreds of meters from each other. It would be another forty-two years before the village was stripped again, but for now it resembled the nest of a weaver bird crammed under an iron roof. This nest of a village had a sad, subdued air about it. Banana and coffee trees stood bravely in the sun, the former waving in the wind as if to draw attention to themselves, the latter staying still, as though to show how tough they were. At the village entrance were a few shabby shops, the type that specialized in the sale of paraffin, matches, soap and salt, their roofs rusting in the heat and humidity. A few curious eyes watched as the drivers wiped the red dust off the cars and as Serenity's party straightened creased fabric and paid attention to their shoe leather and haircuts.

The glitter of the cars seemed to heighten the tension and the intensity of locust nibbles in Serenity's thorax. After all, he was the one about to be weighed, decanted, measured, tested, approved of or rejected.

At Virgin's parental home the atmosphere was formal, reflected in the white tunics and different kinds of jackets the men wore, and in the wraparound, ankle-length, short-sleeved *busuti*s the women donned. The hosts stood in the red-earth courtyard like polished crockery on a polished tray. The weedless coffee shamba in the background looked like a worn decor for an old oft-rehearsed play. The apparent richness of the visitors' attire and the shine of their cars conspired to give Virgin's parental house a woebegone look, the walls looking a century old and the iron roof, red with rust, a century and a half older.

The guests were ensconced in sofas covered with white table-cloths to hide their diversity of make and ownership and present a uniform image. The women sat down on exquisite mats made in all colors of the rainbow, which, combined with the soft browns, soft greens, and soft reds of the women's busutis, challenged the solemnity of the occasion. Extra cheer was lent by a necklace here, a bunch of bangles there, pearls here, a fake gold watch there.

The strain of their life and their beliefs was deeply etched on Virgin's parents' faces in stark configurations, some of which called to mind tribal scars common in the north of the country. The father was small but strong, a frank expression the main asset of his face. The mother was tall and thin, exhibiting great fortitude and perseverence. If they had on broken-heeled shoes, it did not show, and even if they did, the significance would have paled in the light of the black-framed portraits of the pink-faced, haloed Holy Family. The child Jesus had an expression too serious for his age, and the Virgin Mary had soft features encased in thick-petticoated garments. St. Joseph, exhibiting the silent anguish of an aged cuckold too timid to confront his much younger wife with the severity and implications of her crimes, was standing behind his wife and child in his eternal red anarchist's tunic. Any lingering frivolity would have been canceled out by the portrait of Jesus on the cross, all thorns, all wounds, all blood, occupying a prominent position facing the door.

On this occasion, Serenity was not expected to say much, and in fact he hardly said a word, because he had a speaker to plead his case in the court of Virgin's family and friends. While his speaker went about his job, Serenity was being examined by the members of Virgin's family, very carefully but tactfully. Meanwhile, he could look anywhere he wanted, except up at the roof, which revealed coin-sized portions of sky in places—this because a well-bred person never embarrassed others. For much of the time he kept his eyes on the food and drinks, which he consumed or pretended to consume. He could cough or clear his throat, but not so noisily as to attract undue attention. He could not clean his nails, or attack his teeth with his fingernails, even if a piece of meat as large as a pinkie got lodged between his front teeth. In such a case, he could excuse himself, stand up, hold the hem of his tunic and go outside. To pick his nose, he had to do the same. To fart, belch, scratch his armpit or his groin, he had to follow the same procedure. He could not ogle the womenfolk. He could not address them directly. He could not contradict or correct his in-laws, on fact or error. In general, he had to portray a lamb on the way to the slaughterhouse or at least a wolf in a lamb's skin.

As he went through the motions, he became sure of a few things: (a) he was unimpressed, thus unintimidated, by his brothers-in-law; (b) Virgin's sisters and relatives in general would be treated as they treated him; (c) one of Virgin's paternal aunts, if his memory or the introduction was right, was gorgeous. She and he were probably of the same age. She had not looked down or looked away when the power of his gaze made her aware of his eye. She was a bit oval in the face, a contrast to the round faces of the family, and her big clear eyes, her high forehead and her not so severely restrained, hot-comb-straightened hair gave her an outstanding look. Her long, subtly grooved neck reminded him of his sister Tiida. There was an extremely vague resemblance to Virgin, maybe in the set of the mouth, or in the mouth-nose combination, he could not say. Her smile, which he had seen twice, on both occasions directed toward another family member, burst with the flash of a splitting coconut, the white, smiling teeth seeming to flow and brighten the dark brown facial features. To heighten the tension, and to make sure he had been noticed, he ignored her for some time, looking elsewhere, concentrating on the drinks, and then broke the spell by looking her way over his glass. He caught her eye once again. The third time he tried he found her place empty. She never showed up again until the moment of his departure.

Virgin had appeared only once, to welcome and greet the guests. He imagined her standing in the garden or among the coffee trees, dealing with whatever she was feeling. She had not crumbled or cracked under the pressure. For that you could trust the Catholics: they knew how to instill character, and how to hone it like a knife on an age-old whetstone.

It took Serenity a whole week to deal with the refraction of reality occasioned by so much sudden attention. By the time the second visit beckoned, he was relaxed enough to welcome it. Now he felt like a well-to-do teacher addressing a crowd of well-behaved but needy pupils. The nibbling teeth of gastric and thoracic locusts that had terrorized him on the previous occasion were gone. Women were cheap here in the central region, in contrast to the cattle-rearing peoples in the west and the north, where bride-price could rise up to one hundred head of cattle. Here people asked for calabashes of beer, bolts of cloth, tins of paraffin, ceremonial chickens, a lump sum of money and a few other minor things. Bridegrooms often felt compelled to outdo themselves in dazzling displays of generosity. The overriding feeling Serenity had on this bride-price setting and paying day was that these people could use a bit of financial help, if their beliefs allowed it, and the safest way to secure it would be by asking an exorbitant bride-price.

This time around, he and his father were in for a pleasant surprise: these people had no intention of exacting self-enrichment in exchange for their daughter. They asked for very little. It seemed so embarrassingly cheap that when the groom's team withdrew to confer, the two glittering cars swollen in front of them like bizarre money chests, they had no option but to put on a garish display of generosity.

Grandpa wanted to donate a cow and a calf. Serenity, however, wanted something more visibly urgent: a new roof. It was bound to last longer anyway, impervious as it was to *nagana* and other cattle-killing diseases. There was disagreement between father and son. To help break the deadlock, Mbale, Virgin's eldest brother and officiating brother-in-law, was summoned. A firsthand torture victim of roof-leakings and of the recurrent youthful nightmare that they would wake up one night trapped in a roofless house, Mbale sided with Serenity. He was then charged with the task of whispering the gift in the family's ear. Virgin's parents were opposed to this overt desecration of the temple of matrimonial holiness—their daughter was not a cow to be sold for the glorification of Mammon—but the rest of the family moved in with full force. Who among them had not dreaded family visits in the rainy season? Who among them had not thought of helping the family out by roofing the house forcibly if necessary? This was the occasion to do it. Afterward, when the wedding was over, it would be too late.

The majority won, and the gift was accepted. The interesting part was watching Mbale and a few other men, who knew a lot about roofs and the price of iron sheets, capped and uncapped nails, beams, labor and the like, calculating how much money was needed to complete the job as quickly as possible. Virgin's parents, dismayed at having failed to kick the traders out of the temple, could not bear the lugubrious look of the crucified Jesus and left the house. They went for a long, somber walk, bemoaning the shameful hijacking of holy matrimony by Mammon.

Serenity loved the histrionics. For the first time in living memory he did not begrudge the shopkeepers their earnings. He could already see the new iron sheets glittering in the sun. There was another fine twist to it all: the spirit of the corrugated-iron church tower he had wanted to destroy had invaded this house, and was about to shatter or dent this family's very Catholic sensibilities. Here, it would not be a tower, but it would have as much power. Mammon's profanity was going to shine. Strangers in sweaty overalls were going to invade this place, tear down the dilapidated roof and spray the air with rust, broken nails and rotten beams. Buried in the rubble would be the Virgin Mary, with her dead alabaster smell and promises. Up would go the new roof, proclaiming the rise of the new Virgin and her new wine. Up would go the new roof and the thrust of his new life, power and the glitter of his new dream. The heap of banknotes, a mini-tower in itself, made him feel happy. He was not like those grooms who promised heaven and earth before the wedding, and afterward failed to fulfill those promises, bloated with tactical amnesia. Everything was going to be on time: he was a doer, not a promiser.

Virgin watched the roofers, heard their oblique comments and resented them for sprinkling rust in the butter oil her aunt was rubbing into her skin to super-condition it for the wedding. Local butter oil redolent with a faint milk smell was used because it worked better than industrial products. It made the skin browner, clearer and tighter on the bones. Virgin, like most peasant girls not raised around cows and fresh milk, found the scent disturbing, almost nauseating. The fear of carrying a milk smell in her bridal garments and into her marital bed bothered her. One had to make a perfect first impression. One did not want a niggling imperfection wedging itself into the scheme of more important things. She was gripped by the fear that the baths, some herbal, would not defeat the smell.

Although she felt like exploding in kaleidoscopic displays of violent anxiety, she kept her temper under wraps. She wanted to maintain control of what was going on around her. But how could she manage to achieve that amidst all the hammering, the shouting and the leering of the roofers? How could she remain the center of attention when so many relatives, friends, villagers and strangers were milling about, calling, screaming, barking orders, contesting superior knowledge of decorum, custom, tradition, religion and nonsense? All the villagers who owed her parents a favor and those who didn't were there, lending a hand, necessary or superfluous, adding to the madness. Most annoying of all, religion had been chucked to the sidelines. Nobody said morning or evening prayers anymore. People all around her were indulging their lusts without a care in the world. Her parents had given up trying to make them say grace before meals. Local beer was flowing down cheerful throats all day. In short: The Devil was winning when this should have been God's biggest hour. And there she was, unable to do anything about it.

Amidst this physical and mental turmoil, the bride turned her mind to her father-in-law, and she experienced something akin to hot flashes. She did not like the man at all. All the vibes from that direction were wrong. Their two personalities were antagonistic, and yet she was destined to spend a number of years as his neighbor. How was she going to do that? She also worried about Serenity's aunt. She did not like her either. Who could like a woman suffering from amenorrhea? It was whispered that she had menstruated only thrice in her whole life. Such people were often witches, people to be feared. Their tongues were often potent beyond measure, making things happen even if they did not mean them to. On top of it, the woman had had that buffalo dream. What was she supposed to make of it? How could she make something of anything when she was not in control, when the whole world seemed to be milling around on top of her head?

She could have called off the wedding, but who had ever heard of

a peasant girl calling off a wedding? After all this? Who would listen
to her? Which fancy reasons would she give? A bride's sensitivities
and anxieties? She knew nothing would wash with this crowd of lively
souls. And she did not want to call the wedding off, even if she could.
It was her show, her day in the sun. All the impotence and hostility she
felt against Serenity, against herself, the roofers, Mbale, Sr. John
Chrysostom (her erstwhile Mother Superior), and against the world,
was a way of coming to terms with her new position in life, her new
powers, her new expectations, her new dreams.

Serenity was in seventh heaven; Virgin's family were quivering with
the thunder of his power. His success felt even sweeter when put into
proper perspective. As a typical go-between man, always relying on
others to transmit his messages and negotiate on his behalf in matters
of the heart, he had suffered terrible anxiety, a condition exacerbated
by the second go-between's long absences and mysterious silences.
Had she betrayed him and chickened out? That was how people generally let one know that there was no hope. Such people assumed that
it saved your feelings and your dignity a few ugly dents. Serenity always preferred to have the bad news up front: it hurt intensely at first,
but the pain disappeared gradually into the mists of fate or in the vapors of another chance arising. Serenity was not the conquering type;
unlike his father, he found the fear of rejection too real. He preferred
the mediation of others and the time it gave him to digest and weigh all
possible outcomes. He thought of himself as a crocodile, ever conserving his energy by waiting and letting the prey come to him. That
anesthetized him against the guilt some conquerors felt when termi-
nating relationships. He always felt that the prey had seen it coming.
Virgin had delivered herself to him, and the intensity of the fire she
had ignited in him, coupled with the psychological lift he had given
her, should have canceled out any hesitation whatsoever. So why was
she torturing him?

As the nights sat on him and the pressure and the pain permeated
every fiber in his body, Serenity went over the course of his prelimi-
nary dealings with Virgin. He had surely not forced himself on her.
The attraction had been mutual. In addition, he had shown her great
respect. He had not blown his trumpet, or said anything to inflate his
ego. If anything, he had given her the impression that her opinion was

all that mattered. Why, then, was there this horrible news blackout? The weakness of the go-between system was that it left many questions unanswered for too long. How long was he supposed to wait? The days had now gone into high double digits. Anger and frustration had corroded his patience, his understanding, his hope. When the pain became too harsh, he contemplated dropping her. He could do it because he was a man aware of defeat in life; the feeling would not be new. He could call off the go-between, swear never to see Virgin again and crawl back into his father's arms. He gave it three more days and nights. However, just as if Virgin had been spying on him, seeing into his mind and gauging his limit, he got a message from her two days later.

Virgin had felt it necessary to hold nine consecutive novenas to St. Jude Thaddeus, praying for assurance that Serenity was the man for her, because marriage was forever, divorce unthinkable. She prayed for fortitude to deal with Kasiko's devilries, if any, and for enlightenment to guide her through the difficulties ahead. She prayed for happiness and for health. She prayed for twelve healthy, God-fearing children and for the strength to raise them. In the face of the seriousness and the holiness of matrimony, time had ceased to matter. She could have made it ten or more novenas without feeling that she had taken too much time. In her view, a man who had been living in sin deserved to wait however long it took the Lord to answer her prayers. Such an individual had to undergo some mortification in order to achieve the purification necessary to enter into holy matrimony with a virgin.

The wedding of the former county chief's son gathered friends and relatives, strangers and villagers, from far and wide. The three houses in the homestead and the grass huts erected ad hoc for the wedding were filled to capacity. There were three days of intense activity, which climaxed on the Saturday the bride entered the house of her groom in holy union. It was set to be the wedding of the decade in the area. Grandpa made sure that everything was in order, and that there was enough food and drink for everyone. Great fires kicked up monstrous sparks and punctured the dark night with their glow. The air reverberated with singing, drumming, dancing, arguments, speeches, fights and a panoply of human activity left unrecorded. The smell of beer, meat and banana plantain combined to wrench memories back to the days when Grandpa was still in power and people came to feast at his house every fortnight. This was how it had been; how many wanted it to be; how it might never be again. The lukewarm fingers of nostalgia stroked the hearts of the old, garnishing the smells and the sounds and the fires with old truths turned to dull uncertainties in today's environment. Many dreamed about their own weddings, long ago when they were still men among men, when a bride had to be a virgin in order to get married and stay married.

Many remembered Tiida's and Nakatu's weddings. A daughter's wedding was a mild affair, because a family member was leaving, given away, taken away to bring life and happiness to another family. Such celebration was lopsided, and did not last deep into the night. Who would want to celebrate when the children the girls bred were going to carry other people's clan names? But this time, as in all cases when a son brought a bride home, somebody was coming to enrich the family and the clan with children. This was what gave the night its sharp sexual edge, its lewd undertones, its aggressive joy. It was as if everyone were going to marry and deflower the bride, and bite into virgin, undilated, unpolluted meat. It was the reason why the beer went to the head, loosened the tongue and came out in dirty jokes, naughty songs and provocative pelvic gyrations.

For Grandpa this was almost a repeat of his own bachelor-party night. His name was being mentioned a lot around the fires. His old praise songs were being sung here and there. The Red Squirrel Clan anthem was being drummed out at intervals on an old scuffed drum. Prominent clan members and leaders were talking about him, speculating on the remainder of his tenure as clan land administrator, weighing Serenity's chances as possible successor to the post. Clan politics was the unstated theme of the evening and of tomorrow's wedding day. By this time tomorrow, the bride would no longer be a virgin, and her character and fecundity would be the next episodes in the drama of her entry into this house and clan.

My parents' wedding was consecrated in an old Catholic church chosen by my maternal grandparents. There, encased in thick brick walls, amidst dim, colored light falling from stained-glass windows onto a lugubrious Christ, watching the joyous proceedings from his ugly cross; there, amidst pungent clouds of incense which killed off any neurotic insinuations of milk smells and other bodily odors stubborn enough to withstand the fastidious bathing and perfumings everyone had undergone; there, amidst the cheerful smiles and sibilant whispers of witnesses from both families, Sr. Peter Padlock and Serenity became wife and husband.

A good part of the bride's family never made it to the church, or to her new home, because they had insisted on transporting themselves as a group and had turned down Grandpa's offer of a bus. The carcass of a bus they hired broke down. The carcass of a truck they replaced it with got two punctures and, having only one spare tire, could not proceed farther. The sorry and not-so-sorry vans they commandeered, with great ingenuity, could take only the most prominent members of the family, vastly outnumbered by their counterparts who, in addition to cars, had two hardened Albion buses at their disposal.

As night fell, a ten-year-old black Mercedes thrust the newlyweds into the vortex of the celebration. The car was mobbed, the streamers parted, and greedy faces peeked inside at the clouds of tulle to see the bride. It took some time to extract the pair from the car, whose owner's daughter Grandpa, Tiida, Nakatu, Kawayida and some other close relatives felt Serenity should have married. At last, the bride, swimming in tulle, with a white, moon-like crown on her head, orchids in the crook of one hand, Serenity's hand in the other, waded through the mud-thick ululation, clapping, drumming, singing and gobbling eyes. She could hardly feel Serenity at her side in his small-lapelled black suit, white shirt, dark tongue-wide tie and pointy shoes. A crew cut had made his head look severely smaller, his figure taller and thinner and his ears squirrel-like.

The newlyweds were installed on a wooden dais covered with white mats, and seated in sofas covered with white cloth not so much to disguise their diversity of design or ownership as to cater to uniformity and a sense of conjugal purity. A glittering silver hurricane lamp, unbothered by a single moth, flashed as it rocked gently above them to the thunder of the jubilation. Padlock felt transparent, hypnotized and nauseated by such intense scrutiny, but it was the dancers who gave her an asphyxiating sensation in her chest which, at times, made her afraid that she was going to pass out. To the deep, hard beat of the big drum the dancers made the most profane, most horrifying, most beshaming pelvic thrusts she had ever seen. They had comically accentuated their waists with padded long-haired colobus monkey sashes, making their thrusts look disturbingly larger, bolder and more obscene. Man or woman, they gyrated, ground very deep and, with legs spread in the exaggerated way of somebody getting off a high bicycle, drew back, quivering with sexual suggestion. Swivelling waists in which there was no unoiled bone and moving on feet which barely touched the ground, the dancers advanced toward two poles planted directly in front of the newlyweds, grabbed them and smothered them in diabolically frenzied pelvic thrusts. The crowd, drooling like tortured dogs, went crazy, so crazy that the whole booth shook as people followed suit, grabbing poles near them and fucking them in explosions of unadulterated joy.

Virgin could have covered her face but for the crown and the gloves. The sensation of being grabbed by powerful hands swept over her, making the shame of every thrust a very palpable ordeal. The crowd was fucking her, raping her, deflowering her, gobbling the rivers of blood that poured from her cavities. She would have wished to die, but this was her wedding, her show, her path to the new life and the mission she had dreamed of for so long. She visualized Jesus on the cross, all blood, all wounds, all pain. She closed her eyes, and when she opened them the dancers were gone.

Speeches were in progress. Grandpa, in a white tunic and a black coat, welcomed everyone, thanked them for honoring his family with their presence and requested that they stay until the break of day. Other speakers came and went without saying much. Most were more like preachers than speakers. They tried to inflame the crowd with such words as faith, loyalty, forbearance, respect for elders, but they never really succeeded. All these words poured over the bride and the audience like spent bullets. The bride felt like a stonefish extracted from the ocean floor and thrust into a laboratory tank for public display. She had to fight feelings of tension, alienation, irritation and impatience. It was true that she had craved attention, but what she had got was a deluge which made her feel like she was drowning. What were these people looking at so intensely? Her face? The tulle or the crown? Was this happening to her alone, or was it common at every wedding? Had

Serenity caused a scandal and were people wondering how she would cope? Or was it simply her mind playing games with her, seeing things where there was nothing? Why, why were they staring at her like that? Christ . . .

The next thing she saw was the cake and the glittering silver knife. She felt a stiff nudge from her matron. She rose and followed Serenity. He tried to help her with the bridal train and only succeeded in making her balance worse. She stumbled as she tried to keep her eyes on the steps, on the cake and on her groom at the same time. The moon on her head shifted out of orbit. Serenity acted quickly: he checked her fall. The moon returned to its orbit with a few expert touches from the matron. The crowd cheered. The drummer struck a few expert undulating beats. The bride cut the cake in a disembodied haze.

Children with outstretched palms surrounded her, the girls glowing with admiration, the boys alive with curiosity. Suddenly they all looked like Serenity's illegitimate daughter, and were mocking her, sneering at her, openly despising her for supplanting their mother. Suddenly their mother was responsible for the breakdown of the truck and the bus which should have brought her family to this place to be with her. Suddenly she felt isolated, surrounded by children ready to pelt her with rocks, and adults ready to enjoy it. After the shame of those pelvic thrusts, and of the communal defloration, it had come to this: death at the hands of Kasiko's diabolical child! Why was this child, and all copies of herself, smiling so sweetly, so innocently? The matron rescued her: she took the plate from her hands and distributed the cake to the jubilant children who, because their parents were hard by, were subdued and very disciplined.

The cake seemed to have gone to the head of the crowd, which responded feverishly to the assault of the dancers and the drummers. The whole booth was swinging, rocking to the shouting, the clapping and the whistling of the crowd. Amidst this explosion, the bride was whisked away from the dais.

Serenity was nervous, groggy, anxious. He had not been this close to his wife in a long time. He was in the grip of a very vague yet very real fear. His courage, his virility, his self-control were at their nadir. Erections! They seemed to be manufactured in a factory far away in the hemisphere where the black birds, his mascots, came from. The spark he had been gathering, the ball-bursting explosion he had been dreaming of, seemed to have fizzled out. He was now in the bedroom of his bachelor years, the room which had witnessed his best and his worst sexual encounters. Inside these tight walls he had had sex with Kasiko. In the tightness of this room his daughter, God protect her, had been conceived. Outside this room, in the spare bedroom, the same daughter had been born, under Grandma's supervision. The moans of his brother Kawayida's premarital sex partners seemed to mix with the moans of his own women to give this room a strange feeling of looming disaster. He knew that it was imperative to decapitate all those ghastly hydras haunting the room, watch them writhe in death's throes, and then await a new spirit to arise and possess him. Before that, it could only be disaster. He wished he had wedded at a friend's house, some neutral territory unhaunted by the past.

As he waited for Virgin to bathe the day's worries, storms, fears and dust off her body, he inopportunely remembered Kasiko's parting shot: "You are rejecting your Eve, your own rib. If I am not enough for you, why can't you have us both? I will do anything to make you see your mistake . . ." Was that a threat or the purest bluff? The unsettling vagueness of it!

Serenity felt his bowels melt with shock: his bride was being escorted into the bedroom by the very woman he had exchanged meaningful looks with! His throat was parched, his hands were trembling. Was this a trick? Thrust as he now was inside the caverns of many men's dreams, the dreams of being taken care of by two luscious females, he clammed up. This could not be true: who had chosen this woman as the officiating aunt for his virgin?

In that capacity, she was there to help the couple get down to the nitty-gritty of their nuptials, if they needed her guidance at all. She had gunned for the job, not so much for the pair of sheets she stood to gain if Virgin was indeed a virgin, or for the honors, but for more personal reasons. The groom was an interesting person, a learned man whose friendship or acquaintance could be beneficial to her. It had not happened in years that she liked somebody the first time she encountered him. This man was the reincarnation of an adolescent crush, when she had become infatuated with a teacher and done her best to fuck him. Thank God, the man had been old-fashioned and far more sensible than she. It was that admiration that she now wanted to invest in her new in-law.

The first intimate encounter between my parents in many ways typified the whole pattern of their marriage. Serenity wanted Virgin's aunt out of their bedroom: her absence would lessen the myriad thoracic and gastric locusts nibbling at him. And anyway, he was not a virgin; he did not need anyone's help. The woman, large eyes downcast, resignedly left the room, but then had to return because every time Serenity touched Virgin, she pushed him away.

In her mind, Serenity personified the crowd of lechers and perverts who had made her life a hell with unholy pelvic thrusts and booth-pole fuckings. She was not going to allow him to deputize for them. She recalled the teachings of St. John Chrysostom: "Bodily beauty is phlegm . . ." In the convent, they used to call what he intended to pour in her womb "holy snot." The sound of it!

Virgin's aunt, untainted by either the words of St. John Chrysostom or their slow-working effect, restored order by reiterating the importance of the "holy" exercise. Holy snot or devil snot, the deed had to be done. Serenity, now under the eye of the woman he had once played eye games with, fumbled, barely erect, and got cut by the three-day-old stubble, gritty as iron rust, cultivated by the bride, who had just been introduced to the workings of the double-edge razor blade. In the convent they used to pull out those devil hairs one by one, not so much for the less brutal stubble which resulted as for the mortification part of the exercise. Cut, angry, frustrated, the squeaking bedsprings as irritating as locust bites, Serenity boiled in his own anger. The joyless futility of it was magnified by too keen an awareness of his bride's indifference, and the supervisor's eye on parts of his body he never revealed to strangers.

The situation became so pathetic, so desperately insufferable, quiet as it was in the room and in the booth outside as the drummers rested and ate their supper, that Virgin's aunt had to intervene in more than supervisory capacity. Authorized in all ways to get the job done, she, in the politest, kindest voice Serenity had heard that day, called for a break. As Serenity left the bed, she touched him on the shoulder to direct him to the chair where a beer awaited him. That was the key he had been searching for all day: it minced the wall of mist in which his virility had been frozen. It closed the book on his fears, propelled him into rarefied realms of relief and engendered in him a blissful absence of anxiety. The relief swelled to such proportions that he wondered, as he sipped the beer, whether it had not gone beyond the mere healing of his past anxieties. Was it degenerating into desire for his bride's aunt? The possibility that he could have real feelings for her crashed over him, and he felt mud sucking at his feet, pulling him to depths he dared not reach. The temptation was to see the bride and her aunt as complementary parts of one character, one person. If Virgin was the serious, determined, ambitious one, her aunt, then, had to be the playful, happy, lustful provider of fun. He had never been thrust onto the horns of such a dilemma before, and he prayed that this was pure fantasy, the hallucinations of an overwrought, overworked bridegroom.

Virgin's aunt had been whispering things in his ear, but Serenity heard nothing. He shook to the core as he felt the hand on his shoulder again. The charge kicked like a mule. The woman sat down, and a gleaming dark knee caught in the golden light made him dizzy with confusion and pent-up desire. A touch on his calf shot his body full of delicious sensations. If this was not where the fate of the trio was sealed, it was where their lives, like three rivers going down a steep mountain, met, joined and fought their way to the bitter sea behind the mists.

Serenity was back on his way, rejuvenated, energetic, fiery in the thorax, ticklish in the balls, with wells of licentious power pumping from his stomach. He got cut again, but he hardly felt it or cared. The whitewashed walls, the white tablecloths and the white sheets seemed to tremble and quiver. He needed all the energy his stomach provided, for his wife had the hymen of a thousand women. His breath cut his windpipe as he breathed hard, sweating with the determination that even if his wife had a hymen tough as rawhide, he would bore through it.

With the walls cracking and tilting, the mice squeaking and squealing and the sheets crackling and rustling, Serenity tore through the barrier, Virgin a rocking wave of muscle. Three rubies, two big ones and a very small one, were created. The bride's aunt, a smile on her face, congratulated them, happy that the bride had not climbed trees, ridden bicycles or played with sharp objects that would have torn her hymen. The creation was whisked away for examination by a relative or two from both families. Serenity, now all smiles, awarded his bride's family a large, juicy goat, according to custom.

Changed into a crownless outfit, with a stiff, pained look on her face, the bride returned to the booth. The dancers were back with their pelvic thrusts and gyrations. The crowd was afire with expectation. It would be a free-for-all, with everyone dancing or singing along; diehards cursing, catcalling, ferreting for quick sex or fighting, and the remaining old people retiring to make room for youthful excesses. The drummers struck the drums and the fiddlers rubbed the fiddles with great vigor, charged by the food, the beer and the full-throated cheers from the crowd. The bride could have tossed everyone into hellfire, if only to wipe the all-knowing glint from the eyes directed at her. The quick ones had already heard that she had been a virgin, and the drunken imaginings of blood and tight sex seemed to have made them bolder, more provocative.

Serenity was on the same wavelength with the crowd. He was so confident and so happy that he ignored the fire from the deep cuts on his glans. He enjoyed the attention and the congratulations he got from friends, relatives and strangers who came up onto the dais to shake his hand and whisper a few words in his ear. Their excessive politeness reminded him of his father at the height of his power. For a moment he even thought about campaigning for the post of clan land administrator. This was a dream away from the gap-toothed cheers of his pupils on parade or at the football pitch. The wave thrust him into the center of a hot political rally, with the loudspeakers booming, the politicians shouting and the crowd intoxicated with promises of a better life. Independence was approaching, and something coming off the imaginary rally crowd told him that he could not miss out on this chance of a lifetime. All the drumming, the singing, the dancing and the obsequious congratulations told him one thing: to grab the chance and better himself.

Serenity got up as two dancers approached the dais with waists gyrating, bellies jiggling, legs spread wide in anticipation of one of those spectacular splits which cramped amateur leg muscles. He went down to meet them, and they smothered him with bad-woman smiles. They thrust their dancerly pelvises at him, simulating copulation at its hardest and most playful. He shook fluidly, as they grabbed his arms and quivered as if the earth were coming off its hinges. Then, raising their legs as if they were male dogs with cramped thigh muscles attempting to piss on a high section of pole, they quivered their withdrawal. The bride could have shot the whole lot. She could also have shot Serenity for taking off his coat, tying it round his waist, following the dancers and almost tripping over the straw on the booth floor. He was a bad dancer, too stiff, too inelegant, but since he was the groom, the man responsible for the extravaganza, the crowd cheered. He was floating on a new wave, intoxicated with a new daredevil spirit unwitnessed before. He was not sure about the origin of this blaze, and he didn't want to pry too much for the fear of losing it or frightening it away. He hoped, as he pranced, that it had something to do with the rubies, and nothing to do with that magic touch on his shoulder. He was swallowed up by the crowd. They started pouring beer all over him, thrusting banknotes into his pockets and lifting him high in the air. All the drums seemed to be throbbing and thundering in his head. Grandpa was ecstatic. He swayed like a drunken dancer. Tiida and Nakatu were dancing, and shouting for good measure. Grandma was waving a scarf in the air to the rhythm of the song.

The last person he saw was Nakibuka, the officiating bridal aunt, disrobing him, washing the beer, puke and grime off him and ultimately leading him to bed.

Weddings were notorious for their anticlimaxes, and if the evidence outside Serenity's house was anything to go by, something of a small disaster had insinuated itself into the jubilations. There was so much vomit outside the booth and on the veranda and in the road that if it hadn't been too ridiculous to think that some plotter had paid people to vomit, Serenity would readily have believed that there was somebody behind it. All the banana plantain, all the lean meat, all the cow's entrails and all the beer was there, with the least apology of digestion. The latrines and their environs were major disaster areas. Serenity had never seen such quantities of shit in his entire life. The trails of yellowish-green diarrhea were even more unsettling. If a herd of hippos weren't to blame for this prodigal spread of dung, then there must have been something terribly wrong with the banana beer the crowd had consumed. He remembered that, as was usual on such occasions, various people had donated drinks without anyone putting them on a list. What would a list of donors have helped anyway, he thought, and shrugged uneasily.

To clear away all the garbage, all the grass huts, all the muck, would claim a few days, but there was no shortage of volunteers. Luckily, no one complained about the beer or the food, and no deaths had been reported in the course of the week. So it hadn't been a plot after all! So nobody had put bits of hyena's liver in the drinks or in the food! What a relief!

In a social hierarchy where the husband's family ranked above the wife's, any woman hoping to do things her own way had to seize the initiative from day one of her honeymoon and send clear messages to her spouse's relatives, and that was exactly what Padlock did with her glum expression and her taciturn attitude. Serenity's relatives soon found themselves marooned in a steadily contracting sitting room with a noncommunicative bride in front of them and a heavy, oppressive silence. A few wished Nakibuka were the bride, because she was cheerful, talkative and had a very sweet smile. They soon learned not to call when Serenity was out, which was often, because he had many things to deal with apart from resuming his classroom duties.

Serenity's sisters, Tiida and Nakatu, both marriage veterans and very knowledgeable in these matters, quickly realized that their brother had married a woman to keep them out of his house. Like many other relatives, they left for home as soon as the mountains of shit and the pools of vomit had been cleared, the borrowed chairs and benches returned and the booth dismantled. Tiida summed up her feelings: "She is some woman indeed. Another unclimbable Mpande Hill."

"I told you," Nakatu replied. Both further agreed that the mountains of shit and lakes of vomit were indicators of fecundity. They knew that this was a woman to outbreed all. Not that they were in direct competition with their younger brother, but it was still a sign of power to bring many children to your father's house when there was a wedding, a funeral or a clan meeting. Tiida had stopped breeding: the doctor, with his sensitive stomach and nose, could not bear the sight of nappies or the noise of children after a long day at the hospital. He had wanted only two children. Tiida had given him four, after a lot of pleading for the extra two. Nakatu had two children, twins, and it was feared that the pair had damaged something inside her to the effect that, despite many well-timed efforts, she had not conceived in the last eight years. It was she, with her unfulfilled desires, who was not too pleased with the bride's putative fecundity. This was before she met Hajj Ali and his miracle-working semen. Nakatu did not like the bride very much, and in a way was pleased that she had turned out to be such a grouch; she would not need much reason to avoid her.

Padlock, for one, did not miss the company of her sisters-in-law much. Of the two she liked Tiida a little bit more. Tiida impressed her as a doer, someone trying to better herself all the time. The sad thing was that she was going in the wrong direction. The unforgivable affliction of pride and vanity she exhibited made Padlock pity her. A woman who bathed four times a day, fussed over just about everything and boasted about her flush toilet, her marble bathroom and her husband's big post was sick, insufferable and highly pitiable. If Tiida had not been her sister-in-law, she could have sat her down and warned her about her affliction, and even shown her a way of overcoming it. She could have gone on to inform her that vanity indicated a lack of self-knowledge so deep that she would need a lot of hard work to combat it. How she would have liked to hammer it into Tiida's proud head that beauty, especially the type she washed four times a day, was phlegm, blood, bile, rheum . . . She would have rubbed her nose in the writings of St. John Chrysostom, and even used the cane, if necessary, to make her take them on board. But sisters-in-law were royalty, incorrigible and damned to drown in their muck.

From the throne of her new reign Padlock reviewed Nakatu with a sick feeling of disdain. She was like a louse to her. Her insecurity, revealed in her ranting about her twins, her tall, gorgeous husband and the Raleigh bicycle he had given Grandpa, made her nauseated. This was lack of, or weakness of, character, accentuated by a deficient religious upbringing. What had the priests and the catechists done in this parish? Had they left the Devil to take over and eat the essence out of people? At the core of Nakatu was a pool of instability so fathomless that Padlock was sure the woman could be swayed this way and that, to the extent of sleeping with Muslims, marrying them or even converting to their religion. Padlock was sure that Nakatu was being exploited by witch doctors, who promised her children, ate her chicken and stole her money for nothing, soothing her mind with empty rituals which would pave her way to final damnation. She could see her strip, dance naked in front of fires and bathe in all sorts of garbage: the blood of animals, the piss of beasts, anything the witch doctors prescribed. She could see her drink concoctions made of lizard blood, snake eggs, anything. She could see her lie with circumcised witch doctors who specialized in conning women out of their money and their flesh. Her sister-in-law's soul was yearning for a very serious exorcism. How she would have liked to drive all those demons out of her! From behind the wall of her glumness, the bride saw herself fasting, locking Nakatu up for days, entering her demon-filled room, stripping her, whipping her, commanding the Devil to leave her body. She would finally give her enemas with holy water, baptize her a second time and let her go. But sisters-in-law were royalty, incorrigible and damned to drown in their muck.

According to Padlock's battle plan, Grandpa and Grandma were going to be tackled directly, through a show of sublime resentment aimed at discouraging their interference in her affairs. She did not like Grandpa, because he was the only person to make her feel uncomfortable and insecure. Who was he to do that to her? She always felt that, given the chance, he would scheme to reinstate Kasiko or to drive his son into the machismo of taking a second wife. She, however, was going to take the initiative and deliver a son first, one of the many to follow. With a dozen offspring, she knew that she would be invincible and in position to manipulate the situation to her advantage. That would be the best way to wipe the self-congratulatory look off the old man's face. It was the insufferable look of somebody who had cured another's leprosy—she, of course, being the leper, delivered from the leprosy of poverty. This, after all, was the man who had warned his son that he was marrying below his station. This, indeed, was the man who had, ever so un-Catholicly, questioned the quality of her genes. As a Catholic, she had to forgive seven times seventy times, and she had already forgiven him, but she would never forget.

She would, over time, make him eat his words. She would, over the years, extinguish the flash of corrugated-iron sheets she saw in his eyes whenever he looked at her. She still knelt for him, as she was supposed to, and she stayed on her knees as he addressed her with the eternally irritating question "Are you fine, girl?" Did the old man think that she had just been operated on by a team of drunken surgeons, given a defective heart or relieved of a terrible hernia? Or had her rubies, and the goat his son had given her family, put stupid ideas in the old man's head? Did he think that his son was hung like a zebra, and that whenever he did it she had to be revived with cold water and then stitched up? She wanted very much to assure him that his son was quite average, and that from now on he would be in for regular droughts. To start with, there would be no sex on Saturdays and Sundays, on major Church feast days, on the feasts of St. Peter and St. John Chrysostom and during the forty days of Lent, the Holy Week and pregnancy. So if this old man believed in whispered falsehoods, she would correct the error. But for now, like any good daughter-in-law, she knelt, and even smiled when the word "girl" dropped from the old man's lips.

Now, this old man rightly deposed from power years ago spoke with the authority of a despotic chief, giving the word intimations of a blessing, lacing compromise in its sounds: peasant you could be, he implied, but thank God you are not a work-broken hag. There was also a touch of condescension and doubt in it. She knew that, for himself and for others, he approved only of tall women, and she was not a tall woman. She didn't have those excessively wide pelvic plateaus famed for fecundity. She was not possessed of an elephant's back. But she would show him that she meant business. For the moment, as she rose and saw the two depressions left by her knees on the ground, she whispered, "Lord, Lord, Lord, how low have I sunk! How long have I got to be measured against the standards of common women and whores?"

Like all seemingly helpless souls, Serenity was fought over by many over a long period of time. The truth was that even after his migration to the city, many people still argued about the viability of his marriage and the suitability of his wife. On many a sultry afternoon, with a good meal under their belt, the coffee kettle sizzling on the fire, a mild wind combing the countryside and teasing banana trees in their afternoon torpor, my grandparents would discuss his affairs. Grandpa would suddenly change the topic of conversation and say, "He should never have married that girl. A chief's son should never be bossed about by a little peasant girl."

"It was his choice, and as long as they get on reasonably well . . . Anyway, Sere's mother was a chief's daughter, and look what happened to her."

"That was different. The woman had a worm in the head: she could not settle down. She thought that the whole world revolved around her. I gave her the best silks, fed her the best goat meat, treated her the best way I knew, and yet she cheated on me. With that worthless bastard. She left her children for that feckless lout!"

"You did not pay her the attention she needed. She was the youngest woman about, pitted against diehard cases who had already seen everything between heaven and hell."

"Come on, sister. She was my favorite wife. What more did she expect? On second thought, I should have sent a policeman after her and dragged her back here. I should never have allowed her to sleep a single night in that bastard's house."

"You lost her and now you think you've also lost your son?"

"Serenity is uninterested in clan affairs. He is married to a woman who should have been the wife of the pope or the archbishop. Am I not right to fear that I've lost him?"

"Look at it this way: Serenity had a woman who both feared and idealized him. What wouldn't she have done for him? She gave him a daughter and would have gone on to give him many sons, but he sent her away and married this woman instead. Don't worry about him. Worry about his daughter, our granddaughter, whom we have not seen in a long time. I have a feeling that the woman will give her to another man to please him or just to get back at Sere. And think about it: When was the last time Sere visited his daughter?"

"I liked that woman: she knew how to treat people. She was uneducated, but after getting rid of her, Serenity did not marry a doctor or a lawyer either. Well, he married a doctor in Catholicism." He laughed out loud. "I have tried to interest him in his first child, his first blood, but he is evasive every time I mention her. What am I to do?"

"If I were you, I would be looking for a young girl or a decent woman to take care of me. I would not worry too much about a son who is married to a doctor in Catholicism."

"Young girls are nothing but trouble. After the first day in the house they go looking for boys their own age who give them gonorrhea, and then they expect you to pay the doctor's bills. Old women are control freaks, chased as they often are by the demons of their past failings."

"I would still not worry about somebody married to a woman who should have become the wife of the pope." Grandma laughed. "And after leaving me her first child, be it that violently, I can only wish her the best."

"Sere's wife is nothing but poison."

"Watch out for girls swinging their hips when passing by. . . ." She laughed knowingly.

Forty-five days after taking his bride's virginity, Serenity's first sex drought began: a doctor confirmed that I had been conceived. As further proof, Padlock vomited copiously every morning and nibbled at the salty clay from the vast swamp at the foot of Mpande Hill.

As a way of dealing with frustrated sexual energy, Serenity rekindled his migratory dreams and wrote out many application letters to government institutions asking for a job in the city. The country was quivering under the wind of Africanization, or indigenization of institutions, ripping them from the hands of Europeans and Indians. Serenity's hopes were high.

Eleven months into the marriage he still had no invitations for job interviews. Then I was born. It rained so much that week, and so intensely that day, that the swamp swelled and seemed to divide into many smaller, fiercer swamps. It flooded and destroyed the aqueducts and drowned the blue Zephyr hired by Serenity to take his wife to Ndere Parish Hospital. As Padlock labored, the driver climbed onto the rack of his car and held on as the wind rushed and threatened to fling him into the dark, swirling inferno below. The water rose up to the roof of his car, and the driver spoke his last will into the winds, certain that he was about to die. But after two wretched hours the winds relented, the rain stopped and the poor man thanked his gods for saving his life.

My umbilical cord was cut by Grandma with a new double-edged Wilkinson Sword razor blade. Padlock named me John Chrysostom Noel, the last name given despite the fact that Christmas was still far away. Serenity selected a name or two from the ready arsenal of the Red Squirrel Clan. He charged me with the grave duty of avenging Grandpa by becoming a lawyer someday, and to show that the mantle had left his shoulders he added the name Muwaabi (prosecutor) to my weaponry. He could as well have named me Revenge. Grandpa could not become a lawyer in his day, because of racial discrimination. He, for one, called me Mugezi (brilliant, intelligent), the name I kept when the time came to scrap the ballast of my nominal encumbrance. Grandma gave me no names but claimed me from birth, thereby prefiguring my future as a midwife's mascot-cum-assistant (pregnant women, in their eternal quest for sons, preferred a male mascot).

Padlock hated Grandma for it but could not countermand her word because it was Grandma who had cut my umbilical cord. Her belief that Grandma had it in for her increased. The story was that a week before Serenity introduced Padlock to his family as his fiancée, Grandma had two short dreams. In the first one, she saw Padlock standing in a lake of sand with a buffalo behind her. In the second, Serenity was peering at a gigantic crocodile lying at the bottom of a canyon. Grandma refused to interpret the dreams. Padlock asked her fiancé to have a go at it. He based his interpretation on totemic symbols. Padlock belonged to the elephant totem. The buffalo, another bush giant, was a surrogate elephant and symbolized (totemic) power. The presence of the buffalo in the sand was just a further demonstration of its indomitability, he concluded.

The second dream was interpreted along the same lines. The crocodile symbolized extraordinary power, tact, patience, self-knowledge, appreciation of territory and longevity. With a crocodile, not a red squirrel, as his totem representative, Serenity had concluded that his marriage was going to be a partnership of equals. His wife, the buffalo, was going to be the aggressor; and he, the crocodile, was going to be the tactician, the voice of caution, the brains.

Padlock, a more paranoid entity, took a more pessimistic view of the dream. Women who hatched dreams usually possessed a darker side, like the witches of the Inquisition. She believed that Grandma was trying to blackmail her, that she was using the dreams to keep a tight leash on Serenity. Mothers-in-law, afraid to let go of their sons, often did that. Grandma was not her mother-in-law, but Padlock believed that she considered herself to be. Why a buffalo and not an elephant if it was all so innocent? And why the sand? Sand was a bad surface for movement: it was a bad sign. If anything, she reasoned,

Grandma was the sand that would impede her movements, check her actions and make her marriage a living hell.

The feeling that Serenity came from a depraved family grew stronger in Padlock's heart. First, there was his whore of a mother, suspected of killing two of her own baby girls, who ran away, pregnant with another man's child, to escape her network of shame, and who died in disgrace. Then there was his pagan father, who claimed to be a Catholic but had had wives all over the place, and a child of sin, Kawayida, most likely one of many bred and disowned, or bred and lost in the maze of illicit unions. Then came Serenity's two sisters: one imprisoned in her ignorance and vanity, one weighed down with instability, witchcraft, devil worship and apostasy. There was the strange aunt, sufferer of chronic amenorrhea, who delivered babies, prescribed herbs and hatched arcane dreams she feared to interpret. Since the Church no longer sanctioned the public burning of witches, all Padlock could do was keep a wary eye on the woman and resolve to keep her out of her house, her life and the lives of her future children.

Because Padlock had no gossip friends round the village, rumors about her proliferated like weeds after a bushfire. People did not understand her, and since they could not get the information they craved, they supplied their own. This led to Padlock's growing hatred for the village. She felt squashed between Grandpa and Grandma, the centrality of Serenity's house charged with the vertigo of a precipice. She began feeling policed, the invisible eyes nudging her to jump into the abyss on either side of the house. Grandma made matters worse, for whenever she heard me wail or scream for any period of time, she would quietly appear in the compound with a vague expression on her face, as if she had come to borrow something she had forgotten. Padlock would see her out of the corner of her eye and ignore her at first, pretending that she was too immersed in whatever she was doing; then, still fuming with economically managed anger, she would turn, acknowledge Grandma, hold her eye for one long moment and say, "Welcome, aunt. To what great fortune do we owe this unexpected visit?"

"It is not an unexpected visit," Grandma, exhibiting great equanimity, would reply. "It is a courtesy call from an old-fashioned woman."

Later, when the hostility increased and came out in the open, she would add, "An old woman who believes in keeping an eye on her husband." Grandmothers jokingly called their grandsons "husbands" because, traditionally, a grandson of my caliber was the putative protector of his widowed grandmother. Padlock could barely stomach this brutal flaunting of crude paganism in her own yard, especially because there was nothing she could do to stifle it.

Paralyzed and incapacitated, like a legless grasshopper, Padlock could not help turning the fire of her hatred on me for my arrival on that monstrously rainy day, thus helping her worst enemy to gain such a firm hold in her house. Yet all the clashes in the village were just mere curtain-raisers for the epic showdowns that were to come in the charged atmosphere of the city.

Padlock realized quickly that she would never win the war against rumormongers, some of whom had gone as far as saying that she owed her current status to witchcraft. Knowing that they could do worse, she tried to avoid the villagers, keeping quiet even when she wanted to tell off those pagans. As a result, pressure accumulated dangerously inside her, and the need to migrate and leave the dead to bury themselves became even more urgent. It had to happen soon. She was the new wine which needed new bags, but she feared that the old bags into which she had been put on her wedding day would taint her before she got the chance to tear them up.

When she was alone in the house, it seemed to swell, and to press down on her with its old ghosts, old secrets, jealousies and hatreds. When she entered the bedroom, she was hit by a rancid-milk smell mixed with the funk of Serenity's ten years of bachelor exploits, making her aware, once again, of the tainted bed on which she had sacrificed her holy hymen. The bed, with its infernal squeaking springs, seemed to be the source of the unholy smells, the gangrenous sore sowing cancer everywhere. She cringed at the thought that she had allowed herself to become one of its victims. That same bed reminded her that Serenity had not been a virgin on their wedding day, and that his sin was incarnate in that daughter of his, whom he did not talk about but who was somewhere in the countryside, doubtless mocking her and her children. Padlock was happy that the child of sin was a girl, who could never become an heir, but she shuddered to think that one day the girl would perpetuate her sin by having her own offspring, mostly likely out of wedlock.

Padlock kept going back to the days before the wedding. She saw herself being smeared with butter oil by Aunt Nakibuka, who ordered her not to move, not to do anything, because the oil had to be driven deep into the skin by the fire of the sun. While she suffered the smell, the anxiety, the heat, the dehydration, Serenity, tainted as he was, was only having a haircut and a long bath. She would have wanted to thrust him in hot oil and scald all the women from his skin and his mind. She would have wanted to use molten soap, hot like liquid fire, and burn all the sin from his pores, and make him say many prayers, and give him many enemas with holy water. Then and only then would he be ready to take somebody's virginity. But it was too late. This degraded house had to be abandoned, if only for the sake of the children. She had already given Serenity enough time to work things out; now she was going to threaten to tear this stained, stinking bag of a house down.

"When are we going to leave this place?" Padlock, sitting on a fine red mat, asked. She was watching Serenity eat banana plantain with meat. Or was it sweet potatoes with fish?

"I am doing my best," he replied without looking at her. He was satisfied with the way she ran the house, but he was uneasy about important matters being thrust at him during mealtime. Some women, like Kasiko, did this sort of thing in bed; Padlock did it at lunch or at suppertime, and he resented it. "I am waiting for job interviews."

"You have been waiting for a long time. It is almost two years now. Maybe the post office is letting you down by misplacing your mail. Or maybe somebody at school is sabotaging you by sitting on your incoming mail."

"I am going to look into all that," he said flatly, struck by the irony of being let down by an institution he wanted to work for. How many application letters had he sent to the Postal Workers' Union? Very many. He watched as I ineffectually chewed a piece of meat. Two more children and the Serenity Trinity would be complete, he thought. He would then concentrate on his job, and on getting enough money to send his children to the best schools. What more could a father do?

In the midst of his daydream he was struck by something: the second sex drought was already on! The vomiting and clay nibblings had already started! His original plan had been a child every three years in order to ease financial pressures. Now it was too late for that plan.

"Any invitations for job interviews this week, this month?" Padlock asked, a residue of clay on her gums. Last time the swamp from which this clay came conspired against her by drowning the car which should have taken her and her unborn son to the hospital. What was it going to do this time? Was it going to punish her for stealing its clay by instigating a miscarriage or a stillbirth?

Serenity wondered which contraceptive method she would prefer: the condom, the diaphragm . . . "I am planning to go to the city to inquire."

"I am not going to rear my children here," she said rather sternly, the last word dropping like a huge chunk of clay in a basin of water.

"I know," he replied, thinking that she had made "children" sound like a crowd, not just three little individuals. He got up to clean his bicycle. Oh, it needed a proper wash. He put two rags in a bucket, strapped it on the carrier and cycled down to the stream at the other end of the village. Five kilometers in that direction lay the church, the missionary hospital and the school. He cycled past Fingers the leper's house and two others. Children waved at him from the muddy courtyards, their bare feet smudged, their bellies peeping from loosely hanging shirts. They reminded him of his school, poorer than the Catholic school in Ndere Hill, struggling to keep up. It was time to leave it all behind. He had given six whole years of his life to that school, and he felt that enough was enough. He had to leave before he became too old, before it was too late. Quite a few of his colleagues had missed their chances, had aged, compromised their dreams and become stuck like trucks drowned in mud swamps.

"Children are given by God," his wife had fumed when he introduced the question of birth control. "How many people want them but can never have them? Take your aunt, if I may use your family as an example. She will never know the joys of parenthood despite delivering just about every other baby in the area."

"Enough. Enough of that," he had replied with finality. He now felt that he had missed a golden opportunity. He should have put his foot down and insisted that he was not going to breed for the whole barren world. He felt that he would have to create another opportunity in order to drive his message home. He stood a better chance when they migrated to the city. The cost of living was higher there, so it would be easier to convince her to space out the children and to have just those they could look after. It was going to be a hard task, and he wondered how successful he would be.

Serenity had viewed the wedding pictures over and over again, dissatisfied by he didn't know what in his wife's face. Now, with mud sucking at his feet and the water rippling away murkily into the bulrushes, into the stretch of forest and finally into the papyrus swamps on the other side of Mpande Hill, he believed that he had found the object of his musings and ruminations. The bride hadn't smiled in any of the wedding pictures, and in a few she had just grimaced, like somebody with safari ants in her pants. The only person with a constant smile on her face was Nakibuka, the woman who had broken the nuptial stalemate and accessed his past with that magic touch on his shoulder. She smiled sweetly, confidently, as if it were her wedding, as if she were celebrating victory over all her husband's past loves, as if she were quite invincible. The fire that had led him down the dais onto the dance floor, to be fucked by the other dancers and to dance himself, came rushing back. He smiled gratefully. During the honeymoon, Nakibuka had told him all about Padlock. It had not been the best thing to listen to. His wife's background made Serenity wonder whether she would ever compromise and accept contraception.

Serenity knew that the glumness on his wife's face was her eternal protest against the injustice of being denied her firstborn privileges. The hardness in the set of her mouth was a plea for redress. Her parents had ignored her as soon as her brother Mbale was born. The irony was that he had been the officiating brother-in-law, the one who had handed her over to her husband on behalf of the family. The birth of three more brothers had left Padlock doing all the hard work, the digging, the cooking, the washing and the fetching of firewood, because she had to learn how to run a home. As a woman she had to learn to wake up first and retire to bed last. In a short time she had all those boys, all those mini-men, to wash, to feed, to see off to school, to pluck jiggers from, to protect from fleas, bedbugs and mad dogs. She gradually became the swamp that filled with the murky waters of hatred, the steadfast clays of perseverance and the dark green papyrus of obedience and stoicism. Her back creaked with the loads of potatoes, cassava and wood the boys refused to carry. Her hair and her clothes reeked of kitchen smoke and dish soap. Her eyes reddened with too much worry and too little relief.

The two girls, Kasawo and Lwandeka, arrived too late, without any spare oil in their lamps for her. To them, she was like the forgotten bride: too young to be a mother, too old to be a sister, too jinxed to share secrets with and too mysterious to be of much use. So they kept out of her way, associating instead with the boys. Her parents never took her side, always coming down hard on her, because she had to learn to handle the dirty work and lift the bigger load. They seemed to have followed the same philosophy when selecting a name for her. From the arsenal of clan names they chose Nakkazi (strong, robust woman) for her. At first she was happy with it, till she came of age to go to school. There it turned into a bully's dream because with just a little doctoring, excising a letter or two, it meant completely different things. Its malleability was her curse. Nakaza, Nakaze, Nakazi, Nakazo and Nakazu meant female pubic hair, vaginal dryness, female shit, a female cane plant and female nonsense, respectively. So to different bullies she was different things. At the end of each week they put a guava in her satchel, to thank her for her flexible name and her perseverance. At first she ate these guavas unwashed, till she discovered that they were spat on or rubbed against a bully's buttocks before they were slipped into her bag.

In her free time she would go to the garden and stand lost in thought under guava trees, touch their smooth stems and look at their hard fruits. The stems felt like her hands, and she became fascinated, and could hardly stop caressing them. She would have swapped all her nicknames for "Nakapeela" (female guava), but nobody accorded her the privilege. When she complained to her parents, reporting the bullies, some of whom were villagemates, her parents made her say the rosary and asked her to forgive them seven times seventy times. By then she would be dreaming of guava stems, flexing her arms as if they were made of wood and using them to punish her tormentors.

She finally sought refuge in the convent, where she became Sr. Peter, a name, once again, forced on her. She had originally wanted to become Sr. John Chrysostom and rage against the body, extoll the spirit and the soul, but the Mother Superior was called Sr. John

Chrysostom and there could not be two in the same convent. It was considered extremely vain of her to contemplate naming herself after that great saint when she knew that the Mother had been called to bear that mantle. Apologizing to Mother Superior, she settled for the hare-brained action man St. Peter, who, despite his defects, had risen to lead the Church and become the first pope.

The situation had changed in her favor: from behind the cool walls of the convent she watched with satisfaction as her brothers tilled the iron land, whipped by the rains, terrorized by pests, mocked by droughts, and were finally defeated by bad harvests. She knew that they would never come to much and would never rise above village level. Protected by the certainties of the habit, she watched as their wives, married young, labored with pregnant bodies, cooking, digging, washing, giving birth. She watched as they were dragged by fluctuating commodity prices into worry-infested tomorrows. That was her revenge. She sipped it in trim little drafts, and savored it whenever she had time to contemplate their lot. The only remaining step in the drama was for them to brave the sun and the rigors of climbing the steep hill to the convent, and stand, hat in hand, begging for help. She now had the power to grant or deny help. The rosebush of nun-hood, with all its thorns, filled her nose with the holy smell of victory from time to time. At such moments she could not even feel the pain of a thousand thorns.

In those days, Sr. Peter had one big worry, which she prayed over every day. It was the single defect, the one weakness, she could confess to. There were some moments when she felt as if she were being lifted by giant hands and thrust inside a bathysphere which sank and negotiated dark, treacherous reefs on automatic pilot, beyond the reach of everybody, God inclusive. Once in there, traveling at incredible speeds, she lost all control. She felt like a wingless eagle dropping from the sky. By the time she became aware of her lower back, her armpits and her olfactory system, it was too late, the consequences a marvel even to herself.

It had all started long ago, on the day when she decided to fight back. She had grabbed a stick and hit her younger brother Mbale very hard on the shoulder. She went on hitting him even when he fell down. She would have gone on punishing him if two village men had not intervened, grabbing the stick and pulling her away. That was one of the reasons her parents had welcomed her nunly vocation, because peasant men, from whose ranks her suitor would probably emerge, would either maim or kill her if she ever did that to them.

Nowadays the attacks, or "flashes" as she called them, came only occasionally. They were usually triggered by an incident in which her anger was aroused and her temper inflamed. Gravity of transgression did not matter: a boy breaking another's nose, trespassing in the convent garden or coming late to church could trigger the explosion. She would hear sounds and feel lifted up, and automatic action would ensue, followed by sweatings, purgings and the bursting of lemon odor on her whole skin.

It was the purgative effect of those attacks which both intrigued and worried the otherwise no-nonsense Sr. Peter. The explosion, like a holy fire, would pulverize all her inner tension and for a moment bring her bliss. In the midst of it, when onlookers saw and heard only wailing children, an orchestra would be tearing down her walls with music. At such moments of stormy bliss, everything revolved round her and she became the center of that raging, frothing, primordial, infernal world.

As a way of dealing with the resultant fear, she took the view that what occurred at such moments was a revelation, a holy fuse God had left smoldering inside her for His holy purposes which she, in her simplicity, was yet to understand. So she prayed for enlightenment and asked for answers to that mystical riddle. She fasted. She wore a strip of gunnysack on her skin. She worked harder than the rest, feeding the pigs, washing their pens, smelling their shit. She disinfected all the convent bathrooms and washed all the toilets. She won praise all round, and the fuse seemed to die a natural death.

Yet when she reduced the prayers and curtailed the work sessions, she discovered not only that the fuse was still alive, but also that its purpose was still a mystery. She turned to Holy Scripture. Elijah slaughtered four hundred fifty prophets of Baal; Jesus lashed the people who had turned the temple into a den of thieves; God unleashed snakes on His people and massacred thousands to extinguish His anger. But what was the purpose of her fuse? She was only a simple nun.

She finally concluded that the fuse was a test of the strength of her character and her commitment to the call. She started looking forward to the attacks in order to fight them. As a tribute to the lucidity of this new vision, she forgave defaulters, content to let them escape with verbal warnings buzzing in their ears. Sometimes she gave them light punishment, like collecting straw for brooms, raking mango leaves in the compound or helping the cook wash the porridge boilers, but soon she realized that, in the end, she could not spare the rod without spoiling the children. She picked it up once again and wielded it just like everybody else. This time, though, she tried to control herself. She was only partly successful. What happened in the end was that the pupils who got beaten first got off lightly, and those who came last, when the falling-eagle phenomenon had come into play, took the brunt, as if she were compensating for earlier leniency. The children were quick to remark that Sr. Peter had gotten worse, for, if they were all being punished for the same misdemeanor, why were some getting beaten harder than others?

During her week as duty mistress, in charge of school liturgy and general discipline, the inevitable happened. She hurt seven children so badly that in the end, in order to keep the affair out of court and out of the greasy hands of scandalmongers and church-haters, Sr. John Chrysostom, in her capacity as Mother Superior, promised the angry parents that she was going to take swift and decisive action. A few hours later, she disrobed the otherwise industrious Sr. Peter and, in one stroke, thrust her back into the world she despised so much.

The disgraced nun went down on her knees and begged and promised never to touch the children again, but to no avail. In desperation she pleaded that she had nowhere to go. To which her former superior replied, "Everyone has got a place to go. Remember, foxes have their own holes, too." Paralyzed by shame and blinded by rage, Sr. Peter took refuge in the home of Mbale, the brother she had nearly maimed at the beginning of it all.

Within a few days, Mbale's iron-roofed house was oppressed by the cataclysm of his sister's depression. She locked herself in the guest room with a jerry can of water and a plastic basin, and refused to come out. She refused to eat, surviving on two mugs of water a day. She cried and prayed all day, and, spent, she slept all night. In mortification, she slept on the bare floor, and scratched the earth with her fingers till her nails bled. She asked Death to come for her. She rattled heaven's door with poignant novenas to St. Jude Thaddeus, helper of desperate cases. Each morning she scribbled a message on a piece of paper to the effect that she was still alive, and that no one should get alarmed or attempt to interrupt her prayer-and-mortification sessions.

On the seventh day, Mbale knocked on her door with the intention of starting some form of dialogue, but she sent him away. He threatened to break the door with a hammer, and she replied that he would regret it for the rest of his life. Afraid that she would die in there, he hurried to his aunt, a good-natured character whose negotiating skills he hoped would help. They arrived on the ninth day, and found the former Sr. Peter washed, fed, wearing a blue dress and relaxing in a wicker chair on the veranda. A hen or two was pecking at her toenails, mistaking them for maize grains. She agreed to go with her aunt, who found her a job as a filing clerk in a small cotton-buying firm in a nearby town.

Sr. Peter, as she still thought of herself then, attended her first wedding just to get out of her aunt's house. All she was hoping for was a lingering sense of disgust, generated by the dancers' pelvic gyrations and the people's profanity, to buoy her home at the end of the evening. She did not look at anyone. She did not drink anything. She did not participate in any festivities. She would have preferred to hover above the crowd, unseen, and watch foolish people disgrace themselves by rolling in the muck of their lust. She stood outside the booth, arms across her chest, stared into space and let the noise, the cheering, the drumming pour over her like water washing a rock. This went on until a face crossed her line of vision. It disappeared and appeared again. It was the face of a young man who looked as lost as herself. He seemed to be trembling, quaking, as if experiencing something as quaint as a miracle. Looking closely, he discovered that she was radiating sublime calm and perfect solitude with such force as he had never seen before. He was hooked by the fathomless intensity pouring out of her frail bosom. Her apparent sanity in the face of the one hundred and one madnesses around her spoke eloquently to something so deep within him that he could not avert his eyes. It was this sudden awareness of her powers, powers she hitherto believed to have left behind the cold walls of the convent, that made her tremble and almost panic. Afraid that her loss of control had been witnessed by a second young man who came and stood next to the first one, she turned and left, melting into the excited crowd.

Young Serenity could hear himself swearing, through clattering teeth, that he would leave no stone unturned until he conquered, or was conquered by, this woman. He could feel mud sucking at his feet and locusts nibbling at his stomach. What was he getting into? She was not the model of beauty his father promoted, but he felt determined to go his own way. Infected by her solitude, or rather his solitude kindled by hers, he sealed himself off from the excess of booze, dance and funk which the wedding had become. Now she was gone, like an apparition. He could hear his friend laughing hard. The friend knew both the girl and her aunt, and did not think much of the girl: she was too intense, too uptight for his liking. He would have gone on to make a lot of fun of her but for the intensity in Serenity's eyes.

For days Serenity could not excavate the image of the ex-nun from the caverns of his mind. He spent long periods of time recapturing the contours of her face, the lines of her figure and the depth of her solitude, all in vain. At the wedding he had drunk only one beer, but it seemed as if he had emptied a whole crate and that her image, or what he thought to be her image, was just a drunken man's delusion. His friend's caution and apparent lack of enthusiasm unsettled him. The only thing that kept him going was the feeling that he was on the right track. His friend, with a wry smile, agreed to help him.

The ex-nun's aunt had already seen the remarkable transformation on her niece's face. The cadaverous downward warp was gone, consumed by the slow fire of unwinding revelation, replaced with the thinly disguised expectant visage of someone on the verge of great things. Told of the prospective suitor, the young woman's aunt expressed tactical surprise at the news because she did not know the young man involved, but she was happy. Her niece needed a new start, a new purpose in life, intimations of which seemed to be hanging, like a cloud of locusts, in the air.

For Sr. Peter herself, the vision of the young man's face clarified the significance of her name for the first time. She was the rock on which a new family, a new church, was going to be founded. She could feel the poles sinking into the bedrock. She could see the structure going up, coloring the firmament with its magnificence. Her death to the convent, to nunly life, had enabled this resurrection.

As Serenity's go-between and her aunt negotiated off and on for weeks, Padlock felt not a shadow of a doubt about her future role. All she needed was God's confirmation of the same, and Serenity's commitment. There was the matter of his concubine and of his child of sin: St. Jude would look into that. After ninety days the answer came. There was nothing to stop her.

Pedaling back from the stream, Serenity sighed when he remembered the ninety days of hell during which he wondered whether Padlock had turned down his marriage proposal. There was a pattern to his life. He always seemed to be the last person informed about matters concerning him. Things always happened when he no longer had power to change them. Now what was he to do with his wife's life story? Knowing her background was just going to make him sympathize with her even when he should not.

It was dark, and the swamp was pumping its fetid smell over the valley, suspended in the air like a wet blanket. In it one could discern the mingled odors of mud, fish, decomposing grass, wildflowers and frogs. Mosquitoes and other biting insects had upped their sorties on this bicycle-cleaning intruder. Serenity rode home, dead to the world. The trees and bushes along the path took on ghostly forms and grotesque dimensions which rattled memories of childhood stories of witches and magic from the cobwebby rafters of his mind. His father's house was in total darkness. The old man was never home early in the evening: he went off to see friends and to look for female company. The period when the place crawled with no less than twenty people at any one time seemed too far away to rattle into consciousness. It seemed as if a storm had come, swept everybody into the swamps, pinned their heads under the murky water and drowned them en masse, leaving behind this grandiose pod which echoed with the Fiddler's tunes.

He was nearing home now. Through the window he could see his wife leaning over the table, scrutinizing something. A letter had arrived from the city, laden with the Uganda Postal Union logo: he had been offered a job! The sixties were going to be his peak time: first he had gotten married, then he'd had a son, and now he was going to move to the city!

The new wine had, finally, torn the old village bags. The movable parts of the house—the personal effects, the pictures, the wedding gifts, everything needed to start a new life in the city—were compressed into parcels and sullen bundles and shoved into boxes sealed with tape or strangled with string. Wooden chests appeared and, like magic, swallowed the house. Soon only the veteran bed remained, in addition to a stick or two of furniture. All this torrent of activity raged around me, and, like a drowning man, flail as I could, I could not get a grip on it. A stream of people moved in and out of the shrunken house, drinking tea or sipping beer, wishing my parents good luck.

A puke-yellow lorry appeared and swallowed everything. It dawned on me that we were leaving. The house now echoed when one called. But why was I not dressed for the journey? A little crowd had gathered, despite the wet, and they stood in the grass, away from the thick tires, out of range of flying mud kites. It was then that I was told I was staying.

Serenity climbed into the cab. Padlock turned to follow him in. I touched her, smudging her dress. She cringed and, with blinding speed, drove her palm full into my face. I fell back in the mud and, in protest, rolled once or twice. I kicked a few times and then heard the driver's booming voice lamenting that departures were often accursed affairs. Mud had flown onto Padlock's dress. She raised her foot, the yellowish sole flashing, as if she were going to plant it full in my face. Serenity's voice rose, and Padlock seemed to wake from a dream. The raised foot was placed on the steel foothold, and with my father's help she got into the cab. The flash of that sole sobered me up. I sat in the mud, and at that moment smoke blew in my face. The truck growled and groaned like a mortally wounded animal. By the time I opened my eyes it was gone, two thick wet trails the only mark of its passing.

I was mud-soaked, like a piglet after a pretty good wallow. Grandma picked me up. Rain broke out. She lifted me, mud and all, and carried me to her house. It was not the first time that she had rescued me or watched me suffer. She was the only witness to my first thrashing, when Padlock punished me for insinuating my precocious curiosities into the very adult matter of her latrine functions. It was all because of babies: I wanted to know where they came from, but she would not tell me. I knew that she knew the answer. I decided to investigate and surprise her with my knowledge. For starters, I followed her to the latrine that day.

When the door closed behind her, leaving four inches of viewing space underneath, I lay down on my stomach, chin in the creepers, and amid rumblings, gassings and strainings I saw large cylinders appear, get soaked in dust-particled light and disappear down the rectangular hole. I got access to the hairy fleshiness underneath the stomach, and a magic flash of pink reminiscent of nasal tunnels convinced me that my research was going in the right direction. A baby was being born! Although I was seized by the urge to rush in and warn her about what was going to happen, I was too overwhelmed by my curiosity to move. Dust from the grass tickled my nose, but I forced the incipient sneeze back. Now I was thinking: if the baby fell in, it would have to be fished out. . . . The idea of such filth made my skin creep. Why wasn't she squatting away from the deadly rectangle? Did she want maggots all over the baby and inside its orifices? She was pushing very hard now, as if a lance of pain were going through her.

I closed my eyes to avoid seeing a human being drowned in muck. So this was the reason why she was so secretive about the birth of babies!

"You are going to learn never to spy on people again," I heard her saying. I was half-flying, half-walking. We broke up a fight between two hens over a long earthworm. I felt like that worm: the game was over for me. I tried to explain, but the cutting edge of Padlock's anger, aided by a guava switch, could only slash, whack and thrash. Why wasn't anyone coming to my rescue when I was screaming like a piglet being castrated?

Suddenly Grandma was there. At the edge of the battlefield, her head thrown back, arms across her chest, waiting to be noticed. I wanted those arms around Padlock's neck, but on the chest they remained. Is that the best you can do? she seemed to be asking Padlock. I threw the question back in Grandma's face.

Sensing a change in the air, Padlock stopped, momentarily embarrassed at being caught off guard. Snotty tears falling, I escaped and hid behind Grandma. A threat or two followed, and though the glass in Padlock's eyes shone bleakly, I knew I was safe. Swollen but safe.

Now, soaked and runny with mud, I felt safe again. I was happy with the new deal. The millstone of Padlock's temper and the bushfire of her anger were off my back. I wallowed in the mud not because I had been left behind, for children were left with their grandparents all the time, but because I had not been informed of my freedom earlier on.

I started life where most people ended it: in the baby business. Suddenly, as a midwife's mascot-cum-assistant, I was catapulted into adult circles and felt comfortable high up there with dads and mums, heavily involved in the facilitation of the coming of their babies, privy to adult secrets, seeing adults in instances of vulnerability my age-mates would never dream of. Suddenly, I was being treated like a little prince by superstitious women who attributed their safe deliveries and the coming of long-awaited sons to my mascotry, and I had a vague claim to the life of many babies born in the village and a few sur-rounding villages. Suddenly, it occurred to me that I had powers of life and death, because I could give a pregnant woman herbs which might cause a miscarriage or prevent one or help the fetus to grow. All that power was as overwhelming as it was unbearable.

In my new capacity, I attended consultations—that is, pregnant women came to talk to Grandma about their gestation. They described how they felt, how long and how much they vomited and how much it stank. They gave lurid descriptions of their fevers, backaches, fre-quent urination, pile attacks, constipation, swollen ankles and heart-burn. They discussed their appetites, fears and hopes and wanted to know up to what month before delivery they could continue to have sex. In order to deal with the last item, I would be sent off on errands, but anticipating it, I often stood behind the door and listened. Some-times Grandma would ask the women to show her their bellies. I craved to touch those tight-skinned balloons, but I knew that I would never be granted the opportunity. Grandma stroked them, kneaded them, felt them, and advised the women accordingly. If a case needed closer examination, she would take the woman behind the house, and I would hear them whispering or laughing or arguing. They would return with the woman fastening her belt or pulling down the hem of her skirt.

For the herbal medicines she gave the women, Grandma combed the forest, the garden, the bush and the swamps and came up with leaves, bark and roots. I accompanied her with a bag or a basket, and I watched as she worked. She plucked the leaves skillfully, removing the old ones and sparing the sprouting tender ones, careful to preserve the plant. She rarely pulled out whole plants, except when she was going to use the roots, the stem and the leaves. For the bark, she used a knife or a small hoe and removed the outer layer, which would quickly grow back. She always covered the roots with soil and tied banana leaves on stems she had deprived of thick layers of bark. I often grew impatient, urging her to let the trees take care of themselves, but she would not budge and insisted that those trees were our asset, and that it was our duty to preserve them.

Our village, Mpande Hill, and the swamp always made me think of an octopus, the hill representing the head, the swamp the long tortuous tentacles snaking round our village. And my observation of the swamp, and the way we approached it, made me believe it was a living thing, a large snake we warily attacked from the sides. The water, sometimes crystal clear, sometimes black, green or brown, was always cold and full of life: dragonflies, tadpoles, little fishes, leeches, frog spawn in long slimy strands and plants with matted roots that resembled long hair being pulled. As we walked in the shallows we were wary of the sharp-bladed bulrushes and of poisonous plants. This was the least popular part of the expedition, resulting in lacerated skin, wet clothes, insect bites and all sorts of discomfort because some of the plants we needed were in clusters surrounded by relatively deep water and hostile objects.

Among the herbs we collected were some which had to be taken raw, or crushed into a pulp and rubbed on the belly, on the back and into joints. Others we simply immersed in bathwater, roots, spawn, soil particles and all. The rest were dried in the sun and packed in plastic bags for future use. The most important herb was the one which helped to widen pelvic bones, thereby facilitating dilation and delivery. Women had to drink it and bathe in it twice or thrice a day throughout pregnancy. Grandma warned them sternly about the consequences of negligence, which included, among other things, the suffocation or deformity of babies and sometimes the death of both mother and baby.

In addition to administering herbal measures, Grandma advised the women to eat nutritious foods: meat, fish, eggs, soybeans, greens and more. In those days, most women were just learning to eat chicken, eggs and scaleless fish, which up to then had been eaten exclusively by men and despised and denigrated by women. A self-respecting, well-bred woman would deign to cook them but would not bring them any-where near her well-bred mouth.

Tiida was the first woman in the area to take up her aunt's call for change. The conservatives said she broke chicken legs and slurped egg slime like a man, and that her babies would be born with feathers all over them and little wings instead of arms. She laughed at them, and at the greedy men who still denied their wives and daughters these deli-cacies. Everyone waited for feathered babies to be pulled out of Tiida, but she bred only healthy offspring. Now the women were largely con-vinced, with only a residual minority of die-hard skeptics. Aunt Na-katu was among the latter group: she somehow never got over the taboo. She tried chicken a few times, but complained about its smell.

Prenatal care was the glamour part of the baby business. Trouble broke loose with delivery. Babies, those little monsters, chose to come at odd times: deep in the night, very early in the morning or in the rainy season or at Christmas. And some enjoyed making everyone tense: the pangs would begin, the water would break, but then they would refuse to emerge for hours or even days. It was often under those inopportune circumstances that Grandma and I discovered that the advice and the exhortations had either been followed not at all or only partially or badly.

Many women neglected the daily herbal baths and imbibings which helped pelvic dilation. This exercise was called breaking bones. "How often did you break?" Grandma, suspecting the worst, would ask. Horrifying answers would come, dripping from flaky, fear-twisted lips. Hearing the same woman scream and express the fear that she was going to die would make one say, under one's breath, that she deserved every ounce of pain she got, though for us that was no con-solation at all, because the baby still had to come out.

I was not allowed to witness the actual moment of birth. I always left when the woman lay down on her back, a pillow under her head, legs up under the sheet, perspiration dotting her face, fear popping under her eyelids, panic just a breath away, with Grandma combatting waves of hysteria. At such moments Grandma was like a goddess, a priestess, an oracle whose every gesture, every sigh, every twitch spoke volumes. At the flick of her finger, I would leave the arena, an acrid smell in my nose, the picture of the woman's face deeply etched in my mind, the sound of her voice buzzing in my ears, a vague evaluation of her chances coursing through my head.

At the beginning of my stint, I used to be afraid that the woman was going to die. I would quake and quiver, with sharp pains kicking up storms in my breast. Each woman cried differently, and with some it felt as if their blood would be on your hands, and on the hands of your children's children, if they died. The men, gloomy and silent, were not reassuring either. They seemed to be studying every fluctuation, every nuance in the woman's vociferations, as though waiting to pounce on you the moment they were sure that she had drawn her last breath. Half my mind would be busy with the woman, visualizing her anguish and her efforts, and half would be working out the safest escape route, but sometimes it went on for so long that I dozed off and slept, the woman's screams fading away like wisps of smoke in the evening sky, until I would be jogged back into wakefulness.

I would go outside and be whipped by the smell of cow dung or pig shit or goat urine, depending on what animals were kept by the family. On rainy days the pigsties, oozing liquid shit, stank to high heaven, worse than the sodden kraals and the waterlogged cow pens. This stink and the runny shit I often stepped into didn't endear animals to me in general.

It was in everyone's interest for the delivery to go well. If all failed and the woman, with baby head peeping or leg popping, had to be rushed to the hospital, the resultant cloud of tension and anxiety messed up everyone's peace of mind. There was only one car in the village, owned by a scion of Stefano, but it was more often than not out of order. It would often stop dead on the road, and he'd ask us to help push it.

The chronic unreliability of this machine meant that somebody would have to find a van to take the woman to the hospital, because in that condition she was in no position to sit on a bicycle. The most annoying aspect of it all, however, was that most of these cases had had prior warnings from doctors not to risk delivering at home. They always had reasons for not complying.

The transformation adults underwent with the onslaught of pain both fascinated and frightened me. Women who normally worked like horses, digging, fetching water, carrying mountains of firewood, washing hills of clothes and the like, would suddenly be reduced to whimpering wrecks, head turning this way and that, arms beating weakly, legs gone rubbery, self-control in tatters. They reminded me of a dog under attack from thousands of bees or a teetering paper canoe in a stormy swamp.

It was equally fascinating to see the same women after the baby had arrived. They seemed to have sweated out all the pain, all the anguish, all the nightmares, and were open to joy, relief and satisfaction. I would see them laughing, smiling, beaming, shedding tears of joy, as though what had occurred before had been a joke, a mere bit of play-acting.

The cause of all the prior commotion would lie there glistening like a baby monkey soaked in grease or a piglet immersed in crude oil, all wrinkles and purple membrane, the ugly umbilical cord popping with each exhalation. Our ordeal would be over. Dissolving into the air would be all the lost sleep, all the past anxiety, all the fizzled tension, all the sacrificial blood of cocks beheaded, cocks strangled or cocks buried alive at witch doctors' shrines.

My first delivery was the hardest and the most memorable. The messenger woke us up just after midnight. It had rained, and a cold wind was blowing, rustling the iron sheets of the roof and making tree branches wail. Contemplating the discomfort outside made the bed feel warmer and sleep seem sweeter. Hearing the unwelcome caller made me wish the wind would carry him away and bury him in a ditch till day broke, but there was no stopping such individuals; they acted with the urgency of boiling milk on the rise.

Grandma called me several times, and I feigned sleep, like the children in Uncle Kawayida's story who overheard their parents fucking. She shook me and I woke up with a start. She laughed and I laughed too, but that was where the levity ended. I had seen the woman in question twice; she was short and thin, her belly like a sack of potatoes strapped onto her frail body. Why hadn't she gone to the hospital? I wished death on her, and then I revoked my wish because, whichever way it turned out, we still had to put in an appearance.

The messenger, a big adolescent boy with thick calves, had come on a bicycle, but Grandma would not sit on it despite his great expertise (he regularly carried coffee sacks up the implacable Mpande Hill to the mill, and participated in the suicidal downhill races in which one could brake only with one's bare heels). I sat on the carrier for part of the way, but the bumps were so bad that I decided to walk. We arrived caked in mud. I had damaged a toenail on a rock, but there was no time for self-pity because of the turmoil at our destination.

The boy's father, big, dark, tall, was trembling and his teeth were chattering as he bit back his tears. The woman was wailing, thinly, as if she were using the very last of her energy. This was more frightening than the more energetic, full-voiced screaming I heard on latter missions. This was the cry of a woman with a dead baby inside her, heavy like a sack of stones. It was the cry of a dog dying after being beaten by a horde of boys for stealing eggs or for biting somebody. She was calling for a priest, of all people! I peeped inside the room, saw the popping eyes, smelled the long labor and something else I could not name, and I drew back. It took Grandma two hours to deliver the baby. It should have been a large, thick-waisted parcel, but on the contrary, it was as small as a fist. We spent the rest of the night with the family. The puny baby woke us up in the morning with such a screech that Grandma glowed with pride.

The leper in our village, Fingers, was a nice, kind, harmless man. I was not afraid of him, but the scars of his deformity deeply disturbed and haunted me. The fading pink knots on the spots where the fingers had been made my stomach turn whenever I met him. My skin crawled when he touched me, or patted me on the head as he sent greetings to Grandpa or Grandma. I would stand there, not pulling away because I didn't want to hurt his feelings, answering his questions while praying for something drastic to happen to terminate my ordeal. Fingers was a generous man. He now and then cornered me and invited me to his home, and he gave me large yellow mangoes and juicy purple sugar-cane. His children would be playing in the yard, without a care in the world. I could not refuse the gifts; it wasn't polite or cultured to do so. So I ate, putting a brave face on things like the adult I believed I was, but as soon as I left, I would push a finger down my throat. I wanted it all out: all the residual leprosy, all the germs, all the juice. The fact that his wife and children bore no signs of infection did not reassure me: there was the possibility that leprosy was only infectious to non-family members.

Fingers' wife was pregnant, and I believed that this time the baby would get it: our leper could not be lucky forever. My prayer was for her to deliver in the hospital, in the company of nurses and midwives who had medicines to combat the disease. Every time I saw the woman, I would look at her in parts, beginning with the head or the feet and moving my eyes up slowly in the hope that by the time I got to her midriff she wouldn't be pregnant anymore; but the belly would appear only to have grown. Once or twice she asked me about a certain herb, and I gave her two kinds, hoping that they would speed up her delivery. I should have been so lucky.

The messenger arrived one afternoon. All day I had entertained plans to go to my favorite tree and look out for Uncle Kawayida's blue-bellied eagle. I was hankering for his stories. Now I was trapped and paying for my procrastination. To make matters worse, Grandma dismissed the messenger with the news that we were on our way.

"I am not going to participate in delivering a baby with no fingers."

"Who told you that?" She was taken aback.

"Look at its father's hands."

"He was cured, that is why he is back in the community."

"Are you not afraid of catching leprosy?"

"No."

"Well I am. If the leprosy was totally eradicated, the fingers would have grown back on, wouldn't they?" I said, feeling and looking very clever.

"Stupid boy. Fingers and toes do not grow back on, and if you cut off your finger while knifing a jackfruit, that will be the end of it. You will be like him, with young boys developing theories about you."

"Still, I am not going."

"Get that bag quickly. Check the razor blades. Do you want to be held responsible if something happens because you've wasted time with your useless questions?"

The baby was born intact, without any missing fingers or toes, without holes in the face or stomach. I expected something to happen within a month or two. I spied on the family. In the meantime I got a boil, as Grandpa and Serenity were wont to, and had a load of nightmares. My fingers and toes rotted in front of my eyes and dropped off in my bed. Fingers bent over me and asked me how it felt to be without fingers and toes. He laughed long and hard, the sound echoing in a dark corridor. I woke up with the feeling that I had lost my sense of touch and smell. The relief of finding everything intact!

Nasty post-natal cases now and then fell into our laps. A baby's navel could become gangrenous, oozing a sullen yellowish-green pus which worried inexperienced parents a great deal. Grandma provided herbal cures and exhorted the parents to practice more rigorous hygiene. Women who did not dilate enough might have to be cut open, and in some cases would take a long time to heal, as Dr. Ssali's sensitive penis did. Some would come weeks after, leaking, their loose stitches poisoning every sitting and walking movement. Some women, fed up with the pain, would ask Grandma to remove the stitches and concentrate all her healing powers on closing the cut. This was a disastrous idea, and Grandma did her best to explain what would happen to their sex lives if she did what they asked her to do. She would even go to the extent of citing songs hummed by men about "buckets," women who were so wide that a tree could grow down there. She often succeeded in convincing them to return to the hospital to get the stitches redone.

By the time our stint ended, in 1971, we had delivered more than fifty babies, ten of which had died, mostly of measles: three at birth, seven in infancy. Four women had also died during or after childbirth, three of whom had been strongly advised by doctors at the mission hospital to stop breeding. The fourth case was a freak accident, and it turned ugly on us.

The husband of this dead woman came at Grandma with a panga raised in one of the blindest rages I had ever witnessed. Grandma, however, delivered the performance of her life: she did not move a muscle, and to top it off, she bent her head the other way, exposing her neck to the flashing blade. When the blade could not rise any higher, I closed my eyes for a moment. What was going to come off, her head or her arm? I imagined Grandma's head bouncing round the courtyard and blinding everyone with blood in a dramatic show of power which would be immortalized in song. At that moment I wet my pants.

No one knows what brought the man to his senses. Maybe it was Grandma's fearlessness; maybe it was the mechanics of a miracle; maybe murder was beyond him, and the panga was just a token of his cowardice. He was a notorious brawler. I had seen him once in a fight with another man. He was not the kind to care much for his wife, and we heard that he often beat her. My guess was that she died of meningitis, exhaustion or something instigated by his violence, but whatever it was, I was too scared for Grandma to care anymore.

In 1967, at the age of six, I took my first crack at school. The 1966 state of emergency had passed without inflicting much damage on our area. Our school was perched high up on Ndere Hill and had escaped molestation. Serenity had been to the same school, and so had Tiida, Nakatu and many of our other relatives. Every morning children from the villages trekked to Ndere Hill to drink from the well of knowledge. If you stood on top of this hill and watched hundreds of these large and small creatures emerging from milky clouds of morning mist with their breath pluming, geometry kits rattling and feet crushing the pebbles, you could think it was an apocalyptic locust invasion visited on the hill by some angry deity.

I joined the ranks of these green-shirted creatures, bemoaning my fall from the pedestal of my lone status into the abyss of student anonymity. The price of this humiliation was walking five kilometers every day, wheezing and sneezing in the cold for good measure. To ease my pain, I would dream the gigantic church tower anew every morning. Sometimes I saw it flashing in the morning sun; sometimes it stared morosely through the clouds of mist; sometimes it disappeared as if it had toppled and fallen, making me wonder how large it looked flat on the ground, but it was always there, laden with its terrible majesty, steeped in its power, encased in its inviolability. It was fifty-five years old, five years younger than the church in whose shadow our school nestled.

Both the church and the tower had been built by a French priest. Moments after adorning the top with a black cross, some women who believed he could do supernatural things thought they saw him actually flying, impersonating an angel, a bird or Our Lord Jesus, in fulfillment of a promise of a big miracle to celebrate the completion of the tower project. The promise had been made because the tower had collapsed twice during construction before he got the idea of using corrugated iron sheets instead of bricks. People started clapping and singing "Hosannah in the highest" when they saw him spread out in the air, white cassock billowing like full sails, hammer dangling precariously from his belt. It was the parish catechist who first realized what was going on and hurriedly linked hands with another man to break his master's fall. Fr. Lule (a local corruption of Roulet) fell with such force that he broke the four hands trying to save him. His brains oozed out, his back snapped and he died without saying a word. The ladder, which no one remembered in the commotion, followed Fr. Lule down, killing a woman and breaking her daughter's leg. Two months later, a catechist from one of the small subparishes fell from the pulpit and broke his spine, his pelvis and one arm. Some said he had been drunk. Some said he had always been afraid of heights. The majority believed that all the deaths and accidents were linked: every large building had to have a blood sacrifice before it opened to the public, and since no bulls had been slaughtered for it, they said, the church had decided to take its own sacrifices.

Normally, before entering a new house, one slaughtered a goat and sprinkled some of the blood on the walls. If one could not afford a goat, a few cocks sufficed. The owner of the chronically sick village car had sacrificed a cock to it: he chopped the head off and tossed the headless bird onto the roof. It slid down the windshield with spectacular twitches and bled to death on the hood.

When I asked Grandpa if it was true that the church had killed the priest, the woman and the catechist and maimed the rest, he only asked, "What would you think if you were (a) a fanatic Catholic, (b) a skeptic, (c) a pagan?" "Truth has many sides," I concluded after a long moment of reflection.

"You will make a good lawyer," he replied.

School brought me into direct competition with other pupils. I did very well. Thanks to Grandpa, I already knew the multiplication tables by heart and I could read and write, though my handwriting was horrible.

Dull pupils often got into trouble, but so did the bright ones. Large boys, some of them sprouting beards, passed me chits to scribble answers on and pass back. I got caught a few times, and the teacher caned me.

The large boys, whom we called "grandfathers," distributed nicknames. Mine was Sperm of the Devil because, according to

Dummy A, only a devil could know the multiplication tables by heart and spell so well at my age. He wrote "Spam ov Devill" on a piece of paper and pasted it on my bench with a knot of jackfruit sap as large as a fist. I got punished, but the nun commented on the author's appalling spelling, which was some consolation to me.

I tried to induce Dummy B, another large boy, to punish Dummy A for me, but he refused. Dummy A was notorious for retaliation. He could lock you in a cupboard and make you beg for release. He could sit on your stomach and spit in your face. He could thrust you inside an unwashed porridge boiler, or threaten to break your leg in a game of football. We were all afraid of him.

One morning I heard two young teachers saying that bullying was pure blackmail. I decided to try it myself. Before the teacher entered the classroom, I proclaimed, "My grandmother is a witch doctor. Only one word and one caterpillar thrown in the fire at midnight, and the penis of the person who wrote 'Spam ov Devill' on my desk will wilt and grow hairs all over it." I spat thrice in my palm and rubbed my crotch. A cloud of gritty silence descended on the class. At lunchtime, the culprit took me behind the toilets, making me fear the worst, and confessed. I let him roast for some time, funk escaping from the wet patches that were his armpits. We made a deal. I acquired my first bodyguard.

Now it was the girls' turn. Since they had no penises to be turned into caterpillars, they thought they were inviolable. They would shout "Spam ov Devill," laugh and scamper away. Dummy A seized their books, hid their netballs and threatened a few, without much success.

One morning six girls surrounded me. I spat in my palms and addressed their ringleader, a large girl with breasts the size of my head. "You have a man," I bluffed. "You will give birth to a limbless creature, and your breast milk will turn to pus." Contrary to expectation, I was not mobbed or booed. Milkjar just crumbled, like a lump of clay under a millstone. She started to cry. I panicked. I ran toward the blind side of the church, but I was caught by the headmaster. Held by the wrist, I was thrust amidst Milkjar's cronies. I pleaded self-defense, and explained that I had not meant anyone any harm. Milkjar was pathetic: she could not stop crying. The headmaster thrust a stick in her hand and ordered her to beat me. She dropped the stick as though it were a hairy caterpillar. The headmaster dismissed me with a stiff warning never to make penis or breast threats again, and gave me two strokes with the cane for good measure. I was furious.

I expected Grandma to side with me and condemn my tormentors. I was wrong. "Never stoop to their level, you hear?"

"Stooping! A girl large enough to birth me bullies me, and giving her a taste of her own medicine is beneath my dignity!"

"There is a part of the story you have not told me," she concluded. She was right. I had excised the witch doctor part from the story.

One person haunted my early school years: Santo the madman. He was quiet, harmless and as stealthy as a shadow. He always wore a clean white shirt and khaki trousers and never reeked of funk like Dummy A. Sometimes he wandered around, counting the fingers of his hands as if he were putting the final touch to a mathematical calculation. No one bothered him, which was rare, what with the many large, bored boys around. The teachers had warned everybody of the dire consequences—many hot canes and the task of uprooting two thick mango stumps with a hoe—if anybody was nabbed harassing Santo.

We envied Santo his handwriting, a fine, leaning cursive, and his arithmetical capabilities. Teachers often said that if we could write half as well as Santo did, they would reward us. Before going home, we wiped all the blackboards clean, but every morning we would find the legend KYRIE ELEISON, KYRIE ELEISON, CHRISTE ELEISON on every blackboard in the school. The spelling was always immaculate, the display same in all classrooms. It was said that Santo was a genius and that he had gone mad just before leaving for Rome on a four-year scholarship to Urban University. He was destined to be the first priest from our area. The celebrations to mark his departure had lasted five days. Fr. Mulo (a corruption of Moreau), who was Fr. Lule's successor, was going to take him to the airport. That morning a fire woke everybody up. Santo had poured paraffin on his luggage, his bed, his curtains, and torched everything. He never said a word again. All efforts to make him talk, including a few, early attempts at torturing him, failed.

Sometimes he came to school for food. Sometimes desperate boys passed him pieces of paper loaded with difficult sums. Sometimes he helped them out; sometimes he just chewed the papers. The clever ones left complex questions on the board, and if they were lucky, by the next morning the answers would be there next to the legend. It might also happen that the answers would come days later. Some guessed that he had a spare set of keys, others that he just got in through the classroom window.

On a number of occasions, I woke up very early and ran to school, hoping to catch Santo writing on the blackboard or climbing out of the window. I failed. I never solved the riddle of how he got in and out.

The baby business slowed as my primary school years passed. The birthrate plummeted in the villages. Most young men and women succumbed to the dusky seductions of the towns and the city. I could not blame them. They looked different when they returned: they were larger, richer, smarter, and had loads of dirty stories to tell. These exiles no longer made me tremble. They were just poor copies of Uncle Kawayida, and their stories were often pale shadows of his exciting narrations. I no longer listened to them. As a result, I spent much time playing in Serenity's house, in the trees and all over the village. I frequently climbed into my favorite tree to scan the horizon. I sometimes espied people cutting papyrus reed, which they used to make carpets and roofing. I watched them standing in the water, braving leeches and water snakes, and cutting, cutting, cutting, careful not to get lacerated by strips of papyrus as sharp as Grandma's double-edged razor blades. I loved watching Mpande Hill. Now and then I caught sight of a bicycle race in progress, one of those suicidal dashes made by the hard boys from the villages. They were always won by the boys who ferried coffee to the mill, as they were the only ones who could brake a bicycle with their bare heels. I participated in one such race, riding pillion for a friend: it nearly cost me a foot. I was banned from the races then because the boys feared attracting Grandpa's wrath.

After an insufferably long time, I finally caught sight of the blue-bellied eagle gliding down the hill. "Uncle Kawayida, Uncle Kawayida, Uncle Kawayidaaa!" I chanted. I quickly got the key to Serenity's house and opened it. I swept all the rooms with a straw broom. As the breeze cleared the air, I heard the motorcycle roaring outside. Uncle Kawayida had bad news, though.

His father-in-law, Mr. Kavule, had died. Uncle Kawayida was morose and taciturn, making me think that he loved the dead man very much. He left the following morning with Grandpa. They returned tormented by disgust.

The man had died of cancer and was stinking like a dead elephant, but he could not be buried because in his will he had demanded a four-day wake, and a dead man's last wish was binding. The body was kept in his sitting room. When the wind blew, half his village squirmed under the blows of stench hammers. Everybody was hungry, because the stench punished any eaters by clawing all the food and most of the bile out of their stomachs. The man had left a record forty offspring: thirty girls and ten boys. Grandpa openly wondered how the man got the beautiful women he bred with, for twenty of his girls surpassed many people's concept of beauty. Even the not-so-beautiful were beautiful by many people's standards. Kawayida's wife was very beautiful: tallish, brown-black, shapely, done in only by her large ears. The main criticism was that the girls could have done with better manners and more education. They tended to say whatever came to their minds, and some were on the loose side. Of the thirty girls, only nine got married. "Quantity, quantity, quantity," Grandpa said one afternoon, shaking his head with regret. "They are lucky to be beautiful, but unlucky to be so uneducated." That was the only time I heard Grandpa make a comment about Kawayida's wife.

Up to this point in time we had got used to the idea that politics was a disease that afflicted only Grandpa in the family. The general impression was that he provoked trouble and punishment in order to atone for mistakes he had made as a chief. On Independence Day, October 9, 1962, he got into trouble with some pro-government hooligans and escaped with a shallow stab wound and a broken tooth. In 1966, when the constitution was suspended and a state of emergency was declared, he got into trouble once again. This time it was in a distant village where soldiers had beaten up people for violating the curfew. For his criticism, he was immersed in a cattle dip. Weeks later, he was invited to the same village to mediate between the soldiers and the villagers. Grandma told him not to go. He went anyway. This time he was shot on the way back, the bullet lodged in his leg for the rest of his life.

It was thus a total turnaround when politics seemed to come

down hard on Grandma. On the night of January 25, 1971, General Idi Amin, helped by his British and Israeli friends, seized power in a military coup. He overthrew his former benefactor, Milton Obote, the prime minister who had led the country to independence and had gone on to suspend the constitution. General Amin gave eighteen reasons for the coup, among them corruption, detention without trial, lack of freedom of speech and economic mismanagement of the country.

There was dancing, singing and all manner of jubilation in the villages. I personally did not know what to make of it. For some obscure reason, I slept at Grandpa's that night. A fire woke us up. Fierce ululation led us to Grandma's compound in a rush. The house had turned into a dugout canoe trapped in a furious sea of pink, blue and red flame. It tottered horribly and wobbled groggily as the waves surged. Doors and windows collapsed with spectacular fatigue, only to be gobbled up by the swirling waves. The iron sheets twisted, as if in terrible pain, and furled into grotesque funnels. Beams undermined by flame broke off and brought the remains of the roof down. Women, mouths agape, hands on the sides of their heads, looked on, shredded screams cascading down their parched lips. Men, paralyzed, dumbfounded, stared impotently. A mangled mass of words boiled inside me, clogging my mouth, condemning me to the asphyxiated grief of a defeated mastiff. Grandma, submerged, twisted, gnarled, grappled with death after forty years of midwifery.

I could think of only one person who could have done this: the man who had tried to chop off Grandma's head. The coup provided a perfect alibi. A hot yellow stream ran down my leg: I had pissed my pants for the second time in my life.

My life had turned upside down.

BOOK TWO

THE CITY

THE SEETHING, kidney-shaped bowl functioning as the taxi park had originally been a volcanic hill. During the last active phase two things happened: the hill shattered, creating this valley, and the surrounding valleys were transformed into the seven round-topped hills at the core of the city of Kampala.

As I stood on the rim of the bowl, sniffing dirty whiffs from the notorious Owino Market and exhaust fumes from countless vehicles, Uncle Kawayida's stories seemed to burst out of the dramatic confines of his imagery into the polychromatic chaos that washed the bowl like a caustic solution. The corroded asphalt, damaged by a million feet and a million tires, vibrated with its eternal burden of travellers, loafers, hawkers, snake charmers and all manner of other nebulous figures, calling to mind the bowl's early swampy days, before the water was drained or diverted, the vegetation was cut or burned and the animals were displaced or exterminated.

The volcanic fire dormant below and the solar fire blazing from above, the relentless surge of vehicles and all the souls on parade here, turned this vessel of cobwebbed fantasies, this cocoon of termite-ridden ambitions, this lapper of blood and chewer of flesh, into the most fascinating spot in the whole city. My chest swelled when I stood in this brewery of motion, dreams and chaos. I could not help trembling with the electricity of great things to come. I knew that both wonderful and dismal memories were trapped inside the asphalt. Like devil mushrooms, they popped up to give a hint of the past and a taste of the future. Just by looking at the crowd of marauders, van boys, lechers, beggars and other nameless souls adrift here, I felt I was privy to the secrets of things to come. Every visit felt like the first time. It made the air quiver with possibilities.

I witnessed my first live birth here, in the metallic morning air, as the sun rose to pound the bowl into another day of spectacular madness. Suddenly a woman appeared, ejected from the bowels of an anonymous van. The exhaust fumes blew her garments round her midriff, exposing the swollen cavern from which baby after baby dropped. It seemed as though all of the fifty-something babies I had left in the villages had followed me here, to reveal themselves to me in one blinding extravaganza, torment me with their sanitary demands and harass me with the ineluctable power of their presence.

For a moment, the woman was screaming so hard that the whole bowl froze in an eerie silence, and she was racked by so many pangs that her face had the ash-gray serenity of coma. The silence was ripped open by the cry for a midwife or a doctor, somebody who knew what to do. I didn't, wouldn't, couldn't move. I was trapped by the ballast of a past career as a midwife-assistant, and the fate of a life running in reverse. It was then that a wall of muscle and a forest of legs sealed the images of the alfresco birth from my eyes. I saw blood flowing under and around feet, dodging outcrops, filling depressions and getting picked up by tires and soles for transportation to destinations unknown.

The skyline, gawking with architectural indigence, towered over the bowl like a row of stained, gap-toothed jawbones. The buildings re-

sembled cracked, time-whipped relics from a decayed epoch. The
dust-caked walls, the grime-laden windows, the rust-streaked roofs
and the prematurely aged ambience fostered disillusionment in my
soul. The sheer drabness of shape and the utter paucity of any structural fantasy made me reserve my loyalties for the swamps, villages
and hills of my birth. I got the irrepressible feeling that a gang of
demented architects, doubly laden with cerebral malaria and tropical
torpor, had saddled the city with these monstrosities.

A distance away, sweltering in its diaphanous illusions, stood
Nakivubo Stadium, scene of many radio-broadcast football matches.
It presented the bowl with its dirty backside, dripping streaks of stale
piss and blobs of graffiti. The pylon-borne stadium lights, clustered
like the suckers of a giant octopus, overlooked the filthy Nakivubo
River, whose cement-corseted waters were the dumping ground of
dead dogs and cats.

Towering over the stadium was the Muslim Supreme Council
Mosque. Perched on Old Kampala Hill and encased in a fading beige
veneer, the mosque was redeemed by its old Arabic grandeur, but
doomed by a front view dominated by aging residential estates, home
to poor Indians.

On the next hill, Lubaga Catholic Cathedral stood, shrouded in
tall, gracious trees and bombastic history, its phallic twin towers flirting with the nippled dome of Namirembe Protestant Cathedral. The
old rivalry dated back to 1877 and 1879, when the first Protestant and
Catholic missionaries arrived in Uganda. It was a rivalry redolent with
the blood spilled in unnecessary religious and political wars. In their
search for allies, both factions had periodically turned to pagans and
Muslims for support. This part of the city, with its places of worship,
its hospitals and schools, was called the Religious Wing.

Rising out of the bowl and swelling northward was Nakasero
Hill. Lashed by asphalt and boxlike buildings, this was the home of
wholesalers and retailers fighting to prosper in the doomed air of commercial asphyxiation. The cubbyhole shops were grouped like a bunch
of cargo containers vomited by a shipwreck, pounded by the iron
sun, harassed by poison rain and eroded from the inside by the semi-
volitional mode of disintegration favored by stranded pirates. On a
higher terrace, overlooking the shops, were the High Court, a bunch
of lesser courts and a police station, arranged in pompous, tree-lined

lanes dotted with the residences of army officers, whose jeeps farted onto the windows and the file cabinets of these overseers of justice. The majestic tension from this hill seemed to seep into the bowl. I would stand on the rim and try to listen for brewing earthquakes.

For the moment, though, I would hear only the crazed cries of the van boys, the raspy whispers of toothless fortune-tellers and the monotonous chants of snake charmers. Finally, my attention would be drawn away by the needle-sharp call of the muezzin, the iron wail of sirens or the roar of army jeeps headed for Nakasero Hill. Overpowering the fading sirens would be the indomitable crack of the fault lines on which these hills stood in their self-important configurations. I would will them to shift and bury the hills, overturn the valleys and kick up a monstrous mushroom cloud. I wanted Serenity, Padlock and their current dictatorship, whose caustic fumes had brought me here, to go the way of the animals which used to roam these valleys.

By their own standards, the two dictators had done well. They had moved from the rural obscurity of Serenity's village house to the red-roofed pretension of a big Indian bungalow. The front windows were covered in wire net because Indians lived in mortal fear of burglary. The front door, which was rarely used, stood on top of twelve wide steps that lent the edifice the look of a dismal pagoda.

The living room was cluttered with sofas, baby things and other objects which made the air prickly with the dust that nestled on them like ticks on a cow. It was not hard to see that the house had contracted, pressured as it was by the number of people occupying it, by the inevitable expansion of a very Catholic family.

The open backyard formed part of an extended yard, which compressed lives, histories and religions into the shared burden of structural intimacy. I was gripped by the sensation that it was a prison of sorts, with too many regulations and too many pretensions exacerbated by a dictatorial administration that believed in incarceration as a superior form of discipline and upbringing.

For Serenity, living here was a form of upward mobility, because these were formerly segregated areas. In those days this part of Kampala was called Mini Bombay. Serenity had, for some time, luxuriated in his dream of having three children and saving money to buy himself a car and all the other trappings of a secure life, but his dream had been hijacked by the hydra of Catholicism, which he had first met in his wife's parental home. The tortures of the crucified Christ on his inlaws' wall, now safely preserved from the vagaries of a leaking roof, had entered his life. Hydra breath had scorched the thin veneer of his dream, and he was now on his way to having as many children as the Indian civil servant he had replaced in this pagoda. He now had six children, courtesy of twin births, and his head was awash with worries. A man bewildered by the speed at which things had careened out of control, he both feared the future and mistrusted the present.

Serenity preferred to delegate power to his enforcer, Padlock, and shield himself from drab domestic work. He was a man who loved to do things by remote control, as though he were conserving his energy for a holy task. Normally, he preferred not to know what his enforcer did in order to keep his dictatorship going. At the back of his mind he held the notion that his enforcer deserved as much trouble as she got for having insisted on breeding so many children. He kept thinking about a magic escape route out of his current predicament, but he felt too proud to give up and walk away. He was rational enough to remember that it took two to have a big family. He kept trying to trace where and when he had lost control and let Padlock win. It dawned on him that Padlock had waged a very determined campaign, rejecting any form of compromise or discussion. The pressures of adjusting to the city had played into her hands, and before he realized it, he had lost both the contraception battle and the war. The result was his trademark wrinkled forehead, which lent him a scowling, comical look—a look fit for a tormented despot.

Padlock was a changed woman. She had become more confident and assertive because she no longer had to look over her shoulder when enforcing rules in her house. Her mien demanded respect while bearing not a trace of apology. The draconian disciplinarian in her had fully emerged and was grounded in her new status by a new ritual: Padlock had to be greeted on bended knee by all her children. Early every morning, I had to slip into her bedroom, which she shared with Serenity, go down on my knees and mouth a greeting. The alternative was to go out and look for her in the courtyard, where she always seemed to be, press my knees on the chipped cement and speak the loathsome greeting. The thought of calling this woman "mother" made me sick. It made me want to throw up on her feet. Her insistence on making me lie every day by calling her something I never believed in introduced me to fiction and to the delusions of power. It also intensified our clashes.

Looking down at the squirrel grovelling at her sandaled feet, she would or would not return the proffered greeting. Her internal system was wont to reject my offering, which meant that I had to try again till I got it right. Meanwhile, she would be towering in the morning air, her hair looking like a tea cozy.

"I didn't hear you," she would say, looking above as though asking for heavenly intervention.

To a man bursting with impatience to get off his knees and elude the pitying looks hurled by passing strangers, her manner was maddening. It was not that her ears were faulty; no, she had actually heard the greeting, but her dictatorial sensibilities had not been appeased by my tone of voice. The right tone had to embody total acknowledgment of her power, servile gratitude for every little thing she had ever done for you, and unequivocal submission to her will. The right tone of voice got you a reply and permission to stand up. All this was easy for my brothers and sisters, raised in the city, but for me, the free-spirited villager who had never knelt for anybody and who had been knelt to by quite a few grateful mothers, this status was hard to accept. It cost Padlock a number of guava switches to beat me into submission.

I particularly resented this courtyard worship because I did not want to be seen on my knees by our neighbor's third and youngest wife. Knowing that her eyes were on me made me feel like a little helpless bird, beak up and open, tongue quivering, waiting for mother bird to drop a worm down the throat. From the very beginning I saw Sauya Lusanani, the wife in question, as a combination of sister and lover and as the embodiment of the spirit of the city. I convinced myself that, with her in my camp, my plans for revenge would succeed. She was the youngest adult around with whom I could associate, and my present predicament made me want to know her more urgently. Until that could happen, I lived in torment. She was a Muslim, and there was the chance that she would reject me because I was a Catholic. In my desperation I convinced myself that I would convert if that was the only way to get her. I wrestled with the question of circumcision: Was there a way I could convert without getting circumcised? How could I allow myself to be circumcised when there was the possibility of penile cancer? Had I learned nothing from Dr. Ssali's ordeal? I was sure that Padlock would disown me and influence Serenity to stop paying for my education. How, then, would I become a lawyer?

At night I would think of Hajj Gimbi and his three wives, and wonder whether he was in bed with Lusanani. How was I going to supplant him? This man did not deserve that lovely girl. He was more of a father, or even a grandfather, to her. He had a large beard, which burdened his lower jaw and made his mouth look small and nasty. His large eyebrows overshadowed his small piggy eyes, which looked ridiculous in his large flat face. I felt that this man should have been the object of Padlock's vilification for sending away wives of his own age and marrying younger women. I kept thinking about ways of invading his home and taking Lusanani away from him. I knew that it would cost me time and energy, but I was determined to get what I wanted.

Padlock, like many women who produced many children too quickly, hated the sanitary obligations that came with the territory: apart from hating the exercise of supervising her children's toilet, she also hated washing the mountains of diapers and bedclothes. My coming was a blessing for her, and she made no secret of it. In one stroke, I had become the family shitman. Every morning my olfactory glands were bombarded with a string of scatological blasts, my eyes smothered with scatological disasters in different gradations of color and solidity. In the village, I had been above such mundane obligations, and I had got away with leaving visitors' children in their shit. The clients Grandma and I dealt with, those superstitious mothers, wouldn't dream of asking me to wipe their children's butts, but here in the city, I paid for all my earlier prerogatives.

As if compensating for all the sleepless nights I had spent at Grandma's funeral wake, I slept heavily in those days and found it hard to wake up. Padlock did not like this and had various ways of awakening me: she either shook me gruffly by the shoulder, barked in my ear, doused me in cold water or used her favorite tool, a guava switch. She used these methods in rotation, one for each day of the week. On the days she doused me, and on the days she beat me into wakefulness, I could hardly bring myself to mutter the ritual greeting. As a result, it would take minutes to get the tone right as we fought a minor war of wills, which I always lost.

My main task each morning was to wake the shitters and line them up with enough space between them to avoid fights as they shat, because I wanted all the steaming stuff in the middle of the newsprint on which they squatted. In order to avoid catching the scatological blasts full in the face, I would stand a little distance away and watch, shouting at anyone whose rectum strayed from the bull's-eye. The strainings and explosions were not too different from Padlock's performance on the day I thought she was producing a baby destined to fall into the latrine. Anticipating the end of the shitting session, I would tear up rectangles of newsprint and call whoever was done to get his or her ass wiped. I was careful not to spread the shit over their little balls or cunts, because if I did, it was my duty to remove it, for which I had neither the time nor the patience.

Padlock did not trust me. She would lurk somewhere at the edge of the yard, her presence a loud warning to the shitters not to misbehave, her scowl a premonition of things to come if I hurt her children's asses in futile acts of revenge. She stayed in the background till she was convinced that I was doing my job properly and that my hands would not succumb to stealthy temptations of dealing mean tricks, and then she disappeared quietly.

All butts wiped, the shitters would enter the house and leave me to deal with their odoriferous products. If the paper was not soaked through, folding the hills and streams of feces was quick work. Delivering the parcels to their destination was a task I executed with alacrity, because I was eager to leave for school. On bad days, however, the newsprint got soaked through and burst. My temper would flare, but its fires would be quickly doused by the fumes. I would do it all over again, deliver the parcels and take a deep breath as I hurried to my next task.

I always washed myself dreamily, buoyed by the thought of Tiida, Miss Sunlight Soap, the woman who bathed four times a day. Her profile would rise in my mind, and by the time I saw her whole body, I would be through.

I loathed breakfast. After seeing, smelling and handling all that excreta, I felt as if it had metamorphosed into the food before me.

Over time I completely gave up omelettes and avocados, for obvious reasons, and used my share to barter for favors from the shitters, who loved both with childish abandon. They would compete tactfully, begging with message-laden looks. If somebody had seen me doing something wrong the day before, they would feign indifference, sure that I would do the sensible thing. I would then reject the other bids and buy that particular shitter's silence. One or two clever shitters volunteered to do things for me. They spied on others on my behalf, and kept me posted. I did my best to please them, because my survival depended on it, like a mountain climber's life depended on the strength of his ropes.

School was my paradise; there I competed on level ground, and did my level best to reach the top. It was the only place where I drew compliments from adults; I also drew pleas for help from fellow pupils, who regarded tests as I did the heaps of excreta I had to deal with every morning. I would look at the large boys, perspiration on the bridge of their noses, armpits runny with funky sweat, and smile thinly. The real joy came from beating the clever ones. It pumped my heart with zeal and filled my nose with the sweet scent of victory.

Time passed very fast at school, and when the last bell rang, I always felt a load on my chest, heavy as the ugly tasks which awaited me at home. I could already visualize the blood-curdling soaked nappies, swimming placidly like sated crocodiles in the filthy grayish-brown water with blobs of shit. What had the witch been doing all day? I would ask myself. I would kick the basin, but not hard enough to hurt my foot or tip it over.

After cracking the rudiments of the Archimedean principle, negotiating the typhoons of Asia, scuttling across the pampas of South America, climbing the skyscrapers of New York, combing the wine estates of France or ascending the snowcapped mountains of Africa, this sordid task was unbearable. In those days there was nothing I hated more than that demonic creation, the diaper.

One by one, I fished them from the shitty water, averting my eyes from the sight and my nose from the stench. I held them with the tips of my fingers, and shook the remaining muck from the depths of the fabric. The squeezing seemed to last a lifetime, for overused, overstained garments never brightened even if you squeezed them with manic constancy. Padlock was an additional factor; if she was dissatisfied with their appearance, she was always ready to take the fabrics down from the line to soak again, even if they were already dry and stiff, and order you to wash them. "You will wash them till I tell you to stop," she would say, heading for her Command Post. This was the room adjacent to the living room. It was fitted with a Singer sewing machine, and Padlock spent her day there pedaling away and receiving her customers.

I would listen to the rumblings of the treadle and the humming of the needle until the sounds became intermixed, and in my imagination her foot got stuck underneath the treadle, her finger trapped under the furious needle. The din ate up all her cries for help, and the more I became disgusted with my job, the more she suffered. I would look to see whether Loverboy, a twenty-year-old pimpled, arrogant fellow renowned as the only person in the city who gave Padlock the gift of spontaneous laughter, was around. He often came in the afternoon, swaggering like a conquering pirate, looked the place over and entered the Command Post to watch Padlock work. Sometimes he brought her clothes for repair; sometimes he came empty-handed, to collect finished work or just to talk. When he was around, I would sneak to the door and try to catch what they were saying. They mostly talked about the past. Padlock told him about her parental home, her convent days, her wedding and the like.

Loverboy received these morsels of her past with an ironical air, sticking disdainful needles of criticism into the parts which did not appeal to him and rewarding the bits that he liked with loud laughter and corroborating remarks. In general, he waded through her life with the insolence of a lovable pirate. The remarkable thing was that Padlock seemed to enjoy every bit of it. I could hear them laughing, Loverboy freely, Padlock discreetly, as if she were straining a precious liquid through cotton cloth. At first I was at a loss as to what to do about this pimpled figure who handled Padlock as casually as secondhand clothes. I would watch him entering the courtyard, his legs striding, his arms held wide, his chest forward, and wonder, and also feel paralyzed. He looked like a fabulous, gargantuan weapon I could neither handle dexterously nor use crudely.

At first I used to ignore him, looking the other way when he turned up and speaking only when spoken to, but with time I faced him when he arrived and greeted him politely. He would return my greeting brashly, screw his nose up at the filthy mess in the basin or in my hands and trot into the house with a few athletic bounds. Once inside, he would engage Padlock there for long periods of time. Lusanani, who had befriended me by asking whether Padlock was my real mother, would come over and stand at the edge of the yard where Padlock stood to supervise shitting sessions, and we would talk. "She is not your real mother, is she?" she would ask, her head cocked.

This irritated me at first, till I found a riposte: "Is Hajj your real husband?" I would ask, and she would laugh. It was the laugh of mates, of people in almost the same boat, with a shared burden. I would look at her, imagining how she had gone through her first pregnancy, and how the baby had been delivered. Her body was young, firm, supple. I would get sudden urges to jump up, slip my hand up her dress and explore. Then I would be seized by the feeling that I was too young for that, and that even if I asked her to reveal herself to me, she would refuse. I would have visions of Hajj Gimbi on top of her, wheezing, squealing, sweating. Then I would hate her, him too. I would start wishing that on his way home the front tire of his motor-cycle would burst so he would fall down on the asphalt, preferably in front of an oncoming truck, and his little mouth would be silenced for good. I would, at other times, see him on top of a tall building, spilling paunch-first over the railing and flying upside down like the late Fr. Lule. With him out of the way, Lusanani would be mine, and I would not have to wash those filthy nappies, or do anything else I loathed.

Meanwhile, we talked about the city, the taxi park, the Indians in the shops, the soldiers in their jeeps, the children at her home. We would begin eagerly, bursting with words, and then slow down, till we started repeating ourselves like an old couple. Many times she spotted Padlock too late. By the time she dropped out of sight, Padlock would be on me, her guava switch cutting into my calf or backside. I would look at her with disappointment: So she *hadn't* caught her foot under the treadle! So she *hadn't* caught her finger under the needle! So she *hadn't* screamed herself hoarse in tortured solitude!

Padlock misread insolence into my look, and misinterpreted my open-eyed reception of pain as a challenge to her authority. "Village trash! She spoiled you rotten, but I'll teach you a lesson." And the switch would move with the fury of a buffalo shaking egrets off the wounds on his back.

I lamented the dismissal of Nantongo, the housegirl, who was

Padlock's first and last incursion into the vertiginous world of status symbols. No prosperous household was complete without a housegirl. When Nantongo was around, I had less to worry about. She cleaned, cooked, washed—she did everything. During the short time between my arrival and her departure, all household work revolved around her. She washed Padlock's football-field-sized bedsheets. She would rub and squeeze that white cotton fabric till I feared that she would end up like Fingers. She washed nappies and baby clothes with the stoic efficiency of a machine. Her frail hands were always moving, curling and uncurling like crazed millipedes, doing something every moment. Her back was always bent or straining with this or that task. Yet her face remained open, affable, unmarked by bitterness, as if all the labor were mere wind blowing over it. "Your mother is her own worst enemy," she told me one day, as if that explained everything. I waited for her to elaborate, but she didn't, and in order not to appear stupid, I desisted from inquiring any further.

The only noticeable improvement since Nantongo's departure was the subsidence of Padlock's tirades. When the girl was around, Padlock quarrelled with her at length, delivering sermons in a cold, grating, disembowelled voice just this side of a whine. It was as if the girl were driving pins under her nails. "You never wash the stains out of my bedsheets. You drink the baby's milk. You wear my clothes before you wash them. You dribble the sauce on your way from the kitchen to the dining room. You abuse my children, pinching them, threatening them, treating them badly."

"Should I keep quiet when they call me names?"

"She is answering her employer back! What an ingrate! Who do you think is interested in seeing the inside of your mouth or in counting your molars? You teach my children bad manners. How can I keep you under my roof? You look at everybody as if you were going to swallow them. Didn't they teach you to respect authority where you came from, eh?"

"But Mrs.—"

"You are showing me your teeth once again! You are showing me the roof of your mouth! For once, listen to what your superiors have to tell you. What kind of a man would want a girl without manners who eats like a lawnmower?"

Me, me, me, I wanted to say. Others too. I had seen men dallying with one-legged or clubfooted women. I had seen men in love with one-eyed women. Uncle Kawayida's mother had buckteeth. And that was just the tip of the iceberg.

I soon learned that Padlock was not displaying her knowledge of men; she was just carrying out a campaign to drive the girl out of her house.

"Remember when you came here, girl. You were crying. You were desperate to get a job, and a roof over your head. I gave you everything, and now you can't even cook me a decent meal."

To crown the drama, a cup slipped off the tray Nantongo was carrying to the cupboard and shattered on the floor. I had never seen anybody mourn so much for a lousy china cup with a chipped rim, a stained, scuffed bottom and a fading pattern of periwinkles. It hadn't cost much, and would never have made it into an antiques gallery, but it got quite a send-off.

"I knew it! I knew you were capable of things like this! What will be the next move, Nantongo? Botulism, or something more potent? Don't forget there's a lot of rat poison in the shops, and a packet in the house."

Padlock's face bore the chipped strain of a faked rage; the girl turned around to face her, smiled and dropped all the cups on the floor.

"Oh! Oh! Oh!" Padlock struck her thighs and lamented as the cups collided with the cement and disintegrated into bits which seemed to cover the entire floor. Then her face hardened with the intent to cause serious bodily harm. Nantongo, as nimble as an antelope, side-stepped her and said, "I have allowed you to say whatever you wanted to say about me, but I will never allow you to touch me."

Padlock could not believe the quiet vehemence of the girl's words. She was momentarily caught between intoning another futile dirge and wringing the girl's neck. To salvage the tatters of her authority, she blurted, "You are fired."

By daybreak Nantongo was gone. All the remaining china was packed in boxes, and everyone got a mug.

Serenity espoused benevolent dictator tactics to the nth degree. He relied heavily on the potentiality of force rather than its actuality. He loved operating in a web of unuttered threats, restrained violence and low-voiced warnings. He let reports of individual misdemeanors hover round him like flies on a slumbering crocodile. He let it be known, indirectly, that he never interfered with the work of his enforcer, except in the most dire of circumstances. If he ever noticed that Nantongo was gone, he never said or gave any indication. According to his principles, Nantongo was just another ripple on the surface of a pool which would be around for eons. He let that ripple expand to the edge of the pool, where it died, unnoticed. With Nantongo gone, I was the next in line, yet Serenity acted as if he never received any reports about me.

Stiff as a ramrod in his pressed trousers and shirts of the same color, he walked into the compound with a leather bag under one arm, waving to the neighbors with the other like a beneficent general on holiday. If the courtyard was clean, without rubbish or excreta, he would nod and enter the house. If you had done well at school and there were no school bills or letters of complaint from teachers, he left you alone. He often retired to his arsenal of books, or changed and headed for the gas station to meet Hajj Gimbi and two other friends to converse, watch the traffic and bemoan the state of affairs or play cards.

The four friends discussed the post-independence situation, the suspension of the original constitution, the 1966 state of emergency, the 1971 coup, the future of the country, of Amin, the Muslims, the Catholics, the Protestants and the foreigners. When they got bored, they reminisced about their youth, their careers, their dreams.

On the way to the borehole to get water, I would pass this Total petrol station, its trinity of pumps sealed in the dull uniformity of headless statues, the store behind smothered in fluorescent light and the glitter of oilcan tops, the rectangular hole in which greasy mechanics buried themselves to examine the underbellies of cars gaping like a mass grave. The four friends, epitomes of male privilege, would be placidly intoxicated by motor fumes, flying dust and the grating passage of time. Sometimes they seemed lost in the magic of the cards, or dazed by conversation about the feel of a woman or the first smile of a child, or the rush of a successful deal. Sometimes they were rocked by laughter at a rude adult joke.

The mood at the block of African shops hard by was always different. Music from loudspeakers placed on the gas station's veranda charged the air and set the tone for the loud arguments, the hard laughter, the backslappings and gruff chest-thumpings which crowned a successful joke or a clever statement. Sometimes there would be the roar of an explosive quarrel, spiky words carving the air and captivating loafers with their viciousness, outrageousness or acerbity. Sometimes there would be an acrobat, a contortionist or a guitarist picking notes off rotten strings on a rotten guitar. Sometimes the air would whistle explosively amidst a fistfight complete with glistening muscles, rasping gasps like tearing metal, and generous cheers as spectators appreciated the show. Sometimes a travelling quack would be promoting wonder drugs which cured baldness, halitosis, barrenness, bad luck and premature ejaculation with a single dose.

I never stopped there; I had to hurry to the borehole and stand my jerry cans in line, awaiting my turn. There was an old-fashioned British pump, heavy, cumbersome, thick-handled, large-mouthed, impossible to handle on an empty stomach, destined to last a century. The wooden handle always smelled of grease, smeared on to discourage the ubiquitous termites.

If a well-shaped girl like Lusanani was pumping, and you stood two feet behind her, you could see her arms rise, her body bend into curves and her face dip under the handle. You wanted her to pump on for ages because her openmouthed, dilated-eyed expression and her laboring body lighted your mind up with lewd fantasies. Her slender waist; the lines of her underwear peeping through her dress; her thighs, her calves and her legs, taxed by the motion of the heavy pumping action, fueled diverse imagery in my lively mind. As I watched her buttocks opening and closing, and how her panties curved around them each time she bent over the handle, I knew that some adult part of me desired her, and would get her and capture her spirit, and it would infuse the next stage of my life's journey. I felt doomed.

On the way home, with cars roaring on the road and some occasionally stopping at the gas station, the sight of Hajj Gimbi, his white skullcap and trademark beard, would unsettle me. I felt he was studying me, reading my mind. This suspicion was bolstered by the fact that many fortune-tellers were Muslims. It was common knowledge that the Koran was a potent book, full of magic, blessings and curses. Hajj Gimbi seemed to know what I thought of his wife, and that I wished he would disappear and leave her to me. He seemed to be waiting to catch me red-handed with her. I figured he was taking his time because Dad was his friend and he did not want to act rashly without concrete evidence. When we met, or when I was sent over to his home to deliver a message, I would tremble, waiting for him to confront me with my evil thoughts. He never did. He appeared strangely happy to see me, which confused me, although it did not change my thoughts or my feelings for Lusanani.

Confronted with dictatorship, and especially with the lack of freedom of speech for the first time, I thought I was the only one suffering in silence, but the red-ink incident proved otherwise. I had somehow adapted to the blind alley that was my new home. I had learned to keep quiet, to divert my eyes and to not say a thing. It was a new sense of self-preservation, the type I lacked in the village, the type which made your throat scratchy just when you were about to make a dangerous statement. Why the despots were super-sensitive to little things I could not tell.

One morning while I was kneeling down to deliver courtyard worship, I noticed that something was sticking out from Padlock's behind, as though a Quink ink bottle was stuck in her ass underneath her clothes. I knew that this was not a joke, because if Padlock had any sense of humor, it was not of this kind. So what was it? The bulge was too deliberate to be an oversight. So what was going on? Titillated by this rare piece of drama, my spirits catapulted me from my sullenness, and I got the tone right the first time. Padlock, anticipating resistance as usual, was startled by my humility. I quickly moved on to my usual tasks, washed and prepared to leave for school.

Padlock was the family banker, and since I had asked Serenity for money to buy exercise books a few days before, I had to go to her to collect it. This was normal procedure, because Serenity asked us to plan ahead. "Money does not grow on trees," he often said, warning us that he needed time to get it.

I found Padlock in the sitting room. She said nothing when I told her what I wanted, but just turned round and headed for the bedroom, where she kept her purse. And then I saw it: a patch as big as a baby's mouth, red as a ruby! I could hardly take my eyes off her behind. It was not that I had never seen blood before; no, I had seen it many times, and I also knew how it smelled. I concluded that a person this careful had to be in grave danger if she was leaking blood like this. I opened my mouth to alert her, but at the last moment I coughed instead. I had to kill those words. It was unwise to alert a dictator before she had given you what you needed. What if, in shame, she changed her mind and refused to surrender the money? I could not risk getting into trouble with teachers, and ruining a fine day at school, by doing something the consequences of which could only be guessed at. Wasn't I a custodian of Aunt Tiida's secret? Didn't I know too well that silence was golden? Would this new secret be too hard to keep? I didn't think so.

Joy swept over me: now I had something to blackmail my enemy with. I could use the secret against her in future. I could definitely use it to stop her from hammering me. How would I go about it? It was real blood, her very own despotic blood. Let her sit in it a little longer while I thought out a master plan to end my miseries. She could smear the house with it. She could retouch the red dates on the calendar with it. That would advertise the fact that despots were also human and that they bled when you cut them.

Next time around it would be Serenity's turn. He was bound to bleed from the front, in the fly area. He could spray the courtyard, the toilet and the entire neighborhood with it. He could even spray Hajj Gimbi's lime-green Kawasaki motorcycle, the gas station and some of the passing cars.

When I received the money, I did my best not to betray myself by recoiling from her touch. I had the suspicion that her fingers smelled of blood and that the money carried a nauseating whiff. Her fingers were damp and cold, which worried me a bit because Grandma had said that coldness of hands and feet was caused by anemia. How anemic was this woman? Obviously not enough to die before I returned from school, I concluded. I sniffed the money: it had no noxious smell on it.

As I walked to school I tried to imagine what was happening down Padlock's pants. Was she bleeding like a headless cock? If so, what a tough nut she was, hemorrhaging and yet acting as if everything was under control! This should have been the right time to whine, yet she was not giving any inkling that she was in pain. Pregnant women undergoing hemorrhage used to feel alarmed, and call for help. I remembered that cocks used to kick and twitch as they bled to death: Was this woman feigning indifference? Padlock was impervious to pain, I concluded. It was the reason she was so handy with her guava switches. I was then gripped by curiosity. I wanted to find out if Padlock was incapable of feeling any pain at all. What would

Loverboy have to say about that? Maybe it was the reason he liked her so much.

The day conspired against me by thrusting me onto the wings of irrepressible joy. I did very well in class, and during break time I found a ten-shilling note in the grass behind the classrooms nearest the playground. This was a rare stroke of luck, for I hardly ever found anything.

I looked at the note carefully to ascertain that it had not been deliberately planted there by a sufferer of boils or some other communicable disease, to be picked up along with the sacrifice, for ten shillings was a lot of money in the early seventies. Padlock would lash the skin off your back for losing it; Serenity might do the same thing.

By way of celebration, I called together two friends and bought them buns and sodas. As we ate I worked out where to store the rest of my booty. I would have shared my good fortune with my two most loyal shitters, but did not for fear that they might get so excited they would end up betraying us. In a dictatorship, there was no use getting oneself in trouble over superfluous generosity.

The school day drifted away with the speed of rain clouds chased by hurricane winds. In my exuberance I had forgotten to work out how to use my new knowledge against Padlock. And on the way home I could hardly think deeply. Nevertheless, I was feeling happy when I arrived. My thoughts kept dazzling me. I felt anchored in the glories of my academic capabilities and good luck.

The Padlock who confronted me when I entered the courtyard crushed my exuberance like a dry leaf: she looked like a fortress, her moat alive with piranhas, her drawbridge chained firmly to her castle walls. So she hadn't bled to death! So she hadn't smeared anything, even during her most difficult moments! She looked as if she were being eaten alive by so many locusts that the front she presented to the world was moments away from calamitous disintegration.

As though summoned by some worried gods and charged with the laudable task of defrosting the chilly air inside the house, a customer arrived at that moment. She lifted Padlock from the chilly depths of isolated suffering. Padlock asked how she was, how her children were doing, if her husband's van was running again, and if . . . I felt totally useless.

City women, like this specimen, operated in their own hemisphere, even the pregnant and the ugly ones. This woman, whose stomach, thighs and buttocks had been crushed by too much child-birth, was the type who would have badgered Grandma and me to give her love potions and all the dubious charms insecure women resorted to in a bid to win back the spark of bygone days. Here, however, she did not even look twice at the short-trousered classroom terror whose exercise books were wrapped in old newsprint and glowed with the teacher's red marks of academic excellence.

Padlock continued to shower the woman with attention. She rose and turned her back to me for the first time that afternoon. She was headed for the Command Post to take the woman's measurements. I saw the patch. Was this a new one? It looked larger, more dangerous, and in need of immediate attention.

Suddenly, I lost control of the words I had imprisoned and barri-caded in my head. Suddenly, as if the words were fed up with all the cowardly silence of the day, the sentences came out feetfirst like babies at a breech birth. Suddenly, I heard myself say, "You are going to die. Aren't you aware that you've been bleeding all day . . . Ma?"

More words threatened to gush out, but I barricaded them with hands on my throat. Padlock stopped dead, her head thrust forward and then skyward as if yanked by giant hands. She pirouetted with the agility and grace of the dancers at her wedding. Her face creased into a thousand wrinkles. The customer's face, which had gone pop-eyed when I first spoke, fell with the relief of a commuted death sentence, and her eyes twinkled mischievously as she saw the patch for herself. With all manner of nunly and girlish shames mincing her, all vestiges of self-control gone, Padlock snapped. Something like a tree trunk split in two by lightning flew sideways and hit me with such force that the lights went out.

Hours later I woke up with a bad headache and a swollen eye. Not a single word of what had occurred passed between the lips of the par-ties involved. In a dictatorship, the past and the present were Siamese twins, I learned, better left unseparated for the good of public order and family harmony. Anyone who needed a sense of history had to cultivate it in catacombs, where its ugliness could not disgust the eyes of the populace.

For now, I carved the incident in potato. The sweet potatoes I was made to prepare for supper were inedible. Serenity said nothing.

Padlock shot me her warning eye, assuring me that neither was I forgiven nor the act forgotten.

For the next few weeks, I prepared the best meals in my repertoire, because I had seen the clothes Padlock had bled into. I did not want her blood to contaminate the food, so I did all the kitchen work with the fanaticism of a late convert. Because she left me alone for a while, I guessed that she took my enthusiasm for a change of heart, for remorse.

At night I was invaded by a series of bad dreams, which made me believe that Padlock had substituted mental torture for physical harassment. I was visited by the wooden effigy of Jesus on the cross. An image seen uncountable times in church, in prayer books and on rosaries, the Crucifixion had taken on the surrealism of a dream; however, it was not Jesus but Padlock on the cross. All her skin was lacerated, and her blood dripped on the stones propping up the ugly cross. I was the only person watching her ordeal. The look of blame on her lugubrious face was meant to cultivate eternal guilt in me: I was her putative crucifier. On other nights she came to me camouflaged as the Virgin Mary, in a white robe, a blue sash round her waist, in her hands a globe, her feet hidden in clouds. Then she would be crucified with her robe on, torn by whips, and she would start bleeding.

Despite my efforts at rationalization, not ruling out the possibility of my mind playing mean tricks on me, I could not erase the feeling that the bad dreams were somehow caused by Padlock.

In the mornings, as I knelt to proffer my greetings, I would search her face for clues as to whether she remembered dressing herself as the Virgin Mary or disguising herself as Jesus and coming to me, but she betrayed no emotion, no inkling that she knew of my nocturnal terrors. With the weight of night after night of gory visions sitting on my mind, I wondered what I had to do to break the cycle. I wanted her to know that the guilt stuff would not wash with me—it was too late for that. I also wanted her to know that it was better for us to work together, as adults and partners, than to decapitate our endeavors with spurious violence.

I started thinking that she might be one of those people who, when possessed by ancestral spirits, sat in fire, ran around naked, climbed very tall trees, fought and destroyed things with diabolical fury, then denied everything when the spirits left them. Grandma would probably have helped me verify my suspicions, or at least dismiss them. I decided to tell Lusanani about them, but around that time the nightmares dwindled and stopped.

The lasting effect of the bad dreams was to unburden me of the millstone of heavy sleep. I now slept lightly and woke early, before Padlock barked in my ear or doused me in cold water or struck me with her guava switch. I reverted to the schedule of the village, where periodic tranquillity was interrupted by the sudden advent of babies. It felt wonderful to lie awake at night and imagine the world in slumber. It gave you the feeling that you were living in a different time zone, in a different universe, in a place where people awoke as you went to bed and put on their nighties as you slipped on your school uniform.

I sometimes felt the urge to go out and wander through the streets, dark lanes and piss-sodden alleyways, or negotiate my way to the taxi park and watch its midnight emptiness. I wanted to gauge its actual size, walk its length and breadth alone and fill it with my imagination, but it was unsafe. The caverns of darkness crawled with robbers. The mysterious depths of the night hid wrongdoers on the prowl. The length and breadth were alive with soldiers on patrol, in search of nocturnal excitement and illicit adventure. The sky was alive with ghosts of people killed in the coup, killed before the coup, killed during the state of emergency, killed at the dawn of independence as politics wore hideous masks and became bloodier all the time. The night was full of ghosts redolent with earthly smells, ghosts in search of the next world, ghosts saying endless, faceless goodbyes, ghosts flying about for one last glimpse of their beloved, ghosts marking their loved ones with batlike claws. Grandma was one of those ghosts. It was better to spend the night in the same place, in case she located me, in case she smelled me, in case she chose this particular night to reveal herself to me.

Lying awake on my back, I would think about her, and about the despots' lack of bitterness, joy and excitement. Accustomed to the afternoon brawls in which Grandpa and Grandma thrashed every subject under the sun with heat and passion, giving the impression that every line of argument and every word mattered, I found the dull harmony of the dictators sickeningly lacking. They seemed to enter each other's heads telepathically, suck out the necessary information and imbibe it, rendering words superfluous. It seemed like a trick, a clever ploy to monopolize power by keeping everyone else guessing. Could two despots be in such perfect harmony? It was possible, but it was also possible that there was something I did not know, something under my nose, hidden from me by my inexperience or blindness.

I delved into the depths of the latter possibility with the intensity of obsession. I rose to such high plateaus of nocturnal contemplation that when I heard sharp voices one night, my first reaction was to think that I was dreaming, of a fight at the African shops, perhaps, or at the sand patch behind the school playgrounds, where long-jumpers held practice sessions and school toughs held dramatic fights to establish their supremacy.

As the words whistled and the air vibrated with the suppressed hostility of so many heaped frustrations, I realized that I had stumbled onto something. I quickly got out of bed. The shitters, immersed in childish sleep this side of bliss, emitted dull farts and little snorts and innocent groans, as if in lamentation for missing my discovery. I slipped into the sitting room, the smell of tilapia fish eaten that evening kicking my palate. I ventured past the fat green sofas, past the redwood dining set where Serenity ate alone, overlooking us as we sat on the floor, and I was soon at the connecting door which led to the epicenter of the salvoes. This door was usually left ajar to allow the nocturnal cries of the shitters to be heard from the sanctuary of Padlock's bedroom. Now it was open a little wider, and my parents were at each other's throats because they were sure that everyone was asleep. This was tradition transplanted from the village into the present garden of marital strife.

As I stood on the rim of this seething crater, my mind careered off into the realm of probabilities. Had somebody fetched a weapon from the sitting room or the kitchen, and in murderous haste forgotten to close the door? And if so, what damage had been done to the other party? How long had this been going on? Had Serenity finally found the courage to discipline his enforcer? Or was it Padlock dishing out the hard blows? I was trembling with excitement. The sound of breaking glass brought me back to my senses. There were additional heaves, gasps, sighs. A curtain of darkness effectively cut me off from the action, but the thought alone of the despots hitting, clawing and choking each other made it all very real in my mind. I was flabbergasted to learn, when the noise had subsided, that it was Loverboy at the center of the conflagration.

I remembered the day I saw Loverboy sitting on a stool, his arm on the cutting board on which lines of violets were twitching as Padlock sewed two pieces of material together to make a dress. His face carried the merest suggestion of a smile, and Padlock's glowed with the finest patina I had ever seen on her countenance. At that moment she seemed to be in seventh heaven. No one living or dead, apart from Loverboy, had ever taken her that high.

On the strength of that evidence, I couldn't blame Serenity for feeling jealous and hurt by Loverboy's visits. I could see lazy clouds of vicious rumor circling round his head. Townspeople were no different from villagers. They all loved gossip. Except that whereas the latter swigged it from tumblers, the former sipped it from thimbles.

Serenity, who had had his failed trial marriage to Kasiko, could not help feeling that his wife was doing whatever she wanted with Boy, as he called Loverboy, to show him what it felt like when the shoe was on the other foot. Suspected revenge and misguided jealousy had thrust the crocodile and the buffalo onto the treacherous sands.

"You love that boy, don't you?" Serenity asked, quivering like a crocodile with its vulnerable underbelly exposed to the destructive capabilities of a buffalo's horns.

"Not in the way you think," Padlock replied icily. "He is just nice to have around." The words had resurrected her voice and impregnated it with a vein of warmth.

"Why can't you tell the truth about this boy of yours? Do not think that I am a fool."

"I told you the truth. He is just a customer of mine who happens to say things that make me laugh."

Serenity, old shop and shopkeeper prejudices filed to a fine sharp point, momentarily wondered why he had succumbed to the demands of his wife and brought the commercial devilry of sewing machines and customers into his home.

"Wh-what things?" he stammered, as he used to when he was sent to the shops and could not find anybody willing to go there in his stead.

"Compliments. He admires the way I handle material and turn plain strips of cotton into beautiful dresses."

I steadied myself against the door as my knees almost gave way. Padlock, a woman from whose vocabulary the word "compliment" had been expunged in infancy and replaced with "threat," craved compliments! And was desperate enough to lap them from the purulent platter that was Loverboy's mouth! Loverboy, the only creature, bipedal or quadrupedal, to oppose, reject and compliment Padlock and her views and get away with it! I was struck by the way I had misread Padlock, but I felt my chest swell with gratification: despite her indifference to hemorrhage and her quickness to strike with guava switches, she was not impervious to pain. I could hurt her!

"Ah! So, I don't make you laugh! I don't appreciate what you do despite the freedom I give you!"

"It is not the same," she replied, her voice thick with impatience, her tone loaded with a patronizing edge. What she did not put in words was the idea of purity and innocence which nullified the usual man-woman devilry when she was with Loverboy. Loverboy sought only the healing power of words from her. The flattery she got from him was the nearest thing to calf-love and adoration she had ever experienced.

"What do you mean by that?" Serenity asked, an edge of anger to his diction.

"If there are women who can make you laugh, there are also young men who can make a married woman laugh. I know there are many women waiting for something to happen to me so that they can rush over here to occupy my place. But I tell you this: breed your bastards as you like, as long as you know that they will never be allowed a place in this house."

Serenity did not like the matter of his daughter brought into discussion. He did not like being on the defensive all the time. Earlier on he had made it clear that he was too busy worrying about money to go chasing other women. Why was she going back to the old topic?

What she did not tell him was that she kept having nasty dreams about her wedding day, with images of children with outstretched hands, waiting for a piece of wedding cake. The cake crumbled into stones, which the children used to hit her because she had supplanted their mother. She now doubted that Kasiko's child was a girl. In the dream, Padlock was always surrounded by boys who vowed to succeed their father because they were the true firstborns in Serenity's house. She craved reassurance that Kasiko's child was a girl, but she could not find a way to get it without betraying herself.

"What has brought all this on?"

Faced with an educated man who she knew would scoff at the idea of dreams in which a girl became a horde of rock-throwing boys, she felt embarrassed, and so she resorted to what came easily to her: tough talk and threats. "Hajj Gimbi must be arming you with the skills of a polygamist. But that disease will never contaminate this house."

"Leave Hajj out of this. He is my friend, not yours."

"I will never share a roof with another woman."

"I am getting very fed up with all this nonsense. If this is your way of voiding guilt over what you do with that boy, say it and keep quiet. I am not going to listen to this nonsense all night. I have to wake up early to go to work."

"How can you trust those Muslims? Are they now talking you into converting to Islam or Aminism?"

"I told you to stop this rubbish. Hajj is my friend. Take your paranoia elsewhere. Saddle Boy with it, and tell him to drown it in a well. People are talking about you and me and are calling me a cuckold. They think the boy is all over you, like yaws."

"I never want to hear that from your mouth again. Never!" she barked. The bedsprings groaned as she shifted her weight angrily.

"I don't want people talking about us negatively. We are an exemplary family. Don't ruin in minutes a reputation built in years."

"He only flirts, but if those people out there are rotten enough to believe what they think, why should I care?"

"Flirting! In my house! Over my sewing machine! What does he do, sing you songs? Tell him to stop it. Let him find himself another tailor. I don't want to see him here again."

All this was very raw information; I was yet to digest it and find out what a godsend it really was. I was starting to get bored. I even thought of returning to bed because I had gotten more than enough for one night.

"You are not holy yourself. Why did you accuse me of jealousy when I sent the housegirl away?"

"I never said any such thing," he replied sleepily.

"She was staring at you."

"She was just trying to stop you from bullying her. I never noticed her."

"I could not trust her around Mugezi," Padlock put in.

"What is going on between you two?"

"Children have to be obedient; he is not. He thinks he is the man in the house. You let him get away with anything. Don't you worry, I am going to break him myself. I am determined to stop him from turning into one of those people robbing, torturing and killing people. His grandmother spoiled him rotten, but I am going to undo all the damage, whatever it takes. I never trusted that woman."

My legs buckled, and I almost fell against the door.

"You've gone too far. Stop it, stop it!" Serenity's voice was a piercing whine.

Robber! Killer! Torturer! Who was robbing, torturing and killing my spirit every day? Who tortured me with terrible words, with the smell of shit and the fire of guava switches? Who corroded and robbed my spiritual goods in a bid to file me down to the conventionality of a cog in a wheel? A war had just been declared. I had no illusions of winning this trench warfare, but I was determined to become a very costly, very destructive victim. The enormity of the task of controlling myself, and using this new knowledge sparingly for maximum effect, made me tremble and break into a chilly sweat. How was I going to look at my parents, greet them and obey them, as if I knew nothing?

"I want a promise from you that you are not going to leave the job of breaking this boy all to me," she said. "We have to claim him before the evil of this world does."

"I am helping. Who pays his school fees?"

"I mean physically, in a disciplinary manner."

"I will help, and I will also make sure that Boy does not come back here."

"I told you there is nothing between us." Padlock was angry that Serenity was trying to link two separate issues.

"Flirting in my house is nothing?"

"That boy walks miles looking for customers for me, free of charge. Without him I would be redundant most of the time. What could I do without his help and his connections? It is not in anybody's interest to discourage him."

"If you do not stop him, I will do it myself."

"You have made your point."

"It is an order."

By now I could not take in anything more. The voices seemed to echo from a faraway cave. I did not care what happened afterward. I did not care whether he broke her leg or her arm or whether she crushed his kneecaps or caressed them.

My stay in this city had, so far, been a calculated attempt to reduce my stature, to prune my idea of myself and to crush my personality in the mortar of conventionality. I was being ordered to do things without being told the reasons or the purpose. I was being beaten and lathered in contempt. I was only good for washing nappies, cooking, fetching water—for doing all the things that Padlock did not want to do. In other words, the torture rack was grinding and spinning, slowly doing its job of breaking body and will.

My late-night discovery taught me one thing: I had to use as much secrecy as the despots did in plotting against me. I had to strike with the padded stealth of a leopard, hiding my tracks as well as my claws. I had to fight their fire by carefully lighting mine in such a way that when both conflagrations met, they would destroy each other without torching the house. I had to act with the stubborn mischief of a pig.

In the village, when you bought a piglet and did not want it to escape, you put it in a gunnysack, which you tied up and carried home. Even then, some piglets did escape when the sty door was left ajar or when the rope on their leg was not properly fastened. They escaped not so much to return to their original homes as to retaliate for the boredom of captivity. The escapees took revenge by eating the neighbors' crops. Some pigs waited longer: at mating time, sows carried to pedigree pigs escaped and had to be chased around the village. When they were caught and delivered to the males, they twitched out of position, wasted prime sperm and sabotaged the birth of pedigree animals. I was ready to apply some of those pig lessons.

I was restless for days on end, unable to sleep, unable to go to the door to spy again. A wooden stiffness oppressed my chest, crushing down into my abdomen and killing my appetite. On the way home from school, I would go to the taxi park and watch the vans, the travellers and the rootless spirits adrift. I was jostled by youths of my age peddling radio batteries, underwear, exercise books, toothbrushes— anything they could lay their hands on. I was stalked by pickpockets who thought I had pocket money or grocery money with me. I was approached by a phony fortune-teller who promised to divine my future and bless me if I had money to buy his services. I saw con artists leading illiterate peasants to the wrong vans, the wrong vendors and the wrong corners and using colleagues stationed there to rip them off. I saw provocatively dressed women milling around, jiggling their buttocks, twitching their cheeks and doing all they could to catch men's eyes. I saw women who looked lost, unwilling to ask for help, unwilling to go far in case they got more lost.

I concluded that there was a proliferation of rats in the land, because there was such a variety of rat poison and wire traps. In the village, we used to open dry batteries and mix the carbon inside with fish in order to kill the smell, then put the mixture in a mouse hole or behind coffee sacks for rats to eat and die. Here there were plenty of poison liquids, cakes and powders for killing rats. I had enough money to buy enough poison to kill that giant rat called Padlock, but it was the surviving power of rats that worried me. Rats often ignored poisoned food and jumped wire traps. What if, instead of eating the lethal food herself, Padlock passed it on to one of the shitters? I could not live with that. I probably could not live with Padlock's death on my conscience either. There was also the police to think about. Padlock never went out, except for mass, and it would not be hard to find out that her poisoning had been a domestic affair.

I looked at the snakes, especially the gleaming cobras which danced and twitched and puffed out their necks when the gap-toothed charmers blew their flutes or whistled. The glittering magnificence of the scales and the black eyes made my chest swell with the temptation to buy one and deposit it in Padlock's bed. The snakes were fangless and harmless, but maybe she would have a heart attack. Still, I could not see how her death would translate into more freedom or more rights for me, so I walked on.

I smelled rain in the air. The sky was darkening. Heavy clouds hovered above the broken-toothed skyline like vultures and marabou storks. They sealed off the sun, the minaret and the cathedrals on the distant hills. A cold wind bit the skin into goose bumps. The sky collapsed into walls of water, and a stampede erupted.

The deluge rolled into the bowl from the top of Nakasero Hill, sweeping in with the fury of impotent judicial courts and raking the land with the crushing power of mighty army officers. Nakivubo River flooded, regurgitating filth onto its banks, into the roads and onto the nearby shop fronts. Snakes floated in the water, as did a tortoise, a few dogs and a drunkard trapped in the webs of his intoxication. The roar of the water merged with that of the military tanks, rocket launchers and troops involved in the January 25, 1971, coup. Riding on the waves was General Idi Amin.

With the general on my side, I would crush the despots like nuts in a mortar. I saw sodden soldiers combatting the waves as they escorted a high-ranking officer. On their statue-like faces was the fatalism, resignation and utter obedience of worshippers dedicated to the gods of war. It was your head or theirs, when the chips fell. The air trembled with their deadly power, as it had once vibrated with the alfresco delivery of the baby on the asphalt.

If I could recapture the totality of such commitment, and the courage of Grandma at the moment the panga flashed, I would not need poison. I could just walk up to a soldier on patrol and inform him that Padlock and Serenity were Obote sympathizers. They would then be picked up, tossed into a jeep and carried off to the barracks. There they would have their teeth pulled and their backsides massaged with rifle butts or rhino-hide whips. There they would be made to do things outside the realm of even Uncle Kawayida's story-spinning imagination. But if I called in soldiers, I would not be acting with the stealth of a leopard.

I could, if I wanted, join the State Research Bureau, the organization charged with keeping an eye on things, monitoring the enemies of the state, both actual and potential. I could get the Bureau's red identity card, and no one would dare to touch me again. I could flash the card at teachers, Serenity, Padlock or anyone else who stood in my way. Armed with that card, I could strike fear into the depths of Padlock's heart and make her know what it felt like to be at the sharp end of tyranny. There was also the possibility of claiming Lusanani, eloping with her, and daring Hajj Gimbi, or anybody else for that matter, to do something about it. The only problem was that, without Grandma to guide me, power would most likely destroy me. It would seduce me with guns, knives and white-hot threats and catapult me over the edge into vertiginous frenzy. That also would not be striking with the padded paws of a leopard. I put that alternative on hold.

The safest thing to do was to choose Amin as my bodyguard. He was a realist. He never turned the other cheek. He answered love with love, hate with hate, war with war. He was proud to the point of arrogance. Judging from how far he had come, how much he had endured on the way at the hands of the British and of his countrymen, and how patient he had been, his was a deserved pride, a fitting arrogance. This was a man who, unlike many Africans, was not afraid to voice his opinion because he did not fear reprisals, unlike me. He was reprisal itself.

At the Independence Day celebrations that year, he had demonstrated his power. Countless cymbals had ripped the air, countless tubas had farted deep into the stratosphere. He had separated the lake of vapor and sweat with the magnificence of his presence, lulling anxious hearts, soothing doubting minds and massaging parched palates with words of wisdom and the seeds of leadership. Inside him growled the whales of dominance. When he roared, his enemies shivered with the fatigue of crippling defeat. When he smiled, he was a gloomy sky cut by razors of lightning. When he rewarded his cohorts, he surpassed the multiplier of loaves and fishes by multiplying cars, mansions, high-powered jobs, money. I knew it: He was the baby I saw popping onto the asphalt. He was the baby born to rise like a mountain, flow like a thousand rivers and die a thousand deaths. My second guardian angel had materialized.

I rushed home with a snap in every step.

BOOK THREE

BY THE AGE OF SEVEN, I had already become Grandpa's principal audience. I listened to his political discourse and memorized the main points without understanding them; then, at the end, he made me defend the British, the Indian and the African sides of the national argument in question-and-answer sessions. I was his future lawyer, possibly a future politician too, since many lawyers turned to politics: his ideal mini-double. By this time, after many years of contemplation, Grandpa had come to the conclusion that the modern state was a powder keg which would go off in a series of major explosions. It was a house built on the treacherous sands of inequality, strife and exploitation. He secretly lived for the day when it would all blow up, for he truly believed that only then would a new order be born out of the rubble.

The city sat at the heart of Grandpa's dissertation. When he was a young man, Kampala was divided between the Europeans and the

Indians. Africans came from the villages to work there, mostly in minor functions, and returned to their villages. Life was segregated, courtesy of official British policy. The British had first used Indian soldiers to defeat the central part of the country, and when it came to conquering the rest, Protestant chiefs from this region headed armies which fought to spread the tentacles of British colonial rule. As in the case of the Indian administrators, bureaucrats and traders imported to administer the area Indian soldiers had helped to conquer, the local Protestant chiefs were given administrative powers in the regions they had conquered, thus planting the seeds of modern tribal strife.

For Grandpa, the shock of being barred from law school brought into focus the racial inequality at the heart of the colonial system, and he decided to fight back. He campaigned and became a subcounty chief in the forties and a county chief in the fifties. These positions gave him a better view of how the system worked, and he learned how to fight it from the inside. The British were safely at the top, insulated from the Africans by the Indians, and the Indians enjoyed the middleman's role without soiling their fingers. During the forties, Grandpa did two things he detested: he collected taxes to fuel the administrative machinery and gathered conscripts for the World War II effort—young men sent off to die in theaters of war whose names they could hardly pronounce. His only brother by the same mother volunteered; he was eager to go and kill white people, especially British soldiers, because they had stripped and whipped him for loitering near the British Club. Grandpa tried to stop him, asking him to stay behind and fight for change locally, but in vain.

During the war, Grandpa supported Germany. Actually, to him, the war was a European affair he had no interest in. He regarded it as a bizarre game of football, the British and German teams resuming where they had left off in 1918. Because he disliked the British team, especially their colonial rule, he settled for their biggest rival. News from the front line took an agonizingly long time coming, and when it did, it was mostly brief, bad and insufficient. Thousands of young men "returned in envelopes," meaning they died on the front and their families were notified by mail. Many young men returned that way, in soiled pieces of paper passed from hand to hand. He expected to receive his brother's envelope too, but it did not come. The war finally ended and the veterans came home, without any news arriving of his brother.

In the meantime, he backed the raging economic boycotts. It was his way of dealing with his brother's loss. He also felt he owed it to the conscripts who had returned in envelopes. During the boycotts, however, his brother resurfaced. His leg had been blown off by a land mine in Burma. He never said anything about his war experiences, for he had lost the power of speech. He spent his days locked away in the miasmas of his mind.

The biggest achievement of the boycotts was to lessen the Indian stranglehold on trade and put some coffee mills and cotton ginneries in African hands. Yet ruin came hot on the heels of success: somebody accused Grandpa of anti-government activities, including sabotaging the war effort. He was impeached, and his efforts to return to office ended in a crushing defeat at the hands of a Protestant chief. More ruin followed, and his life crumbled round his ears. As the boycotts raged through the fifties, he fought to pick up the pieces of his life, without much success. To begin with, his favorite wife was taken by another man, and not long afterward she died. Serenity, Tiida and Nakatu became orphans. Grandpa's household fell apart: relatives, wives and friends left, and had it not been for Grandma, it would have collapsed totally.

The sixties were ushered in on the back of mounting political pressure. The British Empire was disintegrating from the center, and there was unrest in its constituent parts. The British were on their way out. Locally, they were escaping the flames of the house they had set on fire. Grandpa did not like that. He would have liked them to stay and pay for the sins of dividing the people and heightening intertribal strife, for the economic exploitation of the country and for creating a recipe for future disaster. Protestants had the upper hand in national politics; the northern peoples controlled the army, police and prison services; and the central and southern peoples were peasant farmers and bureaucrats. There were far too many fault lines along which seismic activity could erupt.

By that time Grandpa was more a watcher of than a participant in both national and local politics. He talked at a few small meetings, espousing non-partisan political views, which sounded strange to political neophytes who had been promised opportunities if they voted for this or that party. The local elite had entered the political arena in the process. The Indians, however, stayed out of it, content with their 90 percent control of trade and their royal role as the geese that lay the golden eggs. After sixty-eight years of British rule, for much of which Africans had been more spectators than participants in the political and economic life of their country, Grandpa could see no ground for optimism. He could only see powder kegs smoking, waiting to go off.

Pre-Independence partisan violence, manifested in the cutting of banana and coffee trees belonging to members of rival parties, made Grandpa sure that the house built on divisions and exploitation was going to be undermined by the same, and sooner rather than later. When he was attacked by mastiffs angered by his criticism of the victorious Protestant, northerner-led Uganda People's Congress party, he saw the wound he suffered as a vindication of his theories. It was the conviction that he was right which fueled his quick recoveries, fired his intransigence and empowered his stoicism. The explosion was near, and so was the construction of a new house in which everyone would have a stake. The old house built on British supremacy, Indian collaboration and African tribal strife did not belong to anyone. Nobody felt safe in it. It was a house to be used and abused for petty gain. It was a house to be pulled down, because of the piratical cancer at its heart. At the time he was telling me these things, I thought he had made up some of them.

Grandpa was speaking from experience. When he lost power, and the women left, and the army of relatives and hangers-on dispersed like feathers in the wind, his vision became clear. The cloud of power was gone, but he felt unburdened, liberated from the ghosts of control, unyoked from a parasitic household. His home had been a small island infested by pirates, terrorized by conflicting interests, incessant jealousies. It had been a joyless place. He hardly knew what went on within its walls or outside them. It burst with intrigue, insincerity and competition. He would feel the strife as soon as he entered the compound. He could detect the negativity in the branches of the trees, and in the smell of the soil of his coffee shamba. The proceeds from his crop haunted him, torn at as they were by the claws of greedy hangers-on.

At the peak of his power, awash with worshippers, he could hardly get anyone to tell him the truth. He could feel masks going up as soon as he arrived home from work. Each word uttered was a spear, a costly bullet not to be wasted but to be carefully used in individual or collective battles for favor, for money, for position. Grandpa did not think that the national powder keg would go off in the same way his house had crumbled. He knew it would take time.

Nineteen sixty-six. Four years after Independence. The constitution was suspended, a state of emergency declared in the central region. Armed soldiers were stationed in Grandpa's village for the first time in national history. He believed that the time had come for the national edifice to go up in flames. He stoked the conflagration with the oil of his eloquence. He spoke to the political idiots about their no-win situation in biting parables. He acted with the bravery of a man who knew that destiny was on his side.

When the bastards dipped him in a cattle pool, he believed that he was going to die, and that his death would blow the conflagration all the way to the top. When they let him go, he felt he had missed a historic opportunity. When the villagers invited him back to help them deal with the question of military brutality, he saw it as a golden opportunity to fulfill his mission. When he was shot on his way home after a stormy meeting, he prayed for death to take him, but only one bullet was fired at his leg. He waited for more bullets to come and thrust him into national martyrdom, but in vain. When he opened his eyes and found himself in a bed at Ndere Parish Hospital, without any soldiers guarding him, he felt sad. The day of national reckoning had shifted a few more years into the future. He was afraid he might miss it.

General Idi Amin's coup took Grandpa by surprise: either he had misjudged, or a quirk of fate had manifested itself. He had expected the president, Milton Obote, to lead the country down the red road of Communism or Socialism. He had expected to see the nationalization of Indian businesses, and British military intervention to protect the interests of British capital. The British would force Obote to rescind the nationalization plans; banking on Russian or Chinese help, he would refuse, and he would be taken out in the name of anti-Communism. But before any of that occurred, Amin was there, and Grandma had died in a mysterious fire.

Intoxicated by sorrow and uncertainty, and left on his own without his favorite adviser, adversary and sister, Grandpa suspended his political musings and soliloquies. At the back of his mind was the twitching pulse which intimated that Amin might be the man everyone had been waiting for, the man who would fire the next explosion, or series of explosions. The British pirates had left the political arena to their local counterparts and had concentrated on running the economic show by remote control, aided by their Indian agents. Was Amin the man who was going to smash the whole setup?

Grandpa was plucked from the depths of his nostalgia by the news that the Indians had to leave the country within ninety days. "This is it," he said to himself, sediments of unease gathering at the bottom of his heart. "A few more explosions, and the house will be reduced to ashes and reconstruction can begin." For once, he allowed the bug of optimism to bite him, and he believed Amin's vows to return to the barracks after putting the country back on its feet. Grandpa started going out to drink. There was too much electricity in the air to stay home and moan about the past when the future was looming on the horizon. People sang Amin's praise. He could see the mighty padlocks on Indian businesses falling away like rusty trinkets, opening the way for Africans to storm the bastions of economic power. Voices of apprehension were gobbled up by the noises of jubilation. No one wanted their euphoria poisoned by doubt; they had waited so long that they wanted to imbibe it in its purest form. Grandpa ignored talk about the economic abuses of Indian business owners. His mind was already on the next step, the next explosion, for what had been started had to be pursued to its logical end. Amin obviously had balls, he conceded, but how would he use them?

November 1972. Indians had started to leave. Grandpa did not miss the departing Indians, because he did not have any Indian friends. He had always made big purchases from the same shop, where they served him politely, but that was where the relationship ended, sealed by the tinkle of coins. He had seen Indian shops begin, expand and flourish. He had also seen a few edged out, but it had been an Indian playing field.

Now Indian temples would be desolate, worshipperless; Indian school gates, torn open to allow everyone in; Indian clubs and sporting facilities, penetrated and occupied by new faces. As a group, Indians were too powerful to sympathize with, but he could not help thinking about the old. What were those creaky-boned, triple-chinned old men and women going to do? What would he have done, God forbid, had he been in their shoes? What would Grandma, God forbid, have done in their predicament? What would she have felt and said? He could not imagine how the old were going to cope in Britain, a place he never desired to see, for he reasoned that if the British could cripple his future in his own country, they had to be worse on their home turf, where they had even more power.

Grandpa could see the Indian community splitting like a jackfruit dropped on concrete. There were the rich and the poor, the skilled and the non-skilled, the highborn and the untouchables, the Indians and the Goans. How were the untouchables, despised and discriminated against by their own people, going to fare in Britain, where many of them would look darker than Africans? Had he been in Amin's position, Grandpa would have given the old people the choice to leave or to stay. It was only fair. It would not be new to the country: when the chiefs from the central region were expelled from the regions where they had gone to establish British rule, the people who wanted to follow them left and those who wanted to stay remained behind.

All the Indians were leaving. Already there were rumors of suicide: people setting themselves on fire, eating poison, drowning. Grandpa felt happy that the British could, this time, not escape the boomerang of race which Amin was sending them. He was putting thousands of Indians on their doorstep, many of whom had been kept out of Britain by the immigration quota system. The irony was that British officers had promoted Amin, and Britain had had a hand in his coup, and now the bastard was paying them back. British officers had certainly passed over many more deserving African officers when they were grooming this hydra, and now it was too late to start chopping off its multifarious heads. What had indeed come on the wings of racism and piracy was flying home on the same.

Gripped by fear for the future, Grandpa partook of the bonanza of cheap sales by going up Mpande Hill to the shops. He got himself a fifty-kilo sack of sugar, a ten-liter tin of cooking oil, a twenty-liter tin of paraffin, and cement for repairing cracked graves in the family burial ground near my favorite tree. Grandpa could see that Amin was a robber baron, a corporate raider, a mafia boss, a man who, in other circumstances, would have built himself a financial empire as big as Barclay's Bank, for he had the guts, the luck and the ruthless drive of a successful pirate. What bothered Grandpa, however, was that Amin had far too much power and was too unpredictable. No one seemed to know what he was capable of. The future thus looked overcast.

Grandpa remembered that when Serenity migrated to the city after Independence, he found the place still as segregated as ever, with the proliferation of slums the newest development. Life still went on in diaphanous chambers of adjacent experience, with every race, every class and every tribe separated by a glass wall. This was the post-Independence city, and the former classroom teacher was dazzled by its aggressive energy.

The whites, in their marble fortresses, were locked in their privilege and elitist corporate power. They enjoyed the protection of nuclear arms in silos back home and warships in the Indian Ocean over here. They were the goldfish in mobile aquariums, gawked at as they rolled through the city on the way to their schools, their clubs, their power jobs. Serenity could feel the locusts of envy nibbling at his thorax.

The Indians in "Mini Bombay" were sealed off in their mansions, their schools, their hospitals, ever a mystery to the Africans, certainly a riddle to Serenity, whose feet were heavy with mud as he negotiated the city. The nearest he came to knowing an Indian was his departmental boss, a man who issued orders and directives in a thin high voice. All Serenity knew of his boss's private life was that the man had ten children and that his parents had come from Gujarat, where he had never been.

Serenity was shocked by the ugliness of tribal strife. All the soldiers he saw were tall, dark sons of northern Uganda. The policemen were a mixture of northerners and easterners. There was palpable hostility toward the people from the central region, his region, and mud sucked at his feet and locusts nibbled at his thorax and gut whenever he saw the armed soldiers. They looked at him with envious annoyance because he was a civil servant, with better pay, a better job and more security. They made him feel like a potential victim of armed frustration, money hunger and tribal hatred. Steeped in village civilities all his life, Serenity found it hard to get used to cosmopolitan hatreds. The forlorn arrogance with which his people tried to defend themselves against accusations of colonial collaboration made him uneasy: Serenity had never been an arrogant man. He had always survived by making himself inconspicuous. He avoided conflicts, understated his opinions and ducked the limelight. Now it seemed he was onstage all the time, watched by a hostile audience, playing roles he never cared for. It seemed everyone was onstage, playing roles cut out for them by fate or by strangers. He could sense danger brewing.

The Africans were loosely united by their dislike of Indians and Europeans, by their past of building castles and falling off the scaffolds of mansions they never lived in. Race was class, and class was still determined by race. Africans wanted to emerge from the dregs at the bottom to the salubrious air on top. The majority believed that time was on their side, which in a way was true. But with bills piling up, Serenity did not feel comfortable with waiting. He wanted a worry-free future, a better job and a pilgrimage to the land the blackbirds migrated to annually. Thrust into the vortex of competition, hatred and uncertainty, he faltered, he doubted. How would he make enough money to give his children the best education and still save some for himself?

The post-Independence political elite had what he wanted, but the pressure, the gore, the mire they waded through to achieve what they had terrified him. It was the way of hardened thieves. His neighbor and friend Hajj Gimbi often said that change was in the offing, but what was in it for him? Change for the better was for those who waded in gore, and Serenity was not that desperate.

He had always been afraid and suspicious of authority, and Amin terrified him in a special way. A man who came to power in a coup and led thousands of soldiers and was not afraid of death was to be feared. He brought into sharp focus the contrast between book law, social law and armed law. By the look of things, armed law was in, random arrests and detentions were becoming commonplace, and it all frightened him. His main consolation was that Hajj Gimbi had connections, courtesy of his religion and his friendship with people who knew people who mattered. Hajj Gimbi had reassured him that in case he fell into trouble with the army or the police, he would help him.

The news of the Indian expulsion order left Serenity speechless, the balming fingers of euphoria stroking his thorax. He could smell hope in the air as the horizon trembled with the change and the possibilities it suggested. Serenity was shocked to realize that his childhood fantasy had come true. The conspirators in the destruction of his childhood, and part of his adult life, were leaving! Their dream was over, damaged irreparably! He knew that the Indians would not leave without a fight: the geese that lay golden eggs would claw, and flutter, and bite, and break the eggs if possible. Suddenly things looked different; all the abuse, all the suspicion, all the hatred, all the fear, all the power of money and monopoly, floated uselessly in the air like degraded poison. Suddenly, neither goodness nor evil could save them.

Serenity was puzzled to learn that the British did not want to have the Indians back after all the Indians had done for them, after all the money they had made for them, after the hundreds of years of British occupation of India. For the first time in his life, Serenity realized how precious it was to have a nation, a homeland, a place to go. He fleetingly recalled Padlock's expulsion from the convent, except that this was a far worse tribulation for those involved. As he watched the tears, the fear, the pain, he realized that he had overestimated the nature and the extent of Indian power.

Rumor was rife of Indians taking their own lives, selling all they had, pouring salt in car engines, giving things away. There were moving sales everywhere, anxious Indians lining up for travel documents outside British Embassy buildings. Watching these people in endless lines, pounded by the iron sun, helpless and confused, made Serenity distrust power even more.

He returned home one evening with a beige-plastic-cased, sixteen-inch black-and-white Toshiba television set, which had the peculiar habit of stinking like a mixture of burned leather and rotten fish after only two hours of service. The stench diminished when the set was switched off, but returned fifteen minutes after it was turned back on. This stench intrigued me, because I was not allowed to watch television. Padlock and Serenity believed that television was a subversive entity which could irreparably damage a mind with a propensity for sin by feeding it better ways of transgressing and rebelling. So, to save me from myself, and to save themselves the extra energy needed to police a sophisticated miscreant, they banned me from watching the box. The shitters were charged with the duty of reporting me if they saw me watching when the despots were away or when they were unaware of my presence.

Consequently, I only got secondhand news and impressions of what went on. The shitters outlined what cartoon heroes, boxers, film stars or Korean trapeze artists did, and I imagined the details. As I heard the laughter of the shitters or their fights as they dug elbows into each other jockeying to sit nearer the screen, free from obstruction by top-heavy heads, I tried to visualize the action. Sometimes a very smelly, very stealthy fart escaped an anonymous rectum and sparked off accusations and counter-accusations. I would smile to hear Padlock hollering, issuing threats, calling fire and brimstone down on the culprit.

What annoyed me most was that I could not see history in the making. I could not see decrees dropping from Amin's lips as I had anticipated when I first heard that this technology had penetrated the walls of our pagoda. I longed to see Amin's face, his demeanor, his mood, as the decrees which influenced the lives of millions of people left his body like magic incantations. I had visions of a nervous Moses trembling as he struck the water with his stick to create a way for the children of Israel. How did Amin differ from that Biblical figure?

I now and then entered the living room on redundant missions and took a few furtive looks. Amin's face filled the whole screen, and if there was any fear, any inkling of the gravity of the decisions he was airing, it did not show. His was the face of a master, a magician safe in the knowledge that his wand was omnipotent.

After the television, Serenity decided to buy himself a house of dreams: he purchased a library of books from a desperate Indian man who had been rejected by the British, the Canadians and the Americans and was preparing to go to Pakistan. The dreams came with their own history of violence: half the collection belonged to a man who, weeks before, had eaten rat poison, slashed his wrists and bled to death among his books, ruining quite a few, which had to be burned. Serenity's new acquisition arrived on the back of the puke-yellow Postal Service truck which had brought him to the city. The driver still sported Elvis sideburns, and when he complained that the chests were too heavy, his voice boomed as though it had passed through a fat clay pot.

Serenity discovered Oliver Twist, Madame Defarge, the Artful Dodger and many more ghosts in the Dickensian jungle, but it was the American jungle that stole his heart. American writers, with their migrant's fascination and obsession with money, success and power, spirited him off into a world of dreams where likeable rogues had it all. Ensconced in their penthouses, they cut deals, sipped champagne, participated in orgies with perfect-bodied nymphos and indulged in excesses just this side of madness. They gambled, raced sports cars, flew private jets and went on lust-sodden cruises in the Caribbean. Serenity lapped it all up and turned it over and over again in his head, angry that it was all out of his reach.

Serenity was shocked to discover that character was not a monolithic rock which stopped moving somewhere in one's late twenties, anchored by a wife and children, policed by friends, relatives, colleagues, extended family and strangers. He found himself in flux, and he became aware of unreleased sexual energy in his body. Temptation, liberated by the turbulence of recent events, coursed through him like malarial bacteria waiting to explode into full-blooded fever. He could not remember the last time he had been in bed with a woman whose body attracted him with its power, grace and elegance, combining sight, smell and touch to create a feast of sensory satisfaction.

What was he supposed to make of Loverboy? Was he the reincarnation of the man who had seduced Serenity's mother and led her to her death? If not that, what did the young man represent? Youth, freedom, innocent flirtation? Or uncommitted love? Serenity was swept back momentarily to his bachelor days when he had raided a few marital beds and partaken of ungratified sexual reserves there, free to come and go, free of responsibility for the women, free to give and take what he wanted without a thought for tomorrow. He resolved to watch the Boy carefully. At the same time, he remembered his wife's bridal aunt, seeing her rise from the tombs of unpursued possibility with the supercilious grace of a bored goddess.

The imminent departure of the Indians kicked off furious rows in many an office. At that time an office bully lured Serenity into a trap.

"Do you believe that all the Indians are going to leave?" the bully badgered.

"Yes."

"Catholic, put your money where your mouth is. Some of us believe that you are just pretending, pussyfooting as usual."

"They have to leave. Amin is serious."

"Amin can't do that. The economy will collapse. Britain will bombard him from the air. He can't take the chance on an embargo. He is also afraid of America: American warships are stationed in the

Indian Ocean very near here. My bet is that a reprieve is imminent within a month. Amin is just scaring these people, trying to show them who is the boss. He probably wants more money from Britain and America."

Why wouldn't Britain and America succeed in stopping Amin? Why wouldn't Amin back down? Serenity had no foolproof answer. He could only trust his hunch, but Cold War politics and the fight against Communism being so hot and unpredictable, should he? He decided to go for broke.

"Britain and America won't intervene," he said bravely.

"They will shit on him till he suffocates and relents."

"No, they won't."

"Amin will be hit so hard he will even call back the few Indians who have already left."

"No, he won't," Serenity insisted.

"I give you five hundred dollars if you win; you give me the same amount when you lose." The man licked his index finger, passed it across his throat in a beheading motion and pointed it in the air, gesturing his oath.

All eyes were on Serenity now. Five hundred dollars was a lot of money for a civil servant: if he lost, he would be in trouble for months. The books and the television and other things would have to go. Why should he cave in to this bully? Self-respect? The thrill of tottering on the brink? The indulgent fantasy of doing what people did in books and got away with? He rolled his head like a calf trapped in a quagmire. He struck the table: once for accepting the challenge, twice to vent disgust, thrice for courting Lady Luck. Much to his dismay, the bully pulled out of his front pocket a typed agreement on yellow paper. It had been a setup. He signed the paper, and a neutral party pocketed it.

It was the fear of losing his bet and the possibility of Amin changing his mind that kept Serenity lecturing Padlock on international politics, global relations, the world economy and the strengths and weaknesses of Western capitalism, caustic subjects which filled her with bile. Padlock tolerated the barrage only because they had agreed never to break the sacred code of despotic harmony in front of the children. By delving into the murky waters of Cold War politics, with its polarization, pragmatism and reincarnation as the Scramble for

Africa, Serenity hoped that fate would pick up the tremors in his voice, the fear in his thorax and the fire in his gut, and side with him.

Padlock, on the other hand, felt like shutting her husband's irritating mouth with a vicious slap or a whack with her guava switch. On and on he went, damaging the secret power of despotic silence, committing the unforgivable sin of interrupting the news reader, postponing night prayers and the holy rosary, and shattering her peace of mind.

This relentless assault on her mental faculties by Serenity's obsession with politics reminded her of one crucial matter: her divine duty to break me. She was setting the stage for the first major explosion. She built up an index of misdemeanors, which she recited in full every time she was dissatisfied with my conduct. These days she left many of my sins unpunished. Her tone took on the truculent whine of gathering disaster. She kept on reporting my misdemeanors to Serenity, who, sadly for her, was so wrapped up in the ramifications of the wager that he could not honor his end of the bargain by taking immediate physical action. The more he disappointed her, the more determined she became to see my day of destruction. She started reporting every other evening, at the same time, just before the all-important eight o'clock news, when the stinking antics of the box irritated Serenity and caused a lull in his political soliloquies.

One afternoon, after most of the Indians had gone and the bully had paid Serenity one hundred dollars, the one and only payment he made, the puke-yellow Uganda Postal Service truck returned. This time the tailboard spilled forth a fridge-cum-oven, a mighty spring bed, a box of black tea cozies which were in fact Afro wigs, a few other bits and pieces, and something which greatly fascinated me. It was two-legged like a billboard, had a rectangular shining face and was so burnished and smooth that one could see one's face in it. I watched the driver's hairy hands carefully to see if his palms became wet after touching the gleaming surface. With bated breath I waited for him to wipe his hands on his khaki overalls, but in vain. A smile on my face, I went near Serenity, hoping to touch the object in order to sate my curiosity, but Serenity just growled and said, "If you touch it . . ."

The reverence with which the new imports were handled made it clear that they were dear, much dearer than the stinking Toshiba or

Serenity's suede shoes. I could hardly camouflage my interest as the shiny object was being installed in the fastness of the despotic bedroom.

The hour after the truck's and Serenity's departures passed with grinding sloth. I kept watching the clouds—dusky, foamy horses with heads jammed into each other's rear ends—as they slid across the sky. Was it going to rain?

Padlock was neither in the Command Post nor in the toilet, which led me to conclude that she had gone to the shops to buy cotton, chiffon and other materials for dressmaking. Loverboy had not appeared, and it was too late for his visit. The shitters were either busy with menial tasks or wrapped up in play. This was the time to storm the walls of my humiliation and walk the floor kissed daily or every other day by my knees as I worshipped at the altar of despotic power. This was the time for me to enter the shrine of despotic slumber, on my feet like a pirate taking an island, and, like a conqueror, grab the treasures I desired. This time there would be no one to make me check my step, my manner, my tone of voice, my conduct. I was going to be the lord of the chamber of despotic decree, dreams, love, child-making, nocturnal debate and hidden conflicts. This was my coup d'état, my riposte at my tormentors. I was going to open their drawers and boxes, and examine their clothes and jewelry, and see if they had dirty little books filled with smudged secrets. The magnet at the heart of this putsch was the glittering object. It had razored the darkness at the center of my fear with its lightning swords, and the concomitant blood of courage had birthed this coup, this rebirth of my old days of power.

I stormed past the Toshiba, its pale case dimly beckoning and obliging. The soles of my feet bounced on the hairs of the carpet, whose thickness was alive with the dust that made stiff-brushing it a stone-rolling ordeal. "You will clean it till I tell you to stop," I could hear Padlock croaking. I brushed past her ghost, which never forgave Grandma for dying before a Hoover could be bought, those resources having been diverted toward her burial costs. Serenity had since refused to buy the machine.

I pushed the door before which I had trembled when I heard Padlock's plan to break me, and I was soon inside her bedroom. It was in semi-darkness, as if the walls were bursting with untold secrets. The old bed was bare, stripped naked, its cone-shaped springs facing the ceiling like empty funnels. I sat on the springs, eliciting a few metallic squeaks. The bed resembled Serenity's bachelor bed of old conquests. The springs and the frame cut into my backside. I stood up and turned my attention to the new bed. The thick, prickly blanket looked snake-like in its red and brown patchy magnificence. Face taut with excitement, I ran my fingers across the blanket, static electricity crackling. The silky bulk of the pillow felt like the coat of a sow at mating time, just before misdirected semen jetted over it. On this pillow heads full of horny dreams rested as the despots, and the Indians before them, mated. A stuffy, woody smell floated on the air, combining with loose, lewd dreams to foster a mounting tension in my loins.

Padlock had an intriguing reading lamp: the shade was a black-dotted yellow cone, the stand the effigy of a famous white woman, her pleated skirt billowing round her waist as though she were standing on a fan, and a cheeky full-lipped smile on her face. There she was, this silver-screen veteran, discarded by departing Indians, adopted by the despots. I prodded and stroked her behind, the incongruous obscenity of her presence filling the air with refracted sexual forces. I prodded her behind one more time and moved on.

I brought my nose very close to the glittering object at the head of the new bed. I was disappointed because it smelled like shoe polish, its oily tang lingering on my palate. Succumbing to tactile temptation, I stretched out my hand and touched the gleaming surface, its dry smoothness, the imagined smoothness of Lusanani's backside. I closed my eyes and explored the very cool, very smooth surface, my fingers going deeper and deeper into imaginary orifices, my imagination's eye peeking under the sheet at slick dilated lips. I stretched across the thick pillow, and it moved under me like the back of a sow, and my hand reached the extreme end of the object, very near the wall. The sensation of swimming in a dark pool, warm and slick with swine sperm, was intoxicating. I got the feeling that the Lamp Lady, Nantongo and Lusanani were sitting on my stomach, squeezing a thick liquid out of my loins. As I turned on my back, I saw the box of wigs. One wig was sitting on top of the box like a hen on its eggs. The hairs called back memories of Aunt Tiida's pubic hair. On closer scrutiny, though, the wig was more like myriad black caterpillars sewn together into one monster. I turned to the glittering board, the pressure in my loins more palpable. What was beneath this glittering magnificence, this slick dryness?

Using my thumbnail, I attacked the edge of the board. I worked slowly, trying to attain a good rhythm, but got nowhere. I needed an implement. I thought of fetching a nail or a knife, but changed my mind. I didn't want to leave scratches or betray my tracks. I had to use my fingernail, but with better technique. I wedged my thumbnail between the veneer and the glue and the frame. A piece of veneer as big as a man's fingernail broke off. Beneath the veneer was mere wood! Dull brown, long-grained wood! Sweat broke out on my back: What was I going to do with the broken piece? A dull, anticlimactic feeling assailed me, momentarily stalling panic.

I licked the glued side of the splinter and attempted to paste it back in place. Was there no proper glue in the house? There was a tube of solution used to patch bicycle tubes. A bolt of elation shot through me: I was going to get away with the invasion, the damage and the discovery that below the glitter was banal dullness. I trembled as I had trembled when I thought that Padlock's baby was going to fall through the rectangular latrine hole. Once again I was ahead of her.

A soaring sensation overtook me. I was soaring into safety's bosom, swimming through currents of warm air as thick as morning mist. At that moment a furious palm swept hot air into my face. Two fingernails sank into my lower lip, carefully avoiding my lethal teeth. This was a novelty, for Padlock was a celebrated ear puller. Maybe she was so excited by the occasion that she could hardly contain herself, let alone stick to normal procedure.

"Do you know what you've done?" This woman knew how to irritate me on all fronts: her pathetic country-western girlie whine, xeroxed from a white nun from her convent days, the same nun from whom she had inherited the little tremolos which she sprinkled piously on the last hymn every night, really got to me. If somebody was going to torture me, I preferred it to be done manfully or womanly, not childishly or girlishly, which made it feel as if I had been spat upon by a five-year-old brat.

"Ma-ma-my liip," I said, trying to control my fears.

"Do you think you are still in the village, where they do things mindlessly?"

"No-no-nooo," I replied for lack of a better answer, angry that I had betrayed myself. People didn't do things mindlessly in the village. On the contrary, they conformed to norms. People did a lot of mindless things in the city but were too pretentious to admit it, and possibly too ashamed of themselves to face the fact. In the village Grandma or Grandpa would have told me straight away that the glittering thing was just a bloody headboard for a bloody bed, wooden, veneered, period. Here, in the jungle of pretensions and despotisms, adults acted dumbly, explained nothing, and at the same time believed they were doing a wonderful job. In the meantime, Padlock twisted my lip and slapped me again.

"Do you know what that bed cost?"

I kept quiet. My lip got twisted. Colored dribble mixed with tears ran down my chin.

"Remember this: I am not your grandmother, and I am not going to spoil you like she did. I am going to set you straight. And I am going to hammer sense into your head even if it kills you."

"Yes, yes, Grandma, Ma."

"I am tired of your boorish behavior. I am tired of your rotten manners. I am tired of always getting shamed by your behavior, you hear?" A twist of the lip followed each of those statements, her eyes wells of black, yellow, red fires.

"Stop eating like an ox, you hear? Stop eating as though there was no tomorrow. Do you hear me? Stop it, stop it, stop it."

This was very hard to bear: being reduced to the voracity of a healthy ox in a wire-thin voice was the ultimate insult. The eating habits of city dwellers totally disgusted me, especially when their deficiencies were veneered with brittle respectability. In the village you ate your fill, and more food was forced on you; all that on top of the sugarcanes, the jackfruit and the pawpaws eaten between meals. Here, on the contrary, you were expected to starve yourself or eat as little as possible, work like an ox and be proud of it all! If you wanted a sugarcane or a pawpaw or a jackfruit, you had to buy it. Since there was no money to throw around, many people could not afford to buy fruit, yet they acted as if you were supposed to be proud of that too. If city dwellers revelled in the masochism of measly meals, that was their business, but expecting me to adore it like a sacrament and to strive for it like a Holy Grail was totally unacceptable to me, because I knew better. If the despots found it hard to feed their children, it was their problem. Maybe they should not have migrated. Maybe they should have planned their births better. To expect me to play along, and to worship

deficiency, was to insult my intelligence, especially when I was working so hard, freeing them from their filth. Consequently, I never forgave Padlock for the scalding transgressions of her tongue, the vicious
excesses of her imagery and the despotic myopia of always seeing
things from her side.

As more and more strings of bloody saliva dripped through her
fingers onto the front of my shirt, Amin's words dripped through the
filters of my brain into my consciousness. Amin had exhorted every
citizen to walk tall, to act proud and not to let anyone deny them their
rights, their dignity or their self-worth. Amin called on everybody to
empower themselves and to excel in their chosen fields. He said that as
a boxer, he always won by knockout in order to avoid the traps of bi-
ased officiating and the pitfalls of contested victory. He called upon
everyone to knock down the obstacles in their way, no matter what, to
emerge victorious and remain on top. He reminded us that the axis of
power was always shifting, drifting in the opposite direction, and that
nothing would remain the same, especially for those who were ready
to work hard and realize their ambitions. He said that the main reason
most people were not what they wanted to be was because they were
too timid, too ready to follow others, too lacking in initiative and too
unwilling to take risks. He said that his government was a government
of action, a revolutionary government which would wake sleeping
dogs and pull everybody along. He asked everyone to get involved. He
asked pupils to depose bad teachers, workers to overthrow tyrannical
bosses, wives to divorce bad husbands, children to reject bad parents,
victims to rise up and take power and the poor to take chances, make
money and enjoy the fruits of this country. He reiterated that Uganda
was a free country, for free people, where all were free to do what they
wanted.

I was in chains, and what was I doing about it? I was bleeding,
crying, begging for mercy, allowing injustice to go unchallenged.

If I wanted, I could chin-drop Padlock with the top of my head
and crack her jaw. If I dared, I could gouge her eye, break her nose or
dislocate her knee with a side-kick. If I had the balls, there were many
things I could do to end my suffering. But, like the people Amin talked
about, I was not taking any action. In this case I was afraid of Serenity.
Would he not kill me for injuring his wife? How was I supposed to unite
powerful exhortations of courage, freedom and self-empowerment with

the immediate dangers of retaliation from Serenity's anger? St. Amin, help me. St. Amin, pray for me. St. Amin, overlook my cowardice. St. Amin, deliver me from my fears. With all my attention on Amin, my pain subsided. I started feeling proud that I was not crying out and that I had not pissed in my pants. I was keeping up in my own way.

Amin had said that if you got cheated out of your deserved victory, go home, regroup, train harder than before, return to the arena and deliver the biggest knockout ever seen. He said that for some it took two or three or four trials before the glorious moment came, but that one should never give up, and never accept defeat. I stood very still, apparently impervious to further punishment. I had decided to wait for my chance.

By now Padlock had become annoyed with my lack of attention to her words and her torturings, and with a final shove, she released me. Bloody, like her ink patch of not so long ago, I felt proud. My lip was swollen and devoid of sensation, droopy like a pig's teat, but I carried it like a flag of courage. Amin had to be proud of me.

I was clever enough to realize that my punishment was not over yet. I cleaned the blood from the floor and left the garden of the Lamp Lady with her billowing skirt, fear ticking like a small device in my head.

Serenity returned from work as usual, handbag in hand, his stiff trousers chiseling the air, a detached look on his face. As he changed and headed for the gas station, my fear was a gong in my chest. He returned with a satisfied look in his eyes, stationed himself in front of the box and began his political soliloquy. Padlock was busy crocheting, driving a long hooked needle into fat thread to produce the creased ropes she needed to make tablecloths.

Had he already got the news? Was he toying with me, spinning out threads of torture, waiting for the right moment to go for the jugular? His face was blank, devoid of any inklings. I drifted in and out of the living room with the creaky walk of a locust, my ears abuzz with Amin's doctored voice as it poured out of the single television speaker. The house seemed to contract and dilate like a birth canal, awash with the smell of impending disaster. I felt every move terror made, but I was powerless to stop it. I lifted the sheet of false security to peek at the contractions and dilations of impending doom, but lacking the telepathic capacity to drill through the opaqueness of despotic conspiracy, I failed to read the signs. I took refuge in the kitchen, doing my best to bury my trepidation in the gurgling noises of cooking food, and to fight the guilty feeling of unpunished transgression with the comforting fire of the cooking stove. It was all in vain. Even Amin couldn't bring solace. I wanted an earthquake to arise in the pit of the pagoda and bury us all, but I soon learned that earthquakes, like so many other disasters, only visited places where they were unwanted, and would never come by order or wish.

The two-man tribunal always took place after night prayers, when the residues of Padlock's nunly tremolos were still in the rafters and supper was just minutes away. This meant that most condemned persons were doubly punished: they bore the weals of guava-switch thrashings and entered bed with the gastric howls of unassuaged hunger. Sometimes the latter punishment was commuted and one could eat, but many found the food unpalatable only moments after being thrown about like balls and howling like wild dogs.

As the tribunal passed its sentence, taking time to ask if I knew the cost of a real bed, inflating the sentimental value of freshly acquired goods to a staggering level and bestowing the patina of false newness on secondhand goods, I got the feeling that I was the chosen victim of Indian curses invested in all their forcibly relinquished goods. Was it not possible that the bed and its magical headboard had been abandoned by a family that, out of desperation, had drowned themselves in Lake Victoria, or eaten poison, or thrown themselves in front of an oncoming truck? I was very sure that Serenity, courtesy of his educational sensibilities, had failed to assuage the spirits of the former owners, dismissing such precautions as superstitious mumbo jumbo. There was also the possibility that the red specks I had seen on the leg of the bed were residues of Indian blood, loaded with Indian curses, jetted by an Indian woman assaulted by frustrated soldiers. Serenity, in his educated arrogance, had not sacrificed a large cock or a goat to take away the blood and the curses of former owners. I saw myself as the sacrificial animal, caught between the hostilities of clashing cultures. It was a plausible explanation for my deadly fascination with the veneered banalities of that headboard.

On the other hand, I realized that a despot didn't need the curried curses of dispossessed property owners to explode into murderous excess. A despot did what he did because the time was right, and because he had allowed himself to be goaded into the hard corner of slowly simmering rage.

Serenity struck with the bare-clawed fury of a leopard at the end of a long antelope-stalking session. It seemed that everybody, including me, had seen it coming. The shitters watched to see whether the confrontation would live up to their expectations. Serenity was all over me with his suede shoe. For a moment, I was too overwhelmed to do anything about those scalding blows with cooked rubber. Up and down, left and right it went, guttural groans of you-saw-it-coming issuing from his twitching mouth.

With the first pain barrier cleared, I thought I was going to die. I was not afraid to die, because Grandma was on the other side waiting for me. In fact, I was terribly afraid of not dying and remaining a cripple with an arm broken beyond repair, or my head messed up like poor old Santo's, or my spine damaged like the catechist who fell from the pulpit. There was a man in the village who could not sit or walk. A bull had tipped him into the air, and something had gone wrong. I was being thrown into the air now, but rather than stay handicapped for the rest of my life, pissing and shitting in a bedpan, I preferred to die.

I started to fight back, head-butting Serenity in the shins and the kneecaps. I started aiming for his swinging crotch. I got beaten harder. The audience stopped giggling. Serenity was out of control, answering his enforcer's challenges to his despotic credentials. This was a demonstration beating. I wanted him to go on and on and on. Every blow drained off the chaff, leaving me pure. This was a landmark, a historic pillar in my life, and I wanted it to be so prominent that its scars would fire the boilers of my revenge. I was falling, falling, falling, like water escaping through cotton cloth, dropping into the glass, leaving the accumulated dirt on the cloth. The hammering whisked me off to the slopes of Mpande Hill, where I almost lost a foot in the spokes of a bicycle gone wild. This time I was the rider fighting to keep the bicycle on course, away from the ravine, instead of the boy riding pillion. I was back in the swamps, swimming with peers: I kept going up and down, up and down, swallowing green water as I now swallowed solid air. My friends were calling me now. I got ashore. It was over.

■   ■   ■

I woke up in my bed, bruised all over, the creaky movement of swollen joints a source of pain. General Amin's spiritual help was the ointment which oiled the wounds of defeat and stopped them from festering into gangrenous ulcers of despair. I had lost, and now I had to regroup, train hard and engage the despots in my own good time, at a venue of my choice. War had been officially declared, and I was thrilled by the possibilities of impending engagement. Padlock had never hidden her hand. Serenity had shown his. It was my turn to show mine.

For three whole days I was too sick to go to school, and I could hardly restrain waves of disgust with myself for demonstrating such weakness. All the bones were fine, only the flesh ached. So why was I not at school? Why was I home listening to Padlock's grating whine? Why was I allowing myself to be irritated by the victorious timbre in her voice? This was her moment of glory, a confirmation of her power, and I was showering affirmation on it. She now filled the house with her spirit, humming to herself to fill in the remaining holes, barking orders or working on her sewing machine.

Serenity was scared, though he was too inhibited, too set in his despotic ways, to come to me for absolution. I was ready to grant it cheaply, at the cost of a measly gesture, because I knew how hard it was for a despot to apologize, or to appear to be apologizing, for his actions. However, I was not going to give it to him for free. He had to come and get it, like a man, from a man who had bought that power with his blood, tears and bruises. As a boxing fan, he should have learned that boxers hug at the end of a fight, however hard or bloody, not so much because they like each other, but to acknowledge the other man's role in the convolutions of victory, defeat or otherwise. I was ready to acknowledge him and his role, and to forgive him for losing control, for breaking the rules, for brawling, but he came neither to my corner nor to my bed. He started returning home late from work. He failed to look me in the eye. He ate his meals shielded from me, from his enforcer and the shitters, by the papery walls of a faded red hardcover Beckett book. He was hiding and waiting for the arrival of Godot. He forgot that I had usurped the role of Godot.

Serenity tended to like authors—like Beckett and Dickens—who had had difficulties with their mothers; I don't know what he expected of them in his current predicament. From behind his papery fortress,

encased in despotic stiffness, he looked as chiselled as a latter-day
Beckett. He seemed to be protecting himself from the curse of
Padlock's tongue, the very tongue which had imported the imagery of
murder into his house during their late-night confrontations. He
seemed to be reeling with the realization that he had stayed just this
side of murder. He seemed to be wondering how and when he had
regained control of his senses, for nobody, least of all Padlock, had
raised a single voice of protest throughout the rampage.

During my confinement, I considered returning to the village and
helping Grandpa as he wrestled with age and hernia, but I knew that
he would disapprove and send me back. Had I learned nothing from
his tribulations and lectures? Had he been beaten and immersed in a
cattle dip and shot for nothing? All Grandpa wanted was a lawyer, and
since Serenity had disappointed him, the responsibility was fully mine.
Had I not learned that there was no giving up and that one had to lick
one's wounds and then come back in style? I was ashamed of myself.
I also realized that there was no longer any village to return to. I carried the village with me, and it would remain so for the rest of my life,
although the years with Grandma could never be relived.

With the beating still fresh in their minds, the shitters obeyed orders
with the precision and dispatch of survivors who knew too well what
could befall them. They weren't about to tempt fate or to stir the wrath
of sleeping gods. On a few occasions I caught them talking about me,
but I ignored them. They were wary of me, as if I had contracted leprosy, most probably the leprosy of guilt by association. I could not
blame them for finding it hard to proceed on the treacherous mudflats
of despotic unpredictability.

　　For her part, Padlock acted as if nothing had happened. In her
mind, the score had been settled. I had once condemned her to death,
and she, in turn, had made me peep into the hungry lacunas where
death putatively resided. Her only interest was in finding out whether
my fall from grace had led to a total change of heart. When I attempted
to stir her guilt by pretending to be too sick to do my shit duties, she
said, "Cut out your little games, boy. Remember this: this is not your
grandmother's house." From then on I executed my duties with the
cold efficiency of a soldier on guard.

I avoided Lusanani like the plague. The note she thrust in my pocket on the way to the borehole was dripping with sympathy, the very thing I could do without. It irritated me as much as the sight of her nipples protruding from her wet blouse. It should have been a message of congratulation, for had I not passed the test, survived the ordeal?

I raided Serenity's library of fantasies and lingered about, wondering whether to make off with Beckett. I finally decided to take *Treasure Island*, the most popular book in the house. I hid it for days, hoping it would be forgotten. I was planning to give it to a girl I was beginning to take an interest in. She was younger than I, in a lower class, and I did not even know whether she cared much for pirates, ships or adventure. Serenity ignored the disappearance of the book, but Padlock pursued the matter hotly. She slowed down only when she realized that no chest-beating, confessing fool was going to pop out of the woodwork and own up to the "robbery." She took to saying, "I know who the thief is. God will shame him one of these days. Whatever one does in the deepest darkness will be proclaimed from housetops."

Personal experience told me that whenever Padlock had recourse to Divine Intervention and Holy Scripture, it was not out of piety but out of a sense of looming defeat. I sat comfortably on the book, waiting for a chance to donate it. In the meantime, a friend of mine took an interest in it. It was an ill-fated move to lend it out. An aspirant girlfriend of his who was trying to assert her rights took it, and my friend, who had all along been looking for a chance to lay her, did not ask her to return it.

At school I got myself pocket money by writing love letters for large boys to their prospective sweethearts. It was my favorite hobby, for it accorded me the chance to see how burdensome hormones worked, and to what lengths boys went to appease them. This was also my foray into the arts of blackmail, deceit and corruption, which culminated in my most daring move: writing a love letter to Padlock.

The usual procedure was that a large boy would approach me, mostly at the recommendation of a third party. He would introduce the subject, often beating about the bush, especially if he was intimidated by my academic credentials. I would listen, and he would ask if I knew the girl in question. We would follow the girl. He would sing her praises, even if she deserved none, and I would memorize what he liked about her. Back at my desk, I would write a letter emphasizing the girl's strong points. If she possessed no visible beauty, I would improvise, assigning her qualities which would make her mind spin, but careful not to exaggerate too much. It often worked. If a girl was very clever, I would raid Serenity's poetry books, extract a few catchy lines and stroke her heart with the words of a dead poet. The most accessible source of inspiration, however, was the Old Testament, which most pupils never read, making my quotations all the more impressive.

Seeing how frantic some boys became, buying patterned handkerchiefs, underwear, petticoats, powder, perfume and sweets for girls who did not love them, and sometimes did not disguise their disdain but could not resist the lure of free gifts, one could not help concluding that love was a disease which one chose to ignore and endure, or cure by doing all manner of foolish things.

If we dispatched a letter and a girl took her time reacting to it, the boy would ask me why it took so long, as if I knew and I was just refusing to cooperate.

"Go and talk to her, beg her if that is what she wants. Tell her that I can't sleep, and I can't do anything without thinking about her. Tell her that I will give her anything she wants . . ."

At that point, I would doctor the pleas and the answers, because I wanted to keep my clients happy. If the girl said that the boy had bad breath or stank or that he should drown himself to save womankind from the scourge of his existence, I would say that her parents had threatened to beat her if she ever started dating in school and had put spies on her to make sure that she kept away from boys. My other favorite line was that the girl's parents had vowed to make her drink azure blue to induce abortion if she ever became pregnant, and that afterward they would come for the boy with pangas. I would end by saying that the girl was in love but saw no way out of the situation, at least for the moment. Most clients bought the lie, at least for some time.

If two boys competed over the same girl, I would pocket their money and choose whom to favor. If I didn't like the girl, I would campaign for one boy, get him a date and then tell the other about the rendezvous.

For bullies I had my punishment: I would take the money or the gifts meant for their girls and give them to Lusanani, and then lie that the girl was not yet convinced, or that the reply would be coming soon. If the bully threatened to take action, I would ask Lusanani to write a letter insulting the fellow, asking him to leave her alone.

All this experience in wheeling and dealing proved beneficial later, when I entered the world of business. For the moment it made school the most interesting place on earth for me, apart from the taxi park bowl. Adding to the excitement, on top of the love letters, the deceit, the promises, the successes and the blackmail, there was sports. When the football season began, betting started, and fights broke out as losers who failed to pay up were hounded by angry winners. Large boys were often asked to intervene and frighten the losers into paying. When the hostilities reached insupportable levels, the score could be settled by a fistfight or a wrestling match at the sand patch, where long-jumpers made their sinuous springs. A date would be decided, and after school eager spectators and ready combatants would slip behind the buildings and enjoy the match.

One day, as I was wrestling with a letter to a trainee teacher on behalf of one of our hormonally unstable boys, it struck me that it would be a fine idea to tackle the despots by writing Padlock a love letter made to look as if it were from Loverboy. It was such a daring idea that for days I was restless. I woke up at night to listen through the connecting door and hear whether they were still feuding over him. I didn't want to catch myself in the snares of my own lies. I wanted to strike at the right moment, hoping that the marital harmony of the despots would get a good jolt. I didn't find out anything about the state of despotic feuding: it was as if they anticipated me and fought earlier or much later. The only constant factor in the drama was that Loverboy continued visiting, albeit less frequently than before. My guess was that Padlock had told him to slow down a bit and give Serenity a false sense of security before picking up the old routine. The situation was ideal for me. Serenity was probably not too happy with his wife's intransigence, but because she had done something about the boy, he must have eased the pressure and ignored Loverboy's irregular visits, waiting for the right occasion to put his foot down again.

I consulted *The Book of Letters* and *How Not to Write Your Letters*. The latter helped me most, pointing out the kind of grammatical and semantic mistakes a person of Loverboy's caliber, with his early secondary school education, was most likely to make. It took me two months to write and rewrite the letter, distancing myself as much as possible from my first literary document. It took me a few days to convince my *Treasure Island* friend to ask his sister to type out and mail my letter for me.

It took Serenity one glance at the typewritten khaki envelope addressed to his wife to know that something was wrong. In the first place, in all their time together, his wife had never received a typewritten letter before, and she had not now alerted him that she was expecting one. Second, there was neither ON UGANDA GOVERNMENT SERVICE nor KAMPALA ARCHDIOCESE nor any other official sign to indicate where it had come from. Third, the deplorable state of the print—half red, half black ink, instead of solid black—set off warning bells: who was so pathetic as to not be able to afford new ribbons? He swiftly decided to open the letter.

Serenity's suspicions were vindicated as soon as he read the first line. Boy, that pus-inflated walking pimple, had struck! Serenity had all along suspected that Boy had continued flirting with his wife, and giving her laughs he could never give her, under the guise of a sober business relationship. The fact that his prude wife had accepted, rather enthusiastically, the Afro wigs he had given her indicated that she had fallen into the trap of desirability. Her passive acceptance of the lampshade, with its billowy-skirted Monroe woman, now took on more significance. Arms shaking, throat choking, armpits melting, bum itching, he read the letter again and again.

Dear Miss Singer,

How are you smoking the cosmos in these highly atmospheric days? I am highly honored to dispatch this greatly wonderful missive to you. I supplicate you to recall the wonderful happiness we shared before this highly antagonizing cutout of love lodged itself in our cosmos and disorganized its blissful ministrations.

Permit me to conjecture that by throttling your highly volcanic love, you are disorganizing the workings of the cosmos. I hate to see you that way, you know. Your disestablishment of

our love and its highly vertical thrust can only bring negative
tintinnabulations in our hearts. I supplicate you to remember our
Song of Songs:

> *Your felicitous neck is like a mesmeric tower of gold*
> *Your fantastic nose is like a phonetic monument*
> *Your mellifluous eyes are like grammatical pools of silver*
> *Your wonderful breasts are like aquatic love bombs*
> *Your infatuated body is a volcano of hot juices*

Miss Singer, I supplicate you to recall that I am your best
friend. A wise man said that we make many friends but trust
only a few. The wise man also said that many are married, but
few are happy, remember.

Miss Singer, you are the Queen of my heart, and I want you
to make me the President and the Commander-in-Chief of yours.

Before I supplicate you to sign off, recall that I am yours
amorously, marvelously, dangerously and thunderously,

> *Mbaẓiira the Great.*

Serenity had been there before. He could smell post-adolescent ver-
bosity, flatulence, crass emptiness and immaturity a mile away. In his
day, the letter would have had pink and red hearts festooning it, with
powder inside the envelope.

He found the name "Miss Singer" very disgusting. If that was an
indication of a childish streak in his otherwise very mature wife, he
would have preferred to know through other means. He knew older
men and women who dallied with younger partners, how they grov-
elled, compromised their personality and marital status, just to come to
the level of the younger party. The younger ones in question often spat
on their partners' status and age, giving them childishly younger or sil-
lier names in order to gain a degree of control over them. Now the bug
was inside his house. Had he not warned his wife to keep away from
this fellow? Whom had Boy paid to write this garbage?

Serenity was consumed by the righteous rage of a wronged husband, but it did not last. It was replaced by sadness, a creepy feeling of
missed opportunity and betrayal. Why hadn't he confronted Boy face-
to-face? Why had he felt the need to play the gentleman?

His sadness deepened when expressions like "love bombs," "volcano of hot juices" and "infatuated body" jabbed his mind. For a woman as prudish as his wife, Serenity felt that such expressions could only have come into use with her express encouragement. She was most probably attempting to clutch at the shreds of her faded youth, or the tatters of an adolescence eclipsed by parental sanction and convent rules.

The whole thing was especially pathetic because it was his wife who had decapitated marital passion by announcing so many days of sexless abstinence that copulation had become as calculated an act as going to the beautician.

He deplored the role he had played in the drama. He could have reported her behavior to Mbale, their marital arbiter, but he had felt too ashamed, too compromised, to unburden himself to a man who respected him so much. He had thought about it many times but could not find the right words, the apt opening: "Ah, *muko*"—brother-in-law— "you see . . . my sex life is . . ." or "My wife refused to see to my needs on such and such and such days . . ." or "I can't get my wife to . . ." Serenity feared that Mbale would lose all respect for a man who could not get his conjugal rights from a wife he had married in church. Serenity also knew that a man of Mbale's peasant background would never appreciate the kind of decency which made a man burn for such long periods without trying to get his rights by force. Serenity had also failed to unburden himself to Hajj Gimbi for fear that it might ruin their friendship.

Now he felt doubly sad and angry that his wife had fallen into the traps she had set with her own hands. It was evident that she wanted more sex, but did not know how to break down her barriers without losing face and power in other areas. Serenity believed that his wife's recent obsession with Hajj Gimbi's polygamy and his own putative affairs had been a mere smoke screen to hide her dirty secrets.

At the center of his sadness was the fact of his mother's elopement and all the feelings of abandonment which had resulted. He remembered all the women he used to run up to and welcome home, and the fear at the back of his mind that they might indeed be ghosts disguised as tall women. He remembered the patronizing way they used to pat him on the head before letting him down. Where had he got the notion that his mother had been a tall woman? To a three-year-old, most women must have seemed very tall. He remembered the tall woman who had ended his obsession. He suddenly felt very angry. Why hadn't his father done something about the situation? He had known about his rival's activities but had chosen to ignore it all. Was complacency a family weakness? he wondered. He suddenly wanted to do so many things at the same time. He wanted to prove that he could act, arrest situations and nip trouble in the bud. He did not want to end up wifeless, with all those children to raise alone. He also didn't want his children to be brought up by another woman. He finally realized that a married cuckold with children could not afford family-shattering revenge: every form of retaliation had to be short-term.

Serenity considered disappearing for a week. He could stay in a good hotel, relax and work off his anger, his sadness. He could visit his relatives: he had not seen his sisters in a long time, and this could be the chance to check on them.

It struck him like a bolt of lightning splitting a tree down the middle: Nakibuka! Had the woman not done her best to interest him in her life? Didn't he, in his heart of hearts, desire her? Had he ever forgotten her sunny disposition, her sense of humor, the confident way she luxuriated in her femininity? The shaky roots of traditional decorum halted him with the warning that it was improper to desire his wife's relative, but the mushroom of his pent-up desire had found a weak spot in the layers of hypocritical decency and had pushed into the turbulent air of truth, risk, personal satisfaction, revenge. His throttled desire and his curbed sex drive could find a second wind, a resurrection or even eternal life in the bosom of the woman who, with her touch, had accessed his past, saved it and redeemed his virility on his wedding night. Sweat cascaded down his back, his heart palpitated and fire built up in his loins.

The afternoon was laboring, hotly, toward evening. It was time for the departmental meeting and the weekly review of accounts. He was the first to arrive in the boardroom. He drank two glasses of water quickly and looked out the window. Where was everybody? He wanted to leave as soon as the bleeding meeting ended. He had to look for Nakibuka's house, and that worried him. Impatient, alone, angry, he left the room and rushed back to his office to look in his diary. He hoped he had her address. What if she had moved? He perversely imagined Boy going through the same motions, scheming, debating, wondering. What if Boy was already in the Command Post making his

Miss Singer laugh by praising her love bombs and her grammatical pools of silver? Eddies of anger washed over eddies of sadness. He thought about returning home in the hope of finding Boy in the Command Post and teaching him a lesson, but unable to figure out exactly what he would do to him in case fate tempted him by placing Boy in his hands, he decided against it. He feared he might lose control as he had when disciplining his son. In the name of discipline he had almost committed murder, and had not liked the experience at all. He had vowed never again to let himself go that way.

Thus, to Nakibuka's he would go, even if she had moved, even if her man was home, even if he could not spend the night with her. He found her address and smiled half angrily, half sadly. He disliked Hajj Gimbi's form of polygamy: What was the use of having all the women in one house? Every woman deserved her own house, and it accorded one many more chances of relaxation and escape from the problems, the moods and the quirks of the other women.

Serenity returned to the boardroom. The meeting was already in progress, but it all washed over him. Nothing could interest or irritate him now.

A millstone of anxiety kept my mood oscillating between jubilation and dejection: I was ecstatic at the realization that I had the wits and the discipline necessary to beat opponents larger and meaner than me; I felt oppressed by the irrational fear that Serenity had found out what I had done and was going to do something really terrible to me.

As I pounded groundnuts in a mortar with a wooden pestle polished to a red sheen by years of use, I tried to place myself in Serenity's shoes. What would I have done? There was the possibility of fighting fire with fire, say, by leaving women's underwear in my pockets or taking a woman or refusing to pay bills for some time.

Padlock did not strike me as a woman quick to run away; breeders like her rarely did, which meant that she would try her best to find out what was going on before taking any form of action, and despite my part in the drama, and my hatred for this woman, I did not really want her to go. She, in a crude sort of way, represented stability, provided me with a target for my attacks and chances to hone my wits.

As the eldest child in the family, I knew that my position would not change much even if Padlock left and another woman took over. I would most likely still do the shit jobs, wash, clean, cook and fetch water. But I would definitely never allow another woman to beat me, or to make me kneel in front of her. Was Padlock leaving? Was she even contemplating the same? Or was it all in my head?

Suspended in ignorance, Padlock was akin to a door on a single hinge. She acted with the restless and brittle charm of a buffalo with bees in his ears. She thought that Serenity had decided to break with habit for once and had gone straight to his friends without first reporting home, but he was not at the gas station.

I played along, enjoying the panicky rusty-hinge squeak of her voice and the seized storm of alarm which raged in her bosom each time I informed her that Serenity had not yet come back from work. Her sense of alarm was easy to fathom: a decent, reliable man staying away or returning home late meant trouble. Either there was a prominent death in his family, with all concomitant financial hemorrhage, or something nasty had occurred, say, an accident or a mistaken-identity arrest. Serenity was one of those men who informed their wives about their plans and movements and would never go off without sending a message home.

As night fell, Padlock's face took on the sad expression of a tormented, short-tempered rhino. I fought hard to resist the unfortunate tendency to feel sorry for this woman, because at the center of it all, I wanted her to suffer, to wallow and howl like a bitch in hellish heat.

On the second night, Padlock looked vanquished. The alabaster crust of her face had been replaced by the broken-lined, brittle expression of an adolescent reeling under jilted love. She eyed me with the sneaky, quasi-conspiratorial look of somebody gathering courage to share an ugly secret. Pinned and writhing like a cockroach on a nature-study board, she drew on one's reluctant supplies of pity. Expressions like "volcanic love" and "mellifluous eyes" rang in my ears, amazing me once again with the magic of their success: at school they turned adolescent hearts and earned me pocket money; now they were turning a despotic system on its head and making a despot dance on the hot spikes of her fears. I found myself appraising Padlock to see whether I had exaggerated too much, but she was too immersed in the cauterizing dust storms of her nightmare to be worth appraising. In writing the letter, I had only had Lusanani and the girl I had intended to give *Treasure Island* to in mind.

The sight of Serenity entering the compound, bag in hand, sent chills down my spine. His face looked tranquil, as if he had no worry in the world. I could not tell whether he had put two and two together or whether he had bought the stuff wholesale. He responded to my greeting neutrally and entered the library of his fantasies. I waited with bated breath. In the meantime, I noticed that Padlock's two-day-old stoop had suddenly disappeared, venom had returned to her face and there was an angry snap in her gait. I felt I had done the right thing: this woman was not going to change. If anything, my struggles with her had just begun.

It was evident that there was trouble in the air. For once, the connecting door was locked and gagging rags peeped like petticoats from the space underneath. Serenity had given nothing away all evening, content to hide behind *Godot* as we ate. Padlock had shimmered all evening with a barely disguised rage, which had for once made her night-prayer tremolos sound faulty. For the first time in her married life, she dropped Serenity's plate as she poured soup on it, and she could barely bite back some form of adulterated curse. From behind the papery walls of *Godot*, Serenity did not move a muscle. He was too busy ruminating on the events of the last three days and two nights to mind his wife's tension.

I left my bed at around one o'clock and placed my ear on the keyhole. I heard only whispers. I slipped out of the house and stood outside the bedroom window. Mosquitoes buzzed cantankerously, moths collided against naked bulbs suicidally, a pack of dogs howled lustfully. I ignored it all, plus the robbers and the ghosts and the soldiers on the prowl. Voices rose and fell, and finally my reward came.

"I stayed away for your sake."

"For my sake? How could you say that?"

"My first impulse was to come home and kick your head in."

"What?"

"You have seen the letter. Now stop insulting my intelligence with that innocent-girl stuff."

"It has nothing to do with me."

"A boy calling you Miss Singer is nothing! Your stooping to that stupid boy's level is nothing! And your denying all responsibility is nothing! Your cheating in my house is nothing, eh? It is all nothing, nothing, nothing." Serenity's voice had thinned dangerously, like an icicle.

Realizing how fragile the ice she was skating on had become, Padlock tailored her despotic immunities and said, rather plaintively, "Why can't you believe me?"

"I can walk away, you know that. You are not the only woman in the world." He stopped there, unwilling to reveal the juicy bounty of his escapade. Padlock's aunt had given him the blissful attentions of an experienced mistress in her fastidiously scrubbed little house. The relief of not having to explain himself, because she had always known that he would turn to her! Serenity could almost hear himself thanking Nakibuka's former husband for beating her, thereby opening her eyes to gentler forms of love, his specialty.

Serenity and Nakibuka's impromptu conversation had taken its own course, meandering and coming back on course to concentrate on them. It was untainted with hurried confessions or forced intimacies. The letter had nestled itself very late in the web like a casual thread, till it was drenched with the saliva of laughter, the pangs of anger and sadness severed by mutual understanding. Mythical mellifluous eyes and felicitous neck and volcanic love were transferred from half-red, half-black print to the winsome character of the bridal aunt. By the time the volcanic crater of holy juices was explored, both parties were giddy with passion.

"Somebody wants to destroy me," Padlock said, interrupting Serenity's sweet lapse of concentration.

"Have you created that many bitter enemies? Or is it Mbaziira the Great's girlfriend driving an old rival off her patch?"

"I don't appreciate such crude language."

"Well, what is so refined about an old woman pining for young blood?"

There came noise of a scuffle and long, sulky squeaks from overburdened bedsprings.

"What are you doing?" Serenity said with alarm. "Give me back that letter now. Don't eat the evidence. Are you mad?"

Padlock was lucky that Serenity abhorred violence; otherwise she would have suffered a broken jaw. Serenity swallowed his anger and concentrated his thoughts on Nakibuka. His crucifixion on the joyless cross of a monogamous relationship was over; his thirst was not going to be mocked any longer by the sponge of his wife's vinegary sex. Given a choice between fecundity and beauty, his wife had opted for the former, her aunt for the latter. Two children later, Nakibuka's body was still taut, supple and undeformed. He now desired her more than ever. He dreamed about her and wanted to be with her. She was the best thing that had happened to him in a very long time.

As mosquitoes terrorized my silent vigil, making me think of retiring, Padlock's voice pierced the night: "Where did you spend the last three days?"

Silence.

"Tell me where you spent the past days."

Silence.

"I want to know where you were."

The passionate whinings of mating dogs drooling with the lust of a nocturnal orgy drew nearer. The rustling of dogs' feet, accompanied by sharp panting and heavy sighing, passed two houses away. Somewhere in the darkness were about twenty dogs at the mercy of their hormones, watching or mating or drooling. These were dangerous dogs. A few days ago, an orgy of frustrated canine lust had resulted in the mauling of a drunken man, too heavy-legged to flee, who had run into the pack. I didn't wait for more warning. I entered the house. As I tried to sleep, many long minutes later, shots rang out. The orgy whined dementedly, almost climactically, and then fell silent.

Padlock, I had to admit, was possessed of an intuitive intelligence, but she lacked style. A few days later, she called me to her Command Post and, without looking at me, asked if I happened to know somebody with a typewriter. Apparently, a friend of hers wanted some important documents typed out for her. Expressing fake surprise at being involved in such high-caliber matters, I replied that I knew nobody rich enough to own a typewriter. I hinted that Serenity had access to a typist and a typewriter too. Defeated, she was grabbing at straws to thatch her embarrassment when a customer called. I vamoosed.

Days later, I noticed that somebody had developed the sneaky habit of going through my geometry set and exercise books, and my clothes too. At the same time, I noticed that Loverboy had not appeared in the compound for some time now.

A fortnight later, I discovered that the searches had been extended to my bedding: the mattress was out of place, and had been left like that on a number of occasions. I developed the little habit of pasting old glue and chewing gum residue on my geometry set, on my bed and in the corners of my suitcase.

There are two pits despots naturally fall into: stereotyping and scapegoating. Padlock was no exception. She dropped hints that she knew who the criminal was, which was another way of saying that I was responsible.

Now, if there was something I was raised to despise, it was stealing, especially from parents and relatives, but Padlock did not know this, and she continued suspecting and holding me responsible. Of course, I had stolen *Treasure Island*, but not for money. The interesting thing was that more and more books went missing, and the more it occurred, the more my property was searched. Many shitters complained, constantly, that their pens, pencils and exercise books had gone missing. The truth was that some shitters lost these things at school, as did many other kids, but because of the stiff punishment that accompanied declarations of such careless losses of property, they took the shortcut and made use of the scapegoat.

Brought up on blood sacrifices, I decided to sacrifice myself in a bid to thank the gods who had saved my skin by keeping my name out of the Miss Singer scandal, at least as far as Serenity was concerned. At the back of my mind, I had the feeling that Serenity suspected me but had decided to ignore me because I had accorded him the opportunity to pursue the object of his desire. In sacrificing myself, I also wanted to thank Padlock's gods for their role in my victory. At the bottom of all this, I wanted to reclaim my former constituency, the shitters, who still saw me as a cross between a criminal and an outcast of sorts. I wanted to become their hero and weaken Padlock's hold on them.

Ergo, on two occasions I implicated myself in the improbable pilfering of two pens. Glad that the criminal had been revealed by the working of God's grace, Padlock gave me twenty guava-switch strokes on each occasion. Every stroke was invested with all the past angers, past frustrations and past suspicions, and if I had not been toughened by my mission, I would have incurred serious damage, but on both occasions I acted tough as nails. I did not cry out; neither did

I shed a tear. She swung at sensitive parts, and to divert my mind from the pain, I concentrated on my heroic role, and the tears remained safely in their ducts. I saw the eyes of the shitters widen with admiration, and my face turned cold as stone, veneered with a hero's insouciant arrogance. I was their hero. It felt good. I was back on top. Convinced by now that I would not shed a tear even if she removed my eye, Padlock let me go. I swaggered like a cop after flooring a troublesome criminal. I swaggered like Amin after winning with a huge knockout in a boxing ring. Padlock could not stomach it. She called me back and cut me thrice with the switch on my right calf. It just made me swagger more. She finally gave up.

Furnished with a heroic criminal, the thief did a better job. I started enjoying the game and my part in it. Padlock's wallet was raided a number of times. The thief's sense of timing became spectacular. When Padlock left obvious baits, he humiliated her by ignoring them. He wanted to hunt his prey and work for his booty. He surely knew that only gods expected and accepted sacrifices. When Padlock hid under the bed in a bid to nab him, he never showed up. The house swelled with the pungent arrogance of a clever raider and the bad blood of his frustrated tracker. As if to provoke his tracker even more, the thief extended his finger to "tooth money," sometimes called "rat money."

When one uprooted a milk tooth, after many threats and gruff shakings by Padlock's rough fingers, one deposited the bloodied thing behind the cupboard for the "rat" to find and replace with hard cash. It was that money that the thief started targeting. Padlock was especially annoyed because she had, on two occasions, used silk thread and yanked teeth with such force that the bleeding was so heavy, everyone feared she had cut into the gum. With blood guilt on her mind, she went berserk when she discovered that the rat money had been stolen. In respect for tradition, she had to replace the stolen money on both occasions. In addition to that, she observed that both "robberies" were committed while I was away. So somebody had surely been insulting her intelligence! Ergo, the property of the shitters got raided.

On the day of judgment, night prayers were said as usual and the roof was stained by Padlock's last-hymn tremolos. Supper was just minutes away. This time, though, two shitters were not served groundnut soup, which was appetizingly thick with dry fish. The aroma filled

the house and tickled our sharp appetites. A schooled sadist, Padlock
had taken care to buy quality fish and quality groundnuts and had prepared the food in a quality banana-leaf-thatched pot to heighten the
flavor. We ate our food inches away from the condemned shitters, their
foreheads gleaming with beads of guilty sweat, their eyes red with
fear. We washed our dirty fingers with water poured and trapped by
the two criminals in small bidet-like plastic basins such as I would,
years later, find in a foreign brothel, and which I would always associate with smut, soap, fish smells and poisoned meals. Serenity, high in
his chair like Pontius Pilate, washed his fingers absentmindedly, looking neither at the block of blue soap proffered nor at the trembling
shitter making the offering. Godot, encased in red, tired-looking hard
covers, was the only being on his mind. And, oh, the ever so sunny
aunty of the woman herding his brood.

Determined to register my protest, and to sabotage Padlock's
sense and system of justice, I was the first to rise. An undercurrent of
disgust coursed through me, making me resent the calculated sadism
of official justice. Maybe I empathized too much with the subversive
element. The truth remained that I had played a part in the drama
which had culminated in this, and I had enjoyed the exploits of the duo.
I was troubled by the jangling question of whether I was responsible
for their defense. Padlock called me back.

She reached under the green sofa and removed three finger-thick
guava switches and declared, rather pompously, that she had caught
the thieves who had been terrorizing the household. The duo was ordered to lie down a foot from each other. Serenity, who had so far said
nothing, and in the spirit of despotic harmony was not supposed to say
anything, disappeared behind the red shroud of Godot. Padlock was
all over the shitters like a hungry eagle terrorizing a brood of hens. In
a wan attempt to resurrect Big Brother's machismo, which had saved
them on the two earlier occasions, the duo turned their glazed eyes to
their hero; but my act was too surreal to replicate, and at their age their
hero too would have failed to call forth any macho wonders. The orgy
of howling, drooling, prancing dogs cracked the confines of nocturnal
mating scenery and invaded the house. The resultant mayhem of canine vociferation was punctuated by pleas for clemency, promises never
to sin again and prayers seeking deliverance from the notorious St. Jude
Thaddeus, savior of desperate cases. One of the shitters even went so

far as to call upon the mighty Serenity, probably in the name of Godot, to intervene; but he only got cut more viciously as Padlock made it clear that despotic or non-despotic intervention was out of the question.

General Idi Amin had told us to fight hard and come back each time we fell. And his rise to power had proved that the majority of people needed a savior, somebody to save them from themselves and their fears before they could get in shape to fight. There had to be giants, heroes, like me to save the helpless. It struck me how easy it was to sit back, watch and put your hands hopelessly in the air. Everybody had put theirs in the air the day Serenity hammered me, maybe because they never listened to the general as I did. Maybe it was because they had never drunk from the well of heroism and self-sacrifice Grandpa had shown me. Maybe it was because they had never woken up at midnight to go with Grandma and deliver a baby five kilometers away. I wanted to rise above them and take the blows. I asked myself what General Amin would have done in this situation. He would have intervened to save the shitters, or at least distracted Padlock to give the victims a breather.

Moreover, General Amin was fond of sending messages and warnings to his enemies. He warned imperialists, colonialists, racists and Zionists that their time was over. It was high time somebody sent a message to Padlock that overkill was not the baptismal name of corporal punishment. Above all, for the first time since my arrival in the city, it struck me that I was as much a parent to the shitters as the original providers of sperm and eggs. I, in fact, knew more about these children than the despots. In cleaning them, washing them, helping them with homework, bribing and blackmailing them, I had got close to them. I had grown fond of them.

Anyway, wasn't it known that I was a co-parent? Wasn't it known that I was the third force in this dictatorship? Wasn't it known that I regarded Serenity as my elder brother, and Padlock as his mean-hearted wife who had to be harassed, corrected and damned if she was too crooked to change?

"I am the one who gave them the money," I suddenly said.

"What?" Serenity prodded, gasped.

"I gave them the money."

"They confessed to the crime," Padlock said coldly after giving the duo a few more hard strokes.

I was caught off guard. I hadn't thought of every despot's stock-in-trade: confessions.

"Do you mean to say that you stole the money and gave it to them?" Padlock asked with great fury.

Heroism had tripped itself on its coattails. "No."

Now the more squeamish of the duo looked alarmed. Padlock smelled sabotage and wanted to demonstrate that heroism was synonymous with scars and a bruised ego. She cut me across the back, and an innocent shitter got knocked down as Padlock turned, clumsily, like a buffalo speared through the ass.

I jumped and sat down again. I got four more cuts. It hurt, but I couldn't cry out: I had my image to uphold. Another four switches came my way, this time on the legs. I bit back canine howls, thinking about the shitters. I momentarily feared I had wet my pants, but it was not so. I smiled. Once again I had denied her victory. Infuriated by the unsatisfactory sighs of whacked air, Padlock stretched her hand to deliver solid fire to my back, but something popped and glass poured down. She had struck the electric bulb and its shade. Serenity was infuriated: he hated all interruption of his reading.

"Enough of this," he barked without looking up. "Nakibuka, enough."

"Who?" Padlock turned to Serenity with the stick still held high in the air.

"What?" Serenity mumbled. He had given himself away. I had heard him; so had his wife.

The stick fell from Padlock's hand. The shitters could claim it was a miracle performed by St. Jude Thaddeus. A cloud of silence had descended on the house. Padlock sent everyone to bed, and miracle of miracles, she did not even ask the shitters to thank her for disciplining them.

I slept like a log that night. I had acquired two loyal followers.

I missed Uncle Kawayida very much. He never visited us anymore. Sometimes he met Serenity at his office and returned home without coming over. He had bought himself a pickup van in the heat of the Indian exodus and was raising turkeys. I knew that only a Muhammad Ali fight could lure him to our home, but Ali had not fought anybody worthwhile for some time, and he was yet to appear on the stinking

Toshiba. I did not like Ali, because he was more arrogant than I ever wanted to be and he openly boasted about his victories. I preferred that others sing my praises. However, I would have forgiven him everything if any of his fights occasioned a visit from Uncle Kawayida. The fact that my uncle stayed away was ample proof that the rivalry between his wife and Padlock was still strong. I was worried about him and his family. His town lay along the route to where anti-Amin guerrillas, under the leadership of the former dictator Obote, were operating along the Uganda-Tanzania border. Amin had successfully repelled one guerrilla incursion, inflicting heavy losses on the attackers, but one never knew what would happen next. What if the guerrillas crossed the border and took over Uncle's area?

When I thought about it, the idea of guerrilla warfare impressed me. I liked the risk, the odds, the guts and the sticking of pins into a despot's backside. I realized that what I was doing to Padlock was nothing short of guerrilla activity. It was not terrorism, as I had once called it; since my village days, I had associated that word with dead dogs and Muslim converts living in fear of incurable penis ulcers. "Guerrilla warfare" sounded better.

I decided to raid Padlock's Command Post and incapacitate her sewing machine. To begin with, I had never benefitted from the machine: my clothes always got last priority, even if I reported first. I also wanted to bring Serenity into the equation: he was getting off too easily for my liking. If the raid succeeded, I knew that he would be the one to buy the spare parts for the Singer. I also knew that the Singer agent had already gone back to Bombay, Nairobi or London, which meant that Serenity would have to import the parts. This time I was going to reap revenge plus a bit of money too, but basically I wanted Padlock to realize that brute force had its glaring limits. Moreover, I could not stand the way the despots moaned about Amin and his rule, the firing squads, the rising prices, the instability of the economy and the brutality of some soldiers.

Elsewhere, events were taking place that linked me with a woman whose house I would later occupy, whose keyhole I would peep through in a bid to assuage sex hormones gone mad and whose fatherless children I would try to parent. As I penetrated the Command Post,

General Amin's men were penetrating the woman's house and whisking her off to an unknown destination.

I knocked a tin over in the darkness, held my breath and proceeded. The Command Post smelled of cotton cloth, Singer lubricant, wood and trapped nocturnal heat. In the darkness, the sewing machine resembled a medieval instrument of torture on which sinners were punished by sadistic clergymen and their followers for holy purposes. A perverse joy kicked in my breast and offset the fear in my bones. "She is not your real mother," I could almost hear Lusanani say in the darkness, her breath tickling my ear. What was she doing now? Would I ever be alone with her in the darkness? It would be wonderful to raid the secret of her petticoats right here, in Padlock's holy of holies.

I moved forward. I touched the clothes in the basket, mostly women's clothes: Padlock-made dresses, blouses and bras. The cylindrical wicker basket's bottle-cap-like cover was under the cutting board, just inches from the underbelly of the Singer. I stuck my finger in a small cavern, slippery with lubricant. Polished steel felt perversely smooth in the darkness. I extracted the bobbin. It felt like a steel lemon, and I kept rolling it over and over in my fingers.

As Padlock prepared to enter her Command Post, we got the news that Lwandeka, her youngest sister, had got into trouble with the State Research Bureau. Her whereabouts were still unknown. Fearing the worst, Padlock left immediately. For four whole days, the house felt pleasantly light and birds sang in the nearby trees. Suddenly everyone was breathing pure air, as if a cadaverous stench had just been carried off by a cleansing wind. The shitters chased each other all over the place, threw things, besmirched their clothes, shouted and called each other names. I enjoyed my role as indulgent nanny or surrogate parent and let them have their way, provided they did not do anything to annoy me or land me in trouble. Play reached its climax an hour before Serenity's return from work. In time, selected shitters started cleaning up so that by the time the self-effacing despot arrived home, everything was in order. Serenity was more relaxed. The network of worry wrinkles in his face was shallower than usual, and he seemed keen to put everyone at ease. He let it be known that as long as order was maintained, homework done, school attended, everyone could take a breather.

I was the second-in-command. I relished the power and the chance to do things my way. I was leading my own revolution. By showing the shitters a different way of doing things, with words rather than guava switches, I was turning them against Padlock and the way of life they had been reared in. The squeamish shitter, who now followed me like a puppy, carried out voluntary surveillance work, reporting misdemeanors, which I pretended to note so as not to decapitate his initiative. He was the one who supervised the cooking, listening to the gurgling sounds of the cooking pot, making sure that there was just enough water, not too much so as to waterlog the food or too little so as to burn it. In case of emergency, he had to call me.

I took time off to hold long conversations with Lusanani. She came over, entered the house for some minutes, but left before I could give her a tour of the Command Post. I felt disappointed. I thought that the magic of my dreams would keep her in Padlock's holy of holies, and maybe even voluntarily make her surrender some of the secrets of her rustling petticoats. As she walked away I wondered whether Grandpa had secured himself a girl like this to take care of him. There was an official news blackout I could not circumvent to find out how he was doing.

Four days away from her kingdom seemed like a lifetime to Padlock. Four days under somebody else's roof, following somebody else's schedule, eating somebody else's meals and sleeping under makeshift conditions felt like four eternities squandered in purgatory. The talk her relatives indulged in shocked her with its randomness and lack of serious content. They seemed to be blowing chicken feathers in the air and relishing the effort of catching them. Padlock found herself isolated on an island of dead seriousness, fact and humorless analysis of the tragedy while all around her teemed levity in the face of disaster. Her brothers and other sister made deep forays into the sands and bogs of childhood, history she preferred to leave undisturbed. After stirring mirthful mud pools full of toothless old men, gap-toothed old women, old clothes, Sunday masses, heavy Christmas meals and childhood escapades, they clung to the only topic that interested her: "First children turned out right, later children did not; are parents fully to blame?"

"Lwandeka was a typical last child," Mbale said at length. "She took advantage of Mam and Dad's weakness and grew up thinking that the whole universe revolved around her."

"We are told that the State Research Bureau arrested her for corresponding with German saboteurs. Why did she do that? Didn't she know that Amin meant business? Didn't she know that it was dangerous to write letters to Germans?" somebody asked.

"All of us who were raised right turned out right," Padlock joined in. "You who had it easy are now paying for earlier freedom." She looked at her second sister, Kasawo.

In Padlock's eyes, both her sisters were whores. To begin with, Lwandeka had failed to find a man to marry her, shaming the family by breeding children in sin. Kasawo, the fatter and elder of the two, had not done any better. She ran amok during her teen days; she rebelled against her parents; and she eloped with a crooked man who drank heavily and beat her, almost killing her. She too had missed the honor of holy matrimony, and was now a market woman, that halfway station between a white-collar whore and an eternal mistress.

Padlock blamed her parents for neglecting their duty, especially for sparing the rod on the girls, and she felt that they deserved all the humiliations life dished out to them. At the peak of their rebellion, both girls had gone against parental will, returned home whenever they wanted, dated older men, dropped out of school and refused to do anything at home. Now they wallowed in sin like pigs in shit and made the same mistakes, like dogs eating their own vomit. Padlock was of the view that imprisonment could be the best thing that ever happened to her youngest sister, provided she didn't get raped. Imprisonment would cure her of the urge to correspond with spoiled German women, most probably whores, who did not fear God and fomented rebellion.

Padlock went over her childhood days again. How she had worked for these people, washing, cooking, digging. How her back had creaked as she did chores they refused to do. How thorns had pricked her skin as she went to the forest to collect firewood for the family. How her neck had ached as she carried pots of water on her head. How her parents had always sided with the younger children, always blaming her for the mistakes others made. How she had got beaten for little errors. How her parents had refused to protect her against school and village bullies, rationalizing that it was her daily cross, meant to make her strong. And how, after all that, her parents had gone soft on the younger children!

Padlock now saw her role as that of financier, with much of her money going to pay Lwandeka's ransom. Gratified by her monetary power, Padlock did not air her most radical views on the disintegration of her parents' authority. It was the reason she never pursued the lead when Kasawo hit back and said, "We never had it easy. We just had the guts to rebel, and to stay in perpetual rebellion. That was where we beat you, who turned out according to Mam and Dad's prescriptions. The good thing is that we are all parents now."

"You disowned your first child because his father tried to kill you, so don't talk to us about parenthood," Mbale hit back.

"Your wife has never tried to kill you, has she? Before she raises a panga at you, leave that extremity to me, who has been there," Kasawo said rather calmly, and Mbale kept quiet then.

"We are all getting too excited," Padlock said tactfully. "Why not discuss whether the men we are going to entrust the ransom money to are reliable people?"

That defused the tension. Padlock, having made the most important contribution to the discussion, stopped listening to the chitchat which followed: talk about wives, her nieces, nephews, aunts, uncles . . . Her mind was already back home, worrying whether the roof was still on her house. She had a life to lead, dresses to make and children to think about.

Conversation, however, stubbornly went back to her past. Kasawo, still smarting from Mbale's earlier comments, ganged up with her youngest brother and accused both Padlock and Mbale of childhood mistreatment. She mentioned pinching, name-calling, malicious abandonment when they went to the well at night or to the forest on firewood-gathering errands. Padlock felt like slapping them and forcing them to shut up or to say the rosary. She and Mbale kept quiet under the assault, and the duo's anger was soon deflated and lighter conversation introduced. Laughter erupted, and the place shook with the weight of family history resurrected.

By the third day, Padlock had reached a sort of compromise with her family: she tolerated their chitchat as long as they did not expect her to participate wholeheartedly in it. It gave her a sense of superiority to watch mere mortals grovelling in the quagmires of memory. She was waiting for news about Lwandeka, which was not forthcoming. The carapace of her patience was gradually cracking up. It disintegrated totally with the arrival of the one person she had neither the intention nor the wish to meet: Aunt Nakibuka. The hydra of anger, hate and impotent disgust sank its teeth deep in her, and she had to fight hard to curb the violent upheaval inside. She somehow managed to sprinkle a sheen of civility onto her emotions.

Normally, nieces got on very well with aunts who had seen them to their bridal bed and stood by their side during the turbulent events which led to the first public celebration of womanhood. Nieces usually cherished these aunts, because they had held open for them the portals to womanhood and motherhood and proffered tips on how to control and manipulate a man without his awareness. These aunts were the first court of arbitration, and combined the role of defense lawyer, counsellor, conspirator and judge. Nieces often said things like "Our man has done this or that" or "Our man threatens to divorce us" or "Our man is seeing somebody else." A niece's marriage was also a bridal aunt's marriage, in a sense, because both wanted it to work.

Padlock was not anyone's average woman or niece: the nun in her never died.

She was uncomfortable with Nakibuka, who she felt knew too much about her. Nakibuka had seen her nakedness, which, in her convent days, was anathema. In those days, one never looked at oneself, even as one bathed or pulled devil hair. The body belonged to Christ, and to Christ alone. She felt that this woman also knew too much about Serenity: Had she not courted his erection? Had she not seen him impotent, afraid, defeated? Had she not bathed him when he made a fool of himself on their wedding night, cavorting with low-down drunks and common sinners who smeared him with vomit?

This woman had, worst of all, revealed family secrets to Serenity during the honeymoon period. For this Padlock felt she could never forgive her aunt. Hadn't Nakibuka told Serenity everything about his wife's early childhood, her nicknames, her attack on Mbale, her convent days, her desperation after expulsion from the convent, everything she did not want anybody to know? How dare she betray the family that way? People with loose tongues always got their punishment, and Padlock was sure that Nakibuka's was waiting. Padlock also felt that her aunt was in league with the Devil and was going to destroy her family and marriage.

It had taken Nakibuka a long time to find out that things were not going well between her and her niece. In her estimation, she had done a wonderful job preparing an uptight ex-nun for what was by family standards a very high-profile wedding. It had taken a lot of patience and cajoling, and she had expected some gratitude and a warm relationship in return, but apparently that had been asking too much. Invitations for Padlock to visit her had remained unanswered, and her visits to her niece's home had become progressively colder. Her choice of Padlock as her daughter's godmother had proved a catastrophe of shattered idealism. It was then that the older woman realized that something was wrong, and she withdrew. She consoled herself that her niece's marriage was rock solid and that her counselling duties were redundant.

Years passed without the two women exchanging visits. Nakibuka's marriage became stormy: her man wanted more children, she didn't. She saw no use in having six children just to prop up a rotting marriage. The canings started. She insisted that if he really wanted to beat her, she would rather have it where she had had it before: on "government meat," as they called the buttocks in school, the only place a teacher was authorized to beat a child. She could not imagine herself with a swollen eye or a torn lip or a broken nose.

The beatings on government meat resurrected the slumbering ghost of a platonic adolescent crush from her school days, and amidst its ashes rose the figure of her niece's husband, Serenity. What had begun with furtive eye contact in her niece's parental home and culminated in shoulder touching on the wedding night nurtured Serenity's cheerfulness and attentiveness when she visited or when they met at family functions. At one such family function, a funeral which Padlock didn't attend, they had talked for close to an hour, feverishly, spontaneously. She invited him to visit her and her husband, hoping that his manners would rub off on her man. Serenity never appeared.

Unlike the time when, possessed of adolescent hormonal devilry, she wrote letters every other day to the teacher she was infatuated with, even hinting at suicide, she remained calm. Except when her nights were haunted by the events of the wedding night. When thoughts of that gleaming male flesh cooking in the heat of the bridal bedroom made her tremble. When coincidental resemblances to Serenity of men she met or bypassed made her heart beat violently and seized her muscles with lingering paralysis. When Serenity's form filled her mind as she lay down to be caned on "government meat" and she screamed and begged, swelling her man's ego with the falsehood of love sounds disguised as pain-choked noises. Months and months passed as she waited for Serenity to make a move. She attended every family function, every wedding, every funeral and every clan gathering in the hope of refilling her mind with his voice, the sight of him and his scent, but he eluded her.

The day he appeared on her doorstep, his clothes smelling of the evening air, his shoes coated with dust, dogs howling in the background, she could hardly hide her shock. She hid in the bedroom for a long time, calming herself, preparing to accept rejection, negative reports about Padlock and pleas for her intervention to save his marriage. Rejection had to be taken with dignity; she was ready. Back in the room with Serenity, conversation flowed naturally and almost careened out of control when she discovered that it was not her intervention he craved but her caress. She was not looking for a husband, nor was he looking for a wife. They had both been looking for lovers. With her husband out of the way, they were left to themselves, the dogs in the background harbingers of things to come. There was no going back now. She could not give up Serenity, and neither would he give her up.

The unexpected undercurrent of sweet guilt at this first meeting with Padlock made the older woman's voice shake a bit, but since it was not taboo for them to share a man, she managed to look her niece in the eye. The friction and resistance she read there were expected. A maternal uncle robbed of his wife by his nephew would have worked up the same frustrated intensity, sorry that the robbery was not traditionally taboo. By now Nakibuka had admitted to herself that she was Padlock's rival. Better-looking and more confident, she could afford to be generous and nice to her beleaguered niece, who looked worn, like an old boot. The younger woman was being courted by premarital, post-convent winds, which made her look as if she were shouldering all the world's tragedies. If she did not take care, Nakibuka thought, soon birds would be nesting in her hair, baby hippos snorting in her belly and hyenas rubbing their rumps in her armpits.

Nakibuka concluded that Padlock worried too much, thrived on pressure and misery, and that it was too late to change her. She had learned her lessons badly and controlled her man too openly; no wonder he had turned his back on her. Nakibuka was happy that it was all in the family. If Padlock did not want to share Serenity, she could go to hell.

Padlock did not say much, preferring to keep her feelings to herself, happy to keep Nakibuka guessing. Serenity had betrayed her; so had this woman. She had not taken Serenity to task; she saw no use in quarreling with this whore. The next twenty hours were so wretched that they reminded her of the floating, gorging feeling she had experienced when Sr. John Chrysostom chucked her out of the convent so many years ago. She wanted to wring this whore's neck, but she couldn't stoop that low. She put her tribulations at the feet of Jesus, thinking of Judas Iscariot. The proximity of her whoring aunt made the hours wail with chilly desolation and isolation amidst this crowd of laughing, romanticizing, reminiscing relatives. Each minute sank into her with the force of an eagle's talon. She fought time with her only cherished weapon: thoughts of home, her own home, where she was supreme ruler. The rest—her relatives, their voices, the food, the noise in the distance—became blurred, sealed in a miasma of endless fog.

At night Padlock lingered in the darkness, watching the stars. She suddenly remembered Mbaziira and the Miss Singer letter. What if it was Nakibuka who had engineered the plot? But how had she come to know about Mbaziira? Impossible.

Padlock noticed no one on the bus home; she had not noticed her relatives when they bid her farewell. Vendors assaulted her somewhere along the way, pushing things in her sightless face, but she didn't see them. By the time she entered her pagoda, Padlock was shaking with excitement, as though she had just eluded drooling devils stationed all along the road. The house smelled slightly of fish and of washing soap, but that did not matter: smells, like pests, could always be annihilated. She checked the rooms to make sure that nothing was missing. Everything was intact: she was impressed. She had not expected Serenity to do such a good job, what with his nose always in a book and his heart with his cronies at the gas station. This was real power, she thought, a system which worked despite its enforcer's absence. The stench of diapers drove her from the bathroom; her nose longed for the more cultured smell of sewing-machine lubricant. Her head was already buzzing with the sound of the machine, savoring what inexperienced ears called dreary monotony. The sound reminded her of a train, safe in its singular track, unstoppable in its purpose, single-minded in its labor toward its destination. She felt like a train. She dared Nakibuka to destroy her family: she would be reduced to bits, like any other whore suicidal enough to stand in Padlock's way.

Her nerves fully assuaged with the sounds and smells of home, she contemplated her following task with ease; she had to make a dress for a girl who was going to be baptized in two days' time. If there was enough time, she could also make a dress for a woman who was going to attend a wedding in a week's time. There was various repair work she had to do. Her life was back on track. The girl had top priority: she would probably become a nun, Padlock thought wistfully. Nunhood, the convent and the vows were things that would speak to her for the rest of her life. Nunhood, she said to the walls, makes a woman a woman among women, a priestess, a goddess, a queen of heaven.

If Padlock had not been such a control freak, and had lacked delusions of infallibility, the devastation which befell her when she discovered the theft of her bobbin would have been proportionate. Singer's cold indifference to her coaxing would have been in the realm of possibility.

How in the world could her bobbin go missing? A mere bobbin, and not the precious gray head, the clothes or the scissors, but the bobbin! The cold calculation of it! The devilish timing of it! The humiliating simplicity of the crime! Her head spun with bewilderment and incomprehension. She must have inserted her finger a dozen times into the empty bobbin hole. Once or twice, she almost mangled her index finger as she absentmindedly pedaled, but the hole remained empty.

She overturned every box, every container, she shook every piece of cloth and moved every stick of furniture, but the ultimate insult, the ultimate anti-miracle, continued to stare her coldly in the face.

If armed robbers or drunken soldiers had marched in, ordered her off her throne, taken her money and commanded her to remove the gray head, put it in a gunnysack and hand it over to them with a servile thank-you-for-robbing-me-sirs, she would have understood. Brute force and raw power she understood very well, and appreciated how they worked, but not sneaky wit; especially not when her Command Post still had inviolability written all over it. The excision of the heart from her machine, and the bloodless insult of it all, made her head swell dangerously with a murderous rage.

If Padlock had been a woman of words, she would have cursed holes into the roof and drowned the room in the saliva of her invective, but that was not like her. She just sat on her desecrated throne and let all the anger, the sorrow and the frustration course through her, not bothering to wipe away the despair which mingled itself freely with her tears. She wanted to do something terrible, something horribly cathartic, in order to wash away the debilitating feeling of human weakness.

What kind of animal, human or devilish, could do this just a week after she had beaten the piss, the goo and the blood out of two thieves? What kind of devilish maggot was stirring in this thief's rotten mind? Was this imperviousness to pain or *love* of pain at work? She shuddered at the thought, at the fleeting possibility, that this monster could have burst onto the planet from her belly, carried for nine months in her womb and suckled on her breasts.

As if that line of investigation were too treacherous to pursue, she took the view that the criminal had come from abroad, exploiting her absence.

Padlock grilled us for what seemed like hours. The main question was "Who called while I was away?" She lashed us again and again with the same question, framed differently each time, twisted into all possible configurations, as she dug to conjure the thief from under the floorboards.

Padlock hardly knew what to believe when the answers came. She seemed to sense, for the first time in her married life, the emergence of a new product, hundreds of guava switchings later: a ballless, timid-to-hell breed of shitter had emerged, the kind that could hardly say no to authority. She must have sensed hatred, fear and the fact that truth had become a suspect entity. This made her investigative duties that much more hazardous.

At the height of it all, with conflicting reports swirling in her head, she contemplated the possibility that Mbaziira, alias Loverboy, might be the culprit. Had she not brusquely asked him to stay away from her house? Had he not vehemently denied having had anything to do with the fated love letter, as any guilty young man would have done? Had he not called her accusations ungrounded and questioned her state of mind? And though he had not threatened to do anything, had he not left rather too quietly in the end? He had a motive and possible access. He, like nobody else, knew the ins and outs of the Command Post. Yet the children insisted that he had not called. Had he, then, come when everybody was away?

Amidst the confusion, Lusanani surfaced like a leviathan in the troubled waters of Padlock's mind. A married woman who played with young boys had to have perversity carved all over her psyche, especially if she was married to a man old enough to be her father or even grandfather. In Padlock's mind, those were indicators big enough to pinpoint a criminally unstable mind to which transgression was second nature. She was obviously a callous thief who had coldly befriended Padlock's son in order to gain access to her bobbin, her son's virginity and God knew what else. Lusanani's husband had given her carte blanche to sin by declaring, "My wives never borrow money or anything else. I forbade them."

Padlock could not believe her ears that day; Hajj's words sounded like a huge smoke screen which shielded the sinister activities of his thieving young wife. She now hated and distrusted that bearded man more than ever. She deeply believed that he had something to do with Serenity's dallying with Nakibuka, for it was still true that one's friends said a lot about somebody. She wished that this man and his wives would move to some dust bowl, rotten slum or, preferably, dismal cave, where they would destroy themselves and their ungodly way of life.

Halfway through the investigation, I glowed with hope: yes, Padlock had changed, or was changing. She had exhibited great self-control; she had not touched anybody, and for the first time in living memory she seemed to respect our bodies, despite the terrible distress she was in. She could have lined us up and thrashed us till the skin came off our backs, but this time a new light seemed to have come on inside her head. Was there no way I could secrete the bobbin back in its cave and save her from further suffering? I figured that in the coming days

I could find a way of bringing it back, say, by leaving it in a place where a shitter could pick it up.

The investigation was interrupted by the arrival of the good news that Lwandeka had been released after a short court case. Instead of lifting Padlock from the dungeons of her affliction, the news seemed to plunge her even deeper. It was as if, once again, her sister had got off easily and had not learned any lesson. Instead of filling with the joyous mood of a woman's escape from suffering, the house was oppressed by the cadaverous smell of ill will.

Padlock resumed her interrogation in a meaner vein. All the previous days' self-control had vanished. Her head was awash with the metallic sounds of a train derailing and crashing to bits.

"Did Lusanani come here?"

"Yes, she did," I replied.

"What? What for?"

"To talk," I said softly.

"How many times have I warned you to stay away from that woman? What did you talk about: letting her steal my bobbin?" Her voice was dangerously controlled, almost coldly indifferent.

"She did not steal it."

"You did? Who else? After all, you were in charge of the house, were you not? Or did you let her do her own dirty work?" She was almost off her chair now, muscles taut, like a horse about to attack a high fence. "Who was responsible for looking after the house? Answer me!"

"Dad," I said very slyly, to deflate her momentum and divide blame into more manageable parts, with the bulk at the address of her fellow despot.

Suddenly she was towering over me, blocking my view with the corrugated, trembling grayness of her garment. "You, you, you, you," she puffed, bending over, her breath hot on my forehead. "You, you, you, you, and I said you." For emphasis, she cracked me hard on the top of my head with her knuckles. It felt like a hornbill was up there pecking, pecking, pecking. I almost cried out. I reversed all my plans. I would never return her bobbin. I would never be reduced to the timidity of the shitters. Now she could rant, rave or go on a rampage and break my nose or arm, but the precious bobbin, made even more valuable by the scarcities created by my godfather, General Idi Amin, would remain under cover. It was mine now. I had earned it. If I ever failed to find a buyer for it, I would enjoy the perverse joy of seeing it swallowed by latrine shit and maggots.

"Yes, I had to look after the house," I said in order to appease her.

I was happy that the Indians had gone, and along with them the last Singer agent. I hoped that no Singer owner in the area had any bobbins to spare, least of all to sell to Padlock. I wanted her Singer to gather dust and become a breeding place for spiders.

I was happy that Serenity had been drawn into the situation: he now had to look for a new bobbin or ask Hajj if he knew anybody who could import bobbins from London or elsewhere. It was going to take time. I loved it.

Padlock was going to disintegrate with impatience before my very own eyes. I would have advised her to veer into a less sedentary line of business, say, selling fish in the filthy Owino Market, where she would imbibe the stench of rotting offal and garbage on top of suffering the indignity of competing with market men and women who openly worshipped the Devil and Mammon.

Serenity played his usual low-key game, wondering why and how a thief could take only a bobbin, of all things. He promised to enlist Hajj Gimbi's help in the search for a new one. Hajj, Hajj, Hajj, Padlock fumed, her teeth gnashing, her nose dilating, beads of furious perspiration on the bridge.

The poison of uncertainty sank deeper into her: Who had really written the Miss Singer letter? Who had really stolen her priceless bobbin? Had Serenity really slept with her aunt? Was somebody really hell-bent on derailing her life and destroying her?

Padlock brooded, pumping the house full of poison and putting everyone on edge. She sat on her throne, put thread on the Singer board, placed her feet half on the treadle, half on the floor, and knitted, driving the thick steel needle in and out with the cold fury of someone hatching a sinister scheme. The Command Post brimmed with the ill-omened silence of a haunted graveyard. She became very dangerous: my things were relentlessly searched every single day. She was ever on the lookout for Lusanani's figure on the edge of the courtyard, but I had warned the girl to back off; now we met only on the way to the borehole.

One afternoon, as I was brushing the infernal carpet, I reached under the green sofa and what did I discover? A neat bundle of five half-dry guava switches, carefully cut on both ends! Woe to the thief! Woe to the craggy landscape of Padlock's mind! Woe to any defaulter who would fall on the jagged edges of its crags! How lucky I was to be the real thief! Such predictable plans of vengeance no longer impressed me.

It was evident that this time round there would be no waiting for night to fall; the deed would be done early in the morning, after Serenity had left for work. The thief would be asked to remain behind and skip school. The door would be locked, the key pocketed. Then woe to the thief who would see, if he still had eyes to see at all, switches rising and falling with diabolical fury and orgasmic insistence. I smiled cheekily, patted the bundle like I would a good faithful dog, and continued with my sanitary duties. My only worry was that a frustrated Padlock would use any excuse, say, bad school performance, to cane some defenseless shitter. Was this bundle an indicator of Padlock's predictability, parental incorrigibility or despotic fallibility? Or all three?

Padlock started reading from the Old Testament every evening after night prayers. She started by beseeching God to reveal the thief. When He refused, she beseeched Him to use His tremendous power, the type that had delivered Israel from Egypt, to bring back the bobbin. I noticed that, under the narcotic influence of her faith, she started looking in the most curious places every morning, afternoon and night, as though through her earnestness the Almighty would be moved to let the bobbin drop from above like steel manna and cure her hunger for miracles.

As the searches intensified, they mesmerized me with the power of their blind insistence. At one point I almost panicked. Had she dreamed, like my Biblical heroes, and received the rough bearings or coordinates of the spot where the bobbin was buried? I recalled the blind faith some women had invested in my mascotry not so long ago, and how some were rewarded with sons. What if Padlock's faith was going to achieve its reward?

I started having odd nightmares with Padlock bearing down on me, the bobbin in one hand, a hammer in the other.

• • •

Padlock stepped up her campaign of terror by reading frightening passages from the Old Testament and praying for maladies like leprosy to afflict the thief. I had already seen what leprosy had done to Fingers; I remembered the stumps and the scars. What if Fingers' sugarcanes had secreted bacteria in my body and all Padlock's prayers and curses had to do was activate them?

Padlock hammered us with Exodus 32, emphasizing the sinfulness of the Israelites in making the Golden Calf. She lingered on the three thousand people who died that day as God assuaged His anger, and on the disease among the survivors which God meted out for good measure.

As I was getting used to the barrage, she whacked me with Joshua 7, which was about Achan's greed. She made her point very clear by reading verses 19 to 26 very slowly: "My son, tell me the truth here before the Lord, the God of Israel, and confess. Tell me what you have done. Don't try to hide it from me." Achan replied, "I have sinned against the Lord . . . You will find the cloak, two kilos of silver and a bar of gold buried in my tent." Maybe I should confess, a voice said to me, but then what happened to poor Achan? He was seized and taken to Trouble Valley, together with his sons and daughters, his sheep, cattle, donkeys and tent, as well as the stolen objects. There he and his family were stoned to death and all his property was burned! Then the Lord was no longer furious! In local terms, it would take all the skin from somebody's back, legs, buttocks and arms, and five broken guava switches, to douse the blazing torch of Padlock's anger. I wasn't that stupid. If anything, by reading such horrible texts, Padlock was just shooting herself in the foot. General Idi Amin never said anything about martyrdom. He only preached self-preservation. I would never let him down again by allowing this woman to beat me for nothing or for anything I could get away with. This was obviously a mind game, and I was cleverer than she.

Serenity was also playing a mind game. When his wife bombarded the family with terrifying images of the plague, his own plague of secret love dug deeper into him. When Padlock introduced Achan and his greed, Serenity became Achan, eyed the treasures God had ordered to be wasted and, failing to resist his urges, took some for himself. Serenity relished stories of personal struggle, because they spoke directly to him and highlighted his difficult situation. When he went over to visit Nakibuka, they discussed the Biblical passages, laughed deep into the night and used the images of terror as launchpads for serious lovemaking. Sinning had never been so sweet, nor had it ever triggered such satisfaction. Serenity let himself go, unleashing deep-throated groans which seemed to come from the bottom of his spine. Bred to fear, overestimate and suspect power and authority, he felt free from the shackles of his upbringing and the gaping lacunas of his adolescence. This woman did not need him, did not rely on him, did not pressure him for anything: she wanted only what he could give. And the less she asked, the more feverish his will to give became.

Padlock was not wholly dim: she realized that even the most terrible brutalities pale with overexposure. She abruptly abandoned the horror epics and dived into the slimy waters of the psalmist. She dredged up lines which portrayed her as the good, suffering believer. Her hope was that subtlety, self-pity and a dose of good old-fashioned sentimentality would succeed where bone-crunching violence had failed. Pandering to the myth that the sight of a powerful despot on her knees was enough to unhinge hearts and move mountains, she dipped into the schmaltzy psalms, a tender girlish mask on her nunly face.

The pathetic crassness of it almost made me laugh. After ruthless bombardment, now the slimy kisses! All to extract a suicidal confession which would be rewarded with ruthless punishment. The schizophrenic seed at the heart of her logic made me quite sick with disgust and made me wish I had stolen ten bobbins.

Save me, O God / I am weak and poor / Hurry to my aid / My God rescue me from wicked men / From the power of cruel and evil men / I have trusted in you since I was young / I have relied on you all my life / My life has been an example to many / My enemies want to kill me / They talk and plot against me / May those who try to kill me be defeated and confused / May those who are happy because of my troubles be disgraced / I am terrified and gripped by fear / I wish I had wings like a dove and could fly away / I see violence and riots in the city / Filling it with crime and trouble / Protect me, O God / Punish all my enemies / You know how troubled I am / You have kept a record of my tears / Help, help, help, O God!

The manipulative cow!

. . .

In order to remind the thief that her sickening pleas for God's help had not changed her attitude toward the crime, Padlock introduced the notorious crime-solver St. Jude Thaddeus, detective, protector and rescuer of desperadoes. This man was reputed to put both dead and living sleuths to bitter shame. Among devout Catholics, he was fondly called an "automatic rifle." All you needed was faith and a novena, and the magician would patch up rotten marriages, find dead bodies floating in rivers, make paupers rich, cure frigidity, impotence, gonorrhea and syphilis, and give desperately barren women those dreamed-of wrinkly little monkeys and greased piglets.

Eventually, the hype got to me: I quaked under pressure. I had seen with my very eyes magicians making coins disappear in one's palm and then plucking them from one's neck. What if this guy was a more powerful version of our taxi park magicians? I remembered that Moses had a very hard time with Egyptian magicians who did all the tricks he did. Now all this dude had to do was to give Padlock a vague dream or a crude hunch to turn the garden over, and the bloody bobbin would be hers again. Vengeance too. My immediate plan was to dig up the bobbin and hide it elsewhere. I started waking up in cold sweats. If I got itchy at night, I would wake up with a start and rush to the light, hoping that the sleuth had not given me leprosy. When I cut myself with a razor blade as I trimmed my nails or sharpened my pencil, I feared that the bleeding would not stop till a river had formed and a confession been extracted.

It was my *Treasure Island* friend who came to my rescue. He too was a Catholic. He had an aunt who had once been a fanatic devotee of St. Jude. She had traveled to his shrine on endless pilgrimages. She gave to the poor like crazy. She invited cripples to her home. She offered frenetic prayers every day, prayed on her knees till they got thick calluses, but this was her tenth year of barrenness and bitter disappointment. She had now turned furious critic of the notorious sleuth. She felt taken advantage of. I sympathized.

The first novena passed without anything happening. Padlock's psalmic sentimentality worsened as she introduced another nine days of St. Jude's prayers. She no longer searched in curious places morning, noon and night. The steel manna which she expected to fall from heaven lay safely buried in the garden where she walked every single day. The third novena was a plain embarrassment. The psalms had dried up. Padlock looked deflated. Serenity enjoyed the drama. At the beginning of the daily novena, he would flash his wife an indifferent look, as if to say why bother, and then turn away.

Fully convinced that not even God Almighty would retrieve the bobbin, Serenity bought black-market dollars and asked a friend to import a bobbin for him from neighboring Kenya. Ninety days after the disappearance of the old bobbin, the new one arrived. Padlock was overjoyed despite the initial embarrassment caused by the failure of her prayers.

A few women whose work never got done because of the stolen bobbin had given Padlock a piece of their mind, accusing her of not wanting to help them. They swore never to return, but now some crept back, and Padlock served them without reminding them of their harsh words. The monotonous roar of the machine massaged all the madness in her head and restored her peace of mind. Her train was back on track, and she looked cheerful, her tremendous fits of depression gone. I knew that she was still dangerous, waiting for the thief to go on a spending spree and land himself in her lethal trap. Not me. The bobbin remained buried, like gold bullion awaiting the arrival of a pirate ship.

I was thirteen and it was approaching time to change schools. I didn't want to go to a Catholic school. I wanted to know what plans Serenity, the despot in charge of education, had in store for me. I could not ask him directly, because despotic secrets were never divulged that way. The only way was to spy on him. I asked my faithful shitters to shadow him and listen to his conversations while he watched television and generally do everything they could to get the information I needed. I waited for weeks, asking them every other day what they had heard. There was not much to tell. One day Serenity began to talk about schools just before news time, but the news reader cut him short. Weeks passed. Finally a loyal shitter clinched it for me. He overheard the despots discussing the issue in the Command Post one afternoon.

"It would straighten him out," Padlock said.

"They offer very good education. On the other hand, you can't imagine how bad government schools have become. Pupils go to school with knives, some with guns, and threaten both teachers and headmasters. The children of soldiers have really messed up our schools. Mugezi needs a quieter environment."

"My parents would love to have a grandson who is a priest. He can end up a parish priest, rector of a seminary or even a bishop," Padlock said.

"The church is very rich," Serenity declared. "A clever priest can become very rich indeed."

"You are only thinking about money," Padlock rebuked.

"I do not want my children to suffer. They should be able to drive big cars, live in big houses and have what I could not give them."

"They have to survive these times first."

I was restless for days. I visited the taxi bowl every day for a whole week, losing myself, my blues and my impotent anger in the tumultuous waves of activity there. I dreamed of an earthquake to end it all. I listened to hear if the ground was quaking, preparing us for the next apocalyptic explosion, but alas, only the steady grind of the vehicles and the eternal calls of the van boys, the snake charmers and the hawkers filled my head like an infernal ache.

What use was a priest? And those ludicrous cassocks! Celibacy was definitely not for me. I had already decided to marry three wives in the future. With the earnings of a lawyer, I was sure that I could easily give my trio a comfortable life. The Church, in my estimation, needed ball-less people like the shitters, not me, who was ready to follow General Amin's calls for self-advancement. Amin did not like the Church, and accused the clergy of meddling in politics, as they had done in the past, while doing nothing about the corruption inside the Church.

I had no plans to exchange one dictatorship for another. As a lawyer, I would run into dictators, but I would have the power to fight them, hit them hard and exact my own revenge. If I had learned anything from my years with the despots, it was that it was good to be an expensive victim, but even better to be one's own judge and executioner.

The despotic decision to send me to the seminary was vindicated by the government's announcement of the impending state visit of King Faisal of Saudi Arabia. Suddenly, Padlock talked about her fear that Uganda was about to be Islamized, all the churches closed, the clergy and nuns imprisoned or killed or forced to convert to Islam along with their followers, and that polygamy would become the order of the day. The Islamization rumor was as sinister as the old anti-Communist one spread by the Church in the fifties, to the effect that Communists were going to take power, close the churches, kill the clergy, marry off the nuns and enforce wife-swapping and common ownership of property.

"First he expelled missionaries, then the British, the Israelis, the Indians, and now he is ready to bring in the Arabs, those old slavers who call us infidels. Gaddafi will be spending his weekends here, making sure that the forced conversions go through. Faisal is coming to make Amin speed up the plans."

In Padlock's view, all the Arabs were old slavers, and all the Israelis were the people whose exploits she read about in the Bible. On the same level with the Israelis were the very white peoples, who were blessed by the Book. In her mind, the white races could do no wrong as long as they fulfilled what God commissioned them to do: to go out, conquer the world and save it from the threat of Islam. All the darker races had to do was to accept the deal, offering their labor and resources in return. For that reason, she saw nothing wrong with the old missionary tactics of sugarcoated invasion, fomentation of religious wars and political interference.

Serenity, on the other hand, held more intelligent views about the situation. To start with, he did not confuse the current Arabs with the East African slave traders; nor did he confuse the Israelis with the Biblical people, for whom he did not care much anyway. As for the white races, he admired their technology and wanted some of their power, but he did not adore them or hold them as God's chosen people. He found the concept of a chosen people rather absurd. He knew too well what had happened in the two world wars. The mindless slaughter in the trenches of World War I reminded him of colonial slaughters in the Third World. The cold-blooded genocide of World War II had given him a more skeptical view of the white races. On a personal level, he had never got over the shock of his uncle returning home from the war with his leg blown off. The man used to visit twice a year and make him wash the stump and dress it in bandages. Serenity would not eat meat for days. He would be haunted by the sight and the softness of the stump. The fact that the man did not talk made Serenity afraid of him. What was he thinking? Why didn't he talk anymore?

What did he see when the day ended and people's conversations were replayed in his head? He was the person who had made Serenity abhor violence. Whenever Serenity felt like exploding, he would remember his uncle and desist. In his adulthood, Serenity's fear of the white races increased. He believed that they could easily blow up the African continent if it suited them. At one time he had wanted to correct his wife's view of whites, but he had given up. Like God, Padlock was politically inaccessible.

"Nobody is being forced to convert," Serenity said after what seemed like a lifetime.

"They are being bought," she replied, thinking about Dr. Ssali, her husband's brother-in-law. "They are being given cars, jobs, businesses, promotions, anything to make them convert."

"People choose what they think is best for them," Serenity concluded.

Disappointed, Padlock resumed her lookout for those who wolfed their food, or blew onto it instead of patiently waiting for it to cool like decent people, or ate the meat or fish first, or slurped or munched or let soup crawl through the gaps in their fingers. Thank God, everything was in order.

My conclusion was that Padlock was stepping up her anti-Islamic campaign in order to wean me from Lusanani, which proved a noble but doomed endeavor. Lusanani was my partner in crime. She had already shown signs that she would do practically anything for me, which was more than I could say about Padlock. I was hatching a vague plan to keep myself out of the seminary, and although I did not know what role Lusanani was going to play in it, I was sure that she would figure in the final draft.

For the moment, I was very excited by King Faisal's impending visit. My admiration for my godfather soared. He had got rid of all the foreigners, plus a few foolhardy missionaries, and had turned to the Arab world for sponsorship. Good thinking. I had seen snatches of his visits to the Arab leaders on television. It all looked good. Now I was eager to see King Faisal.

School routine had changed. Every morning we did gymnastics and athletics, sang the national anthem, recited poems and practiced dances and a march-past with the school band.

The city was shivering under the great visitor's spell: shop buildings were pasted with paper flags of Uganda and Saudi Arabia. Many other buildings flew proper flags. All the shops had received a face-lift, and roads were undergoing major repairs. General Amin appeared daily on television and was seen making speeches, supervising road repairs, opening new schools and hospitals and launching multifarious functions. He flagged off a motor safari rally and joined the race in his Citroën Maserati. He was indomitable, indefatigable and as indispensable as air.

Soldiers decked out in new uniforms, new boots and new guns appeared on the streets. On our way to and from school, we passed them, as stationary as trees, as committed as suicide bombers. I felt proud to go past them. They were there for my own good, and for the good of the country. I only had to open my mouth and they, like faithful mastiffs, would come puffing and panting to my aid. They made me feel kind and generous; after all, I had only to summon them and the despots would be in dire trouble.

On the day the great man arrived, we stood on the roadside with two flags in our hands: the green one of Saudi Arabia and the black, yellow and red one of Uganda. Amin, like a bear on a crane, towered over the king, who swayed dizzily in the morning air. A mild sun was shining, creating a sweet haze which touched thousands of years back into the pages of the Bible and thrust onto our asphalt the phenomenon of Elijah going to heaven on a chariot of fire. Every one of us seemed to be saying "Father, Father, don't abandon me" as the chariot swept by. All we got in reply was Amin's schoolboy grin and the king's stationary hand trapped in a salute or a wave. The king's face did not move; if it did, the gesture was swallowed by a mass of crisscrossing wrinkles. A quaint haze of power emanated from the thin old man. I thought of Abraham. He looked at the world with the sublime dignity of somebody totally at peace with life and death.

The king never stopped at our school; obviously we were not important enough to detain life and death on wheels. Personally, I was not disappointed. I felt that I had been touched by the sweep of his garment. I was no longer afraid of death in the real sense. It seemed to have entered and inhabited me. If this man wanted to Islamize Uganda, he could do it. Gaddafi, on the other hand, had not done it, possibly because he was too jumpy, like somebody with too much to prove, somebody with too many balls in the air. This man looked out of the strange eyes of eternity, had nothing to prove, and every word he uttered reverberated with the weight of the centuries and the powers of heaven and hell. I was captivated, because that was what I wanted to be. That was the power I was seeking in life. I wanted to extract some people from the jaws of death, and to condemn others to the bowels of hell. I dreamed about King Faisal for weeks. Harmless dreams in which nothing much happened.

Serenity and his cronies kept abreast of the changes in the country. They ruminated on them for hours on end, searching for the best way into the future.

"I am going to open a shop for my wives," Hajj declared. "Come join me. My bank will finance the deal. There are many schemes to help entrepreneurs. It is a matter of presenting a viable plan, and the bank releases the cash. Let us join forces before it is too late."

"I am not the business type," Serenity confessed. "The mere sight of goods on display sends cold shivers down my spine." His old prejudices were still alive and kicking. He could never get the fear of shops and shopkeepers out of his system.

"The trouble with you Catholics is that you are natural-born followers," Hajj commented as they watched the evening traffic, some of it bearing Saudi Arabian stickers. "You are always looking for somebody to follow, to obey, to work for. You are bred to fear leadership and power and to play it safe. We Muslims are natural-born hustlers, always looking for an edge, a chink to squeeze through. This is a government for doers; those who dither will be left inside a burning house." Pearls before swine; Serenity was unimpressed.

"People do not change their ways overnight."

"For the first time in the history of this country, Muslims are in control, and a Muslim man is calling upon his Catholic brother to join hands and walk into prosperity."

"I want to fight in my own field. I have my sights on the Trade Union of Postal Workers. I want to be the chairman or treasurer of the accounts branch. That is my ambition," Serenity confided for the first time.

"Should I put in a word for you?" Hajj asked, a conspiratorial smile on his face.

"If you can," Serenity said reluctantly. "A man with many mouths to feed needs all the help he can get."

"I know the right people who can nudge the right ribs. Remember, Amin is here to stay. Those who believe that he is here now and gone tomorrow will regret it."

Thoracic locusts attacked Serenity's insides with a vengeance. His wife's paranoid lamentations donged in his ears. What would his benefactors ask in return? Conversion to Islam? Or recruitment into the State Research Bureau? Security organs were infiltrating the civil service; Serenity wanted no part in the game. He wanted to ask Hajj about the benefactors, but he failed to find the right words to carry the message without insinuating that Hajj might be involved with the wrong people.

"I will inform you when I am ready," he said vaguely, keeping the door open without committing himself.

"Nobody will ask you to do anything dangerous. I help you just because you are my friend and my neighbor, the person I can trust with my life." Serenity had not fooled him; Hajj had sensed the caution.

"I am very grateful for the offer. When the elections are ready, I will inform you."

"Take your time, but don't wait too long."

I still had one big pressing problem on my mind: how to avoid going to the seminary. Twice I asked Serenity for permission to go to the village to see Grandpa. My plan was to involve the old man, with the hope that he would nip the ridiculous idea in the bud. On both occasions, however, Serenity sent me to Padlock, who made me kneel in front of her for ten minutes before giving me a cold refusal. I was stuck, and angry too. I had money, from selling the stolen bobbin, but I could not declare my financial position. My box of tricks was empty: Cane, a Dummy A look-alike, had warned me never to use the same trick twice. But what was I supposed to do? I decided to turn to him for help.

My association with Cane had its origin in my letter-writing days. I had helped him write a few letters to girls he desired. Two had fallen into his net, but he never paid me. He just promised to be of use much later. Cane was big, tall, dark, with a conspiratorial charm that left you convinced, or pretending to be convinced, even if you nursed serious reservations. We, his classmates, both admired and feared him because he was a northerner, born somewhere in the harsh northern Ugandan plains, abandoned by his father, a soldier, at a tender age and raised by his mother, who had followed the great asphalt road south to Kampala. Like Uncle Kawayida's mother, she sold food and anything else she could lay her hands on in order to support herself and her son. What a strapping young man he was! Cane bubbled with the angry confidence born of hatred and too much familiarity with society's underbelly. He had an opinion on practically everything. He used to say to the majority of us, who were from the central region, "It was not the British who messed up this country; it was your sycophantic forebears, your greedy chiefs and your king who finally sold the country to Obote." Reared on loyalty, most of us were surprised that he was openly criticizing his fellow northerner Obote. "And those who sold to Obote might as well have sold to Amin. So please don't moan when things go bad. Take your punishment like real men." Unable to figure out what side he was on, we usually kept quiet.

For a long time Cane disorganized Grandpa's political dissertations in my head and almost dislodged them. That I had memorized most of them without really understanding them was an additional problem. I could not analyze them. As soon as I tried to take them apart, they crumbled like rotten paper, but by and by I asked myself the right questions: Did Cane mean that if our chiefs had not been divided—Protestants, Catholics, Muslims, pagans—they would have stopped the spread of British colonial rule and imperialism? Did we, at the turn of the century, have military superiority over British forces in the East African region? What about Captain Lugard's machine guns? No, Cane was wrong; the British would have come in anyway. The chiefs were minor players in the drama. I would have liked to ask Grandpa some of Cane's questions, and taken Cane's side just to tease the old man, but I was not allowed to visit him.

Cane was also our sex educator. He introduced us to the world of pornographic magazines. He had an uncle in the army who smuggled them into the country from Kenya. For the first time in my life, I knew what those white nuns looked like without their habits—some models resembled them so much that I at first thought they were sisters or the same people. Most models were not pale, but gold-brownish like sponge cakes. Others resembled mulattos or half-caste children born of Indian and African parents. We had many questions to ask Cane. How did the magazine makers collect all those beauties? None of them was obese or ugly or unattractive in any way, so how did they get them to pose naked, bums in the air like grasshoppers, glistening pink lips beckoning, brown assholes peeping? Were these people for real, or were we seeing dolls? How unfortunate that Grandpa was old: he should have seen this.

I was privileged to examine the magazines as much as I wanted. Other, less fortunate voyeurs had to pay, in cash or kind. Cane also brought booklets with titles like *All You Need to Know About Sex* and *The Complete Sex Handbook*. Cane loved to watch our reactions as I read passages, surrounded by a group of eager faces. There were intriguing words like "penis," "sperm," "semen," "vulva," "vagina," which Cane made us recite, but which he refused to explain. He was also not good at answering questions. Everyone wanted to know the difference between a vulva and a vagina, sperm and semen, but he refused to elucidate.

It was Cane who told me why Padlock had knocked me out on the red-ink-patch day. "Mothers pretend that they don't bleed, those fakers," he said, laughing. I was too angry to laugh. "And you should hear the childish, sniveling noises they make when they are being fucked." He guffawed and slapped me on the shoulder in the process.

When we went back to the group, he said, "All your mothers get fucked every night, except when they are bleeding. Your fathers pour their . . . in your mothers' . . ." He made us fill in the missing words. Somebody wanted to know how fathers poured their . . . in our mothers' . . . Somebody suggested that they used spoons or funnels. Cane almost slapped him; he couldn't believe that we were so ignorant.

Cane was not afraid of teachers, and he took special pleasure in teasing female teachers who acted tough with pupils. In fact, that was how he got the name Cane, because he used to tell them, "Cane me, bitch." The first woman to fall for it caned him till she started sweating and wet patches appeared in her armpits and between her breasts. She finally gave up. Cane liked lying on the floor for the strokes, and when he got up, he usually had a big erection. He would stand there with arms akimbo, his penis pushing against his fly like a big impatient rat. Female teachers soon learned their lesson. Nowadays, they referred him to the headmaster or to their male colleagues.

I met Cane on the way to school and introduced my problem. He patted me on the back and said it was nothing. In class he tore a precious page out of a porno magazine on which a golden-haired, blue-eyed girl was sitting on a chair, legs apart. He tore a blank page from an exercise book, folded it in two and sketched the head of the biology teacher, accentuating her hairdo, her nose and her lips. He pasted the sketch over the head of the girl. He glued the picture onto the blackboard.

The teacher found the class rumbling with juicy murmurs, which died down as soon as she appeared. She entered the room, put her bag on her chair, surveyed the blackboard and got a massive attack of nerves. "Wh-wh-who?"

"I did," Cane said from the back, double-bass booming.

"Why?"

"Isn't it funny, mistress?"

"Remove this dirt from my blackboard, and get out of my class. Stay out for the rest of the month."

"I prefer to be caned, mistress," Cane said very calmly.

We almost burst out laughing; our hero was going to show her a full-blooded erection, our erection, our riposte. Oh, the gutsy sensation of it!

"I said get out."

"Please, mistress, cane me, cane me, please."

"Out, out, out!" she screamed.

"Cane me, cane me, bitch."

We roared, striking our desks with excitement. Tears flowed from the corners of our eyes. Cane was our avenger. How we loved the humiliation of this big-breasted bully! Normally, she didn't hesitate to use the cane and to make you fetch ten buckets of water and pour it in the grass in front of the classroom, but Cane was untouchable.

In his own good time, Cane sauntered to the front, looked the teacher over, collected his picture and left. The dramatic effect of it! However, misgiving was ticking in my breast: Was this what I was supposed to do with Padlock? Cane was swarmed at lunchtime, but he ignored his admirers. He beckoned me and my *Treasure Island* friend, whom everyone called Island, to follow him. As the school compound quivered with noise and color and the sun hovered above us all like a ball of fire and brimstone, we cut across the football field. Two terraces lower was "the ring," the sand patch where long-jumpers practiced and our fighters grappled in no-holds-barred confrontations. We were swallowed by the cassava trees and elephant grass. Whipped by the dry wind, the bushes crackled and rustled, their sharp blades tickling, cutting and licking our bare limbs. In the valley, giant trees in eternal competition with school buildings shot more than twenty meters into the air, their canopies reminiscent of the papyrus reeds in the swamps of Mpande Hill.

A little distance from the trees and the overgrown path was a dead man in a black shirt and blue trousers, lying on his face, arms outstretched as if he were crawling toward the trees.

"This is what I wanted to show you," Cane announced.

Where were the notorious flies? Why wasn't I afraid? Island, on the other hand, wet his pants and quaked badly.

Farther on was the body of a woman on her back, her right arm across her face as if shielding her eyes from the sun. Was she sleeping? Where were the signs of death or deathly struggle?

"Who killed them?" I asked.

"Maybe our little friend here did," Cane said, pointing to Island.

"N-no, not me."

"Who, then?" Cane asked. "Me?"

My guess was that after the biology teacher had sent him out, he had roamed around and found the corpses and thought of shaking us up.

He glared at me and moved near the woman. He lifted her skirt with his foot. "You want to see her . . . ?" He turned to Island and forced him to say the word. It seemed as if the effort would kill him. Cane grabbed the back of Island's head and pushed him down. A yellow stream, like liquid gold, poured into the grass.

"Coward," he said, releasing him. "These people are dead, yet you are afraid of them. Why, eh? If you weren't my good friends, I would have made you undress them. It is time for class, boys," he concluded, turning serious.

Had he answered my question? Of course he hadn't. I always preferred people who spoke in plain language, but this was tantamount to speaking in tongues, and this time, like many times before, I was lost. I didn't even know why he had shown us the bodies. I could only imagine that he was showing off how fearless he was. Was he expecting me to tackle my adversaries in the same way? Was that it?

Lusanani gobbled my virginity within the walls of the derelict house where we had made our bobbin transaction. We explored our eager bodies and squeezed whatever delight we could out of them. I was finally clearing the last hurdle to adulthood. In the process, I was touched by twinges of regret: I should have asked her earlier, I kept thinking. In an attempt to make up for lost time, I tried to enjoy as much of her as I could.

I was back in my favorite tree, suffused with the smell of ripe jackfruit, salivary glands oozing, a rush of impending gratification bearing down on me. She sighed like ten bushes in a storm, and I tried to discover all the moaning voices of birthing village women, and the terrible voice of the birthing woman at the taxi park, in her vociferations. My biggest success that evening was the freedom to explore and occupy her mystery swampy terrains for as long as I wanted. I smeared myself with her fluids and arrived home smelling like an overripe jackfruit. It was late. Padlock was in a state. She asked where I had been. At the well, I replied, my eyes twinkling impishly with the pride of sexual discovery. I expected her to comment on my new perfume, but she ignored it. I was proud that I had lost my virginity and made it known. Now she would cancel her seminary plans, for I was no longer fit for celibate priesthood. I almost laughed in her face.

I relished the new sense of danger, and I walked about with a swollen chest. I was no longer afraid of Hajj Gimbi, because what he could do, I could do too. Now I wanted Padlock to nab us, but would Lusanani agree? That would mean putting her marriage on the line, although I doubted whether the danger was that great. She was the youngest wife, with the power of desirability on her side. I knew she could get away with a lot.

Lusanani refused to cooperate the first time I suggested the plan. She favored the idea of writing me a love letter. Cane had warned me never to use one trick twice. Above all, I wanted an immediate reaction. We patched up our differences, though, and I returned home smelling to high heaven. Padlock ranted and raved but failed to address the issue at hand. I felt I was in control.

On the scheduled day, I bathed all the shitters except one. Night fell rapidly. I ordered the unwashed shitter to remain in the bathroom. I went to the edge of the courtyard. Lusanani took her time, but finally showed up. When most people had entered their houses, we crept to the front of the pagoda, the steps pouring in front of us, the city winking in the distance. I had my back in the direction Padlock was going to come from. We pretended to be having sex. Hajj was away for a few days. Serenity was at the gas station. Everything was on schedule. We talked about our former schools. I dreamed about the university and a law degree.

"You will have forgotten me by then," she whispered.

"Never," I said sincerely. "I promise."

We were standing in a corridor between two pagodas. Suddenly she said, "Allah akbar!" The tip of a stick had struck her on the head. Padlock flung herself on me in order to reach her, but Lusanani fled. Padlock concentrated on me. She was holding a thick stick and was hitting me on the shoulder, on the back and on the legs. I could only defend my head. I did not want her to take out my eye. My arms soon became paralyzed by the heavy blows. I tried to gore her in the stomach, but she hit me with the stick on the back of the head. She won the day.

My left hand remained numb for a week. I was scared that it might wither. I prayed to all the gods that it wouldn't, because I did not want to resort to violent retribution. As luck would have it, feeling trickled back after ten days. Within a fortnight it could lift again.

My stint with the despots had begun with blood—Grandma's— and had almost ended in blood—mine. Serenity stopped Padlock from pursuing the Lusanani side of the business. I told him that it was all my fault. I also told him why I had done it. By now he was more or less sure that I was responsible for the Miss Singer letter and the bobbin mystery. He and Padlock wanted me out of their house. Serenity proposed sending me to Kasawo's, but Padlock refused. The seminary was only forty days away. I was finally sent to Aunt Lwandeka's. I was relieved.

The conflicts had worn me out. I felt brittle and cracked like an old boot. There was no time to waste. The seminary was a detour I wanted to pass through quickly in order to get back on my lawyerly track. Although my stint at home couldn't precisely be called an explosion, it had given me an inkling of what Grandpa meant by the expression that the modern state was a powder keg which would go off in a series of explosions. My secret wish was to have nothing to do with any of those conflagrations.

BOOK FOUR

THE HYDRA at the heart of the autocracy commonly known as the seminary system bore three venom-laden heads: brainwashing, schizophrenia and good old-fashioned dictatorship. This Infernal Trinity of venoms worked jointly; the erosion of old, unacceptable ideas and the infusion of new, approved ones were meant to lead to the gradual breakdown of the relationship between thoughts, feelings and actions, which would result in a malleable subject ready for use by and for the clerics in charge of the system.

In theory, seminarians were orphans, lowly bastards plucked from the dirty, sinful world and shepherded into purity by clerical fathers whom, God willing, they could one day join in holy priesthood. Therefore a seminarian's mandate was to please, obey and be docile and trustworthy. A seminarian had to surrender his personality and sexuality and become a voluntary eunuch. He had to dedicate himself fully to his calling, and in return he would be entrusted with the treasures of the kingdom come ordination day. A seminarian was the closest thing to the ancient apprentice temple whore: he entrusted himself and his rights to Mother Church, who was free to do whatever she wanted with him, including dismissing him summarily. If he persevered and cleared all the hurdles put in his way, he got his reward: one hundred percent compensation for everything he gave up on earth, and one hundred percent reward in the life to come.

Just as in the dictatorship I had left behind, at the seminary I found myself in acting school, because survival here depended on how well you adapted to your new role and how wonderfully you performed it. You had to second-guess your superiors, tell them what they wanted to hear, show them the face they wanted to see and feed them the best cues, for they too had a role to play. The sooner you learned the stage value of fine delivery, the longer your life span in the seminary and the more likely you were to make it to the altar and to the time when the faithful would grovel at your feet for blessings, exorcism and deliverance from sin.

The seminary was like any other mildly wild school in the seventies, and certainly not a holy garden full of angelic children who watched butterflies and picked flowers in between lessons. It was true that there were no boys with guns or butcher knives in their schoolbags, but the common, less lethal weapons they had, they used very well on us newcomers. For many long nights we hardly got a chance to sleep. Gangs of second-year bullies, still smarting with the previous year's sufferings, swooped down on us soon after dark, and especially after lights-out, doing considerable damage.

This kind of attack was not unexpected. The bullies exercised their newly acquired powers by inventing nicknames for newcomers, or reusing old ones. They kicked newcomers around, whistled at them and called them "Bushmen." That was for starters.

On the first night, boys armed with canes, mallets, electric cables and anything else they could find woke us up—we had not been sleeping anyway—and took over from where they had left off during the day. The few who pretended to be fast asleep got drenched with cold water before being pulled out of bed. We were divided into small groups and led to the end of the dormitory, where there was a platform resembling a long podium (the dorm had once been a recreation hall). We were made to kneel on the floor, raise our hands in the air and re- cite Psalm 23: "The Lord is my shepherd . . . He prepares a banquet for me . . ." This was the banquet our masters had prepared for us for over a year. We were made to recite the Our Father, the Hail Mary and a number of other prayers while we knelt, sat, stood, bent, held hands aloft or spun around. Those who were slow to react were either kicked or prodded with sticks. Someone produced a huge aluminum bucket full of cold water and a fat jug. We were told that the baptismal cere- mony was about to begin. We stood at one end of the podium and waited as a chair was installed at the other end. A boy in church robes, or what looked like church robes, sat on the chair with a paper miter on his head—he was the High Priest in charge of the ceremony—flanked by the bucket man. A boy in a cassock, holding a piece of paper, ap- peared and signalled to one of us to crawl to the feet of the High Priest. The cassocked boy shone a flashlight on his paper, read out a name, turned to the Priest and whispered the candidate's new nickname in his ear. The Priest got the jug from the bucket man and drenched the candidate with cold water as he said the following words: "I baptize you in the name of the Father, the Son and the Holy Spirit. From now on you are 'Hornbill' "—or any other selected name—"God bless you my son, and go in peace." The cassocked boy then told the victim to recite his nickname once, thank the Priest and crawl back to the other end of the podium.

There were four dormitories, officially named after patron saints but popularly called Vatican City, Mecca, Cape of Good Hope and Sing-Sing. I was in Sing-Sing, the most notorious dormitory, abode of truants, rule benders and bullies, the chronic victim of negative pub- licity, neglect and dirt. The same initiation ceremony went on in all four dorms, with varying intensity. Sing-Sing, with its unique position at the back end of the sleeping quarters, very near the bathrooms and the acacia trees and the seminary fence, topped them all. Every bully there lived dangerously and made every "Bushman" wonder why the priests let all this happen, for surely they knew about this and other ini- tiation ceremonies.

At two o'clock, as sleep gradually took over and the tin roof dripped with dew in tiny, tortuous rivulets, there was commotion once again: we were being woken up. Clad in pajamas, we were made to stand in the corridor between the two columns of beds. After a check to see that we were all present, we were marched off to the bathrooms, ten meters away. The timing was deliberate: the air was ice-cold and windy, and fat clouds loomed in the sky, as though it was going to rain. We stood under the acacia trees, a mat of dead leaves underfoot, our bodies quaking as much as our teeth clattered, and awaited our fate. Dew dripped from the leaves above, driving all semblance of sleep from our eyes and fatigue from our bodies.

Bullies armed with sticks lined up in front of and behind us, and their leader issued our orders: we had to do pushups, situps and then frog-kicks. We were reminded that we were completely in the hands of these boys, and that the more cooperative we were, the better for us it would be. I kept my head down, determined to survey the lay of the land before deciding how best to go about striking back. The weak and the slow, tormented by cramp and semi-paralysis, got kicked and cracked on the head. The drills went on for a long time because we were generally slow, unused to such rigors. The bullies exercised sadistic patience, making sure that everyone got there with time.

Finally, with leaves and dirt on our clothes and in our hair, we were lined up and ordered to open our flies. "Play the fiddle, Bushmen. The fiddle, you nincompoops. As soon as you ejaculate, you retire to bed." How on earth could one get even a mild erection? The penises looked like shriveled worms, sprouting mushrooms or coiled centipedes.

Two Bushmen left early that morning, one saying that he had come to become a priest, not a criminal, but the priests didn't seem too impressed. After all, many were called but few were chosen, and he who loved himself more than God was not worthy of the call. Didn't the chaff, in the end, separate itself from the grain? Didn't the dead bury themselves? Ships which broke up after the first storm weren't fit for the voyage, we learned.

On the fourth night, just as the extravaganza hit its peak, someone pulled my left arm, dislocating it. I screamed. The boys panicked and fled. The infirmarian was eventually called, and I got the necessary attention. I was haunted by the fear that this time my hand was going to remain paralyzed and would wilt and become totally useless. I moved my things to the infirmary. I exaggerated my affliction and enjoyed temporary immunity. This was my salvation from the horrors of Sing-Sing. Ensconced in the stark pale blue walls of the infirmary, overlooking the woods, I was safe. Nobody ordered me around. Nobody teased me or forced me to do anything for his pleasure. I slept as much as I wanted. I dodged mass and any other activity I did not like. For the first time since my arrival, I had time to think.

I wasn't very interested in finding out exactly who had pulled my arm. Given the circumstances, it could have been anybody. After all, boys were doing what the staff let them get away with. What could I do about it? How could I lay my hands on the staff? For the time being, all I had to do was survive and wait for a chance to act.

I was already thinking about getting myself a bodyguard, someone like Dummy A or Cane. I had noticed a shabby, loud bruiser called Lwendo. He went after the newcomers with a vengeance, beating them, calling them names, confiscating their things, forcing them to carry his bathwater to the bathrooms, eating their food and making them wash his clothes on the weekend. My uneducated guess was that he was screaming for attention, somebody to make him feel big. I decided to give it to him in exchange for protection.

I went to him one afternoon and volunteered to do for him all the things he found too demeaning for a second-year student. I promised to sweep under his bed, to clean his shoes, to wash and iron his clothes and to fetch him water during the drought.

"Bushman, you are out of your mind," he said, laughing derisively. "You are a cripple. You can hardly wipe your own bottom, and yet you are volunteering to work for me? How will you do that?"

"This arm is going to heal sooner than you expect. I can already move my fingers. In a fortnight I will be at your service."

"Go and work for Jesus in exchange for a miracle cure," he said, laughing smugly.

"I am serious." Silence descended on us. The first bell had rung for class; within five minutes the second one would ring, and everybody had to be in class by then. Black-trousered, white-shirted shadows wheeled past us with a crunching of shoes.

"I've got it," he said, flaring up. "You are a spy, Bushman. Who sent you to keep an eye on me? The rector or one of those bloody priests? Do you think I am stupid? Get out of my way, Bushman."

"I am not a spy. I would never even think of it. I swear by my broken arm."

"All right, Bushman. I accept your offer, but I am warning you. If you fool with me, I will throw live coals on you one good Saturday afternoon, you understand? Now, what do you want from me?"

"I want your mates to leave me alone. One of them dislocated my arm, and he hasn't even got the decency to come and apologize. I don't expect him to. But I don't want any of them in my way."

"I will see what I can do, Bushman," he said, smiling victoriously. Behind his back, in the middle of which a trail of sweat showed, I said, "One day you will stop calling me Bushman."

As soon as Lwendo agreed to swat my flies, I started planning my liberation. I wasn't going to be his lackey for a whole year. Blackmail was in my blood; it was just a matter of time before it ensnared him. Above all, I didn't like him, and I didn't value his company. He was too loud, too shabby and too tactless for my taste. My plan was to use him, abuse him and then drop him in the gutter where he belonged.

I despised manual labor. My stint with the despots had cast my attitude in stone. My next maneuver was to get myself a white-collar job, say, in the library, sacristy, infirmary or laboratory. I needed to find some priest to impress with so much false enthusiasm that he would recommend me.

The priest in charge of the sacristy was too much of an actor to be ensnared by the wiles of an amateur. He did not encourage familiarity either. His big, small-eyed face had an eternal frown on it, and his long frame made him seem as if he were always looking for something on the ground or in the air. Stolen altar wine and steel balls, boys said. He was an incurable grouch who believed that we were having a very easy life. He often said that the seminaries of today were watered-down versions of the old ones, in the days when priests were men. I, like many other boys, detested his sourpuss attitude and kept out of his way. The common joke was that he had pissed all the steel out of his balls because it could not stand the temperature of his displeasure.

My most realistic prospect was Fr. Kaanders, a retired Dutch missionary, who was in charge of the library. The library was not a popular place: most boys would not be caught dead reading a book which was not compulsory. I felt that if I turned on my charm, the old man would eventually be trapped in my designs.

I attacked the library with a vengeance. I was always the first person to arrive and the last to leave. When I entered, I would walk very slowly along the bookshelves, stopping now and then to pick up a volume. I would wipe it quickly, almost absentmindedly, open the pages and pretend to be absorbed. I would look at a picture page, think private thoughts or simply kill time, and hope that Kaanders was watching. When I felt that it was time to replace the volume, I would close the book, carefully part the other volumes and put it back. I would then move to another shelf and do the same thing all over again. After making the rounds of the shelves, I would remove two or three volumes, place them on a desk and read a favorite book. In the meantime, I pretended to consult the bigger volumes.

At other times I came with a notebook and read while pretending to stop and make notes or copy diagrams. I gave every impression that I was squeezing the maximum amount of knowledge from every volume I touched. Whenever I wanted to flee bullies, to think or to nap, I would go to the library. When the bell for class rang, I pretended not to have heard it. I stayed on till Fr. Kaanders came over, tapped me on the shoulder, then tapped on the face of his watch, at which I would start as though I had seen a ghost. I would smile at him, excuse myself, hurry to put the volumes noisily back, collect my things and rush out of the building.

In order to win the library vote, I knew that I needed more support. I targeted the literature teacher. Literature was still not more than an elevated sort of English grammar and composition lesson to many. I myself knew nothing particular about literature, and for a long time I could not even define the word. I looked it up, memorized the definition and lost it again. I knew for sure that hypocrisy would not win the day here. This man was the soberest priest I had ever met. He was also the most educated we had: a priest with a degree from a secular university was still a rarity in those days. This man was viewed with suspicion by some of his colleagues. Why would a university graduate join the priesthood instead of getting himself a good job in the city?

they wondered. This lean, ascetic man had the uncanny ability to look right through you, making you feel that he knew everything about you and that lying to him was useless. It was for this reason that few boys chose him as their confessor or spiritual director. Boys disliked priests they could not effectively fool.

Since I knew that I could not fool him, I decided to take genuine interest in his subject. I asked questions and tried to make him break down this literature mystery for us. I read the books he gave us, and tried to really understand what they were about. Deep analysis was not my forte, but I did my level best and used my Longman dictionary a lot. Somebody nicknamed me Longman Dick, because he claimed that I handled that book more often than I did my penis.

In a subject treated with suspicion, my good marks started to make me stand out. However, I did not try to catch the teacher's eye. I wanted him to notice me, to court me, to make the first move. I often finished my assignments ahead of time, but I did not hand them over, waiting for the day when they were collected. The strategy bore fruit. Although I was thrilled, I tried to remain indifferent.

Two months into my library campaign, Kaanders came over to my desk one afternoon and said, "You love books, boy. Oh boy, boy."

"At home we have a library with very many volumes. The only toys one gets at home are books."

"Books are unpopular here, boy, boy," he said, surveying the shelves in their cold, straight lines. "Do you want to come and help here, boy, boy?"

"Yes, Father," I replied, trying not to show too much excitement.

"Good, boy, boy. That will be so good, boy."

This was the most irritating characteristic of his fading years. He called everybody "boy." The priests in particular resented it. He would be talking to the rector and would say, "Boy . . . I was saying, boy." He would go to the bursar's office and say, "When will the books we ordered arrive, boy?" At table he would lean over to the priest in charge of the sacristy and say, "Boy, I didn't find any wine in the side chapel where I say my private mass, boy." Or, "Would you pass me the salt, boy?" The younger priests with egos as large as houses never got used to being called "boy." Each time the word came, especially when there were boys around, they looked as if they wanted to cuff the old man. The innocuous look in Kaanders' time-harassed face would both confuse and annoy them. It was not a word intended to injure, let alone annoy anyone, but why was the man so obsessed with it? One young priest attempted to correct him and bring it to his attention that he was not a boy, but the very next sentence the old man said began with the word. Everyone laughed, and the priest gave up, and boys called him Boy until he was transferred. There were a few nuns living in a small convent attached to the kitchen and the food store. Kaanders, to everyone's amusement or despair, also called the nuns "boy" all the time.

Kaanders' battered body bore the scars of his long battle with the polygamists of Jinja Diocese. In the midst of his running battles with paganism, polygamy and ignorance on the marshy, tsetse-fly-laden eastern shores of Lake Victoria, he had contracted the sleeping sickness. The disease and the nervous breakdown that followed had both been treated and pronounced cured, but in his dotage the tsetse fly struck back, reminding him of its residual juice in his blood. Nowadays he dozed off in mass, in class, on the toilet seat, in the library, anywhere. He could be teaching us French, and out the lights would go. We would watch him with boyish glee, his head tipped precariously forward, loose mouth open with a string of saliva in one corner, arms on his thighs, sleeping. He would wake up as suddenly as he had knocked off, and would say, "Boy, oh boy, boy, that fly . . . Where were we?"

During mass, especially in the course of a very long Sunday sermon, he would float off to dreamland on the wings of the fly. The sermon would end, everyone would rise and he would stay seated, chin dug into his chest, a puddle of saliva on his seat. Somebody would finally nudge him, and his lips would begin to work. Kaanders was very bad at remembering names, except those of great writers. He hardly knew the names of his fellow staff members; however, he clearly remembered the name of the boy who cleaned his office.

Amnesia made Kaanders the most popular priest with students, and most especially with truants and other chronic rule breakers. Whenever he caught somebody doing wrong, he would ask the name, which he faithfully wrote down and presented to the rector, saying, "Boy, this boy was breaking rules, oh boy, boy." The rector would make a show of seriousness while suppressing laughter, for none of the names were known to him. Sometimes he was presented with names of army officers, famous singers or other characters the boys had come up with at the time of their apprehension. Whenever he was in the mood after a Kaanders visit, he would mimic the old man: "Oh boy, boy, I found Captain Jona, Father Adriga and Sister Pants behind the fences . . . Oh boy, boy, what bad things they were doing there, boy!" He would laugh, hammer his desk with his fists and tap his feet on the floor as he rocked.

On his bad days, Kaanders would totter under a hood of amnesia so strong that he would forget that he had already had his breakfast. He would return to the dining room and ask any priest he found there, "Who has used my cup, boy? Oh boy, boy, nobody has any respect anymore, boy. My cup! I have used it for the last twenty years, and somebody has used it and forgotten to wash it and replace it. Boy, oh boy!" Most priests would just look at him, shrug resignedly and let him simmer in his own quaint soups. He would pace the room back and forth, coming very close to the wall on one side and the fridge on the other, before stopping and saying, "Boy, somebody ate my cheese, too! Oh, boy!"

It was remarkable that Kaanders never forgot or confused French grades. It seemed as if his mind went out of its way to accommodate French. He spotted each and every mistake and underlined it in red ink and penalized it with half a point. He taught us the following seven French adjectives in song form, which became his nickname: *"Bon mauvais méchant / grand petit joli gros."*

It all went well when the boys were in the mood for such little songs. When they were not, especially before lunch, they would deliberately mess up the sequence of words and almost drive him crazy with red-faced, foot-stamping frustration.

Every other afternoon at the library, at opening or closing time, he would ask me my name and spend a minute or so turning it over in his head, stretching every syllable phlegmatically in an attempt to wrestle it down, but there were so many small holes in his sieve-like brain that, come next time, he would ask me again what my name was. He memorized my face, though. That was not too difficult, since every other day, during manual labor time, I went to the library, swept, checked in books returned, made a list of those overdue and set aside those destined for repair.

As other boys toiled in the fields, mowed grass in the compound, scrubbed the refectory floor, hunted cockroaches in the scullery, killed rats in the food store and did one hundred and one other chores, I nursed the books and ministered to the needs of the library.

At first I was bored. I had achieved my goal. I did not really like books. The dust tended to get on my nerves by irritating my nose and making me sneeze. I dreaded the time when Kaanders repaired worn-out volumes: all the measuring, the cutting, the gluing, all the pressing and the caressing and the breaking of dry, crisp, newly repaired volumes consumed so much time and energy that it drove me crazy. Kaanders' eyes watered slightly when he surveyed the work of his hands. He had given a new lease on life to a mutilated object. He had given an anonymous treasure hunter a chance to dig into those refurbished volumes. The perverse joy of it made him whistle and stroke the books like lapdogs.

In the meantime, I was busy hatching a scheme to get rid of Lwendo. I wanted to blackmail him and maintain a stranglehold on his dirty neck. I eventually intended to focus my attention on some particularly nasty staff members, whom I was deliberately ignoring for the moment because I wanted to set my house in order first. It was my belief that as long as I was dominated by that shaggy rat Lwendo, I could not be free to do other things.

Long before I was asked to work in the library, Lwendo was in charge of the charcoal store. This made him a very important person, because we all needed his services on Saturday afternoon, when we ironed our clothes for Sunday mass and the whole week. We all flocked to his barn, a small, faded brick-red building with a large rectangular chimney, which had been a kitchen in the days when seminaries were seminaries and priests had balls of steel. Lwendo, the man of the moment, had to fill everyone's box with live charcoal, but the demand was usually greater than the supply, and both competition and discrimination were high. Second-year students got first priority, those they recommended second. The Bushmen who had no one to vouch for them got the last small half-dead charcoals, often served with more ash than fire.

Whenever he wanted a bit of fun, especially on wet days, when he found it hard to gather enough wood to make enough charcoal for everyone, Lwendo would withdraw after serving the privileged ones and let the Bushmen jostle and nudge and fight over the remaining half-dead coals. He would stand outside in the trampled grass, spade in hand, sweat dripping down his face, and watch the scrum and laugh till tears trickled from his eyes. "The Bushmen are killing each other over charcoal, ha ha ha haaa, hehehee . . . ," he would go, joined along the way by a few other second-year students whose ironing needs had already been catered to by newcomers in return for protection. Lwendo was lucky that no one got seriously burned in the scrums, and that the boy who got pushed into the hot ash never put the blame on him.

Lwendo's job gave him freedom and brought him in contact with the nuns who cooked for the staff and for us. During manual labor he was to be found in the kitchen chatting up a nun or two, pretending to be making plans for his Saturday chores. In between visits to the kitchen, he would gather firewood, old sticks of furniture and anything else he needed, or pretended to need, for lighting the Saturday fire. Lwendo also spent much time with the pigsty gang, boys who looked after the seminary's pigs and were responsible for slaughtering them on chosen Saturdays for the fathers' table. Leaders of this group kept back some pork and smuggled it in buckets to Lwendo's barn, where it was later roasted and devoured. All this was illegal and could lead to one's immediate suspension or expulsion, but no one was eager to report these crimes.

Rumor reigned supreme here. If one needed the truth, one had only to follow the noses of the gossipers. One such character linked Lwendo to Sr. Bison, a fat little black nun with very round legs, very round arms and a very ample behind on which fantasizers said one could stand the fat Jerusalem Bible without its falling off. This same nun was linked to the Rev. Fr. Mindi, the disciplinary master. I was only interested in the former connection.

I started shadowing Lwendo in the evenings, in the hope of nabbing him while he was eating the forbidden fruit. If not, I wanted to catch him in some very compromising situation. I failed. What I knew was that whenever the food was bad, and it often was, he would go to the kitchen and eat leftovers from the fathers' table after supper. During the cooking weeks of nuns with whom he did not particularly get along, his visits to the kitchen were less frequent. I had two options: either to link him with stealing pork and roasting it in his barn, which meant enlisting the cooperation of an interested priest, or to catch him fucking Sr. Bison or some other nun.

It took me eight weeks to nail him. I shadowed him every evening during the night study, which began at 9 p.m. One evening he was not in class or in his barn or in the library. He could only be in some father's office or in the kitchen. I went to the kitchen at 9:30 and found it vacant, the sooty boilers staring dolorously through the grimy windows. I stood outside the kitchen and thought hard. The food store, a long, cold room full of sacks of maize, maize flour and bad beans, was to my right. Normally, its heavy wooden door bore the weight of two large fist-shaped padlocks. I looked. The door was closed but not padlocked. I decided to chance it and go in. This room was out of bounds, except for those with special permission. I did not wait for permission. I was the librarian, after all. I could always say that I was looking for Fr. Kaanders, or that he had sent me to the bursar to see if some books had arrived.

A thick, weevil-impregnated smell befouled the still air, making the long, cold room feel smaller and more forlorn. The pregnant gunnysacks on their stumpy wooden stands reminded me of Grandpa's sacks of coffee, stuffed and ready for the mill at the top of Mpande Hill. The sacks, like the beds in Sing-Sing, were lined against the wall, creating a wide cement corridor in the middle which looked like a long, dark tunnel into a big hill. I stood and listened, fighting the sudden need to sneeze, afraid to be found here alone in the darkness. It was very quiet. A dead stick fell from the trees near the convent onto the corrugated-iron roof with a long, thin scratching sound. I started as though jabbed in the ribs.

I thought I heard other sounds, this time coming from the back of the tunnel. They were more like squeaking rats. Maybe there were other prowlers in here. I thought I heard a dog sniffing repeatedly. The sound was sharply controlled and entered the body like needles or tongues of fire. Lusanani suddenly came to me, her bosom drenched by a leaking jerry can, her nipples erect under her cotton blouse. She suddenly filled the darkness, although this was certainly not her song. Hers was a more sophisticated rendition, garnished with a staccato chorus and blessed with flowery, praise-laden stanzas. This sound was genuine, clean, urgent and maddening. On tiptoe, the burden in my trousers a sweet hindrance I vaguely thought was donging like a church bell, I advanced toward the sniffer dog.

Lwendo stuffed the nun with powerful, deliberate, loaded thrusts.

A cheeky ray of light from a choked ventilator fell dully on red panties heaped around a work-conditioned ankle. Lust-glazed nunly eyes saw me first, and the gasp that burst in the darkness tore through my groin with the corrosion of sulfuric acid. Lwendo, well aware that the damage had already been done, would not be denied. He pressed to the juddering end with the preening insolence of a stud in a corral. Realizing that it was not a priest but me, his lackey, he laughed, and in his eagerness he tried to shake my hand.

I had bought my freedom and his friendship, on top of helpings set aside from the fathers' table during the grateful nun's cooking week. In my excitement I thought of Uncle Kawayida, the magician, the charmer, the storyteller, and of his story of the man with the three sisters. I would have liked to tell him about this coup, and about seminary life in general, but communication between us had faded badly since I left the village. Did he read books? No, he was too busy running his business, raising turkeys and broiler chickens. Had he forgotten about the old days? I didn't think so.

I was a free man now. I toyed with the idea of going after a bully or two, but the bullying had cooled down. I decided to go after people larger than me, the real bosses of the place. I still found no pleasure in beating people of my level. I relished the challenge of reaching above myself and winning, albeit with more bruises. My attention had already been drawn by Fr. Mindi, the disciplinary master, and now probably solo fucker of efficient Sr. Bison. This man not only caned boys, but also went after them, hiding in bushes and behind buildings, high walls and fences, everywhere, to catch those breaking stupid rules like talking during silence time or eating between meals. He knew all the paths used by truants, and often hid behind the acacias overlooking Sing-Sing in the hope of catching hungry boys who escaped and returned to the seminary with bananas, corn, pancakes, sugarcanes, anything to keep hunger at bay. Some truants had a business instinct: they took orders and delivered foodstuffs at a profit. Fr. Mindi went after these "traders in the temple" with missionary zeal. He called them to their dormitories at odd hours in the hope of finding contraband or money in their boxes.

Officially, all pocket money was kept with him, but many boys hid most of it in places where they could get at it freely, without first going to Fr. Mindi and explaining why they needed it. Sing-Sing suffered most of Mindi's money-hunting "police checks," as they were called.

Die-hard truants and money hoarders fought back. They spread rumors and set him on the trail of the wrong people. With Mindi thus diverted, they made good their escape. He fell into this trap a number of times, till he discovered that boys were laughing at his gullibility. He caught some of the pranksters and punished them harshly. Information about police checks somehow leaked from the fathers' dining room, and many of his raids were pre-empted, with the result that on days when he planned to surprise the real criminals, he found their lockers and suitcases empty.

The role of disciplinary master hinged on his self-image, and on the perceived image the boys had of him. As far as Fr. Mindi was concerned, both were poor. This only served to make him harsher.

I often wondered why this educated man couldn't see the ludicrousness of his position. Boys fed on bad *posho* (corn bread) and weevilled beans stayed hungry and had to supplement their deficient diet. Wouldn't he have done the same? Couldn't he see that he was enforcing impossible rules? Couldn't he see that he was the Pharisee who preached total rest on the Sabbath, yet rescued his donkey when it fell in the ditch on that day? It was easy to say that no one should eat between meals when your stomach was full of pork, fish, Irish potatoes, greens and the other goodies priests ate.

I also hated the lack of self-control this preacher of self-control exhibited when he caught his man. If he was indeed enforcing impersonal rules, made in Rome and imported by the bishop into the country, he had to exhibit some impersonality and impartiality. On the contrary, he enjoyed his successes, especially when inflicting pain on miscreants. It was personal after all. He was demonstrating that although some got away with it, anyone caught would pay a high price. Pride, ambition, future career prospects and power were in it for him.

Fr. Mindi was the most hated man in the seminary. Boys called him the Grim Reaper, and they prayed for him to get into a car accident and live the rest of his life in a wheelchair. They prayed for him to become blind, to get cancer and to be afflicted with every purulent disease on earth. The feeling was that as soon as he left, things would improve dramatically, for it was believed that he was deliberately keeping the situation bad. Nobody could understand why the food remained terrible when there was land, and possibly money to develop it. We had come to believe his philosophy was that bad food made good seminarians and ultimately good priests.

"He should die," boys often said, especially when they watched him dribbling the ball at the football field. He could move with beguiling swiftness. He was the patron of Vatican dorm, and thanks to his participation and coaching, they won most annual inter-house competitions. Whenever they won, Fr. Mindi would allow two pigs to be roasted and would give us abundant food for one weekend.

"No, no, noo," others replied. "He should live and suffer forever and ever."

"What should we do about it?"

There was general agreement that the man should be left in the hands of the gods, who should see fit when to break his leg or inflict a car accident or subject him to armed attack.

Fr. Mindi penetrated my thought patterns. I tended to think of him as a brother to that constipated gorgon Padlock. Both had had a religious call. Both had responded to it. One had dropped out to become a real parent, while the other remained behind to become a symbolic one. Both believed that the harsher, the meaner and the more mysterious you played it, the better your children turned out.

It eventually struck me how limited Fr. Mindi really was. Padlock, in her nunly, peasant-girl constrictions, was more like a sore-infested buffalo hardly able to keep thousands of egrets and ticks off its festering back. Mindi, on the other hand, was bloated with theology, philosophy, Latin, Italian, Church history and all manner of other clerical and secular learning garnered from both local and foreign seminaries. The four years he had spent at Urban University in Rome had sharpened the edge of his conservative Catholicism, reinforced his harsher traits and dulled his empathic and self-analytical capabilities.

Yet, this was a man we were supposed to call Father and emulate and put on a pedestal. If scholarships to foreign universities and all that learning resulted in this barren role-playing and regurgitation, what was the use of it? This was a man programmed to obey, and to be obeyed. This was a man who had suffered and was now making others suffer so that they in turn would make others suffer. This was Mindi's version of one hundred percent priestly compensation on earth and one hundred percent reward in the life to come. His material things, especially his car, were part of this package, this compensation scheme for having responded to the priestly call and given up the family life the damned enjoyed. He bragged about it, thinking that he was encouraging us to persevere. His dream was not different from my lawyerly one, taking into account the power he enjoyed and the rumors about him and Sr. Bison. It was only the oil of holiness and of predestination which he poured on his that put me off. My aim was to rub off that oily sheen and expose the dull, grainy core underneath.

I was back to my old sleepless ways. It felt scary to be up in the small hours of morning, but there was an exciting edge to it, a marauder's adrenaline rushes, that made it worthwhile. I left Sing-Sing at around two o'clock. Dorobo, the newly hired night watchman, very tall, very strong, soot-black, lethal with his giant bow and arrow, was out doing his rounds, or sleeping. It was the image of his huge bow that etched itself in my mind like a diamond half-moon and followed me around as I moved from shadow to shadow. I praised the Lord that we Africans never idolized dogs: How awesome would this man have been with a huge German shepherd at his side? But there was not a single dog on campus.

The seminary stood on top of a hill, arranged around the chapel, accessible from all sides. It was easy to move from Sing-Sing, at the extreme end of the compound, to the chapel because of the protection accorded by the trees and a pine-tree fence for most of the way. I found Dorobo behind the chapel, crammed into a nook, roaring in his illegal sleep. My destination was to the left of the chapel, ten meters away. It was a long, slant-roofed building used partly to store tools and partly as a garage for the fathers' cars.

I crossed the gravel-strewn stretch to the tool area and opened the side door with a key used by the student in charge. I found myself inside the long, cold building with heaps of scythes, hoes, pangas, rakes, defunct lawnmowers and chain saws reeking of dust, oil and neglect. I picked up a blunt panga and weighed it in my hand, remembering the maniac who had threatened to decapitate Grandma. I set it down again, careful not to let other implements slide and make noise. I proceeded to the connecting door.

The hinges squeaked, making me afraid that Dorobo might hear me. I got inside the garage, and was confronted with the smell of cars: a tangy combination of oil, steel and rubber trapped in a confined space. There was Mindi's blue Peugeot, Kaanders' white Volkswagen, the rector's beige Renault and an old grayish car left behind by a priest friend of the rector's. In the far corner was a huge, full-bellied motorcycle on its flipper-like kickstand, seemingly leaning against the wall, a pool of oil under it.

It took me a few minutes of sweaty-palmed poking and fumbling to get into Fr. Mindi's car. I imagined Aunt Tiida, dressed to kill, watching Dr. Ssali trying to get into their Peugeot and fussing with camouflaged pleasure as their neighbors looked on from behind parted curtains.

The stench of tobacco, however, brought me back to my senses. I was inside the car of a chain-smoker. I thought of pouring salt in Fr. Mindi's engine and wrecking it for good, but that seemed uncalled for. I was not here on a rampage, but a courtesy call. I was principally here to send a modest message to the big man, something a touch above the average seminarian's idle fantasy revenge. I had eaten a few pawpaws, bought from a truant, and combined with our weevilled beans, the stench they gave my excrement was overpowering. I held my nose as I opened the plastic bag. I had delved into Uncle Kawayida's archives and pulled out a football hooligan's weapon: shit. I used a trowel to smear the seats, the roof, the floor, the steering wheel, the gear shift, the dashboard and all the carpets. I locked the stench inside the car and worked on the door handles. I left the offensive plastic bag on the bonnet.

By now the whole garage was alive with stink-hammers. I hurried out of the contaminated air, closed the connecting door as carefully as possible and tiptoed around the heaps of scythes, pangas, hoes. . . . I was aware of the precariousness of my position: somebody could smell me from a mile off. I made my way to the bathrooms, cleaning myself along the way with odoriferous pine needles plucked from the fence.

I had visualized a more sophisticated aftermath to my painting job. The staff members were typically very equivocal about the attack. "Somebody vandalized Fr. Mindi's car." "Somebody did terrible damage to a certain staff member's property." "Somebody acted very disrespectfully and uncharitably toward our bursar," they said. The details finally leaked out via the boys who were made to clean up the mess. Fr. Mindi had found them talking during silence time and had charged them with the horrible task of scrubbing, washing, wiping and drying his desecrated status symbol.

Finally, Fr. Mindi told us officially. He dressed his anger in curse-laden threats, ultimately announcing that if the culprit did not give himself up within three days, something was going to happen to him. I was in familiar territory, hardly able to believe how similar dictatorial thought patterns were. This man with an ego as large as a cirrhotic liver expected the culprit to crumble under its holy smells. If this was what that Urban University conservatism had come to, then I didn't envy him all the lasagna he had eaten in Italy. His experience with truants should have warned him that not all miscreants were in awe of his university curses covered in Bolognese sauce.

Fr. Mindi paid us a second visit, this time at the refectory. "What sort of a seminarian can do such a thing? What did he come here for? Does he want to become a priest? How did he enter the system? It is in your interests to denounce this character. I am sure he said something to somebody, criminals often do. Please, let me know. If this sort of behavior is left unpunished, we are all in big danger. This is the kind of person to set the whole place on fire." I wasn't turned on; neither were the majority of the boys, who felt that Mindi deserved every dose of pain he got.

The rector, as somber as a judge with piles, asked us after a day to surrender the culprit. Like Mindi, he believed that somebody had heard something or seen something or smelled something. He hinted that somebody might have a grudge against the bursar, but that the manner in which he had expressed himself was beastly and unworthy of somebody destined for the altar. He laid on the syrup: "Come and talk to us if you have a problem. We are here for you. Without you we would not be here. This is a family, and if one family member hurts, the whole family suffers. Remember, one rotten orange can corrupt the whole basket. If you know anything, tell your spiritual director, or slip a piece of paper under my door. Don't let anyone see you. I assure you: nobody will be penalized for giving us the necessary information.

And if anyone threatens you, trying to keep your mouth shut, come directly to me and he will be dealt with." I had heard all this in my former life. It left me cold.

Four days after the attack, amidst a cloud of speculation, Fr. Mindi announced, rather triumphantly, that he had caught the culprits. The staff was divided. Mindi wanted three bully boys expelled with immediate effect. Others wanted the boys punished but given a chance to continue with their education. The skeptics questioned the manner of the discovery, because they found it too plausible: somebody commits a crime, names are anonymously given on a piece of paper and heads roll.

Lwendo and his classmates were in an uproar. They went around saying that a Bushman was responsible for betraying the trio to the staff. There were threats against the Bushman and vows to squeeze them till they squealed, but when one of the trio was expelled and the other two were suspended for a fortnight, the furor died down.

So much for justice. I never succeeded in finding out who the smart Bushman was who had punished the bullies by saddling them with responsibility for the crime. I didn't mind either. My neighbor in the dorm said that I often laughed in my sleep.

Books took over. It was bound to happen anyway. Life was too regimented and too boring. Sports were dull, picking up their only blast of annual excitement during inter-house competitions. The dominance of church activities and liturgy was generally asphyxiating. As others caved in to total submission or to sporadic fits of bravado, I turned to books. I was intrigued by the secret universe under the dust-laden covers and thrilled by the endless morsels one could extract from the most unlikely volumes. Between some very dull covers were the most spectacular wars, adventures, murders, love affairs and characters, whole terrae incognitae to explore.

Given the faking, the pretense and the fear that stool pigeons were lurking everywhere, collecting news, marking every critical word one said, books offered a reliable escape route into a safer reality crammed with fantasy and ideas.

As in most dictatorships, secular books were unpopular in the seminary; they were considered subversive. Good seminarians distrusted such books, because they contained demons that made you critical of the good fathers and of Mother Church. They made you rebellious and arrogant, deaf to your vocation. They gave you a mind of your own and made you ask the wrong questions.

I remembered World War II and the men Grandpa had conscripted. I spent days looking through war records to see if the local contribution had been recorded. All I learned was that Africans had died in that war. There was nothing specific about the Ugandan contribution to the effort. The slaughter of tens of millions of people in Europe just nineteen years after the end of World War I, plus the deaths of the twenty million who had succumbed to the Spanish flu soon after, apparently did not include blacks and seemed another of the whitewashed versions of modern civilization sold to us here. It was as lopsided as the gloss the Church put on the carnage of the Crusades, and on all the other Church wars right up to our own Religious Wars at the turn of the century.

Fr. Kaanders gradually began to make sense to me. He had spent a good part of his youth fighting polygamy to uphold standards he believed were universal and crucial, and had ended up almost dead from exhaustion and sleeping sickness. It was while in the grip of death that he had realized the forlornness of his attempts, the stupidity of his sacrifice and the impracticability of putting the clock forward thousands of hours. Wisely, he decided to freeze the clock and let time take care of itself. I would do the same. I would embrace death in a timeless hold, look it in the face and turn it into an ally. I was delighted. I ruminated on my discovery for days.

It was on one such woolgathering day that Fr. Mindi caught me reading during prayer time. In fact, the bell had just rung. The boys had just started marching to the chapel, and I think he was smarting to get somebody. I hadn't moved quickly enough or shown any sign that I would. He had already put the painting job behind him and had reverted to spying and stalking around the compound with a vengeance, as if to say he would not be forced to change by a bunch of snotty boys. Now he stood before me, the cassock making him look taller than he really was.

At the end of the morning I went to his office for my punishment. Music was playing in his cozy little office, the pop sound fluttering in the background like butterflies on a windowpane. I thought about Sr. Bison and wondered whether this was the music he played as she made her maddening fucking sounds. All the furniture was in good order, covered with clean cloths to avoid staining. I lay down to take my punishment. The hairy carpet tickled my fingers and took me back to the infernal carpet at the pagoda.

I got my three on "government meat." The memory of my painting job anesthetized me totally. I was struck by the fact that this man had learned nothing. He was knowledge itself, thus ineducable. I thanked him for punishing me with a docile, contrite look on my face. His eyes lit up.

"Good boy. You are very quiet, very humble, and you never cause trouble. I am sure that one day you will make a very good priest." I could hardly believe what was coming out of the mouth of this Urban University alumnus, but I politely said, "Thank you, Father."

The main topic of conversation among us was still food: it was becoming worse. The posho was half-cooked, or simply bad, made as it was from wormy maize flour bought in bulk and stored for too long. The beans were weevilled and hardly responded to the cajoling of boiler fire. They remained hard and indigestible, and made us fart like hippos. The staff constantly complained about ill-mannered boys who farted in church, in class and in the hallways. Served them right. Truancy increased, and the price of black-market pawpaws, sugarcane and pancakes skyrocketed.

The drought came, turned the grass from green to gold, terrorized our water supply and made the smuggling in of foodstuffs a little easier. As we trekked the one kilometer down to the seminary well with our buckets, basins and jerry cans, the experts slipped into the bushes to meet waiting vendors. Some smuggled the contraband home inside their water containers. Others hid the stuff in secret places and fetched it during supper time or night study. That was how the unlucky ones fell into Fr. Mindi's net.

There were two expulsions, one from Sing-Sing, one from Mecca. They were accompanied by a plethora of curses aimed at Fr. Mindi. There were idle threats to beat him up and set fire to the garage in order to punish the whole staff. Nothing of the kind happened, de-

spite the genuine belief that all our suffering was the main responsibility of Fr. Mindi, the seminary bursar, embezzler and torturer.

Since the finances of the seminary were a mystery to me, my
main concern was to discourage Fr. Mindi from spying and persecut-
ing black-market food traffickers. If he stopped getting in our way,
well, I felt we could let him do his own thing, but the man was like a
demon, driven with the blind insistence of a psychopath. The only way
to deal with him was on his own terms.

For a librarian, stalking a priest was as simple as pie. The library
was at the end of the office block. I could always go along the offices and see which priest was in or out. I was free to go to the fathers'
residences, even those behind the offices, in fictitious pursuit of Fr.
Kaanders. I knew for sure that Mindi's favorite spying hour was from
nine to ten in the evening, when every seminarian had to be in class for
the night study. It was actually the safest time to tackle him, with little
chance of unexpected intervention.

There was a network of paths through the football fields behind
Sing-Sing which led to idle, overgrown seminary land, all the way
down the valley, into the forest, up to the main road and the villages
beyond. The main road was one kilometer away; one part of it led to
Jinja Diocese, the theater of Kaanders' old nightmares, the other to
Kampala Archdiocese, under whose wing the seminary was. Fr. Mindi
had worked in the archdiocese for six years before getting posted here.
He had had less trouble from archdiocesan polygamists, who, unlike
their die-hard counterparts in Jinja Diocese, kept quiet about their second or third wives. His scourge had been bold women who, fired by his
good looks and his football prowess, openly solicited him.

Now, in the midst of the drought, Mindi was always out, enjoying the cool night air while waiting for his prey. These nocturnal walks
reminded him of parish work, which had entailed waking up at night
to go and give last sacraments to dying parishioners. Fr. Mindi was
fiercely proud of his profession, and he firmly believed that priesthood
was the noblest profession on earth. He had more or less worked out
the next ten years of his career. He envisaged four more years here,
after which he would return to the parish, grow maize and beans to sell
and make enough money to live a comfortable life independent of
parish funds. In his spare time, he would coach the parish football team
and drive it slowly to the top of the interparish league. He regularly

fantasized about his shambas, watching the maize grow and the bean leaves turn from green to gold. He dreamed of bumper crops and rich financial rewards.

His current thoughts, however, were rudely interrupted by sounds emanating from the other side of the pine fence, a stone's throw away from the acacia trees. He heard a hiss and wondered whether it was a snake. The second hiss was human, deliberate, insolent. This was something new: truants always ran away from him and never drew his attention. Who could this person be? The night watchman, whom he had chastised for letting his car get vandalized? Yes, he had even threatened the man with dismissal if he did not stop sleeping instead of keeping watch. The next sound was a dog whistle. Somebody was whistling at him as though he were a dog! He was nobody's dog. Not here, not even in Italy. He stopped and weighed the temptation to jump over the fence and tackle this bastard from the air in one lithe move. Much to his surprise, the whistler shook a pine tree to make his position clear. Having decided to jump, Fr. Mindi moved closer. He raised his head above the fence to see what was really going on, and to make sure there was a safe landing. He sensed the obnoxious stench too late.

"Oh, my God!" he said as the two-day-old parcel burst open in his face. A wet slapping sound suffocated the second and longer exclamation. A soggy mass covered his face, then dripped down his throat, the front of his shirt and on to his trousers. Instinctively, his hand went to his face and got messed up. He plucked pine needles and frantically rubbed his face and clothes. He ran wildly to the back of the chapel and all the way to the refectory, but the aluminum water tanks were empty. He careered downhill to the piggery and used the drinking water in the pig troughs to wash. The stench would not go away. He tried to vomit, but only strings of bile dropped from his mouth. He went up the hill again and finally sneaked into his bedroom via the back door. The stench filled the room. He sprayed himself and the room with deodorant and went about cleaning the mess properly.

Fr. Mindi wasn't the first dictator to be blinded by his own sense of unquestionable power into making the wrong diagnosis of a critical situation. He could not break through the membrane of despotic outrage to come to the root of the problem. He believed that the attack was an act of hate, which was wrong. It was a lesson in not striking out in anger. The attack had been coldly calculated and executed, the way proper punishment should be, but swollen with his sense of power and self-righteousness, Mindi could not see that. His priestly oils kept his vision glazed and served to infuse him with paranoia. He firmly believed that a mad seminarian was out to kill him. He remembered the shock of his father's poisoning. His body had turned soot-black in death. Fr. Mindi could now see it floating in front of his eyes, black shit oozing out of its rear. The idea came to him that death by poisoning might be a hereditary curse cast onto his family by some unknown individual. If so, he was next in line. This really shook him up. He was not ready to die so miserably. He suddenly felt very exposed, very unsafe. For the first time since his return from Rome and his ordination, he felt that he could not win. How was he supposed to fight this faceless enemy? How was he supposed to tell his fellow brothers in the priesthood what had happened to him? And what would they make of it? Were they training psychos or diocesan priests?

Fr. Mindi reported in sick for a few days, and ultimately left the campus for a week. There were rumors that he had an ulcer; later ones claimed that he had asked for a transfer. He returned to the seminary looking sick, hardly able to drum up even a brittle arrogance. He hated the boys. He hated the seminary. He hated his secret tormentor. Boys remarked that he had stopped spying and prowling. Another rumor circulated that he had purchased three huge dogs to bolster the security of the seminary. The most interesting part of all this was that nobody knew why the bursar-cum-discipline master had decided to neglect his responsibilities. The whole turnaround was so unexpected that nobody dared celebrate openly. There was a feeling that his withdrawal was a trick, a ruse to draw rule-breakers out, but why had the bursar taken to travelling so much? Why was he staying in his office most of the time when he *was* around? Why was he no longer attending communal mass? The boys smelled a rat.

Censorship was firmly in place. Our letters were opened and read before we received them. When we wrote letters, we put them in unsealed envelopes for the rector to read before he sealed and posted them. We were allowed to write letters only on the weekend, and it was against the rules to post them ourselves.

One evening, I got a message that the rector wanted to see me. My heart palpitated. Was the game up? Had somebody really seen me executing the second attack? For sure I did not care about the seminary, but I did not want to be dismissed mid-term. I wanted to go at the end of the year after taking the national certificate examinations. Ah, Lusanani might have written. If so, what was I going to tell the rector? What clever lie was going to save me? Trepidation took over.

"You look scared," the rector said before I could even open my mouth. "Did you do something wrong?"

"No, Father, but . . ."

"But what?" He was in a talkative mood tonight despite all the paperwork strewn on his desk. There was a pile of open letters, and I wondered why this man was going through our mail. Did he really believe that it was wrong for boys of our age to communicate with girls? Did he really believe that ordained virgins made the best priests? What did those people in Rome think they were doing, giving such directives? Here was a man approaching middle age, quite a likeable fellow with a good sense of humor, reading our mail like a dirty old man in search of cheap titillation. He always told us funny little stories, and we liked him for that. Now I wondered whether he did not garner some ideas from our letters. "Have you got something on your conscience?" he asked, dramatically raising his brows.

"Don't we all?" I bravely said. "I lied to somebody yesterday. I took a new exercise book from his desk and used it without telling him. He asked who had taken his book, and I said I did not know. I replaced the book in the evening, but I could not confess to him what I had done because of his temper." This was pure bullshit, but plausible bullshit in our situation. This was the kind of calculated lie we told in the confessional. We usually first discussed among ourselves the kinds of sins to confess: lying, calling others names, using other people's things without permission . . . Now I was looking for an opening, baiting him with my putative frankness.

"How do you like your job in the library?"

Relieved, but also aware that he was looking for an opening, I said, "I like it very much. My grades have improved greatly since taking the job."

"Any problems?"

"Sometimes we cannot trace who steals our books."

"Have you done your best to plug all the holes?"

"The most annoying thing is when some boys steal books borrowed by others."

"I guess you hear a lot of things in the library."

"Sometimes."

"Did you hear about the terrible thing that happened to Fr. Mindi?"

"Yes, the vandalization of his car was a shame to all of us aspiring to become priests."

"I did not mean that. I meant what happened to him recently."

"No. Yes. I heard he has got an ulcer."

"Didn't you hear about the attack?"

"No, Father. What attack?"

"Haven't you heard anybody talking about it?"

"No, everyone is talking about the ulcer and how the bursar must be working too hard."

"I am not talking about ulcers. I am talking about a physical attack."

"No, Father, I haven't heard anything to that effect. Fathers are above such things."

"In our day, lawbreakers used to brag about their exploits. That was how they got caught. Are you sure that you have heard nobody bragging about teaching Fr. Mindi a lesson? Don't think I am not aware that some boys don't like the bursar."

"I have not heard anything, Father. But I am sure the culprits will get caught. Last time the net got them. This time too they will not escape."

The rector seemed to think that my answers were too glib. He also knew that I knew that he did not know who had carried out the attack. He resented the fact that he could do nothing to extract a clean confession from me or from anybody else.

"If you hear anything, come and tell me. This kind of appalling behavior cannot be allowed to go on. The seminary cannot be allowed to degenerate into anarchy like some secular school. This is in your interests too. If priests get attacked, seminarians will be attacked as well. And if such people escape, what kind of priests will they make? Who would want to serve in the same parish with them?"

I wanted to say that every newcomer had been the subject of

physical attacks for a whole year, and had been forced to jerk off at two or three in the morning at one time or other when the priests were in bed enjoying wet dreams. I wanted to say that maybe a priest getting attacked was just a case of chickens coming home to roost. I was aware that I could not say that without getting expelled. I pitied the man for underestimating me. I was nobody's stool pigeon.

"Oh, some other matter," he said, showing me the letter I had written to Aunt Lwandeka. "Why did you seal this letter? Is it a bad letter?"

"No, Father. I just forgot. I must have been absentminded at the time. The addressee is my maternal aunt. There is nothing bad or secretive in the letter."

"You forgot? Do you often forget to post your letters through the right channels?"

"No, Father."

"What is in this one?"

"Amin's men arrested her once and she gets nightmares about them. I wrote to advise her to say novenas to St. Jude Thaddeus."

"Should I open it?"

"You are welcome," I said, putting on a brave face. There was nothing in it about the notorious St. Jude Thaddeus, but I took my chances.

"All right, you can go. But if you hear anything, don't hesitate to inform me. I am relying on you, son."

"I will do my best, Father," I said as a way of telling him to cut out the father-son bullshit.

I was very relieved. Thank God it was not a letter from Lusanani. How would I have explained my relationship with a married Muslim girl in this most Catholic of places?

Starved of rumors which could give us a clue as to what was going on with the bursar-cum-discipline master, the boys started targeting individual staff members. They asked them leading questions during lessons. The black priests, veterans at this kind of trickery, left us high and dry. I interpreted that as a sign of solidarity with their suffering colleague. It was also revenge on us, for surely they knew that whoever had punished Fr. Mindi had come from within our fakely smiling, open-faced ranks.

It was Fr. Kaanders who came to our rescue. After the usual *bon/mauvais/méchant* nonsense, when his mind was clear of its formidable fogs, boys lurched in and asked him what was going on. After much sweeping back of the few strands of hair on top of his domed head, he said, "Oh boy, boy, boy . . . Father Mean-dee is going away, boys." Naturally, there was an inquiry as to where the bursar was going. After a series of "Oh boy, boy, boy"s, he informed us that Mindi had been transferred to the parish. What intrigued me was that the old man seemed to be in some anguish over the question. I kept wondering whether he had learned the details of the grisly contents of that plastic bag and was just wondering who among us had planned and executed the attack. We tried to ask him who was going to replace the bursar, but he would not tell us.

A week later, the vicar general paid us a surprise visit. He was a tall, fat man with a hanging belly, large buttocks and a clumsy gait. He spoke too quickly, disguising a lisp and a stammer, and it was hard to hear what he had to say. Despite his less than satisfactory locution, he loved the sound of his own voice. He slapped us with a fifty-minute sermon, to which we listened woodenly and throughout which Kaanders slept soundly. We were inundated with the same drivel about our vocation and what it meant to be a priest, how special we were, how we had to preserve our honor and the like. Many of us agreed that the vicar general had sweet, albeit empty, words to say, but we were irked that our breakfast had been terrible—thin, wormy porridge with dry bread—while the staff had feasted on goodies that had filled the corridor with wonderful smells. Here, the importance of a visitor was gauged by the changes his presence effected on our table. When the bishop came, the bursar gave us the best meals, because the big man often came to look in on what we ate. We wondered if he was dumb enough to believe that what he saw us eating was what we usually ate or if he just wanted to see whether we were grateful for not eating the usual hog feed. This guy, though, had not bothered to look at what we were being fed, and for that reason most of us did not care a damn about the wise words he had to say in his lispy, stammering sermon. The chapel came alive only once, when he failed to wrestle down the word "boss" and slid precariously: "Jesuth is the both, I-I mean the bosh, er, th-the boss of this inshtitution." After that he spoke very slowly. We were overjoyed when the mass ended.

During such visits, the priests were also on their best behavior, punctually holding mass, wearing their cassocks everywhere, abstaining from smoking in public and putting on a show of being the most docile and most exemplary priests in the whole diocese. They had personal files at the diocesan headquarters which they wanted to keep as clean as possible, because the cleaner the file, the better the chances of being posted in the best parishes.

The vicar general disappeared after mass and left incognito. Eventually we learned that Fr. Mindi had been transferred. The big man had come to meet the staff and introduce the name of the new bursar because, being a controversial move, it needed a bit of sugarcoating. All we learned was that a white missionary was coming to replace Fr. Mindi.

For a while there was feasting, and for the first time the boys looked cheerful. There were no more spyings, no more police checks, no more fear of lurking stool pigeons. The truants enjoyed the time of their life. Now their contacts came and brought the contraband near the football fields behind Sing-Sing and traded pawpaws, sugarcanes and anything else they had. This was what I had intended to happen, and I was happy that it had worked. A lot of food was being thrown away now, the euphoria of wonderful meals in the offing sharpening the rebellious edge even in the truly docile.

I watched everything from a distance, wondering why the night watchman and the priests were letting things rip. At the height of the frenzy, I saw a symbolically violent act taking place one hot afternoon. Somebody had somehow procured an enlarged picture of Fr. Mindi, pasted it on manila paper and nailed it onto a tree trunk. A group of boys with sticks were hurling accusations at it and beating it. I left after the face had become mere bits of torn paper. The euphoria of change had stirred pools of reservation, even misgiving, in the pit of my stomach. What would happen to all this emotion if the new man failed to deliver? I did not want to speculate too much. I felt I would cross that bridge when I came to it. So far, the only reflection in the water coursing under the bridge of change was the dull, disappearing image of the former bursar, who seemed to sleep by day and pack at night.

∎ ∎ ∎

Fr. Mindi's replacement was Fr. Gilles Lageau, a French Canadian missionary from Quebec. Far from being the stereotypical bearded greaseball missionary, Fr. Lageau was a good-looking, straight-nosed, blue-eyed man with a keen awareness of his looks, his power, his influence and his fail-safe mission. He arrived with a decent suntan, which did nothing to disguise his ruddy complexion and matched his reddish hair and the golden fluff on his thick, meaty arms. One could detect in his walk the swagger of American silver-screen heroes. The fluid movement of his well-tended body was a lucid announcement of naked power, in whose perquisites every optimistic seminarian hoped to share. If the priest had arrived looking faded and woebegone, with the years trickling down his face, every seminarian would have been disappointed, but the combination of American power and French arrogance made the man seem the personification of the anti-lethargy cure everyone had been hoping for. His reputation had travelled far ahead of him. By the time he arrived, we knew that he was a financial whiz kid who had all the tools to fish us out of the quagmires of poverty, malnourishment and the opportunistic diseases that fed off underdevelopment. This made him an instant hero, and his arrival an event awaited with the anxiety of a conquering messiah.

The man was unusual, but so were the circumstances in which he came. The era of white missionaries had ended. They had started the Church in Uganda almost one hundred years ago. Before disappearing, they had cultivated a local Church and a local clergy in most dioceses, except Jinja Diocese, where the die-hard polygamist culture held sway and stopped people from sending their offspring into the barren heartlands of priesthood and nunhood. The indigenous Church they started expanded very quickly. By the time they started leaving or dying, the Church had an indigenous archbishop, later a cardinal, many bishops and the full administrative cadre that manned the Catholic Church. The missionary element eventually dwindled, depleted by death and the demise of the Church in Europe. There was, in fact, a genuine fear among conservative missionaries that black people might one day rise and lead some of the formerly purely white missionary organizations, because most of the work done now was in Africa and vocations in Europe were almost gone.

At the moment, some of those organizations had their own local seminaries. The diocesan seminaries were all under the leadership of indigenous priests, with the help of a white missionary here and there. Whenever a white missionary left, he was generally not replaced, because there was no one to replace him with. A white missionary replacing an indigenous priest was a rare occurrence. However, Lageau was anything but ordinary.

Lageau's instant heroism was rooted in the fact that we, the seminarians, the downtrodden, believed that this new and energetic white man was going to offer a direct challenge to the black priests and, with his enormous zest, pull them toward a total revision of the administrative, financial and liturgical system. There was a lot of speculation as to Lageau's motives for coming here. Some thought he had been sent as punishment for some big mistake, for, they reasoned, nobody could willingly leave the beautiful plains of Quebec for our little hill. Others said that Lageau had requested the transfer himself because he needed a challenge. As a corporate raider, he needed a sagging company to transform into a soaring eagle in order to soothe his ego. The third theory was that Lageau was an ombudsman sent by Rome and other financiers to investigate corruption inside the diocese and in the seminary system before making recommendations for change. There were also those who said Lageau was a cowboy in search of adventure, and that as soon as he got bored he would move on. The little we knew was that he had worked in parts of Asia and Latin America and was now in Africa. Whatever the truth was, Lageau had moved onto the scene in a big way and had become the dominant force in our little universe.

At long last we heard from official channels that Fr. Lageau had come to handle the seminary's purse strings. There was singing and dancing in our streets, and especially in the open spaces between the beds in the dorms. Armpits ran with sweat as adolescent anticipation of fabulous meals got everyone excited. No more rotten beans. No more maggoty maize meals. No more half-cooked rice on Sundays. Come in, *matooke*—plantain—and meat. Come in, sweet potatoes and fish. Come in, fantastic meals all week long. What wouldn't this rich North American do in this cheap-priced land of ours!

Food was the most important element in our secluded environment. We ate to live and to void our bodies of redundant desires. We went to bed with food on our minds and awoke the same way. How we envied the priests their daily treat and their Sunday banquets! The nuns cooked for the priests with all their hearts and all their throttled sex drives. They indulged the priests as they would a super-lover, somebody they wished to drive to new levels of erotic madness by baiting him with condimented recipes that inflamed every zone of his body. In those days, priesthood was equated with good food. It was something worth suffering for. It was at table that one realized how words were divorced from reality: there was a lot of talk around the theme of equality, but those sweet words disappeared in a miasma of pig food when the bell rang for our lunch. I, for one, wasn't too badly off, not after blackmailing my way into priestly leftovers, but the contrast was staggering nonetheless, especially on those days when I didn't get any.

At times I felt I was living within the covers of certain books. I was glad I had not been selfish. I could have sat back, munched my morsels and done nothing about the Mindi menace, but I had done all I could, as if I were one of those worst hit by the food crisis. No wonder I walked around with the feeling that the whole seminary owed me: after all, it had been my parcels that had, in part, brought about the arrival of the French Canadian millionaire who was going to revolutionize everything as we knew it. I had the feeling that good things always came wrapped in mysterious parcels.

Fr. Kaanders was very excited by the arrival of Fr. Lageau. The macho man in him peeped through his old liver-spotted skin, and his dull eyes lit up. He now walked with a twitch in his step and pulled his trousers up to his belly button in an almost showy fashion. The arrival of Fr. Lageau energized him. It gave him a feeling of being young again and of going into battle to tackle ancient problems. With a young man at his side, he would not be alone in his whiteness. He would have someone to drink a glass of wine with and talk to about the other side of the world.

Fr. Gilles Lageau looked very much like Sean Connery portraying James Bond. Beside him Kaanders resembled a panhandler soliciting pin money from a hunky Californian windsurfer. Straw-haired, arthritic, incontinent and bad-toothed, Kaanders could hardly keep up with the flashy North American. It became clear from the beginning that if any kind of relationship was going to exist between the two, it would be up to Kaanders to sustain it. We watched the two white men with almost anthropological fascination. The contradictions of the Western world held us spellbound, at least for some time.

Both priestly and seminarian narcissism generally found an outlet in a keen interest in material goods. The cars, the clothes and the furniture the staff had were analyzed to the last atom for information pertaining to quality, manufacturer, cost and durability. Lageau increased this activity. He boasted about his golden Rado watch ("the champion of chronometers"), which, putatively, lost only one second in ten years. Such Western reliability! Such Western precision! Wags spent time calculating the mountains of foodstuffs the watch alone could buy for the two hundred boys on campus. Others tried to figure out where Lageau bought his short-sleeved pastel shirts and the pastel trousers he wore. A boy helping in his office finally divulged the secret that Lageau wore French clothes, exclusively. Much was made of the expensive belts, checked socks and genuine leather open-toed sandals he wore in class. There were bets as to whether he possessed a cassock or not, for he and Kaanders never wore those cumbersome things, not even when the bishop visited.

The sudden appearance of this flamboyant man in the midst of poverty-stricken souls struck a blow for the rich: we developed a finely tuned idealization of them, accompanied by a deliberate transfusion of generosity into their veins and a conscious defeatist effort to justify or overlook their shortcomings. Few thought it strange that a man in his forties was openly boasting about his watch, coming as he was from a region where such watches were common; we felt that such little faults were the fleas on an otherwise powerful dog.

Local politics were also at work: you never bit the hand that fed you, or was most likely to feed you. Consequently, there was much turning of the other cheek and much patience in the hope that everything would turn out right in the end. After all, didn't rivers flow toward the areas of least resistance? This force, this Western river coursing through our midst, was more likely to take up our burdens if we laid ourselves at its feet.

Ignorance was another ingredient in this concoction. There was little real-life knowledge about how the West, or the rich, carved out chunks of wealth for themselves. Hardly any of us knew how the magical Western economic machine, personified by this man, operated. The tendency was to glorify the unknown. So the Westerners, in this case Lageau, were glorified to a sickening degree at times. Most of us believed that Lageau was our God-sent conduit to the benefactors in the West. The doors he could open! The dreams he could fulfill! Fantasy perquisites ranged from pocket money to quality consumer goods to good meals, to begin with. From experience we knew that priests who had benefactors enjoyed a better standard of living than those who did not. They had decent cars, cash to spend and nice clothes. Occasionally, they also went for holidays abroad. Therefore, the magical hundred-percent-compensation scheme for having left both mother and father to follow Jesus flashed whenever Lageau's blue eyes appeared.

A plethora of guessing games went on for quite some time. The priests were cautious; we were optimistic. Didn't good things come to those who waited? A little more patience would certainly not kill us. And it surely didn't, but neither did it bear the envisaged fruits.

Lageau demonstrated his aristocratic credentials in good time: he was impervious to opinion, anybody's opinion. Tears of anguish flowed, falling into shards of dashed idealistic dreams. We felt a painful reluctance to revise our attitudes, our dreams and our scanty inventory of knowledge. No one wanted to admit that they had been wrong in expecting too much, for surely what could be too much for one who operated in a charmed circle of money power like Lageau? But reality had to be faced: Lageau said, "Some people think that there are money mines in Europe." The wink which followed that statement made hearts jerk with excruciating pain. If there were no money mines in Europe, where the fuck were they? Here? In Siberia? Or in heaven? Shouldn't he have said that money was not the problem but how to spend it? The wink, as we soon found out, had been a way of turning us into quasi conspirators, quasi confidants. He elucidated: "Priests come to me all the time begging for cars, hi-fis, money and benefactors." This was delivered in the oblique manner of an aside. In reality, it was a condiment to flavor the harsh mathematical dish he was serving us. He taught us mathematics. When no laughter came, he winked, screwed his finger against his temple and awaited peals of laughter. We were supposed to laugh at the naive, greedy, materialistic priests, but the laughter that came was both lopsided and painful, because everyone realized that we were not conspirators and that, if anything, we were laughing at ourselves.

A dull, heavy feeling akin to bean-weevil-inspired flatulence per-meated me and threatened to decapitate my keen interest in this man. All my feelers were out: this was my first encounter with somebody who had it all, and I wanted to learn as much as I could. I felt I had beaten Serenity to the finish line: I had come face-to-face with one of the "millionaires" he had met only in books. This was the first man to make me question the sense of power I had grown up with. In times of crisis, I always heard the cries of fifty babies in the background, re-minding me of how special I was, had been. At the seminary, I often thought I was in the wrong company, among toddlers Grandma and I had delivered. I felt I knew something priests didn't: I knew what to do at the hour life came into the world. Lageau was the first man to make me aware of another sort of power, a more devastating power that controlled millions of lives by remote control. I almost felt ashamed of myself: my former power lay in amniotic fluid and blood and the smells of birth. His power, however, glittered with the sharpness of silver and the richness of gold. It frightened me and held me hostage in its glare.

My faith in him, though, became dented very quickly: I have never been a man of faith. Weeks passed and the diet remained as re-volting as before. My view was that any new leader worth his salt seized the initiative quickly, effected changes, even if only cosmetic, and swung people onto his side. The principle remained that a dictator was only as bad as his successor, but Lageau showed no sign of im-proving things, which was both very strange and sickening. Where was the money? Had he come empty-handed? If so, what was the dif-ference between him and Mindi?

Just as discontent set in, Lageau seemed to divine the situation, and he deigned to ask what we thought about the seminary. I almost felt ashamed for having doubted the man's democratic credentials. Since I had been bred on tyranny, my belief that all authority con-tained in it the seeds of tyranny could be excused. I noticed that my co-seminarians were reluctant to open their mouths and speak up. I raised my hand, proud to be fearless. I went for the jugular. *"Mens sana in cor-pore sano,"* I said, quoting my Latin teacher. "My belief is that the bur-sar is aware of the deplorable food we eat every day. The beans are weevilled, tasteless and far from nourishing. The maggots in the maize flour have become very fat and look fatter on our plates. We would like to have better, more nourishing meals. We would like to have a more balanced diet. We would like the nuns to take more care with our food, especially on Sundays, when the rice is usually half-cooked and has pebbles in it. We would also request the bursar to buy the seminary a water pump to get water up the hill during the drought."

Lageau, clad in light blue attire, looked at me and narrowed his left eye to a slit. I felt a bit uncomfortable. He then raised his eyebrows, as James Bond does before setting off an explosion with a remote-control bomb activated by his wristwatch. The thunderclap followed soon after: "Do you think that money grows on trees or runs in gutters in Europe? Let me tell you this: your total school-fees contribution amounts to only eight percent of the annual budget. We pay the lion's share for your stay here. If anything, you should be grateful that budget cuts have not been effected over the years. I came here to work out a compromise deal between the seminary and its financiers and to make sure that the seminary does not close down for financial reasons. Thanks to sources in Europe, I cannot see that happening during your time."

I quaked. My knees went rubbery, and my armpits trickled with sweat. If I had not been backhanded and guava-switched for challenging authority before, I would have gone on to ask him what the fuck his flamboyance was all about. Europe, his financier friends and his wealth did not mean a crock of shit to us as long as we ate pig food. Good food was the least he could do for us. We could always fetch our own water—many of us had done that all our lives. But the food! I could feel public opinion turning against Lageau.

The news spread quickly. His attempts to solicit opinion from other classes were met with indifference. There was an element of local wisdom in it too: people who just talked for the hell of it were never respected, especially if boasting was part of their repertoire. Lageau was now being seen as an empty braggadocio who did not even have the decency to make good his boasts by at least rewarding us with good meals. Lageau's popularity sagged, and Kaanders, in his faded glories, regained his.

The immediate result of Lageau's revelation was to drive me deeper into the library. What did I need from these fake people? It struck me that one of the worst aspects of dependency was the deplorable company one had to keep. General Amin, whom I had neglected for a long time, suddenly surfaced like a leviathan. He still preached self-empowerment. I realized the importance of making my own money. I was happy it tied in well with Grandpa's exhortations that I become a lawyer, but maybe I would not be a lawyer and would instead raise turkeys and broiler chickens like Uncle Kawayida or brew liquor like Aunt Lwandeka. I was determined not to live like the priests. I was determined to beat dependency, and all the humiliations that came with it.

To be honest, I was one of Lageau's few detractors, for despite his apparent uselessness, many boys still admired him. In a defeatist kind of way, he was held high: He was at least richer than our clergy. He acted like a star. He enjoyed all the arrogance and the privilege many seminarians dreamed of exercizing on the lowly faithful after ordination.

"Look at our priests," Lwendo said to me. "Aren't they pathetic? Aren't they asking him to buy them cars? Aren't they asking him to get them rich benefactors?"

"Well . . ."

"They envy him his power, don't they? Lageau has repaired those lawnmowers which lay dead in the tool room. The seminary no longer spends money on electricians. How much can one person do?"

"I don't care how much the seminary spends on anything. As long as the food is terrible, it is all wasted money."

"I work with him. The electrical system is as good as new nowadays."

"You also admire his shouting as if everyone were deaf? Or is he deaf himself? Sometimes you hear him from a kilometer away, just asking for a hammer."

"We are a slow people: boys do not often react quickly enough to his demands. They should know better."

"I do not care for his manners or his fortune," I insisted.

"The problem with you is that you are just as bad as he is: both of you have got egos too big for your own good," Lwendo divined.

"My ego is not the problem. It is the glass-balled attitude of people around here. Have you noticed how quiet the black priests are when Lageau is around? It is as if they are afraid to make mistakes. They are like women who gladly let men bully them, waiting, in turn, to bully children."

Lageau had replaced Mindi as the patron of Vatican dormitory.

He was a fantastic volleyballer, and Lwendo pointed that out to me. "See how he has breathed life into volleyball, a game which was dead. It has become the second most popular sport. Imagine!"

I enjoyed watching a spectacular volleyball game, but I valued a good meal more.

"Look, the man does not spy on anybody. He lets us break the rules as much as we want."

"Ha, ha, ha," I said tersely.

"I wonder what really happened to Mindi, though. He lost steam too quickly. People don't change so suddenly."

"He was, er . . ." I stopped short. "Oh, maybe somebody put a knife to his throat and scared the goo out of him. The same might happen to Lageau if he does not stop boasting emptily as if he owned the whole of Europe."

"Nonsense. Nobody can touch him. Where will they find him? I seem to detect double standards here. You are sore because a white man is boasting, but let me ask you what you did when Mindi was lording it over us?" He laughed.

"I hid behind a fence and . . ." I almost said it.

"Hiding, hiding, hiding. You did nothing special. All we seem to do is hide."

I gave up.

My attention had started wandering homeward. A loyal shitter kept me informed about developments there. He wrote describing Serenity's old craze: Muhammad Ali fights. Serenity was spellbound by his hero's comebacks. The Rumble in the Jungle fight had taken place in Zaire. Ali had become world champion again, and Serenity could not stop praising him.

On fight nights, Serenity hardly slept at all. He woke up after midnight and waited in the sitting room, watching previews and interviews till four in the morning, when the fight started. He marveled at Ali's generosity and outspokenness but worried about his health. Padlock was sick to death of Serenity's daily boxing monologues.

I had done my best to avoid Serenity and his Padlock, but events in the Catholic world finally brought us together. One Sunday morning, when Lageau had become just one of the main actors on our center stage, the rector broke news which had already whipped Catholics across the country into a frenzy. He announced to placid-faced seminarians, most of whom were thinking about the pig food awaiting them at lunch, that the Holy Father had declared 1975 a Holy Year and called upon Catholics all over the world to join a pilgrimage to Rome and the Holy Land. The rector, who had already found a sponsor and was going to represent the seminary, explained that the Holy Year was announced once every twenty-five years. He promised to offer special prayers for us during his pilgrimage. As if most of us cared. Registration of potential pilgrims had already started in every parish, and the rector asked us to pray for the archbishop and for all those involved in organizing the pilgrimage to do a good job. Big deal.

In order to limit discrimination, bribery and foul play, every diocese had been allocated a quota of pilgrims. Chances were good for the rich from poor parishes, because most peasant farmers and civil servants could not pay for the journey and didn't bother to register. Serenity registered himself, and his chances were good. Padlock wanted to go too, but her efforts ran into trouble because one had to register in one's parish of birth, and only one person per family could register in each parish: Mbale, her younger brother, had already registered in theirs. Her situation was further complicated by the fact that even if she managed to secure a place, there was no way Serenity could finance her journey as well as his own without filing for bankruptcy.

Padlock dreamed of being the first person in her family to kiss the hand of the pope, to be pictured with the Holy Father, to step on Holy Land, and to touch and taste and feel the soil Father Abraham, Joseph, Mother Mary and Jesus Christ had walked on. She wanted to be the first in her family to breathe the air that had carried inspiration to the authors of the Holy Book, but once again Mbale seemed about to sabotage her plans and poison her dreams.

Padlock's mood swings came back with a vicious bite. She brooded and filled the house with the stench of her depression. She felt like a bobbin trapped inside its slot, unable to get out unless somebody decided to remove it. She had attacks of hyperventilation. She feared she was about to burst or explode. She remembered the bitter prayers and fasting she had offered at Mbale's home soon after being regurgitated from the convent. She wanted to fling herself on the cold floor and claw it with her fingers till the nails bled. She could not now go into voluntary solitary confinement and offer novenas, because she had a family to lead. She put her arms on her chest and entrusted her burdens to God. In the meantime, she hammered the shitters with guava switches whenever they transgressed, and put Serenity on emotional tenterhooks.

Serenity was pinned firmly by the horns of a dilemma. On the one hand, he wanted to give the mother of his children a chance, because he knew how much it meant to her. On the other hand, he wanted to surprise his wife's aunt with a gift all her former lovers could not: he wanted to fly her to Rome and Jerusalem and tattoo his name forever in her heart. Serenity had insomnia attacks. He tossed and turned in bed. He listened to the sounds of the night and became infuriated that dogs howled so much when mating. He felt disgusted with his financial impotence and his inability to please both his wife and her aunt. He got out of bed and consulted his library. He revisited Godot and other characters, wondering what they would have done in his predicament. He got angry that Muhammad Ali could have so much money, when he, a loyal fan, was writhing on the torture rack of poverty, unable to exploit incoming chances. Serenity was wrapped in his reveries for weeks, sauntering through life with dreams cooing on one side and reality heckling on the other.

Serenity's sisters, Tiida and Nakatu, had in the meantime kicked up a storm of controversy in the village. Largely uninterested in Catholicism, they had no ambitions for themselves; but in a bid to turn the tables on all families in the village, especially the formidable Stefanos, they had decided that Grandpa should go to Rome. Both women's Muslim husbands had promised to contribute to the pilgrimage fund, and so had Uncle Kawayida, who was doing very well in business. Grandpa's chances of securing a place were good, for the local people were generally poor and places were left over after the initial registration heat had died down.

Tiida and Dr. Ssali had won their battle with the Conversion Committee about a year earlier. They had been awarded an oily-white Peugeot, which was washed daily and looked after like the sole remnant of an endangered species. Tiida enjoyed being chauffeured to important meetings in the car because it was new and elegant, and also because the leathery smell of its cool gray upholstery imbued her with the heady feeling that she was as tough as leather. One day her husband drove her to Serenity's home during his lunch break. She stepped out of the car full of the leather smell, feeling that her opposition had virtually no chance. Her mission was to pressure Serenity into contributing to Grandpa's pilgrimage fund. She could have met him at the office, but she had decided that her larger-than-life presence in the pagoda would be the best way to clinch a resounding victory.

As Tiida surveyed the pagoda, with the chaotic events of the Indian exodus bubbling at the back of her mind, she felt proud that her family had done well. Here was Serenity, or Mpanama, as she fondly remembered him in his short-trousered, tall-women-accosting days, in a house built by Indians which was indeed a far cry from the obscurity of his bachelor cottage. Here he was in the middle of the city, abreast with new developments and furthering his ambitions. The postal union move had been a very brilliant maneuver, she conceded. At one time when they were growing up, she had worried that Serenity was too sleepy to come to much in life. She had feared that he would end up poor, with patches in his trousers and debts up to his neck, simply because he didn't seem smart enough to put winning moves together; but now, after all those years and all the changes in the fortunes of the family, she felt that they were better off than the Stefanos. Here were father and son about to go to Rome, and Kawayida and she both owning vehicles, and Serenity involved in the leadership of the Postal Workers' Union. The Stefanos were now a family of the past. Old man Stefano was battling the ravages of a stroke that had left him paralyzed on one side. The star of the scions of the Stefano family had stopped rising.

Aunt Tiida knew that Serenity did not espouse this kind of family rivalry, but she was ready to work on him, to stir guilt in his heart and make it clear that he owed his father this last favor as a show of gratitude for all he had done for him. She would remind him of the land Grandpa had donated for him to built his bachelor cottage, and the role the old man had played in organizing his wedding. She felt that she had Mpanama in her grip. She had left nothing to chance. It was the reason she had come to neutralize his wife and pin her down in her pagoda. This village girl, whose parents were saved from the terrors of a rotten roof by her brother, could not defeat Tiida. She was ready to put Padlock in her place—at the bottom of the pile, where she belonged.

Like most people who have just acquired new status symbols, Tiida believed that the brand-new Peugeot had given her a sharper edge in relation to everybody else, and it was true that the village girl her brother had married had nothing in her possession with which to counter the glitter of the French-made machine. It looked very unlikely that Serenity would ever buy himself a new car. Not with so many children, not with so much responsibility. All this made Tiida feel high up in the air.

What she did not know was that Padlock had not changed over the years. She still was indifferent to material goods, she still felt utter contempt for shamefully acquired possessions, and anybody who exchanged his foreskin and his religion for some spray-painted piece of metal was utterly despicable in her eyes. In her scheme of things, the Peugeot had been acquired from the Devil, by devilish means, and its owners deserved no respect and would never get any from her, least of all in her own house.

Padlock greeted Tiida with insulting politeness, as though she were a lunatic to be handled with great care. She played the cowed village girl in the presence of visiting royalty. She blocked avenues of conversation with terse, very polite replies. She retreated to her bridal tactics of unapproachable gentility, which left Tiida stranded and looking for ways of lifting the blockade. Tiida was not intimidated— she rarely was—but she felt embattled, confused, unable to operate in these icy conditions. There was a kink in her cable which blocked the flow of her power, her charisma, her ability to stun. This was not the kind of woman who normally fazed her. On the contrary, it was only richer women, more elegant ladies or younger sophisticated girls who made her heart pump, and even then she fought back. The strange thing was that she suddenly felt as if she had done something wrong in the past for which she was paying now, but in her living memory she felt she had never double-crossed her brother's wife. In fact, she was one of the few people in the family who ever defended Padlock, usually pointing to her fecundity.

Refreshments were served with great care amidst a silence that seemed to howl and oppress both the house and the afternoon itself.

Tiida looked in her glass and saw minute pieces of squashed orange swimming in the yellow liquid. It occurred to her that her mind was in the same liquid state, unable to form a plan of attack or defense. It also occurred to her that her brother's wife had not even asked about her children. Was this because they were now living in the city, where village civilities didn't rule, and where housewives behaved like little queens? Or was it because Tiida was married to a Muslim and her male children had been circumcised, and her brother's Catholic wife did not approve? This kind of treatment was new to Tiida, and it made her very angry. She remembered that a certain nurse at the hospital where her husband worked had tried to disrespect her and to undermine her position, possibly with fancy dreams of taking Dr. Ssali off her hands. Tiida had confronted the woman only once. The next she heard, the woman had asked for a transfer. All she had told her was to keep her dirty hands off the good doctor if she treasured them. What did the woman think? That she was going to chop them off? Anyway, it had worked, but nothing seemed to work now; even her mounting wave of anger seemed self-defeating.

The sight of the richly dressed but highly confounded Tiida strengthened Padlock's resolve to go to Rome. This woman had to be shown that poverty could be defeated with honest labor, and that Catholicism was still the paramount religion in society. She wanted to show this woman, together with Kawayida's wife, that she was powerful in her own right. Padlock remembered clearly that on the day Tiida and her husband had visited Kawayida and his wife in their newly acquired Peugeot, Kawayida's wife had said, "It is a shame that Nakkazi does not have the brains to make dresses out of chicken feathers. It is the only way they can get a car, if you ask me." The same woman lamented that Padlock's brothers lacked the brains to use turkey shit to make bricks and tiles and build a respectable kitchen for their parents. Padlock was awaiting a confession from Tiida, but Tiida was not about to weaken her already precarious position by kowtowing to her brother's terrible wife. She had her pride, lots of it; kowtowing to peasants was where she drew the line.

Padlock made her intentions clear by backing out of the sitting room as soon as she had served the refreshments. Leaving Tiida on her own, she retired to the Command Post and sent the sewing machine chugging. As the needle bit into cloth, the Singer filled the house with the monotonous, train-like sound of its immobile journey, sprinkling the compound with the joyous revenge of its mistress. When the children came home from school, she ordered them to maintain a deathly silence and not disturb the guest for any reason or else she would tear the skin off their backs. After long stretches of time, Padlock would go into the sitting room to check on her visitor, the way one checked on a poisonous snake coiled inside one's precious china pot. She would mutter a few words of mock civility, then leave Tiida to languish in the heat of her discomfiture.

At five o'clock, when the national television program began, Padlock deigned to ease her sister-in-law's solitude by switching on the stinking Toshiba. Tiida got annoyed with the fleeting nonsense of American cartoons and their nasal chatter, which was all mumbo jumbo because she didn't understand a word of it. The black-and-white things flew, collided with each other, clobbered each other, ran themselves over with cars and did all sorts of stupid things only a child or a moron could appreciate. To soothe her biting rage, Tiida thought about Dr. Ssali. She wished he would come for her. She wished he would run her brother's wife over with their Peugeot. She wished he were rich enough to finance Grandpa's journey on his own and save her the humiliation of dealing with her brother's peasant wife.

By the time Serenity returned home, in the evening, Tiida was silently mourning the fact that she had decided to stay and wait for her brother. Her usually clear eyes were bloodshot. There was perspiration on her brow and on the bridge of her nose. She wanted to scream and to call her brother's wife all the names that swept through her head. But she was so enraged that she could hardly speak, let alone order her thoughts.

Serenity took his sister for a walk. Night was falling. A thin mist was descending in the distance, hovering over the tops of tall buildings and on the peaks of distant hills. They did not go toward the gas station, because Serenity did not want to introduce her to his friends. Serenity explained that he was very tired because he was in the middle of campaigns for the post of treasurer to the Postal Workers' Union. He talked about long meetings, canvassing drives and visits to workers' homes. He said that the campaign had robbed him of his sense of reality. He complained about his insomnia. He expressed his wish to win and gain access to extra resources. He was angry that somebody had edged him out for the chairmanship, but he could not really complain, because Hajj Gimbi's invisible friends had intervened, pushed aside a Muslim candidate and supported his candidacy for treasurer.

Serenity monopolized the conversation and lectured his sister as never before. Tiida found herself playing second fiddle. She was amazed at how eloquent her younger brother had become; he had finally come into his own. She could now see him representing other people, a bit edgy but capable. Before she could say why she had come to see him, he told her that he had absolutely no money to spare. He was going to Rome to boost his leadership image, he said. Tiida agreed with everything he said, sadly wondering whether the first thing she had met that morning had been a woman or a dog: this was too much bad luck to be coincidental.

"Is your wife also going?" she valiantly asked, seething with suppressed rage.

"She wants to, but she has neither the money nor a parish to register in."

"They have never been strong, money-wise," Tiida couldn't help chipping in.

"But her younger brother has registered himself," Serenity said proudly.

"Where did he get the money?"

"He is going to fly on his pigs," Serenity said, laughing, remembering a joke about flying pigs, but his sister totally missed it. She flinched, because in her husband's religion a pig was a filthy animal. She found herself thinking that her brother's wife's family were like pigs to her: she did not want to have anything to do with them.

The crushing sense of defeat Tiida felt was almost akin to that dating back to the days of the plague of flies, the dogs' heads and the villagers' claim that her husband's conversion to Islam was a curse. She wished she had not come. She felt encumbered by the bad news she had to bear, and by the ballast of spurious negotiating power and insulted personal charm she had to jettison. She heard Serenity ask again how they had finally won the car, and she felt angry. He was just asking for the sake of softening the hard edges of her defeat.

"Conversion Committee politics. Heads rolled, and the new man cleared the backlog during the euphoria following his victory," she said, languidly thinking about Nakatu. She had probably foreseen the defeat, and that was why she had refused to come along.

Tiida's visit only served to highlight Serenity's almost impossible financial position. Where was the money going to come from? He had a sneaking feeling that Hajj Gimbi could be of help, but how could he go to him after all he had already done? Serenity was like a viper eyeing a juicy rabbit: in order to swallow it, he would have to break his own jaws and suffer the pain of ingesting the animal and of realigning his jaws afterward. Was he ready to take the risk? Serenity felt he was, but how was he going to broach the issue? There were also more worrying considerations: What if Hajj's friends got fed up this time and asked Serenity to do something grisly in return? What if they asked him to transfer big amounts of union money to secret accounts? Serenity was tormented for weeks.

Nowadays, when he joined his cronies at the gas station, he spent long periods of time brooding, saying nothing, responding late to jokes and exhibiting a surly absentmindedness that annoyed his friends.

"I never knew that treasurers slept during the day and counted money during the night," Mariko, a Protestant friend who talked little himself but won most card games, teased. They all laughed, Serenity too.

Hajj Gimbi started talking about his pilgrimage to Mecca and Medina five years back. As he talked he became very animated, as if each sentence brought him closer and closer to the glowing heart of the pilgrimage and its significance to him: "People were like grains of sand on a gigantic plain!"

"And all dressed in white!" Serenity wondered aloud. He felt alive for the first time in weeks. He pictured angels milling around on some celestial plain.

"Tell us, what does it look like in Rome?" Hajj asked.

"I wish I knew," Serenity said.

"Tell us about all those women in short dresses who mill around anxiously waiting to see the pope," Hajj pressed on, smiling mischievously.

"Well . . ."

"By the way, why don't you go and find out? We could always use eyewitness accounts. Buy a camera and take some nice colored pictures for your cronies," Hajj suggested, to immediate corroboration from the others.

"Money," Serenity said uneasily, to the roar of laughter.

"There is always some obstacle, money or whatever. Look, your pilgrimage comes only once in . . ."

"Twenty-five years," Serenity said.

"Yes, twenty-five years. Ours is annual. What will you tell your grandchildren? That you failed to go because of money? There is always money, but chances come only once in a lifetime."

Everyone agreed.

"I have an idea," Hajj said, his little eyes sparkling.

"Yes?" Serenity jerked forward. It was clear that he wanted it to be a secret between him and Hajj, but Hajj was no lover of secrets. He had nothing to hide, he always said.

"Apply for three thousand rolls of cloth from the government textile mill at Jinja in the name of the union. Sell the cloth on the black market, and fly 'Hajjati' to Rome with you," he said, referring to Padlock. They all laughed.

"Money," Serenity said unhappily.

"Money!" Hajj Gimbi zoomed in ironically with his booming voice.

"Money," the other two cronies said together.

"To be on the safe side, apply for five thousand rolls. Don't worry about money. You only have to sell the delivery note to the black-marketeers. They do the rest."

"The State Research Bureau . . . ," Serenity said, half with levity, half with genuine fear.

"The State Research?" Hajj asked, as if he had never heard of them.

"The State Research!" The others took up the joke, and the laughter too.

"You are a real leader, with many delusions of grandeur," Hajj said to Serenity. "Those boys are too busy doing more important things to notice you. Ha, ha, ha, haaaa!"

Like a good husband and a sensible man, Serenity kept everything secret. Padlock, stung by his apparent indifference to her anxiety, was pressuring him to listen to her and do something before it was too late.

"You have not even registered!" he countered as he wondered whether the next morning State Research boys were going to drag him out of his office, jam him into the trunk of a waiting car and take him to a forest, or a river, or a filthy cell.

"Do something."

"We will see," he said.

" 'We will see' is not good enough. You know that."

"We will see," he reiterated for the umpteenth time. "I said, we will see."

General Amin played his cards well. He knew that if he allowed Catholics total access to subsidized government-priced dollars from the Bank of Uganda, he would lose vital political capital. He wanted Catholics, for once, to acknowledge his importance in their life, and especially in this pilgrimage. He devised three quotas. In the first quota, he placed five thousand people, who received the necessary travel documents and dollars and were made to understand that they were the country's official representatives. Unofficial government sources gradually let it be known that there were extra places for those who could secure foreign currency on their own; this was the second quota, composed of the elite, people with both money and connections.

The government sources warned that if any pilgrims sold government-priced dollars on the black market, they would be arrested and their passports torn to pieces. Catholics felt insulted that the government could suspect them of doing something so base. Serenity was exhilarated, Padlock dejected. The chosen five thousand were going without having to sell the clothes on their backs to pay for foreign currency! Being among the chosen ones, Serenity was in seventh heaven. The deal had paid off: he had sold the delivery note and secured the cash, and the buyers had neither pointed guns at him nor pushed him into the trunk of a car! It had been a revelation. In gratitude, he had bought Hajj Gimbi a very large goat with teats hanging almost to the ground. He also spent a weekend with Nakibuka. He bought her clothes and gifts for her children, but he did not tell her how he had made the money.

▪ ▪ ▪

Serenity boarded an Alitalia jumbo jet with three hundred forty-nine other passengers one late afternoon. The most impressive sight he remembered was a view of Lake Victoria as they rose in the air: the lake resembled an oblong pool of quicksilver. The next morning he was in Rome, reborn, his life transformed. The city was alive, sighing and heaving under the crush of pilgrims from the world over, the ubiquitous tourists and its own dwellers.

Serenity was very interested in ancient sites, the Colosseum, the museums, the cathedrals, anything that could breathe new life into the characters he had encountered in the history lessons of his childhood. The Renaissance, the Reformation, the early Church and the Roman Empire all came alive now in a living context that linked past and present. Serenity felt strangely at home.

He stood in crowded St. Peter's Square. Filled with wonder, Serenity ate holy bread from the hands of the aging pope, marvelling at his hooked nose and the glamour that still failed to dispel the dimness of his features, and found it hard to believe that so delicate a creature could be the head of so vast and powerful a corporation as the Catholic Church. What did this man know about him? What did he know about Catholics in Uganda? What did he know about the people who took him most seriously? Apart from feeding them dogma, what had he really ever done for them? Yet he influenced their lives as though he knew them personally!

In Serenity's mind, the man resembled an armadillo that controlled his territory from underground, crawling occasionally to the surface, carapaced in dogma, to be seen and to confirm that he was still in control. Loaded with layers of exquisite garments and priceless jewelry, this monstrous armadillo seemed to have emerged from his hole ready to shine. He spoke with the calculated sloth of those assured of an eternal audience, and his magnificent raiment had the gleam of garments washed clean in the blood of imperial power. The holy armadillo moved with arthritic grace. His body breathed the air of sublime indifference. His demeanor oozed with the contradiction of preaching sadistic negation of the body while bedecking oneself in gold. He operated in the supremely detached ambience of holy dictators, tyrants who feared nothing, imperial despots who controlled the lives of hundreds of millions of people far away.

■ ■ ■

At the turn of the century, agents of an earlier holy armadillo had come to Uganda, locked horns with agents of other religions, got involved in bloody wars and poisoned politics with religion while the armadillo slept. Now Ugandans, descendants of those who died in those Religious Wars, were jostling to touch his successor, to kiss his ring, to be blessed by him, to be pictured with him, everything forgiven and forgotten. Serenity thought of his wife. He was annoyed that this man, whose principles and dogmas had scarred her forever and turned her into a rigid, frigid bundle of inhibitions, knew nothing about her and the troubles he had gone through in accommodating her and her implacable beliefs.

Serenity spent the nights in his hotel room, ruminating on what he had seen during the day. Richer pilgrims went out whoring. One got mugged. Another lost his way and spent the night searching for his hotel. Female pilgrims stayed in their own hotel, where some were joined by their male counterparts for wine-drenched fornication while a few others were fondled and flashed by city freaks who posed as photographers.

From his hotel window, Serenity could see whores walking the street, parading their wares, accosting men, bargaining, getting in and out of cars or simply looking bored with the waiting game. He found it curious that they were very expensive. They aroused supreme indifference in him. It was beyond him to contemplate flushing his precious black-market money down some sordid whore's drain. He wished Nakibuka were with him, helping him to capture and savor the special moments. He ate just one meal a day to save money, but he felt filled up. He seemed to be feeding on dreams—Jesus in the desert, temptation galore, capitulation never an option.

Serenity bought souvenirs, but his heart was stolen by a bronze plaque depicting the legend of Romulus and Remus. This was what he had subconsciously come to get; this was what the blackbirds carried unseen in their beaks. In the middle was the wolf, big, dominant, her snout pointed menacingly at unseen intruders. Her large puffy teats were hanging down like strange fruits. Her eyes looked glazed with what could only be the joy and sensuousness of breastfeeding. The twins, nude and silky like hairless piglets, were sucking the diabolical milk as the wolf protected them with the arch of her body.

This was overwhelming for a boy abandoned by his mother to the wolfish quirks of his dad's wives. He held the plaque as if somebody were about to snatch it from him. The vendor, an old man with a thick mustache and little gray eyes, was intrigued. Serenity was his first customer that day, and how strangely he acted!

Thoracic and gastric locusts nibbled at Serenity with gusto. He almost forgot where he was, in a cramped side street with tourists in shorts and mini-skirts passing like paper ghosts all around him. A river of mud seemed to carry him away from these people and their city and their wares, past the tower of Ndere Parish and the swamps at the foot of Mpande Hill, back to the bosom of the village.

The vendor offered him a good discount if he bought three of the plaques. Serenity seemed to wake up. The vendor reminded him of the old Fiddler and the breasts between his legs. Barrel-organ music was coming from the end of the street. He remembered how he had wanted to learn to play the fiddle. The vendor repeated his offer, looking at Serenity closely and hiding his growing sense of unease behind a large smile. The message of the plaque was too personal for either Hajj Gimbi or Nakibuka to really comprehend. No, he wanted only one plaque, for himself alone.

The rest of his stay in Rome disappeared in a speedy haze. Time oscillated between lucid bursts of euphoric consciousness—say, when a painting talked to him—and a groggy flow of tide, traffic, people. The bus rides, the monuments, the holy masses, the visit to Lourdes— all had something surreal about them. He felt it all slip away.

Serenity had bought a gigantic, meter-long rosary with wooden beads as large as tomatoes. He hated the thing, and the clapping wooden noise it made as he walked, but it was the height of fashion: all his fellow pilgrims wore them to show that they were not common tourists. He lacked their sense of pride and conviction. He thought they all looked like walking billboards for clerical commercialism.

Serenity woke up in Israel. It was hot and dry, with a sandy-gray haze clinging to the air. He looked at the embattled city of Jerusalem, which had suffered violence from time immemorial. He envisioned its destruction and reconstruction, its rises and falls. He pictured the seesawing between peace and war that had gone on over the centuries. He wondered how the city contained the pressure of all that history within its walls.

Serenity flew to the Old Testament. He recalled some of the wars, the internal struggles and Moses' leadership ordeals. As a leader himself, albeit of a much smaller caliber, he appreciated Moses' impossible position, squashed as he was between the will of God and the wishes of the Israelites. He remembered the story of the Golden Calf, and the snakes, and he wondered why God chose to operate in such a climate of violence. Serenity now appreciated Jesus' rebel credentials much more. Stories of the poor, the dispossessed, the victims of Roman colonialism and local greed, made an impression on him. The people of Jesus' time needed a charismatic leader to chip away at the bedrock of oppression and misery.

Serenity felt a bit like Jesus. He wished he could also be mythologized. He wished the peasants of Uganda could tell stories about him and his family from one generation to another. He realized that his childhood wish to learn to play the fiddle had had grains of mythmaking desire in it. He had wanted to be somebody to outlast time, a Jesus-like ghost who would sprinkle his name on the sands of time, a free spirit who would inspire strangers with the universal seeds embedded in its home-grown fruit. But what did he have to offer the peasants of his village and the slum dwellers of his city in return for eternity? His exploits as treasurer of the postal union? His father's chiefly acts? His late aunt's baby-delivering achievements? What universal seeds lay embedded in the jackfruit called Serenity? he wondered.

Some pilgrims wept when they arrived in the Holy Land. It was almost too much for peasant folk who had never dreamed, as they dug in the fields, as they plucked their coffee, as they fed their goats and pigs, that they would ever come here. All the powerful people in the world had been here, and now, wonder of wonders, they were here too! They marveled at the power of modern technology which enabled Israelis to grow crops in the desert. It seemed miraculous, like many Biblical stories of their childhood. Serenity also marveled at the level of technology here, but he noticed that the owners of this capability had lost that precious sense of wonder. They took everything for granted, like a peasant finding beans in a pod. It seemed sad to him.

The nights were cool and calm, a far cry from the hot, hectic days, and he looked forward to them. They enabled him to withdraw and to rest. It was three weeks now since he had last touched Nakibuka. He felt the miracle of her fire burning, testing him to the limit.

Serenity's arrival at Entebbe Airport was anti-climactic. Ugly meter-long rosary dangling round his neck, the knocking of wooden beads a monotonous, raucous song, the iron links clinking like dog chains, he and other returnees vacated the plane and headed for the check-in gate. On the second floor, overlooking the tarmac and the silver-gray lake in the distance, excited relatives and friends waved and cheered with a mixture of ululation, rapturous song and the shrill calling of names. Serenity waved like everybody else, a dazed expression on his face: home, he was back home. Padlock, Kawayida, Nakatu and Hajj Gimbi were among the people who surrounded him and smeared him with the oil of their happiness, relief and joy. The gloom that had enveloped him all night on the plane lifted and dissipated like morning mist.

General Idi Amin's pragmatic fist had been cocked for more than a fortnight, and now it hit Serenity full in the face. During his absence, the general had made an additional four thousand places available, including foreign exchange benefits. Padlock had hardly slept a wink during the last five days: Mbale had secured her a place in their home parish! The suddenness of it all had thrust her into the immortal terror that something might go wrong to balance this unexpected good luck. She became gripped with the fear that Serenity would not return. Planes blew up or fell or hit rocks frequently these days, but now he was back! Alive! Where was he going to get the money for her journey, though? "We will see, we will see," he had kept saying. The impatience in her bones and the fear of disappointment in her bosom made Padlock tongue-tied and a touch sullen amidst the joy of Serenity's return. Blind faith had kept her going before Amin's surprise turnaround, and it was blind faith she was counting on once again to seal her victory. Beyond it she dared not look: the lacuna of analysis and speculation was too deep and too vertiginous to dive into. Now the sight of Serenity, her Serenity, looking so distinguished made her proud. She tried to be happy, hoping that her happiness for him would be rewarded. Had he really been to Rome? And Lourdes? And the Holy Land?

The journey home was a bittersweet ordeal. Everyone was talking at once. Hajj Gimbi's voice boomed, and Padlock was proud that pagans were giving praise to God: stones were indeed shouting. She felt an absence of hatred for this bearded fellow, for Kawayida and his wife, and for Nakatu, who remained a dull enigma to her.

At home there was cheerful pandemonium. A delegation of postal workers from the union was there, Catholic, Protestant, Muslim, pagan. They had hijacked the occasion and taken over organizing the celebrations. The pagoda seemed to belong to them now. They barked orders and served drinks and food with ease. Now and then they burst into song. Padlock had looked forward to a low-key event, but these fellows had no regard for jet lag or anything else. They were here to eat and drink and dance and show allegiance to their new leader. As the drums rolled, both Serenity and Padlock found themselves thinking of their wedding day so many years ago. The celebrations gathered momentum rather quickly, and by the time night fell there were drunks swearing and cursing and brawls Serenity dared not break up for fear of annoying his constituency. He reveled in the cheerful disorder.

During the small hours of morning, Padlock tabled her request. Serenity resented the timing. She had not left him any room to maneuver, any chance to go behind her back and give the opportunity to her aunt, whom he was dying to see. He agreed to finance his wife's journey, especially because the dollars were government-priced. To test her, he said that he was going to borrow the money from Hajj Gimbi, but Padlock raised no objection. As a matter of fact, during her desperate hours, when she feared a plane crash or some other disaster involving Serenity, she had also thought of that alternative. All that was behind her now: she was going!

Everything had fallen into place for Padlock. She left a few days before Mbale, because he still had some things to straighten out. She waited for him at the airport in Rome, showed him the few places she knew by then and warned him about con artists, fake photographers and guides who flashed pilgrims and tried to rob them.

In the air, looking at clouds stacked like cotton wool dropped from great heights onto empty fields, she felt like the Virgin Mary. She could see herself standing in those cottony clouds, globe in hand, eyes raised to heaven, balancing the evanescent with the eternal, heaven and earth, life and death. She was sitting next to the window, and her neighbor did not see the tears of joy furtively trailing down her cheeks.

She wanted them to flow and flow and flow, and etch tracks in her flesh, and drench the cottony clouds outside. She pushed her childhood away when it tempted her with negative feelings. She focussed her mind on peace and virtue. As she wheeled across the cottony celestial plains, she espied a small old woman. It was Grandma. She remembered Jesus' exhortation to settle disputes with neighbors before offering sacrifice. She whispered the end of her grudge and vendetta into the stratosphere. She hoped that Grandma had forgiven her, too.

Padlock had discovered that, locked in this hermetic sarcophagus, flying at a thousand kilometers per hour, it was easy to forgive earthly wrongs. She remembered that in Grandma's dream she had been standing in front of a buffalo in a lake of sand. She now understood it. Sand was the clouds, and she was the mighty one-ton buffalo. If only she had known that the old woman was only mouthing prophecies! If only she had known that the old woman was only a harbinger of the greatest triumph in Padlock's life! If only she had known! But all that was in the past now. She was headed for the future.

As they flew over Israel Padlock saw the sand and remembered that she was the mighty buffalo who had come from a humble village to consummate her Biblical relationship. She was the virgin raised from the mud and the bush of a lowly village to the triumph of birthing God's son and bringing salvation to all. She was the Virgin of Nazareth, a place where nothing good was expected but where the greatest man had lived before starting his preaching and healing career. She could feel the monstrous power of Biblical history moving under the land of Israel, crashing to a climax at the portals of Jerusalem. As she walked on this holy soil she could feel herself swelling with all the prophecies, all the miracles, all the trials and victories of the Israelites, for she was the new Israelite, with a circumcised heart, embodying the bread of life that had come from Nazareth. She wanted to go into all the little villages Jesus had traveled through and talk to the people, taste the wine, eat the bread, touch the palm trees and search for the essence of the phenomenon that had begun here and burst upon the whole world. She wanted to go to the well where Jesus sat and talked to the Samaritan woman. She wanted to watch people drawing water and carrying it on their heads, as in Uganda. She wanted to sleep in a tent and listen to the music of this land. She wanted to get to the very bottom of her faith. She wanted to go to

Golgotha, and walk up the hill of skulls, and sweat as Jesus had done. She wanted to pray at the spot where the crucifixion occurred. She wanted to pray at the spot where Jesus ascended to heaven. She remembered the woman who for years had been tormented by hemorrhage. Such faith! She felt Jesus' healing power inside her.

Brother and sister held a joint thanksgiving ceremony in the village of their birth. Mbale, the catechist and the gifted talker of the two, told of what they had seen during their pilgrimage and how it had felt to meet the Holy Father and to be in the Vatican. He tried to describe what it was like to see the crowds in Lourdes, the mountains and the edifices in Jerusalem. The day ended in drinking and drumming and singing.

However, all those things could not fully drown out Mbale's worries. He had financed his journey by borrowing against the coming harvest. His living, breathing collateral was a healthy tomato crop sprawling over a big stretch of land. In his absence, his wife and children had sprayed the plants and chased off curious monkeys and hungry birds. Three fantastic harvests were behind them, and this one promised to be even bigger. Mbale saw it as God's gift to him, a sort of repayment for all the good work he did in the subparish. Nobody disputed that, not even his critics. They all agreed that Mbale was the hardest-working man in the area. The family woke up before six, prayed, ate breakfast and braved the dew and mist to tackle the day's work. Come rain or shine, they worked the whole day, with just a few breaks to eat lunch, drink water or snack on sugarcane. This was a regimen for boy and girl alike. Mbale's family worked like donkeys, and everyone agreed that the man deserved every cent he milked from the land. The villagers used to say that Mbale's sugarcanes smelled of his sweat.

In addition, Mbale was the subparish catechist, teaching and preaching the Good News, counselling married people and preparing those who wanted to receive the matrimonial and other sacraments. His faith was rock solid, and the biggest insult was to tell him that the Virgin Mary menstruated or that St. Joseph might have been impotent. All skepticism concerning the Bible was anathema to him and could fetch one a sharp remark or even a slap when he was loaded with enough banana beer.

No pilgrim was prouder of his journey than this uncle of mine.

He retold the story a thousand times over. The meter-long rosary became his personal trademark. It reminded everyone that he was not just another peasant farmer breaking his back on the land, crawling with sweat in the iron sun, but somebody who had conquered space and traveled to the Vatican, Lourdes, Jerusalem and other places mentioned in the Bible. His sermons on Sundays became legendary. If in the gospel Jesus had been to Cana, Capernaum or Jericho, Mbale would tell his hearers: "When I was in Cana . . . I felt the power of the Lord inside me, moving like a raging fire. Then God commanded me to go home and preach to you my people. . . ." When talking about the pope, he often said, "The Holy Father commissioned me to tell you that he loves you. He wants you to repent, because the end is near. . . ." Two months after his return, vicious winds ravaged the village and a big part of the countryside.

The winds, when they first whistled down the hills, sounded like many wooden rosaries clapped together. They found Mbale in the beer hall listening to a song some women had composed in his honor for putting the village on the world map by conquering space. The winds swept down the hills into the village, carrying with them the fury of forty-two years of dormant disaster. They tore the roof off the beer hall, wrapped it into a jagged ball and deposited it two football fields away. They decapitated wind-blocking trees, spreading the crushed canopies all over the place. They aimed lower, uprooting or breaking banana and coffee trees. They terrorized fragile houses, blowing holes into walls, ripping off doors and carrying them to unknown destinations. The subparish church was a sturdy edifice; it put up a good fight. The winds whipped it from all sides, dumped coffee trees uprooted so many meters away onto its roof and hammered its doors with flying banana trees. The winds dived under the roof with the evil intention of furling it up obscenely like the Lamp Lady's skirt, but all they got off were bits of tired rafters. They rampaged to the anemic little school affiliated with the church and crushed its much older buildings, ground to liquid mud the pit latrine and flooded the yard with Sunday-service and school-week excreta. Water completed the demolition job, washing away crops, paths, dogs, rats, sheets and anything else found in open space. The paltry remains of Mbale's tomato plants were found in the village well, jamming its surface and sabotaging its flow.

No one was more nonplussed than the pilgrim, who had narrowly escaped decapitation in the storm. The rosary got lost in the process, much to his chagrin.

"God tests those he loves," he said philosophically, wondering how he was going to pay his creditors.

Padlock, who would one day meet her end in the nearby forest, returned to the village to survey the damage and to see what she could do.

The natural disasters which were going to dog their family and their in-laws' families had just begun to show their hand. Unlike the locusts, which had come in the thirties and had almost been forgotten by the villagers, the new disasters would leave scars that would last through the ages.

To begin with, though, the people fought the battle of reconstructing their village. Mbale spent the next seven years struggling to pay his creditors.

Holy masses were said copiously throughout the land, and if prayer alone were enough to turn things around, the country would never have undergone the catastrophes that dogged it in the coming years. At the seminary, we seemed to be attending one long, unending mass. Morning light seemed to be doing perpetual battle with stained-glass chapel windows, holding us hostage to a self-repeating drama. Seminarians, faces upturned in sublime boredom and lips moving somnolently, were like baby birds waiting to be fed. The rector, minus meter-long rosary, told and retold the story of his journey in apparent perpetuity. The Vatican, Jerusalem, Lourdes, or was it St. Peter's Square, Jerusalem, Lourdes, or some other peripatetic configuration? Nowadays, when he caught defaulters, he called them to his office, asked them why they had broken the rules and then clinically passed sentence. "Give me one good reason" became his leitmotif and nickname. Some staff members were annoyed by this leniency. They openly wondered how long this road-to-Damascus conversion would last.

In the meantime, Lageau's popularity waned, and we finally found him a nickname: "Red Indian." He was ruddy, after all, but the name was actually a passing reference to the fact that, despite his Wasp roots and apparent wealth, to us he could have been a marginalized Red Indian on a reserve. We mostly called him Red.

In the midst of this teacup storm, the *Agatha* controversy arose and kept us on tenterhooks till the end of the year. It was as if Lageau were issuing a riposte.

The seminary was built on a hill three kilometers away from the nearest stretch of Lake Victoria, the same lake on whose eastern shores Kaanders had fought polygamy and contracted sleeping sickness. The lake provided good fishing and swimming facilities in these areas. The locals combed the waters with nets dropped from wooden canoes and caught both small and large fish, but did not think much of swimming. Seminarians were allowed to go swimming once a month, but the prospect of walking three kilometers to take a dip, get wolfishly hungry and then return to the hill for ghastly meals never appealed to many. The only people who made use of this dispensation were the die-hard truants; they used the chance to meet their contacts, and sometimes their girls.

Lageau gradually came to personify both swimming and boating. Whenever he was not in the mood for volleyball, he would get in his car and go swimming. On the weekend, he got permission for a few good swimmers to accompany him to the lake. It was to this select group that he revealed the imminent arrival of *Agatha*.

The news spread like a gasoline fire in a wooden shack. The materialists among us praised the man to the sky. They could hardly wait to cast their eyes on *Agatha*. Someone stole a picture of the boat, and it changed hands faster than porno magazines in a military barracks. Eyes devoured the swan-like contraption with a mixture of admiration, awe and cold envy. The Red Indian was sending a big message, putting everybody, including the rector, with his Vatican-Lourdes-Jerusalem stories, in his proper place. This boat, still hundreds of miles away, was like a Holy Grail full of elixirs for a national plague. The quick ones pointed out that our meals were finally going to improve.

"With all the big fish he will catch, we will certainly get a share."

"God has remembered us at long last," the optimists intoned.

Lageau basked in this glory without directly fanning it. He struck an uncharacteristically reticent pose and let the boys and a few loose-tongued priests do his dirty work. I kept aloof of the drama. At the time, Kaanders and I were busy nursing old books back to health: cutting, gluing, pressing, trimming the finished product and hallucinating on the fish glue. Normally, Kaanders' hands trembled, as though little electric currents were passing through his veins, but inside the bindery, amidst mountains of paper, the odious paper guillotine and the tattered, needy books, he became steady as a surgeon. He worked nonstop for long stretches, disregarding mealtimes and looking almost frantic in his zeal. He kept a block of cheese in the drawer, nibbled it like a rat nibbling a cake of soap and returned to work. Nothing seemed able to break his concentration. We worked all week, including during sports time. He kept on saying, "Oh boy, this has to be completed, boy."

By the time *Agatha* arrived, a gigantic swan edging uphill in the dusk, a white bolt of light in a gloomy evening sky, she was already community property, dripping with the saliva of communal speculation. A glossy twelve-footer, she sat on her dolly, awash with fluorescent light, and glowed like a new alabaster Virgin. As cameras flashed in the dusk, Lageau stood in front of her, fascinated, like an inventor awed by his invention. He beamed and glowed, as if to say priesthood was the best profession on earth, as if every ordained priest got a twelve-footer at one point in his career. He had waited for *Agatha* for a long time, and now that she was here, he felt a boyish impatience to try her out.

Weeks of expectation followed. Everyone was watching. An African priest famous for his sycophantism drove *Agatha* to the lake with his car, affixed the engine and waited for Lageau to arrive.

Sometimes Lageau took a boy or two along to help with the boat. Dressed in white gym shorts, white canvas shoes and a white T-shirt, Lageau resembled a debonair tennis player. He began fishing with rods, then turned to nets. He first caught tilapia fish, then he started netting thirty- to seventy-kilo Nile perch monsters. The fathers' fridge and deep freezer filled to the brim, but rotten beans continued to be part of our daily diet, except once a month, when we got Nile perch.

I thought about attacking Lageau head-on to ask why he was not giving us more fish, but I held back. I wanted somebody else to make the move. I didn't want to appear to be too food-minded. I did not have long to wait.

We started experiencing frequent power failures. At first we thought it was a national or regional problem, and that it was the Energy Board's fault, but it soon became apparent that the seminary was suffering many more power failures than other local users. Lageau became extremely angry, because on top of being forced to use lanterns, he had to spend time tracing the source of the problem.

At first the saboteur just pulled out wires or fuses. Fr. Lageau fitted them back easily, a curse or two on his lips. Then the saboteur decided to raise the stakes. He ripped parts out of the system and drove Lageau almost crazy with frustration. We would have a situation where the fathers' block was in total darkness while ours enjoyed sparkling fluorescent light. A week after that was rectified, the whole school would be plunged into darkness. Fr. Lageau then built boxes over all the transformers and kept the keys in his office. He told us that he had defeated the bastard this time. The bastard must have been listening and was not pleased. He waited a week or so and struck again. These power failures affected our night study, but the advantage was that we slept longer. In that sense, few seminarians ever got angry with this enigmatic character, and any anger toward him disappeared in the blaze of the deep-freezer dramas that followed. After every successful attack, the bursar would order the freezers to be emptied, and we would feast on the fish. The saboteur would wait for the freezers to fill up again, and then he would rip a part out of the electrical system and the bursar would be forced to give us the fish. In the meantime, all efforts were directed at catching this fellow, but in vain. I was intrigued by him. I wanted to know who he was: he thought so much like me. Serenity would have liked him too, for he seemed to spring out of the pages of a good novel.

The fourth, fifth and sixth times the power supply was sabotaged, we spent a total of twenty days without power. The rector addressed us on each occasion and warned the saboteur to stop his subversive activities. It was interesting that he made no threats of divine vengeance or anything like that. He must have known that this fellow was impervious to all matters divine. I waited for the rector to call me to his office and try to ask me if I knew who the saboteur was, but he did not.

After the sixth campaign, things changed a little: we now got fish thrice a month. The attacks stopped.

My indifference to the *Agatha* drama did not last long. One morning, Fr. Lageau woke up to find a two-inch scratch on *Agatha*'s second rib. Since she had not been to the lake for the past three days, there was only one revolting conclusion to be drawn. A tomato-red Lageau, Elvis hair standing on end, concluded that *Agatha* had been assaulted, her pride chipped, her inviolability compromised. Who in this godforsaken place had dared to lay his hand on her? Who had marked her? After all she had done for these wretched boys and their wretched priests! Which senseless clod had done this? What was he trying to achieve or prove? It did not, could not, occur to Lageau that it might have been a mistake, an accident. After what the power saboteur had put him through, Lageau believed that accidents never occurred in this place. Everything was planned, and where *Agatha* was concerned, Lageau was not ready to hold back. He had had enough. At the back of his mind was also the idea that beautiful boats, like beautiful women, never got accidentally hurt. They were purposely assaulted. His car, his flowers, his person, had never been vandalized. Why did it have to be sacred *Agatha*? Who did not know that Agatha happened to be the name of his mother, his first girlfriend and his ideal woman? Who did not know that *Agatha* brought out all the protective instincts in him?

Like many powerful people who operated inside their own bubble of inviolability, Lageau was terribly hurt and offended. Excruciating pain seared him, making him afraid that he was going to have an improbable heart attack. He felt the approaching pounding devastation of a migraine, his mother's staple affliction. He lived in perpetual fear of inheriting it. Too angry to give word to his emotions, he rushed to his room and locked himself in. He took a shot of whiskey. It burned with a familiar relief-laden fire, quickly cooled by dejection. God, he thought, it was not his week to say mass for the boys! He dressed quickly and hurried to the sacristy.

A golden hue suffused the interior of the chapel. Boys were mumbling prayers prior to the Angelus and the mass. The golden hue might have been a crimson bolt of fire. Fire was the only thing on Lageau's mind when he asked the rector to let him say mass that morning.

"It is my week," the pilgrim protested weakly.

"But I have a special message for the boys."

"Can't it wait till after mass? Couldn't you address them in the refectory?"

"No, you have to understand the special circumstances."

"Spiritual?" the rector asked, wondering whether the bursar had seen an apparition or had a road-to-Damascus experience. He looked so red!

The rector capitulated despite Lageau's refusal to say whether the special message was spiritual or otherwise. How Lageau's ears glowed! the rector thought.

Two minutes into the holy mass, the rector understood why Lageau had been in such earnest. The bursar launched his attack: "Animals!" All the priests and boys eyed him curiously. What a strange intro! We were not the natural audience for animal-rights speeches: we beat our cows or let our herd boys beat them when they strayed; we whacked pigs on the head with pestles or cut their throats to prepare them for the pan; we persecuted squirrels for eating our groundnuts; we murdered rats with poison and traps; we kept dogs and their fleas outside the house; we had a love-hate relationship with monkeys, and if they eluded death for raiding shambas, it was thanks to their sensibilities. Animals were animals here. So what the fuck was Lageau talking about? After acquiring the boat and murdering fish, was he now turning champion of animal rights?

"Monkeys, black monkeys. Monkeys with no regard for aesthetics or property. How could anyone desecrate *Agatha*? What had she done to them? Why would anyone cut her rib? You know why? Because they are monkeys. During this mass, join me to pray for these monkeys to gain a modicum of respect for other people's property."

The priests, taller than lampposts in their immaculate robes, stood round the altar and behind Lageau like camouflaged bodyguards, their black, sheeny faces inscrutable in the morning air. Were they as coldly detached inside as they looked outside? Maybe, maybe not. They seemed protected, elevated above Lageau's words. Surely their colleague knew how materialistic most of them were, and was aware that they could never raise a finger against *Agatha*. They remained as placid-faced as statues of the Virgin, and as taciturn.

Many seminarians, at least those who had been fully awake to hear this most controversial of intros, were too shellshocked to react. I heard a few shuffles of angry feet, and a hiss or two. Maybe I was not fully awake either, as I had just been released for a day from the bindery and its glue. Yet I was sure I had heard him. I was sure that most of us were warding off the stinging effect of Lageau's words with the shield of docility and deference to authority. Wasn't everyone reacting in the classic good-seminarian way? Turning the other cheek? Letting the spittle run till the spitter ran out and then walking away? Wasn't this the ultimate test of our fortitude?

Someone had once said that *Agatha* was too beautiful not to be the cause of someone's downfall someday. But what had happened to her? Had someone copied my trick and painted her? Had someone taken a knife and cut her just to see if she was wooden or plastic or carbon fiber? How many kids cut their parents' sofas just to see what made them soft? Hadn't I chipped the despots' bloody headboard? How many kids ripped arms off dolls just to see what made them squeak? Had the saboteur taken his campaign up a notch and done a number on *Agatha*? I almost smiled. This fellow really had steel in his balls. I could understand Lageau's frustration: the saboteur who had made a mockery of his electrical skills was still on the loose, and now somebody, possibly the same sod, had done a number on his *Agatha*! I gave Lageau the benefit of the doubt, because I believed that somebody had made a long, deep, vicious cut into *Agatha*'s rib just to drive the poor "Red Indian" mad.

The whole mass seemed to be taking place inside a submarine, away from solid ground and reality. Normally, during these early morning masses, many boys were not aware of what took place till communion. Everything ran on automatic pilot, because the structure of the mass was the same; but now everyone was awake, as though receiving messages from tiny transmitters hidden inside the altar. In a way, everyone was struck by Lageau's courage and self-righteousness. Your average white man, faced with two hundred glum black faces, would not call them monkeys so arbitrarily without a gun at his waist. Your average colonialist would have thought twice about going this far without a detachment of sharpshooters behind him. But this unarmed, boy-faced man was rubbing shit in our faces with absolute impunity! This was the tough guy many of us wanted to be: clean-shaven, soft-spoken and average-looking, but endowed with balls of steel. I felt like cheering. This guy was delivering blows to the faces of priests I had wanted to slap a few times! Yes, yes, this was great. I could feel the heat spreading in my chest.

Lageau reminded me of Jesus cursing the Pharisees, calling them adorned graves filled with rotting flesh and terrible stenches. Yes, this man was some reincarnation of Jesus. He seemed transformed, too.

Soft golden light fell on his gold-wire spectacles and burst into twin-kling stars that multiplied when he moved his head. At the moment, he was the quintessential personification of power and glory. When his hand slashed the air, his Rado burst into liquid arcs of gold that nego-tiated the air like lithe surfers on colorless waves. When light fell in-side his mouth, tongues of gold flashed from each gold tooth like distant suns. This was fantastic stuff. I was hooked. I could feel my knees go rubbery, because I realized I was in the presence of somebody special. I felt attracted to this man's sense of power and who he was.

In Fr. Lageau I saw the might of the Catholic Empire, advancing, conquering, subjugating, manipulating, dictating, ruling. I experi-enced the awe the lowly faithful felt when faced with the gods of the empire. This man also gave off intimations of the World Bank and International Monetary Fund hegemony. He personified cast-iron rules forged in golden rooms, immortalized in gold-edged books with thick golden pens in faraway gold-sprinkled cities. He had that rigid, straight-backed, take-it-or-leave-it attitude of the almighty when they had their man on the ropes. This man, encased in gold, towered over raggedy-ass, snot-nosed republics and used or abused at will. He twirled his golden burden on his gold-ringed finger and commanded them to catch and service it. With a few slashes of the golden pen in the golden room on the gold-edged page, he could double, triple or quadruple somebody's burden or if, for whatever reason, he decided to reward a minion, he could halve or quarter the load. This was real power as I dreamed of it. This was real power as I wanted to have it in my hands. This was the ideal power which shielded one from the ghastly sight of dying babies, emaciated adults and stinking geriatrics. This was the ideal power that let one go to bed at night smelling roses and wake up in the morning unbothered by anything.

I was on my knees. I was sure that many boys believed I was praying. Far from it: I was worshipping power in its glorious isolation, juggernauting down the hill like the winds that had devastated Mbale's village. I wanted to stay here for the rest of the term, for the rest of the year, maybe for the rest of my life.

It was the sound of boys singing the last hymn that woke me. Or was it the sight of boys vacating the church? Everything seemed topsy-turvy. I became aware that I was locked in dreamy isolation from the herd. Snot was creeping ticklishly down my nostrils. My mouth was parched from exposure. I slowly regained my wits. Exorcised by my increasing consciousness, the demons of power retreated. I started asking questions.

Wasn't arbitrary use of power on the weak the reason I hated Padlock? Hadn't Lageau done exactly the same thing? If so, why was I so hypnotized? Wasn't I worshipping color, some semblance I did not know? Beyond the power of his heredity, what had this man ever created? Had he ever carved his name in diamond by writing a wonderful book? Had he ever expanded somebody's moment by composing a song? Had he ever invented a machine or some mathematical formula to increase the world's knowledge or to relieve its pangs or its wastefulness? Not to my knowledge. He was just a masquerade. As Padlock had not created the uterus, Lageau had not invented money—or knowledge or power, for that matter. Like most of us, he was a scavenger, a user of other people's remains. His excessive show of arrogance was the guilt-ridden chicanery of an inheritor. Maybe he had money, maybe he could buy a town, maybe he could own half the land in Uganda, but he was a mere cog in the money wheel, a mere spoke in the power hub, and as for his color and his nuclear-arms-secured prerogatives, what had he added to them? Nothing. Like many intelligent people, he had fallen into the trap of defending an old perspective, exploiting the weakness of others; he had not discovered a new way of thinking. In other words, he was merely regurgitating hundreds of years of philosophical, social and political vomit.

I felt very disappointed, and weary too. Lageau, like many people I could no longer learn from, had lost his allure. One day I would be greater than him, just as I would be greater than Serenity, his Padlock and other little despots. I felt nauseated, as though all the fish glue I had inhaled in the past week had been rejected by my system in one stabbing jolt. Despite his missionary education, Lageau had missed one chapter in cultural anthropology. To us, the monkey represented cleverness, curiosity and the sort of intelligence he boasted—it defended its own standpoint. As a matter of fact, among the fifty-two totemic clans, the monkey figured prominently. Girls of the monkey clan were known for their alertness, nerve, quick wit and loving care. Lusanani, the gobbler of my virginity, belonged to the monkey clan. The superficial disdain for monkeys, with its origin in the missionary-colonial era, was ludicrous, simply laughable. It was the hollow cry of uprooted people dancing to strange tunes and breaking their legs. All these white people believed they were scoring a point with the monkey thing, but they were not: they were just scratching their own assholes.

This man standing in church displaying his ignorance was scratching his behind, smelling his finger and screwing up his nose. Monkey business. This man baring his shallowness at the altar was nothing original; he was mimicking his forebears, the agents of the holy armadillo who had waged wars and poisoned our politics with religion. Hadn't General Amin, time and again, charged that the Catholic Church was built on murder, terror, senseless war, genocide and robbery? This fresh slaughter of the innocent and the not-so-innocent was an old tool, and it shocked only the dim-witted among us. For a church that glorified pain and torture and raised the cross as its banner, this was insignificant. If, like Fr. Mindi, Lageau believed that he was showing us something to emulate, he had fallen far too short of the Church's high psychopathic standards. It all just breathed the quaint air of the principle on which Lageau had stood to call us monkeys. I wasn't turned on anymore; I was just irritated.

Not too long ago, Serenity had beaten me nearly to death just hours after Padlock had tortured me and bled my mouth for tearing a strip off a banal secondhand headboard cast away and accursed by departing Indians. I had, from then on, become a non-respecter of property. Now *Agatha* no longer awed me. Her sweet, smooth curves no longer made my heart race with suggestive thoughts. She had descended from the stratosphere of idealization to the lowly status of mass-produced consumer item barely saved from the dilapidation of secondhand dinginess by a clever reconditioning job. Some generous soul in Canada had paid for *Agatha* with no intention of turning her into a whipping post for the seminarians among whom she was going to live. Maybe a few dim boys believed that *Agatha* was brand-new and that Lageau had acquired her with his own cash. Wrong. *Agatha* was an old shoe, a cute little whore who covered her history with glossy makeup.

What did all this say about us seminarians and the priests we were supposed to emulate? Were we indeed pussy-whipped and glass-balled? Were those wax-faced priests indeed money-awed turds? There they were, sitting, standing, as a fat blue-green fly wiped his feet on their stupid faces, laying eggs in their gaping mouths which would soon be gobbling a rich breakfast as we lapped thin, worm-infested porridge. Was that why they remained silent? Apart from their color, what had they added to priesthood? Had they expanded the vision of life and spirituality? Had they combatted suffering or added to human knowledge in any special way? When they opened their mouths, they merely regurgitated rotting Church rules, worm-infested dogmas and slimy platitudes created in the burrows of the holy armadillo. They were just perpetuating the stink-old order: white, nuclear-warhead-privileged priest above the black, shit-scared peasant priest, who was above the shitty-assed peasant nun, who lorded it over the wormy peasant faithful—man, woman, child. Hundreds of years of Catholic dictatorship later, ninety-five of them home-grown, had come only to this! What a waste!

Lwendo's reaction to the incident mortified me. I found him at the water tank. He was waiting to draw water in his yellow plastic basin, at the bottom of which was an old loofah brush and a worn cake of Sunlight soap. Ah, Sunlight soap! A triumphant glint touched my eyes when I remembered that long ago I used to draw water and take it to the bathroom for him.

"Many bastards here have no respect for property," he said. "Do you know how much that boat cost?"

"As if it was Red's own money! Do you know the kind of stories he told the benefactor who paid for it? And the missionary organization which shipped it here? Yet he acts as if he paid for it all by himself. This is a simple boat, not a yacht."

"Whatever it is, canoe or whaler, it deserves respect. A priest is supposed to look after the assets of his parish. Charity begins in the seminary."

"What an original thought!"

"They did not have to injure her."

"How sensitive of you! And how sensible of Red to shake his little monkey buttocks like that! Next year he might not have anything to sit on."

"What should he have done? Called us saints?"

"He should have looked for the culprit, found him and dealt with him accordingly. But indulging in collective guilt is like licking his thin monkey lips—it didn't come to much."

"But at least you agree that he had cause to be angry."

"Of course he had, like he had cause to swear at the power sabo-teur who is still at large," I said, laughing.

"You talk like a supporter of the bastard."

"Before he did something, all the fish ended up rotting in the freezer. Now, thanks to him, we get to see some of it on our plates." I burst into laughter again.

"Maybe you are the power saboteur," Lwendo said, grinning. "Maybe I should report to Father Lageau that I have caught his man."

"It is good to see Father Red Indian turn crimson and swear at ninety miles per hour."

"The bastard will get caught, and he will regret it."

Lwendo's conventionality in some respects defied my compre-hension. This was the same fellow who used to grab other people's things and use them without permission. This was the same one I nabbed fucking our very own Sr. Bison. Yet now he was defending Fr. Lageau's indulgences. Was it obeisance to "might makes right"? Had Lwendo's wild-man stint been just a type of inverted conformism? His reaction made me think that maybe I was the only person from a screwed-up environment and that I smelled rats where there were none. Why was nobody else experiencing a sense of outrage? Had I originally expected too much from Fr. Lageau and was now just work-ing off my frustration?

I retired to the library. I wanted to stab Lageau and his ego, but which word could I sharpen like Dorobo's monstrous arrows? Dirty words were out of the question: they would just confirm Lageau's be-liefs about us. Irony was the best ship home across the swirling waves of frustration and outrage.

I stole a cassock-like vestment from the pile used by altar boys, hid it behind the chapel and later moved it to the storage area where we kept old books. No one noticed the theft. A cassock was crucial for night raids: it was the insurance that Dorobo would not shoot you be-fore issuing three loud warnings. Truants had their own cassocks, and often got away with their misdeeds because wandering priests mistook them for fellow priests and did not disturb them. Most priests, how-ever, would not bother anybody roaming the night in a cassock be-cause truants had, on a few occasions, thrown red pepper in the eyes of inquisitive priests in order to make good their escape. Fr. Mindi had been a victim of the trick thrice, though it had not stopped him from snooping.

I rehearsed my moves a few times and struck early one morning. *Agatha* was in a dangerous spot: she was lit up on all sides. The chances of being surprised by a sleepless priest or even the watchman were great. The hardest thing was to get to the hallway and the offices, which were twenty meters from the chapel, seventy from the classrooms, ten from the refectory and three hundred from Sing-Sing.

The night was pitch-black. I started my journey at the bathrooms, via Lwendo's barn till I made my way to the back of the chapel, the only place with a winking light inside. Because there were no dogs on campus, I walked without fear of sudden attack. Having come this far, I walked bravely from the chapel to the hallway, opened the door and held my breath when I entered. *Agatha* was in front of me, emitting an oily whiff, her alabaster skin super-smooth in the fluorescent light. If caught fondling her, I would be dismissed outright, but I did not think about it. I looked at the damage: a faint, timid, tentative line, not the vicious gash I had expected. This was curiosity. Viciousness would have been deeper and louder.

I removed a long nail from my pocket, chose a spot near the middle and went to work on *Agatha*'s belly, four ribs from the top. My cuts were deep and long. Etching five letters and an exclamation mark seemed to take an eternity. In reality, it was a quick job. OH GOD! proudly stood on *Agatha*'s belly. I was shaking. I drew back and stood behind the door, listening. I watched the way to the chapel carefully. I followed the same route back to the bathrooms.

Fr. Lageau had his first real migraine that morning. One half of his head, neck and side felt paralyzed. He was too entangled in the web of his anger to think straight. He retired to his bedroom, incensed that everyone was going to see the evidence of his humiliation. The migraine was horrendous—he felt like vomiting, diarrhea grated in his rectum, light hurt his eyes—and he lay down in darkness. "Oh God!" he mumbled. The irony of it! The priest who drove *Agatha* to the lake took him to the hospital.

Lageau was down but not out. A few days later, he took a bale of secondhand clothes he had received on behalf of poor seminarians to

Lwendo's barn, doused it in paraffin and set it on fire. The flames and the thick smoke drew a crowd of boys and a few nuns who came to see what had happened. Lageau stood in front of the barn, at the spot where Lwendo stood to watch Bushmen fighting for charcoal, and watched without blinking, without saying a word. The nuns put their hands on their mouths when they saw what was burning, but said nothing. The boys stood a respectful distance away from Lageau and whispered among themselves.

That same evening he came to our refectory, and in a calm, toneless voice announced that he was going to catch the culprit even if it meant going to Mars. He said this standing two meters away from my table. Everyone knew that he had burned the clothes in revenge, and many wondered why he was still pursuing the case after releasing his anger in the bonfire. I was not the only one who had fantasies of stoning him with chunks of the loathsome posho we were about to eat.

The literature teacher, who had not attended the fateful Monkey Mass, as we called it, referred to the incident obliquely, by exclaiming "God!" at unexpected intervals in the lesson. We prodded him for comment, but he kept on saying, rather ironically, "I reserve my comments. Silence is golden, speech is silver. I would rather keep the gold."

The seminary was awash with speculation as to who had shamed Lageau. I kept out of it. Lwendo tried to talk about it, but I showed no interest at all.

The line of investigation Lageau took scared me. He collected specimens of our handwriting and promised to feed them into a computer. I hurried to the library to find out what a computer looked like. I tried to find out how different computers worked, but I got no wiser in real terms. Kaanders noticed my sudden interest in computers and said, "Oh boy, boy, Father Lageau is going to catch that bad boy, boy."

"It was a shame what they did to *Agatha*, Father."

"Oh boy, boy."

"I hope the culprit gets caught," I said to test him. "It is probably the same person who steals library books."

"Yes, yes, boy."

I asked Kaanders how a computer could be used to catch the culprit, and he said that it would look for similarities in letter patterns. I now had to cover my tracks by sabotaging Lageau's efforts.

Like most dictatorships, the seminary was locked in a web of rumors and mystery. Days later, Lwendo came and said that Lageau had already caught his man.

"A staff meeting took place last night. But the staff is divided about what to do with the culprit."

"How was he found out?"

"Somebody slipped a piece of paper under Father Lageau's door, and it might have helped the computer. The same fellow is said to have been seen entering the dormitory in a cassock some nights ago."

I was now sure that I was not alone in my hatred for Lageau. This sounded very much like "Fisherman," as we called the secret power saboteur. I became more and intrigued by this fellow. I suspected that he was a bit like Cane, always out to challenge authority. Had Fisherman really seen me, and was he now just enjoying the game of fooling Lageau? And if so, why was he fingering certain individuals?

"To me, it looks like only bullies get fingered," I said, feigning indifference.

"Lageau is different from Mindi. Bullies, well, they are the ones who commit crimes, aren't they?"

I felt I had to do something quickly. There was a chance that the boy would not be expelled. For the moment, though, I was banking on the possibility that Lageau was concentrating on a number of things and would not keep too keen an eye on *Agatha*.

In the morning, the boy was dismissed. He told his friends that he would be called back because he was innocent. This was unlikely; hardly any dismissals were reversed, except if one came from a very powerful family with diocesan connections, which the boy's parents lacked. I became more determined to throw a spanner into the works.

This time I first checked on the watchman. He was asleep. I approached the hallway from the refectory side. The smell of *Agatha* excited me. *Agatha*, like a sorceress casting her stones for divination, kicked up images in my head. I could see her on the lake and hear winds moaning all around her, above the monotonous purring of her engine. The noise seemed to rise to a crescendo, fill the whole hallway and make the floor vibrate.

I sank onto one knee, ready to gore anybody sneaking up on me in the gut. I etched the words RED INDIAN under OH GOD!, which was still there. Cold sweat trickled down my back and armpits. I rose suddenly, thinking that somebody had tapped me on the shoulder. False alarm.

Relieved, I walked out of the hallway, leaving the rusty nail behind. I had played the same trick twice and got away with it! This time I went via the refectory to the back of the classrooms. The neat rows of desks had something almost divine about them. They represented a little world, complete in itself, with its own rules, rewards and punishments. I could see the acacia trees in the distance. Home, I was almost home. The trees, the squeaky insect sounds, the forest in the distance, all reminded me of the village, the swamps, the hills, Ndere Primary School, the church tower, the nuns and Santo the madman.

The bathrooms were nearer now; I could see them looming like decapitated statues. They suddenly reminded me of the three gas pumps at the service station where Serenity and his cronies congregated. I negotiated the corner of the last building and almost collided with Dorobo. I thought he was smiling, because I could see a white burst in the pitch-black ball of his face. I froze.

"Gud morning, Faza," he boomed.

"Good m-morning." I could not remember his name. I wanted to bait him with the sound of his name and acknowledge him with the most unique feature about him, but I could remember only "Dorobo," the name of a Kenyan tribe given to him by the boys because he was so black. How tall he looked now! He reminded me of awesome American wrestlers in cage matches. I might have been inside a steel cage, slipping and sliding on the sweat- and blood-stained canvas, trying to figure out how to escape this monster. There was not much I could do except to wait for what he had to say, and maybe beg for mercy. What would I trade in return for clemency? Dorobo then surprised me with a touch of humor: "You no sleep, Faza?"

"Ah, I-I sleep . . ." I was tempted to add the highly patronizing "my son" to my answer, but how dare I? He could book me for truancy, cassock-stealing, raping *Agatha* . . .

I suddenly thought of Cane and the corpses: how big Cane must have felt, standing there and showing us the corpses as though they were dolls! How powerful he must have felt while pushing Island's head down toward the dead woman's stomach! It occurred to me that there might have been something sexual in it for Cane. Wasn't that why he lifted the dead woman's skirt with his foot? I was glad I hadn't looked. I was glad I had not seen what was underneath.

"You no sleep, Faza, eh!" the giant said and laughed.

I wanted to join in the laughter, but I did not know what exactly he had up his sleeve. "Yes, too much worry about exams."

I was in for a bigger shock. He said, "Sank you fa *Agasa* job, he-he-heeee."

"Ah . . ."

"Sank you fa Mindi job too, he-he-heeeee." And he rocked with more laughter.

I was now sure that he was beating me with my old stick: blackmail. But why, if he knew all along, had he waited this long? To gather sufficient evidence and leverage? I knew it. He wanted me to forge and stamp documents for him. He probably wanted a recommendation written out on seminary stationery, stamped and signed in the rector's name. I could do that, with some degree of difficulty, of course. My guess was that he had found a better job but did not want to alert the staff about it.

"Are you thanking me?" I said, waiting for the bombshell.

"Ya, ya, tough, eh? Faza Mindi no gud. Faza Lago no gud. You? Ha ha haaaa, tough. Otha boyz coward, but you?" He roared again and made me uncomfortable. "Faza Lago ask about boat and I say I watch fa thief not fa writer, ha haa . . ." The giant doubled up, clutched his thighs and roared away.

My fear now was that some troubled priest who might have heard us was about to catch me.

"Very clever of you to look out for thieves and not for writers!" I unsuccessfully tried to laugh.

"Me writer too," he said, pointing to his huge chest with the quiver full of his odious arrows. "Me put dem pepaz wid name in Mindi and Lago orfice, he he heeeee." He went off into one of his huge laughs. This time I joined in.

"You?"

"Ya, fa Dorobo game."

I laughed hard this time, for now I understood. A group of boys used to tease this man by pretending that they were involved in a sentence-making game.

"I met a Dorobo warrior yesterday," one would say.

"Did you know that Father Mindi's mother was a Dorobo woman?" the second would ask.

"What a coincidence! The bishop's uncle was a Dorobo warrior too!"

Those boys were the ones who took the blame for the damage done to Fr. Mindi's car. None of them knew who had done them in. The watchman had fooled us all!! It all made sense, because both Fr. Mindi and Fr. Lageau had talked about firing him, but the rector had vetoed the decision on all occasions.

"It late now, Faza. Sleep, sleep." He made a snoring sound and melted into the shadows. I kept thinking that he was Fisherman, the power saboteur. A real fisher of men. I hurried to the bathrooms. My teeth still clattered as I lay down in my bed.

There was confusion and incredulity when morning uncovered yet another assault on *Agatha*. While he condemned the action, the rector showed us the nail the attacker had left behind. Fr. Lageau had another migraine attack and ate pills and stayed in bed the whole day. There were threats from staff members loyal to him, for they were afraid that their cars and other properties might be attacked too.

Agatha was repainted, and a German-made monster of an alarm was installed on her. There were rumors that Lageau had put in an order for a ferocious police dog. As if I planned to attack *Agatha* again! The dog came after I had left the seminary. Years later, government soldiers sent to hound guerrillas from the forest cut its throat and barbecued it.

"*Agatha*'s alarm could feed you for a whole year," Fr. Lageau was quoted as saying by his volleyball playmates. We could live with that, because there were no more expectations from him, and the hope that he might improve things had died. Boys now made jokes about *Agatha* and the dog.

"How is *Agatha*?"

"Oh, she is fine."

"Who is Agatha?"

"A little yellow-haired Canadian whore."

"Where did she spend the night?"

"Whoring and cheating. Her pimp cut her up in retaliation."

"What did her boyfriend do about it?"
"He bought her a police dog."

Almost at the same time as the events at the seminary, Padlock lost her parents to natural causes. At the moment I was facing the night watchman, a large, flamboyantly patterned puff adder was being attacked and displaced by safari ants. He moved his headquarters to a sweet potato garden and buried himself under the soil and the sparse leaves left by the hot season and the first harvests. A few hours later, the old woman woke her husband for morning prayers, the rosary and a hymn to welcome God's new day. This was like second nature: they had been doing it for the last forty years. They loved praying to the God who had sent both their children to Rome and the Holy Land and brought them safely home. The old woman prepared tea on an open fire in the kitchen and served it quickly. She left her husband in the sitting room under the supervision of the crucified Jesus and the Holy Family, and went to the garden. It promised to be a hot day. The sky was clear, and she could see all the way to the forest. One part of the forest still bore the ravages of the recent storm. Godless people blamed Mbale for causing the storm. She found this ludicrous, pitiable too. Those people needed a foundation—God. The storm had come but had not done much damage to her house and gardens. She believed that it was not the hill that had protected them, but God. Mbale had got off badly and now had debts to pay, but it was all for the better: he would work harder and pray harder. There was nothing God could not do if asked with a sincere heart.

The old woman bent down to rake up the sparse potato leaves clinging to the thin, snaky stalks. She became aware of the sharp pain in her lower back. It had been there for years. She had dedicated it to the Virgin Mary. She stepped over potato mounds, gathered the leaves and heaped them at one end of the garden. She surveyed the naked mounds, survivors of wind, rain and the first harvests, which had been done with digging sticks. She grabbed her hoe, ready to dig up the mounds, collect the last potatoes and prepare the area for another crop. The pain shot up again. She thought about asking one of her grandchildren, probably Mbale's, to come and live here and help her with some chores. She raised her hoe and cut deep into the mounds, spreading the soil over her feet and collecting the potatoes one by one with her fingers. Last harvests were usually mediocre, and this was no exception: the potatoes were small and stringy.

She felt a scratch on her right foot. She ignored it. It had to be one of those red safari ants she had seen near the latrine. As she dug up the mounds, she thanked God for the blessings He had poured on her family: her children bringing home the pope's blessings and pictures in which they stood near the Holy Father was more than she could ask for. It made all the hard work of raising them rise like a cloud of incense to the portals of heaven. Her own children! Children who used to go barefoot to school, who were teased for being poor, who were taught the hard way. Her children had flown to the Holy Land! The blessings Nakkazi had brought back were a sign that God had forgiven her sisters for living in sin, for rebelling against His will, for shaming everyone by begetting children of sin and for spurning holy matrimony.

The second scratch was almost imperceptible: the pain was swamped by the thoughts swirling in her head. She was remembering Nakkazi's wedding. She could see the whole place crawling with people: relatives, friends, strangers. She could still hear the builders hammering, taking down the old roof and putting up the new one. She could see the bride glistening in the sun, butter oil sinking deeper and deeper into her skin. She remembered feeling a bit pressured by the inlaws, and had been instrumental in turning down the transport they had offered. Then their vehicles broke down on the wedding day, and most people remained behind! She remembered feeling worried that Nakibuka would create a rift in her daughter's marriage: the way she eyed the groom had been unhealthy. Thank God nothing had happened, and Nakkazi had been happily married for years and had never said a word against her aunt. Now one of Nakkazi's boys was going to become a priest: what an honor! The old woman felt she had fulfilled her mission on earth.

The third scratch jolted her: it was very sharp, as if it had been made with a long thorn or a large needle. In a bid not to interrupt her thoughts, she did the natural thing; she lifted her left foot and used the heel to rub hard and kill the red ant without having to look at it. Her heel, however, landed on a thick, soft, rotten-potato-like thing. She jumped in the air and saw the viper's tail swing like a thick, dirty rope.

The arrowhead attached to her foot was magnified by fear to the size of a pumpkin. Jesus, Joseph and Mary: What was happening? She screamed and fled the garden. The snake still clung to her foot. She could feel the poison entering her bloodstream. The whole leg already felt heavy. Regaining her wits, she stopped, retraced her steps and reached for the hoe. She battered the viper and in the process almost chopped off her big toe. She could see her husband trudging toward her and the neighbors approaching. Who would look after her husband when she was gone? She had to live. The energetic neighbors got to her first. They pulled the viper off her leg, calmed her down and helped her as best they could.

On the way to the hospital, with the furious sounds of battering, crushing, marauding winds in her ears, she succumbed to the poison.

Her husband didn't attend her burial. Her death released the chained winds of a ten-year-old malarial storm which surged in the very core of his being with diabolical intensity. The winds sent him vomiting, sweating and laboring for each breath. After only two days he was given the last sacraments by his son. After administering the last rites, Mbale returned home to lead his mother's burial. As the first mourners returned home, news came that the old man had died.

I didn't attend either burial: I left the dead to bury themselves, because of exams. Besides, I had to help Fr. Kaanders collect seminary books from the already restless boys. It was a hectic, hunger-ridden, truancy-bitten week. We got help from some volunteers, but the progress we made was slow. We checked each book for both the seminary stamp and the serial number. There were many lost books, but there was hardly much I could do about it. Kaanders kept dozing and drooling into the books he was working on. During the few moments of free time I had, I forged my own expulsion letter, signed and stamped it with the seminary stamp we kept for library purposes. I also recommended myself to the best schools I knew.

Lwendo could not understand why in the world I was quitting. The next time we met, he was a lieutenant in the army. A guerrilla war had been waged and won, and the guerrilla forces he had belatedly joined following his own expulsion had become the nation's armed forces.

BOOK FIVE

THE SEVENTIES were dominated by self-made men who, defying their limited backgrounds, rose to vertiginous heights of power before dashing their chariots into the abyss. Names that came to mind were Richard Nixon, Chairman Mao, Emperor Bokassa and Elvis Presley. They reminded me of yellow moths which flew long distances in the dark to come and dance round Grandpa's hurricane lamp. Bewitched by the luminescence, most would circle the glass, avoiding direct contact and keeping away from the lethal ventilators above. The intrepid ones, however, could not resist the ultimate temptation, to explore further. They got sucked into the ventilators and were roasted to death. Others eventually were scalded by the hot glass, and more collapsed with fatigue. The apparent connection between luminescence and death puzzled me for years.

■   ■   ■

My childhood was undergoing a death of sorts, sloughing into adulthood, the carcass of blind precocity disintegrating in the new light. I was moving in a new direction. My eyes were opening to the world, taking in vistas they had hitherto been blind to. My flirtation with General Amin had ended, killed by the murderous light of truth. I felt I had more or less outgrown the fight with Serenity and Padlock. I realized that I had all along dammed my disgust with the way the affairs of the country were being conducted just to keep fighting in my corner. This peeling away of old skin hurt. I felt sore, lost, trapped. The way to the future seemed bleak. I experienced alternating feelings of jubilation and desolation. I shuddered to think about the task of redefining myself. I shuddered at the thought of confronting the world within and without. For a long time I thought I was chasing a mirage.

During school holidays, I always got the impression that at the seminary we were living inside either a charmed circle or a blind corral. The world outside was a harsh, formless, convoluted chaos in which success was for the fittest. The rules of engagement had to be worked out by intelligent observation and intuition, the very tools we were discouraged from developing. After being told what to do and when to do it for months, we returned with a sick feeling of detachment and debility to the real world of ruthless survivors. The fathers called the world "a den of lions," and it must have been so in many ways; but along with the fear, it contained the genuine excitement of exploration. This was the only place where we could get to the bottom of our feelings and thoughts, because the type of acting demanded was different from the cut-and-dried roles offered at the seminary. This was the school of hard knocks, but buried under the heaps of chaff were precious grains of wheat, without which the bread of life could not be made.

I always spent my school holidays with Aunt Lwandeka. It was to her house that the tyrants had dispatched me after the incident of feigned sex with Lusanani. Like many students, I looked forward to the holidays. The ordeal of collecting hundreds of library books at the end of each school term meant that I always arrived home burned by exhaustion. I would spend the first few days in sweet bewilderment, trying to find my feet, fighting to regain my strength. In a way, I was like a tourist who came with the season and left as soon as his appetites had been sated. I enjoyed the anonymity of living in a shrinking industrial town with a past larger than its present. I enjoyed watching people who were totally different from the seminary crowd, and I was fascinated by their stories. I relished the feeling that I was temporarily part of this doomed crowd, savoring the ways of Sodom and Gomorrah with no real danger of perishing with the lot. Images from Uncle Kawayida's descriptions of town life careered through my mind again. I would refresh them with news of Amin's latest capers, fluctuating prices, stories of bribery, murder, military mayhem, rape, betrayal, bravery, love . . . and try to work them into a composite whole. At such times, I gorged like a bear preparing for the arrival of winter.

It was during these school holidays that I realized how powerful the poison of the hydra at the heart of the seminary system was. All the work the fathers put in at the seminary, telling us how special our call was and how different we were from the sinners in the world, paid off now. It was hard to really feel part of what was going on around us. Reality was a Pandora's box of conflicting loyalties. Amin's capers became things happening in a cartoon film. The people found dead in forests became characters playing dead. The scarcity of essential commodities and the general hardship became transient phenomena that would vanish as soon as the picture was over. The stoicism needed to endure attained a heroic luster. The air of creeping doom acquired apocalyptic echoes. It became the last turn of the screw, foreshadowing the arrival of the savior. Self-preserving as this refracted view of the world was, it exacted a heavy tax on its espousers. I was neither the first nor the last seminarian to groan under the tremendous burden.

I approached Aunt Lwandeka like a puzzle, a split persona I had to reconstruct in the quasi-surreal circumstances of the time when many things were not what they seemed to be. To begin with, she never gave me any details of her abduction, imprisonment and subsequent release. Occasionally, she spoke of being pushed into a car, interrogated, threatened and taken to court, but she provided only the merest outline. Aunt Kasawo and Padlock and other adults knew everything. I wanted to join that exclusive club. If I was not going to get what I wanted from the horse's mouth, I knew I had to tap other sources. It cost me about two school years to put the final piece of the puzzle in place.

At the beginning of my holidays, I always hoped to find some new document, some loose rumor or story adding to the original. My biggest find so far had been a chit written by Aunt Lwandeka in fat, girlish letters on a page torn from an exercise book belonging to one of her three children. I found it tucked away in a small Good News Bible at the bottom of her suitcase. It read:

> 7/3/73   allest. ballaks. intallogeson. snek. tall man. knife.
> bligadir. fleedom.

The first time I saw the chit, I laughed. I had never seen such a childish interpretation of the English language by an adult. This kind of writing could crack up a classroom for days. The names Cane would give this unfortunate individual! But this was my maternal aunt. This was the peasant girl who had rebelled against her strict Catholic parents and refused to finish school. How I wished she had kept a diary, with all the juicy details! But like many peasant girls, she never kept details of her life on paper. She had written this chit to aid her memory, and I knew that the decision had cost her a lot of thought. Her childish English suddenly made me feel protective of her. I felt closer to her because I knew her secret, her weakness. I also felt that I had the power to redeem her.

I added the new facts to the sketch of events I already had. Now I knew that she was arrested on the seventh of March, 1973, and was taken to the barracks, where she was interrogated by a tall man with a knife. She referred the tall man to a certain brigadier, who influenced the subsequent course of events. The case was taken to court, and she was finally freed. Who was Snek? Was "snek" an anagram? If so, was he a foreigner or some home-grown bruiser? Was Snek the tall man or the brigadier? Maybe Snek was none of the above and she was the woman who had written Aunt the trouble-causing letter. I was tempted on very many occasions to casually mention the name Snek and watch Aunt's reaction, but I valiantly restrained myself. I did not want to get into her bad books.

When it finally dawned on me that "snek" was not a person but a reptile, I felt angry that Aunt had not told me what had happened to her. I knew that she lived in mortal terror of snakes, but I wanted to know why. Had the thug made her eat raw snake meat? Or fuck a snake? What was this snake thing about? I felt that she had locked me out of a vital secret.

Aunt Lwandeka's involvement with politics started after her release. Something had changed in her during those weeks of proximity with death. One could even say that the snake poison had gone to her head. Her handwriting might have remained girlish, but girlhood had ended for her. Her involvement, however, remained low-key and only became open in the mid-seventies, when guerrilla activities across the border in Tanzania increased. She gradually told me about it. She was a member of the National Reform Movement, or NRM, as everyone called it. The NRM was a small organization within the blanket guerrilla movement in Tanzania fighting to oust Amin. It was charged with the task of executing small anti-government operations like blowing up power lines, wrecking bridges, attacking military roadblocks and disorganizing government figures.

From the little she told me, I learned that Aunt's role was to supply information about local troop movements, roadblocks and the whereabouts of key local government officials. She was also part of the group that housed NRM guerrillas in secret locations and supplied them with travel documents, graduated-tax tickets, identity cards and the like. All this was playing with fire, of course. If Amin's men arrested her again, they would not let her go: they would torture her, rape her, possibly kill her, or make her beg them to end her suffering. I was sure they would make last time seem like a schoolyard prank. It was no longer a secret that the State Research Bureau, military intelligence and other security organs were scared of whatever was brewing across the border. Aunt knew what Amin's men could do, but she thumbed her nose at them. She had already crossed and burned the last bridge: fear of death. All this did not make me feel very safe. At the seminary, there was this thing about all authority coming from God; I did not believe it, and yet I felt there was some truth in it. The jigsaw puzzle I was putting together at times seemed to form some devilish configurations. I did not like it.

The first time Aunt got into serious trouble, the time when Padlock left her domain for four full days and I remained in charge of the shitters with the bobbin already in my possession, it was a letter from a German lady that triggered the whole thing. Dr. Wagner had come to Uganda with the intention of setting up her own practice. She first worked for a Catholic hospital in order to acclimatize, and that was when Aunt ran into her. Aunt worked as her housekeeper. Later, after being impressed with her diligence, Dr. Wagner made plans for her to go back to school in order to improve her English as a precursor to further schooling. Aunt was very enthusiastic about the plan, and being in the proximity of a learned person motivated her more. She admired Dr. Wagner and found her easy to live with because the rules were clear-cut and everything happened at a fixed time, in a fixed order. The 1971 coup did not bother Dr. Wagner. She knew that whichever regime came to power, doctors would be needed. The Indian exodus shook her but did not unhinge her: she was a professional, after all. If anything, the exodus hardened her resolve. The scope of her duties could only widen, as there were all those patients formerly treated by Indian doctors to care for. However, the Economic War—the effort to indigenize the economy—bred instability, which worried her. Since the mission hospital she worked for had been standing from the beginning of the century, she did not fear for her job, though she now doubted the feasibility of striking out on her own. Then the hammer fell on Britons, Americans and Germans. She was allowed to stay, but things went from bad to worse. Two hospital vans were stolen. Staff members disappeared and wouldn't say where they had been when they returned. Dr. Wagner's view was that somebody in government was harassing the hospital because the archbishop was very critical of the Amin regime. The hospital took measures and employed security guards, and staff were advised not to go out at night or open doors for anybody after curfew time. Dr. Wagner believed she still had a chance. She was not yet ready to return to Germany; her mother had died of cancer, and she was too shaken up to go back just yet. Then she got notice that her work permit had to be renewed on a monthly basis. She thought of going to neighboring Kenya, but she had not liked the racial climate there. When, out of the blue, she was given twenty-four hours to leave the country, she flew home in a huff.

The letter she wrote to her former housekeeper had to be rewritten several times, each time diluting its venom, but she refused to erase certain elements; for example:

The soldiers at the airport stole my money. They also wanted to steal my watch, but I would not surrender it. I advised them to ask General Amin for a salary raise if they believed they deserved more money for terrorizing people. One tried to butt me with his rifle, but his colleague held the gun from behind. This makes me wonder how you are going to live in that kind of environment. You are on your own now. Work hard on your education, and make sure that you get some certificates. Send me information about your activities and about the country; and if it is important, I will circulate it among friends and among the country's well-wishers. Take care of yourself, and remember: Ugandan soldiers are very dangerous. . . .

The policy of opening foreign mail had reached its zenith about then, and overzealous underlings, eager to impress overbearing bosses and win scanty favors, fell upon Dr. Wagner's letter like a famished pride of lionesses on a giant buffalo. Within a day, they had traced Aunt's whereabouts. She was still at Nsambya Hospital, where the letter was addressed. They rushed to the junior staff quarters, pulled her out of bed at 3 a.m., tossed her into the boot of a car and drove her two kilometers to Makindye Barracks, where they had an office.

Aunt Lwandeka ate all the threats as they were served to her. She had already realized that hers was an important case, one most likely to be tried in court as a testimony to German infiltration, spying and slander campaigns. It would bolster the claim that mission workers and others in the employ of the Church were spies for foreign governments. Aunt's captors wanted a confession obtained without visible bodily damage to her, because she had to appear in court, but the confession was not forthcoming. Tempers became dangerously inflamed.

Normally, women talked quickly, but Aunt would not talk at all. She kept swallowing their insults and threats with a calm, almost vacant look. The "tall man" asked his men to strap her onto a table faceup. He drew his knife and threatened to cut her up, in vain. He then pulled a spitting cobra out of an iron box. He put it at her feet, and it bit her several times. That really unhinged her. She remained conscious by an act of will pinned on the belief that the fangs had been blunted and the poison milked. The horror made her scream, and the men laughed and stroked her face arrogantly. The snake bit her again and again, but she still had enough willpower not to tell them anything. Mad with rage, the man picked up the snake and slid it inside her clothes via her cleavage. She started shouting like mad. She tugged at the ropes, and the men laughed and slapped each other on the back. They danced around, shouting, *"Amin oye, oyeee! Amin ju, juuuu!"* At one time Aunt thought she was going to faint. The reptile kept wriggling as though entering the depths of her body in order to terminate her and her future children with its lethal poison. All horror had a limit, and the thugs knew that. The man at last retrieved the reptile and petted it. He rubbed it in her face one last time and asked her to talk. He wanted answers to the following questions: What were the names of the spy organizations Dr. Wagner worked for? What kind of spies was she recruiting? What sort of military aggression was her group planning? Was she at all linked with the failed 1972 guerrilla incursion into Uganda? What kind of secret information did Aunt send the German spy? Which of the remaining hospital staff were spies? How long had this spy ring been in existence?

Aunt refused to talk. The knife was now brought close to her face, but her lips remained sealed. She knew by now that they would not cut her. She, on the other hand, was working out when to spring a surprise on them. When she felt that the time had come, she asked them to talk to a famous brigadier. Immediately.

Who the fuck did she think she was? Who the fuck did she think she was talking to? Who the fuck did she think this brigadier was?

She said time and again that she worked for him. Baiting dissidents, foreign spies and their benefactors.

Why the hell hadn't she said so before? There was plenty of confusion and suspicion and a touch of fear. Longevity in the security agencies, as the tall man and his cohorts knew, depended on not stepping on big men's toes, and on knowing when to relent. However much the tall man might have liked to teach this woman a lesson, he knew that it was suicidal to press on, especially if her claims were true. That was Aunt's salvation. Even if the brigadier took time to do something, Aunt knew that she had already frightened the thugs enough to be left alone.

The brigadier ordered her captors to take her to court. She was taken dressed in flowing robes to cover legs swollen with snake poison. The case files, however, were stolen or lost or both. The letter also disappeared. The judge got angry that court time was being wasted. The case was dismissed after a fortnight. Aunt's brothers and sisters, with the help of Padlock's money, bribed the thugs and the policemen to drop all "investigations." Aunt was released a week after. The brigadier later defected to Tanzania to join the exiles and guerrillas.

Padlock and Kasawo used the incident to implore Aunt to turn her back on politics and involvement with dissidents. As a survivor of an attack on her life, Kasawo believed that she was a credible expert on how to survive in hard times, and she expected her younger sister to swallow her admonitions and advice whole. Kasawo also believed that her younger sister's involvement in politics was a form of compensation for failing to find a man to marry and settle down with.

As a good younger sister who had just escaped the jaws of death, Aunt Lwandeka did not defend her position, showing the expected deference to her elder sisters. She let them exhaust themselves with talk.

"You must stop all this political nonsense," Padlock ordered.

"We were worried sick about you. We were afraid that something terrible was going to happen to you. Have you got no feelings for others? How can you even think of dragging us through the same nettles by saying that you cannot give up?"

"Get a man, marry and settle down." Kasawo dropped her favorite line with a smile. "If your own children are not enough for you, go and care for orphans."

"Stop writing to foreign spies, sister," Padlock said angrily. "What will that German woman do for you? She was using you all the time she was here, making you wash her knickers and towels. Wasn't that bad enough? Now she is back in her country and has left you to languish. She doesn't even know what you have just been through. She doesn't even care. Can't you see that?"

"Listen to your eldest sister's words," Kasawo said.

"I know you are smart but also naive and unguided. Ever since you gave up religion and stopped praying and putting yourself at the feet of God, things have gone bad for you," Padlock began, her voice rising without her face muscles reacting. It could have been the miracle of the talking statue. "The first educated man who came along fooled us all, and in the end, he dropped you to marry a more educated woman. What has he done for you and your son ever since? What have the other men done for you and your children? You work hard for them as if they were orphans. Now you are gallivanting with politicians who will dump you as soon as you have done what they want. Stop trusting people. Invest your trust in the only one who will never desert you: God."

Aunt took her punishment in silence. She gave her sisters her demurest look but did her own thing in the end. There was no turning back. She considered going to Tanzania to join the NRM guerrillas, leaving her three children with their fathers. She communicated with the brigadier a number of times about it. He wanted her to join him in Tanzania because the NRM could use all the help they could get. A close friend who was also involved in the struggle took her aside one day and warned her that she was putting all her eggs in one basket. He asked her what she knew about fighting, if she knew how long the struggle would last. He asked her if she was sure that the NRM would get a big chunk of power when the struggle ended, if she was sure that she would be given a big post after the struggle. He asked her if she believed that all those guerrilla groups loosely united against Amin would remain united after he was gone. He asked her if she was really determined to throw her life away as though she had no other alternatives. Then he asked her to make and sign her will and hand it over to him.

Finally, Aunt Lwandeka came to her senses and stayed. She saw the wisdom of fighting from inside, giving information to the NRM and housing NRM missionaries before they did their job. It proved a more satisfactory option. It did not take her away from her children. It did not disrupt her life; in fact, it gave her the chance to remain in control.

After being haunted by the wooden faces of the tyrants, it was almost a revelation to be near someone with a living face. Aunt Lwandeka had a fluid face which could project her emotions with ease. She could smile, laugh and cry. Her face could also project seriousness, toughness and anger in telling measures. It was a shock to discover that a woman who had come from the same Catholic peasant womb as Padlock could be so different. She used a warm voice when greeting you in the morning, when talking to you during the day and when asking you about your day in the evening. She played with her children, and asked them what was or was not wrong with them. She told them foolish stories and sang them meaningless little songs. She put them at ease but also demanded discipline from them.

Aunt bathed all her children herself, scrubbed their backs and examined their feet carefully. She held them and let them vomit in her lap or shower her with diarrhea when they were ill. When they had measles, and their eyes went red, and they refused to eat, and they cried incessantly, she would plead with them, ask them to be quiet and tempt them with nice little things. She would show a high degree of patience even if she herself was feeling very tired.

Ballasted with Padlockisms, I took up arms to save these children from what I believed was the wrong way to be raised. I drove them hard to do their homework. I drilled them to memorize the multiplication tables. I loaded them with spelling tests. I shouted at them to wash up and to move quickly when ordered to do something. I advised Aunt to discipline them, meaning to beat them and to stop them from talking back. I asked her to discourage them from finding excuses for the wrongs they did. I wanted them to be docile, obedient and trustworthy. I wanted them to stop playing ball, throwing things, tearing paper and chasing each other round the house. Playing seemed to liberate a laxity that had no place on the table of virtue.

I took it upon myself to father these fatherless bastards whose only common parental bond was their mother. Where were their biological fathers? Wasn't Aunt a sort of whore? Wouldn't the Biblical Jews have stoned her to death? Deep down I must have been titillated by the word "whore"—it made me remember Cane's nudes, labias gaping and beckoning to both customers and voyeurs. Aunt was doing it with many men, I thought. The thought both infuriated and excited me. I loathed seeing her talk to any man. I would get seizures when she talked to her man friend. The way she paid attention and responded to him, even if the subject was as banal as diapers, fever or sunshine! As the "man" in the house, as the "dad" of the children, as the number two in command, I felt both insulted and eclipsed.

I would not have minded if Aunt had been ugly, obese and nasty, but she was petite, elegant and attractive. She made me think of Lusanani all the time. When she smiled, the gums did not jut sheathless in the air, deserted by lips pulled brutally back. Instead, the lips stretched just up to the top of the teeth and stayed there in a controlled, almost self-conscious smile. I wanted her to smile over and over again.

Her smile was the dearest feature I preserved and clung to when the tide turned against her and riddled holes into old dreams.

I started entertaining murderous fantasies when I saw her with her man friend. I wanted him to be crushed by a car. This man lived in his own house, a distance from Aunt's house. When he came over, he brought good things with him and tried to be nice, but I wanted nothing to do with him. I wished impotence on him, because I knew that after the smiles and the gifts, he would lie on top of Aunt, push his large penis inside her and make her emit silly sounds. I could see him with his hands all over her, dipping his fingers into all manner of orifices, pushing with all his might. I was in the clutches of the impotent anger suffered by the righteous who get trapped in compromising situations.

I felt invaded and demeaned by his presence. Here was a man who could father the fathers of the three little bastards. I did not like the urge I felt to watch myself when he was around. I wanted him to be the one to watch himself, ask himself questions and doubt his self-worth. I wanted him to fall off his pedestal and break his limbs. If not, I would push him off. In order to catch him with his pants down, I took to keyholing. It was at this time that all the morsels I had plucked from library books came alive. I would put my ear to the keyhole, dying to catch a wet whisper, a broken sigh, a sharp moan. I wanted to compare Sr. Bison's simple, clean, very effective sounds and Lusanani's elaborate songs with Aunt's unknown repertoire. Time stood still in boggy confusion whenever I was rewarded with a sound of sorts. Celibate priesthood was in the balance. If this was how a seminarian gathered information and life experience without breaking celibacy rules, it became clear that it was a ship full of holes I was sailing on. I could feel myself drown, snapping for air. I eventually gave up keyholing, feeling lucky that I had not been nabbed.

On such mornings, Aunt would emerge looking radiant and strangely calm, almost apologetic in her niceness. I kept imagining the storm that arose one day while Jesus slept in a boat. After all the humping and grinding and vocalizing, Aunt's storms seemed to have dissipated. Mr. Storm Crusher himself always emerged looking nonchalant, as though all he had done was swat a fly. Aunt would take extra care with the breakfast, as though she had to appease everybody. A strange unease would overshadow the meal. It was as though something wrong had happened, and everyone knew the culprit but could not speak out due to conflicting loyalties. Aunt would resemble somebody juggling hats on her head. After the meal, she would change from lover and mother to NRM operative, market supervisor, liquor brewer and church volunteer. Some act. Mr. Storm Crusher's departure thrilled me.

I could appreciate all the different hats Aunt wore except that of church volunteer. Her reconciliation with the Church seemed quite dramatic in the context of her teenage rebellion and independent adult life. It seemed a calculated decision to incorporate a part of her past into her present life. She went to church every Sunday and was a member of the Catholic Women's Group. It did not occur to me then that she might have stayed near the Church just to milk information for the guerrillas, because many Catholics sympathized with the cause.

During the week, she spent the biggest part of the day at the market fulfilling her duties as a market supervisor. In the process of settling disputes, handling applications for stalls, collecting stall dues and liaising with local government officials, she conducted NRM business. She exchanged messages with contacts, guerrillas who came disguised as customers, potential traders and favor seekers. In addition to this, she brewed liquor once a month at a friend's place in the suburbs. It was a very dangerous undertaking, whose crudity repelled me. I would compare it with Fr. Kaanders' book bindery and feel dismayed. Why was Aunt taking such a risk? Were there no better ways to supplement her income? It was only much later, after contact with the soldierly Infernal Trinity, that I reconciled myself to the business.

For the time being, things went well. I enjoyed the holidays very much, save for the occasional worry when Aunt was late coming home in the evening. I would start speculating. Had her luck run out? Had the security forces caught her carrying NRM documents? But she always came back, and apologized for keeping me waiting.

My wish came true. Aunt's man friend stopped spending nights at her place during school holidays. I had pushed him off his pedestal. I did not care how often Aunt went over to his place, as long as he stayed out of my way.

During my second holiday, I saw a picture of the famous brigadier. It was again in that Good News Bible, where Aunt seemed to hide things dear to her. I had seen the man once on television and three times in the papers. I started suspecting that this was more than guerrilla business. Soldiers never gave photographs to civilians like that, except for very personal reasons. I felt excited and at the same time repelled by this move. So my maternal aunt was fucking one of the leading men in the country! What nerve! The picture had been taken with a Polaroid camera, a very convenient thing for such a man, who must have mistrusted photo studios. But why keep it in the house? Was that not the height of girlish folly? I remembered her fat, girlish handwriting. Was my family doomed to cross paths with soldiers? I was also consumed by hero worship. I would have given anything to know what this man was like as a person. What made him tick? What did it feel like to be in government and at the same time sympathize with guerrillas?

With Mr. Storm Crusher confined to his house, I felt secure in Aunt's house. I no longer had reason to bully her children. I had grown to like them. I thought of them as the outspoken version of my old shitters, whom I had not seen in a long time.

Early in 1976 I went to the village for the first time in years. The hills and the swamps and the forests were as magnificent as ever. The village had shrunk. It was like a desert island eroded by gales, before being revitalized by a new population of pirates. The old part of the village was trapped in an abyss of desolation, while the new part exhaled the harsh air of dubious wealth. I found drinking places in the most unlikely spots. Loud dance music emanated from the obscure corner where Fingers, the leper, had his house. There was a new house now, with a new iron roof that glared like trapped lightning and a huge loudspeaker on the veranda that spread musical mayhem all around. Strange youths in bell-bottoms and large, ugly platform shoes swayed past me as they struggled with intoxication from imported liquors. Loud drunken boys walked with thick-bottomed drunken girls in thick shoes, Afro wigs and gaudy jewelry, mouthing obscenities formerly unknown in these swampy areas. Where had all these people come from?

A clutch of new houses with red bricks and iron roofs had loud advertisements dangling on the verandas: SUPERMARKET, HOTEL, RESTAURANT, CASINO. In front of these "supermarkets," "hotels," "restaurants" and "casinos," youthful gamblers slapped smudged cards hard and loud on gaudy tables to the roar of the spectators. Expert nostrils produced double-barrelled nicotine fumes. Alcohol flowed among the tables. It impregnated brains with fights and groins with frustrated hard-ons. I glimpsed a mini-brawl. A card game had gone rancid. Cards flew in the air. The table lost its limbs. A platform heel ground the middle of a fallen face, to the cheers of the inebriated, thick-bottomed girls. Hard by, three youths were trying out small Honda motorcycles, revving them and pumping blue smoke into the eyes of the cheering girls. Somebody with a large hat was collecting money for a race as I walked past. Sodden noises tickled the back of my head, as though pulling me back into the fray. A little farther on, three motorcycles passed me in a bend, splashing me with mud as they tore past to the other end of the village. They were being followed by a puny Honda Civic filled with noisy youths banging the windows, the seats and the roof.

I hurried to the old village. The old people were cowering in the shadow of desolation. It seemed as if the explosions predicted by Grandpa had begun by sucking the village into whirlwinds of violent change, dividing it into irreconcilable parts. The nostalgia that had marked the early years, when the oracle of Grandma and Grandpa invoked stories from the lacuna, was gone, erased by the aggressive energy of the young smugglers and their friends. A touch of fear had crept into the area.

Serenity's house was wrapped in webs of decay. The windows were sealed from the inside by termites, and the doors were being sawn off their hinges by ants. The roof was flaking and reddening in the incessant rain and sunshine. Serenity had obviously lost interest in the house, and in the village, and was ready to see the past crumble into the dust of decrepitude. I opened the house as I used to in the past when a visitor emerged from the lacuna. I was greeted by a musty cloud of heat, dust and bats. I handled the doors and the windows carefully lest they fall from their hinges. I did not remove the termite tracks. I did not sweep either. What was the point? I watched as the wind picked up the dust and swept it into the branches of the nearby trees. In the sitting room, tucked away in a corner where Padlock used to keep her mat, was a two-foot anthill. In Serenity's bedroom a large snake had sloughed under the bed of memories. The bed was dusty but still on its legs, thanks to anti-termite varnish. I emerged into the backyard in a rush. Weeds had overrun the place, colonizing the bathroom and the fireplace where I used to boil water for Aunt Tiida's four daily baths. Somewhere here I had received my first thrashing, somewhere there Grandma had stood, planning her intervention. The latrine from under which I had spied on Padlock's genitalia had shrunk like a can in the fist of a giant.

Grandma's place still bore the marks of the fire. The puny cottage built by a relative near the site of the old house was empty. The yard was overgrown and full of old leaves from the trees under which Grandma and Grandpa used to fight after lunch. I stood at the spot where the crowd was on the night of the fire. The bottom seemed to fall out of my bowels. I no longer belonged here. I had to find a new center of existence. Oppressed by the weight of the past and the brutality of change, I walked away.

Grandpa's house still looked big and impressive, but carried the sulky air of a deteriorating monument. The coffee shamba was battling with weeds, the windbreakers with mistletoe, the terraces with erosion.

Grandpa had aged too. All those beatings, and the shooting, and the stabbing, and the turmoil of his political and personal life had taken a big toll. If you were looking for him, you could find his old warring self only in the eyes: the candid, questioning gaze was still there. His ears had weakened, especially the one slapped by goons in 1966. Now you had to shout a bit to be heard. He cocked his head to favor the better ear. We were very happy to see each other. He was struck by the fact that I had grown. He kept asking when I would conquer my lawyerly studies, and I kept explaining that I still had a long way to go.

We visited Grandma's grave. Stiff-backed, Grandpa stood and watched as I effortlessly pulled weeds, rearranged stones moved by erosion and straightened the cross bent by the winds. The same unspoken question went through our minds: Who killed this woman? Who judged her, sentenced her and executed her? I remembered all those babies we delivered and all the herbs we collected in the forest, in the swamp, everywhere. I again felt like wetting my pants, a strange feeling after all those years. I waited for her ghost to rise and shake the leaves of my favorite jackfruit tree. I waited for some miracle to happen. Nothing happened. She had left me to finish the job she had begun. My medium of communication had changed from amniotic fluid and gore to lawyerly ink and saliva.

We left the burial ground. The coffee shamba could do with better maintenance. Many trees needed trimming. Grandpa relied on hired labor both to weed and to pick his coffee. He still got enough money from it to look after himself, although the mills took months to pay, blaming the government for the delays. It seemed as if Serenity's dream had come true: Grandpa's estate was no longer as profitable as before, but he did not mind. He had not wanted to go to Rome. He rarely travelled these days, except to attend funerals, important weddings and big clan meetings. Clan land had gone to other families. Grandpa was now free, no longer the arbiter of clan disputes, no longer the custodian of clan property. He was just a man who sat and watched the fluctuations of the political climate.

He asked me to shave him. It took me time to find the razor blades. He sat in his easy chair, with his legs stretched out, his thin, deeply etched Beckett face upturned. The razor crackled and filled with stubble as I dragged it across valleys and ridges. Birds chirped fussily in the tallest gray-skinned *mtuba* trees. They jumped up and down on one branch.

"Snakes," Grandpa said irately. I nicked his throat. "It is a black mamba up there. This place is full of black mambas."

"Green mambas too," I said, cleaning the stubble and the blood.

"All this bush," he said, sweeping with his hands. "It is full of snakes."

"Are you still afraid of snakes, Grandpa?"

"Who isn't? Of course I am still afraid of them. My worst fear is finding one in bed, sitting on it and getting bitten." I suddenly remembered Padlock's mother and the puff adder that had killed her. I did not laugh.

"Snakes replaced all the people who left the village," he continued.

"How about the newcomers?" I asked eagerly. "I can hardly recognize a familiar face in this village!"

"I told you the village is full of snakes. It is the coffee-smuggling madness that is the cause of all this."

"When was this area taken over by smugglers?"

"A few years after you left. It was good that this happened in your absence."

"How did it happen? I mean . . ."

"In the sixties, your parents migrated to the city to look for work and a better life. Now young people leave to join coffee-smuggling gangs and to get killed by anti-smuggling patrols."

"Tell me about it, Grandpa," I said, almost salivating.

"Young people discovered a way of making quick money, without having to go to school. They smuggle coffee across the lake to Kenya and exchange it for American dollars. They come back laden with consumer goods: bell-bottom trousers, radios, Oris watches, wigs, all that junk, and behave like maniacs. They discovered that this little village was a good place to hide and to cause mayhem without attracting undue attention from the authorities. The nearest military barracks is fifteen kilometers away, so they have nothing to fear from the army. Now and then, a few soldiers escape from the barracks and spend a weekend here, drinking and fighting over women. The smugglers can live with that. The chiefs lost control and let the youths have their part of the village and destroy themselves in peace. But sometimes they hold motor races through the old village, scaring children and women out of the way as they tear past at great speed. All those boys are gamblers. Anti-smuggling patrols are killing them in ever-increasing numbers. Others kill their colleagues when they see so much money and greed sets in. It all seems to make the survivors more reckless. They come home, spend the money like lunatics, go broke and go back. Most survive only a few trips before getting killed. Most of the boys who used to take my coffee to the mill are dead. You just hear that so-and-so's son or grandson 'drowned.' "

"What a waste!"

"Keep your nose in the books, my boy."

"It is all I seem to do, Grandpa."

"I used to tell you about the coming explosions and you sometimes looked incredulous. You were too young, I guess. But I think now you see that I was right. Things cannot remain as they are."

"What will happen afterward?"

"That is for you to work out; you are the lawyer, aren't you?"

I smiled sheepishly and said, "Yes, Grandpa."

"I don't need all this coffee, all this land anymore. It is for you and your brothers. I have a feeling that you will not come back to the land. Go out into the world and make a place for yourself. A big lawyer does not need to be tied to the village, especially if it is full of the wrong people."

"Thank you, Grandpa."

I thought about asking him to challenge Cane's view that it was our chiefs who let the British into the country and destroyed what remained of it, but he seemed lost in thought, as if communicating with people I could not see. I already had my send-off; what more did I need?

There was a relative of some sort, a careless young girl who laid things all over the place—kettles in the doorway, pans in the yard, the kitchen knife on the table—who was responsible for Grandpa's householding. She cooked, cleaned, washed and did some work in the shamba. On the weekend, Uncle Kawayida's mother came over and helped her. I found that a very interesting turnaround, but again I did not ask Grandpa what he thought of it. I pitied the woman a bit. She must have worked like a horse, cleaning up this girl's mess. The girl was semi-illiterate, polite and very hospitable. When she brought tea, my cup had traces of hurriedly wiped dirt, and Grandpa's was in no better condition. I was caught between insulting her hospitality by asking her to immerse the cups in a mountain of suds, thrice, and closing my eyes to take the torture. The cup smelled of fish. I engineered a little accident, pretending that an insect had crept up my leg. I spilled the contents of my cup and refused a refill. I started suspecting that Grandpa's nose was in trouble too: in the past, he would not have touched dirty utensils with a barge pole.

Grandpa reminded me of King Faisal of Saudi Arabia. Although he lacked the look of absolute power and total harmony with death of the king, Grandpa too had reached that stage where the old looked frozen in their dessication. His cane looked like a thinner extension of his hand. He had prodded me a few times with it when I annoyed him and tried to get away. He volunteered to show me round the village. It was very good weather: mild sunshine was drying the rain that had fallen the day before. The sky was very blue, as it mostly was here, with a few scanty clouds. Vegetation was glossy with constant rain. The air was laden with earthy smells mingled with whiffs coming off different plants. It was quiet here.

Grandpa got into a gray trench coat, a white tunic and soft slippers and grabbed his cane. He was going to show me off, his prize bullock. I felt proud. I would be the first lawyer from this village. We followed the main path that went round the old village in a semi-circle.

We went over to the Stefano homestead. It was a large compound that used to be full of people, sons and daughters and their families living in smaller houses built round the main house. I was always afraid to go there: the courtyard used to look enormous, and with all those eyes looking, it felt intimidating. Now it was like a deserted football field long after the match, with just a handful of people looking for souvenirs in the stands. Mr. Stefano, once a big, tall, fat man, lay paralyzed by a stroke. His infirmity haunted the place. It felt dead. "My only competition," Grandpa said. "What a sad way to go!" I was thinking about Tiida and her efforts to take Grandpa to Rome. How idiotic the whole enterprise looked on the ground!

I wanted to see some of the children Grandma had helped to birth. I wanted to see the tanner, whose courtyard used to be haunted by the stench of drying cowhides stretched and fastened onto wooden frames with pieces of string. He was a tall, gaunt man I used to associate with the Biblical Abraham. He had a lot of jackfruit, mango and avocado trees, but no child wanted to eat his fruit because of the stench in the yard. He used to live with his old wife, whom we called Sarah. I asked Grandpa about him. He said that he was alive, still tanning his hides.

I also wanted to see Aunt Tiida's first lover, the one who gobbled her virginity but would not marry her. I did not ask about the man, because Grandpa did not like him.

The path was wide but uneven, with potholes here and stones there. Grandpa stepped into a pothole he had not seen and made one prolonged wince. He had hurt his bullet leg. I did not know what to do. I suggested he sit down, but he refused. He bent forward, clutching the leg, his face a twisted mass of lines. I could hear loud music from the other end of the village. It was a Boney-M song, and the crowd was singing along. After some minutes, when the song had ended and another had started, Grandpa stood erect, held my hand, and we headed home. End of tour.

I had a lot of time on my hands. I climbed my favorite jackfruit tree and studied Mpande Hill. It seemed to float in the wind, drifting past stationary clouds and carrying with it a lake of papyrus reeds that resembled pale green umbrellas. This hill was our Golgotha. Two or three bike riders had died on its slopes. I remembered breathtaking downhill dashes by the area's tough guys, two hundred meters of the steepest ride one could get. The only time I participated, riding pillion, it was a five-bike race. We stood at the top, the front wheels in a line, the riders' faces masks of concentration, the valley below a yellowish-green mess, the spectators dwarfs on a giant plain. I sat on a gunnysack folded in four. My underthighs were already chafed. The rider's bare waist was slippery, and I held on to it and fixed my eyes on his back. I kept wondering how he would brake with his bare heels—all race bikes had no brakes as a rule. We shot downhill at a blinding pace, pebbles pouring into the ravine. The hillside tilted. The trees and papyrus reeds rushed at us. The wind wailed horribly, whipping and cutting my skin. Two riders shot past us in a ghostly blur. We went faster. Oh, the thrill! The front tire wobbled as it hit a stone, and displaced gravel poured in golden rivulets down the roadside into the valley. The rider bent forward to exert more force, opening my face to the wind. Tears and snot and saliva flew in thin threads. I ate an insect or two and spat into the wind. The front wheel skidded, filling my mind with broken limbs, torn guts, endless days in the hospital, countless injections, overflowing bedpans and blood-soaked bandages—the phantoms of my fear. I was now sitting in empty space, the carrier gone, my hands on the wet pants of the rider, a shredded scream in my sore throat. He was fighting to avert disaster, every muscle taut and soaked. We went sideways, cutting across the road, floating on air. In a daredevil over-take move, a rival drew abreast of us. I felt a sharp kick to my leg as he went past. Helped by the momentum of the kick, my rider got the wheel back onto the road. We came in last. His back was running with vomit. He didn't complain. Some boys did worse: they wet and shat themselves. His left heel was raw, skinless; the right one was angry red. He limped.

"Thank me for saving your foot," the man who had kicked me said. "The spokes were just about to chew it off, and I guess we would never have retrieved it."

"His Grandpa would have killed you," they said to my rider as he stoically tended his heels.

"I would not have waited," he said, grimacing. "I would have taken the boy straight to the hospital and fled the area."

Everybody laughed. I didn't. My legs still felt independent of my body.

I never told Grandpa about the ride. Why weren't the young smugglers in the new village organizing such races? Scaring villagers did not seem that much of a thrill to me.

Uganda was in a state of siege, writhing like a dying moth on the floor. The bugles of defeat were poised, waiting to blow the walls down. The inside of the country was like a grenade whose pin had already been drawn. There was an explosive feeling in the air. Catastrophe or catharsis?

To the north, in Sudan, the Khartoum-based Muslim government was busy fighting the Juba-based Christian-animist rebels in a war that had little prospect of ending. Bombs and guns devastated the land while circumcision razor blades terrorized virgin vulvas. Now and then, Sudanese refugees camped at our border. It seemed about time to return the favor. To the northeast, in the Horn of Clitoris- and Labia-lessness, the Ethiopian Ogaden war was going through its surges and ebbs, breathing violent drafts over harsh desert tracts and scalding both combatants and non-combatants, many of whom fled to neighboring countries, Uganda inclusive. To the east, in Kenya, Uganda's goods were embargoed and piled sky high in the harbors. Smuggling operations based there, aimed at bringing down Amin's regime by crippling the coffee-based economy, were reaching an odious climax. To the south, in Tanzania, the refuge of General Amin's predecessor, Milton Obote, anti-Amin guerrillas were gathering, whipping themselves into attacking form and making brave incursions into Uganda. They were rehearsing for the final showdown. Using Radio Tanzania, their leaders called upon the Ugandans to get rid of Amin.

■ ■ ■

By the start of 1976, the meetings at the gas station had taken on a grimmer look. It was clear to Serenity, Hajj and Mariko, their Protestant friend, that the country was headed for stormier weather. To begin with, the State Research Bureau and other security agencies had become omnipotent, arresting whomever they wanted at any time in any place. Across the border in Tanzania, the exiled dictator Obote was making a lot of noise about his desire to topple the government that had ousted him. The exodus of Ugandans fleeing for their lives, which had begun with a brain drain as educated Ugandans quietly departed, now reached epidemic proportions as spy organizations became more paranoid and picked up more and more people suspected of helping guerrillas. Once abroad, a few of these exiles talked about the appalling situation they had left behind. Amin was not amused. Hajj Gimbi's friends in the security forces told him of their fear that Uganda was going to be attacked, a fear vindicated when the Israelis rescued their countrymen at Entebbe Airport, hijacked by Palestinian fighters and brought to Uganda because of Amin's sympathy with the Palestinian cause. The renewed fear of attack had become an obsession, which was exploited by pirates within the army and the security agencies for personal ends.

Nowadays my father and his friends dispersed early. One day an army jeep had stopped at nightfall and men in civilian clothes had jumped off, ordered them to lie on the ground, kicked them a few times, accused them of plotting against the government and proceeded to empty the till and demand more of the day's takings. If Hajj Gimbi had not dropped an important name, it might have been worse, because there was no more money to take. The pirates had made do with the trio's watches.

After the attack, Hajj Gimbi started looking for land in a rural area fifty kilometers away. He found it, bought it and started building a house there. At first, Serenity thought his friend had panicked and should not have bought land so far away from the city. Hajj disabused him: "The good times have ended. The city has become a den of killers. It is time to move back to the village."

"Why?" Serenity asked vexedly.

"Amin's fall is not going to be tidy. From now on, things are going to get much worse. Armed robbery is already on the increase. The soldiers are becoming more desperate. The future looks bleak."

"Hasn't it been like this for the past two, three years?" Serenity, anchored in suburban daydreams, asked rather obtusely.

Hajj was becoming impatient, almost angry. "What I mean is, woe to those who will be trapped in the city in Amin's last days. Woe to families without any place to hide."

It struck Serenity that if war broke out the following day, his family would have no safe place to go. In other words, apart from his dilapidated bachelor house in the village, the only accommodation his family had was the government-owned pagoda. Serenity felt ashamed of his myopia. He did not like rural areas, he did not like farming, and that had affected his way of seeing into the future. He was among the few people to whom the notion of land ownership did not appeal. He associated land with the bad people clan land had attracted to his father's house, and his father's inability to control them. He nursed a secret fear that the moment he secured land and a house, his home would be overrun by people, probably from his wife's side. More still, he remembered the drama in his sister Tiida's home when somebody left fly-attracting entrails and dogs' heads near her house because of a land dispute. It was true that landowners were often dishonest and greedy, unable to resist selling the same land to a second party if the price was right, and the proliferation of guns had turned land disputes into fatal or near-fatal clashes. His worst-case scenario involved somebody hiring soldiers to shoot his children just to drive him off a piece of land. Up to that moment, he had believed that, if things got bad, he could always move to another suburb. Now he realized that he needed a quiet place far from the city where they could stay if a protracted campaign of terror or even war broke out.

The city was the seat of government, the center of power, and if it meant fighting for it to the death or bombing it flat, those caught in the cross fire would certainly perish. Serenity, who had not been too shaken up by the robbery at the gas station, found himself shivering. At the same time, he felt eternally grateful to Hajj, whom he saw more and more as the elder brother he never had. That fate had brought them together, first as neighbors, then as bosom friends, made Hajj seem like a gift from above.

It now occurred to Serenity that with the fall of Amin, he might lose his trade-union post, and maybe even his job. He started thinking very hard about the future.

Mariko looked with smug amusement at his two scheming friends: his family owned large tracts of land in several rural areas and one or two in the city. He volunteered to give free accommodation to Serenity's family in case war broke out. Concealing his irritation, Serenity smiled at him.

Serenity asked the man who had helped Hajj find a clean piece of land to do the same for him. The era of the magical delivery notes had ended: army officers had taken over the management of state factories, most of which had been decimated by mismanagement and corruption, and it had become virtually impossible to fool them. Serenity, who had no death wish, had quickly adapted to the times. He discovered a safer way to make money: by saving on trade-union purchases like gas, he amassed a small fortune. The incompetence of his new boss played into his hands, although, with characteristic restraint, he took only what he could account for. After getting the land, he commissioned a house plan, bribed somebody in the land office to get it quickly approved and within two months of the purchase, the builders had started working. After the house had reached window level, Serenity realized how wonderful it was to own the roof over one's head.

The year ended well, and the new one started rather quietly. Nothing special happened, and the friends hoped 1977 might be better than 1976 had been. Till Hajj brought some very disturbing news.

"One of the big Christian leaders is in trouble," he said one afternoon.

"The Catholic archbishop, you mean?" Serenity asked. Not long after the honeymoon of Amin's coup, the Catholic primate had become Amin's most outspoken enemy and critic. He had criticized the killing of priests, one of whom had been the editor of a Catholic journal; the expulsion of missionaries; the rape of nuns; the kidnapping and killing of prominent Catholics; the killing of people in general; the breakdown of order; and abuses of power by the army and the security agencies. There had been rumors of attempts on his life, house searches and other forms of persecution, but so far the campaign had remained at that, and it had not stopped him from talking.

"I do not know for sure," Hajj admitted.

"Surely it can't be the Anglican archbishop," Mariko said uneasily. The Anglican Church had taken a middle-of-the-road course and had not been very openly critical of Amin's government. Although prominent Protestants had also disappeared, it had not been particularly bad in a bad situation. The Protestants had always tended to be pragmatic in their politics, and it was that pragmatism that had won their party, the Uganda People's Congress, power at Independence. A large number of Ugandan exiles in Tanzania were Protestant, and therefore linked to the UPC, but there was no direct contact between the exiles and the Protestant religious leaders.

"Recently there has been much noise from Tanzania, and the impression is that the exiles led by Obote and the Protestant faction are up to something," Hajj explained.

"Exile always means that somebody is up to something, doesn't it?" Mariko, feeling the need for desperate reassurance, said wearily.

"I am talking about infiltration. There are rumors that guerrillas are already inside the country. Some of their leaders slip in and out of Uganda and boast about their escapades on Radio Tanzania. What this means is that there are collaborators who have not yet been unearthed."

"I don't want to think about it," Mariko said irritably.

"Nobody wants to think about it," Serenity said.

Politics and religion were hand in glove: theoretically, every Muslim was behind Amin, every Catholic behind the banned Democratic Party and every Protestant behind the hibernating UPC. As a result, religious leaders had the patina of demigods, controlling people's minds and souls. It also meant that antagonizing or harming a religious leader would bring the wrath of his followers on your head.

"The Anglican archbishop is untouchable. He is archbishop not only of Uganda but also of Rwanda, Burundi and Zaire. He is an international figure. Amin dare not touch him."

"He is also an Acholi, and Acholis and Langis have not done well, since the Obote connection makes them possible allies on a tribal basis," said Serenity, now getting the hang of it.

"All this saddens me a great deal," Mariko said.

"This is not about religion," Hajj explained. "It is about politics. Many Christians think that the Muslims have been immune to Amin's interference and are therefore safe. Nobody is safe. Look, Amin created the Muslim Supreme Council to control Muslim affairs, and he has not hesitated to depose council leaders when it suited him. Some even lost their lives. So if he plans to interfere with the Christian churches, it is because he sees it as the only solution to his political problems. Remember, it is coming on a hundred years since the advent of Christianity in this country. This very year, the Protestant Church is going to celebrate its centenary. Amin and his henchmen must be worried to death about the implications, both local and foreign, of such a big event."

"Exiles and other forces using the chance to destabilize the country, eh?" Serenity suggested.

"Yes," Hajj replied grimly, his beard swaying morosely.

"The hands of our religious leaders are clean," Mariko said, vexed, almost shouting at his friends.

"You remember the Islamization rumor, don't you?" Hajj said.

"Yes, it was said that Amin was going to declare this a Muslim country," Mariko replied, looking suspiciously at his Muslim friend as though he were a government spy trying to trap him.

"That rumor had unexpected repercussions," Hajj continued. "It drove more Christians to church. This being the centenary year, the churches will burst at the seams. In two years' time, it will be the Catholic centenary. All this mounting excitement is leading to sleepless nights in high places."

The three friends did not have long to wait. News came that the Anglican archbishop's residence had been searched for weapons. As tensions rose, especially among the Protestants, government radio admitted that the search had taken place. The Anglican Church fought back by writing a strong letter to Amin, washing the Church clean of involvement in anti-government activities and mourning the growing insecurity in the country.

As things started to cool down, it was announced that the Anglican archbishop, together with two cabinet ministers from Obote's home region, had been arrested for stockpiling arms, with the malevolent intention of killing President Amin and creating disorder.

"My worst fears have come true," Hajj Gimbi declared. "This is just going to worsen Christian-Muslim relations. All Muslims are going to be painted with the same brush. I don't trust the people handling this affair."

"But what does he want to achieve by this?" Mariko, burning with the genuine anger of the apolitical, asked. He was a mild Protestant who regularly went to church, obeyed the law, helped the needy and hoped that the sum total of his good deeds guaranteed his safety.

"He wants to intimidate the Church and keep people on tenter-hooks," Serenity suggested.

"If there are snakes in your house, or if you think there are, you smoke it. Your household may have to stay outside for hours, but you do what you have to do," Hajj said, raising his palms in the air. "I am afraid that is how our leaders think."

The trio watched the television appearance of the three detainees on Serenity's stinking Toshiba. There seemed to be hundreds of soldiers everywhere. On display were the neat piles of arms the plotters had intended to use. The meeting took place on the lawn of a famous hotel, which some people said was also partly a torture chamber. The arms displayed had been found near the archbishop's house. Other collaborators had been arrested, but the three men were the lynchpins. A letter written by Obote, implicating them in the plot, was read. At the end of the meeting, the soldiers said they wanted the three men dead, and indeed they died in a car crash while trying to overpower the army officer who was driving them. Of the four people in the vehicle, only the driver survived the crash, escaping with minor injuries.

Serenity and his friends, like the majority of people, read between the lines, but they still felt very sad. This was history writing itself in front of their eyes. It was a nasty experience. These were some of the saddest days in the history of the country; worse things had occurred, but it was the small happenings that exposed the extent of the rot.

Aunt Lwandeka was demoralized for a day or two. It was not that the country had lost its political virginity—that had happened long ago—but that it was tottering on the brink of brinks and everyone seemed to have an idea of what was going to happen next. The general lesson was very clear: if it could happen to the big fish, it could happen to the small fish anytime, anywhere.

The three friends did not have any more words to say about the incident. They just sat and played cards or talked about other things. Hajj and Serenity drove the builders harder than before, and it was not very long before their houses were completed and they moved their families away from the eye of the storm.

■ ■ ■

The move from the city to the village was Padlock's dream come true. She had hated the city, its noise, its profanity and its disorder from the beginning. She had had a love-hate relationship with the pagoda. She felt that the house, like Serenity's bachelor bed, was tainted, this time by the pagan spirit of the Indians who had been there first. Over the years, she hankered for something pure, something virgin, something she could fill with her own spirit. The violence of the city, the kidnappings, the rapes and the insecurity had disgusted her village sensibilities. The absence of punishment for offenders almost drove her mad with outrage. In her book, crime always meant punishment, and yet here was a situation where sin was being tolerated with impunity, even rewarded.

For years she had lived in fear of being raped. She had a feeling that the soldiers would do it one day. Consequently, she tensed up when she saw those tall, dark figures walking or driving by. Her head swam whenever they stopped a vehicle she was travelling in. She felt asphyxiated. One time, she almost jumped out of a taxi van when a soldier popped his head inside to take a closer look. She happened to be sitting near the door. The man never noticed her and never asked her to show her identity card. He concentrated on other passengers. Yet she felt terrified. She broke into a sweat, her eyes reddened and her lungs strained for air. The feeling of beleaguerment had worsened after the pilgrimage. She feared that her holiness was about to be obliterated. She feared that her name was about to be erased from the book of saints. She feared that a group of soldiers would do terrible things to her, decapitate her and drag her defiled body through the streets. She feared the effect the deed would have on her children. At the height of her fear, ambivalence insinuated itself into her thoughts. The dropping-eagle syndrome recurred. She started feeling purged. She started feeling bad about getting purged. The purges made her afraid that the Devil was winning. When the fear came without concomitant purges, she felt driven close to the edge. When the soldiers ignored her, as they always did, she wondered if they were not standing in the way of destiny. When they seemed to notice her, she quaked and asked that the cup pass from her. She suffered in silence.

All this confusion left her hankering for a place in a village: a virginal place she could impose her will on, a peaceful place where she could pray and meditate. She thought of herself as a desert plant, a cactus which defied the desolation, and when she moved into the new house, she felt that her very deep roots had sunk into the foundation and permeated the land. Virtue would triumph over decay, the cactus would prosper in desert sand even if the water had to be sucked from tens of kilometers away. The local priest could not come to bless the house; he deputized the catechist, who sprinkled the house and the compound and the garden with the water she had brought from Lourdes in a plastic bottle made in the shape of the Virgin Mary. The meter-long rosary hanging in the sitting room was her talisman against evil, the leather-bound Bible her sword and shield against the enemy. She felt that she had entered the house she had been born to live in.

The size of the little town suited her purposes well. It was a small, one-street, one-market, one-dispensary trading center serving a small population. Nobody stood out, or at least not by much. The children went to a good school four kilometers away. The teachers kept their pupils under constant observation and were quick to report if the latter misbehaved. Padlock could not have asked for more. The Catholic subparish church was one kilometer away, and the priest visited once a month to hear confessions and to say holy mass. The catechist, a hard-working man of Rwandan origin, treated her family with respect and Christian love. Padlock liked the man and was generous to his six children. She made them dresses and shirts at no cost from remnant pieces of cloth. Whenever the priest visited, Padlock got a place in front of the altar. It made her feel that the priest was talking directly and exclusively to her. She watched everything he did. She listened carefully to every song the choir sang. It was her show. She contributed to the big meal cooked for the priest on such occasions. She liked being consulted by the catechist on various matters. She liked her new position in life. She had finally found her center, and she had no plans to relinquish it.

Serenity, on the other hand, was a townsman and remained behind in Kampala during the week. He vacated the pagoda and moved into a smaller house with one bedroom, a sitting room, a kitchen and a bathroom. It was linked to two other houses of the same type, all wrapped inside a fence. His neighbors were people in their forties and fifties, looking for peace amidst the turmoil of the city. Now Serenity could enjoy the anonymity of the city with the convenience of being at the center of things. In the evening he read his books and listened to the radio, mostly BBC or Voice of America. During the day, he dealt with trade-union affairs at the office or at meeting places in town. He never invited colleagues home: it was his own private space. He usually ate at a small restaurant in town, and only prepared himself tea when he returned home in the evening. Nakibuka came for a few days each week and served him carefully prepared meals, as though she were courting him. On the weekend he would board a bus to visit Padlock and the children, taking them commodities they needed. Serenity fulfilled the duties of a provider with guilt-laden efficiency, floating between the world of the married and the unmarried and bouncing between wife and lover with somnolent ease.

During the last quarter of 1978, that diabolical mathematical invention, the triangle, made its first appearance on our historical scene. A few years later, it was to return with enough fire and brimstone in its hold to torch the entire country. The first, the Kagera Triangle, was a seven-hundred-square-kilometer tract of land on the Uganda-Tanzania border. It was captured by Amin's soldiers in a matter of hours. In a blitz that rolled like magma from a fuming volcanic crater, tanks, Mig fighters and foot soldiers poured fire onto Tanzanian border forces and unsuspecting villagers and captured the Triangle in an extravaganza of killing, looting and burning. The quick of foot and wit evaded the hoofs and the marmorean horns of these buffaloes and fled; those who dithered perished. In this original triangle, as in its mirror reflection years later, the buffaloes of aggression claimed that they were looking for anti-government elements hidden in the forests, in the bushes, on the hills and along the rivers. Guerrilla Radio condemned the attack and the annexation in squeaky susurrations that reached us from behind the cupboards where we hid to listen.

Safe in my aunt's house, I could feel excitement rising like a fever, waking all the specters of past wars I had discovered in the dusty shelves of the seminary library. I could hear crackling fires as houses burned, plaintive cries as people begged for their lives, clopping hoofs as cattle were driven onto army trucks and clattering aluminum and silver as household goods crashed into green army sacks.

A gush of bombastic government diarrhea akin to Amin's honeymoon broadcasts smothered the implications of the annexation in cheap-thrill yarns intended to confound. The lies were diaphanous, but a balm to the weary. It was not easy to dismiss these boasts, because this was the staple food on which Amin had subsisted for the past eight years.

Things, however, continued to move from bad to worse. Prices escalated as hoarding and black-marketeering hit a new peak. The country's imports rotted in Kenyan ports, where they had been impounded for months, some for years. The little gas there was went to the army, leaving the country's transport system paralyzed. Food could no longer be moved from the villages to the city. As a result, Aunt Lwandeka started preparing the hated posho—better-quality stuff than the seminary hog feed, but posho all the same. As it became almost impossible for people to go to work, poverty settled firmly in homes and tormented large families with incurable hunger, reducing most to one meager meal a day. Quite a few people got shot while stealing food from shops or government depots. War was at its worst now, coursing through arid alimentary canals, sapping energy, fertilizing vengeance and breeding scapegoats and collective guilt.

As worries stampeded through people's heads, trucks loaded with goods looted from the Triangle coursed by, dirty and overburdened, on their way to the north. Army officers and men who had been bent on mutiny now appeased their hunger with curse-laden booty that had intimations of doom charted all over it.

Weeks went by, and the number of trucks trekking to the north decreased. Guerrilla Radio informed us that the buffaloes of aggression had turned tail, bringing the primordial beast of war onto Ugandan territory. The marauders in the Triangle were being mauled. The cacophony of blood-soaked words that were exchanged by the leaders of the two countries heightened the sense of danger. The national tragedy that had begun eight years before, under the master director, Idi Amin, had come to an end.

Uncle Kawayida sent us a Christmas message in a hurriedly written letter: war had started at the border, and Tanzanian forces and Ugandan guerrillas had pushed deep inside the country. He, however, assured us that civilians were well treated in the "liberated" areas, and that the only real danger was from Amin's fleeing soldiers.

Schools were closed, and the remaining foreigners left the country, including Fr. Gilles Lageau, who bequeathed his big dog to the seminary. Trucks loaded with stained furniture, frightened goats, chickens in wicker baskets, gawky women, sad-faced children and groggy elders trekked north in a cloud of fear, despair, malice and dust as soldiers and their families escaped. Where was Cane in all this? Was he in the army now? Had he fled? Did he take his porno with him? All this reminded me of the Indian exodus back in 1972. In those days, gap-toothed schoolchildren stood along the roads and sang songs praising General Amin, reciting the crimes of the Indian community, especially monopolization of the country's economy. Now there was no singing, except the groans of the overloaded vehicles, but the message was clear.

Obote's overthrow on January 25, 1971, had turned my world upside down, robbed me of Grandma and sent my childhood in an unexpected direction. Eight years later, I watched the anniversary celebrations with cynical interest. January 25, 1979, was as mean, morose and menacing as the face of a pedigree bulldog. Everybody, soldier and civilian, was on edge, as though chilled by the trumpets of defeat. I looked closely at the soldiers, the men who had charmed me on the day Amin divided Lake Albert in two and who had generally made me feel protected. They looked haggard, harassed, as if they had been fed on poisoned food for a month. I knew that among them were men who had committed the most horrendous crimes, torturing, mutilating and killing people. How was the chaff going to be separated from the grain?

I now saw Amin as a ghostly specter who had come to destabilize and pollute the nation by accentuating the evil within. My uninformed view was that the seeds sown were going to germinate, and that the worst was yet to come. Optimists said the opposite. The only thing most people agreed on was the desire for Amin's head on a platter.

I thought of the Spanish flu that had killed almost twenty million people in Europe in 1918, well after the war was over. I could see Amin survivors being tortured by some violent epidemic, say cholera. Aunt thought otherwise. She was a die-hard optimist. For her, the fall of Amin seemed to mean everything, the end to our problems. I started suspecting that the brigadier had given her assurances of a good future.

As a taste of things to come, Aunt Lwandeka's guerrilla colleagues attacked power lines and immersed the city and many other areas in a blackout. They reminded me of the power saboteur at the seminary. City houses became death traps in which people choked on putrid toilet fumes. The water shortage exacerbated the trial and made the city uninhabitable. Fights erupted at water taps, boreholes, anyplace where some water could be drawn.

Explosions rocked the city's foundations one evening. The same night, soldiers banged on our door around nine o'clock. I had put the children to bed and was just waiting to switch on Guerrilla Radio. Harsh soldierly voices ordered me to open up. I did so immediately. Two very tall soldiers stormed into the house. One rushed into the sleeping rooms. The house was filled with the stink of sweat, dirty boots and bad breath. I was asked where my father was, and I explained that he was dead. I showed them my identity card. My heart was beating wildly as I remembered the picture of the brigadier in the Good News Bible under Aunt's mattress. I held my breath as one soldier ripped Aunt's sheets from her bed. He poked the mattress, but instead of lifting the front part, he went for the foot of the bed. Finding nothing, they got bored and stormed out. I felt as if it was my charisma that had averted disaster. Others were not so lucky. I heard screams as people were beaten up in a bid to make them surrender all the money in the house. A few houses away, two men with no identity cards were picked up, prodded with rifle barrels, hit with rifle butts and thrown onto a jeep. Operation Hidden Guerrilla moved on with the crunching of boots, the kicking of locked doors and the barking of nervous soldiers.

Where the hell was Aunt now? I was beside myself with rage. Why was she still risking her neck for the guerrillas? What if the soldiers had found that bloody brigadier's picture?

Aunt must have divined my rage even before she entered the house. She flashed me her girlish smile, apologized and calmed the storm. NRM guerrillas were all over the city, she said. But none had been apprehended, because they all had proper documents.

The texture of the nights changed when Guerrilla Radio stopped. How we had come to depend on it! At first the broadcasts became choked with claptrap. Then they simply died away. The advance of the beast of war now became a matter of conjecture and scrappy rumors. I resisted taking Aunt's stories at face value, because I suspected that she was administering reassurance therapy to the nanny of her children. Large numbers of trucks packed to the rafters with dirty soldiers brought the message home better. Officers zoomed past in jeeps with very long aerials and spears mounted on the radiators, as though directed at enemies in the sky. One day I thought I recognized Dr. Ssali and Aunt Tiida's Peugeot at the tail of a fleet of cars laden with army officers. People put their cars on blocks and hid the wheels in dark places. In my mind, Aunt Tiida was the kind of woman to veto such action. I could not see her caving in to the desecration of their gorgeous machine, but maybe I was wrong. Had she not stood by her man in his darkest days? Miss Sunlight Soap had her unpredictable side too. In a similar situation, Padlock would have had the wheels removed in a jiffy. How she would celebrate if Tiida's car got repossessed by the Devil or his agents!

Roadblocks increased, but Amin's soldiers were oddly subdued. There was no wind in their sails. Randomly selected travellers were stripped in search of telltale rifle-belt welts on their shoulders. The rest suffered the piracy of losing armies: ransoms. Roadblocks started moving, as though by magic, from place to place—here in the morning, gone in the afternoon, back late in the evening. At times it felt like I was watching a game.

The flow of traffic to the north choked to a trickle and dried up. Within a fortnight the road was dead, oppressed by the vacancy of the grave. I thought of Grandpa and the explosions he had foreseen. I wanted to be at his side, but the lacuna between us widened by the hour, resounding with bombs. In what seemed to be the climax, there was continuous fighting for two weeks, two days, two nightmares. As bombs exploded and empty stomachs growled, the city center, the National Radio and the Parliament Building were finally overrun. Amin's government had fallen. It was April 11, 1979.

There was sporadic shooting in our suburb as remnants of Amin's forces covered their retreat. The front line dissolved in the distance with the formlessness of a bad dream. The "liberators" arrived and moved on, pushing their enemies farther and farther away toward the north and the east. Behind them a Pandora's box of old conflicts opened up. It was the afterbirth that really showed me the realities of war.

Amin, the man who had come in a haze of mystery, disappeared in the mists of rumor and the vapors of war to unknown foreign borders, howling, ranting and raving, with no one the wiser as to his future. His legacy, though, had just begun to take root and flower.

The village sealed between Mpande Hill and Ndere Hill was gored and kicked as the buffaloes of aggression thundered to their northern havens. Soldiers from the nearest barracks swooped down on the new part of the village, as though in the mood to resurrect old carousals. They grabbed and made off with the women in bell-bottoms who had come with the phony wealth, the joyriding Honda Civic and the racing motorcycles. The remaining youths were swallowed by the swamps and the forest, where they joined the inhabitants of the old village, who had taken no chances. The soldiers could be heard firing randomly at empty houses as they retreated. At Ndere Parish a crowd from the villages had taken refuge under the protection of the cross. Amin's soldiers rampaged to the fathers' house, took money and valuables and grabbed a van and a few girls. They exacted ransom from the displaced people and in the process broke somebody's arm. The soldiers wanted more and more money. The priest interceded on behalf of the people, and for some reason the thugs relented. As always, they shot into the air as they departed. They spied madman Santo as they drove away. He seemed to be writing in the air with his index finger, oblivious to everything. He was moving back and forth between two classroom blocks. They hailed him to stop. He did not hear them, or if he did, he ignored them. A soldier let off a burst of rifle fire with a laugh. The bullets spared Santo, and the thug did not bother to try again. Santo disappeared behind the classrooms, waiting for his favorite hour to write KYRIE ELEISON, KYRIE ELEISON, CHRISTE ELEISON on the blackboards. Nowadays, he wrote and erased his own words.

Martial music underscored the change of government. Now and then, the extravaganza was interrupted by the announcer, who promised the listeners peace and security. The masses were waking up, rising to the new day with the force of a huge bull. Bottled optimisms burst forth and mixed with vertiginous hopes in blinding kaleidoscopes of emotion. Statements like "Never again will we be ruled by the gun" and "We have paid the final price, and now peace is ours forever" swished in the air.

Our liberators, a mixture of Tanzanian soldiers and Ugandan exiles, eyed the masses calmly. They dispensed the type of superior kindness one reserves for degenerates. The people mobbed them none-theless. The shameless way the men and especially the women almost salivated over them! I felt lucky that I had been protected from the brunt of the past eight years and could afford to watch with amuse-ment. The liberators, speaking smooth, polished, singsong Kiswahili, were hugged, dry-kissed, lifted shoulder-high and showered with im-measurable gratitude. There was frenetic dancing and singing every-where, up crowded streets and down stinking, piss-sodden alleys. This was the purest expression of joy I had ever seen, free from religious bias or political pollution, the joy of King David dancing before the Ark of the Convenant. Euphoria, like a potent drugged wind, blew over the people, including yours truly, to a degree. It intoxi-cated them with the magic of what could be, should be, had to be, and thrust them deep inside the colorful pages of their most secret fan-tasies. It left them panting with a level of expectation unknown in the last eight years.

In the sea of jubilation, one saw floating islands of masked anxi-ety: the very dark, sometimes tribally scar-faced, northern-born civil-ians. They were doing their best to look cheerful in the hope that they would not remind their southern counterparts of their tormentors, the killers on the run. One could see them praying not to be lacerated by the flashing pangas of revenge. Each jubilating hand had the potential to vivisect, each hailing mouth had the power to condemn someone to death. For the moment, the joy of the masses was too intense to be sul-lied by such base sentiments, and vengeance remained sealed in the kaleidoscopic casket of euphoria.

I felt weak in the knees. Aunt was jumping up and down. I held her very tight and felt her body quaking with feverish joy. Tears of happiness flowed down her face and tickled my neck. The energy from the crowd seemed to sweep me up in the sky. I suddenly felt part of the monster, moved by its shouts, intoxicated by its cheers, tears and laughter. I was now sure that war had left the gun-mounted hills, the soldier-infested valleys and the cordite-stained skies and was coursing through us all. I did not know when I let go of Aunt. I remembered being offered free liquor by a group of men who urged me to drink, drink, drink. It was some sort of competition. Drums were throbbing, accompanying lewd songs. The lights made me feel very intoxicated. I became dizzy, went out and puked against the wall. A vendor who bought Aunt's liquor wholesale invited me in. I knew she liked me, but she was no spring chicken. She cleaned my face, my clothes and my shoes. She had fine knees, which gleamed like polished and varnished wood. I looked at her fingers. Aunt said that one could tell a woman's age by her fingers; I could not, and thought she had said that because she herself had smooth, beautiful fingers. As the vendor woman maneuvered me onto the sofa I was overwhelmed by her beautiful knees. I grabbed her with all my power and came in my pants. Her curse was the last thing I heard.

Two days passed. I felt sick. I couldn't rest fully because of the noise and the firing of guns. The din and gloom were shattered by the arrival of Uncle Kawayida. I was very happy to see him. He was reticent, as if he was not happy to see me. He was wearing dirty clothes and mud-stained shoes. I had not seen him in years, but he had not changed much. He was still thin, tall and alert, his oval face with its big eyes giving him a wily, charming look. He refused the long greeting formula I had begun unravelling. That meant big trouble. Had one of his women got gang-raped by soldiers? Had his in-laws lost members of their large family in a fire or a massacre or an accident? Mr. Kavule, his late father-in-law, had after all left forty children, thirty girls and ten boys. Had something happened to them?

Danger was closer to home. Grandpa was missing!

Grandpa had left the village a week before the fall of Amin's government in order to meet a clan elder. The man who foresaw national explosions thought that the time for the big one had not yet come. In the village, far away from the theater of war, things had still been quiet. He believed he could go and return before the city fell. He met the clan elder, settled some important clan affairs and left three days before the fall of the city. He was last seen ensconced in the cab of an overloaded pickup van which was to take him straight home.

I felt sick with grief. I asked Uncle Kawayida what he thought had happened, but he did not want to talk about it. He was waiting for the arrival of Serenity to make a plan for a detailed search. In the meantime, he asked what I wanted to do in the future, what I was doing for money. I told him about Aunt's monthly liquor-brewing activities. He made calculations by scratching figures on his hand with his index fingernail.

He shook his head and said that it was a good business. What did I think of taking part? I said it was too dangerous. He replied that it was dangerous businesses that paid. I found the suggestion repulsive. How could I, the former seminary librarian, the ouster of Fr. Mindi, the terror of Fr. Lageau, the future lawyer, do something as crude as brewing liquor in a discarded oil drum over a wood fire? I was cut out for white-collar jobs that earned clean money. I said I was planning to do part-time teaching jobs. He screwed his lips into a pensive pout. No money, he implied. How long would I continue to depend on Aunt? I felt tongue-tied and misunderstood. I asked him about his turkey and chicken business.

He said that he had made a lot of money because he had done something different: where others had rushed into retail business, he had cut his own path. He added that in order to succeed, one had to make one's own way. I wanted to ask for advice in love matters. I wanted to know more about his escapades with the sisters of his wife. I wanted to know his views on polygamy. I looked for the right words which would accommodate both titillation and the real quest for knowledge, but failed to find them. All this was good distraction for both of us. Looking for a way to pose questions about sex, I asked him about his mother. He said that he was happy that she was looking after Grandpa. But where was Grandpa now?

Serenity arrived: it was evident that he was expecting the worst, as though a monster had leapt out of his favorite book to torment him by kidnapping first his father, then his wife and children. I had not seen him in a long time, but it felt as if we had parted only yesterday. The two men set off almost immediately. They rode round the city on a Kawasaki motorcycle Uncle Kawayida had borrowed from a friend. He still dared not use his van for fear that the liberators might impound it for military purposes.

I was immobilized for days. I felt like a stone on a riverbed: events eddied all round me. I had to look after the children because Aunt was busy meeting her National Reform Movement colleagues and, I suspected, the brigadier too. There was a loose coalition of exiles which was going to form a provisional government before the elections. Aunt was very optimistic, saying that the National Reform Movement was going to play a big role in the coalition. I asked her whether she wanted to get into politics. She said that she wanted financial help from the

NRM in order to launch her own business. She obviously still treasured her independence. Rumors, however, had it that the coalition was a front for the return of Obote, who had spent all the years of Amin's rule in Tanzania. Aunt said that the rumors were wrong: Obote could never come back. He had had his chance, and the exiles would block his return. I was not convinced. Aunt did not want to go into objective analysis. She seemed to believe that all the Tanzanians had come to do was to help Ugandans get rid of Amin. But who was going to pay for the war? Uganda, of course. Who would guarantee the payment? I was thinking about the Versailles Treaty of 1919, made to guarantee that Germany paid war indemnity. Was Uganda going to make a treaty with Tanzania, or was the return of Obote going to be the guarantee of payment? Aunt did not want her optimism sullied by such callous speculation. I sensed that the "snek" woman was annoyed by the theories of somebody who had not been part of the struggle, somebody who had never been threatened with torture and death. She had her faith in the National Reform Movement, and in the brigadier, whose picture was still under her mattress. Who was I to make her doubt her instincts? What if she knew something I did not? I backed off. I might even have been bothering her just to forget Grandpa's disappearance.

At about the same time came the news that Aunt Kasawo, survivor of a life-and-death chase many years ago, had been attacked by uniformed men—a popular euphemism for Amin's thugs. I speculated wildly, and the event distracted me from the search for Grandpa for a while. The attack had occurred not long before the fall of the city, which meant that Amin's men had already left her area. I had a hunch that it was our liberators who had attacked her. If it had been Amin's men, I reasoned, the news bearer would have said so, since Amin was gone and there was freedom of speech. The euphemism pointed to the reluctance of the public to believe that the liberators were also capable of these acts, especially now, as the euphoria was still high. This time, though, I knew that I would get the details soon. I already had my theory; I was just waiting for confirmation. Locally, I had heard rumors about liberators "begging" women to service them, and on occasion using force to get what they wanted.

• • •

Three thousand and ten days of oppression, murder, mysterious disappearances, kidnappings and torture-chamber excesses had to erupt from the dungeons of memory into the sunlit streets. Euphoria, like every other drug, had worn off, and withdrawal symptoms like ravenous hunger and vengeance made people look around for scapegoats. Post-liberation food shortages did not help the situation, and the corny radio promises now sounded spurious, insulting.

The sudden, unbelievable absence of the tyrant and the convenient reluctance of our liberators to assert their authority, lest they be associated with the men they had ousted, increased the power vacuum gathering force in the land and empowered the masses in the worst way possible. Suddenly everyone, if they were forceful enough, could become inquisitor, judge and executioner. Far away in the villages, houses belonging to northerners and to some Muslims had gone up in flames. A crowd had swooped onto the home of Aunt Nakatu and her husband, Hajj Ali, accused them of being Amin supporters and asked them to come out lest their house be burned down and their coffee trees cut. Hajj Ali came out of the house, confronted the crowd, explained his position and asked them why they were turning against him. Luckily, the voice of reason triumphed. The elders in the group persuaded the hotheads to relent. Hajj Ali sacrificed two goats to the crowd. Others were not so lucky. They were driven from the villages, their houses burned, their goats and chicken slaughtered. In the village, the youths of the dubious wealth marched to the barracks and looted it clean.

Closer to home, I opened my eyes and thought I was dreaming. The majestic greedy road, which had eaten the fleeing northerners and Amin's henchmen, was clogged with people bearing the weight of fridges, squeaky beds, greasy motor parts, new and used tires, rusty and new iron sheets, slabs of clear and stained glass, hissing sofas, bales of cloth, boxes of medicines, cartons of laboratory mercury, gigantic office typewriters, hairy sacks of rice, sugar and salt, greasy tins of cooking and motor oil and more. Men with bare torsos were pushing thirsty cars and vans and motorcycles, some with crushed tires, creaking under mammoth loads. Full-scale looting was on: the first purgative phase.

Here and there, people crushed by ill-gotten loads sprawled in the roadside grass, panting, heaving, perspiring, farting and begging for water in razor-sharp, staccato gasps. Next to the gaspers, smartly dressed hustlers with bulging neck veins haggled with prospective buyers, eager to make quick sales and return to the city for more booty before the liberators put a stop to the looting bonanza. The liberators, bunched in little groups or spread out at ineffectual roadblocks, watched with cynical smiles as government property trickled or flooded past their posts. There was a perverse logic to the bonanza: since these people were the current non-existent government, they were just taking home what belonged to them, property formerly used to oppress them. As long as they were busy, they could give the liberators no trouble. There was also the issue of cooperation: allowed to loot, even the worst elements could be relied upon to report the remnants of Amin's henchmen who, the liberators feared, might hit them from the back.

It seemed as if troublemakers knew that this would be the last time soldiers with loaded guns would look on as shops and government offices were emptied. As a result, they grabbed this chance with both hands.

The shock waves of liberation were ripping through the city. Banner-carriers, with caustic words flying and flapping in the toxic air, marched, declaring support for the yet-to-come coalition government. They hurled abuse at Idi Amin, and demanded food, essential commodities, peace and democracy. Flag-wavers, bellies growling with hunger or looted rotten foods, demanded capitalism, free education, better housing and Amin's trial. Students, balled fists punching the air, circled the city in long, multi-colored lines, a cacophony of hopes, dreams and demands cascading from peeling, parched lips. Criminals, eyes needle-sharp, limbs snake-nimble, prowled, seeking to get whatever they could in the confusion. Traders, red-eyed and loudmouthed, demanded an immediate stop to the looting and a return of the looted goods or compensation from the government.

Buildings hit during the skirmishes smoldered morosely, pouring thick columns of toxic smoke into the saturated atmosphere. Shop fronts battered by trucks and tractors gaped sadly like desecrated tombs. Lakes of glass shards, not unlike greenish-blue frozen water, flooded pavements, trailing into gutters and splashing into roads. Trails of sugar, salt, fertilizer, oil, forlornly advertised the routes chosen by the more vigorous looters. The sky was filled with flying paper, which the ghostly winds coming off the dead and the dying twisted in the air as though teasing onlookers with classified and unclassified information.

Here and there, in gutters, alleys, roadsides, doorways, both stale and fresh corpses oozed red-yellow fluid, faces rigid, mouths battered by untold secrets. I saw neat wounds caused by very sharp objects; I saw independent body parts liberated by bombs, heavy objects and bullets; I saw blobs of flesh and bits of bone and large patches of blood shaped like the world's lakes and continents.

Through the relentless heat, the sun-sharpened fetid stenches of decomposing flesh, garbage and emotion, I somehow made it to the taxi park, the orifice from which all the mayhem seemed to gush with apocalyptic ruthlessness. Bullets, like giant popcorn, exploded as the outnumbered liberators tried to appear to be doing something about the chaos without actually tarnishing their good image and reducing the immense credit they had amassed with the people. I now and then caught a snatch of their singsong Kiswahili as they endeavored to break up fights.

I stood on the rim of the bowl. I felt overwhelmed and afraid for my safety. The earthquakes I had dreamed of when I first came to the city, and Grandpa's predicted national explosions, seemed to be rocking the bowl from all sides. A mighty stench from the notorious Owino Market bearing the putrescence, the intoxications and delusions, of both past and present blew over the taxi park and stirred more madness and confusion. The gawky skeletons of architectural decrepitude that formed the gap-toothed city skyline seemed to tilt and fall over like uprooted teeth, the roots obscenely exposed. The grime-laden windows, the rust-streaked roofs and the dust-caked walls seemed to mix and gush down the hill like discolored gore pouring out of rotting body cavities. The filthy Nakivubo River seemed to be running with blood and tears and refuse that rained down from the mosque, the Catholic and the Protestant cathedrals, the high and low courts and the residences of dislodged army generals.

I was prodded by passersby and found myself descending the steps into the center of the bowl, where there were hardly any vans. It was open court there, with privatized justice and insane retribution on offer. Two very tall, very dark men dressed in the paraphernalia of the

State Research Bureau—platform shoes, bell-bottom trousers and reflective sunglasses—stared at the jury from behind silver goggles. Somebody flipped them off, calling for respect of court as the goggles got crushed.

"I know you. You were a member of the State Research. You took my father away from me. You and your colleagues bashed his head and dumped him in Namanve Forest. Do you remember that?" a large woman shouted.

"Kill them, kill them, kiiill theeem," the crowd roared avidly.

"Amin is gone. You and your friends are going to pay the price," someone hollered.

"Pay, pay, paaaay." The word was passed round.

The verdict was unanimous. The Bureau, a mountain of killings and torturings on its doorstep, was not a name to generate mercy, even among the levelheaded. The most lethal weapon at this time of chaos was to accuse somebody of collaboration with the Bureau or with some other Aminist security agency. "Guilty" platformed feet were swiftly swept off the asphalt, with hard objects meeting the pair midair and striking with the vengeance of three thousand and ten days of woe. By the time the two men hit the ground, they were half-dead. The circle, like a giant sphincter, closed to a fleshy dot, and the duo were flattened like the chapatis the Indians had introduced here.

"The bastards did not even beg for mercy," somebody said as he went past me. With the tension dissipated, I squeezed my way to another spot.

Portraits of Amin, defaced but discernible, lay stamped into the asphalt. Effigies with limbs torn off smoldered pungently in gasoline bonfires. Near the spot where I first saw a live birth, a crowd of onlookers was watching smoke rise from piles of tires. I could faintly make out four human figures, constricted and twisted in death. The story was that they had been caught trying to get into a van. They had denied being Amin's henchmen, but on examination showed telltale shoulder weals caused by rifle straps. They were almost instantly necklaced with tires and set alight.

My attention, and the attention of almost everyone in the bowl, was attracted by the blaring of a bullhorn. The man with the horn was being followed by a group of emaciated, ragged, ecstatic, skeletal men and women, freshly vomited from the torture chambers on Nakasero Hill, just beyond the High Court. The skeletons were dancing and waving twigs as measly tears ran down from their protruding eyes. They were cheered as they marched through the bowl. Vendors, impressed by their escape, gave them buns, drinks, anything they had, free of charge. Others gave them money for the fare home. Many of these people were dazed, staring glassily as though they could not believe their luck. They walked as though they were still shackled and intoxicated by the stink of incarceration, and the vomit, the blood, the excreta and the violence of torture chambers and detention centers. They walked with the full weight of freedom on their shoulders, and for some it seemed too much to bear.

It suddenly struck me: Where was Grandpa? Was he lying wounded in a pit, a building, a bush, waiting for someone to hear his cries for help? So far, his sons had failed to locate him, or even to meet anyone who had a clue as to his whereabouts. They had been to morgues, hospital wards, makeshift refugee centers, military barracks and the homes of relatives, all in vain. They had hardly rested in the past week, and seemed totally at a loss as to what to do next. Aunt Lwandeka had asked her National Reform Movement colleagues to look for Grandpa, but they had not returned any news.

With the sharp stink of burning rubber in my nostrils, mad curiosity in my head, rifle shots and joyous shouts in my ear, I pushed my way through the crowd. I went past charred remains and mutilated effigies and headed for the cathedrals. I was going to check at the Catholic Cathedral of Lubaga and, if necessary, at the Protestant Cathedral of Namirembe. It was hot and humid, and the heat stuck to the skin like a layer of ointment.

Near the edge of the bowl, another court was in session. Tribal facial scars were on trial: diamond-shaped scars, vertical slashes, horizontal scars and swollen dotted scars on foreheads, temples and cheeks had betrayed their northern owners. Anyone seen with the same was a potential suspect. Three women with vertical slashes on their cheeks were in the dock, tried by a group of ragged boys young enough to be their adolescent sons. The crowd was savoring this delegation of judicial powers to these dregs of society with the demeanor of a boss watching his minions exact revenge.

The boys, heads lice-tormented, groins crab-infested, brains glue-crazed, eyes aglow with that rare total power occasioned only by war, chanted, "Witches, witches."

"Witches . . . burn them, witches . . . fry them, witches . . . fuck them . . ."

The accused, red eyes popping, nostrils dilating and faces warping with deathly vacillation—that terrible indecision between humility and disdain, supplication and condescension, frowning and fawning—mumbled and jabbered, appealing to emotions hardened by the last three thousand and ten days of wrath.

The ragged kids, as if commanded by an infallible leader, closed in on the trio. They ripped soaked fabrics, razored open cesarean scars, invaded stretch-marked territories, laid waste anything in their path. The flashing of metal and the snapping of bone rose above the animal grunts as life struggled with death. I did not wait for the final outcome.

The Catholic cathedral, perched high on the hill like a new Golgotha piled with skulls and bones, was strewn with people without destination, people awaiting overdue redemption like forgotten goods. Many had come from as far away as fifty kilometers, fleeing advancing Tanzanian forces and discomfited Amin troops. To these people the archbishop was a hero, and the sins of the clergy were merely the inevitable fleas on a useful dog. These survivors had neither the maniacal look of the Crusaders nor the defiant visage of the martyrs: they were scared, unsure, hesitant. It was as if they believed that war had only taken a break and would return as soon as they left for home. I went all over the compound in search of Grandpa and checked the list in the administration office. In vain. I left the cathedral, with its phallic towers, the cook fires, the bawling children and lost adults, and headed for the Protestant cathedral. It was a wild-goose chase. I could hardly focus on anything now. I seemed to be as dazed as the skeletal people I had seen at the bowl, and as hypnotized as a drugged mouse. As I was leaving I stepped on somebody's clothes, spread out in the grass to dry, and heard angry voices calling me to stop. I just strode on.

The headquarters of the Muslim Supreme Council, the place I associated with Dr. Ssali's conversion, was crawling with Muslim refugees. Anybody who feared reprisals stayed here, under the mighty shield of the great edifice. I thought I saw Lusanani among the unveiled women. I followed a woman and whistled at her, sure that it was Lusanani. A strange woman turned round, startled. I apologized. I should have known that Hajj Gimbi, expert reader of the times, had moved his family to the rural area where few people knew him and were unlikely to cause him trouble. I saw quite a few anxious faces here. There was genuine fear of a backlash against Muslims among these people. They had seen what had happened to some of their colleagues who had been accused of harboring Aminist sympathies. But their leaders exuded the confidence that nobody would dare assault them here at the giant mosque. As I left I felt a big sense of failure: I had not located Grandpa.

Evening was approaching. The sun had gone down quickly on the day's mayhem, and order had crept back.

The city looked empty, as most people had hurried home to beat roadblocks, the curfew and henchmen searching for victims under the cover of darkness. Everyone knew that the first weeks after the war were more dangerous than the last weeks of the war itself, and acted accordingly.

I was exhausted, crazed by the day's failures. I wished it were all a dream and I could blow life back into the corpses and make Grandpa hear my voice. As in Grandma's case, reality had its own harsh, unbendable plans that did not respond to the urging of even the most powerful minds. I was so famished I thought I was feeling the hunger of the dead and of those far away whose crops had been destroyed in the war. I knew that I could not bear all the sufferings of the last three thousand and ten days of Amin's rule. I was even reluctant to take stock of the damage: Grandma dead, Grandpa disappeared, Aunt Lwandeka threatened and tortured, Aunt Kasawo gang-raped . . . and I was afraid it was not over yet.

I found myself walking along the corsetted banks of Nakivubo River, the hunger and thirst I felt turning the filthy water into a crystal-clear waterfall. I kept on walking toward Owino Market, remembering my fantasy of seeing Padlock working there. I saw vultures and marabou storks lazing on the garbage dumps, sated, ready to leave after another successful day at the office. The market was built in two sections, one with cement stalls, one with makeshift ones where commerce spilled onto the pavements. It was like walking through a sooty ghost town. There was a side road that came down from the cathedrals and cut right across the slums and the market. I walked toward it. People hurried past me like ghosts, unnoticed. Then I saw a woman turn and hold her nose, but she did not spit. I knew there was a corpse nearby, because one never spat at a dead person.

I had in fact bypassed four bodies lying in the shadow of the market office building. The power of the stench made me feel as if the roof of my nose had been ripped off. Two corpses were lying faceup; one was facedown; the fourth was headless. I was the only onlooker; others just hurried by. The woman who had held her nose had disappeared. I did not recognize any of the dead. I was about to walk back to the taxi park before it was too late, when I was struck by the familiar look of one dead man's bloodied brogue. I had brushed that shoe many times and wiped the polish off with a piece of white cloth. I knew where the cracks were and how carefully they had been repaired. I bent down to look more closely, the stench almost knocking me back. The man lying facedown was Grandpa! My bladder voided itself, releasing a few drops. Suddenly I was no longer hungry or thirsty. I was just dazed and groggy. Why had Serenity and Kawayida not looked here? Had they looked and failed to recognize their own father?

I somehow made the journey home. Aunt Lwandeka went to her NRM colleagues, got a jeep and moved the body to the morgue for immediate attention. She then drove to Serenity's suburb. The two brothers were lying in bed, exhausted by yet another day's futile search. They were relieved because the search had ended, but angry that they hadn't discovered Grandpa's body sooner.

The clan gathered at Grandpa's house. The last time there was a crowd like this was at Serenity's wedding. Aunt Nakatu had become older and fatter, though unmarked by her recent tribulations. Hajj Ali looked distinguished in a white tunic and a gold-threaded Muslim hat. Baby Sulaiman, their only child, was already attending primary school. Aunt Tiida and Dr. Ssali could not get over the loss of their beloved Peugeot. Amin's army officers had commandeered it, over Tiida's protests that theirs was a Muslim family which should be exempt from such aggression. The car had broken down one hundred and fifty kilometers from the city. Dr. Ssali's mechanic found it in a roadside ditch with the engine blown up. Tiida told the sad story over and over again. I saw Uncle Kawayida's wife for the first time in years. She looked tall and majestic, exuding the energy of well-being. If it had not been for her thick lower jaw and large feet, she would have been the most beautiful woman there. She had come driving their second van, and was proud to oblige the mourners. Uncle Kawayida did all the driving now, but for some reason, his wife kept the keys, which kept getting lost. At one time, all people seemed to do was to look for the keys. Uncle Kawayida's wife liked the game. She kept finding the keys and feigning surprise.

Grandpa's body arrived two days later because of the intensive work that had to be done on it. Grief apart, I felt proud of the man. He was one of the few people I knew who had practiced what he preached. I felt proud that he had taken those beatings, and the stabbing, and the bullet in his leg. He had lived in a self-chosen political battlefield, and had died in it. I now associated Independence Day, the 1966 State of Emergency and Amin's fall with him. To me, he was an encyclopedia of our political history, and without his dissertations and my efforts to regurgitate them, I would have been a political ignoramus. He had pursued his political ambitions and paid the price. He had made the predictions of national explosions and died in one. He had led the life of a rebel, speaking his mind even if it meant suffering for it. He had been an island of outspokenness in a sea of conformism. Whatever others said about him, I did not mind.

The forlorn drama of death was highlighted by the head-shaving ceremony. Aunt Tiida turned this banal ritual into a spectacle. According to custom, the heads of all the orphans had to be shaved stone-bald. Tiida saw her brothers' and her sister's hair collecting at the shaver's feet and decided to rebel. When her turn came, the old man with the razor blade did not even look up. He just extended his arm, beckoning her to come forward.

"I am keeping my hair."

"What!"

"You heard me," she said, laying on more authority than she really commanded. "I am not mourning my father with a bald head. If you want, I will cover my hair, or even dirty it, but it is not going to be shaved off. Dad never cared for such scruples."

"Do not hold up the ceremonies, woman. Come here and get it over with," the old man, now surrounded by a phalanx of supporters, commanded.

Serenity and Kawayida, both red-eyed with grief, seemed about to explode. They looked at their sister with vehemence, waiting for her to change her mind. Angry voices were gathering volume. Dr. Saif Ssali, a man who knew how small things could cause big problems, moved forward to forestall trouble. He led Aunt Tiida out of the circle of mourners and talked to her. Crestfallen, she returned and offered her head to the razor.

News of the incident circulated quickly, feeding the thirsty gossip machine that ground incessantly to lighten the prevailing mood of doom and gloom. Another popular topic of conversation was the recent looting spree which had occurred in the towns and in some rural areas. Survivors from the youthful section of the village who had attacked the barracks and brought back army bunk beds, tents, boots, biscuits, corned beef, fridges, incubators and bullets joined the mourners and told their stories. Now and then we heard explosions from their end of the village. Idle youths put live bullets on lighted coals and cheered the explosions.

Serenity had looked at me with a mixture of envy and anger when he learned that I was responsible for the discovery of his father's remains. There I was, once again, weakening his position as first son. He felt particularly defeated because on three separate occasions, Kawayida and he had passed through Owino Market on their way to the cathedrals. He could not figure out how they had missed those bodies, which had been so near the road. I was not in the least preoccupied with his concerns. I was only interested in seeing his first child, the daughter who was one year older than me. I pictured her as endowed with the elegance of Aunt Tiida, the mild temperament of her mother and Grandpa's ambition. My hopes were dashed by Aunt Nakatu, who revealed that the girl would not attend the burial. She had boycotted all family functions attended by Serenity. It was clear now that Serenity had not been much of a parent to her. I suspected that he might have offered occasional financial help, say, when the child was sick, but no more. My feeling was that he did not hate her, but he simply did not know what to do with her, what to offer her. As a man brought up by female wolves, he must have assumed that all females had the wolfish capacity to take care of themselves, an assumption backed by Padlock's independence and Nakibuka's confidence.

I had already met Kasiko, the girl's mother. She was far better looking than Padlock. She carried her years well, and compared with Padlock, time had been very kind to her. I liked her. She had not treated me like an enemy, her supplanter's offspring, the way Padlock would have done. I would have liked to know her and to meet her daughter, but I did not know how to proceed. Ours was a family trapped in decay, the fibers binding us corroded by lack of contact, the dislocations of modernism and the vagaries of undigested Catholicism. If Serenity had not estranged this woman, there would possibly have been a way in which she would have enriched my life. There was something accommodating, sweet and mild about her, a grace in defeat, a glowing inner strength I would have liked to investigate.

Yet there was something ugly in the way Padlock and Kasiko avoided each other. They sat miles apart, eyeing each other warily like scavenging birds. If Kasiko were to fall into a pit, I was sure the ex-nun would not help her out. On the other hand, if Kasiko found Padlock in a pit, I was sure she would pull her out, if only to enjoy the revenge of being her savior. To me, the two women seemed two sides of the same coin: Padlock had strong principles, but as sole role model, she was defective, in need of a balancing element, somebody with heart like Kasiko. Kasiko in turn needed something of Padlock's independence. Serenity knew this, but it was too late. He also knew that Hajj Gimbi's children had better female role models than the shitters, who had to do only with the reclusive Padlock. "She is the mother of my children," I heard Serenity say to Nakibuka several times.

Nakibuka was also present. Had Serenity ever had so many women with him at the same time and yet looked and felt so lonely? Kasiko, Padlock and Nakibuka seemed to be three hot pebbles in his boot. Hajj Gimbi would have called the women together and made them do things whether they liked it or not, but Serenity was walking a tightrope, doing his best to avoid the trinity, as if by ignoring them publicly, he was honoring some old agreement or diluting the gossip about the fact that Nakibuka, his mistress, was his wife's aunt.

I was impressed with Nakibuka's charisma and stage presence. She acted like the first wife of Serenity's wifely trinity. She was oblivious to backbiters and moved confidently among the mourners. She organized a cooking brigade, sent loafing youths to fetch water and made sure that nobody had more than their fair share of food. She was back in her role as the bridal aunt, taking care of both the uptight bride and the nervous groom, welcoming relatives and visitors, making sure that everything was running on schedule. She had first come to this village eighteen years ago. Now she was back as a conqueror, going straight to Serenity when she needed something, helping out Aunt Tiida where necessary, moving with the consummate ease of a fish in water.

I could not get enough of watching her. I was mesmerized. I could see what self-love had done to her: she looked at everyone, friend or foe, as if she were on the verge of breaking a secret or reciting for them a love poem. She looked at the mourners with friendly eyes, ready to welcome the wandering stranger, reassure the weary of heart and send off the hopeless with a smile. She was so good that even Aunt Tiida got irritated. "Who does she think she is?" I heard her say to Aunt Nakatu. In a sea of grief-stricken mourners, Nakibuka stood out, but so would she in a crush of joyful celebrants. There was something flirtatious about her, the very reason her husband used to beat her: she used to make him tremble to the core with insecurity, too aware of his own inadequacies. Serenity's insecurities and discomforts were not exacerbated by Nakibuka, and neither would they be cured by her. It was the reason that, despite having this powerhouse in his corner, he still had the manner of an animal with caustic grease up the ass.

I did my best to keep out of Nakibuka's way, because I did not want to become a messenger boy delivering messages to Padlock, Serenity or whomever else she wanted to contact. I kept out of Padlock's way too. She looked pathetic, with her pouty, pinched-faced nun look. I disappeared whenever I could, returning only at mealtimes.

Sleeping arrangements caused a stir. Uncle Kawayida wanted Serenity's "wives" to occupy his bachelor house. Nakibuka and Kasiko moved in, joined later by Aunt Lwandeka. Padlock, however, asserted her position and refused to enter the house with Nakibuka and Kasiko. Uncle Kawayida, assisted by Tiida, carried out negotiations with Padlock which ended in a stalemate. Serenity tactfully kept away. Padlock won the day, sleeping on the bed on which she had lost her virginity. Nakibuka and Kasiko, like allies in a trench war, slept outside, as though planning to storm the house at the crack of dawn.

I slept outside under the tree of Grandma and Grandpa's afternoon arguments. I listened to the howls of dogs in heat, the snores of sleepers and the calls of nocturnal creatures. I remembered the night I was confronted by Dorobo, the seminary watchman, the power sabo-teur. I could see him towering like a tree, wide as a wall. Fr. Gilles Lageau had left the country. Fr. Kaanders had died and was buried at the seminary. Lwendo was still pursuing his priestly vocation. Where was Cane? I remembered the two clean, stenchless bodies he had shown us so long ago. Memories of Grandpa lying in the shadow of the market office came back. The stench too. The slimy finger of nau-sea crept up my stomach and I retched, thinking about the bullets that had killed him. I could not sleep again. Tomorrow was the burial. The grave was dug, the last nail in the coffin of the past ready to go in. I became very restless. I walked to the youthful end of the village. The "restaurant," "hotel" and "casino" were wrapped in darkness. The youths with their bullet-on-coals games were asleep. The coffee-smuggling business had died a natural death after the fall of Amin. The place where joyrides, card games and drinking bouts used to be held was strewn with plastic wrappers coming off new mattresses, ra-dios, shirts and other goods looted from the barracks. The looting spree was over now. In its place was a lacuna of inactivity. People seemed to be waiting for oracles to pronounce on the future of post-Amin Uganda.

The burial took place early in the afternoon. There were two puke-yellow Postal Service trucks filled with Serenity's trade-union members. Hajj Gimbi was there, together with many other people I did not know. The only thing I remembered was the two trucks coming and going. The rest of the day was wrapped in a sickly yellow film full of fading images. I kept wondering whether they had finally removed the bullet Grandpa had carried with him for thirteen years. I wanted to keep it as a souvenir. I remembered Grandma's dream of the buffalo and the crocodile. I wondered where I fit in the past and the future.

The political picture eventually became clearer. Tanzania's gray-haired leader, President Nyerere, was calling the shots. A coalition government incorporating old political forces and many diffuse new ones was in power. Nothing was getting done because of the infight-ing and interference from Tanzania. Aunt did not like her colleagues' chances. She had discovered that the National Reform Movement was small compared with the giants roaming the political arena. The brigadier had got only a small post: he was one of a team in charge of repairing military barracks and recruiting soldiers. Already there was talk of elections. Nyerere's old friend Obote was free to participate. It was clear that Tanzania was finally ending his exile and using him to guarantee payment of war costs. Inside the country, expectation was low, disillusionment surging. Democracy built on old forces promised to be no bed of roses, and even at this early point there were rumors of impending civil war. The tidbits Aunt got from her colleagues pointed to a murky future as the infighting in the government mounted. For the moment, people eased doubts about the future with actions to improve the present. Parent-teacher associations sprung up and opened schools while the government dithered. It was evident that getting rid of a tyrant was one thing, setting the house in order quite another. I was kept from political musings by the string of tragedies that struck the family.

Female liberators were the latest sensation; they now controlled most roadblocks. I had seen them, behinds bulging in tight military pants, breasts bouncing in green army bras, hair peeping out from under sweaty caps. They were the direct response to the growing complaints about harassment at roadblocks manned by their male counterparts. The honeymoon between the populace and the liberators was over. Calls to remove all roadblocks were made daily, because the liberators too had succumbed to the temptation of ransoms. Plans were under way to send the Tanzanians back. In the meantime, many tried to acquire material things they could not get in Communist Tanzania. Roadblocks stayed because there were still people with guns used in armed robberies, a few of which got impounded at checkpoints.

For some, though—Aunt Kasawo, for one—the introduction of female personnel had come too late. Kasawo lived in a strategic little town between Kampala and Masaka. They called it the Cervix. It was taken by the liberators after a fierce battle and was used as a base for forces marching to Kampala. At the height of the campaign, a large contingent of Tanzanian forces was stationed there, waiting to be sent to the front line or back to base in Masaka.

Discipline was high among the soldiers, courtesy toward civilians was of the type Ugandans had never seen in their soldiers, and the harshness of punishment for defaulting soldiers was chilling in its severity. Two Tanzanian soldiers had been shot soon after capturing the town for raping a sixty-year-old woman. The local citizens witnessed the shooting and could not believe their eyes. Amin's men would not have lifted a finger against the rapists; they might even have promoted them, to spite the people. From then on, the citizens relaxed, leaving their doors unlocked, because nobody stole or robbed anymore. For three months, the people lived in a sort of utopia, which they hoped would outlive the fall of Amin.

In the morning, people went to watch army drills and to listen to the soldiers singing as they panted and sweated. Afternoons passed colorfully as civilians put their dreams for the future into words while they waited for news about the progress of the liberation war. In the evening, they gathered in groups and listened to Guerrilla Radio and cheered as Amin was called names, and sang along as popular tunes aired, and broke into discussion at the end of the broadcasts. Some of the programs were made in that town: Guerrilla Radio personnel came over and interviewed people about life in liberated areas. Local people heard their own voices on the air for the first time and enthused over the peace and the good relations between the liberation forces and the populace. Top military personnel also visited, and people saw with their own eyes the individuals who held the future of the country in their hands. Army personnel carried out light politicization campaigns, stressing the importance of self-help projects.

Outside the barracks, everything was fine; inside, the men left behind to guard the town got bored. With boredom, repressed, deep-frozen demons thawed, throbbed into life and started pounding on internal doors. Consequently, more and more soldiers thought they could do with a little booze and a little sex. After all, they were about to go to the front line, and this could be their last chance. Anyway, hadn't they put their lives on the line for these very booze makers and booze sellers and booze-drinking women? They pounded on the glass wall that separated them from the juicy, big-bummed women they had come all the way from Tanzania to liberate and protect, but whom they could not touch without getting whipped, incarcerated or even shot dead like their two comrades.

It was one hundred and fifty days since the seven brothers had had their last meal. They had been ten brothers at the time: three of them had died while fighting Amin's forces in Masaka. The seven remaining formed a close-knit unit that planned its moves with the care and patience of a weaver. They were a family, and family was more important than its constituent members. They had sworn on their life that if one of them ever got caught, he would shoulder the blame on behalf of the whole group. Originally, they operated in two groups of five, but after the death of their brothers, they had merged into a single unit. For the moment, they watched as stupid soldiers escaped to drink booze and get laid, only to be caught and brought back in handcuffs for incarceration or dispatch to Masaka or back home to Tanzania. The seven brothers had watched the execution of two soldiers with sadness. What a waste! In effect, that was the fifth execution since the beginning of the war. They had no intention of getting caught; they would not act with the clumsiness of Amin's men.

The brothers had decided years ago that quality and quantity were not mutually exclusive factors. Every year they made do with a certain number of meals whose heaviness compensated for the dry periods. While stupid soldiers thought in terms of women, they thought of one woman, a single meal. Hastily gotten women talked, resulting in lineups and floggings. A woman feasted on by the brothers had trouble pinpointing the responsible parties because of the way the whole thing was organized. They had never been caught and could not see themselves getting caught here in this little town.

When Aunt Kasawo went out to try her luck on the black market one afternoon, she walked into a well-set trap. Behind a line of unroofed edifices originally meant to house Amin's army personnel, a soft-spoken young man in jeans, a clean T-shirt and a straw hat stopped her. He offered to sell her quality rice, beans and beef at a price she could not refuse.

"Beef from America! Real beef, madame. Rice from Japan, thick-grained, factory-washed rice that goes straight into the cooking pan! I will give you a discount, madame."

Kasawo liked this affable young man with his clear skin, his clean teeth and his unscented breath. She liked being called "madame," and he was the first person to say the word like he meant it. She enjoyed the young man's enthusiasm. She wanted black-marketeers to work and to smile for their money the way she worked and smiled for hers.

"I am not here to buy air, young man," she said, assuming a superior air. "Show me the goods."

"At your service, madame," he said with a cute smile. He picked up samples from his raffia bag. "Bite on that fat-grained rice, madame. See! Look at that beef: a whole bull crammed into this small tin! A word of advice: open the tin carefully, you don't want to be getting gored in the face by an American bull."

Kasawo was impressed by the sense of humor, the quality of the samples and the price asked. The young man should not have wasted any more words, but, like all starving souls, he could not believe that a meal was standing in front of him begging to be taken. The brothers had been warned about the arrogance of Ugandan women, which made the speed of this victory even more astounding. Then again, Aunt Kasawo had not been the first woman to come by. The man had let quite a few pass by because the vibes were wrong.

"I have not sold a thing today, madame. God must have sent you in answer to my prayers," he said, flashing his white teeth. Aunt Kasawo liked the clear pink gums too.

By the look of things, he was her lucky star too. She was buying low and was going to sell high. She thought about establishing regular contact with him and sidestepping the black-marketeer who took every chance to hike prices by hoarding commodities and creating artificial scarcity.

"Show me the rest of the goods, young man," Kasawo, still not believing her luck, said with mock brusqueness.

"They are in that building," he said, pointing with a long, beautiful finger.

"Afraid of army raids, are we?" she said with the complacency and complicity of a black-marketeer.

"You said it, madame. Those liberators accuse us of selling their beef, but they don't ask themselves how we get it." He smiled and then broke into a belly laugh.

For the first time in fifteen years, Aunt Kasawo thought about the son she had disowned after his father's attempt on her life. He must be big now. Was he this articulate, polite and smart? She hoped he wasn't. His father did not deserve such a son. He deserved a three-foot, drum-headed dwarf. She stood outside the edifice, looked around to make sure that no one was coming, and waited. The black market was built on trust. How she trusted this young man! When establishing risky business contacts, Kasawo worked on instinct, and this one felt right.

She heard him ask from inside the number of kilos she wanted. He showed her a five-kilo bag of rice and a carton of canned beef. She decided to enter and make sure that she was not getting shortchanged. Give a black-marketeer a finger, and he will rip off the whole hand. Aunt Kasawo remembered her childhood parish priest cautioning his flock on Sundays against the Devil.

One moment she was thinking of asking him to become her regular supplier; the next, she was engulfed in the darkness of the tomb. Launched by a leg sweep, she was suspended in air, the vertigo amplified by the darkness of the bag over her head. Still calling her madame, the young man asked her not to make noise. She twitched and kicked and thrashed about on the sleeping bag she was lying on. The cold feel of a knife put an end to her efforts. She felt two extra pairs of hands on her, disrobing her. This was organization at its most efficient. She interviewed herself: How many men violated you? Two, three, four or more? I do not know. Think, make a guess, madame. The army is against all acts of aggression on civilians, and we will punish anybody you identify. Can you tell us what the man you saw was wearing? He was wearing a hat and a T-shirt and jeans . . . Any more clues? No.

First there were one, two, three, four, five, six, seven explosive, thick-porridge-like spurts. Then there were one, two, three, four, five, six, seven not-so-explosive, not-so-thick leakings. Last, there were one, two, three, four, five, six, seven protracted, non-explosive thin leakings. The grim statistics showed half a liter of semen discharged in sixty-eight minutes of non-stop action. The cervix got addressed more than two thousand three hundred times. The breasts got pinched one hundred ninety-five times. The clitoris was touched a paltry five times.

The seven brothers vacated the scene one by one. The decoy left first in order to make his alibi foolproof. They arrived at the barracks in time for the evening roll call. The picture that kept going through their mind was the lightning cross-border attack Amin's forces had made on the Kagera Triangle a few months back.

The irony or perverse logic of the situation was that it was an army doctor who worked on Kasawo and helped her through the medical part of the ordeal. The same doctor went on to ask her who she thought her attackers were, and she said that she did not know. He asked her what language they spoke, and she said she did not remember. Had she seen any of them? She only remembered seeing a straw hat, a white T-shirt and a pair of blue jeans. Had they taken her money? No. She refused to answer any more questions. She had already decided to get the demons of rape and trauma exorcised by a famous medicine man and not to waste any time in highly embarrassing investigations. How would one hold one's head high in such a little place when everyone knew that one had been raped by seven soldiers? Aunt Kasawo was no one's fool. As her childhood parish priest used to say, silence was golden.

A fortnight after Grandpa's burial, Aunt Kasawo put on her best clothes and her fanciest jewelry, ready to go. She was picked up from her home by a Postal Service van sent by Serenity. It drove her to the city and from there to the place where Padlock had been living for the last two years. She looked at the soldiers with a smile full of ill will. She was happy that they were being sent back home to Tanzania, where she hoped they would rape their sisters and mothers. She wondered where the soldiers she knew in Amin's time were now. One had offered her money in exchange for shelter. One had proposed marriage. One had cried in her house the whole night, begging her to smuggle him to the islands in Lake Victoria and to hide him there till the end of the war. The trio had sold her goods, which she peddled on the black market, up to the time the Tanzanians captured the town. Where were those men? Her guess was that they were hiding in northern Uganda, in Sudan or even in Kenya. The sense of inviolability their friendship had given her made her realize how low she had sunk. It dawned on her that the times had changed and that her bad luck with men, which for years she thought she had overcome, was still dogging her.

Kasawo was impressed by the bungalow and the chunk of land owned by her sister. She had always wanted to own a house, a little place she could paint and decorate as she wanted. She greatly admired Serenity's sense of vision: buying this land and building this house just in time. Many people who had made money in Amin's time were now languishing in poverty because they had foolishly believed that Amin would be in power forever and had not saved anything for a rainy day. She, for one, could have built a big house with the money she had made off the black market, but she kept procrastinating. Now she felt ashamed that she was still renting the same place after a dozen years.

Kasawo was struck by the bronze plaque depicting the legend of Romulus and Remus. It had acquired more meaning here. On the dining table was a plastic bottle made in the likeness of the Virgin, with crown, heart on the chest, clouds and all. She felt envious of her sister, who had been to Rome, Lourdes, Jerusalem and many other places in the Bible. The girl they used to call Nakaza, Nakaze, Nakazi, Nakazo, Nakazu! Time had not diminished Padlock's achievement. Aunt Kasawo kept thinking that Padlock was lucky not only with men, but also with children and money.

The place was run like a military barracks. The courtyard was very clean; the children obeyed their mother's orders without question and knew exactly what was expected of them. One after the other, they all knelt down and welcomed their visiting maternal aunt properly. They did their homework quietly, and Kasawo noticed that their grades were very good, even the relatively dim shitter's. As she watched her sister wield the scepter, she remembered the conversation they had had about aging parents years ago when Lwandeka was abducted. Padlock was an exception: age had not undermined her disciplinarian tendencies in the least. If the last-born child was going to get any leeway in comparison with the firstborn, it was not going to be by much. Padlock still used the guava switch with grim determination and was not above sending a defaulter to bed on an empty stomach.

A beneficiary of parental laxity, who at the eldest shitter's age was drinking alcohol, keeping late hours and refusing to mess up her hot-comb-straightened hair by carrying water pots on it, Kasawo could hardly believe her eyes. This kind of cast-iron discipline she had not seen in a long time, and she wondered how her sister was able to keep it up.

As a guest, Kasawo did not have to do anything but eat and sleep. The shitters surprised her with the quality of their cooking, and if she had not seen the two boys peeling the bananas, thatching them in banana leaves and preparing the fire, she would have credited her sister for the meal. The shitters were at her beck and call, and warmed her bathwater whenever she wanted it. In the afternoon, she went for short walks. There had been no looting here, and the shops were running. She felt tempted to step inside the dispensary and get a quick examination by a civilian doctor. It was a whim, for she was all right and the pain had long gone. Kasawo got irritated by the fine Kiswahili spoken by the liberators. It reminded her too much of the decoy who had led her into the trap. She wished she could blow up the shop building the liberators used for military detachments.

The most significant change in her since the ordeal was her tendency to blow up over little things and to belabor insignificant points. If, say, there was too much salt in the food, she would go on and on about it the whole day, unearthing obscure plots to starve her by killing her appetite, dehydrating her and giving her ulcers.

Aunt Kasawo went over the why-me aspect of the rape so many times that she almost drove the stoic ex-nun crazy. It resulted in a visible hardening of feelings on the latter's part. Two opposing forces had met. Padlock had God and Catholic stoicism in her bag, while Kasawo had only her stubbornness, her anger, a vague sense of justice and the belief that the exorcist would solve her psychological problems. Padlock devised the system of letting her sister belabor the whys for something like thirty minutes and then cut in with an unhelpful "It is God's will." This had the adverse effect of infuriating Kasawo and making her more recalcitrant and strident. Kasawo eventually got the impression that her sister thought she had deserved the violation. Padlock viewed the deed as part of a divine plan to save Kasawo's soul. Kasawo felt that she was being listened to but not heard, that her sister was like a know-all doctor ready with the cure before the patient even opened his mouth. She was enraged by the realization that her sister was viewing her as a potential convert to conservative Catholicism. Padlock was talking to her in the patronizing tones of a church elder, and it made her feel like hollering. She was now sure that Padlock believed herself far better than Kasawo.

She was not wrong. After her twelfth child, Padlock had given up even the little sex she used to have, and felt that she was better than all the people around who smeared themselves with devil snot. Secure inside the armor of die-hard Catholicism, she climbed up onto a pedestal, from which she looked down on those wallowing in sins of the flesh. Now firmly installed on her puritanical throne, she felt it was her duty to judge the sinners in the hope that they would cling to the tentacles of her verdict and personal example and pull themselves up from the cesspit of their doomed lives. As Kasawo retold her woeful tale, divulging details of her ensnarement, violation and abandonment; as she recounted her struggle to get up and crawl out of the dungeon of defilement; as she gave details of how she lay half-dead in the path, Padlock felt sublime delight coursing through her. At her feet lay the body of a sinner stripped naked, crawling out of the sty of sin into the path of salvation.

"Sister, why do you persist in sin? Why don't you heed God's warnings to our family?

"God began by sending you your first man, Pangaman, sweetening his lugubrious evil character and making him say sweet things in your naive ears. This man inflated your little ego and led you onto the bumpy path of rebellion and self-destruction. You rebelled against our parents. You drank alcohol. You became unruly. You flaunted the clothes he ensnared you with. You bragged about the sexual sins you committed with him.

"Despite all that, God did not abandon you: He gave you another chance, but you ignored Him. You went on and had other men, sinned as never before, and completely forgot Him. You built a new life for yourself, disowned Pangaman's son, acquired a new name and lived in safety. To make sure that Pangaman would not pursue you, you befriended Amin's soldiers and created an artificial security wall around you. It worked as long as God allowed it to stand. God let you walk unmolested through ranks of killers, rapers and robbers, and you felt inviolable. God gave you access to goods and money, and you felt ten feet tall. You watched as women cried and lived in fear of Amin's henchmen. You wondered why they did not wise up and befriend soldiers to protect them and punish anybody who touched them. God gave you another chance: He spared you the filthy hands of Amin's henchmen but put the sting in the tail of liberation. He sent you the seven brothers. He struck you with the very stick you thought you could not live without. He drenched you with the very waters you believed to be the elixir of life. He struck you down and let strange men piss down your throat. You now retch at the mere thought of it, why? You pissed down God's throat too and wiped your bottom on His plans for you. The violation was the last sign, the last warning before the death of the firstborn. There will be no more locusts and no more storms and no more violators. This is your last chance to repent and turn to God."

Out of frustration, Kasawo asked her sister what she had done about Nakibuka.

Padlock winced for a split second, then bounced back. She had committed that whore into God's hands. Nakibuka too would get her warnings and her just punishment for defecating on holy matrimony. Everybody got amply warned, Lwandeka too. Up to the time of her arrest, she believed that she was Babylon: big, important, impregnable. God sent Amin's henchmen to wake her up from the complacency of sin. God would not hesitate to do the same thing again if she refused to change. She knew the rules from the start: a woman who had carnal knowledge of more than one man was a whore, and whores who don't repent in time get stoned to death.

Kasawo was in tears now. Padlock smelled victory and pressed her advantage.

"You are moaning about your violation because of your apostasy. You are crying about how Amin did this and did that, and didn't do this and that, and shouldn't have acted this or that way. A nation of moaners and whiners. A nation of foolish, ungodly people who cry when God raises His big stick, Idi Amin, to hit evil, disobedience, greed, selfishness and vice out of its fibers in preparation for justice, virtue and salvation. Just like you, this nation did not heed the voice of the prophets and the warnings from God's mouth.

"The white man, thinking that he was God, came, subjugated the land, imposed his laws and way of life on the people, and sat back to relax and enjoy the fruits of his iniquity. He had Indian assistants to help him milk the resources of the nation. Together they shared the milk and honey God gave this nation. They made laws to protect themselves from the wrath of the people. They built bigger and bigger castles. They built higher and higher monuments. They amassed deadlier and deadlier weapons. They flaunted their political, economic and social power. Until God decided that enough was enough. He stirred the formerly docile people. He turned the white man's black collaborators into his worst enemies. He cut the white man with his own sword. He crushed his huge empire in His fist. White men started looking over their shoulders as they drove through the city, as they walked their dogs, as they went to their godless temples. The white man was no longer absolute master. The white man was no longer in control. The white man had been defeated by Jesus' words: he who gets much will have much demanded of him. He finally turned tail and absconded like a thief in the night.

"The Indian, imprisoned in his greed, did not heed God's warning. In 1971, God raised a new sword, flashing with a new wrath. A year later, the Indian was bleeding, whimpering, wallowing in his sorrows. God took away his home, his security, his peace of mind. God turned his former ally, the white man, against him. Suddenly nobody wanted him. He was kicked from border to border like a dirty ball. The black man rejoiced: God had judged in his favor. Instead of learning a lesson and turning to God, the black man took everything for granted. He took over the booty left by the Indians. Muslims and Christians took to eating, drinking, fornicating and indulging the flesh like the white man and the Indian before them. Castles built on sand never survive big storms. The house built on godlessness was shaken by internal storms, and by the wrath of God's sword, Idi Amin, and it fell on its occupants. From within the ruins, people cried out for salvation, and God heard them. In 1979, the sword was dislodged. But as soon as the sword stopped flashing, the people reverted to their old ways. The nation had not repented or learned from the past. Kasawo, you and the nation have not learned and have not repented and will once again be put to the test.

"Don't cry, Kasawo; don't cry, nation. God tests those He loves the most. Look back and you will see that St. Bartholomew was skinned alive, St. Lawrence grilled, St. John boiled in oil, St. Erasmus disembowelled, the Uganda Martyrs wrapped in reeds and burned alive. All of them were God's beloved, yet He did not spare them. Today's people act as though they were the first and will be the last to taste the bitter chalice of God's test. Why don't you, Kasawo, and all of those whiners out there look at the Holy Land, a land I walked with my humble feet and touched with my humble fingers? I found it in flames, and I left it aflame. During Jesus' time, the stones groaned and wailed under the feet of Roman soldiers and the air trembled with the deadly clangor of Roman swords. Nowadays, the ways and byways of the Holy Land lament under the steel soles of modern soldiery. The Holy Land is, true to history, still a battleground in many ways. Did God test this nation more than the birthplace of His only son?

"Kasawo, the Lord rewards His own. He rewarded me. He revealed His glory to me in St. Peter's Basilica. I felt the great walls quake with holy fever. At consecration, I saw chains of white doves dropping from the golden window behind the altar and collecting round the altar itself. I saw the papal chalice and the candles melt and flow in golden rivers down to the feet of the altar. God showed me all these wonders so that you can believe and repent and give up Devil worship. I am your last warning, Kasawo. There will be no more storms, no more violators, no more verbal warnings.

"God saves, God leaves no prayer unanswered," Padlock said, making her sister believe she was experiencing a trance of sorts.

Kasawo felt something akin to disgust, pity and reluctant admiration. Her sister was so convinced of her righteousness that Kasawo, despite her skepticism, could not dismiss it as mere madness or delusion. Padlock seemed so attuned to the divine that she had lost contact with mere mortals. Kasawo had not come to be converted, and her sister's conviction only served to convince her that she was on the right path. She would always be a God/Devil worshipper. The combination worked for her, as Catholicism did for Padlock. All the niggling doubts and guilt she felt were gone, buried at the feet of Padlock's fanatical faith. She could never see the world in terms of black and white. The shades of gray she had negotiated from the beginning felt more real than ever. She had gone to the depths of hell and was now convinced that the worst was over.

Kasawo had always found Catholic dogma both abstract and deficient, unable to stand on its own in the real world. Catholicism did not provide practical ways to confront evil, and its dismissal of witchcraft was too complacent in its essence. As a businesswoman, she could never afford to be complacent about evil. The business community was infested with ruthless Devil worshippers and practitioners of the worst witchcraft. In business, luck was a holy sacrament which was sought both in the grandest cathedrals and in the dimmest witch houses. Kasawo consulted witch doctors, burned mysterious herbs on hot coals and mouthed incantations. On Sunday, she went to church, because it was good for her image and also because she had never managed to dismiss Catholicism as a total hoax. She felt comfortable with keeping a leg in both worlds, because deep down she knew that God and the Devil were two sides of the same coin, and she wanted to play it safe.

There was another side to it. In her desperation, Kasawo had visited her parish priest soon after the violation, wanting some neutral party to talk to. The good man had advised her to commend the rapists into God's hands, and to hate the sin but not the sinners. Such complacency had left her feeling betrayed and more determined than ever to go to a witch doctor, who would assess the possibilities for revenge and purification. Kasawo was itching to get it over with and to avoid suffering for years as she had after the Pangaman escape. Now, as she looked at her sister, she was sure that if she had relied on her and on her parish priest in her darkest moments, she would have ended up raving mad.

Kasawo felt asphyxiated, as though her sister's house were a sealed box. She felt the need to take a walk and never come back. She looked at her watch. She was glad that she was leaving early the following morning.

The Kasawo that came to visit Aunt Lwandeka and me, two days after re-enactment therapy, was not my picture of somebody who had been gang-raped. She was brimming with confidence and energy, and talked almost non-stop. It was evident that her days of self-pity were over. Her ordeal seemed to be just one more hurdle she had cleared. She talked a lot about politics, expressing her skepticism over the new coalition government. She said that she was very happy the liberators were being sent back home to Tanzania.

As she talked I kept thinking about all those men on top of her, and I wondered at how resilient she was to bounce back so quickly. I kept thinking about how African women were Olympic-medalist camouflagers of pain: my mind was filled with twenty-minute pissings, drop by drop, through infibulated holes by women in the Horn of Clitoris- and Labialessness. I watched her closely to see if she was just putting on a show for us. But halfway through her four-day visit, I was convinced that it was for real. The Vicar General had performed wonders for her.

I knew the man they called the Vicar General. Nobody called him by his real name. He was given that title because he was one of the few Catholic witch doctors, the majority being Muslim. He first caught my attention when I came to live with Aunt Lwandeka. At the time, I thought he was the tall, dark man who had threatened to damage her with a knife and a snake. Later the man reminded me of a Catholic parish priest. He had a lot of land, a new car, and lived in a huge house on a nearby hill. He knew many influential people. He had a big practice and had that pompous air of conceited priests. I felt a sneaking admiration for him for posing a direct challenge to the Catholic Church and for pointing out to them that, despite being in business for the last one hundred years, their teachings had left a big, unaddressed hole in many people's lives.

If Kasawo was any example to go by, people were cured by what they believed in. The psychology behind the Vicar's therapy was that those who came expecting pain got painful treatment, and those who came expecting sweet words, blood sacrifices, incantations or cuddles got exactly that. He had such wide experience that as soon as a client started talking, he knew what would work for them.

Kasawo had arrived at the famous man's headquarters feeling special and anticipating immediate attention. She felt she was the big man's special prize, because she had just rejected her sister's Catholicism and opted firmly for him. She also had the feeling that she was the only champion survivor of a vicious gang rape to arrive at the headquarters that day. She expected to find about a dozen people waiting in line. She knew that by using her trader's tongue, she would quickly get the attention she felt she deserved.

It came as a shock to Aunt Kasawo to realize that she had greatly overestimated herself. She arrived at around ten o'clock to find a crowd whose size reminded her of her primary school days. If all these people had not come from nearby, then some must have arrived when it was still dark. She thought that some might even have spent the night waiting in line. The long lines strangely reminded her of the sick, the blind, the deaf and the infirm who travelled long distances to go and meet Jesus in the hope of a miracle cure. The place had the ambience of a school compound: there was the main building, a registration office, a dispensary, dormitories, a kiosk, playing spaces for children, clotheslines, water taps, lines of toilets and of course the many assistants keeping order. This was the most pompous and most organized witch doctor Kasawo had ever seen. She was awed by the thought that all these people had come to meet only one person. She felt proud, in a way, because this man had rescued the business from dirty little places run by dirty old men and shrivelled old women and elevated it to the realm of modernity.

The quarter-kilometer walk up the hill had left Kasawo sweating. The wet-look grease in her hair was trickling down her head, and she kept wiping it off her neck with a large handkerchief. She kept looking at the many well-dressed women, who far outnumbered the men. It struck her once again that if women abandoned the business, witch doctors would run out of work.

She was annoyed that there were so many people ahead of her. She was irritated by the bawling children and by the arrogant airs pulled by some of the visiting women. She could tell the die-hards from the beginners by their indifference. The first-timers looked around nervously to make sure that nobody they knew could see them from the road. The discomfort they felt about being here also came out in the way they shifted uneasily, coughed or blinked as though their bodies were in open rebellion.

Quite a few of these people were supposed to be in a hospital, but they were awaiting clearance from the Vicar General of the Devil's Diocese. Western medicine had been around for more than a hundred years, but many people trusted their witch doctors more than they did medical doctors. Kasawo could understand their reaction. There were many greedy medical doctors who milked people's money without telling them the truth. It was a question of trust. In her case, though, she knew exactly when to consult medical doctors. A little education is not too bad, after all, she thought sourly.

From her experience, Kasawo knew that half the people here had not come to be relieved of physical ailments; they were here in pursuit of luck, success, revenge, love, power, favor and divination. There were housewives who wanted love potions to make their husbands love them more than other women; and some in search of evil magic to cause car accidents, illness or other disasters to their competition. There were barren women desperately searching for babies after combing every church and hospital for help, and fecund women who wanted more children in order to ensure their position in the home. There were mad men and women tormented by "voices" which told them to walk naked, to attack people, to sit in fire, to climb roofs or to talk to themselves; and men and women who wanted to drive some-body they hated mad. There were people with psychosomatic and psy-chological ailments, and others with migraines, cancers, swollen legs and broken limbs. There were people in search of themselves who needed the big man's magic touch to peel away layers of self-delusion, self-pity and old pain before moving on to a better life. Last but not least were those who had lost loved ones in the recent past to deep forests, swollen rivers, dank dungeons and mass graves. They wanted to locate the remains, lay wandering spirits to rest with a proper funeral and, where possible, make the killers pay.

Kasawo sympathized with this group, because all the killers had fled or were in hiding, and no one had been brought to justice.

As Kasawo sat, patiently watching all these people, she wondered whether this was not a nation of gullible moaners and corrupt mythmakers. The Vicar of the Devil was certainly a mythmaker, an enigma, but Kasawo did not agree with her sister that this was a nation of moaners. The pain was real. It was just a nation in search of proper leadership. She too needed guidance from time to time. She wondered whether her belief in enigmatic characters was not a nostalgic search for another man, a resurrection of the Pangaman of her pre-elopement days, the Pangaman who took charge of every aspect of her life. The nation, she felt, was in need not of repentance but of proper stocktaking and action. She personally fantasized about a good man to grow old with, somebody to take care of her. She could not help thinking that after the purification rites it would be that much easier to find him.

Kasawo waited for half a day. By the time her turn came and she passed through the polished wooden door of the consultation room, to be immersed in the crisp redness of the new bark cloths covering the roof, the walls and the floor, she was trembling with nervous irritation. Her center had been hollowed by fatigue. The dry woody smell coming off the bark cloth made her feel drowsy. The man in front of her looked bigger and more imperious. His huge eyes, guarded by hard-bristled caterpillar eyebrows, made her more restless. The wide round nostrils made her believe she was looking down a double-barrelled abyss. The woody smell made her fear that she was being chloroformed. This man was a new force, a juggernaut that fed on dirty old witch doctors and would not stop before engulfing all their customers. This man with his enormous wealth and imposing personality inspired instant faith. Kasawo felt like an old disciple.

"Give me all the details." The words dropped from his despotic lips like heavy gongs whose reverberations were accentuated by the red darkness they were uttered in. Kasawo was grateful for the darkness: it made her feel less self-conscious. Unlike the time she went to see her parish priest, for the Vicar she did not reduce the number of her attackers by four. Kasawo told the man everything she remembered and even felt like adding elements from her imagination. At first it felt strange to hear herself in the darkness; then she got used to it. By the time she came to the end, words were flowing of their own accord. Her anxiety doubled during the subsequent silence. Her heart raced madly as she waited in the darkness for the big man's verdict. He grunted and snorted and finally said that everything would be all right. The relief she felt was phenomenal.

Kasawo was sent to the dormitories, which turned out to be long buildings with either single or double rooms. There was a small shop selling soap, razor blades, bandages, cigarettes, salt, maize flour, tea leaves and other items necessary during a stay. Behind the kiosk, one could get cooked food, tea and porridge. The thought of porridge made Kasawo's stomach turn. She hurried to her room.

There was a spring bed, a cupboard, a basin and a cement floor to rest her feet on as she contemplated the cost of all this. The Vicar was one of the few modern witch doctors who gave credit, because clients could not contemplate cheating them. Kasawo felt that the man deserved every cent he got: she had been here for only half a day, but she was already feeling better. As she lay on the bed waiting for night to fall, she wondered whether this was not a mental asylum where patients checked in whenever the burdens of the past and the present became too much to bear. She sat up in one fluid movement: the thought that her rape could be the figment of a diseased mind horrified her. No, no, no. It wasn't, it wasn't, it wasn't, she said out loud. She lay back slowly, happy that she was not mad. She thought about a boy she had seen that day. He had been brought in fastened with ropes. His father said he was possessed by spirits. She remembered the boy's blank eyes, so fathomless yet so shallow, and the way he fought when they untied him. It took three men to hold him before the Vicar came. She remembered the Vicar's taking him by the hand and saying a few words to him. She remembered how he stroked the sick boy and led him inside. The power, the tenderness, the confidence, the many sides of the Vicar kept Kasawo thinking for a long time.

Dressed in black, a dry leopard tail in his hand, the man entered Kasawo's room. He ordered her to undress, wrap a black sheet around her and follow him. It was past midnight. The compound was quite dark except for lights here and there in the sleeping rooms. They entered a banana grove and ended up behind a massive tree that loomed like a diabolical tower of terror. There was a cave under the tree, inside which were three basins full of cold water. Incantations poured into the air as water from the three basins dripped down Kasawo's shivering body. Bits of herb stuck in her hair and on her body.

Back in her room, the man motioned her to spread a mat which was leaning against the wall on the floor and lie on it. In twenty years Kasawo had not lain down for punishment. It felt strange. Seven strokes of a dry bamboo cane found their mark. Confused, and in strange pain, she was led back to the cave. She bathed again. The water felt very cold, and she could not stop the tears which came with the quivers. The black clothes gave the man the arcane dimensions of a ghoul and made her feel both afraid and reassured. A man born to wield power. A man born to exorcise demons and conquer women.

On their way back, Kasawo became more convinced that God and the Devil were two sides of the same coin. They even used the same methodology in combatting opposition. So many years ago, when she had just met Pangaman, her mother had taken her to the parish priest under the pretext that they were going to buy rosaries. Kasawo was afraid of the white man. She became more afraid when her mother reported to him that she was fornicating with a man, drinking alcohol and treating her father with insolence. Her mother asked the priest to exorcise the demons tormenting her. The priest stood up and said very many Latin words. The expression on his face was deathly. He did not seem to see her or her mother. He finally reached for a cane and beat her. But not even he could beat Pangaman out of her.

The second time round, her mother took her to the mother superior of the parish convent. The nun listened in dead silence, a very sad and terrifying expression on her stern face. She looked at Kasawo for a long time, at the end of which she asked both mother and daughter to kneel. She led the rosary and the litany of the Virgin Mary. She dismissed the mother and asked Kasawo to stay behind. She locked the door and pocketed the key. She drew all the curtains and ordered her to strip. Kasawo did so woodenly. The nun asked her to lie on her back. She took a leather belt and whipped her twelve times between her legs. Kasawo cried out. She had never tasted such pain before. "Think about the nails your sins are driving into Jesus' wounds and keep quiet," the nun commanded. "Aren't you ashamed of the pain your behavior is causing Our Lord?" The nun did not ask her not to tell her mother. She knew that the girl wouldn't. The nun administered the same treatment every day at the same time for a week. It did not work. Soon after that, Kasawo eloped with Pangaman.

Back in her room, seven hard bamboo strokes found their mark again. The man ordered her to go to bed. She was bothered by the repetitions in her life, and especially by her inability to squeeze some usable wisdom out of them. Her thoughts could not coagulate. They flapped around like frog spawn in a swamp. The ordeals and the tears, however, had a very soporific effect.

Kasawo woke up late the following afternoon. The red tiles of the Vicar's residence peeped at her from her window with the seductiveness of a sweet fading fire. She was overwhelmed by the noise of activity in the compound, and she wondered how she had slept through it. As night dropped like a dark veil she went to the kiosk to buy some food. Moths had appeared. They circled the lamps in dizzying yellow arcs. She sat on her bed and ate. She retrieved a moth's wing from her mouth. She spat and threw away the food.

As Kasawo waited for the man to arrive, she thought about how the therapy worked. She had told him everything about the attack and much about her life. It seemed that he had picked out salient elements and used them to make her relive her pain and move on. It hurt more than she had expected, but she felt it was all for the better. Now more than ever, she wished she were more educated and thus able to tie the different strands of her life together. She remembered confessions in the cupboard-like confessional. At the beginning, she really believed that the white priest was Jesus, and she quaked with holy terror, not daring to tell a single lie. But gradually it had struck her that if the priest was indeed Jesus of Nazareth, then he surely did not need to be told anything. She started telling him small lies and omitting little details. "Jesus" swallowed it hook, line and sinker! The terror went away, and she started smelling the man's tobacco breath. From then on, she stopped saying prayers of contrition. The Vicar knew better. He guided his clients through the rituals. He is a Catholic, Kasawo thought; he must have fooled the priests himself. Send a thief to catch a thief, her primary school headmaster used to say.

His massive frame filled the doorway. He beckoned her to follow him to the cave, where she took the same long, cold bath. She had never shivered so in all her life. Her teeth rattled badly as she walked back to her room for the final installment of lashes. He administered them and turned her over. The cold hand of the wind pushed inside her and shook the very marrow of her bones. She was so cold that she started feeling a dull heat building inside her. She closed her eyes and succumbed to the convoluted meanderings of her mind. She was awakened by the fire of his latex-sheathed penetration. He rubbed the stretched membrane of her rejuvenating self with the hellfire of her worst pains. He reminded her of the professional brutality of bone-setters who broke badly set bones in order to correct the mistakes. Her mind worked on and off between bitten-back screams and tears as she tried to hold on. She thought of Pangaman, of her fear, hatred and even love of him. She thought of her father, of the parish priest who had beaten her, of the nun who had whipped her, and of Amin's soldiers, and of her violators. Her face was wet with tears. He asked her if she was crying. She felt shame over it, but she could not lie to the ultimate confessor and admitted that she was. He laughed. She felt relieved.

Back at the cave, she was ordered to fill a bucket with water. He sprinkled herbs in it and ordered her to carry it on her head. This time they headed for the road. They stopped in the junction. She eyed the three arms of the road with trepidation. She prayed that it would remain empty, desolate, dead. He ordered her to strip and bathe while saying the following words: "I leave the world's rapes here. I leave the world's ill luck here. I leave every evil here. Let the winds carry it all to the ends of the earth." He stood at a distance, and she could hear him mumbling. They walked toward the compound in silence. She was glad that part was over. Her body was still burning, but she felt calm. She did not care whether another seven lashes were awaiting her. She had broken a psychological barrier. She felt invincible, fearless, ready for anything.

At the door he stood aside and let her enter. He stood in the doorway and watched her shiver, the black cloth tight on her steaming body. He seemed wreathed in priestly isolation. "It is over, girl," he said in a thick voice. He stood there as if waiting to be thanked. She found herself on her knees, thanking him as though she weren't going to pay him.

The Kasawo that rose from her knees was a woman full of a fresh fire and a blazing, peppery zeal. She dominated all conversation during her visit to us. Aunt Lwandeka looked cowed by her. Kasawo was not my favorite political analyst, but I agreed with her that the departure of the Tanzanians was good for all parties. She swore that the exiled dictator Obote was about to return. This greatly disturbed me, for all along I had been holding that as an abstract possibility. Aunt Lwandeka did not like the news either. It made her sacrifices in fighting Amin look futile. She angrily responded with the view that a guerrilla war would break out as a result.

"Governments are there to fight guerrillas," Kasawo said smugly. I kept thinking about those words long after her departure.

Within a few months, most roadblocks were gone and most Tanzanians were back home. A new army was being formed. The curfew now started at eleven o'clock and ended at five in the morning. There was much talk about elections, democracy and development: the magic trinity.

I was feeling inviolable once more. I had survived the dark days without a body scratch. I was going to the university to study law. I never bothered the few female liberators who were manning the last of the roadblocks. They did not seem to notice me either. I kept slipping past them as though by magic. Within three weeks they would be gone, I had heard on the news. Every other evening, I visited a friend, a fellow student who was living on his own. We enjoyed weighty discussions, especially about politics and women and power. Sometimes I took him a little liquor, which loosened his tongue, and he talked as if the world were coming to an end. We both felt that we could change the world. We talked as though we were in parliament or in some national forum where our words turned into law.

One evening, I was stopped by a voice emanating from the front of an old factory building where surprise roadblocks were sometimes staged. There had been no roadblocks there or in the suburb as a whole for the last five days. I stopped in my tracks and saw two bricks on the shoulder of the road. Sometimes they used a car tire or an oil drum, anything. I was very apprehensive: these people could be up to no good at this hour. To make matters worse, I had neither money nor a watch to bribe them with. Three uniformed women came toward me with rifles casually held, muzzles down. Each rifle had three magazines held together with rubber bands; each woman had ninety bullets with her. What I saw next made my lower lip fall: I thought I recognized the large girl as one from Ndere Primary School whom I had told that she would birth a limbless creature. . . . It seemed logical that she had joined the army to avoid the risk of having such a child. When had she crossed the border to join the guerrillas? When had she recognized me? Had she been stalking me? How long had she waited for this moment? How many men had she shot in my stead? I could not tear my eyes from her. I wanted to make sure that it was her. I tried to look under her cap. Had she changed so little over the years?

I was given little chance to complete my investigations. The Infernal Trinity mistook my questioning look for ogling. But who in their right senses would dare ogle three women armed with two hundred and seventy high-velocity bullets? I was accused of disrespect, disregard for military procedure, subversive activity and more. I was dazed by a sense of impending doom. Shtudent? Yes. Amin shtudent, he-he-heee. In the meantime, I looked around for a drunkard, any passerby, who could distract the Trinity with his arrival. This was the road that had eaten the northerners: How come it was so dead now? I was ordered to produce my identity card. I had never been asked to show my card at any roadblock before, and I wasn't carrying it. I explained my predicament and volunteered to take them home if they deemed it necessary.

"You sow uss to do worrk?" one who had so far said nothing burst out. I turned to address her. At that moment, a whooshing sound and a kaleidoscope of hellish colors exploded. I felt my knees go. In fact, by then I was already on the ground, my back in the gravel. I had not been knocked down like this in years. I looked groggily at the night sky. I could hardly move. I wasn't feeling any pain except for a heavy, dull pulse in my head. The women looked very big from where I was. I was vaguely aware of how afraid I was of getting disfigured by the muzzles or the butts of those rifles.

I was half-dragged, half-carried into the old factory. I tried to think about my first day at the seminary and the jerk-offs in the middle of the night. I tried to think about my campaigns against Fr. Mindi and Fr. Lageau, and the way the night watchman had surprised me. I remembered the two corpses Cane had shown us. Grandpa had lain like this, I thought, looking at those terrible muzzles and large-toothed boots. I was slapped a few times into a reasonable wakefulness. At about the same time, the air was invaded by the mustiness of dirty underwear and dirty bodies. Pigs, I thought. No. Hyenas. When had these hyenas had their last proper bath? A week, a fortnight, a month ago? I kept my mind on the worst possible scenarios just to get through the ordeal and not to vomit into their genitalia. I kept thinking that these women had raped other men before. I was sure the men had kept quiet about it. I was also going to keep my mouth shut. This was a secret never to tell, even inside a torture chamber. In the meantime, I collected some grim statistics: the ordeal lasted approximately twenty minutes before I was thrown out of the building. My face got ridden two hundred and twenty times. My penis got pulled very roughly some forty times. My balls were kneaded very violently twenty times. My skin got ripped thirty times. I ejaculated once. I ended up with a broken nose and a lump on the temple. I nursed sore ribs for a fortnight.

I spent that fateful night at my friend's house. The next morning, I told Aunt Lwandeka that I had been attacked by thieves. A nation of moaners? No, I never moaned. It could have been worse, I kept saying. How ironic that Kasawo had left not long ago! For a day or so, I kept thinking that Kasawo had brought her bad luck to our house and left it on my shoulders. Nonsense. The only pattern I could discern was that I had become another statistic in our family history. I too had been violated, and my tormentors had escaped unscathed.

A week after the attack, roadblocks were removed from all roads.

In the space of a year, we had three caretaker governments, the first lasting just over two months. The exiled dictator returned. He contested and won the elections. There was disagreement among the foreign observers as to whether the elections had been rigged. The innocents, who believed that the observers had the power to tell one political tree to plant itself in the sea and one political hill to move to another location, got slaughtered. Amin had proved such innocence to be fatal; the hopefuls should have known better. Guerrilla war broke out. Aunt Lwandeka's National Reform Movement was among the first fighting groups to join.

The hurricane-lamp-and-moths syndrome had started all over again: all that luminescence, all that death.

BOOK SIX

THE FIRST TIME I stood at the top of Makerere University Hill, with Mulago Hospital reclining in front of me and two cathedrals and a mosque piercing the deep blue horizon in the background, Grandpa's old lawyerly dreams boiled inside me. I felt I had stepped onto holy ground. Grandpa's spirit seemed to have been transported, transformed and spread over this hill to drive a new generation of knowledge seekers to the limit. A son at university was the culmination of many a family's dreams of a better future. I could feel general expectation rising from the ground, swelling like the city's seven hills and willing every candidate to get in through the narrow gate of elitist education. The university's main hall, breathing the supercilious airs of grandeur, intimated entry into a secluded fraternity. I could feel myself grow wings to fly into the rarefied ranks of those chosen to reach great heights. These were the eighties: the burdens of the seventies were behind us, so it seemed. You felt that the worst was over and that shrewd individuals could at last stretch their arms and pluck the fruits of a progressive future. I surveyed the hill again. I waited for clues to my future with bated breath.

Makerere University had emerged from the seventies bearing the motley scars of a survivor: during the last decade, it had neither advanced nor expanded. The days when it was sacred ground were long gone, alive only in memories of alumni like my laconic literature teacher at the seminary. In his capacity as the chancellor, President Idi Amin had done his best to stamp his authority on the institution. On several occasions, the army was dispatched to quell campus riots and opposition. One vice chancellor, an Obote supporter, had not survived: he disappeared in the aftermath of the abortive 1972 invasion. Many lecturers had fled, and the dim economic prospects of the eighties had not enticed them back. Those who stayed saw their status and earnings plummet, the former eroded by the low esteem education suffered in the seventies, the latter by inflation. Now many lecturers held jobs outside the university in order to make ends meet. Scarcity of scholastic and other materials plagued the campus. A culture of corruption had set in at the top: political appointees did their best to enrich themselves while their benefactors still held the reins of power. But all these factors had not diminished the zeal with which students did their best to make the most of a bad situation.

By the time I joined this highest institution of learning, the pressure on its capacity was asphyxiating. The residential houses had swollen, burst and overflowed into the puny annexes where six students shared a room. Top A-levels alone did not guarantee one a place in the most coveted faculties. Over the years, competition had risen to a murderous level. Political influence and bribery moved things faster, but you had to know whom to contact, and that did not always guarantee positive results either. Like the majority of hopefuls, I could only count on the gods and on the selection committee's favor. Both let me down.

The radio had summoned thousands of us to the campus, and we swarmed the main hall like locusts, perusing endless selection lists. My heart went to my mouth as my eyes combed the coveted Law List. Historical precedent paralyzed my limbs: the first lawyer in the family! It was not to be. My name was not on the list. There was, of course,

the lame recourse of the damned: appeal. It did not work: so many ex-
planations, so many justifications, so many technicalities.

My first reaction was to consider giving up education altogether.
And do what then? I was kidding myself. I had to keep sharpening my
intellect. I was finally dumped in the social sciences section, that no-
man's-land between the real sciences and the humanities.

I was doomed to become a teacher. Like Serenity! And have to
take rear-guard action to work my way into better jobs. I was disgusted
with myself, with life, with everything. I knew one thing for sure: I
was not going to be a committed teacher. I was going to be a sort of
nanny for secondary school children. I would need a lousy day school
with a laissez-faire policy. There were quite a few of those around the
city. The government encouraged the opening of day secondary
schools in order to give more primary school leavers the opportunity
to pursue secondary education near their homes. Gone were the days
when secondary education was chiefly a boarding school affair. I already had a school in mind.

Having set my priorities, I concentrated on making money and
fighting my private wars. I still had the legacy of the Infernal Trinity
to deal with. As a non-resident student, popping in only for lectures
and use of the library, I had both time and freedom. Above all, education was not a hard course, at least not for me. I went to the campus as
little as possible. I kept out of campus politics and wrangles over
cramped accommodation, bad food, books and the excesses of a big
student body.

The Obote II regime wasn't having things its way. The party and its
leader had achieved a first by returning to office by the ballot box after
an ouster, but it was a tainted victory whose genuineness was questioned by many sections of society. The same people who were terrorizing the new government now sympathized with the guerrillas. At the
time the guerrillas went to the bush, there was a famine in northern
Uganda. World Food Programme and Red Cross trucks trekked north
via the famous road. I saw them going in flag-waving convoys. The
government did its best to keep news of the famine low-key, a situation
helped by the activities of the guerrillas in the south.

The day belonged to the government and the army, the night to
the guerrillas and their sympathizers. At night, the guerrillas moved

from their hiding places and attacked army barracks, detachments and roadblocks, and on occasion, police stations too. The aim was to capture arms and other supplies. Soldiers lived in perpetual fear of attack and ambush. The army, composed mainly of northerners and easterners courtesy of Obote II government policy, found itself fighting in strange and hostile circumstances. The troops were drawn into lethal campaigns in ominous valleys and on isolated hills, in gigantic swamps, endless grasslands and dank forests, and they had a hard time hitting mobile targets. The mathematical configuration of death, the triangle, which had first appeared in 1978, returned to haunt us. Ours was now called the Luwero Triangle, hundreds of square kilometers of land locked between the three lakes: Victoria in the south, Kyoga in the north and Albert in the far west. The core of the Triangle was a sparsely populated grassland area of massive papyrus swamps, huge marshes and thick forests. The uncanny quality of this triangle was that it contracted and expanded at will as guerrillas moved from place to place attacking or fleeing government forces. This magical quality was helped by the fact that the Triangle was near enough to the heartland, allowing easy access to the city, the seat of government and the big army barracks, while also offering a gateway to both northern and western Uganda. Thus, sometimes the Triangle stretched precariously to within a few kilometers of the city center, and sometimes it contracted devilishly to its wet core, hundreds of kilometers away. The village locked between Mpande Hill and Ndere Hill was among the many areas on the periphery of the notorious Triangle.

The army made some very basic errors that alienated the people within the Triangle. As the soldiers became frustrated with the little success they were having, they began taking it out on civilians, accusing them of harboring guerrillas. Some of those accused did not sympathize with the guerrillas, but the soldiers never believed anything they said. In this way, many people were driven into the arms of the guerrillas, swelling their ranks. The rest were displaced and either moved from town to town until they found a peaceful one, went to live with relatives outside the Triangle or chanced it in the city, where peace still reigned.

The population of our little town started burgeoning. Every day, every week, people at various stages of exhaustion and emaciation arrived with little parcels wrapped in stained tablecloths, bedsheets or rotting bags. They bore the additional weight of countless tales of bravery, survival and atrocity. Many had experienced horrors first-hand; others had moved before horrors could happen to them. The character of our town was changing. Joblessness and food prices increased. The old factories, which had been abandoned by the Indians and were now rotting in the sun, got an unexpected puff of life as some souls tried to find shelter behind them. Housing prices shot up, and I flirted with the idea of building shacks and renting them—people would rent practically anything. Houses without plan or approval from the town council went up. Council officials would come, pretend to threaten them with demolition and walk away with their cut of the action. Landowners hired people to make mud bricks and erect fragile structures thatched with papyrus carpets and plastic sheeting, which newcomers rented even before the doors and windows were installed. Many such structures had no toilet facilities, but it did not matter.

By the time I started attending lectures at the university, I had taken over all of my aunt's brewing responsibilities. She no longer found the time to do it, as her guerrilla activities had escalated. She gave the guerrillas so much of her time and attention that it sometimes seemed as if they were going to emerge from the Triangle the next day and overthrow the government. At first, Aunt was reluctant to allow me to take charge of the brewery, because she did not want to antagonize Padlock, who was still making noises in the distance like a disgruntled volcano. Accidents happened. Cooking drums burst and killed brewers. Most were careless accidents, but Aunt did not want to tempt fate. I assured her that working at the brewery was what I wanted. I felt I had a pact with death. Death was a demon locked in the Triangle, where it would remain. The Infernal Trinity had imbued me with a crass bravado bordering on a death wish. I channelled it all into the brewery. People loaded with untold woes would drink practically anything. There were hardly any more complaints about bad brews. Many retailers bought our stuff and diluted it with large quantities of water, and still they sold it. Boom-boom Brewery, as I baptized the enterprise, was well on its way.

The brewing process was simplicity itself. My job was to buy fifty-kilo sacks of jaggery, deposit some of the sticky brown-sugar mess in a hundred-liter drum of water, throw in the fermenting soap, cover the drum and wait for seven to ten days, occasionally stirring to aid dissolution. When the sugar solution was ready, I would transfer it to the brewing drum, which had to be in excellent condition in order to avoid accidents. I would screw on the cover and affix two winding copper tubes to the other end, fastening them with long strips of rubber to make sure that no steam escaped when the cooking started. The copper tubes would be immersed in a pool to cool them and aid condensation. The brewing drum would then be fired till the solution boiled and gave off steam, which condensed into hard liquor.

Once the fire got going, you had plenty of time to think, to talk, to do nothing. It was time full of temptation: you could go off for twenty minutes without the fire going out. Brewers would return to find the screw covers loosened by the heat or the copper tubes blocked. Most accidents occurred while brewers tried to rectify the situation. I spent my time by the fire thinking, planning my future. I fantasized about roasting the Infernal Trinity, I revisited the places of my past, and at the end of the day I would return home purged.

As the population increased and the market widened, I decided to expand the operation. I got Aunt to rent a piece of land, and I built a shed and a cement pool on it. I bought new drums and new copper tubes and hired the cheap labor that floated around to do most of the work. During the brewing process, my job was to supervise my men and to make sure that no liquor got stolen. At the end of the day, I checked the drums and the tubes into the shed and locked everything in. I handled all the sales.

At that time, in my early twenties, when I started teaching, I was making in one week the money a secondary school teacher made in a year. The government paid a teacher the equivalent of about $20 a month, calculated at the government exchange rate, which was many times lower than the black market, or *kibanda*, rate. That salary was only enough to buy groceries for a week, which meant that teachers had to do other jobs or find supplementary income. In some schools, the parent-teacher association supplemented the salary, but not by much. I got about $30 a month. By then the business had expanded, and I was netting a profit of about $1,000 a month from it.

I was seeing a number of teenage girls at the same time. I preferred teenagers, because older women wanted children as a way of ensuring commitment, for which I was not ready. My only worry was venereal diseases, especially the mysterious new type which slimmed people to the bones before they died in pools of green diarrhea and hellish sweat. The girls floated into my life as casually as the stories they told. Some claimed to have lost all their relatives in government mop-up operations. Others said their families had split up when guerrillas entered their areas. Yet more said they had seen their parents and brothers and sisters get shot. Most claimed to have hidden in the bush while their relatives and friends got killed. I believed them all, in a guilty kind of way, and accommodated their wishes because I could afford to. Some used my money to help family members pay their rent and buy food and clothes. Others spent it on drink and personal effects. Still others claimed they sent financial help to relatives still locked in the Triangle. I enjoyed playing the role of generous benefactor on one hand and spoiled lover on the other.

In the meantime, it was getting hotter in the Luwero Triangle. The government was doing a lot of shopping. The Koreans, who had made their first appearance on Serenity's Toshiba as trapeze artists, supplied the army with Katyusha rockets, which boomed and burned areas suspected of harboring guerrillas. The government boasted that the guerrillas were finished, and for some time nothing was heard of them. Some of the jobless boys who had planned to join them changed their minds. Aunt was scared. She told me that the brigadier was ill. I surmised that he had got shot. British helicopter gunships worked together with the Katyushas to clean the forests and grasslands of the fighters. Infantry troops were sent in afterward. A scorched-earth policy was in full swing, but I did not know which areas were affected, because the Triangle kept changing, contracting and expanding like a birth canal.

Hundreds of fighters and people accused by the government of being guerrillas—scrawny, bearded, ragged stick people—were transported into Kampala and shown at a government rally at the city square. It was claimed that their leaders had abandoned them and fled to Europe. If this was true, it concerned only one of the small guerrilla groups; the main force, including the brigadier, was still intact, hiding somewhere in the mysterious Triangle. The army kept up the pressure; the politicians were happy, the people anxious.

At about the same time, Aunt had two very narrow escapes. A man we knew to be a guerrilla came to town in broad daylight. A government spy tipped off the army, and soon plainclothesmen arrived. They were suddenly all over town. The man was surrounded in a fenced bungalow used now and then by National Reform Movement guerrillas, the largest group in the Triangle. He was ordered to come out, but he refused. He shot at the soldiers through the main gate, killing one and wounding another. The house was rocket-grenaded. Aunt had left only minutes before, with a jerry can of water on her head.

The second time, the army closed in on the market and checked everybody for identity cards. Three guerrillas were there at the time: two men and a boy. The boy panicked because he had no identity card. Aunt told the army officer in charge that the boy was her cousin. The officer asked people in the market whether they knew the boy as Aunt's cousin. Silence. Until one of the guerrillas said that it was true. The boy was taken aside all the same. The officer wanted to know why he was so scrawny. Aunt explained that he had been on the run in the "danger zone." "Then he is a guerrilla." Aunt denied this vehemently, going into detail about innocent people who had been caught in the cross fire and had to flee hundreds of kilometers before coming to a safe haven. She said that this was the boy's safe haven and that she would die for him if the need arose. "The boy can take no more." "Of course everybody can take a little more," the officer replied, smiling. Everybody was eyeing the officer and Aunt rather warily. Many believed that Aunt was going to bring trouble to the whole town, but the officer wanted to paint a benign picture of the army. They were not all compulsive killers. They could be reasonable. He slapped the boy on the cheek and told him to go.

Aunt was genuinely shaken for about a week. She had recruited the boy herself. She had also warned the trio not to appear that day, but they had disregarded her warning. They needed money very badly in order to transport some medicine they had stolen from a small hospital somewhere on the edge of the Triangle. Nowadays, Aunt financed a limited range of guerrilla activity with some of the money we made from Boom-boom Brewery. After the two narrow escapes, I thought she was going to take a long break. Wishful thinking. On the eighth day, she was back on duty, supplying information, helping guerrillas on their way to the city and recruits going to their appointed venues.

Newcomers from the Triangle, driven out by the Katyushas and

the helicopters, reassured people that the guerrillas were still alive—
their silence was a ruse—but the government spokesman continued to
say that the "bandits," as he called them, were finished. Then, as if to
counter his claims, the guerrillas shot down a helicopter carrying the
leading military operations officer and his entourage somewhere deep
in the Triangle. The government reported the deaths almost a week
later. The army was back on the run, suffering a morale crisis. The
guerrillas captured some of the Katyushas and killed a good number of
the Koreans who were manning them. The rest of the Korean merce-
naries cleared out. The army was now on its own. The British instruc-
tors never participated in the fighting, and the army had to deal with its
fears of the bush, the guerrillas and the people by itself. More military
hardware continued to arrive from Britain, Belgium, the USA and
Eastern Europe, but the army gained no great advantage. A string of
humiliating broad-daylight attacks kept them dancing on hot coals.

For my teaching duties, I chose Sam Igat Memorial College, a newly
founded secondary school crammed into two long buildings and a
two-story flat. It was the brainchild of the crafty Rev. Igat. An Obote
supporter, he used his political friends to persuade CARE and other relief groups to put up the long buildings as a memorial for his thirty-
year-old son, who was killed during Amin's time. The government,
eager to help create schools outside the city for poor children, gave the
college a grant and its blessing to get going. By virtue of its location,
eight kilometers from the city center, the school had good teachers and
plenty of students, but organization was its greatest problem. The
good reverend did his best to meddle in the affairs of the school, in
order to safeguard his position as its founder and owner. He wanted to
appoint or approve headmasters and make them do what he wanted.
For a long time he sabotaged the founding of a parent-teacher association because he feared that it would overpower him. Consequently, the
growth of the school was blocked by the very man who claimed to love
it to death. If a teacher or headmaster became very influential, the reverend would spread rumors to the effect that the individual was a child
molester or an embezzler or a guerrilla supporter. The last accusation
being commensurate with a death sentence, many of these individuals
fled his school rather than risk the consequences.

By the time I joined, the school was in one of its confused phases.

I liked it. There was no parent-teacher association to collect money, augment teachers' salaries and keep an eye on things. The staff was divided. A very weak headmaster had just been brought in, and he had decided to do nothing. He let the reverend address the students, going on about his son and his political friends and what he had done for the parish. It was noted that the parish had retired him for committing adultery and siring children with parishioners' wives, but the old man had discovered early on that shame was a sentiment unfit for politicians. He acted as though the charges were merely malicious fabrications.

For a long time, the school had no library. There were about four hundred students, most of whom did not have the money to buy the necessary textbooks for themselves. Teachers used their own books or borrowed some from other schools or from friendly teachers elsewhere. The few available teachers' textbooks were kept in a big cupboard. One day news spread that the school's bad days were over, for the reverend's American and Canadian friends had sent all the necessary books. The excitement was phenomenal, not least among the teachers. But it was all dampened when a load of useless books was delivered one early morning: blueprints of 1940 computers, books on the rudiments of aeronautics, zoology, Greek, marine fish and the American army. The reverend made a long speech, showing off the gravid boxes. He collected a number of well-dressed students, made them wear their best smiles and posed with them for a group photograph, with the boxes in the foreground. "Toilet paper," the teachers said when they saw the books. The students felt cheated. Word spread. Reverend Toilet Paper became Igat's nickname henceforth.

The parents were generally happy to have a nearby school to take care of their offspring during the day. We were their nannies, making sure that no harm came to their sons and daughters before the end of school. The classes were crowded, because the policy was to recruit as many students as possible and not to disappoint eager, hardworking parents. There were some very keen students in the lot, boys and girls who would have performed well in better schools. Some had come from the Triangle. They worked hard at first, but lethargy eventually set in.

The choice of a deputy headmaster always says volumes about a school. Ours was a licensed teacher who had done some teaching when

SIMC, as we called the college, was still a primary school. Now he did all the headmaster's dirty work. He opened and closed the school. He collected the fees, saw to discipline, caught latecomers, did some accounts and doled out money to teachers. He checked breast pockets to make sure that the school badge was well sewn on, not just affixed with pins, as adolescents liked to do. He checked girls' faces for makeup, for tiny, sexy earrings and forbidden hairdos. He also checked girls' fingers for nail polish and faddish artificial claws. He was a man dizzy with his role, out to top himself and justify his position to all.

The headmaster, an evasive elephant seal of a man, spent most of his time on the slide rule, figuring out theoretical mathematical problems. He had little to do, because his deputy literally ran the school. On many days, he did not put in an appearance at all, preferring to attend meetings and see to his business interests in the city. His trick was to assure the reverend that he was not a threat to him, while he did his own thing. The headmaster, like the Invisible Man, acted and moved incognito. Sometimes he entered his office and no one knew that he was even there.

This cavalier spirit extended to school accounts. They were a mess or a maze to the average eye. It was as if a mathematician were creating work for himself to fill his lonely hours, or a crook were disguising his hand. To begin with, most teachers had financial problems. They would go to the headmaster and explain their positions, and according to the need, he would decide how much to give them as a supplement to, or an advance on, their salaries. He would dole out the money and write the amount on a piece of paper. In the meantime, the deputy was writing his own pieces of paper, which ended up on the headmaster's desk. There was such a big heap of famous pieces of paper that many got lost or confused. The only conclusion one could draw was that the headmaster was exploiting the system for his own good; otherwise there was nothing to stop him from acquiring an accountant or a better system. Consequently, clever teachers always had a problem—with the children, the wife, their health, anything—and drew whatever money they could. Sometimes the deputy referred these cases to the headmaster, who, being a nice man, could not find ways of denying them and ended up giving them money and writing on pieces of paper.

The headmaster liked me, because I never asked for money. My guess was that he was writing somewhere that he had given me so much and pocketing it. Whenever I went to his office, it was to ask for permission to go home, ostensibly to the clinic or hospital for my headaches, which later became migraines. This headmaster did not mind a sickly teacher as long as he did not ask for financial assistance. So whenever I had business to settle in town, I would ask for permission to leave. And I would get it. This of course meant that students were suffering, but ours was not a student-oriented school, at least not in the academic sense. There was no use pretending. Most teachers taught in other schools to supplement their deficient pay, and others had jobs in town. As long as one came and taught, one was not obliged to stay on campus. Sometimes teachers came, went to the staff room, had tea, conversed and left, as though their lessons were over. It was a free-for-all, with many students also dodging and staying home to fetch and sell water or do other things to earn money to support themselves and pay school fees.

The old system of sending school inspectors to keep an eye on teachers had died an excruciating natural death in the seventies, and the new government was too busy fighting guerrillas to bother about such banal things as school inspections. Teachers got paid three months late, and in order to appear to be fair, the government did not put them under pressure.

The best thing I could have done for our boys and girls would have been to teach them sex education—we were, after all, keeping them there to grow up before going out to become parents—but that was taboo. Our biggest problem was not alcohol or drugs, but unwanted pregnancies. Strangely enough, many parents believed that sex education would only exacerbate the problem. Most parents did not want their daughters swallowing pills or interfering with the procreative process in any way, and they resented anybody who divulged such information to their little ones. The good reverend, supported by the conservative element among the parents, resisted the introduction of "godless information" into his school with all his might. That just about sealed it.

Under the circumstances, the school could only expel pregnant girls. The culture of shame and secrecy had a lot to do with it all. Most parents never talked about sex to their children—good Christians left such matters to sort themselves out. In the past, paternal aunts used to take their nephews and nieces aside and tell them everything, but with the breakup of extended-family structures, the gap had been left yawning. For the majority of youths, peers were the educators. I now and then intercepted chits and cuttings from pornographic magazines and love letters as they changed hands. They reminded me of Cane lecturing us, and making us complete sentences with words like "penis" or "vagina." I was not such a hypocrite as to feign anger or shock. I often made one student read a chit aloud. Then I would ask if there was anybody with questions on the subject of sex, pregnancy, contraception or abortion. Suddenly everyone would become alert. Once, the deputy took me aside and requested that I not corrupt young minds. I bowed my head, but did the same thing when I intercepted the next chit.

A few hundred meters from SIMC was a small primary school, kick-started for the sons and daughters of the area who could not afford better Muslim schools. Behind the compound was a small, dilapidated mosque, where the faithful held prayers on Friday. The imam, who taught Koran education at the school, lived nearby and ran both places. Looking at the rough mud walls and the leprous roofing set in a bare, pebbly compound chipped out of solid rock, one would think that nothing good could creep out of this wretched environment. Compared with dear old SIMC, and the Catholic school and church not so far away on the same ridge, the place looked dismal and oozed decay. It seemed like a sandy island awaiting the storm that would blow it to oblivion. At break time, however, the joyous screeches of the children filled the air, and their pink uniforms fluttered in the wind like so many large flags. They played and sang almost as hard as the imam drove them to memorize the Koran and the Arabic texts he wrote on the chipped blackboard.

On school days, he would strut from class to class, stick in hand, a frown on his face, and woe to anyone found messing around. The secular teachers who found themselves at the place often gave him a wide berth, not because he would beat them too, but because he believed in respect and discipline more than the teachers did, and he was not into theoretical discussions. "I am a man of action," he always said. If pupils did something wrong, they got punished on the spot. They could plead, and maybe even get a reduced sentence, but the punishment came all the same. "Action, character, responsibility, is all I teach," he always said before and after dishing out punishment.

A friend who taught at this dusty place to supplement his SIMC salary asked me to accompany him to the school. It was among the prancing, rope-skipping, screeching multitude that I first saw Jo Nakabiri. I stared. Her dark face was gleaming in the sun, as though she had used too much facial cream that morning. I looked at her limbs and frame, and I found myself wondering if she was Lusanani's sister or cousin. Her wasp waist and solid bum had me bursting with excitement. Sweat broke out in my armpits. I was intrigued by the uncanny feeling that I knew this person, had at least seen her somewhere before. But where?

We found her shouting at a group of little girls, and when she saw us, her voice dropped, as though we had caught her saying obscene words. It was then that I saw her eyes: large orbs full of bottomless joys and sorrows and mysteries I suddenly felt eager to explore. She extracted herself from the group with the stiff grace of one being watched, then came and greeted my friend and me, in that order. They ignored me for some time as they recited the litany of inadequate salaries, unfulfilled plans, impending holidays, local weddings and the like. She seemed uneasy, as though talking about school affairs, the imam and the pupils in the presence of a stranger were a breach of trust or a form of betrayal. I kept looking at her and at my friend, camouflaging my desire to look only at her. I was already thinking that I had enough money to take this girl away from this place and maintain her in relative comfort.

My impression was that she was working here for respectability, and probably because it was her profession. If so, who was paying her bills? Ten government dollars, which came after three months, was hardly enough for a tenth of monthly expenses. It was likely that she had a man or was living with her parents. If she was a refugee, there was a big possibility that Husband had joined the guerrillas and was somewhere in the Triangle facing the elements, the Katyushas, the helicopters and the army. The idea shook me up a bit. Some of those guys returned with bloodlust in the head and the maddening suspicion that their wives had been screwing all over the place, and they would not think twice before putting a bullet between another man's eyes. In a few of those cases, the woman never divulged that she had a husband; you only saw the fellow standing in the doorway furious as hell and lethal, like a wounded buffalo. Maybe her man had died in action and she was a young widow. There were many juicy widows walking around these days, some from the Triangle, and since they wore no distinctive dress, few people got to know who they really were. I would not mind dating a young widow, or a woman whose husband was fighting in the bush, as long as she told me the whole truth from the beginning.

I decided to ask my friend. Friends helped each other out in this way, even if it was their sister in question. He knew something about her; they lived in the same area. He owed me for bailing him out of endless financial problems.

He told me the little he knew. Yes, she had come from the Triangle two years back and now lived with her grandmother. She had been married once, but no one knew the whereabouts of Husband or whether there had been any children. I would have preferred to hear that the man had died, since now I did not know whether he was alive and still interested in her. That type was quite dangerous: they first mistreated the woman, and when she left them, they realized what they were missing and tried to get her back. When, in many cases, the wives refused to go back, the men grew bitter. Some turned to sending emissaries or to witchcraft, some to stalking or writing threatening letters. What about the other possibility? Maybe this girl was ill-mannered, loose and mean-tempered, and her man had got tired of her bad ways and moved on. Maybe she was the one trying to go back to her old life. In which case the man was waiting and making her stew a little bit longer in the juices of her iniquity.

The campaign to win Jo took many weeks. She rejected all my friend's efforts, saying that she was through with men. I did not believe her. If it had been true, she would have been in a convent flagellating herself and removing devil hair with her bare fingers like the Padlock of old. I wrote her letters, but she returned them unread. Taking into account the ease with which Triangle girls surrendered themselves, her behavior was annoying. I asked my friend to give up the assignment, but he was determined to see it through. He finally succeeded, after I had given up hope. He got her to invite me to the end-of-term concert given by the children of her school.

I sat on a bench behind her and watched her as she watched her pupils' performances. I kept thinking about how my friend had pleaded with her, saying that I was a decent person and that she was making a big mistake by treating me like dirt. She had countered with her suspicion that I had many girlfriends, but my friend had denied it vehemently because he did not know of my Triangle girls. He kept saying that I had just broken up with a bad-mannered girlfriend and that Jo was making my suffering worse by rejecting my sincere courtship. Jo said that she had no intention of being used as a stepping-stone to another relationship. To which my friend swore that my intentions were honorable.

At the end of the concert, she had to talk to some parents who were inquiring about their children. I waited. As the sun was going down she finished, and we walked down the road to SIMC. We sat on the veranda of the two-story building, with the school compound stretched out in evening silence, and talked. She told me that her father had died when she was young, and that her mother had brought her up. At seventeen, she had got pregnant with a daughter, whose whereabouts she refused to divulge. At nineteen, she had gone to the teacher training college to become a primary school teacher. Then the troubles in the Triangle began. Her school closed down and was later occupied by the army. When the guerrillas attacked, she, together with most people in the area, fled. She explained that, earlier on, she had not been playing hard to get, but that she wanted to date only serious people.

I told her a little about myself, and about Aunt Lwandeka, the seminary, the university, SIMC and Boom-boom Brewery. The evening quickly turned into night. We walked down to the main road, and she saw me off. From then on, we started meeting regularly. I got rid of the other Triangle girls, even though I continued to financially help out one or two of them.

On chosen Sundays, we would go to the Catholic cathedral and hear mass. Neither of us was that devout, but sometimes one got information about what was going on in the country, especially what the papers missed or just hinted at. The Catholic Church was still playing chief political critic of both the government and the guerrillas. We would have lunch at a decent restaurant and then go to an alfresco bar and sit and watch the people and the soldiers. She liked beer. By the fifth bottle, she would start singing nursery rhymes and some of the songs her pupils sang in the end-of-term concerts. I enjoyed the show and the childhood it invoked. It seemed we were both looking for an anchor to steady us in these turbulent times.

At such moments, the war faded to the oblivion of the Triangle and its phantoms, suffering and wantonness. We were in our own small world, locked behind steel gates, allowing in those we wanted to see, barring the undesirables. Soaked in beer, we would tell stories that evaporated with the stupor and remained on the sheets where we made love. Lovemaking itself was an act of war, an expression of the tension ripping the country apart. By trying to create something new and beautiful, we were firing our weapons, opposing forces of evil and destruction, throwing a lifeline to something on the other side that had to be redeemed. By driving ourselves to the limit, we were steeling ourselves for battle, for all those confrontations ahead of us, and making sure that we would have the capacity to survive the most painful ordeals. We were both orphans, people from whom something dear had been robbed. The common bond drove us further into the search for fulfillment.

As I thrust deeper into the marshes of love and the triangle of life, I kept wondering where her child had passed through, because this was one super-tight woman, the tightest I was ever to encounter. Had she lied about the child and the marriage? Was she just another myth-maker and I her gullible victim? I knew almost immediately that even as I was savoring the splendors of my paradise, I was also witnessing the beginnings of my doom. This was one experience that would not be duplicated, one act that would be almost impossible to follow. My joy was bruised with sorrow, my happiness touched by fear. I had hit the sexual jackpot: if I lost this, I would only have memories to ruminate on. I savored the sweet torture of her excruciating contractions with unease. I felt that loss was inevitable. I could feel her slip away. Such marvellous things never lasted. If they did, they enslaved their owners and turned them into drooling fools. I had either to enslave her or to pass her on. One side of me wanted to chain her, to tie her on a leash, to saddle her with bells that would betray her every movement. One side wanted to set her free to go out into the world and inflame and torture and madden others with the bruising grip of her hidden treasures. I could see old men drooling and getting heart attacks on top of her. I could see young men driven insane by her flame, getting rid of their wives and girlfriends and ending up bankrupt and alone. I could see men walking round and round, asking themselves where it had gone wrong, how and why they could not stop this pearl from diving back into the depths whence she had come. I loved it.

It would have been easy to ask Jo to move in with me, but I was into the torture games of letting her go and welcoming her back, watching her vanishing backside and embracing her when she returned. I was steeling myself for the loss, preparing the trap for other men to fall into. When she left, I kept thinking that she would never return. When she returned, with the smell of the school on her hair and the heat of passion in her veins, I kept wondering whether she would ever leave. I kept wondering how Husband was taking his loss of this woman or girl or phantom or whatever she was. In the midnight hour, when the bed or the trench or the ambush turned into a torture rack of lust, he must have pined for her. His lust for her must have turned into lust for blood. He must have embraced her in his dreams, but on waking up cold and alone, his head must have spun. I hoped we would never meet.

My time with Jo helped me gain insight into the ways other people conducted their love affairs. Had Grandpa not lived with Uncle Kawayida's mother's buckteeth? Had he not known that Serenity's mother had fallen for another man? Had Serenity not accommodated his wife's ways? Had Padlock not accommodated the fact that her husband was in love with her aunt? Was Aunt Lwandeka not in love with the mysterious brigadier, keeping his picture in her Good News Bible under the mattress? Didn't they maintain trust in each other despite the distance and not hearing from each other for months? Wasn't Uncle Kawayida in love with three sisters? Affairs of the heart had never been perfect; imperfection was part and parcel of the package. I was prepared for the worst. In the war to find and free myself, Jo was one big skirmish, not the final battle.

Midway into the decade, it was clear that there was a stalemate in the fighting. We would see army trucks, as indifferent as sealed coffins, carry their stiff, blank-eyed cargo into the Triangle. We would see dishevelled soldiers returning from their nightmare campaigns with the look of death in their eyes. We would see intelligence officers, walkie-talkies sticking out, eyes red with fear, legs stiff with uncertainty, moving up and down our little town in a frenzied daze. There were rumors, corroborated by Aunt, that the guerrillas were about to start an urban campaign, focussing on the city. After many weeks, they attacked a big army barracks near the two cathedrals. They caused considerable damage, as the army, despite all outward show of vigilance, was caught unawares. In retaliation, the army picked up people from around the city and detained them and interrogated them and tortured them. The dragnet netted few, if any, real guerrillas.

This was when the running games, or Olympic Games, as wags called them, began. During office hours, a report would suddenly circulate that the guerrillas were in the city, and people would stream out of offices and businesses and dash to their cars or to the bus and taxi parks. The pandemonium would be heightened by rumormongers who claimed that even as they spoke, a few suburban towns had already fallen. I was once caught in the wave. People poured out of the filthy Owino Market, Kikuubo, Nakasero Hill and everywhere, and made the taxi park tremble with the noise of their cries and the stamping of their feet. I got knocked in the back and spun around, but luckily got pushed upright by those behind me. Everybody was clearing out. Supercilious snake charmers, trapped in their flaccid dignity, saw their boxes kicked into the air, the reptiles ground into the asphalt. Rat poison merchants saw their goods flying all over the place. Hawkers ran with cardboard boxes on their heads. Van drivers made incredible turns, cutting through the masses before the doors could be ripped from their hinges. Lost shoes, torn bags, shirt buttons, roast maize, white bread, were all ground into the asphalt as people ran from the invisible enemy.

Hordes of unemployed youths who paraded the bus and taxi parks quickly got the hang of the game. They would come to town ready to snatch bags and fun whenever possible. They would stand in little groups by the roadside and watch well-dressed women and men wobbling down the hills, blowing like cows chewing cud at the fireside. They concentrated on women who fled with high heels in their hands, burdened with vanity bags and sacks of clothing, tongues protruding out of parched mouths.

"Lady," they would chime. "Are you a sprinter or a marathon runner?"

"She is a marathon runner."

"How long have you been training for this race?"

"Every day, once, twice, thrice a week in bed?"

"Are you going to be the first Ugandan woman to win Olympic gold?"

"Take this, it is my lucky towel. It will help you come in first. I don't really mind following you."

Like many times before and after, false alarms set the games rolling. At the back of most people's minds was the feeling that there was really nowhere to run, but that they had to keep moving. In the Triangle, people fled toward the city. In the city, people could only flee toward their homes. These panic alarms went on for a few months, till people began to question them. Mission accomplished, they finally disappeared as quietly as they had started.

It was during this time that the guerrillas were moving out of the Luwero Triangle to western Uganda, in the direction of Lake Albert. In the city, there were rumors that the guerrillas had given up and had cut a deal with the government. The army itself was confused: in the Triangle, the troops found only ghost towns and deserted villages loaded with the stench of the dead and the decay caused by aerial bombardment, mop-up operations and the elements. There was nobody to fight. The emptiness of their former hunting grounds was the last warning that they had lost both their prey and their grip on the situation. They had recurrent nightmares of getting ambushed and hit from the back. The eerie silence emphasized the fact that they had let "the bandits" escape to a place where they could hardly be reached. Already there were divisions in the army, and morale was dwindling rapidly. Many soldiers had not been paid for months and were tired of having to loot and kill in order to get money. The casualties—comrades who lay on their sickbeds knowing that somewhere in the Triangle their blown-off legs, arms, jaws, ears or balls were rotting—brought the desperation of the situation closer to those on the front line and those waiting to be dispatched to the war zone.

It was not long before the guerrillas started attacking and taking over big towns in both the west and the south. Mubende, Hoima, Masaka and Mbarara fell. The guerrillas set up a provisional government. The country was now cut in two. For some time, Aunt was left without anchor. She started brooding, wrapping her worries in few words. She was very afraid that she might never see the brigadier again, for the possibility of a protracted confrontation with government forces looked imminent. She tried to look cheerful and hide her suffering. Then one day she told me that she was going to Masaka, deep in guerrilla territory. At this time it was still possible to go and return. Ostensibly, she was going to visit Uncle Kawayida. In reality, she was going to check on the brigadier. She was gone for a week. My fear was that she might get trapped on the other side. Government roadblocks were bad, but she survived them and came back. "It is peaceful on the other side. There is no shooting in the night. People leave their doors open. There is nothing to fear," she said very excitedly. "As a matter of fact, I am going back."

I was both alarmed and angry. I told her that it was sheer madness. How could she push her luck like that? "I have been doing it all my life." Off she went. This time, however, the guerrillas denied her permission to leave Masaka. They did not want their secrets betrayed to government forces, voluntarily or otherwise. They were highly suspicious of anyone coming and going. Aunt pleaded that her children needed her badly, but they countered that they badly needed her to organize women in the liberated areas. The brigadier, however, made a plan for her to escape. She went by boat and landed at a port near the city. She had picked up a fever, but she was so relieved to be back with her children that she never complained about it or the hardships on the way.

There were upheavals in the army. A leading faction of the commanders wanted to negotiate with the guerrillas, end the fighting and form a coalition government. The smallest guerrilla groups, which had remained inside the Triangle on a knife's edge, came out and handed over some guns and signed papers. The group in the west, half a country under its control, did not budge. There was a lot of political shadowboxing and jostling for power, which I ignored as I concentrated on Boom-boom Brewery and on Jo. Money was still coming in, and I could afford to seal myself off in my little cocoon.

The war that dislodged the Obote II government and buried the remnants of the army in both northern Uganda and southern Sudan took the same route as the one that had ousted Idi Amin. The guerrillas followed Masaka Road. They pushed toward the city step by step, town by town. On many occasions, the army tried to use tanks to break through the advancing ranks and reoccupy the liberated areas, but to no avail. At best, they recaptured areas for a few weeks but were later driven out of them. Their hearts were no longer in it, and hardware alone never won a war.

Pressured by powerful army officers, the government asked for negotiations. A cease-fire was called; both government and guerrillas took turns violating it. In the meantime, more civilians were getting killed in sporadic fighting. The triangle syndrome was spreading elsewhere. With bated breath, the nation watched the negotiations. When the fighting reached Aunt Kasawo's little town, everyone knew that it was now or never. Twenty-five kilometers from the city was as near as the guerrillas had ever come to accomplishing their goal. Weeks of negotiations and accusations and counter-accusations of cease-fire violation followed.

Finally, the agreement between the guerrillas and the government was signed. Within a matter of weeks, however, the fighting picked up steam, and the guerrillas captured Kampala on January 25, 1986. It was almost like a repeat of the 1979 show, with government soldiers fleeing both north and east and a new force in power. This time, though, the city had been captured by units with many child soldiers, little boys with uniforms too large for them. It was simply amazing to watch these often ragged units marching through the city, hard on the heels of the retreating army.

Anticipating a repeat of the 1979 bonanza, the looters came out in full force. They were mistaken. Orders had been given that there would be no looting, no duplication of the lawlessness of the seventies. Brave looters got warning shots fired in the air above their heads. Those who persisted got shot. News spread that the guerrillas meant business. Everyone got the message, and the looters returned home wondering what government takeovers had come to.

There was jubilation in the southern part of the country, albeit a little overshadowed by what had happened in the Luwero Triangle. The celebrations were muted; there were no wild drinking parties and ceaseless drumming. Jo came to see me, and we spent the day talking, theorizing about what would happen next. What did the future hold for us? She was thinking about returning to the Triangle to survey the damage and see what she could salvage from the ruins. I was wondering whether Boom-boom Brewery would keep on growing.

Aunt Lwandeka was overjoyed. She told me that she would never get involved with guerrillas again. She was happy that the victory had come when it had: she was tired of waiting and fearing for her life. "I have been reborn, son, given another chance. Nobody gets born thrice." Recalling what had happened in 1971 and 1979, I became gripped by fear: What was I going to lose, or rather, whom was I going to lose, this time? Jo, Aunt Lwandeka or someone else? I could not face the idea of going to the Triangle: I didn't want to know what had happened to the village. It felt better, at least for the time being, not to know. Already estimates put the death toll in the Triangle anywhere between two hundred thousand and four hundred thousand. I preferred the dead to bury themselves.

The most remarkable change regarded security: one could sleep at night without fear of getting killed by robbers, raiders, soldiers or unknown people. One could travel and stay out late. The roadblocks were tough but fair; there was no stealing or raping going on. The people gained confidence in the new government, and their expectations rose. At first, sleeping peacefully at night was enough. Now they found out that you cannot sleep peacefully on an empty stomach or without knowing what has happened to your home, your people, your history. Those who had come from the Triangle wanted to go back; those who had people there wanted to know what had happened to them. They all made excursions to their ghost towns and came back depressed. Their old homes had no roofs or windows or doors, and the dead lay where they had fallen. The shrines of their gods had been desecrated, and there was a big lacuna between the past they knew and the present that faced them.

The task of reconstruction was enormous. The government promised to help devastated areas, but the help did not come quickly enough. People with money decided to go it alone. They bought building materials, transported them to the Triangle on rickety pickup vans and rebuilt their houses. Most waited, going there only to do a little work like digging and clearing the yards.

I sponsored Jo's journeys to the Triangle but refused to accompany her. After each visit, she would come back feeling sad. Her former school lay in ruins. She wanted to be part of the restoration process, but the government was finding it hard to provide the necessary materials. It bothered her a lot that so much had been destroyed. She could hardly understand or let it go. She would go on endless tirades about why it should not have happened, going back to Obote II, Amin, Obote I, up to the colonial government and its local agents. She blamed all Ugandans, all colonialists, all arms manufacturers and dealers and dumpers. She blamed the hatred and the indifference and the inequality that made all this possible, until I either ran out of the house or shouted at her to stop. The tirades helped her to jettison her frustration, but they ended up getting on my nerves and making me ponder things I preferred to leave frozen.

Aunt was still waiting for her reward. She frequently went to the city to meet the brigadier, who was organizing the guerrilla forces into a regular army. He had promised to help her set up a business by recommending her for a low-interest loan from the bank. He asked her to marry him. She said that she would think about it; she had never thought about marriage after her adolescent fiasco with the veterinary officer. He gave her a ring. She at first wore it shyly, and her friends made jokes about it, but she took it in her stride. To start with, she was given the task of organizing women. She set up clubs and held meetings. She worked very hard, and she was as happy as I had ever seen her.

All this time, I had been wondering where Lwendo was. It was months since the takeover. I went to the city and inquired at the cathedral whether he was still in the seminary. He had been expelled. When? At around the time when the country was cut in two. A month later, a military jeep came to SIMC while I was away, and a soldier asked to see me. He refused to leave a message. A week later, Lwendo came. He was clad in military fatigues. He was a second lieutenant now. We embraced. He had learned my whereabouts from a former schoolmate. There was so much catching up to do. The underlying question was, was it curiosity that had impelled Lwendo to come, or was there something else? It was more than curiosity. He wanted me to join him. In what capacity? As semi-spy, semi-ombudsman. I was shocked. It did not make much sense. I had left the seminary to escape dictatorship, and I was not going to get involved with military or security agency dictators. He reassured me that we would be working for an individual, a big boss in government whose task was to fight corruption. I detected clericalism, and sure enough, the man was an ex-priest. It was the reason he had been put in charge of rehabilitation and reconstruction: Catholics still had a reputation for honesty. But what about me, and my former mate Lwendo? I could detect the danger: What would the people whose corrupt plans we would be sabotaging do? Would they try to bribe us or attempt to pop us off? I rejected his offer. I had a good income. What reason had I to get involved in such dangerous stuff? I changed the subject of conversation. I wanted to hear his personal story.

Lwendo was an orphan. He never knew his real parents. He had been brought up by a kind Catholic couple with a big family as one of their children. It was while he was in the seminary that he discovered that his benefactors were not his real parents. By then, they had mapped out his life for him: he had to become a priest, help the needy and repay God for what He had done for him. Lwendo had never liked the idea: his childhood dream had been to join the air force and fly planes. His benefactors could not entertain such un-Catholic vanity. His misbehavior in the seminary had been geared by his resentment of the choice his benefactors had made for him, and the feeling that he had no way out.

After my departure, he had soldiered on. By the time guerrilla activity started, he was in the major seminary, but the regimen was harder than he had anticipated. He quickly got fed up with the place and the staff. He started playing truant and flirting with girls when he went out for pastoral work. He opposed priests in the open. He asked sharp questions about the existence of God and gave political speeches. To work everybody up properly, he supported the Uganda People's Congress and the actions of the Obote II government in the Luwero Triangle. When asked about the killings, he quoted the old Biblical line: "All authority comes from God." He also referred to the time of the Crusades, when the Church waged genocidal wars. The conclusion many priests drew was that he had no vocation. Others defended him, seeing his attitude as residual adolescent rebellion, which would wear off. He was warned to change his ways and pay respect to the fathers and stop political agitation. He refused. They set spies on him. He was caught returning late to campus one evening. He was expelled.

At that point, Lwendo had two options: to go home, across Lake Victoria, or to stay in the liberated areas. Home: Where was his home? Would his benefactors receive him well? If so, what was he going to do in the troubled city? He had no job, no money, no immediate prospects. The theological education he had garnered could only land him on the sidelines of teacherdom or in some function related to religion, which he was not ready to countenance. Above all, the stories that trickled into the liberated areas from the city, with a dose of good old exaggeration, said that people were dying like flies at the hands of desperate government soldiers. Having tasted the relative peace and order reigning in the liberated areas, he was not ready to face whatever lay on the other side.

He decided to stay and join the guerrillas. Already he knew the ex-priest called Major Padre or simply Padre by all, who was a prominent personality in the guerrilla movement in that area. He had visited the seminary twice, trying to sell guerrilla ideology to the priests and seminarians. In what to many seemed like a strange ideological turn-around, Lwendo had been the only seminarian to express interest in his message and to hail the guerrillas for fighting the murderous regime. The ex-priest had given him a faded visiting card, the only one he gave away on both occasions, because the others were uninterested. Not one to hold back, Lwendo used the card as his talisman, and boasted to fellow seminarians that he was the only one with vision.

"You are a chameleon," they said, "with no sense of loyalty or principle."

"I am a child of the darkness," he countered. "I sense where the wind blows." They laughed at him. He shouted guerrilla slogans on campus, alienating even the few priests who believed that he was only suffering from arrested adolescence. Not long after, he said that if he were the leader of the guerrillas, he would have closed the seminary and sent both the seminarians and the staff for military training. Before joining the guerrillas, he visited the padre and talked to him about his intentions. He got the green light: the padre needed people he could trust, and Lwendo, with his big mouth, looked like a perfect tool.

Beset by transport problems, Lwendo entered the training camp at night and almost got shot at the quarter-guard. The soldiers on watch barked at him, ordered him to put his arms in the air and took him in for interrogation. The guerrillas were very wary of sneak attacks from the remnants of government forces they had driven from the town, and of infiltration by spies masquerading as aspiring fighters. Lwendo spent the night in a filthy room guarded by two soldiers, because the padre could not be disturbed at that late hour, not even by those bearing his talisman. Salvation arrived early the next morning. The padre vouched for him, and he was immediately sent for training. Afterward, he did guard duty and patrol, and twice his unit was dispatched to flush out government soldiers who had turned into highwaymen. After lying in ambush for a week, he and his comrades killed four of them. This did not go unnoticed. The padre was happy that his ward could get the job done and appreciated his communication skills, a far cry from those of most Triangle veterans, who only obeyed orders and spoke only when spoken to. Lwendo exaggerated the part he had played in the fight. "When the thugs started shooting, I thought I had been hit. Then I started shooting, and the sound of my gun charged me up and everything changed. It was the best feeling in the world. I wished there were fifty of them out there. I would have killed them all," he told the padre, who had asked him to secretly report back to him. A shadow of doubt passed over the man's face, but he said nothing about his ward's declared interest in killing. He could always use a good story.

On the way to Kampala, when the guerrillas started pushing government forces toward the city, Lwendo had seen some fighting, but only as a quartermaster, supplying ammo. The padre had put in a good word for him. Already that had caused some friction and accusations of favoritism, but Lwendo's advantage was that he was educated, whereas most of the veterans, especially the child soldiers and ex-peasant farmers picked up from the Triangle, were at best primary or lower secondary school products. The movement needed brains in addition to brawn. He was among the most highly educated, and with his Latin expressions he caused much resentment. When annoyed by his fellow fighters, he would smile and say, *"Non compos mentis."* They knew he was insulting them, but not how much, until one sneaked up on him and put a bayonet to his throat and asked for an explanation.

After the war, the padre sent Lwendo to the Triangle, where he fought retreating army forces passing through on their way to the north. He did not do much fighting, but did well the few times he saw action. That was how he had ended up a second lieutenant. Now his benefactor wanted him to keep an eye on goods destined for the devastated areas: iron sheets, cement, brick-making equipment, blankets and the like. Judging by the dedication with which he had handled ammunition and other supplies as a quartermaster, the padre believed that Lwendo could be trusted with larger things.

The post-guerrilla-war economy was in shambles, inflation was very high, there was a chronic lack of production and the thriving black market did not make economic planning any easier. Fighters used to the hard life and discipline of their bush days were now out in the world, open to temptations of quick money and personal enrichment. Many felt they deserved opportunity as a reward for facing death and hardship in the Triangle and elsewhere in order to liberate the country.

Lwendo made it clear to me that he did not intend to stay in the army for long: "I hate being cooped up in the barracks. I hate the lack of freedom, the power of the officers and all those drills. I want to get out early, but with something in my pocket. I have many plans for the future."

"You mean . . ."

"I intend to get my cut of the action."

"What is the padre's attitude to that?"

"He is high up there; I am down here at the bottom. He can fire me if he does not like my modus operandi."

"How about the hostility of your colleagues?"

"It is there, but it does not deter me from doing what I want. The sooner I get what I want, the sooner I quit."

"This whole thing scares me. I am not a soldier. If things go wrong, I will be the bad guy."

"Let me worry about that."

"I already have a job . . ."

"Getting twenty, thirty dollars a month! Come on, man. How long will you stay in that rotten profession?"

"I have no intention of getting beaten and locked up by soldiers accusing me of corrupting you, Mr. Liberator."

"I need you. The moment the padre appointed me, I knew you were the right person to work with. I need somebody I can trust, somebody who won't stab me in the back."

"What if we get caught?"

"Discretion will be paramount. We are not going to do things carelessly, you can take it from me. I am a different man now. I am systematic, patient, wary. You don't have to worry about that," he said earnestly. "Think about it and about your future and then come to me. I won't accept the job unless you cooperate."

The temptation was huge: the smell of adventure and daring, the exploration of unknown territory, the squaring off against bigger guys! The sense of danger had something magnetic about it, a feeling of beating the odds, a feeling of chopping heads off the hydras left in my garden by the Infernal Trinity. I was tired of teaching and achieving little in my profession. The seduction of piracy was like a lantern to a suicidal moth on a cold, dark night. I craved being on top, not in a little brewery where everyone called me boss, but in the larger world. The prospect awakened old seminary ghosts: the raids on Fr. Mindi and Fr. Lageau. I missed the adrenaline. I had done nothing like that in years. I felt that Lwendo and I could hold our own against security agents. It was a mind game, and my brain was afire with images, moves, feints which would bring us victory.

After a week, I forgot about it or, rather, shoved it to the back of my mind to cool off and gather a little dust before I chewed on it again. Had Lwendo really changed? Had he dropped his clumsiness and developed a more cunning, patient manner? Would he listen to me when necessary? How far was I ready to go? Most of us had imbibed the lawlessness, the everything-goes spirit of the seventies. The temptation to undermine some stolid, impersonal, bureaucratic force like the government was dazzling. Most of us were small gods, cuts above those bumbling government agents and stuffy authorities. The urge to test our omnipotence was irresistible.

I did not tell Aunt about Lwendo's proposition. She had warned me long ago never to get involved with soldiers. In the meantime, things were going very well for her. Her women's wing was expanding. For the first time in years, women felt validated, listened to and heard. She settled their disputes and presented their needs to her superiors. Her relationship with the brigadier was moving from strength to strength.

Every weekend, a car came and took her to the city, where she joined the brigadier and his friends for drinks till late in the night. That way she met quite a few of the people at the top. They asked her what women really thought of the government, and what they expected from it. This did not surprise her, because she knew that many of these people were surrounded by yes-men and now and then needed frank opinions.

Like an army of vultures and marabou storks, the International Monetary Fund and the World Bank swooped down on the Ugandan carcass with drawn talons. Not that they were newcomers; no, they had been surveying the skyline for years and had been around even during the last regime. But now they moved with lethal determination. The climate was better. They had a list of conditions as long as the river Nile. The government, eager to fight inflation, stimulate production and inject cash into the economy, obliged them. The IMF tweaked the tail of the new government: if it wanted money, it had to return the property of departed Indians. Thus, the Indians had to return and claim their property after more than fifteen years. The rumors created a buzz in Uganda, especially in the city.

To begin with, old currency was made non-legal tender and had to be exchanged for new. Schools served as currency exchange centers, and for once SIMC was used for something directly relevant to the community. The good reverend went around boasting about the indispensability of his school. In the morning, people with bulky bags of cash stood in line in front of the two-story building to hand in their old money.

I dodged getting involved in the program. I had never liked the look or the smell of the old notes, and neither was the smell of new money something I wanted to douse my senses in. I came to school only to exchange Boom-boom Brewery proceeds which had not been in the bank, then went home. The allotted time for the currency exchange passed before the job was completed. There was panic that people's money would be nullified in the name of fighting inflation, but an extra week was allocated. For people used to the large denominations of the old money, it was horrifying to receive the puny new bills they were given in exchange for their worthless millions.

A fortnight after the money-exchanging exercise, I was at school teaching when the deputy called me outside: "There is somebody waiting for you in my office." I thought Lwendo had returned. However, it was a man sent by Aunt.

"There has been an accident," the scruffy, sad-eyed man announced.

"What kind of accident?" I asked, getting goose bumps.

"She did not say. She just told me to inform you to come as quickly as possible."

There was a crowd outside Aunt's house, and among them some very angry people. It turned out that one of my brewery employees had been burned by the cooking drum. He had not died, but the skin had peeled off the front of his body like a banana skin, and he looked as yellow. The bastard. He was not supposed to brew that day—I had suspended all work pending the stabilization of new-currency prices—but the bastard had gone ahead and done it behind my back. He had started the fire, gone to sleep and not seen that the copper tubes were blocked. He was awakened by a massive explosion. The drum had risen in the air like a space capsule and burst open like a dry pod. If it had stayed on the ground, it would have killed him right away. Instead, he got scalded by part of the contents, the rest spreading in all directions.

Aunt had organized transport to take him to the hospital, and she had also accepted the responsibility for the accident. That had cooled some tempers, but not totally. She promised to foot the medical bills and to help as much as she could. She thought the matter was settled, but the brother and brother-in-law of the victim went down to the brewery and destroyed the equipment and burned down the shed. I went there, and the fire reminded me of another fire fifteen years before. I decided right then that I had had enough of the business. Lwendo had won.

The accident made me look at my relationship with Jo a bit more closely. Who was this girl? I did not know any of her people except her grandmother. As we sat eating supper one evening, I told her that I wanted to meet her mother. She did not seem too happy about it.

"If you are really serious about me, the lady is supposed to know me, and I should know her."

"I will think about it."

"There is nothing to think about," I said.

"How will I introduce you?"

"As Mr. Muwaabi, secondary school teacher and future lawyer."

"As who?"

I repeated my full name casually, a smug smile on my face. I never used the name Muwaabi. Everybody called me Mugezi, and even the government knew me as such.

"The lady would then ask about your parentage."

I was too excited to sense the danger in her tone of voice. I proceeded to talk about Grandpa, the village, Serenity. . . . She suddenly stopped eating, put her palm across her mouth and closed her eyes. I thought a fish bone had lodged itself in her throat.

"*Katonda wange!*" she exclaimed. "My God!"

"What is the matter?"

"I always suspected something. Now I know."

"Know what?" I said irritably.

"We are related. You are my brother, or as the English say, half-brother."

"What is wrong with you?"

"My biological father's name is Muwaabi, and he comes from the same village and went to Ndere Primary School. You are his son. I now see that there is a slight resemblance between you. He got rid of my mother in order to marry in church. And after that, he did not pay much attention to my welfare. It was the reason I always said that he was dead, but I know that he works and lives in the city. I resolved to keep out of his way for the rest of my life."

I could not eat anymore. I felt myself sinking into a big hole full of howling ghouls. I looked at the girl with new eyes. I could see Aunt Tiida in the upper part of her face. I could see a bit of Kasiko too, and Grandma in a very faint way. Maybe it was the presence of all these familiar features that had made her so attractive to me. I was no staunch exogamous traditionalist, but something had gone out of our relationship. It did not feel the same anymore. We drank a lot but said very little that night, and for many more nights. I never touched her again. The magic candle was dead.

It struck me one evening that this was a God-given chance for revenge on Serenity, my chance to repay him for that near-death beating. I should look him up and tell him that I had found somebody to marry and then introduce Jo. Yes, I would do that, as a piece of theater. Sadness permeated all this, because I felt I would never find another girl like Jo. I already was jealous of whoever would marry her.

"Will you do something for me?" I asked her.

"What is it?"

"I want to introduce you to my father, our father, as my fiancée."

"What do you want to do that for?"

"I have my reasons."

"You do not believe that I will marry you, do you?"

"Well, of course not," I said irritably.

"Then what are you up to?"

"Let us say there is some unfinished business between me and my father."

"Why bring me in?" Her directness made me cringe. She was doing her best to look into the future; I was reluctant to abandon the mires of the present and the past.

"There is much unfinished business between you and him too," I answered.

"Why would I want to meet him that way?"

"Are you not angry at how he treated your mother, and you in particular?"

"Of course I am. But that is not how I want to play it."

"How do you want to play it?"

"By ignoring him the way he ignored me."

"Don't you want him to squirm with embarrassment?"

"What use would it be?"

"It would be something to me."

"Give it up. There is no future in it."

"What is your idea of revenge?"

"Marrying a rich man in a stunning wedding ceremony, with a motorcade, ten flower girls, a long bridal train, a troupe of traditional dancers and a feast for days."

The conventionality of it! How could a girl so mistreated by her father be this conventional? She wanted to make Serenity feel a pauper vis-à-vis his son-in-law. What if Serenity did not give a damn about such things? What if he saw it as a waste of capital? It all sounded so shallow. Would Serenity not pity this girl, because such rich men usually had other wives and she would have to wait for him for days?

"Do you want to be one of several wives?" I was thinking of Lusanani, wondering whether these two women had the same views. A Hajj Gimbi look-alike, potbelly and all, handling this cute girl! I could see him sweating over her and wheezing like a steam engine. I could see him fighting hard to maintain his erection in her super-tight cunt. I felt both sick and angry.

"As long as a man gives me freedom to do what I want, I do not mind about the rest of his business."

I felt quite rootless now. I could only drift into Lwendo's claws. How lucky Serenity was! Once again he had escaped.

I met Lwendo at the Ministry of Rehabilitation office on Kampala Road. Everything was in disarray. There were dusty file cabinets, a few sticks of old furniture, an overused typewriter and a black telephone that made a very loud screeching sound. He took me outside to the General Post Office building, and we sat on the railing and talked.

"You don't know how relieved I am," he said. "The man was getting impatient and was about to suggest somebody else. But now we can go ahead."

"Where do we go from here?" I asked. "Do I have to meet him?"

"No. He only has to have your particulars. Write an application for a job in the ministry, which I will deliver to him. Leave the rest to me."

"To whom do we have to report?"

"A certain rehabilitation officer."

"And what are we supposed to do?"

"To double-check the applications, the sites and the relevance of the materials requested. After that, to make sure that the goods have been delivered. Don't worry about the rest; I will be in charge."

We went to a restaurant on Luwum Street and had a lunch of matooke, meat and greens, washed down with a beer. Good start, I thought. At SIMC, there had been no lunch. Lwendo talked about his present girlfriend, but I was not too interested. She was older than him, a nurse at Mulago Hospital, and they were having their ups and downs.

After lunch, we went to the shops and bought foolscap paper.

These were the Indians', those pirates', old haunts, which the IMF wanted returned to them. Time had frozen the stores in stagnancy. The tenants, knowing that they were dealing with other people's property, had not effected repairs, and the Custodian Board, intent on getting its piece of the action, had not insisted on maintenance and repairs. The rust-streaked roofs, the cracked pavements, the grime-ridden windows, summed up the situation well.

Inside, a shop was shared by about twenty people, each with a small space at the counter. Many traders rented the space just to display their goods—imports from Dubai, sometimes from London—and when a customer came, they took him or her behind the shop, or to a place where the real stock was. A few people had made money here, but for most, it had been a question of improvising and surviving. Now the original owners were poised to return. The talk in town was what the traders in these shells were going to do about it. How were the Indians going to play it this time? Last time they had enjoyed complete monopoly, but now Africans had moved in on their turf. The whole thing was heating up.

The industrialists returned first. The small fry, the retailers and wholesalers, followed tentatively. You could see them in business suits or in light safari suits walking in groups, looking all over, trying to dredge up clogged memories, wondering how they were going to pick up old threads. The second generation, who were children at the time of the exodus and had grown up in Britain, were less impressed. You could see their parents desperately trying to kindle the dream in their skeptical hearts.

As one looked at the city, with some buildings hollowed out by bombs, others peeling in the sun and more bearing hurried face-lifts, one wondered how it was going to accommodate all the different forces bubbling inside it. Many among the trading class had hoped that the government would favor them and keep out the Indians because "everyone" had contributed to the guerrilla war and lost people; but the government was more concerned with long-term development, a thing which did not figure in most traders' scheme of things.

Lwendo and I spent the first few weeks walking all over the city, visiting different sites connected with our job. We went to rehabilitation warehouses in the industrial area to study the invoicing system. We visited Radio Uganda offices, where one of our key people worked, and proceeded to other places.

I was relieved that Lwendo was in mufti: green trousers, a green shirt and black shoes. He did not carry a gun, and we walked through the busy streets just like any other people. Army jeeps now and then drove by, but they had no sirens and did not push vehicles off the road. The taxi vans were busy as usual, and now some took travellers to the Triangle, where they had not been in years.

Our first assignment was to cross-check an allocation of blankets destined for Nakaseke, a former guerrilla hideout deep in the Triangle. We got on a bus up to Luwero, forty kilometers from the city. Just ten kilometers from Kampala, we started seeing fruit stands along the road, with skulls arranged in neat lines at the front, shin and thigh bones and the rest in piles at the back. The skulls had no jawbones, and many had cracks and holes on top where bullets or axes had penetrated them. Polished by the rain and dried by the sun, they could have been playthings in a morbid ritual game; but with the ghostly, desecrated buildings directly behind them, where signs of life were just beginning to show, curious faces emerging from behind the ruins to peek at the passengers getting off buses, there was no fun in it. The bus stopped at every little skeletal town and dropped off a person or two, sometimes with a bundle, sometimes empty-handed. Heading toward the ruins, the arrival walked through paths and roads choked by five-year-old grass, some of which grew inside the hollow buildings and poured through the roofs and doorways, windows and ventilators. As one saw these individuals heading for old settlements hidden behind the bushes, one wondered what they would find there: Skulls to add to the collection on the fruit stands? Villages wiped out? Or a thing or two to hinge old memories on?

In less devastated places one saw shop buildings left undesecrated. Mostly the strategic spots where the army had stationed its detachments to monitor the surrounding areas, these surviving buildings had escaped looting because the army had left too quickly or too late to loot. In such places, there were more people, and next to the old skull-laden fruit stands were new ones with pineapples, pawpaws, bananas, sugarcanes and potatoes. The tarmac road chiselled through the forests, swamps and elephant grass like a huge blade. The tarmac itself was chewed at the edges by the tanks and army trucks that had used it incessantly during the guerrilla campaign. There were huge potholes in places where bombs had landed. The silence of the passengers in the bus, broken by a coughing child or a toddler asking something from its mother, was eerie. It increased the feeling that the dead were lying just beyond the road, waiting to be discovered and buried or displayed. The lushness of the grass and the majesty of the tall trees made you think that all that green had been fertilized by the blood and flesh of those who had fallen in battle.

I was becoming more convinced that the afterbirth of war was in ways worse than the actual fighting itself, and that winning the peace was harder than winning the war. Now the guns were silent and the howling of ghosts had taken over, interspersed with the sighs of the survivors, most of whom could not wait to reclaim their land; but the gaps in the silence were punctuated with a sense of anti-climax, a certain lack of direction.

Luwero and Nakaseke were sister towns bound together by the guerrilla war and past history. To get to the latter, you had to pass by the former. At the beginning of the war, both had housed thousands of people and had been fertilized by hinterlands of tens of thousands who brought money and goods. Luwero, the survivor, was showing signs of life with a growing population; Nakaseke, the unlucky sister, was yet to get over the rape, pillage and scars of the fierce fighting she had witnessed. Luwero struck you as a surprise, for, having seen stalls of skulls along the main road, you almost expected to find a mountain of them at the town gates, yet there were none. Nakaseke, on the other hand, struck the imagination as a tragedy, for it emerged from the rich forests, marshes and sprawling grasslands with the halo of a martyr. Her returnees fended for themselves, building temporary structures near the old town or moving into the surrounding villages to await government help and a hard road to recovery.

"What a lucky bastard I am!" Lwendo exclaimed. "I can't imagine the hardship those who fought in these sodden areas experienced."

We had travelled from Luwero on an old Toyota pickup van loaded to twice its capacity, and we were bumped black and blue. I didn't want to think about what these people had gone through, because I didn't want to think of the village of my birth. I was a tourist here. I had come to check a few documents, after which I would leave as soon as possible. The leaders of the people trying to dig this town from the ashes had stayed here throughout the war and had witnessed the grimmest skirmishes, but said little of their experiences.

"Bygones are bygones," one told Lwendo, who had been trying to get details out of them.

They led us on a tour of the town, showing us where the soldiers had camped on different occasions, where they used to torture people, and where they had positioned their guns on the day they bombed the town for the final time.

"We were like traffic wardens observing and sometimes directing very dangerous traffic," the leader said.

"It's unfair," Lwendo said later. "The war zone should have been called the Nakaseke instead of the Luwero Triangle."

"Some people have all the luck," I replied.

The drama of war had ended, leaving behind the harrowing task of putting it into words for later use. Our job finished, Lwendo and I could not wait to return to Kampala. The dead of Nakaseke would have to keep themselves company a little longer. As I watched the towns along the main road flying past, their stalls of skulls, gaping roofs and hidden histories a blur, I was excited. The city was where I belonged.

I was happy that the first mission had gone well, but when I considered what we were going to be paid for it, I became sad: people working so hard and dealing with so much responsibility and temptation deserved more. Officially, they were paying us a hundred dollars a month, a tenth of my brewery earnings. I kept seeing huge bales of new blankets, glittering bolts of virgin iron sheets, warehouses full of cement. I knew that I was back to where I had started: we were going to either convert these to money, or malinger.

It took me a few days to get over my Triangle experience. When I saw the one Triangle girl I intended to keep on seeing, I felt she had edited her story a great deal. She had probably seen more death and destruction than she admitted. I wanted to penetrate her mind and get to her secret. Had Jo told me everything? No, she had not. Her daughter had probably died in the fighting or in flight, dropped in a river, claimed by fever or crushed by stampeding feet. It was also possible that Jo had no daughter, and it was the death of many girls in her area that had impregnated her with the fantasy. We all walked around with skeletons rattling in our cupboard-like souls, editing carefully what we revealed, depending on whom we were talking to. We always second-guessed our audience and told them what they wanted to hear, or what would cause the least damage or best enhance our image.

The first deliveries went well. We went back to Nakaseke and found the goods there. The people were happy. They thanked us as if we had supplied them from our own private stock. Some had already begun repairing their houses. The sound of hammers falling on wood, the chatter of excited builders and the glowing eyes of expectant women touched something in us. People were back in their old ways: doing things for and by themselves. The general feeling was that the dead had not died for nothing, the living had much to look forward to and the children had a future.

Things started changing around the fifth mission. First we travelled to Kakiri, a small town on Hoima Road, and to a few other places, surveying both the damage and the needs. That went well, and the journey was less arduous. In a few weeks' time, we understood that the goods had been delivered: bales and bales of blankets and truckfuls of cement. At the Ministry of Rehabilitation, we were shown the papers. When we returned to Kakiri and the other places, though, cooperation was slim. All signs were that only part of the goods had been delivered. Someone in this little hollowed-out town knew something but did not want to talk. We had to go back to the source. In Kampala, we managed to get reliable records in duplicate. We went to Radio Uganda, and our contact filled in the gaps. He was always a step ahead. I kept wondering which spy organization he was part of.

It transpired that a truckful of goods had been sold to the Kibanda Boys, our own version of the mafia. They had begun with currency speculation in the early eighties. Now they had taken over business operations in Kikuubo, a strip of old Indian shops and warehouses between the bus park and Luwum Street, and were moving from strength to strength.

Kikuubo was crawling with people, traders and customers jostling one another in the narrow street in which Tata trucks were being unloaded. Lines of naked-torsoed young men were being loaded with bags of cement, sugar and salt, bolts of cloth and iron sheets and taking them inside warehouses behind grubby-looking shops. Looks misled: this was serious business. Instead of expanding Indian shops, the Mafia had chosen to use the warehouses and garages as shop fronts. It saved money, and considering how brisk business was, it was obviously a smart idea. Facilities were bad—hardly any toilets existed—but then traders and customers came here to make money, not calls.

Our target was, in City Council terms, an illegal structure: a garage converted into a shop front. We asked for Oyota, and a big, fat man in shorts appeared, eating corn on the cob. Lwendo had brought a gun with him. He had not allowed me to handle it. The only thing I knew was that it was heavy and loaded. The man invited us to the back of the shop, a dark little cubicle we found piled with money: heaps of local currency and stacks of American dollars. Lwendo swallowed hard. My palms itched.

"We would like to search your warehouse, sir," Lwendo said.

"No one is allowed to do that."

"We have a search warrant."

"What are you looking for?"

"That's our business," Lwendo said nonchalantly.

"You cannot just walk into my shop and ask to see my stock. I can call security, or one of the chiefs running this area."

"The law is on our side."

"We are the law; we fought the war; we lost people," the man said disdainfully. At the front of the shop, business was going on as usual. We could hear porters calling to each other, feet crunching, trucks roaring, car engines grinding and high voices warning pedestrians to watch out lest they get crushed. In and out of the shop came people with big bundles of money. They ordered large quantities of merchandise. Everybody paid in cash.

"I know what you boys are looking for," the fat man said coldly. "You want money, and I can understand it. You went to the bush to topple the old government, and now that you are in power, you realize that a man needs cash to enjoy victory."

"We just want to search your store, sir."

"I can understand your frustration. Here are traders who never seem to have done anything for the country. We never went to the bush. We were rich before you went to the bush, and we are richer now. Yet you who went hungry and thirsty and faced death have nothing. But remember, we financed the war."

"Show us your stores, sir," Lwendo said, toughening, evidently unimpressed with the lecture.

The man was biding his time, probably waiting for somebody who had not shown up. He finally took us to the store, whose location Lwendo already knew because of the tip. He also knew the license plate number of the vehicle which had brought the goods, and many other details. I felt a chill going down my spine as we followed the man. Somebody might be hiding in the corridors with a knife, or one of the naked-torsoed men could dump a fifty-kilo bag of cement on one of us, making it look like an accident. It was all in my head. The place was stacked with goods up to the rafters. Lwendo was looking for a little logo, nearly invisible, on the blankets. They couldn't have removed it; it was almost impossible to do so with poor technology. Cleverly enough, the goods were at the very back, and some men had to come in and move bales of things before we could get to them. We were all sweating: the men with effort, me with nerves, Lwendo with the excitement of the scoop. When the man realized that the game was up, he sent the men away and made his proposition. Lwendo calculated how much the things were worth in dollars.

"The best thing would be to take you to Lubiri Barracks and get some of that maize kicked out of you," Lwendo said coldly. "As you said, you have been having too much of a good time all these years."

"No, no, please. You have to understand. I am not the sole owner."

"Do you want to tell us who sold you the goods and how the deal was cut?"

My impression was that the man, like many traders, had a few contacts in government or in the army, but that they were weak. Also, no army officer or government official liked his name getting splashed around in criminal circles. The deal always was: once the goods left one hand, it was every man for himself, good luck to all involved. In the past, the man would have made only one phone call and we would have got picked up and made to look like the criminals. Things were different now. Lwendo considered how the people in Kakiri had created a wall of silence, and he decided that if he took the man in, the investigations might go on forever. He asked for a few thousand dollars, and he got it. We had crossed the line; there was no turning back.

I had never felt so exposed as on the way out of that building. The skin on my back tingled. When people pressed against me, I expected the cold blade of a knife to sink into my ribs. There were even more people now, because it was lunchtime. There were men carrying saucepans of boiling meat and fish to places where women sold food to traders and laborers. What if somebody emptied a seething pan on us and made off with the money? It was all so easy in the confusion. Why hadn't somebody thought of that? Out on Luwum Street, overlooking the taxi park on one side and the mosque and Nakivubo Stadium on the other, Lwendo said, "This is why I insisted on working with you. You can never cut such deals with somebody you don't trust one hundred percent. You see how easy it is to betray someone?"

I laughed, and he slapped me on the back.

"I am on my way out of the army," he said joyously.

"Provided our luck sticks," I cautioned.

"It will stick like hell, don't worry."

The pattern was set: we reported two out of every three cases; the third was ours, and we pocketed the money. Did the padre know about us? I never knew, but he would have been naive to believe that we were angels, especially when the official government line was that corruption was dying in the top echelons, though still pervasive at the bottom. The political cadres, of which Lwendo was not a member, brought in to root out police corruption were not doing well either. Many of them had taken the Lwendo line and were feathering their own nests.

It came as no real surprise that when our game was picking up, sudden changes were made. Almost all the staff at the Rehabilitation office and the warehouses was transferred, and new people were brought in. We were among the few survivors.

"Business" slowed down for some time. We went back to making those long, arduous journeys to obscure places on the back of rotten trucks and in terrible, overloaded buses. One of the worst was to Mubende, one hundred kilometers from Kampala. The first forty kilometers were on tarmac, the last sixty on hellish seasonal roads that disappeared in storms. At one place, a truck had jackknifed into a swamp, and another truck that tried to outflank it had ended up deeper in the swamp. The cargo on the second truck was being unloaded and placed in what was left of the road. We had nowhere to go, and there was no transport anyway at that late hour. We spent a chilly, hungry night in the bus, waiting for a tow truck.

The case here concerned iron sheets which had disappeared without a trace. Our guess was that they had been sold at Mityana, a fast-growing town which was a magnet for all sorts of crooks. The padre was sore because he knew these areas very well, having worked here as a Catholic priest for many years and briefly as a representative of the guerrilla movement. He wanted the case thoroughly investigated. By now we knew that the Kibanda Boys probably had something to do with it. They had found more and more friends in government and in the army, people with Lwendo's frame of mind.

At Mubende, we discovered that indeed the sheets had been sold at Mityana. We hurried back. The eerie thing was that the two men we arrested never begged for mercy or threatened us. What was their secret? Was it pure stoicism or knowledge that they would get us later?

"I don't like this at all," I said to Lwendo as he smoked one cigarette after the other. Here we were, in this strange town, sitting in a small restaurant that still smelled of paint, and there were people out there who wanted to get us.

"Don't worry about that," he said confidently, as though he were bulletproof. "Nobody can touch us."

"How are we going back?"

"By taxi," he said cockily.

"Why don't we use a government vehicle on some of these missions?"

"That would blow our cover."

I looked outside: Mityana was a dynamic little town. New buildings were going up all the time—the whole place seemed to be one big construction site. There were bare-chested men going up scaffolds with pans of concrete, and others coming down. Concrete-making machines were spinning their fat bellies ceaselessly, and foremen's voices agitated the air with supreme impatience. Trucks and buses were rolling in, together with overloaded pickup vans full of people and merchandise. Shoppers from Mubende and the surrounding areas poured in and out of town in hordes. Outside Mityana, level with the horizon, was Lake Wamala. The serenity of its silver-gray surface did not calm my nerves.

To come here, you had to pass through monstrous forests and open grassland for much of the way. The army had suffered big losses in these areas. How would we fare?

"Cheer up, man," Lwendo said. "This time we couldn't let the bastards go. Next time around, we will have our cut."

"It is dangerous money."

"That is what it is all about: beating the odds."

At about three o'clock, our business was finished. We got papers from the police, who would keep the men till they were picked up by the fraud squad, and we prepared to leave. We knew that a few heads had to roll on local reconstruction committees and at the Rehab office in Kampala. We got into a taxi van and set out for Kampala.

We entered thick forests where the sun was cut off for miles by the giant canopies, and emerged at little sodden towns with fruit stands and dilapidated buildings, some of which had been used as torture chambers by the army not so long ago. We went up a hill and descended a steep slope. Halfway down, we heard a big explosion. The van rolled over and over, and we were dumped in the grass below. I felt disembodied. I had banged my head on a seat and was cut on the left arm. Lwendo was unscathed, except for pain in his chest and in his right leg. Some people had been cut by flying glass and lay in the grass whimpering, calling for their dear ones. A man kept on about his wallet till he got exhausted and shut up. Some people thrashed about; some lay dead still, with only trickles of blood and light moans to show they were alive.

I was not afraid. I had been expecting something nasty to happen, it had happened and I felt relieved. I kept wondering: Was this an accident or a setup or a warning? We got help from a truck on its way to the city. Lwendo and I refused to go to the hospital. We went for a checkup at a small private clinic run by a doctor Lwendo knew.

"It was an accident, pure and simple. If they wanted to harm us, they would have done it more easily."

"Maybe they wanted to hide their hand," I said.

"No, they don't have to."

I lay low for a few weeks, trying to make sense of the accident. Had somebody shot at us, or had a wheel simply burst? I no longer felt so adventurous. I had the option of working with Aunt, who would soon need somebody to manage her business affairs: she was planning to make cooking oil from cottonseed. The Reconstruction Bank had already approved the loan and the plan.

The accident had made Lwendo meaner, his ransoms higher. It had also made him realize that we had to stop soon, before our luck ran out. I appreciated his logic. Greed and corruption were not going to end with us. It was wiser to do our thing and check out. His girlfriend was pressuring him to settle down. The Lwendo of the Sr. Bison days had not changed, and the woman wanted to pin him down as soon as possible. A number of women had smelled the money, but he had so far not sunk his claws into any of them because of our peripatetic lifestyle. His girlfriend wanted things to remain that way.

The deal that made us involved cement and was born of an ambitious government promise to repair all roads and to bridge all rivers in the devastated areas, beginning with those that had been destroyed as an immediate result of guerrilla activity. That was how I gathered courage to go to the village of my birth. I had already heard that it had been wiped out. The guerrillas had laid an ambush on the spot where the taxi driver who was supposed to take Padlock to Ndere Hospital for my birth got trapped by the rain and the storm. They first attacked the nearest barracks, fifteen kilometers away, in order to draw attention from the spot of the big ambush.

It had become evident early on that the army's approach was reactive; and even when they seemed to take the initiative it was in response to earlier guerrilla attacks. Carpet bombing had not worked in many places. Sweeping arrests and torture had not rooted out genuine guerrillas. The army was growing desperate and needed a big morale-boosting trophy.

One day the guerrillas shot at army trucks near Mpande Hill and disappeared into the bushes. They did it several times and sent radio messages to the effect that they had taken over a triangular piece of land between the barracks, Mpande Hill and Ndere Parish. The army, believing they had intercepted crucial information, planned a major offensive to sweep the area clean.

On the scheduled day, the army sent six trucks full of soldiers headed by an APC and machine-gun-mounted jeeps. This was during the reign of the Katyushas. When the vehicles were stretched out a full kilometer in the swamp, with Mpande Hill looming inaccessibly in the air, all hell broke loose. Those at both ends were taken out in big fire-balls, trapping the rest on the road and proving the strategy of travel-ling close together catastrophic. Rocket-propelled grenades blew up vehicle after vehicle, and the surviving soldiers were locked in a gun-fight that poured walls of lead and fire all around them. In all, the army lost two hundred fifteen soldiers on that lethal spot, and many others were wounded. Casualties among the guerrillas were minimal: they withdrew in time and escaped through the swamps into the village and the nearby forests.

A few hours later, as burned-out army trucks lay on their sides in the road or swam in the swamps and bodies swelled in the sun or floated in the water, tangled in the papyrus reeds, helicopter gunships arrived in force. Katyusha rocket launchers were mounted on the two hills, and the counter-attack began. By then, though, the guerrillas had already escaped, having had no intention of getting involved into a protracted battle with the better-equipped army. Almost all the local people had fled as well. The choppers and the Katyushas blasted every-thing anyway: shells landed in the forest, in the water, in the valleys, on houses, everywhere. The temperature of the water in the swamps went up, killing fish, frogs, horseflies, mosquitoes; burning papyrus reeds to a sick yellow color, and inducing a hippopotamus clan at the extreme end of the river to migrate. If it had not been for the inaccu-racy of the bombs, no house would have been left standing within a ra-dius of ten kilometers.

A few days later, as the forest smoldered and the houses lay in ruins, the army sent in mop-up operations to look for stray guerrillas who might have survived the blitz but been unable to get away. A few old men and women who had refused to flee, believing that their age might save them, had their elbows tied behind them in the triangular *kandooya* configuration. They had nothing to say, no information to give, and were killed. Those wounded in the fighting were brought to rooftops and pushed off. Anyone who could be fucked was fucked and killed. Any remaining scraps of doors, windows and iron sheets were looted. Thus the village of my birth was consigned to the caustic dust of oblivion.

The looting reached its peak at Ndere Parish. The soldiers would have stripped the church tower bare, but they did not want to share the

fate of its builder, the late Fr. Roulex Lule, by falling down and cracking their skulls. So they pumped a number of rocket-propelled
grenades into it until it folded and crumpled like paper. They blew the
remaining roof off the church and picked the fathers' house and the
school buildings clean. During the weeks of occupation, they broke up
desks and chairs for cooking fires. Lovers of barbecue, they looked for
animals to roast. This was around the time that their colleagues barbecued Fr. Lageau's German dog after attacking and looting the seminary of my secondary school days.

On what would have been the last day of the operation, a local
priest who had hidden in the forest was captured. He was arrested, together with a catechist, and the pair was hanged by the legs on the
smoldering rafters of the fathers' house. Saliva and blood and brains
trickled out of their heads until they died, and birds pecked out their
eyes.

Rain always followed severe bombardment. Rains poisoned with
the wrath of the dead fell, and the swamps swelled, flooding and sub-
merging the surrounding areas. They undermined house foundations
and made the ruins rot and crumble. They carried the ooze to the bottom of Mpande Hill in swirling waves and washed away the history of
the village. Thunder and lightning struck and, coupled with the relentless rain, broke open burial sites, filled them with water and destroyed what remained of that legacy. Elephant grass eventually took
over, growing over courtyards, graveyards, everywhere.

By the time we went to investigate the need for aqueducts to control the mighty Mpande swamp, the village was no more, its memory a
dark ooze seeping from the sides of the two hills. Grandpa's house and
the burial grounds were gone. So were Serenity's house, Stefano's
grand one and the nominal restaurants, casinos and supermarkets of
the youthful village. My favorite jackfruit tree was no more, cut to bits
by the bombs. There were hardly any returnees.

Aunt Tiida and Nakatu came to salvage the tattered memories of
their birthplace and early life but, horrified by the transience of what
they had believed to be eternal, fled to the safety of their homes.
Serenity came to see for himself what the cycles of history and war had
done, and what he could do about it. He too fled, with palms over his
eyes: the realization of the vengeful dreams of his youth horrified him.

The house of his nightmares was gone. Clan land and its exploiters were gone. His very own bachelor house, with its conquests and less savory memories, had also been obliterated. On his way out, he went to the place where the Fiddler used to live. The remains of the house were invisible, and he could only vaguely make out where his childhood refuge had been. Now he understood why the city and the towns were so swollen with people who, despite the terrible conditions, did not seem eager to respond to government calls to return to their areas. Many members of his trade union fell into the same category.

This time it was much easier to steal a truck or two filled with the cement intended for the aqueducts. The Reconstruction Committee in charge was weak because of the thinness of the population of returnees. Literacy among the committee members was low, and the honorable members got lost in the maze of mathematical calculations required. The records at the Rehab warehouse showed that ten trucks had been delivered. On the ground, only five had been received. Aqueducts were being built in Mpande swamp with less concrete than was required. The pirating pattern was the same, except that those involved in the syndicate had become greedier. I was outraged, and Lwendo appreciated my frustration. "No mercy this time," I told him. "If we get them, we bury them deep." He at first agreed, but then realized that this could be our last chance. He did not tell me directly. A few days later, he said, "Don't get carried away. Don't let feelings get in the way."

"What do you mean by that? My village got wiped out. Do you want me to sit back and watch?"

"That is not what I was saying."

"What the hell were you saying, then?"

"That this could be our lucky break. You know well that we can't keep on doing the same thing forever. This is our last time. The destruction of the village and the disappearance of the cement are omens. You are the village. It lives in you. The cement will never be recovered, and the criminals will probably walk once arrested. Better take the cash and go than let some policeman or detective blow it away on booze or pussy."

"No, not this time."

"Yes, this time."

Acting on a tip from our Radio Uganda man, who this time wanted to be paid much more—he claimed he was getting threatening letters, dead rats, headless geckos and such garbage on his front door and wanted to clear out—Lwendo got a jeep and a rifle, and we went to Jinja Road, behind the Radio Uganda building.

The house was a fabulous bungalow, hidden by a fence, facing a sprawling golf course and Kololo Hill. Our man was at home: a small, well-dressed, intelligent man who had made his money in the early eighties by speculating on the dollar. It was striking how ordinary these white-collar criminals looked. He might have been a staff member of Sam Igat Memorial College. He looked almost underfed, but he owned warehouses in Kikuubo and had business connections in London and Dubai.

He gave us what we wanted without much argument. It looked almost too easy.

After taking the money, we had to lie low. In the meantime, I took stock of my situation. I did not want to go back to SIMC, whatever happened. I could sit back and do Aunt Lwandeka's books while making up my mind about the future. I could travel: Where? Abroad: there were many young people leaving for Britain, Sweden, the United States and Germany to try their luck at odd jobs in the hope of earning enough money to build houses and buy cars. The trick was to ask for political asylum, since that was the only way they could secure the right to stay in the West. I had no plans to join their ranks. I couldn't bear the humiliation of the camps, especially because I could avoid it. Maybe I would go as a tourist.

The man we squeezed was no fool. He used his friends in high places to blow the whistle on us, and the padre finally got the news. He called Lwendo to his office one day and, like a father to an erring son, expressed deep disappointment. He said he had had very high hopes for Lwendo and could not understand why he had fallen prey to the hydras of bribery and corruption. Lwendo, like a prodigal son, kept his head down, as though offering his neck for decapitation. The padre, a man of not too many words who knew the temptation of money, said he would not lock him up. Instead, he was going to send him to work as a Rehabilitation officer in the north. In other words, Lwendo was being flung from the Garden of Eden into the fires of the harsh world outside. Already thinking of his escape, he accepted his punishment with a bowed head.

It was indeed Eden that he was being banished from. Living in the south, it was easy to forget the fighting raging in the north. True, big parts of the north had been conquered by the new government, but guerrilla-style fighting was still going on. A hard core of Obote fighters could not accept the fact that an army from the south had taken over power in the north. They tried to stir up the people, and when they failed, they attacked villages and terrorized the locals. Knowing the terrain well, they could move quickly, do damage and disappear before government forces could do something about it. It was ironic that after fighting a guerrilla war against northerner-dominated governments, the southerners were now involved in a similar predicament. And as the northerners had been scared to death in our forests and swamps, the southerners did not know what the dusty, harsh plains would reveal next time they searched for the elusive fighters; but unlike Obote soldiers, they were not allowed to torture civilians. Soldiers who were caught raping and pillaging got shot by firing squads, which made international human rights organizations holler. However, the government remained firm, and when a soldier raped or committed acts akin to those Obote soldiers had perpetrated in the Luwero Triangle, the death penalty remained a very likely punishment.

Lwendo trembled when he considered the dangers of working in a virtual war zone. His luck had held during the guerrilla war: Would it hold in the north, a region he did not know and feared like hell? He feared getting ambushed more than anything else. Lwendo also imagined himself in a Rehab Ministry van or truck, flying in the air on the wings of a land mine and losing his limbs. The thought of becoming handicapped for the rest of his life almost made him lose his mind.

As a government representative, he would have to bend over backward to oblige the people, because the government wanted the northern people behind it in order to avoid looking like a southerner-dominated force of occupation.

Lwendo told me of his banishment and asked me for advice. I didn't think he needed advice. He only wanted to hear his voice reflected in mine.

"Did you agree to go?" I asked.

"A soldier has to obey."

"But you don't have to. Drop out of the army."

"That is what I am thinking about, but in the meantime, I have to act as though I am committed to going north."

"Scary, eh!" I tried to make a joke of the situation.

"I would not want to be one of our boys fighting there. The army is extra strict on them in order to avoid vengeful atrocities on innocent civilians. I thought I had escaped all that mess, and now this bastard orders me to fly straight into that hell!"

I shook my head sadly.

"I would like you to do something for me," he said, looking me in the eye. He had not shaved for a week, and he looked scruffy. I am being asked to pay for the money we made, I thought sickly.

"Yes?" I said none too cheerfully.

"I would like you to accompany me to the north on a scouting mission."

"Are you mad? Do you want me to get killed?" The possibility loomed large of our vehicle rolling over a land mine that had been idly lying around for years. There were attacks by former Obote army brigands, meaner than ever because of the defeat and the hard times they had fallen on. I went over the map of northern Uganda in my mind. It was one thing to know the names of towns, the cash crops produced and what people did and fed on, but it was terra incognita in real terms. Beyond Lake Kyoga and the Nile River, every spot seemed to be full of brigands and hardened Obote fighters. "Do you want me to die?" I demanded.

Lwendo laughed hard, strangely. He was enjoying this bit, or he was just afraid that I would let him down. "Why are you so afraid of death?"

"I have eluded death all these years. Why do I have to go looking for it in the north?"

"That is putting it a bit too strongly. Most of the north has been pacified, except for some pockets of resistance. As it was here in the eighties, the fighting is confined to only a few areas. Elsewhere life is more or less normal." He was saying this to reassure himself, not me. I convinced myself that I had no choice. I wasn't feeling too loyal. I was just under a curious spell. I wanted to see part of the north for myself, and the truth was that I did not fear death, only the pain that might precede it.

Within seven days, we were on our way. I did not tell Aunt Lwandeka where I was going. She assumed that we were going to some Devastatated Area on some survey. We rode on a Ministry of Rehabilitation truck, which was part of a convoy taking supplies to the north. We had an army escort of four young boys around seventeen years of age. They were armed with AK-47 rifles, which reminded me of my nocturnal encounter with the Infernal Trinity. This was the first time in years that I had associated the attack directly with those ubiquitous guns. I looked at the curved magazines, the tapering muzzles and the shiny wooden bits and imagined the power that came from tickling the trigger. It wasn't that glamorous. The price was indeed too high. As I looked at these boys who were the age of my SIMC students, I wondered how many people they had killed, and what their future would be like. Did they think about the people they shot? Would they think about them as they grew older? What effect would it have on their lives? Would they become compulsive killers? Here they were, escorting us, looking as though they could piss on a land mine and disarm it. I estimated that at the time they entered the bush, they must have been no older than thirteen. They had grown up in the bush. How were they adjusting to barracks life? They loved the power they had. I could see the swagger. They had been promised things, but what would happen if those promises were not fulfilled? I was more afraid of these kid soldiers than of their adult counterparts. The older soldiers seemed corruptible, a bit more cognizant of the problems of life: you could negotiate if you had something to offer them. These kids seemed addicted to obeying orders.

I remembered the time I was the age they were when they joined the guerrillas, the time I was having so much trouble with Padlock and Serenity and their despotism. If I had had the chance, or if the circumstances had been right for joining the army, I would have become a soldier. Where would I be now? Rattling in my cupboard would have been a few actual skeletons. I felt lucky that things had not come to that. I might have killed many Padlocks in proxy while the real Padlock was eating and breathing and raising her shitters in the pagoda. Maybe I would have doubled back and tortured her to death, consuming each gasp of blood-soaked breath with gusto. Well . . .

There was not much talk on our truck, or on the others for that matter. Lwendo, particularly, wanted to maintain his distance from the kid soldiers. He always warned me to keep away from soldiers.

"It is not worth it. When the chips fall, a friend will shoot you if ordered to."

The other people on the truck also preferred to entertain their own thoughts. The boys, too, were afraid of the north and were trying to reassure themselves that the fear was in their minds. We were inside the former Luwero Triangle, speeding along the famous Gulu Road. I had never been this far before, and I was excited in a strange way. We stopped several times to piss, and to buy bananas, roasted corn on the cob, sweet potatoes and banana juice from peddlers along the road.

At Masindi, which was approximately at the latitude across the middle of the country where the old southern kingdoms came in contact with northern peoples in the seventeenth and eighteenth centuries, I started feeling that we were on foreign territory. I felt like a southern raider going north on some sinister mission. At the turn of the century, our grandfathers had come this far to help spread British colonial rule. Now we were on our way to see if the north and the south could live together after all that had happened. Lango District, a plains region, was just a river away. Its most famous son, Milton Obote, was seeking refuge in some foreign country, well away from the troubles he had caused the area and all of Uganda. Almost thirty years ago, he had left these harsh plains, crossed to the south like a true raider and, manipulating a political system riddled with faults, arrogance and ignorance, captured the biggest booty: leadership of Uganda. Now he had hung up his guns and his boots, leaving his people to their own devices. I tried to see what he had done for them. There was not much evidence of anything.

The ubiquitous green of the south had gone, giving way to open, dry land of short, sparse grass, puny trees and endless skies. It was hot and harsh here, and just looking at the dry, bare soil made me thirstier. The sun pounded down directly from the sky, without anything to catch it, and concentrated its fury on the land and the people. Winds picked up the dust and spun it in the sky in seemingly playful whirlwinds. This was tough country, where food and water and life had to be fought for every inch of the way.

We had some scary moments when one truck in the convoy broke down. While the problem was being fixed, everyone was on edge, as though brigands were going to surface from the earth and mow us down. The boy soldiers no longer looked so confident. I could see my friend Lwendo sweating hard under his armpits and looking this way and that, as though the place were haunted by vampires.

We finally arrived at Lira Town. It felt as if we had just been air-dropped there. The town seemed to have mushroomed from the ground, isolated, open on all sides. It was just like any other African town: the frugal facilities, the smallness of the building structures under the open skies, the cheerful disorder. From here Kampala, with all its defects, looked like paradise. As in any war zone, there was a considerable army presence, and we were warned never to go out at night. The soldiers tried to look relaxed, their paranoid tendencies on a tight leash. The feeling of nakedness and exposure was overwhelming. After our forests and tall vegetation, this place made you feel prey to unknown forces. That feeling was increased by the presence of displaced persons in the town. Seeing their searching faces and tired expressions made you more aware that danger was lurking out there, waiting for the right moment to snap or to explode.

Part of the convoy continued deep into Acholi District, with Gulu its final destination. We watched it take off the following morning, and felt lucky that we were staying behind.

The local people, many of whom were struggling to lead their lives, scared Lwendo. The displaced people, in their search for redemption and peace of mind, made him jumpy. He imagined them pulling triggers at him, but they had no guns, not even spears or pangas. He saw, hiding among them, rebels and rebel sympathizers who would tip their friends off to come and slaughter us. It evidently did not pay for a soldier to have a brain: Lwendo's worked overtime, plaguing his days and nights with soldierly nightmares. Local rehabilitation officials spoke English, shared information about places where help was needed and were friendly, reassuring. It was in the people's interests to keep up good relations with Rehabilitation officers, because they needed all the help they could get. I trusted them; Lwendo did not. At night he told me a little about the trenches he had slept in. "The trench would turn into a large cunt in which we swam with fire burning in our loins."

"What would you do then?" I said, curious. He gave his combat stories in such measly doses.

"Fuck anything with a cunt," he said and burst into a hard, loud laugh.

"Anything!"

"I tell you, those are moments of madness, of crazed urges," he said, biting his lower lip meaningfully. "The ugliest female would look like a wet-dream goddess. I think some people could even fuck dogs."

At this we both laughed. I slapped him on the back, and he returned the favor.

"Those are flashes of states civilians will never know. The disintegration of consciousness into component parts and the reassembling of the parts in split-second intervals!"

"Did it make you feel special?"

"I felt I had been to hell and back all in one bittersweet moment. Time travel or some other magic. I felt special, a cut above every civilian."

"And how about when—"

"Oh, it made the actual shooting pale in significance. Here you were, waiting, fearing, and then the moment comes. It is a sort of anti-climax, and you want it repeated: the terrible fear, the loin fire, the climactic anti-climactic shooting, the target falling. Punching is more satisfactory, physically speaking. The thing I remember most is the gun smoke and the explosions."

Aha, I wanted to say. Should I ask him how many people he had shot? And where? He saw me looking at him stealthily, and knew I was evaluating him, marking him up or down on my scale, maybe comparing his words with those of others I had heard before. He smiled, and burst out laughing. I thought he was going to volunteer and give me the numbers, but he did not, and I failed to find a way to ask without being too invasive. I was also protecting myself. I did not want to look at him when he became angry and think, He killed so many people, what if he snapped and popped me too?

The return journey was less scary, the landscape more familiar. Lwendo had already made his decision: he was going to resign. He only had to bribe an army doctor to discharge him. He had a history of stomach trouble and piles. The former would become an ulcer, the latter bleeding sores in need of surgery.

■　■　■

Since the end of the guerrilla war, a mysterious disease which slimmed people to the bones had started killing in big numbers. Judging by the sneaky way it operated—recurrent fevers, rashes, blisters—it looked like witchcraft. Many people went to the Vicar and to other witch doctors for consultation. It had started in southwestern Uganda, in the remote Rakai District, about fifty kilometers from Masaka. The theory was that this witchcraft was punishment meted out by Tanzanian smugglers who had been cheated by their Ugandan counterparts in the seventies and eighties when smuggling was rife in those marshy areas. Business being the pigsty it was, and for lack of a better explanation, many people bought the theory. But then, what about those people dying in the city?

Not long after, the disease got a medical name—AIDS—but remained Slim to us. It gave a completely new slant to the theory that war is always followed by other disasters. World War I had its Spanish flu. This was our meaner, more devastating version of it. It slowly ground the most productive people to dust and burdened old people with the millstone of raising orphaned grandchildren. It struck at the heart of the social fabric and stretched to breaking point the tenuous bonds of extended family. It made towns quake with the fevers of arrested development, and the villages sob with the woes of unfulfilled potential. It made cities retch with the talons of unassuageable pain, and the villages writhe with the stench of green-black diarrhea.

At first most Slim victims were strangers, but inexorably disaster came nearer to home, and a string of calamities struck Uncle Kawayida's household with apocalyptic vehemence. We were all stunned, especially yours truly, who admired the man for conjuring banal things into the wonderful stories of my village days.

It was strange that his trials and tribulations seemed linked with the departure and return of Indians: his fortune had come when they left; his fall began when they returned.

Uncle Kawayida was the first of Grandpa's offspring to own a car. He had always had a business instinct. When he was a boy, he used to sell bananas, sugarcane, pancakes and boiled eggs at school. Whenever there was a school day or a district inter-school football competition or other athletic meeting, he would bring his mother's cooking gear and help her with the preparations and the sale at rush hours. It was this early exposure that gave him the edge. When Amin came to power, he realized that times had changed. He sold his motorcycle—the blue-bellied eagle—borrowed money from a friend and raised enough cash to buy a piece of land in Masaka. By the time the hammer fell and the Indian exodus became a reality, he was going around town looking for the best business prospects for a man of his capabilities.

He knew that he could work very hard, especially if he was doing something he loved. He was looking for a simple business that demanded local input, a local market and quick returns. He looked at the Indian shops and the few African shops in between, and realized that he did not like being cooped up in a shop with dead merchandise, worried to death about the month's profits. During his travels as a meter reader, he had explored the surrounding areas extensively. He had been greatly impressed by the swampy settlements of Rakai, especially by Kyotera town, which he imagined to be the upgraded version of the village between Mpande and Ndere hills. On selected weekends, he would ride to Kyotera with friends from the area to drink and to watch the long-distance truck drivers who stopped there on their way to Tanzania, Rwanda and Zambia. Sometimes he caught them on their way back, headed for Kenya, the great road taking them to Masaka, Kampala, Jinja, Tororo, Malaba and Mombasa on the Indian Ocean coast. Most of the drivers were either Somalis or Ethiopians, thin, tough men who seemed oblivious to distance or time. They were like safari ants, going back and forth. At Kyotera they camped, cooking, washing, repairing their vehicles, before continuing on their great journeys. Goods, legal and illegal, exchanged hands across the borders, Ugandans selling to Tanzanians and vice versa.

Isolated in the swamps, Kyotera town had given Uncle Kawayida a sense of connection with the big world. Several times he thought about settling there and joining the cross-border trade of the seventies and early eighties. One could take a chance on gold or diamonds from Zaire. One could deal in fish or clothes or shoes or jewelry. At the time, though, the idea of striking out on his own had scared him.

One late afternoon, while he was on his way home, he heard turkeys croaking and preening inside a closed compound. It struck him: poultry farming was what he was looking for. During the shopping frenzy that saw the Indians off, Uncle Kawayida bought a secondhand pickup van which the desperate owner had decided to set on fire. His friends jeered at him, saying the van would collapse carrying only two turkeys. He laughed. Using his land as collateral, he borrowed some money and hired a place which he filled with feed before going on the hunt for turkeys.

At the end of his efforts, he had little money left, but enough resources to keep the birds going for a year. He installed troughs and lights, and the birds ate day and night. During office hours, his wife took over. When he returned home, he cleaned the troughs, stirred the sawdust to cover the droppings, refilled the troughs and proudly watched his birds.

By the time the euphoria induced by the departing Indians had subsided and people had begun jostling for the shops, he was selling his birds to hotels around town. By the time most traders had settled into their new businesses, he was already experimenting with growth formula to make the birds grow faster and heavier. Soon the first batch of broiler chicks arrived.

That was the start of his prosperity. He expanded his broiler and turkey operations. The walls vibrated with the calls of frustrated turkeys which could not skip the fence to go and terrorize the women who passed outside their house. The pens filled with the tolerable stench of chicken shit, and at peak hours the rafters and the iron sheets rattled with the calls of chickens competing with one another for feed. The market for chickens and turkeys, contrary to prediction, expanded because very few individuals had taken the risk of investing in poultry farming when the old farms collapsed.

The journeys to buy supplies and sell birds liberated another trait in Uncle. He felt oppressed by the need to multiply and spread himself around. A single child, he felt he was one of a kind, threatened with extinction, impelled to reproduce himself. As though intent on imitating his late father-in-law, he went after beautiful women in town with the fever of obsession. Uncle's reproductive rate, however, left much to be desired. It led some to say that his wife had bewitched him. They overlooked the strong possibility that he was dealing with worldly-wise women who knew the secrets of drinking azure blue, taking overdoses of aspirin or inserting bicycle spokes up birth canals to induce termination of pregnancy. They may also have been experts at tying their cervical necks, eating pills or going to the likes of the Vicar for traditional birth-regulating herbs. Uncle Kawayida never looked into that; he was an eternal optimist in that sense. Each time he hoped to win. For all his troubles, he produced only three bastard children, all girls. His wife had four girls already.

Uncle's wife had grown up around children and did not find it hard to do a good job raising all those girls. She sometimes cried because she could not have a son. She envied Padlock for having so much of what she craved: sons. She could not help idealizing sons in her daydreams, but much as she called upon all her gods, sons evaded her yearning womb.

At one time she became consumed with the fear that one of her sisters was going to give her husband a son. How could she trust any of those girls? She thought about putting spies on them, but could not trust her would-be spies. She was her own best spy. She invited her two suspect sisters to stay with her in order to calm her mind with the reassurance that under her watchful eye, they would not commit the ultimate outrage. A son from an outsider was more acceptable; a son from either Naaka or Naaki would give her a heart attack. The girls, unaware of things, could not believe their luck. How generous and nice their half-sister had become!

Barren women and women seeking to influence the sex of their next child receive and take a lot of advice. Uncle Kawayida's wife was advised that the key might be in the diet. She took up eating in the hope that her body's constitution would change favorably and aid her in her quest for a son. She went to bed with food on her mind, and woke up with food steaming in her thoughts. As a consequence, she started expanding. Her body swelled like the turkeys they sold. Her head grew smaller, and her legs labored under the new burden of her weight. Her ankles swelled. She started wheezing and sweating profusely at all times, and especially during the act of trying to make a baby boy. She employed a housegirl and, left with less to do and so much to eat, swelled even more. At first people said it was money, well-being, but eventually they realized that it was a disease, a burden.

She asked her husband to build a family house. The money from the barracks took care of that. Entry into the new house came with another worry: heart disease, which was common in her mother's family. It was at around that time that Uncle had his first son, with Naaka. She had moved out, because her sister had monitored her so much that she had become disgusted with her hospitality and decided to pay her back by falling in love with Uncle. Uncle swore Naaka to secrecy, afraid that hearing of the birth of the first son in the house might indeed give his wife a heart attack.

In the meantime, Naaki, who had stayed behind and entered the new house with the family, got enchanted by Uncle's stories, his easy manner and generosity. She followed him round the house with her eyes. She polished his shoes and smelled his socks. She ironed his clothes and made his bed. She made him snacks. She lingered in his presence. Her eyes misted over when he entered the room, but he resisted her charms for some time, even going to the extent of trying to fix her up with one of his cronies. For the girl, there was no turning back. She was determined to give him the greatest gift she could offer: her love and the promise of a son. Uncle caved in. They did it in front of the turkeys when he went to see them for the last time at night and she sneaked out of the house to meet him. Uncle and Naaki took their love to the chicken house too; the stupid broilers were too busy eating and drinking to mind. When Uncle's wife sent her sister to the shops, they did it in the famous old van, and in an unmarried crony's house. For fear of rumors, they never went to hotels, but did it in the dressing rooms behind the football pavilion where Uncle, a sponsor, had free access. Uncle stopped philandering. The sisters had him under their spell. He felt happy to be inside their loving triangle. The secrecy, the cunning, the planning involved, spoke to his mind. He loved it. He loved wearing one hat with his wife and another with the two sisters. One moment he was concerned with his wife's heart murmur; the next he was playing, laughing, romping with Naaki, or Naaka and his son. For a long time, he felt he was the happiest man alive.

At the start of the eighties, guerrilla war began far away in the Luwero Triangle. Throughout this time, Uncle was having the best of three worlds: his wife's, Naaka's and Naaki's too. He had little to complain about. His business was running, his wife had accepted herself and he was having children with the two young women.

Around 1985, the guerrillas came and assimilated the town into their sphere of influence. Peace and security reigned. Just like the Obote II soldiers, to whom he had also sold birds, the guerrillas never bothered him. He had long ago stopped going to Kyotera. The town was now in the grip of a bone-grinding nightmare. People were dying of a mysterious disease, the so-called *muteego*—an incurable, evil spell which had the power to kill the perpetrator and his entire family. He was happy that he had not joined the cross-border smuggling frenzy, and that there was no chance that any Tanzanian would want to inflict the muteego spell on him.

It was too late for the town that used to remind Uncle of home. People were dying daily; there would be burials in several places in a single village. Nowadays burials were conducted quickly. Gone were the long eulogies of the past. Orphans were multiplying. Parents were burying their sons and daughters and mourning a looming lonely old age.

There was no one more worried than Uncle Kawayida. The gradual return of the Indians passed him by. It all began with Naaki's third child. It came prematurely, very underweight, and died of diarrhea. At the burial, it looked like a baby rabbit and had a blue membrane that passed for its skin. Uncle had never seen anything more disgusting. Then Naaki, a woman in her twenty-second year, whom he loved as he had dreaded his mother's buckteeth, started darkening, with very black patches marking her skin. The itchy patches began on her thighs, proceeded down her legs, climbed to her chest and back and then infested her arms. She resorted to wearing long-sleeved shirts and trousers, scratching herself and dousing her body in ointment. Every change in her appearance cut Uncle like a razor. Feeling for another had never been so costly to him. The affliction threatened to devalue all the great times they had had and to poison love with doubt, regret and terror. He watched the woman become a recluse, a hostage to her house and fears. The hide-and-seek games they had played in front of raging turkeys and feeding broilers haunted them with a vengeance. Naaki ate every concoction every witch doctor prescribed, but in vain. Each time she sank deeper into the morass of deterioration and etiolation. Six months later, she dried up and died.

Uncle's brothers-in-law held him responsible for the death of their sister. They strongly believed that he had been dishonest in his dealings with Tanzanian customers, and had sold them sick turkeys and given the proceeds to their sister. They spread rumors that Uncle Kawayida had made his money from smuggling under the guise of raising birds. "Birds have never made anyone that prosperous. He must have been smuggling gold on the side." They barred him from attending the funeral. One threw a rotten pawpaw at him, cursing him for what he had done to their sister.

However, the disaster that struck the late Kavule's family was bigger than anything Uncle's mind could dream of immortalizing in story form. Within three years, twelve of the twenty-one unmarried beauties had succumbed to the slimming disease, making people wonder how many men had been ensnared in the fatal dragnet of doomed copulation. Four of the ten sons followed their sisters to the grave.

Uncle was devastated. The spotlight was firmly on him: When was he going? Was he sorry? Who was going to look after his children? He faced his trials like a man and went about his business as usual. He grew thinner than he had ever been. The demon of worry terrorized his home with diabolical abandon. His wife succumbed to its wiles. Naaka was still alive, but was she going to be the thirteenth female victim from the same family? His wife now believed that she had also been infected. How unfair it all seemed to her! The more Uncle thinned, the more weight she lost. People started saying that she was next in line. At night, when the lights went out, the demon of worry took over. Kawayida had no peace of mind: awake, death stared him in the face; asleep, the ghosts of the dead and the living dead snatched meaningful rest from his eyes.

To my amazement, years passed. The true nature of the disease became public knowledge. I began thinking that Uncle had a freak chance, some special gene. In reality, it was worry that had been torturing him, not the virus. Naaka was also still alive! Gradually, people realized that worry was as bad as the real thing. Now even the real victims survived longer by keeping the devil of worry at bay, but why did Naaka survive while Naaki died? How did the medical people explain Uncle's survival? Was some other man involved in the tragedy? Or did some people have special resistance? Now I hoped that I, Aunt Lwandeka, Lwendo and all the people I knew had this special gift to survive the viral plague.

In the meantime, Uncle's business had lost steam. He now encouraged people to eat his chicken because he was a survivor. Some people believed him, and he attracted others with discounts. People drowned his birds in cauldrons of soup, licked the last drop and cracked the last bone, and they felt better. A new market had opened. They said it was chicken soup that had saved his family, and that it would save theirs too. His back became bent with overwork, his lungs clogged with the sawdust from the pens. He worked harder than ever before. His ambition now was to save Kyotera, the whole of Rakai and Masaka, the entire country. He built another house for his birds. He worked so hard that he barely had time to change his overalls. The doctor warned him that he was going to kill himself in no time. "A good soldier dies on the battlefield," Kawayida replied, and smiled. He collapsed in the chicken pen one afternoon. Chickens gathered round their master to wake him up: the troughs were emptying fast. The birds were hurting their beaks by pecking at the wooden bottoms. They scratched and pecked at their master, who remained motionless, frozen in his ambition. They pecked out his eyes and burned his skin with the heat of their best shit, in vain. His wife did not miss him at first. She thought he was at Naaki's looking after her children, who still loved him. Later she found him in the pen, drenched in chicken shit. Her lamentation almost drove the birds mad. She had become a sonless widow.

I missed the man terribly. I had visited him several times during his darkest hours. I was impressed by his courage and tough-mindedness.

"Humor is man's best friend. It sleeps and wakes with him," he told me when I marvelled at his capacity to shrug at the world.

"Why aren't you defending yourself? Why let your in-laws treat you like that?"

"They lost their sister in addition to the many others. It is their right to be angry at whoever they want."

"Maybe she had another man," I suggested hotly.

"Never speak evil of the dead," he cautioned. "I loved her dearly, like I love her two sisters. I am among the chosen few who find true love in three different women. I really enjoyed myself. Life is just balancing itself out, son."

"If you insist," I replied reluctantly.

"Son, do whatever you want in life," he said, touching me on the shoulder, "but know when it is over. And never bicker about the price."

Customers were waiting for him. He dismissed me. It was the last time I saw him. Nine months later he was dead.

Lwendo did what he had vowed to do: he resigned from the army. He bribed an army doctor who recommended that he be discharged for health reasons. We celebrated the occasion with a drinking party. For a month or so we roamed the city, enjoying the freedom of not having to look for work. We would meet toward midday, go to a favorite restaurant on Kampala Road, eat, drink and watch the city.

"I am going to open a carpentry workshop and hire a manager to run it. I can't stay there all the time," he said. "I have to hustle some money from these returning Indians. I need to do something intellectual."

"How?"

"Well, they won't find the necessary papers to reclaim their property waiting for them. It is a mess in those offices, and many Indians are afraid to go there. Many fear they will be attacked or robbed or exploited, which plays into my hands. They need people to chase their documents and contact people for them. I have the expertise."

"Sounds like you will be working harder than at the Rehabilitation office."

"I can pick and choose my clients," he said smugly.

"Then what?"

"Look at the streets. What do you see? Haven't you seen the hundreds of Development Aid Organization vehicles all over the place? They are like sharks following the smell of blood. Many come here but don't know how to chase work permits. I can do it for them, as long as they are ready to pay."

It was a brilliant idea, actually. Peace was indeed a bringer of foreigners: during Amin's time, you hardly saw a white face on the street. During Obote II, whites started coming, tentatively. Now it was a wave: tourists with backpacks, white women in mini-skirts, men in shorts and boots, groups in tourist vans, Japanese men in business suits and more. The city was abuzz with American charismatic preachers who addressed frenzied crowds planted with preprogrammed fainters and swooners. They spiced the show up with spectacular miracles in which the lame broke their crutches, the blind ground their spectacles into the floorboards, and the deaf, who had nothing to destroy, shouted like lunatics with ants up their assholes. Some preachers promised to cure the viral plague by the power of Jesus; others promised to eradicate every affliction from the face of the earth. For the first time, there were vigils where Pentecostals and Baptists congregated and prayed and sang all night long under the watchful eye of video cameras. The traditional churches found themselves in competition with lay preachers in expensive suits who jumped, danced and rolled on the floor for effect. The era of televangelism had dawned, and the old padres, stiff as arthritics, were worried because they had been caught snoring and left in the blocks.

Fortune hunters—seekers of gold, copper, diamonds, red mercury (illegally dug out of meteorological towers), animal hides, rhino horn, parrots from Sese Island; merchants of inferior goods; toxic waste dumpers; passport and dollar counterfeiters—all came disguised in one form or other. Africa was represented by the flamboyant Senegalese, who came dressed in gold-thread *boubous* with wide trousers and big watches. They bought legal and illegal merchandise, and exchanged both real and counterfeit dollars.

Lwendo was right: money was there to be made.

I did not play any part in his new plans. They were too peripatetic for my liking. I also knew the mess he was getting into. The story in most offices was the same. The filing system was horrible. Documents had been heaped on top of each other for years like tobacco leaves at a market. Everyone who touched them had to be offered something for his trouble. That was how the system worked. There was sense in it, too, since the salaries were horrible and everyone knew that the Indians had come to make money. If one did not want to pay, as some Indians did not at first, one could stay in one's hotel for weeks without anything getting done; but once money changed hands, and somebody's lunch and supper were assured, then the piles of dusty files and loose paper were ungummed for the first time in fifteen years, and one got what one wanted.

Lwendo fed me stories of his adventures with Indian returnees. He often accompanied them to inspect their property. Some were moved to tears. Others were angry that the edifices were run-down. Most were glad, because they already had a game plan. It had performed miracles for those who had arrived before them, and it still worked: renovation, rent-hiking and eviction. The city was slowly washing its face. The rust-streaked roofs got a gloss. The old pirate haunts took on the look of cherished sea chests bursting with fresh consumer life. What had come on the wings of piracy was leaving by the same means.

In the meantime, the brigadier—who was actually a major in the new army, although friends addressed him by his old title—again, officially, proposed to Aunt Lwandeka. One evening, she asked me whether she should accept the proposal. What did she expect me to say? I told her to accept if she was happy with it.

"I have already accepted," she said, beaming. For many weeks, our life was turned upside down. The impending wedding consumed all our time and energy. I was exhausted from travelling to buy a thousand and one things, to inform relatives and her friends, to do this and that.

The women in the area took over the cooking, cleaning and caring for her children. Everywhere one turned, there were people eating, drinking, singing, arguing, ironing, bringing in or carrying out things. We woke up early and went to bed late. The affair became bigger than it should have been because the women of the area decided to celebrate liberation from past oppression on the same day. In her joy, Aunt had allowed people to hijack her day and turn it into a community affair.

The couple got married at Christ the King Church in Kampala. Mbale, Padlock, Kasawo, Serenity and Tiida were all present. Aunt was as happy as I had ever seen her, radiant through her layers of tulle. The makeup and the occasion had made her look very young, her naturally very smooth skin glowing. I caught Aunt Kasawo saying, "Who would have thought!" The tone betrayed her—it was punctured by too much envy. She was digesting the fact that she was the only one of the trio of sisters who had never wed. She saw Pangaman and his successors as vampires who had sucked the life out of her without even honoring her with an official ceremony. She fantasized regularly about turning down a marriage proposal, but no man had ever put himself in the position to be rejected by her, and the one she was seeing currently had made it clear that marriage had never crossed his mind. "I would buy a pickup van or build a good house with the money people waste on weddings," he always said. His reaction to this wedding had been no less cynical: "The government tells us that there is no money for reconstructing the country, yet soldiers are wedding every Sunday." Kasawo felt that her love life had been a potholed plain with one or two molehills but no real high points. She felt the hole at her center palpitate with unrequited ambition.

The brigadier's army friends attended in big numbers, and the bridal pair walked through a glittering arch of swords on their way in and out of the church. The place was filled with light and music and the smells of incense and well-tended bodies.

The most redeeming thing about this wedding was that the reception took place at the Sheraton Hotel. I had nothing to do except enjoy myself. I was happy for Aunt. She seemed to have it all: money, fame, power, love. For a girl who had come to the city with nothing, she had risen to the top the hard way. She could now snap her fingers and get what she wanted. She was thirty-six, a stage of life when most of her contemporaries were bogged down in dreary, diaper-ridden lives, and yet she was just getting married. And not to just anybody: the brigadier was a good-looking, presentable, powerful man. He reminded me of my former rector, and I could not help wondering whether he did not run a small spy organization. He was a mystery to me. Despite his dating Aunt for some time, I had never come to know him. Since Aunt did most of the travelling, we had met only during the preparations for the wedding. "I hear good things about you," he had said on two separate occasions. Beyond that, he was a closed book. They both looked very happy as they cut the cake. As they distributed bits of it, I thought about Jo Nakabiri.

True to her word, she had refused to attend. I was sad about what had happened to us. I wondered what it might have felt like to see her in tulle. Jo and I hardly knew what to do with each other now. Strangely enough, our relationship had etiolated with the knowledge that we were linked by blood. I did not love her as a sister, I did not feel she was my sister, and my status as a brother had been compromised in both our eyes. To her, I had become as strange as the man who united us: Serenity. She was now struggling to resurrect her school from the ruins of war. The last I heard, the government had allocated the school iron sheets, cement and other necessities.

Food was in abundance, and I ate my fill. I drank a lot, partly to drown out thoughts of Jo, partly to celebrate Aunt's luck. Lwendo did his fair share of demolition work. I could see his girlfriend eyeing him furtively, probably imagining herself in tulle beside him. I doubted that he would ever wed her—ten years' difference in age seemed a bit on the high side—but since I had never taken much interest in their romantic life, I stopped myself from further speculation.

To get away from the anti-climactic post-nuptial atmosphere, I resorted to drifting, roaming the city, visiting the taxi park, as I had done of old. My favorite spot was now crowded with hawkers behind wooden stalls on which they displayed baby wear, shoes, plastic basins, cheap jewelry, anything. The park was fuller now, with more vans, more travellers, more fortune-tellers, more rat poison sellers, though fewer snake charmers. The snakes and their bosses had returned to the nooks of the Triangle from where they had come.

I went to the pagoda: it had been renovated and sprayed with a cream color. I thought of Lusanani and me, feigning sex and getting whacked by Padlock. I thought about all the madness that had gone on inside those four walls, especially the Miss Singer letter, and I felt both happy and sad. What kind of life had gone on here before Serenity and Padlock moved in? What kind of life were the Indians who now occupied the pagoda leading? It looked as if Serenity and Padlock and their brood had never been here. Hajj Gimbi's house had suffered the same fate—old memories washed away with new paint and glittering fittings. The little decorative dragons on the awnings seemed to have come alive and guzzled every strand of the past. I left.

An idea that kept me occupied was a plan to rebuild the burial site under the jackfruit tree where I had spent so many childhood hours looking at Mpande Hill. I bought cement and got someone to do the job. We set off. The aqueducts had been built, and vehicles crossed the swamp without drowning. There were more returnees now, but I did not know any of them. They were mostly from the youthful part of the village. Life was boring, to say the least. Accommodations were bad. Food was deficient. Many people ate posho and beans as they waited for their matooke, sweet potatoes, cassava and millet to grow. When I lay down to sleep at night, I felt disconnected, floating like a piece of wood on a lake. I knew that this was my last time here. So many ruins, so little life. I had swallowed the village, its spirit, every worthy bit of it, and my job was to rebuild it elsewhere. I was glad when the builder poured water on the completed cement graves in order to give them a sheen. It was time to leave.

■ ■ ■

Things took another turn. Many people around the city were dying of Slim. Aunt consoled the bereaved and attended funerals and sometimes organized transport for those who had to be buried in the villages of their birth. One day I overheard a group of market women talking about her. At first, they did not recognize me. When they did, they stopped abruptly and pretended they had been discussing somebody else. "She does not look well . . . our leader does not look well," one of them had said time and again, to the mutual agreement of her somber audience. I knew what they meant, though it was hard to accept it. A woman who had got married less than a year ago! I went to visit her with bees buzzing in my ears. To my relief, I did not notice anything different about her. Her skin was still as smooth as ever. She had not lost any weight, and she was in a very good mood. On the second visit, though, I found her in bed with a fever. It had tortured her for a whole week.

"Don't worry about me, son," she said, smiling. "I will be all right."

Had I looked too worried? She was sitting on her bed, a gown over her nightie, a cup in her hand. Her dark tan knee peeping out of the gown looked luscious. She talked about her business plans, the women's group, her children. She asked me to stop what I was doing and become her business manager. I remembered the man burned by the oil drum at the now defunct Boom-boom Brewery. He had recovered, and nothing had come of his supporters' threats, but I did not like dealing with workers anymore. I wanted freedom to roam and drift. I did not have to work, thanks to the little fortune I had accumulated. Yet I did not want to disappoint Aunt. She had taken me in during my hour of need: Wasn't I supposed to help her now that she needed me? Given the fact that I no longer taught at SIMC, Aunt could not understand why I was not taking up her offer. The truth was that I feared being left with a millstone round my neck when she became too sick to supervise her affairs. But how was I to communicate that to her?

"We will discuss it when you become better."

"I am already feeling better, son," she said, setting the cup down. She reached for a file lying on the bedside table. Healthy or not, there was so much work to do. She used to say that she wanted to give up politics, yet now she seemed to be sinking deeper and deeper into it. Should I remind her? I resisted the urge.

A few weeks later, I returned and found her in bed. A monstrous pimple had attacked her right cheek, which had swollen to the size of a fist. She looked deformed, tortured, scared. I was chilled to the bone. This whirlwind of a woman seemed embattled. What was the brigadier thinking and saying about all this? She did not mention him, which was strange, but then, she had been independent all her life. This time around, words were hard to find. She seemed to be thinking about what I had to be thinking about her. She told me about the fevers and the paralysis in her neck, which had subsided. "I sweat like a hunter," she said.

"Have you been to the doctor this week?"

"Yes. He did some blood tests. He told me not to worry."

The pimple disappeared as mysteriously as it had come; she got well again and started working. People were talking. She had lost some weight, but with good food, she regained it and looked her normal trim self again.

The next attack was around the waist: people called it "the belt of death." From the waistline up to the middle of the stomach, skin lifted as if burned. It burst and formed blisters and sores. It was one of the ugliest things I had ever seen. I got goose bumps just looking at it, and felt my skin crawling like a string of worms. She could have got help in time, but she was so ashamed of the belt that she decided to treat it with ointment and pills in the hope that it would disappear. It did not. By the time she saw the doctor, it was too late. The doctor could only treat the sores. She could hardly sleep, and when she did, she woke up to discover that cloth had bitten deep into her sores. It was a no-win situation which carried on for weeks on end. She shrunk a little bit more this time. Eventually she got well again and started to work. It was like a game.

The fevers returned in full force. They made her shiver and her teeth chatter. Her sweat soaked through the sheets to the bottom of the mattress. Her skin was like a sieve, letting go of the fluids she took in. She shrunk more visibly now. Diarrhea came, burned sores in her rectum and never let go. By this time, her urine had become a mixture of red and yellow.

"Don't cry for me," she said one day. "Take care of yourself and your brothers."

Matters moved from bad to worse. She refused to go to the hospital. All the shames of her past gushed back. She became a sinner earning her rightful punishment for straying and rebelling for so long. She became so ashamed of herself that she could hardly bear to look in the mirror. She hated the burden of her fame and influence. When she locked the door to her room, the whole world invaded. She could see some people laughing at her, some sympathizing, some pitying her, some totally indifferent. All the people she had worked with at the market, in the movement, in the war, were there. Her parents and brothers and sisters never left her side. As the first person in the family to catch the plague, she could not bear the shame.

The brigadier took her away for some time and hired nurses to look after her, but she felt like a fish out of water; she wanted to return to her house. She was brought back one night, and she did not leave the house again. The house stank with the heat of fever and the fumes of green-black diarrhea when she became too weak to wash her things. At the same time, she refused all help. When the few people she wanted to see dropped in, she loaded the air with bottled perfumes and hot incense, and from behind the curtain, she said firmly that everything was fine. The fire in her bowels and the talons in her flesh were nothing compared with the raging inferno in her brain. She could no longer bear to look at her children: she felt she had betrayed and shamed and stigmatized them forever. She would hear them moving round the house, handling pans with great care, running the tap as quietly as possible, and burn with sorrow. She no longer prepared their food for fear that she might revolt them or pass on to them her horrible disease. She wished they could bang the pans and break the cups and run the taps full blast and play loud music. She wished they could piss on their beds and shit in front of her and vomit in her lap as of old. But now only her stenches rattled the roof and terrorized the ventilators. Now the children tiptoed round the house as though a leopard were lurking behind the cupboard. These new changes made her burn with the caustic fires of regret. In her chosen solitude, she wished she had been conventional and malleable enough to marry early and lead an obscure life and meet a banal death. She would close her eyes and wish she were the Virgin Mary flying to heaven without leaving a trace of her life on earth. She passionately wanted to erase herself from the face of the earth, from the annals of the village, from the heads of all who knew her. She could see her grave next to the refurbished ones of her parents, and wished she could just disappear through the roof and strike everyone dumb with disbelief. She was haunted by the feeling that she had let everyone down. All the evils of guilt the parish priest and her parents had inculcated in her invaded and smothered her in their sulfurous blaze.

The next time I went to see her, she refused to open the door. She had already sent the children to their fathers. She was determined to go through her last days on her own. From behind closed doors and curtains, she said that I should understand. She wanted me to remain with a certain image of her: "Son, I am a skeleton out of the Church's devil books."

"I don't mind even if you looked like the Devil himself."

"I never did anything right," she said dryly.

"You have helped countless people. You fought for freedom, for common good. You sacrificed yourself in many ways. What more could you have done?"

"All that does not matter, son."

"It is what really matters. Am I hearing you, or is it somebody else speaking?"

"Maybe I am losing my mind, son."

"I am going to get an axe and break this door down. I have already contacted your best friend, Teopista. She is going to help you personally. First we have to take you to the doctor."

She did not object to this woman; she had come from the same village, and both families knew each other well.

"No, I am not going back to the doctor. Not with all those people watching."

"They are going to die one day; why do you worry so much about them? We will cover you up and walk you to the car."

I kept remembering the red-ink-patch day and my belief that Padlock was bleeding to death. The thought that Aunt was oozing to death almost paralyzed me. Why wasn't she blaming anyone? She believed she was responsible for everything. Looking at all this misery, Dad's family history of dying violent deaths seemed glorious. It seemed more meaningful than this diabolical, slow disintegration of everything one has been. Faced with the decomposition of beauty, the eclipsing of good memories, the trashing of fortitude and the disintegration of dignity in a pool of futile suffering, any other death seemed better than this torture rack of poisoned afflictions.

It was total mayhem. Padlock and all the rest of the family arrived in force. Padlock looked haunted by her own prophecy. She firmly believed that God had spoken through her, although the physical deterioration of her sister shocked her. Kasawo was moved too, but she was more interested in what was going to become of Aunt's business affairs. She started interrogating me about a hundred and one things. She seemed to believe that I had plundered Aunt's safe, bank account and treasure box. I did not like it, but the fight had been taken out of me. I bent with the wind. I wanted to extract myself from the whole grisly situation, but first I had to see this through.

In her last days, Aunt dreamed and talked many times about snakes. She would scream that her bed was full of snakes, and that a big snake had entered her mouth and was swallowing her intestines. Her helper would stroke her and reassure her that there were no snakes anywhere in the house. It was painful to watch. The woman I had once desired, spied on through a keyhole and felt protective about had gone, leaving behind a skeleton barely covered by rubbery skin. Her eyes were floating partridge eggs. Her nose had shrunken; her lips had tightened like rubber bands around her mouth. The neck was gone, the vertebrae protruding. The arms and legs had dried up. The kneecap was like a stone balancing precariously on high, gale-whipped ground. She jabbered a lot about snakes, but when she recovered from her delirium, she told cheerful stories in a squeaky, scratching voice. She had become a smiling skeleton, a talking bundle of bones. I remembered the skulls on fruit stands I had seen soon after the guerrilla war. They had been removed and taken away by government workers, some for burial, some for preservation in a museum of national history. For me, they had all been dumped inside Aunt's house, and she was fighting their legacy with the forced demonic smile of the tortured living dead.

On the last day, her friend Teopista took me aside and asked me to fetch a priest. I refused. What was the use? The woman had undergone her purgatory and hell here. If anything, she was a saint who could do without frocked platitudes. But I finally caved in. In the meantime, the brigadier came with some of his relatives. He looked embattled; they looked vengeful. The priest came. In his black clothes, he looked like an undertaker, or a gangster after a painful point-blank execution. The bundle of bones was buried by multitudes. The burial ceremony and its aftermath remained one blur of ungummed images. Aunt Lwandeka had got it right: "Nobody got born thrice." The virus had denied her a third chance.

Lwendo came to my aid. "You need to go somewhere and sort yourself out, man," he insisted. "Go to Britain or America for a long holiday. You can afford it."

"I don't know anybody there."

"There are many Ugandans there. Some of our old schoolmates are already there. Go and meet them."

"No, I want to stay here." The brigadier had offered me a job on top of pledging to settle his late wife's business affairs personally.

"You have to go. You look more dead than alive. You are so absentminded that I am afraid a car will knock you down one of these days."

"No, no, don't exaggerate." I knew he was right.

Help came from unexpected quarters. There was a Dutch aid organization called Action II which had landed in trouble over child pornography. A government official had found controversial pornographic material in the house of one of the aid workers, along with pictures of orphaned children taken while they were swimming naked in Lake Victoria. The man who made the scoop concluded that the aid worker was a pedophile who must have come to this country to indulge his perverted tastes. He recommended that the group be deported. Lwendo, who knew a few people who mattered, got wind of the affair and stepped in. Serious negotiations took place. Money changed hands. Even then it seemed the organization was going to be closed down as an example to others.

In the end, the deportation order was cancelled. Lwendo invited me to accompany him to the city that day. The man handling the case was Cane. He looked tall, big, sluggish. He drank a lot. He had maneuvered his way into the civil service and landed in different government offices.

"Been to the north yet?" I said, for lack of better words. A chasm separated us, and my salivary libation did not seem to improve things.

"No. Too much fighting," he said laconically.

"Things are improving. We both went there about a year ago," Lwendo explained.

"So you did see where I came from, eh!" he said pensively. He was an important man and seemed to be weighed down by his responsibilities. Too much work, too little pay. I knew all about it. The occasional big bribe always ended up drained by long-standing debts and commitments.

"Sure I did," I replied. I would have liked to remind him of his sex lessons and the erections he used to get in order to embarrass female teachers, but he looked too old to be interested. The terror of hard female teachers excused himself. His secretary had tapped on his desk meaningfully.

"Hard-bargaining bastard," Lwendo said as we descended the Crested Towers building. "Almost broke the balls of those Dutch fuckers."

Action II had worked briefly in southeast Amsterdam, or the so-called Bijlmermeer, which was a sprawling black ghetto on the fringes of the great city. They told us that there were many illegal immigrants there, a few Ugandans among them. They offered to give me a few connections, a few addresses, but I had no interest in becoming an illegal immigrant. I wanted to go on holiday and come back.

"You can go there and meet people who speak your language," one Action II worker said. He offered to make travel arrangements for me, including supplying the invitation letter needed for a visa. In return for their troubles, I could fund-raise for them for a fortnight. I would get free accommodations and food. The deal was done.

The aid workers kept their word. All parties needed each other: they wanted Lwendo close to them, and me to fund-raise for them. I got invited to Holland by their parent organization. Within two months, I was on a plane to Amsterdam.

BOOK SEVEN

GHETTOBLASTER

GETTING ON THE PLANE was one of the best things that had happened to me in years. I travelled first class, a bait used by my sponsors to inflate my ego and make me fund-raise as if the destiny of the whole African continent depended on it. I studied the golden liquid in the four-sided liquor bottle and wished that my own brew had been good enough for bottling and export, in which case I would have been going to Europe as a businessman. In my jean suit and canvas shoes, I did not look business-like. I was turned out like a rebel on a vague mission, which I was. Already I felt I would need all my rebel credentials to get by: I was on my own. Lwendo would have been handy here—together we would have done better—but he had stayed behind to supervise his carpentry workshop, to enjoy the peace he had fought for and to await the arrival of his first child.

Those seven solid hours of flight were like purgatory; I felt like a soul hovering above its bleeding corpse, caught between the shreds of the man I had been and the vague outline of the man I wanted to become. I thought I was free. The tyrants, the family, the wars, all past joys and pains, everything was receding, burying itself behind the jagged skyline of old experience, where I wanted it all to stay forever more. I felt weightless, giddy with the confounding dimensions of new freedom. The liquor penetrated my system and augmented the lack of gravitational pull and my frightening ebullience. I felt magical powers coursing through me, and I believed I could do anything. I closed my eyes, and the last quarter-century sank deeper into the sarcophagus of volitional amnesia. I erased myself from its annals, hell-bent on believing that I had played no part in it, and that it had all been just a figment of someone's diabolical imagination. Before I fell asleep, I dreamed of the plane exploding, mincing the little that remained of a fading past and sprinkling the dust in the clouds, which would burst into rain and wash our chopped remains over oceans and strange lands.

Eventually, the liquor wore off, and consciousness seeped back. I reoccupied my body, repossessed my faculties and looked outside. The sky over Brussels was dusky, the airport blazing like a ship caught in a blizzard, calling attention to itself by flickering multi-colored lights. My kingdom was wrapped in somber mists and a terrifying beauty. It was a magic grotto gaudily lighted like a thousand Christmas trees.

The countless souls filing through it in a somnambulistic trance emphasized the magic. This alien world was one gargantuan foe I would have to vanquish if I was to get my way. The enormity of the task made my gait that little bit heavier. Cold sweat ran down my back and I swallowed hard as the familiar individuals from the cabin melted into the crowd. I tried to look for friendly faces, eager to save the crumbling strands of the communion of our airplane, but everyone seemed wrapped up in thought, dealing with a hundred and one things.

Dazzled by the light, I groggily walked about the grotto to see if there were any gifts dangling from the Christmas trees, tokens of the salvation I was seeking. I went to the duty-free shops to look at the watches, the cameras, the jewelry. Trapped in a glaring white light akin to burning magnesium, the gizmos breathed the harsh air of aggressive marketing and lay under the pressures of their short life span. To buy one such article on my former teacher's salary, I would have had to work for five years. I stumbled away from the snakepit, my tail between my legs. People floated past in a relentless surge, the tapping of their feet a hymn to the gods of itinerancy.

The plane that was to take us to Amsterdam was small. Day was breaking, the mist eaten by a cold light that revealed hundreds of cars, many waiting planes and busy airport personnel.

The most memorable sight that morning was the bird's-eye view of the polders, green blocks of reclaimed land resembling carefully made drawings on a chart. The grotto in which I found myself was even bigger; it was suffused with a dull golden light and armed with more tunnels than a magician's diabolical maze.

Two Action II workers picked me up at the other end of the airport: I felt like I was being vomited from the lukewarm comfort of a leviathan's belly into the cold waters of an accursed sea. The man had small green eyes in a slab face, a cropped beard, a soft voice and large, clumsy hands. The woman had ash-gray eyes, a snub nose and a long mouth in a horsey face. They were very enthusiastic about my visit, and the good work they were doing. For the moment, I thought I was in safe hands. They asked me about the journey, the situation in Uganda, my prediction of the country's future, the welfare of their colleagues and many other things.

The man fixed his eyes on the road, mouth ajar, and sometimes nodded but said nothing. The sea of cars floated past us, buildings loomed up and highways dived in and out of the landscape. We penetrated the city of Amsterdam in a cold sunlight that did nothing to warm the chilly air, which razored through fabric like a knife through butter.

I was installed in a small hotel opposite Central Station, and from my window I could see thousands of people pouring out of the station gate. They reminded me of the crowds at the taxi park in Kampala. Cars, trams, buses and trains rumbled on in a ceaseless hubbub that was occasionally penetrated by the roar of a monster motorcycle. Old, thin-faced buildings with gables mounted on them like magic triangles lined the canals in the grim manner of eighteenth-century soldiers awaiting another looming battle.

My euphoria lasted only till the following morning: flies had ambushed my new paradise. And like Dr. Ssali, Aunt Tiida's husband, who had to deal with the terrorism of those terrible creatures with a raw circumcision wound, I found myself fighting a war on two or more fronts. The irony of travelling in luxury, only to arrive and not only confront flies but also have to recount fly-bejewelled tragedies on the first day of work, was not lost on me. The harsh anti-climax gave me nervous diarrhea. The worst in international beggary, image pillage and necrophilic exploitation waited for my seal of approval. Pictures of children more dead than alive, with flies in their eyes, on their mouths, in their nostrils, on their clothes, ambushed me. The loud pleas for help festooning their heads like demonic halos completely deflated my ego. I found myself trembling and in need of a stiff drink.

My opinion of my hosts took a U-turn. The crassness of the propaganda said volumes about both them and their audience. I was in the midst of pirates far more cold-blooded than I was, and I felt the need to revise and jettison much of my old knowledge. I tried to place myself in the shoes of their so-called donors. If somebody came to me with those pictures, especially the ones with children twisted like constipated chicks, I would have asked them why they had waited that long to act. But then the business was run on expedience and was meant not to prevent but to patch up festering wounds, with flimsy, pus-soaked bandages. I had made the mistake of coming at the end of the feeding frenzy which had peaked in the eighties, when fund-raising organizations wielded powers of life and death over nameless millions and did whatever was necessary to extract money from the calculated indifference of the wealthy West. They not only targeted geriatrics, but also spread the shrapnel over a wide field, hitting the constituency they believed had to be rubbed with shit and flies before releasing a dollar here, a dime there. The caustic magnesium burst of Reaganomics and Thatcherite liberalism had penetrated deep into the aid cartels and empires, and finding myself in its residual glare did my eyes and my sensibilities no good.

The cartels and the sharks of the aid industry had fed to surfeit and at the same time nailed their backs against the wall. The indifferent had become super-indifferent, numbed by the necrophilia, the fly-bejewelled beggary and the grandiloquent appeals to crippled magnanimity. Some sharks had, in the meantime, put two and two together and were trying to inject a humane element into their necrophilia and fly-flaunting extravaganzas. I felt that it was the duty of my hosts and their colleagues to rectify what they had demolished. Yet I did not feel in any way inclined or obligated to lend them a hand. I enjoyed the spite of not telling them that I was taking no further part in their plans. They showed me the fund-raising schedule, packed with activity like a tin of beans. I was scheduled to make twenty speaking appearances and do a dozen newspaper interviews. I endorsed it all, and even thanked them for caring so much about the faceless millions. I called them the Good Samaritans, and they blushed; the irony was not totally lost on them.

Back in my hotel room, I buried my face in the pillow and screamed. How could anyone expect me to sell Aunt Lwandeka down the road? It was not the dead children that had impelled me to withdraw. It was the picture of a young skeletal woman, set with huge letters—screaming, begging, nightmare messages—that had taken the will out of me. In the picture, she was lying on a mat, her cadaverous face upturned, her eyes swimming in mucusy holes, her knees rudely exposed, her stick limbs a perfect picture of a slow, torture-ridden death. The money this cadaver would raise would trickle down to the continent, and then it would double back in the form of international debt servicing and repayment. So the continent was like Aunt in her last days: the little sustenance that went in via the mouth oozed out of the rectum. I now wished Lwendo had squeezed the pedophile very hard and kicked other aid organizations in the groin. These were not essentially evil people, at least not comparable to some of our murderers ranging free in these climes, but they were keeping bad company, company I no longer wanted to be part of, even for a day longer.

I packed my bags the same night. I went down to a phone booth outside the hotel and made a call to the ghetto. As the phone rang on the other side, my heart raced. I was banishing myself from a hostile Eden. As the phone rang I could hear flies buzzing, jumping off the pictures awaiting my fund-raising saliva in the morning and colliding with each other. The vision of blue-green flies and the small black ones colonizing carrion, shit and putrescence filled the booth with a cadaverous stench and made me nauseated. Alas, I had left nothing behind. I had buried nothing in the clouds. I had brought it all with me, coded secretly, gnawing away in the dark like the virus that had killed Aunt Lwandeka. I felt beleaguered, encumbered, enervated. I was too aware of the whiteness of the people around me, on the streets, in the buildings facing Central Station, in the bistros on the Damrak, everywhere. I wanted to find my feet, and to put the horror of the flies behind me.

I felt the money in my pocket. How much worse did it feel out here if one was penniless? Or if one had to scrape it off the floor? Or if one had to sit out one's hell in detention camps awaiting acceptance or rejection following pleas for political asylum? As I ruminated on this somebody said, "Aallo?" Yes, it was the flat, Lugandanized English of our people. I felt like jumping up and knocking myself out on the booth ceiling. Little Uganda, that cocoon of Ugandans in exile, was calling right in the heart of white Holland! This was what returning Indians must have felt when talking to people in Gujarati or Urdu in the middle of Kampala.

"*Osiibye otya nnyabo?*" (How are you, madam?)

"*Bulungi ssebo*" (All right, sir), the voice replied. How sweet it sounded in the cold night air! And what a relief to know that Action II had given me real addresses! The rest of the conversation, and the introductions, and the inquiries about where I could rent a room for some time, occurred in a dream. I could already see the flushed faces of my hosts on discovering that I had disappeared, especially since they hadn't a clue that I hated what they did, and how they did it. I left the booth laughing, the taste of revenge burning like liquor in my breast, the prospect of staying with people from my country lending wings to my limbs. Outside the hotel, the canals were gleaming with multicolored light emanating from the windows and the streetlamps stationed along the banks. The dark, glittering water was moving, wriggling like a serpent pinned at both ends. I had pinned mine, and I felt invincible.

The map of the metro track that chiselled through the sprawling ghetto looked like the letter Y or a broken rosary, the beads forming the sprawling ghetto. In summer, the sight of the towering buildings is softened by the lush green of the roadside vegetation: flowering bushes, trees and grass that lead the way from the steel track. In winter, the trees are stricken bare like fleshless limbs, the sky as gray as the concrete in its brutal upward thrust. I arrived in summer, and the green bewitched me, coloring my first impression of the place. I emerged from the metro, bags in hand, and surveyed the vista—the hulking buildings, the trees along the paved roads and the walkways. It was not bad, at least not as bad as the word "ghetto" had first intimated. There were groups of youths in baggy clothes with canvas shoes and baseball caps turned back to front standing along the metro station, under the culverts and beside the buildings like soldiers contemplating an advancing war. I was excited as I walked past them. I kept thinking that these should have been my students at Sam Igat Memorial College. But what kind of students?

My destination was a few hundred meters from the metro station, reached via graffiti-strewn culverts that doubled as a drug market at night, a square that was used as a flea market on Wednesdays, grocery shops in long, reclining buildings, and a police station housed in a squat, box-like structure. The high-rises, behemoths that could house anywhere from eight to fifteen hundred souls, were configured in large compounds named after the alphabet. The biggest ones were divided into three or more sections, built in semi-circular formation. From now on, the center of my life was going to be Compound E in the behemoth called Eekhoorn.

In 1966, when Grandpa was suffering at the hands of goons during the height of the state of emergency, Amsterdam's ghetto, conceived as a garden of Eden, was being built to house people from Holland's colonial past: Antilleans and Surinamese. Covered walkways connecting the main structures to garages were constructed, paths were paved, pipe water and flush toilets installed; and the apartment buildings oozed the arrogance of newness. The Garden was carved into parks, which rubbed shoulders with highways, metro lines and bridges and sprouted large bushes which burst with flowers in spring and summer. Towering above the bushes were trees that called to mind forests on the South American mainland, from where the majority of the immigrants would come. On summer evenings, the smell of flowers filled the paths, and one could hear the last birds singing and insects preparing for the night.

Dream realized, the Garden was peopled with dusky former colonials, who walked among the trees that hid the forbidden fruit and the grass that housed the serpent which would poison the whole dream. Akin to God, the Dreamer withdrew, and the Garden was invaded by addictive weeds and the vicious serpents of disillusionment, isolation and legalized crime in the true spirit of prime-time capitalism. Mountains of reports on the proliferation of crime, drugs and unemployment piled up in the government offices, but because it was all inside the secluded Garden, not much was done. After all, the soothing waters of welfare benefits were still flowing over the blaze, and the children attended school, and policing was mild. There was freedom of movement from the ex-colonies to the Garden, and everybody was free to do whatever they wanted, in the true spirit of democracy. "A reasonable balance" and "It could have been worse" were the mottos gracing the walls of the government offices. Indeed.

As I entered the ghetto I saw black men, women and children entering and emerging from the behemoths, going about the normal business of everyday life. I couldn't help but smile. The shop attendants in the groceries were mostly black, Caribbean or African, with a sprinkling of Indians and whites. My new home had been recently painted a cream color with red strips on the sides, and it looked fine. The corridors inside were huge and long and windy, and some nooks ran with stale piss. Officially, eight hundred people resided in this behemoth, but unofficial figures ran up to fifteen hundred. Nobody knew exactly how many people lived here. I liked the idea of anonymity, the air of low-key lawlessness and the fantasy touch of the Wild West. I was feeling inviolable: bad things could happen here, but not to me. I had washed my robes in the blood of the bitter wars I had been through and felt that the lukewarm violence of the ghetto would not touch me. Here I could live a quiet life, responsible for and to nobody, and if I got tired of it, maybe I would return to Uganda.

My new home was a four-bedroom flat on the seventh floor. My landlady, Keema, was a thirty-two-year-old woman who had left Uganda and her moldy marriage and gone to Kenya before arriving here on a tourist visa almost ten years ago. Her network of old friends had helped her find work, accommodations and solace, and when her period of illegality ended, she got a Dutch passport and collected her three children. In this flat lived about ten people, most of them coming and going at odd times. When I arrived, there were six regulars. I rented the smallest bedroom, which was next to the sitting room and faced the toilet and bathroom. At night, the sitting room doubled as a bedroom for those who were passing through or had just arrived or had stayed over after a party. The only lesson my landlady seemed to have learned in life was never to turn people away. The place was a clearinghouse for those in transit to Britain, a hub for Ugandan exiles in the country and a party zone where birthdays, Christmases and all manner of obscure feasts were organized, because, unlike her friends' white neighborhoods, the ghetto had no noise limit. Here you could blast your stereo and put the television on at such a volume that the furniture vibrated. If a neighbor was disturbed by noise, all he could do was to return the favor by organizing a party and making as much noise as possible. Police never looked into such matters. In fact, the white policemen never left their box-like structure at night. There were flat wardens in each building who were deputized. And favoring a laissez-faire mode of policing, they kept out of people's hair as much as possible. If burglars struck at night, you had to hold on, hoping that the wardens would come in time to lend a hand. If you got held up by rough youths or some deranged junkie, you had to rely on your own resources. If you were stalked or terrorized by shadowy characters, you had to work out your own defense system. Consequently, quite a few people here carried knives.

Keema's house was a popular place. There was always somebody coming and going. The kitchen was going at all hours, and the toilet seemed to flush non-stop, the gurgling cistern making noises reminiscent of Uncle Kawayida's turkeys. The children attended school, and when they returned, they did their homework and went out to play. My landlady did not see them until evening, because she worked in a greenhouse outside Amsterdam and sometimes returned home late. She always arrived dog-tired and irritable, and if she found a cup broken or a misdemeanor committed, then she would explode into the tension-breaking rages of stressed parenthood.

Most misdemeanors were committed by her middle child, who was about ten. If something went wrong, Keema immediately suspected her. And if the girl did not move fast enough, Keema would whack her with an umbrella or with her hands. Her only son, who was also the youngest, was the apple of her eye. He was stubborn as hell and liked farting when visitors were around, but Keema either ignored the noise and the stink or found some way of excusing him. I took a special liking to the eternal scapegoat, and she exploited the situation. When she needed pocket money, she would come and dance for me, duplicating the pelvic thrusts of the American rappers she saw on television, and I would give her some money. I was far from her only victim. At parties, she would grind in front of male guests with an insistence that left female guests squirming with embarrassment, till she got rewarded. Keema never punished her for these rather provocative displays. She even seemed perversely charmed by them.

During the first weeks, I went to downtown Amsterdam a lot, visiting museums, the red-light district and other places of interest I had both read and heard about; but as the novelty of the city waned and I got used to its sights and sounds, I started staying in the ghetto. At home, I found myself playing my old role of nanny. The children often asked to be helped with mathematics, and I did lend a hand, but for the most part, they watched television and fought and argued and enjoyed their childhood. They made me think of Serenity and Padlock's shitters, and of Aunt Lwandeka's orphaned children.

I met Ugandans of all sorts. There were Ugandans who had been to Sweden, Britain, America, before coming here: everyone called them Swedes or Scanias, Brits and Yankees, because of their tendency to talk a lot about those countries. There were Ugandans who had fled Amin's terror and were now naturalized Dutchmen. There were runaway wives, gold diggers and women forced into prostitution on the side because of their illegal status and failure to get better jobs. There were former Obote and Amin torturers who had deep-frozen their pasts and become harmless family men, some of whom had white wives and half-caste children. There were petty criminals and school dropouts rubbing shoulders with very well educated people who could not get jobs in their professions. There were Ghanaians and Nigerians who masqueraded as Ugandans, or at least had done so when they came here to ask for political asylum in the seventies. There were also Ugandans who had registered themselves as Sudanese, exploiting the war between north and south Sudan and the Dutch government's insistence on allowing in only political refugees from countries with a bad human-rights record. This diverse mixture of history and experience created an air of suspicion which tempered the general friendliness. People did not want to tell you much about themselves before they found out who you really were. There was a feeling that the government might have sent spies abroad to monitor what Ugandans said and did.

At first it was very exciting to hear people's edited versions of themselves, especially how they had got money for passports and air tickets and what they had experienced in Sweden, Britain or America. But as it became a weekly and sometimes daily event, with bored souls coming to Keema's just to watch television and to listen to music and to gossip, it became tedious. They were almost all economic migrants, despite the political-refugee guises some had donned because it was the only way to enter the country. The majority of them had washed their garments in the humiliations of the camps and were marked by the years of waiting in limbo for permission to stay, but they were now brimming with resilience and optimism. Most of them did back-breaking jobs in greenhouses, on farms, in meat-packing factories and in all sorts of dirty places. They arrived at Keema's with the blaze of hard labor in their eyes and the anvils of fatigue grinding their over-worked limbs. I could appreciate their need for frequent visits to such a popular haunt. I gradually appreciated their reluctance to take me in, for who was I to them? How could I survive without working? What was I looking for here? What was my secret? How could I be trusted?

Privacy was a rare delicacy, which I savored in measly portions. Nostalgia-laden conversation from the sitting room penetrated the walls of my bedroom and made it impossible to rest or to think while the visitors were around. I was forced to join the group and masticate the cud of jaded conversations. The parties were a torture. Thirty or more people would invade the house, smother it in perfume and aftershave, and make the walls vibrate with noise, music, dancing, ar-guments and the endless gurgles of an overworked toilet. The ar-rangement suited Keema very well: during the week, she left at seven and returned at seven; on weekends, she wanted to party, to please her friends and to meet her contacts because, as I found out, she got paid for housing these people in transit to Britain or elsewhere. The prepa-rations alone took a day or two, what with the shopping for drinks and eats, the cleaning of the sitting room and other rooms, the cooking of meals and the frying of chicken to be eaten through the night, and the whole energy-consuming atmosphere of a bar before opening time. The meals would be eaten early, and then people would start arriving, ushering in the drinking, dancing and feasting that would last until the small hours of morning. A big quarrel or a fight between two women over a man or two men over a woman would stir up lingering passions and gossip.

The ghetto resembled Uganda during the guerrilla war: the day belonged to the forces of law and order, the night to pirates and their minions and victims. In order to gain a taste of both worlds, I gradually took to nightcrawling and visiting the haunts of small-time drug dealers and users. From around eight o'clock on, the culverts, certain nooks of the behemoths and some well-known cafes came alive with customers. A customer came in, whispered something, handed over cash and got a little parcel wrapped in plastic. At the culverts, some customers could wait no longer and just turned round, faced the wall, opened their parcels and rubbed the fiery powder into their mucous membranes.

Crack users had their own haunts, often derelict houses, where they squatted, lighted a fire and put the rock on a spoon, which they put over the flame. It was quite an experience to watch bliss grab a face, permeate its fibers, soothe its bones and then turn around and desert it. The tight muscles would then slacken, the mouth would gape and drool, the eyes would glaze over and the body would furl like a deflated balloon. Souls passing through this purgatory looked frighteningly tormented. They resembled a viral-plague victim in the throes of a hellish fever. Finally, as the talons of hell sank in, the souls would ooze from both terminals or climb to groggy feet to look for another fix. That was when switchblades flashed. I always extracted myself from the spot before flashing steel could be pushed under my nose.

Along the culverts, in spaces about meter apart, stood youths in baggy clothes with caps pulled over their eyes, waiting for customers. They reminded me of crocodiles ambushing their prey, immobile and dedicated to the point of letting flies go in and out of their mouths. And sure enough, the prey would come looking for the powder of ecstasy. These were dangerous places, and the worst thing that could happen was getting caught in the cross fire of some little fight or stickup. The police never lifted a finger. Police policy was to arrive after the flames had died down, or rather when one of the combatants had been knocked out cold or killed. They never concerned themselves with threats: if somebody threatened to harm you, the police never did a thing till he honored his threat. And many criminals were released as fast as they were arrested. This sort of danger, this uncertainty, added an edge to my prowls.

The knife was the symbol of respect here. Youths with baggy clothes often had one, mostly two- or three-inch devils. I was more afraid of being cut up than of getting shot, but whatever little fears I had did not keep me from going out at night and watching junkies shoot drugs into blue veins in defunct lifts and under the stairs, women sucking or fucking men for money, and men and women fighting over drugs, money or nothing.

The scariest thing about the ghetto was that people were moving every day. No single day passed without somebody moving in or out. Starved of intellectual occupation, I would sit on the railing at the entrance and watch men and women lifting furniture in and out of vans. The junkies I saw sleeping or reclining in pools of urine and vomit and saliva under the culverts on Sunday mornings seemed to rise, shed their degraded bodies, don muscular ones and move fat, hissing sofas, creaking double beds, glass-fronted cupboards and bulky suitcases out of waiting vans and up the endless stairs. Later, the muscled figures whisking furniture up and down stairs seemed to wilt under my gaze and become the blank-eyed zombies craving their fix day in and day out.

Gradually, I started reaching out to Africa in diaspora. It was hard because of the language barrier, and because I did not work or go to nightclubs or do drugs. I looked around for a library where I could borrow some books and hopefully meet people, but there was none. I finally asked Keema's naughty girl to arm me with the rudiments of the Dutch language in exchange for favors and a little money. I built up a crude arsenal of everyday Dutch, waiting for my chance, and when one night I came upon a woman who was being stalked by the crocodiles under the culvert, I was happy. My reaction to the situation was perfect. When I saw her, with the crocodiles a few meters behind her, I said out loud, "I am sorry for being late, darling. I should have met you at the station as I had promised." My view was that the boys had not really wanted to do her any harm. If they had insisted, they would have caught up with her long before I met her. Instead, they followed her at a distance, called her names and asked her to blow them. I found her perspiring and out of breath. She could hardly think quickly enough to mouth the words, "Yes, where have you been all this time?" but when she did, the crocodiles stopped, looked at her and me for one long moment and then slowly turned back. It was the night that had saved her from further humiliation. The boys could not see me clearly, and neither could I make out their faces. They must have considered the possibility that I had a gun or connections in the underworld. They just played into my hands.

The woman thanked me and invited me home for a drink. Her name was Eva Jazz. "I have to be somewhere, I am sorry," I said, just to test her. She insisted, and I knew that she was single or a single mother determined not to work through her horror alone. I dreaded the prospect of being greeted by two or three sullen children who had been waiting all evening for their mother. It was a two-hundred-meter walk through a park softly lighted by spaced roadside lamps, and I could see her eyeing the flower bushes warily.

As it turned out, there was nobody at home. She was thirty years of age, starting to bulge at the front and the back, and I kept thinking about my maternal aunt Kasawo. Eva was half white, half black, but looked whiter than some white people I had seen that week. She had a flat face and silky jet-black hair, which she covered with a dark blond wig. She confronted the world and its lechers, marauders, crocodiles and strangers with a cold look. Yet she could deploy a nice smile that made her face inviting. I liked the smell of flowers that hit me when I entered her flat. It was quite a departure from Keema's overused air.

Eva had fat furniture, a huge hi-fi, a big collection of records and videos, and many pictures of herself and her family on the wall. I was disappointed not to find any books in the house, except for her telephone directory, television guide and a heap of fashion magazines. Her bathroom was filled with skin-toning creams, perfumes, powders, shampoos, toothpicks, nail files and many bizarre-looking objects of body care whose purpose I could not fathom. I was amazed. The stuff could fill a small boutique in Uganda. I kept imagining her in there feeding her skin for hours, and the trouble she took to select the day's facial weaponry from such a formidable armory.

The first meetings were easy. We kept skirting each other, hiding behind the banalities of weather, life in the ghetto, talk about drugs, young people and music. She was surprised to hear that I was from Uganda. She thought I was American or Jamaican. I asked her whether she knew where Uganda was, and she just laughed. I got the message. I did not pry or try to force information down her throat. The spotlight was mostly on her. She was working in a retirement home on the white side of Amsterdam and had a son, two sisters and three brothers in the Caribbean. She had been in the country for the last fifteen years and generally felt at home. Her life revolved around her work, a few

friends, visits to clubs and not much more. She was generally not interested in what went on in the country or in the city or in the world. I
was disappointed. What, then, was I going to learn from her?

At that juncture, I tried to say something about myself—my education, my teaching experience, the wars, my experiences in the
Luwero Triangle—but she was not interested, and I quickly gave up.
It was American pop music that turned her on and made her explode
into flame like the torch of a fire-eater doused in paraffin. She could not
praise Gregory Hines, Lionel Richie, James Ingram, Michael Jackson,
Prince and Aretha Franklin enough. My knowledge in that zone was
shallow, garnered as it was from old magazines, but I was only expected to listen. She inundated me with details of their personal life. I
tried to change the subject to literature but got no response. Hollywood, though, made her sing. Her knowledge of Hollywood films and
film stars was endless. She knew when films were made, and by whom,
and who had starred in them. She knew the difficulties they had had in
shooting or marketing this or that film, and which releases deserved
being hits and which were simply overhyped. Romantic comedies, mu-
sicals and adventure films were her favorites. At such times, I wanted
to leave, but she was not done yet. The catwalk had to be stormed. I
had no interest in clothes and who made them and who modelled them,
but once she got started, there was no stopping her. At the back of my
mind was the idea that I too would get my chance in the sun and inun-
date her with information about places and facts and books she did not
know. I would make *her* writhe and squirm. I was wrong.

The moment liquor was introduced, conversation, or rather the
monologues, started glowing with passion. I learned that she had taken
to drinking when she gave up smoking, which had done nothing for
her weight, in addition to making her sweat and puff. Frequently, in a
frustrated reaction to her weight and her work, she would attack men.

"Dogs, dogs, dogs," she said in a very American accent. She
might have been a character from a Spike Lee movie.

"And what does that make you?"

"They lie all the time."

"And you swallow the lies," I said excitedly. This was our first
real dialogue. "And in turn you lie to them."

"Now you are defending your kind," she said, almost angrily.

"I love a good discussion. Monologues work better on stage."

"At least you should have supported me and waited for me to give you the details."

The women I dated back home found it hard to tell me about their conquests and defeats. They felt it was much better if a man did not know everything about a woman's past. Eva did not care; she liked it. It liberated something in her. She quickly got very deep into the subject of men, and, with eyes glittering, she idealized six-foot-six types, men who towered over her like lampposts. My impression was that she was always waiting or looking out for one. To begin with, she had bought a huge bed, and in her spare closet were two huge robes and an assortment of fancy but very large sandals. I looked at the pop posters on her wall and knew that it was not alcohol but the real Eva talking. I felt lucky I wasn't her ideal man. The preparations she had made for the arrival of her Prince Charming were enough to give more cautious types an impression of desperation.

Amidst alcohol fumes, she invited me to share her bed. This rather surprised me. Why hadn't she waited to know me better? Were there no six-foot-six types waiting in the wings? It came as no surprise when I almost failed. My thoughts were elsewhere. Jo Nakabiri suddenly invaded my head, would not let go, and instead of transforming this woman beside me into a wet-dream goddess or at least something I could drool about while I did the job, thoughts of Jo just made me softer. Of course, I could have put on my pants and left, but that would probably mean it would be my last time here. I still wanted to know more about this woman. I turned to those marathon foreplay maneuvers and licked all the sweat from her neck, her arms, her stomach and every dash of her stretch marks. I attacked her armpits and sucked all the hairs, ingesting her bottled perfumes to the point of feeling dizzy. I inflamed her with calculated thrusts of my tongue. After a good half hour, with her squirming, sweating, oozing and puffing, I finished the job. Older women are nefarious drainers of younger men's energy; they are hard to satisfy, and are vocal about jobs half done. During those gruelling sessions, I paid for all the food and alcohol and water I had touched. As I growled with a mediocre orgasm, I knew that Eva would be my last older woman ever.

I started seeing her regularly, doing her shopping and cleaning her house, vacuuming her carpets and emptying her garbage. This was not what I had come to do, but it was a respite from the racket at Keema's. I had to give up any idea of interesting her in the country of my birth. Uganda sounded too obscure a place to merit even cursory interest, and Africa was a Pandora's box of horrors and shames best left untouched and condemned to the depredations of dust, termites, cobwebby neglect and calculated silence. Whenever I tried to show that there was more to a people, a continent, than its sum total of ills, she would slap me repeatedly with female circumcision. I had seen an anti-circumcision campaign poster on a wall at the metro station in Amsterdam the day I entered the ghetto. Eva was one of the colored people mortally wounded by this other horror from what she considered to be the place of horrors. In fact, she told me once that she wanted to burn up all the posters and all the offices of organizations mounting such shaming campaigns. Eva's impression was that all women in Africa were infibulated, and that Africa was one and the same from Egypt to South Africa.

"You torture women, for Christ's sake," she said in her American accent. "And I guess you would have liked me better if I had been circumcised."

"Of course," I replied immediately. This was not a woman to inform that I did not even know what a circumcised woman looked or felt like, and that I would not care to find out. She had saddled me with the cross, and I was ready to carry it with a smile on my face. "There are 29,999,996 circumcised women in Africa. If you and your mother and sisters had been born there, you would have made it a cool 30 million, ha, ha, ha." Her body shook with laughter, and we high-fived.

"All the wars, all the death of babies, all the backwardness," she moaned while changing her tune. She resembled an aging star of a bad soap on hearing that her man was having an affair with a much younger woman.

"Yes, all that and more, and we are still standing."

She threw me a superior look.

"You have no television, no MTV and no CNN. People over there don't even know Michael Jackson!"

"No, they don't. In fact I first heard of Michael Jackson on the plane," I said, putting on a sad expression. She patted me on the cheek!

Up to that point, I thought she had seen through my lies and appreciated the fact that this was a game, but I was mistaken. She was serious as hell.

"Poor you!"

"Yes, indeed," I replied, resisting the urge to laugh out loud. Who had sanctified pop culture to this extent? At this juncture, she went to her collection of records and started a long lecture on her favorite artists, feeding me with the years the albums came out, who wrote the songs, who played the instruments on them and which songs had been big hits and which had not but should have made all the charts.

Secure as to who I was, I found it amusing to be playing the barbarian knocking down the walls of Castle Europe or rather Lady Eva's palatial residence. But what was the booty? Popular music, Hollywood films, liquor, Tampax and perfume. Not the most inflaming of finds. I kept thinking that if Eva had been Lageau's sister, I would have made her pay in more ways than one, but I had nothing to prove to this woman.

Then came the rages. They began slowly, like winds picking up momentum to cause mayhem. This was what I had been waiting for, but when it came, I almost got swept away by the deluge. It was evident that her anger had been boiling for some time, simmering on a slow fire, waiting for a chance to explode. Her old friends had heard it all before and could take no more, and it was my turn to help her air the dungeons of torture lurking in her mind.

As a regular fixture round the house, I got the full report of what went on at her workplace, details of human infirmity, dirt and suffering that made me happy I had never wanted to be near hospitals. The most recent government and City Council budget cuts and the concomitant sacking of staff had put extra pressure on the remainder, and it made her roar. Eva came home swollen with the shit and urine of white people, the dirt she washed off them and the food they dribbled onto her lap as she fed them through their false teeth and trembling jaws. It kept building up all day, and as soon as she reached home, it exploded, opening sluices of old pain.

"I hate all those motherfuckers, all of them. I want to break the neck of every single geriatric and their sons and daughters and grandchildren who leave them to us. Who do they think they are? Do they think that because we work for them, we are their slaves? At the least discomfort, a ninety-year-old bitch calls you to her cell to take her to pee. You help her with her nappies, all wet and disgusting. You sit her on the toilet, wipe her wrinkly ass, dress her, and then she complains that you're handling her roughly! I am a qualified nurse, but those white bitches think I'm a kitchen skivvy. Come here, Eva, go there, Eva. This bitch is complaining about the way you fixed her false teeth; that motherfucker is moaning that you tied his shoelaces too tight. I am tired of this shit. I am tired of the way those nursing bitches swing their empty bras and their sorry flat asses. You would think there was a million dollars hidden in there! They think they're the best thing that ever happened on the planet. God, what is wrong with these people? Can't they see that they are not all that?"

At first I sympathized and tried to calm her down, but the more she went into the looks of the girls, the more convinced I became that it was her insecurity that was wreaking havoc. I appreciated the fact that she found herself in a terrible profession, but there was little I could do about it. I slowly began to enjoy her displays. They were theatrical, entertaining.

Men did not escape the lacerations of her tongue. "Those white bastards. They believe they own the whole world, even if they don't have two quarters to rub together. The geriatrics whose asses I wipe look at you as if you were there to suck their flaccid dicks. They don't know how pathetic they look with their pancake butts and wrinkly pissers. I hate it. My mother was married to a Dutch motherfucker in Paramaribo for ten years, until he died in his sleep. When she came to Holland and tried to introduce me to the family, a woman threw dishwater in her face. I never forgave them."

My opinion was that if she examined the dark part of herself properly, maybe she would not have to fill her house with skin-toning creams that did nothing to heal the festering wounds in her soul, especially since during the creation process her nose had remained wide and her bum protuberant. At that point in time, I did not ask whether she had considered rhinoplasty or liposuction. The fact I stumbled on later was that she was not a qualified nurse; she had attended a course to help elderly people in the cupboards built for them to await the Grim Reaper. Her dream had been to become a singer and dazzle millions with her voice. She now and then did impressions of Aretha, filing her voice to a high pitch that made her neck veins bulge and her eyes pop, and holding notes for what she believed to be sensational intervals. She would move round the room with a spray can in her hand, head bobbing, body shaking, lip-synching to favorite oldies. I liked it, she loved it. She said that she used to sing to men in bed, especially to Richie, to whom I had not yet been formally introduced. But not anymore.

In her shoes, I would not have told the story the way she did, but Eva was a modern woman for whom nothing was too embarrassing. Anyway, in a country where sanitary pads were advertised on television every single day, giving details and reasons as to why one should buy this or that make, shame was a thing of the past.

"I hate those black American motherfuckers," she said in her very American accent. What she really meant was that she hated the black American man who had crossed her path, raised her hopes and then dumped her. Even then, I doubted the hate thing, because she still kept pictures of him. I was sure that she still fantasized about him, and even loved him, and was urgently looking for a successor, American or European. He was well proportioned, hard-bodied, very light complexioned. He towered a whole six feet five inches. He resembled Lionel Richie like a twin, and, to expand the illusion, Eva had the singer's posters up next to her old lover's pictures. He had a charming ear-to-ear smile and the greasiest wet-look do I had ever seen on a man. Beside him, Eva had felt like a queen on a throne.

On the day before they were scheduled to leave for Houston, she got the shock of her life: Richie disappeared, leaving her bankrupt, jobless and without a house. At first, she thought he had taken a walk to inspect the ghetto for the last time, but then she realized all his things were gone. She looked for him under the bed and behind cupboards. She asked neighbors if . . . She went from apartment building to apartment building checking, in case he had got confused by the strange names. It was a wild goose chase. "The motherfucker left me high and dry," Eva raged. "I should have bitten off his fucking dick and spat it in the fire."

The rages were followed by binges, large helpings of apple pie, eggs, offal, meatballs and french fries with mayonnaise. My feeling was that she was inviting me to leave. I was right. I got replaced rather quickly. I went to see her one evening, and the door was answered by a very tall, very dark, very hard-bodied man who momentarily reminded me of Amin's soldiers. The man had a nasty, menacing look, exactly like Badja Djola portraying the killer Slim in the film *A Rage in Harlem*. I was gruffly informed that Eva was away, and as I lingered, just before the door was slammed in my face, I heard her laughing in the background. I left with my replacement's foul breath in my nose. There was too much marijuana and garlic on it for my liking.

Stripped of a place to rest, I took to drifting. Keema's house was teeming with people, and I felt stifled by the cheer and optimism of migrants busily reinventing themselves. There was too much talk about jobs, jobs I would not have touched with a barge pole back home and which I resisted even thinking about now. Among the visitors were some who had slipped through the net and were now bookkeepers or partners in aid organizations or clerks, but the majority were in the blue-collar sector, and I was repelled by the stories they told, especially about how cruelly some of their bosses treated them.

I could not stay cooped up for ages. The red-light district, like a diabolical hurricane lamp, kept tempting me, just as it had tens of thousands of others before me. I joined the stream of pilgrims to the shrine of the sex industry. The revenue from the videos and the magazines alone was enough to reconstruct the whole of the devastated Luwero Triangle. There were booths for watching videos and live sex shows sold by smart pimps in suits and leather shoes. I ignored all that and joined the current flowing toward the cages where women both displayed and sold sex. The lines of cages were endless, and I could only think of slave buyers parading the selling blocks, the men fingering cunts and the women feeling men's genitalia to see if they were well-endowed enough to warrant a buy.

My buy cost me forty dollars, almost two whole salaries at Sam Igat Memorial College. I felt a twinge of remorse as I paid it to a Latina moth who had flown all the way from the Dominican Republic toward the lethal luminescence of the red-light district. The little island was the biggest supplier of whores to Holland and some of the surrounding countries. Among the Dominicans were Colombians, Thais, Eastern Europeans, Spaniards, a few Africans and a few Dutch women. This clash of continents at the selling block lost all irony whenever the buy turned out to be bad, as in my case. If anything, the whore reminded me of the despots' hypnotizing headboard, and once again I got burned for taking things at face value. My whore was well formed and, locked in her cage and bathed in the dull red light with a come-hither look on her pleasant face, she looked outstanding. She could have been any of Uncle Kawayida's sisters-in-law or the mixed-race children left behind by the Indians as they departed in 1972. This mingling of blood and the gyration of continents to the tinkle of dollars made my head swim. I thought I was in the middle of something special, probably standing at the epicenter of some cultural or historical or even metaphysical tornado. I followed her into her room.

All her life was crammed into that single room. In a corner was a huge leather bag with airline stickers. Under the sink was a statue of some deity of money or prostitution, a dinner plate overflowing with quarters at its feet. I resisted the temptation to sacrifice to this deity in exchange for a good, clean hard-on. For lack of a bidet, there was a small plastic basin, blue like the one we had had at the pagoda. A foot away from the makeshift bidet, the shrine and the big bag stood a small table with three conspicuously arranged pictures: the whoring mother, flanked by a mulatto boy and girl. The implications almost made me puke. Here were ghosts of children thousands of kilometers away, keeping mother company as she sold it day and night to buy them clothes, to send them to school and to pay their medical bills. Every month or two, Grandma got a letter from Holland, and possibly some money too, and in turn she sent news of the children. This whoring of the children's pictures disgusted me more than anything else. I felt the urge to strangle this woman and throw the pictures in the fire. I wanted to leave this cage, but I felt that she had played the trick on so many other decent men that it was foolish to throw away two months' salary like that. I undressed with the disgusted impatience of Fr. Lageau on the day he delivered his monkey sermon. She watched me like a dutiful sacristan directing a priest where to place mass vestments. I kept looking at the children, imagining how they waited for Mum to return with goodies from Europe, smelling of all the fishy perfume, the rancid semen, the slimy lubricant and the greasy dollars. The girl was beautiful, and I could see her being approached by hawkish agents, checked for cesarean cuts and big scars, and then offered a job as a dancer in a European nightclub, only to end up selling it like her mother before her. Obsessed with the children, I was not unsettled very much by her disaster.

In the village that got wiped away by the war, men would have called her a bucket: she was so loose, there was simply no traction at all. It was pure robbery. She was like a tantalizing jackfruit that, when cut open, is found to be watery, spoiled, sour. As a former midwife's assistant-cum-mascot, I knew what had happened: after the birth of the brats that looked at us from the photos, the woman had not bothered to be sewn up, probably with an eye to exploiting her condition.

I had learned my lesson: prostitution was a business where the packaging was better than the goods, and being ripped off was part and parcel of the trade. More annoying still was the fact that the white men I saw emerging from these cages wore the satisfied looks of money well spent. What was their secret? Either they knew the secret of telling buckets from wholesome whores, or they were built like zebras, or maybe they just buggered their buys. I remembered the soldier women and the silence I had kept about the attack. There was a possibility that these white men were getting ripped off but felt too ashamed to admit it. I left in a huff.

I returned after two months. I wanted to make sure. I tried a whore who seemed to wear the sun on her head and the Virgin Mary's alabaster complexion on her face. Were these women using too much lubricant? No. It was the fucking dildoes, spiked plastic cacti on which they sat during practice sessions in this red-lighted desert of theirs. I had had enough of these greased tombs in which men buried their doomed treasures in exchange for the pleasures of a pissoir. White men had been in the business for ages; I left them to navigate the cesspools of the flesh market.

The news of the demise of the despots reached me in the ghetto during the chilly silver days of winter. It was a severe winter, and the old heater could not chase the chill away from Keema's large house. We wrapped ourselves in thick clothes and waited for the freeze to grind to its end.

Padlock and Serenity were seventies people, and the eighties, with the guerrilla war, the turbulence and the changes of government, had left them feeling bewildered. It made them realize that the cancer was not all Amin's doing, and, forced to look further, they felt their sense of optimism flagging. The idea of a strong man holding the roof on the house had made sense to Padlock; didn't the pope do the same thing? However, with Amin's departure and the escalation of the killings, the bickering among Coalition members and ultimately the advent of a weak and murderous Obote II government, the despots were attacked by the locusts of pessimism and indifference.

It was during the depth of his suffering that Serenity came up with the only political statement he ever made. He said that Uganda was a land of false bottoms where under every abyss there was another one waiting to ensnare people, and that the historians had made a mistake: Abyssinia was not the ancient land of Ethiopia, but modern Uganda. Buoyed by intermittent bouts of optimism, he would go over his statement, looking for ways to improve it and make it attractive enough for ambitious politicians to pick up, for he believed that the time had come to change the name Uganda to Abyssinia.

Serenity lived in the exaggerated fear that his crimes would be unearthed, as though he were among the mass murderers and torturers who had escaped with Amin and Obote II. He would spend hours staring into the distance, working out how to cover his tracks, what to tell arresting detectives, what to deny. He thought about writing down his exploits in a story that took place in the legendary land of Abyssinia, changing the names of the characters, but he balked at the idea that some clever detective might dig into it and finally make him confess to the fraud at the center of the story. The other reason he refused to write an account of his crimes was that his opening lines sounded pitiably inadequate when compared with the tone, rhythm and power of the best of the novels on his shelves. He could not bear the idea of making a fool of himself in front of knowledgeable readers.

Serenity told Nakibuka on many occasions that he was afraid of the future. This was at the height of the guerrilla war, when government propaganda claimed that the guerrillas were just a bunch of fanatic Communist maniacs out to kill people, take their land and nationalize everything. The message sounded familiar, and having been spread by skillful government agents, not soldiers, it seemed plausible as well. In the sixties, the Church had been part of the anti-Communist campaign, to the extent of saying that the Communists routinely nationalized people's wives along with other property and that they had to be fought in a holy war. Serenity bought the anti-guerrilla line for a short time at the height of his despair: the war was not going anywhere, people were dying, and he believed that negotiations were the best way out of the quagmire. At one point, he no longer cared who won—both sides were killing people, and the situation looked very grim—he just wanted them to stop fighting, and when rumors had it that the guerrillas were defeated, he was happy. Then he heard that they had instead migrated to western Uganda, captured towns and divided the country in two, and he gave up; he realized that he did not understand what was going on. He stopped listening to the news and the rumors. He resigned his post at the trade union and disappeared out of the limelight. He followed Hajj Gimbi's advice and bought cattle, hiring a herdsman to look after them. Padlock's job was to supervise the man and make sure that he did not steal or dilute the milk or keep the animals hungry or thirsty.

On weekends, Hajj Gimbi and Serenity compared notes on cattle. They no longer talked about politics. Hajj Gimbi had given up on politics, because he could not trust the current players; he adopted a wait-and-see attitude. Serenity was not too fond of the animals, especially when they broke the fence at night and went out and ate other people's crops and he had to pay fines and apologize to angry neighbors, but he knew that they were a good investment.

Hajj Gimbi had resigned his job at the bank and concentrated all his efforts in the village. What he feared most was being linked to Amin's notorious State Research Bureau because he had had friends there. Hajj had come to the conclusion that the best hiding place for a Muslim was deep in the village, away from all the hustle and bustle of the city and its temptations. The new guerrilla government was strict, and he wanted to be away from where someone might finger him for one reason or other. News of anti-corruption units had spread. They allegedly looked into fraud and corruption, but did not specify how many years back they went in their investigations or what they would do with the culprits. Nothing much came of the anti-corruption units, but they scared those with a past like Hajj Gimbi's. Together, the two men watched as the Indians returned: first the industrialists, and then the small traders. They marvelled at the way history wrote, erased and rewrote itself. Both men were estranged from what was going on in the city. It was apparently being repossessed by pre-Independence forces.

It was painful to ponder the fact that things were moving in circles. Hajj Gimbi had more immediate worries anyway; he was having trouble keeping his family together. Lusanani, still the favorite wife, had run away on two separate occasions, and he was afraid that the next time round, she might not return. The move to the village had not pleased her, and she was secretly trying to find herself a place in the city.

The disappearance of the old village and the oozing of the houses into the swamps had hit Serenity hard. The day he returned to his father's house and found it gone, he lost his center. He felt as though a vital part of him had been stolen. He felt unstable, as if walking on one leg. As long as his father's house had been there to hate, he had been fine; now that it was gone, he felt bad about the disappearance of the past, the killings, the lootings and the bombings. He got depressed quite often, and Nakibuka did her best to keep his spirits up. He worried about himself and Padlock: the mud that always sucked at his feet during difficult moments made him giddy, and now he feared that he might lose his leg, or legs, like his uncle, who left his in Burma. The memory of washing the man's soft stump filled his mind with horror. His uncle had vanished one day without telling anyone where he was going, and he had never returned. Serenity feared that he might share the same fate. His uncle had told him once that they had a special bond, which he did not divulge. What made it even more eerie was the fact that those were the first and last words anyone heard the man say after World War II. Serenity never told anyone about it. He had nightmares when the man disappeared, but they stopped after some time. Now, after many, many years, they returned and disordered his sleep with blood-curdling images. He would see his uncle fighting and killing many white people; he would see him helping howling, blood-soaked comrades; he would see him getting shot to bits; he would see him lie still as though dead and then suddenly sit up and call his comrades; he would see him dressed up for a wedding without a bride, and then see him eaten by thick mists; he would see him smiling at him and thanking him for washing the remains of his amputated leg, and then see him fix the worm-filled leg onto the stump and walk away happily. The man came to him differently each time, and he could not understand why he haunted him. Nakibuka's assurances that his uncle loved him did not help. He would wake up feeling bad, and sometimes the mood stayed with him for the whole day.

Padlock was laboring under the strain of a vicious menopause, which had begun prematurely. The monstrous bleedings I had dreamed of long ago in the pagoda, when she came to me as Jesus on the cross, had become a permanent fixture in her life. They sapped her strength and left her feeling beaten up most of the time. She never complained about her cross, but each week it seemed to become heavier. Her worst fear was to bleed to death and be found by one of her sons in a pool of her own blood. She could not bear the thought of her sons seeing her that way. She had taken precautions by forbidding them to ever enter her bedroom, which was hers alone now, since she and Serenity slept in separate rooms. She washed her clothes at night and dried them in her room. She was still commander-in-chief of her home, but she somehow felt that the days of her reign were numbered. It was just a gut feeling, but it kept her thinking about the future. She was happy that she had raised all her children well and sent them to school. The rest she knew God would take care of.

The developments in the country did not interest her in the least: God's people always survived. She felt happy with the choices she had made in life, and felt that, given another chance, she would go down the same road again. The moments of relief, when she had no pain, gave her a foretaste of what she believed heaven to be like; she lived them with the intensity of a martyr about to die for the faith. The evenings were her favorite time: she would go out and look at the cows in the kraal, smell the cow dung and watch the big animals chewing their cud while they swatted flies with their long tails. She would examine their bellies and teats and check for ticks. She would order the herdsman to collect a heap of cow dung and light it with hot coals, ostensibly to keep flies away, but in reality for her enjoyment. The white odoriferous smoke reminded her of church incense, the acrid smell of holy mass. She would stand at the edge of the kraal like a statue and wait for the winds to blow the smoke her way. She would inhale very deeply and feel life creeping back, burning from head to toe like a bolt of lightning connecting heaven to earth. At such moments, she felt anchored at the center of the universe, holding things in place.

Shortly after my departure for Holland, Padlock decided to take a long break, the first in her married life. She wanted to enjoy the serenity of her parental home and the solace of the parish church of her childhood and youth. Her brother Mbale was shocked by the degree of his sister's deterioration. In her eyes was the bottomless expression of holy sorrow he had seen only in the faces of Italian madonnas. It reminded him of the days after her expulsion from the convent. Had she come back to lock herself in her parental house and starve herself to death in one last spurt of religious fervor? The house was not in use at the time. The iron roof had aged, and Mbale had to organize a group of villagers to clean it and make it habitable. He sent one of his daughters to look after her aunt, because Padlock refused to live with him.

Early every other morning, Padlock would wake up and walk to the parish church, four kilometers away, and hear mass and receive holy communion. She took the way via the hills behind the house where, as a little girl, she used to go and hunt for grasshoppers in March and November. The rolling hills, sometimes shrouded in morning mist, reminded her of Golgotha and of the Passion of Jesus. It calmed her to imagine herself back in Jerusalem, walking where Jesus had walked. Feeling the dew on her legs as the grass touched her feet, and the wet mist in her face, made her imagine she was at the center of the universe. At such times, there was no pain, even if the secret disease was at its peak; only peace, serenity, the wish to stay in the hills forever. At such moments, she felt reinvigorated and could not understand why many people believed she was unhappy. She felt the most indescribable contentment coursing through her, and when Mbale tried to dissuade her from taking the hard way via the hills, she just smiled condescendingly at him. He got the message. He also dropped the idea of giving her a chaperone or somebody to take her on a bicycle.

Mbale was not the only person to find Padlock a changed person. People in the village remarked about how laconic she had become, how old she looked, how hardened she came across, like an old, mad nun. The sound of music or voices came to her quite frequently now. People would see her look up as if attempting to frighten off predatory birds, and wonder what was going on inside her head. "She is mad," they said to themselves. Padlock had kept the secret of the music and the voices from everyone. Serenity had long noticed that there was something wrong with his wife, but she would not tell him what was ailing her. And she did not tell Mbale or any of the other villagers what she was hearing. Eventually, everyone let her be, especially because she was not throwing stones at people or eating butterflies or excreta.

The power and pitch of the music had intensified over time, making Padlock feel as if she were inside a musical tornado or at a crowded conference where everyone talked at the same time, at maximum volume. When the music and the voices subsided, she would say her rosary and do her chores. In the meantime, Mbale went to Kasawo to get her opinion of her sister. Kasawo, who was doing well in her little town and had not seen Padlock in a long time, came to see her at their parental home. She was not taken aback by either Padlock's appearance or her behavior. She was sure that her elder sister had always been like that: living in her own world. She dominated the conversation, because Padlock was not in the mood to talk and seemed strangely absent. Kasawo made it a point not to mention the late Aunt Lwandeka, or other victims of the plague. She talked only about how good life was at her place. Her business was doing well, she had a man and her eyes were firmly fixed on the future. Just before she left, early the following morning, she invited her sister to visit her. Padlock was going for mass and never understood what Kasawo was jabbering about. However, she smiled dryly, almost maliciously. Her eyes glinted as she saw Kasawo's big body disappear in the mist on the way to the main road to catch the morning bus. She wished she could force her to go to mass with her. How she would have liked to drag her sister up the steaming hills and down the dewy valleys at breakneck speed and fling her broken, sinning body at the doorstep of the church of their youth! How proud she would have been to break and deliver her to the Lord on a plate and hear her full-throated entreaties for God's forgiveness! But now Kasawo was going back to her godless life, and she might go the way Lwandeka did: to damnation. Damnation, damnation, damnation . . . Obsessed with her only remaining sister, Padlock lost her way in the hills for the first time and arrived at the parish just before mass ended.

On her last day, with her prematurely gray head shaking like a ball of cotton in the wind, Padlock went to investigate why the orchestra was playing non-stop and with such intensity. She heard the crushing and tearing and hammering and banging and donging of things, and mixed in the cacophony were what sounded like the painful screams of a torture chamber in full swing. She left her room in a temper. When she stepped outside into the courtyard and looked at the forest in the distance, her legs buckled with holy fright: before her was the altar of St. Peter's Basilica, above which doves hovered for a minute or so before dropping out of sight in blinding white arcs. There were so many doves that the whole sky looked white.

In the beginning, there had been a locust attack, and then the post-pilgrimage storm. Now there was the miracle of the celestial doves, come to wash evil from the forest and the village. The music crescendoed to a wailing wind's pitch with breaking sticks, cracking iron roofs and splitting trees in the foreground. Then she heard the unbearable rustle of millions of locusts, and the sky filled with the violins of dropping doves.

It was almost ten o'clock in the morning. A sweet, toothless sunshine, golden to the eye and pleasant on the skin, was shining and flirting with the senses. Farmers were already in the garden with backs bent as they dug with hoes, which kept rising and falling to a deliberate no-nonsense rhythm. They worked inside the shambas, a distance from the path. Padlock could see them, but they could not see her. Now and then, the voice of a child lying on a bundle of banana leaves near the diggers came to her and resurrected the image of her dozen offspring. The diggers were busy tilling the land and planting or preparing to plant beans, maize, cassava, potatoes, tomatoes and greens. The children were either helping their parents in the garden or already at school.

Padlock found herself alone on the path. She turned off into the bushes leading to the forest of dropping doves, walking through the man-high elephant grass in a daze. She moved reverently, like somebody approaching holy ground. The elephant grass gave way to shorter grass interspersed with little umbrella-shaped trees. The forest was only meters away, the holy spectacle enticingly within reach. Her chest boiled with the feeling that she was not alone. Distracted by the egrets, she had not seen the mighty buffalo, over which the birds fussed whenever the ants inside his nose and head tickled his brain and made him shudder. The buffalo was extremely happy to receive her. He had been wounded days before by hunters who, in their inexperience, had failed to catch up with him and finish him off. Crazed with contained rage and energized by the discovery of a soulmate, the buffalo charged at Padlock from under the little tree where he had been waiting in ambush.

With consummate ease, he picked her up, tossed her into the air and made her fly upside down like the Korean trapeze artists she had seen many years ago on the Toshiba. Bushy ground rushed madly toward her. Falling and screaming, she landed with both shoulders on the gigantic marmorean horns, feet in the air like St. Peter on the cross. The buffalo took off at great speed, tearing through the singing, wailing, weeping bushes, a flock of egrets in his wake. As they penetrated the forest the undergrowth clawed at her. The foliage looked so green, the air smelled so heavy, her body felt as light as a child angel's wing. She was back in the clouds, headed for Rome and the Holy Land.

They arrived at a clearing in the middle of the forest, dark because of the wall of giant trees which cut off much of the sun. The buffalo tossed her into the air, and she sprawled in the dewy grass; then it ran to one end of the clearing and, taking off at high speed, tore to the other end. The dank air vibrated with hoof-chopped clods and the thunder of its breath. Everything—the sky, the trees, the undergrowth, the ground—seemed to quiver and shudder under the assault. After sixty-three sprints, the buffalo collapsed on the tiny remains of its companion and rubbed slowly with its enormous belly. It made seven more such dashings and rubbings. After the last dash, it fell so heavily that it did not rise: there was nothing more to rub into the ground. It died of massive exhaustion and heart failure. The November rains, which the farmers had been waiting for, came the same day and started erasing the hoof marks with torrents that almost washed away the freshly planted crops. After the rains, the grasshoppers came, and the whole area quivered with efforts to catch this flying delicacy.

The girl who helped Padlock around the house came from school to find her aunt gone. She immediately knew that something was wrong. The fireplace was cold. The food she had left on the fire stones for her aunt to cook was cold. The girl was hungrier than usual and was hammered by the feeling that trouble was in the air. Had her aunt collapsed somewhere? Had she lost her way in the hills? Had she gone to the well and got carried away by the water? She already missed her. She had not liked her aunt at first sight, but had grown fond of her. She had got used to the strict but fair ways of the older woman. There was something sadly likeable about her. There was something oddly impressive about her determination. To a young girl, there was something amazing about the total independence from everything that the woman enjoyed. She seemed to have an unlimited capacity for reflection, meditation, prayer, or whatever she did during those long stretches of uninterrupted silence when she seemed totally cut off from this world. With tears in her eyes, the girl rushed to her father's house to inform him of her aunt's disappearance. She somehow expected to find Padlock there, talking or listening to her father, or even lying down with fatigue. She willed her to be there. She prayed to God that she be there.

Mbale received the news with a wooden face, his only betrayal of emotion the slight drop of his mouth and the furrows that appeared on his forehead. He went round the village asking about his sister. He ended up at the parish church, where nobody had seen her that day. He walked back to the village through the hills, which were quivering under the assault of grasshopper catchers. Nobody seemed to remember seeing her that day, or any other day for that matter. Many said they believed she had returned to her home long ago. Mbale organized a big search in the area, but no one thought of going to the forest. They checked wells, water holes and ditches to make sure that she was not lying somewhere waiting for help.

In the meantime, Serenity got the news. He arrived in the torrents of rain, looking like a chick fished out of a pool of crude oil. Plagued by the failure to locate his father in 1979, he suffered from a massive lack of confidence. Memories of his one-legged uncle filled his head. Had all those dreams about the man come to this? Was it his wife, and not him, who was supposed to share the one-legged man's fate? He felt momentarily relieved. Then he thought about the children and decided that he had to find his wife. She must be somewhere in this village. He pictured her back in the days before the wedding. He remembered their first meeting. He remembered the wedding ceremony, and the preparations, and the big day itself. The woman had to be found. The enormity of the task made him shudder. He knew that it would take a miracle to find a person who never got lost in all her life. Nakibuka joined the search party, but she could bring no new insight to the task. The evenings were the hardest. Exhausted, wet, sad faces gathered round the fire, which was not a funeral wake because a body had not been found, and not a bonfire because of the uncertainty that clung to the air. Days ground into weeks with the tortured sloth of an old steam engine. In the midst of the gloom, somebody suggested searching the forest. Serenity was vehemently opposed to the idea—the woman could not be there—but the forest was attacked the next day all the same.

There were no clues as to Padlock's whereabouts. The tiny threads which had clung to undergrowth and thorns as she rode the buffalo had been washed away. The river of trees and its mysteries made Serenity tremble. The darkness, the wetness and his fear of the forest made him wish he could turn back. He felt like somebody walking to his own death, somebody about to be swallowed by wells of boiling mud after being crushed by the gigantic trees.

Nakibuka placed a hand on his shoulder, and they pushed on. In the clearing, everyone was flabbergasted by the rivers of maggots and the armies of flies which cascaded out of the gigantic buffalo carcass. The flesh had caved in; the ribs resembled a hollowed-out mountainside. The hunters told their story, but no one placed Padlock anywhere in its framework. To begin with, Padlock never went to the forest. Most people believed this to be a different buffalo, because the other one had been speared seven kilometers away. They reasoned that if the wounded buffalo had wanted to kill people in retaliation, it would have had plenty of opportunity in the other area, which happened to be more heavily populated. Most people in the search party wanted to go back to the village right away. They saw no use in prolonging the wild goose chase in a section of the forest known for harboring big-game traps. Mbale and Nakibuka insisted that the group proceed to the other end of the forest, and told everyone to look for pieces of cloth. It was a very unpopular decision. The long, grinding search provided neither a solution nor any clues. Not a single piece of cloth was discovered. People grumbled all the way back. At the clearing, the hunters bravely moved the gigantic carcass. Maggots climbed up their legs and arms, and flies made the air crackle and buzz with the protest of their wings. The wet stench made Serenity feel as though he had a huge hole in his head. At that juncture, he ordered the men to stop moving the carcass.

His wife was definitely not under that filth. Not his Padlock. Not his Virgin. He also discouraged those who were crawling on the ground in search of any minuscule clues.

Many theories sprang up. Some said Padlock had been eaten by a stray leopard, and her polished bones were hanging a forked tree somewhere in this forest. Some said a stray pride of lions had eaten her flesh, and a pack of hyenas had ground her bones in their powerful jaws. Some said she was carried away by the river on the other side of the parish. Some said she fell into a secret pit. Somebody even suggested that she had gone to heaven on the way back from hearing mass.

Serenity's depression increased after the failure to find his wife. As a distraction, he became fascinated with water. He remembered the Tiber River in Rome, where Romulus and Remus had lived. He talked about water and bodies of water all the time. Of all the theories flying around about Padlock's disappearance, he believed that she had been swallowed by a river. Cornered by her lover's obsession, Nakibuka encouraged Serenity to visit the shores of Lake Victoria on a regular basis. They started going every weekend, frequenting certain fishing points where they watched canoes go out to lay their nets. They would sit and listen to the waves and the winds as they sang and wept. The fact that Nakibuka was his wife's aunt helped bring the image of his wife closer. Serenity started thinking about the Virgin Mary.

At first he had adored her, and even asked her to mother him, long before he found his own Virgin, his Padlock. In order to deal with the pain, he united the two virgins, and the belief grew in him that his virgin was going to return to him via the lake. She was the crocodile his late aunt had talked about. She was going to emerge from the lake's canyoned depths to soothe his aching heart. The miracle-working demons of religion Serenity had resisted for the better part of his life plagued him now, teasing his mind, twisting his dreams, enhancing their allure by insidiously referring to the miraculous way he had got the money to finance the pilgrimages. Nakibuka would see him lost in thought, his soul on the waves, combing the horizon for the virgin, and she was happy that he was not alone. He no longer read his books. The long wait for Godot had ended in disillusionment. The holes that had not been plugged could no longer be patched up by imported fictions.

Serenity's world had narrowed down to the house, the cows, the road and the pilgrimages to the lake.

Hajj Gimbi tried to help, but Serenity no longer said much. He was back to the taciturn days after the mysterious tall woman had pushed him away and healed his obsession. On occasion, he saw the returning Indians: they were like shadows to him now, beings from an alien planet. He no longer feared or disliked them; they simply did not exist for him. Nakibuka was the only person who could reach him. She had moved into Padlock's dream house in the village. She now looked after the few remaining shitters who were not in boarding school. On a number of occasions, Serenity made Nakibuka swear that she would look after his children like her own. She did, not caring whether the shitters liked her or not. Serenity started going to the lake every other day. Nakibuka could not accompany him all the time because of the duties of running the home. Alone, he felt braver: he was discovering the world and molding it through his own words and vision. He also knew that his wife would reveal herself on the waves only when he was alone. The reunion would definitely begin as a private affair, and he believed that each solitary excursion would be the last.

One afternoon, he realized that he was lost. He simply could not remember where he was. He started plodding through the bulrushes, headed for a fishing point on the other side of the lake. He went deeper into the marshes, the saw-edged grass cutting his skin. Leeches leaped out of the water, bit him and drank till they fell off, bloated with his blood. At one point, he nearly fell down a slippery rock into the lake. His destination seemed to recede as he approached it. His clothes were sodden, and his shoes full of water. Mud was sucking at his feet. Locusts were gnawing at his thorax and stomach. The sun was going down, hovering dangerously on the horizon; it seemed about to fall into the lake and drown.

His attention was quickly snatched by a floating piece of wood, no, a floating desert island, jagged, ribbed, magnificent in its desolate antiquity. He was back in Rome with Romulus and Remus and the Wolf. Were those jagged edges not the erect teats of the wolves which had reared him at his father's house? Suddenly the sharp edges multiplied, as though there were many wolves floating upside down, erect teats provocatively exposed. He could hardly tear his eyes from the bizarre spectacle. A gigantic flash or wave, or both, burst, blurring everything. It lifted as arrows of water pierced his eyes and washed over him.

The huge crocodile had caught up with him. He had taken to patrolling this territory only recently, because a group of smaller males had tried to oust him in a little coup, which he had nipped in the bud. Now he took his time combing the shore, overturning a canoe or two whenever possible, making sure that he was the sole ruler of his territory. It was a month now since his last decent meal. This would be one of the fifty large meals he would have this year—not bad for a creature fifty-eight years old, seven meters long and so many hundreds of kilograms in body weight. He opened his gigantic jaws, and Serenity saw pink and red kaleidoscopes amidst the boiling wavelets. For a moment, everything was froth, boiling waves and furious action. Three final images flashed across Serenity's mind as he disappeared into the jaws of the crocodile: a rotting buffalo; Nakibuka, his longtime lover, who was also the aunt of Padlock, his missing wife; and the mysterious woman who had cured his obsession with tall women. In that final instant, he suddenly realized where his wife's bones lay, but because the ancient art of communicating with the dead through dreams had been killed off in the family by Catholicism, Western education and abject neglect, Serenity's knowledge did not leave the belly of the crocodile, not even when it died ten years later.

Hajj Gimbi and Nakibuka believed that he had drowned, and they commissioned fishermen to look for his body and notify the police as soon as it was found. However, Serenity's was to be a cenotaph burial too. The body was never found, and to their last days, Hajj Gimbi and Nakibuka could not agree as to how Serenity had met his end.

After the death of the despots, it dawned on me that sooner rather than later, I had to make a decision about what I wanted to do with my life. I still had a few thousand dollars, which I could spend on hand-to-mouth living or on some investment. I took the latter option and, throwing all caution to the wind, got in contact with a man who sold European passports. He was reliable, but expensive as hell. He was generally called Chicken Shit, because he always said to people who complained about his prices that you cannot make chicken soup from chicken shit. He prided himself on delivering quality product, as opposed to those who sold cheap, fake-looking booklets which led many customers into trouble with the police. I needed a good passport in order to start infiltrating Dutch society. I was already thinking about getting a job in order to practice the language and earn a little money as I worked out my next moves. Chicken Shit offered me a choice of becoming a British, American, Spanish or Portuguese citizen! A few months in the country, and by the power of money, I had qualified to become a European! It was hard to take in at first, but eventually it dawned on me that it was soon going to happen. The powers that had parcelled out Africa among themselves at the Berlin Conference in 1884 had done it without even stepping foot on the continent. Me, I had travelled all the way to Europe, paid for everything I used and now was about to pay for my citizenship. I realized that what I was about to do was not the most extraordinary occurrence—I was just going to become one of the ants in the subterranean passages of the underworld which kept much of the economy going—but I still had a few questions. Would I exist in any particular country's records? Of course I would: Chicken Shit was using existing particulars for the booklets. What would I do if the police needed a birth certificate? He said he could provide one quite easily. First I had to choose which nationality I wanted. I chose to become British.

After a fortnight, my new identity was ready. When I went to collect it, Chicken Shit gave me a little test. He gave me two booklets and asked if I could identify the one he had made. I failed the test. I paid over a thousand dollars for both the passport and the birth certificate. Adrenaline hit my system as I pocketed the booklet. I had been reborn: my new name was John Kato. My new surname was a common name for the second male twin back home in Uganda. Somewhere in Britain there was an ant going by the same name, unaware of the existence of a twin brother negotiating the wetness of the Dutch polders.

To test my new powers as a citizen of the powerful West, I went to the City Council cemetery to ask for a job. My nerves jangled, but I called upon my acting capabilities. I veneered my agitation with a serious and eager expression. The time had come to lawyer for myself. The cemetery was on the edge of the city, secluded in a wood with tall, thin trees, paved walkways, clipped lawns and neat graveyards arranged in rectangular configurations. It was very clean and very quiet here among the dead. I walked among the graves, marvelling at the variety of headstones, the messages written on them, the lettering, the little flower patches round the graves and the atmosphere of peace that dominated the place. There were water taps and green watering cans to carry to the plants and flowers. I had found a place to relax and think. The job negotiations went on in English. They wanted a cleaner and gardener. Would I be interested? The pay was bad, but it was enough to take care of my needs. The man did not find anything wrong with my passport. I had passed my first test.

I worked with the fanatic drive of the newly liberated. I was after catching somebody's eye, to make a connection that would help me reach out for bigger things. Would I get them, as I had got their fellow countryman Fr. Kaanders? I observed quite a few burials: very quiet, very decent, very clean affairs. No blood-curdling wailings, no flailing of arms, no tearing of hair or gnashing of teeth. Dressed in black, the mourners would congregate in the hall, say a few words about the deceased, listen to a song or two and proceed to the graveyard, the coffin in the hands of the black-clad undertakers. I knew somehow that my salvation lurked among the mourners. After lowering the coffin, people would leave in neat lines, some whispering, most silent, and go back to the coffee room for coffee and cake or a biscuit before driving home. It was hard to come into contact with the mourners, even those who came singly to water the flowers round the graves of their beloved. The closer I came to penetrating this new world, the further it seemed to recede.

A few months into the job, I learned that the real money lay in disinterring long-dead, long-forgotten people whose rent had expired and burning their remains or reinterring them in specially designated places. I had never liked gardening that much; it seemed a mockery of Uncle Mbale's back-breaking efforts and his children's tough shamba life. Disinterment was pretty disgusting, but it released something in me. I felt a deep curiosity to see what happened to the dead after ten or more years under. It was heavy, dirty work, in some cases worse than what Keema's cronies did, but it exhausted me enough to make me sleep like a crushed log.

The first time I raised my hand against the dead, I felt the freakish energy of discovery course through me. I first attacked the graves reverently, but with time I acquired the reckless pleasure of the more seasoned demolishers. As going up a mountain makes people giddy, going under the earth made me feel more grounded, like a rock. The graves opened up like sea chests split open by a pirate's axe. The legacy degraded—curious, sad, hard to make sense of. The skeletons, the skulls, the crumbling cloth, the brittle hair, in a way reminded me of the Luwero Triangle and the aftermath of the guerrilla war, of people who had rotted into the earth so completely that only skulls and skeletons had remained at the end. Sometimes there were rings, remains of shoes or necklaces, some objects which had been nice in their own time, reminders of values, tastes, customs. These would be piled onto the remains of their wearers and taken to the incinerator. The burning of these remains, these relics of past lives, touched something inside me that burned brutally and pointed to the invaluable role of memory and the fragility of the past.

I did not know anything about these people, but the confrontation with their obscure pasts, terminally locked in the mists of time, touched me. From the filth and the dirt of stinking or crumbling bits and pieces, something glorious seemed to emerge, akin to the resurrection of a dead person come back to tell old stories everyone thought left in the grave. I was no longer working with the dead: in them I was resurrecting those I thought had gone forever. I was back to my library days in the seminary. Graves were my bookshelves loaded with dust-caked secrets. Stories started arising, knocking about in my head, making me wonder what I should do with them. The dedication with which I worked surprised both my colleagues and my boss. They seemed to think that I was morbid, feeding off the dead in an uncanny way. The ghosts of the dead seemed to fill me with indefatigability. I would out-work my more sturdy colleagues, race them till they sweated like sprinters. Most were whiners, going on and on about the dirt and the terrible work. I never contributed to their dirges; I was onto something special. In my mind, I reconstructed our victims' lives, deaths and burial ceremonies. For some I created glorious pasts, for others dismal days in which death was a liberation from a life of tedium, routine, misery. For some I painted a gray life which was neither good nor bad, glorious nor obscure, painful nor joyous.

In the meantime, things were picking up on other fronts. It was while I was working here that I met the woman, the ghost, that seemed to rise up out of one of the old graves we had demolished and wind my life up another notch. The power of the original spark made me believe that there was something deathly about the encounter and its aftermath. It was a gloomy day, and there had been no disinterments and only one burial. I had stayed on and volunteered to look after the watering cans, wanting to take time to think and just have a quiet moment. I found her kneeling at a new grave, a lone figure who seemed to be intent on resurrecting whoever lay under the tombstone. Her body was shaking with sharp sobs. Most white women stood in the sand like trapped buffaloes and mourned their dead with the calculated pomp of a priest at high mass. She, however, did the opposite, and for a moment she reminded me of Padlock clawing the floor of Mbale's house after being thrown out of the convent. As I approached, my eyes went to the tombstone: the deceased had been forty-four years old, the current average life expectancy in Serenity's Abyssinia. Her boyfriend, I thought uneasily. Yes: older-man, younger-woman scenario. I was suddenly gripped with the terror that my find was in her late forties or early fifties, and that it had been an older-woman, younger-man scenario. With every step I took, the mass of dark hair shielding her face blew slightly in the scented wind. I was quite close now. I stood a meter away and waited for her to turn. She did not. I coughed, bowed a little and asked if she wanted me to water her plants for her. I still had not seen her face. She turned her eyes to me in one slow, querulous movement. A decent tan had given her face great depth and solidity and pulled it out of the mass of dark hair to hold its own against her dress and the surroundings. By the look of her, we were about the same age, and I found myself swallowing hard, but then how could such a person be unmarried or unengaged? There were four rings on her fingers, fingers which had never tasted the harshness of the hoe or the smoothness of a pestle. How was I going to get through to this spoiled person, who possibly had a thin country-western pin of a voice? The only souvenir I had ever got from the demolished tombs was a golden wedding ring, and the sight of this woman's rings now disgusted me to the point of wanting to throw my trophy in the trash can. Everything seemed like a game to these people. Four rings bought for the hell of it!

I was about to convince myself that this was Padlock's ghost come back to torment me one last time when I heard her voice. The contempt and confusion registering on my face in that brief instant had made her believe that I was mourning her dead or empathizing in some spectacular way. I was not. Yes, I could water her plants for her. The tone of voice was not too supercilious or too matter-of-fact. It could be interpreted as vaguely friendly or indifferent. Of course I had met types who smiled just because they were bloody scared to death of you. She, on the other hand, was in command of herself. The remains of her makeup had trickled down her face with the serpentine configurations of a bush trail, but what lay underneath was quite attractive. My mixture of lame Dutch and perfect English seemed to disarm her. Given an ear, her mouth loosened and grief flowed out with the sinuousness of a sloughing serpent. Halfway through the flood, I started thinking it was probably the usual detoxifying confession to a stranger. However, I picked up a few vital strands of information: she had the jinx of being deserted by men. Her father and two brothers had died of cancer. We were standing at the grave of the latest victim, a brother. That shook me to the roots, but did not intimidate me. If the disease was perambulating her system the way the plague had hijacked Aunt Lwandeka's body, what the hell, as long as it was not contagious. Death had brought me here; it might as well take me away. I fathomed what she must have been going through: all those deaths, all those fears. The winds of the dead bound us to each other with fearsome intensity. In a matter of weeks, we were together. I was plucked from the ghetto and the racket at Keema's flat and placed in her roomy apartment on the outskirts of the great city. The front window looked out on part of the city, a collection of roofs and spires and towers. In the mist-laden distance I could feel the ghetto beckoning, pulling me back to Little Uganda. But deep down I knew that, having come this far, I was not going back. And I had never belonged there anyway.

Magdelein de Meer literally owned me: I was the first person she truly felt belonged to her. A few white men had passed through her life, all melting in the distance like ghosts. I believed most were scared off by the cancer in the family, especially those who wanted children. Me, I was a fantasy, a dream which, if carefully refrigerated, could be made to last and live up to expectations. I relished the role at first, expanding my horizons under the new skies. In a way, I thought the affair was a victory, then a revenge: revenge on the despots, on Lageau, on the white world, on the black world and so on. But through the ordinariness of two people trying to live together, it dawned on me that there was no revenge, no victory, just another chapter in life, just another psychological barrier broken down, scraped and found, like the glittering headboard, to be of plain wood.

Magdelein had a junior post in a local bank, but she spent like somebody living on borrowed time. She decked me out in fine clothes, which made me uncomfortable, and showed me off. I have never liked formal dress, stiff suits and hard leather shoes, and now I had to put them on at parties. In a place where people dressed informally, I was turned into a fish in a bowl. I was being watched instead of watching. I was often like the corpse at the last service: dressed for burial. She had good intentions and quite a degree of idealism. She did for me what she would not do for a white man, I guess. I was not required to spend my dirty money on anything, except on gifts and language courses. She cooked and cleaned, although she did the latter better than the former. I believed she was competing with mythical black women, invisible specters who could rob her of her dream by cleaning and cooking their way into my heart. Cunningly, I edited Eva from the story I fed her. As I watched Magdelein cooking and cleaning, I kept thinking that I had done as much for Eva. The irony often had me laughing in the bath. Magdelein had a good plan: to mother me and pamper me till I felt obligated to stay. A banker's mind: long-term investment. Two of my white colleagues had me laughing in secret: they complained bitterly about their white wives, who apparently did not cook or do anything round the house.

I had a few more things to laugh about: before moving in with her, we had been obliged to register ourselves with the local police. I showed my British passport and the birth certificate. There was no hitch. She asked me about my passport, and I told her that I was born in Britain before my parents migrated to Uganda when it was still a garden of Eden. She swallowed the tale in good faith, and like many mythmakers, I felt my chest swell. I told her that Serenity worked with the Energy Board in a managerial capacity and that Padlock had been a primary school teacher (flashed by Cane after beating him into an erection). Then one day Serenity got picked up by Amin's men, was locked up and driven from his job. He finally got a job in a small tool-making company, where he worked till his death. Magdelein was a curious woman, and I made sure that I kept the story simple to avoid catching myself in my own traps. I knew that one day she might want to visit the country, but since that was far into the future, I did not mind. It had not been my intention to lie to her; I just got carried away by the yarn. Her curiosity opened wells of imagination in my mind, and fictions flowed out.

She started telling me to stop working. She must have felt uncomfortable recalling the way we had met. There was also the possibility of another vulnerable mourner's taking me off her hands. But it was the thought of my opening up crumbling graves during the day and her box of secrets at night that disorganized her self-image. It brought the idea of death too close to home.

For my part, I thought she just wanted to pull the noose tighter by making me totally dependent on her. On the other hand, I enjoyed what I was doing, especially because I did not have to do it. No two graves were the same; each contained its own secrets. The fire of the incinerator reminded me of my brewing days, and the fires that had raged through Serenity's Abyssinia. There was something spiritual about the fire, a sublimating quality which liberated what was important from the past. I was comfortable in my job and saw no reason to give it up. There was also another side to it. What if she threw me out? I had no plans to get caught unawares and have to return to the ghetto. I resisted all attempts to hijack my independence. I was most irritated when she attempted to do that on the embers of a particularly good afterglow. Sex had never weakened my resolve or mental capabilities; it would not start making me do handstands now. I always found tenderness as a form of bribery particularly revolting, especially as it reminded me of Padlock's attempts to extract confessions by way of slimy psalms.

My ego was also slowly popping out of its can. As time went on, the fence we had made round ourselves developed gaps. I started resenting having to wear suits for Magdelein's benefit. At parties, I started to resent having to defend the whole African continent, or the whole of Uganda, or the entire black race. I refused to become a self-styled ambassador, the eternal explainer of Amin's or Obote's or some other tyrant's atrocities, as though I were partly to blame. I was supposed to explain away droughts and famines and the atrocities of the International Monetary Fund and the World Bank and other pirates with a smile on my face. After all, hadn't I been taken in by these white people at this or that party? When walking down the street with her, I started getting irritated by furtive looks from some old women, who implied that they knew what was going on. I resented the cold stares from white men, especially old men living in dusty, lily-white pasts.

Summers were the worst time of the year: the whole white world came crashing onto my head. I was often the only black person in the hotel, in the park. I started seeing ghosts of the Infernal Trinity in un-expected places, with rifles cleverly concealed under their robes. I started seeing Lageau behind counters, in restaurants, at the beach, preaching his monkey sermon through his thin monkey lips. The past was mingling with the present and contaminating the future with its sly poison. The sexual side of racism disgusted me: there were some women who, when they saw us together, reacted as if I desired them all and could hardly wait to rip off my clothes in public to assault them. This poisoned my thought processes and soured my mood, because most of these women were quite unattractive, too thin, too pale, too fat, too flat or too old for my liking. Maybe there were men who de-sired them madly; I was not one of them. I was mostly thinking about books and how hard it was to capture the essence of the past, but sud-denly there I would be, imagining I was Lwendo, fully armed with a machine gun and the license to kill without compunction. I knew right then that the coffin for our affair was lying open. I was not going to sacrifice sanity for a white woman, or anybody else for that matter.

The white world invaded our nights. At the beginning, we had made love with the fire of sizzling passion. We strangled and burned demons from the past with the relentlessness of youthful energy. It struck me that in a bathysphere, where love would be assaulted by the waves in vain, we would have lived happily ever after. In the real world, love was a feeble thing, terrorized by the sun and washed away by the rains. The line on the sexual graph fell drastically. I would lie there and think of Cane's brown-labiaed nudes and feel sick with dis-gust. I had quickly graduated to the knowledge that it was not she and me against the world.

My past of raiding and defeating bigger enemies had taught me to be discreet, cunning, elusive, solitary. The fact that the enemy could strike so casually, with a look or a negative gesture, wore me down. Most of my enemies were smaller than me physically, psychologically and mentally. There was no fun in engaging them, and I could not plan raids. The man who had flattened the mighty Lageau felt impotent. It was a fact that when I went out alone, everything was fine, but when we went out together, it was hell. I hated the visibility Magdelein accorded me. I hated the fact that I could not discover the world peacefully and dream and redream it at all times. Like Serenity, I knew when I was defeated; all that remained was to end it. Like Uncle Kawayida, I was not going to bicker.

I attacked the Dutch language course like a madman. I attacked the subsequent job course with the same zeal. I was among the few black people who got a decent job. I missed the gory disinterments, but I had to move on. I got a job with a large weekly magazine. I was not a journalist, but I was near where words were beaten into weapons, and I was gradually forging mine.

There were many things I never told Magdelein—mood-souring experiences in town, for example. I would return home and keep quiet, happy to fight my own wars. I discovered later that she kept a diary, which was almost exclusively about me. One day I took a look at it and felt like throwing it in the fire. To me, life was lived day by day, and the actions of yesterday might have nothing to do with what happened the following day. Life was a journey of discovery, and character was a variable that kept veering left and right in search of the perfect way for a particular day. To Magdelein, character was unchanging, life a balance sheet to be rigorously monitored. I realized that the union between a fastidious banker and a free spirit with piratical proclivities was fraught with danger. In this respect, I preferred Eva, with her egomaniacal tendencies. With sweat trickling down my back, I read: Jay—as she called me—has changed . . . Jay moody . . . Is Jay still interested in us? . . . Jay drank tea with milk . . . Jay talked for thirty minutes with somebody in the ghetto. I didn't understand a thing, because it was all in his language: Luganda. Jay hasn't touched me for . . . Is some old ghetto flame beckoning in the background . . . ? I bought Jay a fifty-dollar tie. He did not appreciate it, saying it was a waste of money . . .

We had a row. She accused me of not paying sufficient attention to her. I accused her of monitoring me like a spy. She said she refused to be ruled by bigots and insisted that we go out more frequently, hold hands, kiss in public and make them suffer. I refused. Billboard intimacy had never been my thing and never would be. She questioned my motives. I said I was tired of the pressure. She said we would win. I said I did not want a pyrrhic victory. She ran out of the house and came back with a packet of cigarettes. She lighted one and smoked it clumsily. I said I did not like the smell of cigarettes, and that it was bad for her health and her breath. She said she was free to do what she wanted. I agreed. The damage had been done. The tears didn't mend the rift. I was determined to go out and be my own man. She was determined to change me and still be her own person. It could not work.

I left on a beautiful spring morning. She looked like a puppy fished out of a pot of porridge. I looked like a pirate thrown off a ship.

I returned to Central Station, sat with my bags at my feet and watched the multitudes. The sun was shining, doves were fluttering about, three youths were banging out a rock tune on scuffed instruments. I tapped with my left foot. Half-naked youths were watching, travellers streaming past, trams rumbling. People of all nations and colors poured into the great city like ants streaming toward predestined locations in subterranean tunnels. As I looked, my head began to spin: I was getting dizzy. People seemed to be walking upside down, the dead rising from their graves, the living diving into fresh graves. There was motion and inversion everywhere: the invaders were being invaded, the partitioners being partitioned, the penetrators getting penetrated. The mixing and juxtaposition of peoples became mindblowing, the destinations and points of departure mythic. I held on to the cement bank in order to stop myself from spewing or getting spewed. I had found myself a stone to lay my head on, an enchanted hilltop made of boulders from all the corners of the globe. I was back in my element: watching, planning, waiting for the right time to strike. Abyssinia was on my mind; so was my new foothold on this precipitous hilltop. It has always been a Herculean task for Abyssinians to get their foot in the door, but once in, they never budge. I was in.

ACKNOWLEDGMENTS

My book has been fertilized by other books, among which the following deserve a special mention. *Uganda Now*, by Holger Bernt Hansen and Michael Twaddle, and *Lust to Kill: The Rise and Fall of Idi Amin*, by Joseph Kamau and Andrew Cohen, helped me to deal with the chaotic events which I and many people I knew experienced during the years before and after the fall of Idi Amin. Mahmood Mamdani's *From Citizen to Refugee* shed light on the fate of the Indians in Uganda.